PRAISE FOR

AT THE GOING DOWN OF THE SUN

"Told with authority in an imaginative blend of fiction and history, this many-layered family story offers poignant pleasure."
—*Publishers Weekly*

"A moving blend of history and fiction."
—*Library Journal*

"Brilliantly evokes the special horror of a war for which the civilized world was philosophically unprepared. The contrast between the innocence and complacency of the relatively long period of peace that preceded the first World War and the complete destruction that followed makes a fascinating subject. . . . The novel is the kind they don't make any more, old-fashioned melodrama with larger-than-life characters and incidents. Its style is perfectly suited to its subject, and it proceeds mesmerizingly to its ironic ending."
—*Romantic Times*

At the Going Down of the Sun

Elizabeth Darrell

St. Martin's Press
New York

Acknowledgment: The publishers wish to thank Mrs Nicolete Gray and The Society of Authors on behalf of the Laurence Binyon Estate.

First published in Great Britain by Century Publishing Co. Ltd.

Mass market edition/July 1986
ISBN: 0-312-90044-9

10 9 8 7 6 5 4 3 2 1

They shall not grow old, as we that are left grow old:
Age shall not weary them, nor the years condemn.
At the going down of the sun and in the morning
We will remember them.

Laurence Binyon: Extract from
FOR THE FALLEN (September 1914)

1

THE SHERIDANS came home for the long holidays that summer of 1914 older, of course, certainly wiser, but basically the same as they had always been.

Rex was the first to arrive, as usual, roaring through the valley lanes that divided sloping meadows full of sheep, scattering those grazing nearest the hedges, setting lazy dogs onto their paws barking, and drawing the glances of farming men out in their fields, who shook their fists at him. But it was done in a good-natured way, and the men still had broad smiles minutes after he had passed. The barking of the dogs was more joyful than aggressive, and the sheep soon returned to their juicy patches alongside the lanes. The village of Tarrant Royal had taken Rex Sheridan into its heart from the day of his first childish escapade, and there he was destined to stay.

It was as if the entire village had been listening for the sound of his motor cycle, for his progress along the winding, undulating way was acknowledged by waving, smiling people who had all come out into the June sunshine to see him go by. But, as he approached the centre of the village, his heady speed of more than thirty miles an hour was slowed until he could maintain no more than a walking pace, keeping himself upright by using his legs in scooting fashion each side of the noisy spluttering machine that came second only to one other in his pride of possession.

Plump matrons left their shopping baskets in the middle of the lane in order to crowd round him, questioning him, bringing him up to date with village news, showing him the newest additions to their families. Old yokels waved their walking-sticks in gladness, and called out affectionate reprimands about noise and fumes, whilst secretly eyeing the fabulous machine with rheumy envy and longing for the youthful clean-limbed strength of the second of

Branwell Sheridan's sons. Small boys tumbled from doorways and the branches of spreading oaks, eyes glowing with hero worship and excitement, to beg a ride on the wonderful self-propelled bicycle. Each one was swung up, in turn, onto the fat petrol tank before the rider and allowed to squeeze the rubber horn, whilst shrieking, 'Brrrrum, brrrrum,' in imitation of the engine that was now only softly popping, with an occasional backfire that made all the matrons clutch their bosoms with fright, then laugh delightedly at their own silliness.

But, in the background, were other observers. Young, pink-cheeked farmers' daughters, and buxom maidservants, who hung from upstairs windows or stood shyly in doorways, peeping through rose-covered trellis or huge hanging wisteria blooms. They had waited since the Easter vacation for this day. Their hearts beat painfully fast at the manifestation of their dreams of this figure in boots, breeches, leather jacket, and long flying scarf as he sat astride his speed-machine. The leather helmet hid his bright hair, but he had pushed the goggles up to reveal those merry green eyes, and just one glance at that heartbreaking smile was enough to reaffirm the knowledge that the passion they had felt at Easter was even stronger now the days were hypnotic with sunshine and sweet-smelling briar roses, and the nights were hot and full of temptation. Two months or more of painful ecstasy lay ahead of them. Of the three Sheridan boys Rex was the least handsome, but he captured hearts along every path he recklessly drove, and if he broke them, it was never deliberate.

Impatient though he was, Rex allowed himself to be waylaid by people he knew well and liked for their simple approach to life. He was genuinely glad to see them all—the women who had mothered himself and his brothers through most of their childhood and adolescence; the men who had substituted for a father rarely at home and with whom he played skittles at the inn and cricket on the village green; the small boys who shared his passion for machines; and the young girls who willingly let him kiss and cuddle them during his vacations. As he finally escaped and drove off toward Tarrant Hall, he spotted the pretty faces amongst the wisteria and roses and winked his acknowledgment of their blushing greetings. The blushes deepened and he laughed with the joy of youth and freedom as he turned into the narrow uphill lane that led to his family home.

It was not to the house that he went, but to the flat meadow above it that ran for half a mile across the top of Longbarrow Hill. As he began to bump across the turf of that meadow toward a large wooden barn, his heart began to thump every bit as painfully as those of the village girls who had greeted him so covertly. His passion was inflamed by what stood inside that rough building.

Jake was expecting him. He waited by the tall open doors, grinning his delight and pride in displaying his charge, unharmed and in spotless condition, for inspection. Rex was lost for words, just shook Jake's hand warmly with both his own, then walked right round the aeroplane, worshipping it with eyes that had darkened to emerald with excitement.

'Oh yes, she's worthy of her name,' he breathed with the bliss of seeing the machine again. 'A real "Princess".'

But the eulogy was short-lived as he tugged off his gauntlets and began a spar-by-spar, joint-by-joint examination of the bi-plane he had bought from an airman's widow and rebuilt from the wreck it had become in the crash that had killed the flier. One hour lengthened into two as Rex and the orphaned ward of the village curate talked of the mutual love of their lives—the flying-machine. It did not matter that one young man was wealthy, privileged and virile; the other a charity child, wary and crippled in one leg. When they united in praise of aerial exploration, they were equals.

Rex had taught Jake all he knew about engineering, had lent him textbooks and manuals, and perfected the lad's skills by placing complete confidence in him—something people rarely did. The result was not hero worship from Jake, but admiration, loyalty, and a respect that did not fear honesty. Sheridan money had bought the bi-plane, Rex was the legal owner, yet it belonged to both of them in a way no outsider would have understood. Enthusiasm took all men to the same level. When covered in oil, a gentleman looked the same as a guttersnipe.

After every inch of 'Princess' had been scrutinised, Jake made tea on the oil-stove within his rough quarters above the barn, and Rex sat beside him on a bale of straw to drink it while he told the lad he had abandoned his studies at Cambridge and secured himself a job in the workshops of an engineering firm, which he was due to start in August.

Despite his middle son's aptitude and passion for things mechanical, Branwell Sheridan had insisted that he go from public

3

school to university as befitted the son of a gentleman. Protesting strongly, Rex had nevertheless done as he was told. But he had soon realised that he would never gain a degree in *anything,* much less the sciences. This last term had sealed his determination to follow his star, and he had applied to a northern firm specialising in aircraft production.

There were two blocks to his becoming an ordinary apprentice, however. At twenty he was much too old for the firm's ruling conditions, and he already knew more than the students in their last year. But he could not be employed as an engineer because he had no certificates of qualification. However, his attractive personality, his flair for the trade, and his personal wealth persuaded the directors to yield to his plea to be allowed to work at their benches while he romped through the various stages of examinations that would give him the qualifications he needed. But they could not agree to his offer to take no wages. The union men would never allow it. So the issue was circumvented by engaging him as a general handyman, then letting him do whatever he wanted, within reason. The directors knew when they had a future genius on their doorstep: the young man's father was not yet aware of the fact. Rex meant to keep quiet until forced to confess. With luck, the examinations would be behind him, and he could back his confession with laudable qualifications. His deception did not worry him. Nothing did. Life was full of adventure and promise. He was eagerly seizing every minute of it.

June days were long, so there were maximum daylight minutes to seize. But, when he finally roared up to the house, it was to hurry inside, swing Priddy, the housekeeper-cum-nanny, off her feet in a bear hug, practically crush the hand of Minks, the aged butler, and thump the three dogs with boisterous reunion, before running upstairs with them at his heels, winking at Chester, the grey-haired parlour maid who had bounced the Sheridan boys as babies on her knees.

'Don't bother about dinner,' he called over the bannister.

'But Mr Rex, Cook has skinned a hare, and prepared your favourite asparagus,' came Priddy's protest.

He flashed her a smile. 'If I kiss her soundly on both cheeks, d'you think she'll give me some eggs and sausages, instead? I'm working on "Princess" tonight, and Jake'll cook them later.'

'In the morning, more like,' grumbled Priddy. 'Once you get

4

round that danged flying thing you forget everything else—even eating. It beats me how you ever grew so big and strong!' She shook her head with pride and affection. 'You try kissing Cook after she got that hare in special, you'll more'n likely get a box round the ears, young man.'

Laughing Rex turned away, but found the top stair occupied by a slim girl in a dove-grey cambric dress, starched white pinafore and mob cap, who was looking at him through large brown eyes as if she were gazing at something extraordinary.

'Hallo,' he said, thinking she should cover that body with something more exciting than dove-grey cambric. 'Who are you?'

She bobbed quickly. 'The new upstairs-maid, sir.'

'What happened to Mary?'

The girl blushed pink and said nothing.

Rex grinned. 'Dear, dear! That's one piece of news they didn't tell me as I came through the village.' He looked her over from head to foot. 'You're even prettier than Mary, so be on your guard . . . whoever you are.'

Blushing even pinker she said, 'Evie, sir.'

'I'm Rex Sheridan,' he said with a saucy bow. 'The middle one.'

'I know.' She swallowed, and rushed on, 'I've seen your picture in the sitting-room ever so many times—the one in the cricket clothes.'

'Very observant,' he teased softly.

Suddenly, she blurted out, 'I heard what Mrs Prideaux said just now about Cook being angry. I'll . . . I'll get you some eggs and sausages from the kitchen.'

Highly amused, he put on a martyred expression. 'I couldn't possibly expose you to Cook's wrath, my dear. I must be a man and brave the kitchen myself.' He mounted the top stair and stood beside her, a tall figure looking down into her intense upturned face. 'If I kissed *you* on both cheeks, Evie, would you box my ears?'

The girl looked as if she were about to faint away, so swiftly did the colour recede from her face. 'Oh, no-no, sir.'

He smiled as he tweaked her nose gently. 'Well, you should, my girl. That's what I meant about being on your guard.'

With that, he walked off along the corridor to his bedroom, forgetting the girl and everything else in the anticipation of spending the night with the 'Princess'.

The next day dawned blue and gold with a frolicking wind. Perfect flying weather! By eleven Rex was ready to go. He and Jake wheeled the aircraft from the barn, and the mere act of pushing it along the flat turf of a hill high above the surrounding countryside was enough to put the thrill of elation in Rex's breast. He could not wait for that lurch of the stomach as the machine left the ground, the dizzy sensation as it rose and banked in a turn, the surging sense of mastery as the patchwork landscape took on a distant enchantment and hills no longer hid what lay beyond.

Then it was reality, and he gazed over the edge of the cockpit as the whole of Tarrant Royal passed beneath the wings several hundred feet below. Completely possessed by the effervescence of flying he circled the village several times, waving to those who stood, faces upturned, in meadows and gardens he knew well. They waved back, the men flourishing caps, the women and girls using their aprons or items of washing newly-dried from the line. At the sight of old Mrs Hart brandishing her husband's combinations at the end of her tangled garden, Rex laughed boisterously, waggled the wings in return salute, then headed off to follow the river toward Dorchester. If he turned north at the abbey and chased the railway for ten miles, he knew he would fly over Gunwater Lake, which was due north-east of Tarrant Royal. A good round trip.

But he never reached Gunwater Lake. Five miles along the railway the engine began to cough, and oil started spattering Rex's goggles. He pushed them up swiftly, and looked for a suitable field to come down in. Most of the meadows were low-lying and marshy, so he ruled them out. Once 'Princess' sank into ground of that nature it would take cart-horses and irate farmers to get her out again. They were losing height fast, and he was just beginning to wonder if trains along that line ran infrequently enough to allow them time for repairs when he spotted the perfect landing place. It was a pity it happened to be the well-tended lawns within the enclosed grounds of a large stone mansion, but there was really no alternative.

Turning his head toward Jake in the rear cockpit, he pointed downward to the beautifully-mown park of the manor. Jake nodded understanding, and they were soon gliding low over the walls. Taking into account the need for haste and the way the engine was spluttering oil over his face, Rex made a very creditable landing,

6

and the machine rolled to a halt no more than fifty yards from the house.

Rex clambered from the cockpit, pulling his gauntlet from his right hand so that he could wipe the oil from his vision with the back of his wrist. A voice came from behind him.

'You've made some nasty tracks on the grass, Mr Sheridan.'

'Umm . . . pity,' he replied carelessly, more concerned with the state of his engine. 'I don't understand how we could have worked on this for most of the night, yet failed to spot a fault in the oil-feed.' He put a hand on the young man's shoulder as Jake clambered awkwardly to the ground. 'But it's no blame to you. *I* was checking the engine, if you remember.'

Totally engrossed in the complications of engineering, Rex had twice to be told that someone was approaching before he really heard and looked up. He promptly forgot all about oil-feeds and choked ducts. She was dressed in cornflower-blue summer voile, and her eyes were the same colour. They looked him over from head to foot in the most promising way, while her mouth curved into an admiring smile.

'Hallo,' greeted Rex, smiling back. 'Sorry about dropping from the skies unannounced. Couldn't help it, I'm afraid.'

'Do you make a habit of it?' she teased.

'Only when the angels down here are more beautiful than those up there.' He put out his hand. 'I'm Rex Sheridan.'

She wrinkled her nose at the sight of the oil blackening and greasing his fingers. 'I think I'd prefer a bow of introduction, Mr Sheridan.'

They both laughed, and he quickly wiped his hands on some rag from the cockpit. 'Sorry, one tends to become as oily as the engine. Don't ask me how.'

'Face too? Here, let me.' Taking the rag from his hand she stood close to him and began to wipe his cheeks and forehead. She smelt delicious, and her flaxen hair stirred in the warm breeze that touched her curls.

Rex did a quick mental sum. It would not get dark until nine or ten. He could stay for lunch *and* tea, with plenty of time for the return flight.

'Do you have to mend it right away?' she asked softly, concentrating on his chin now with tender ministration.

'Well, I . . .'

7

'Couldn't you come up to the house for a rest after that hazardous landing?'

He put on a suitably heroic expression. 'Well, I . . .'

'Perhaps have some luncheon.'

'Luncheon?' he repeated with just the right blend of dubious wistfulness.

'Please,' she begged persuasively. 'It's just a little chicken with macedoine of vegetables and baby potatoes, followed by a good Stilton and home-baked bread. Besides, Grandfather will be angry if I let you go off again without taking you up to meet him. He's fascinated by aviation.'

Grandfather, eh? No protective father to ask his intentions? He smiled. 'In that case, I can hardly refuse. After all, I *have* ploughed up his immaculate lawn somewhat.'

Turning to Jake, he said, 'It's a faulty non-return valve. Won't take you a moment to fix. Then I daresay you'll get a cup of tea and something to eat round at the back. Give the cook your best smile, but wipe all that oil from your face first, lad, or she'll think you've arrived to cut her throat.'

He began walking toward the house with the girl, leaving a bemused Jake to tinker with the engine. He pulled off his helmet and loosened the thick scarf.

'I'm not really dressed for luncheon,' he said.

The blue of her eyes deepened as they took in the unexpected rich red of his hair, the face she had so tenderly wiped free of oil, and the width of his shoulders.

'You look very nice, to me,' she commented, a dimple in her cheek appearing provocatively.

He studied her just as candidly. 'And so do you . . . Miss . . . ?'

'Amelia Merrydew . . . *Mrs,*' she told him wide-eyed.

It was an unexpected blow, but he tried not to show it. 'Is your husband also fascinated by aviation?'

Her fair curls bounced as she shook her head. 'Not in the least. He's something in the City.'

'I see.'

He wished he had stayed with the 'Princess' now. What he had seen as an entertaining afternoon was fast collapsing into several hours of probably lunatic questioning by a grandfather who was certain to be deaf, while a ravishing girl he was forbidden to touch sat beside him chattering about her respectable husband. But they

8

were almost at the house now, and there was an elderly bowed man waiting on the terrace for them.

'Your grandfather appears to be expecting us,' he said gloomily.

'That's my husband,' she confessed with a giggle. 'He is very deaf, and takes a long nap every afternoon.'

And that was why Rex was not back in time to greet his older brother when he arrived home just before dinner.

Roland Sheridan's progress through Tarrant Royal was more sedate than Rex's had been the previous day, because he was in the pony-and-trap Dawkins had taken to the station to meet his train. Branwell Sheridan's eldest son was destined to become a surgeon. There had hardly been a time in his memory when Roland had not been filled with this burning desire, and he had talked his father into allowing him entry into a teaching hospital on leaving public school. At twenty-three he had one more year of general medicine to do before starting on his specialist subject, and he had brought home a trunkful of books to study during the vacation.

Not that he intended spending more than an hour or two each week on the subject, because being at Tarrant Hall meant he could indulge his love of riding to his heart's content. In local and county circles Roland Sheridan was known as a very fine horseman and rider to hounds. His dashing style, his superb understanding of the relationship between horse and rider, and his blond good looks ensured that he was greatly admired and respected amongst the equestrian set.

Yet it was into horses' ears that he spoke of his innermost longings and emotions; never into those of his fellow men or women. His friends were not close friends, and girls found him no more than quietly polite. A few had found the combination of muscular prowess and personal shyness irresistibly attractive, so romance had blossomed. But the buds had never opened to full glory.

Apart from horses, he also had deep feelings about his brothers and his country. Having seen a great deal of the Continent, he was unshakably convinced that England was the greatest nation in the world. He loved every wall and hedgerow, every meadowlark and spring lamb, every ancient oak and sleepy village, every awesome cathedral and country church, every sprawling city and dusty highway. He would also claim the people of his homeland as the most honest hardworking stock one could find. He was equally loyal to his brothers, and would defend them with his life, if need be. If he had one serious fault it was that he was totally unforgiving if his trust and loyalty were betrayed. There were only two instances when this had happened, but the people concerned had never been given a second chance.

As Dawkins took the pony-and-trap through the approaches to the village at a spanking pace, Roland gazed around with pleasure at the green hills. It was here in this Dorset countryside that he most loved to ride, with the smell of wind-whipped trees filling his nostrils, and the thud of hooves on the rich green meadows filling his ears. Nothing could beat the man-horse relationship when both topped a hill and there was nothing in view but quiet, empty verdant countryside stretching as far as the eye could see. To Roland such moments were supreme and he looked forward to three months in which to enjoy them.

Progress through the village was spasmodic, since he stopped to chat to the Rector, Ted Peach, the blacksmith, and the landlord of the George and Dragon. So it was inevitable that he should tell Dawkins to pull up again when they approached the mansion with a tiny surgery attached and a long rambling garden, and he saw the daughter of the village doctor by the gate, cutting honeysuckle. She glanced up at his approach, and a surprising suggestion of a blush touched her cheeks when she saw who it was. They had known each other all their lives, yet even with this girl Roland was never generous with his private thoughts.

'Hallo, Marion,' he greeted, stepping from the trap and going across to lean on one arm outstretched against the rustic arch above the gate. 'The garden looks even more colourful this year than last. After the prize again?'

She smiled up at him with a shake of her head. 'You can't have noticed Mrs Hobley's wonderful delphiniums as you passed. They'll take a lot of beating.'

'How is your father?'

'Out delivering Mrs Baines' fifth. But she doesn't really need him. She has them so easily she could almost do the job herself.'

The discussion on a subject like childbirth caused Marion Deacon no embarrassment, because she helped her father in his surgery. When her mother had died very tragically two years before during a complicated multiple birth late in life, the doctor's daughter had left her nearby school to comfort her bereaved father. It had seemed natural for her to act as nurse and dispenser under his tuition, and her gentle nature seemed eminently suited for the cloistered life of the village which she loved. In crisp buttercup yellow blouse and long grey skirt she made a beautiful picture framed by an arch of creamy honeysuckle, and Roland smiled with pleasure.

'I can see you turning into a midwife before long,' he teased.

Before she could respond the three black labradors rushed round the corner of the house at that point, and raced to greet him with barks and flailing tails. Despite her order to get down, they still bounced up and down at the gate in excitement.

Laughing, Marion said, 'They never heed me, as you know. It takes Daddy to make them obedient.'

Looking up from fondling their sleek heads, Roland smiled. 'You spoil them, that's why. They know they'll always get a pat and a tit-bit from you, whatever they've done.'

'That's not true,' she protested. 'Anyway, how many times have I seen you give your horses a sugar lump and a pat of encouragement even after baulking at a hedge? Yes, and I once caught you kissing a horse, remember?'

He avoided her eyes and said offhandedly, 'That was years ago.'

'And you never do it now?' she teased.

'Shall you be riding with us in the morning?' he asked to change a subject he felt was becoming too personal. 'I'll look for you in the usual place.'

She shook her head. 'Damsel has gone lame.'

'I'll lend you Shuba,' he offered immediately. 'Be ready at seven and I'll bring her down for you.'

'That's extremely nice of you, Roland.'

'Not at all. That's what friends are for.'

Silence fell for a moment or two, then she said, 'Rex arrived in a cloud of exhaust yesterday. Daddy says he'll break his neck one of these days.'

He laughed at that. 'Not on your life! You know Rex. He has the luck of the Devil.'

'So he's always telling me. But he went off in that flying contraption of his this morning, and I haven't heard him come back yet.'

'That's nothing new. It's probably broken down again. Give me the horse any day. You know where you are with them.'

11

'You certainly do.' She put up a hand to push back a wisp of hair. 'I always feel presumptuous to dare ride beside Roland Sheridan.'

'Will you feel more at ease to ride beside Doctor Sheridan?'

'So long as I'm not too old to ride then,' she said with laughter in her eyes. 'It takes so long to become a top surgeon.'

Missing her teasing note he said seriously, 'I've brought some stuff home to study during the vac. I mean to pass the exams first time.'

'Daddy wants you to come to dinner soon. He's longing to talk to you about the new anaesthetic.'

He smiled. 'Are you sure it's not really about that new rifle he asked me to price for him in London?'

She grinned back. 'Yes, it is . . . but don't let him know I've told you.'

'All right. Give me a day or two to settle back, and we'll arrange an evening during our morning rides.'

She bent to stroke one of the dogs which was nuzzling her skirt. 'I thought you might have travelled down today with Chris.'

'He's gone to the Greek Islands with a schoolfriend and his family, and won't be here for another month.'

She looked up quickly, rosy from bending over the dog. 'Oh! Priddy didn't say anything about it when I saw her yesterday.'

'She didn't know. You know what Chris is like—scribbled a postcard at the last minute, which I only got yesterday.'

'I suppose he was too full of excitement over the trip.'

He nodded. 'The family won't see much of him, I suspect. He'll probably wander off on his own to chatter to the Greeks, little thinking that the average Greek peasant won't understand the language of Socrates.'

'Poor Chris! It must be terrible to be so brainy.'

It surprised him. 'Why?'

She shrugged. 'With everyone else so dull, in comparison, he must feel very lonely, at times.'

'Oh . . . I don't think he minds. Books are the only friends he needs.'

'Some people might think that very sad.'

Still surprised, he shook his head. 'He doesn't.'

But the thought stayed with him when he reluctantly left her and carried on up to the house. What a strange thing for her to say! His brother had any number of friends. Yet, on reflection, he had to admit that Chris somehow drew people to him like a magnet attracted iron filings, yet managed to remain complete without them. Was that what she had meant? If so, she had mistaken aloofness for loneliness.

Tarrant Hall looked symbolic of all Roland loved as the trap came in sight of it at the end of a long curving uphill drive bordered by horsechestnut trees. Square, crenellated, covered in ivy, its stone walls hardly touched by the two centuries that had passed since it was built, the house was part of England's wild and colourful history. Roland regretted he could not claim Sheridan ownership back through the ages, for his grandfather had bought it only a few years before his death. But the house, with its advantageous view of the surrounding area, had been built on the site of an old Norman castle by one of England's eighteenth-century noblemen, and had been sold only when the line ended back in 1888. The air of past grandeur it exuded thrilled Roland and made him thankful he was the eldest son, who would inherit it by right. His brothers treated it as just a home; he loved it as part of a national heritage of which he was inordinately proud.

The dogs rushed to greet him when he entered, but sank obediently onto their haunches when he ordered them to sit.

'Hallo, Priddy,' he said warmly to the woman who had practically brought them all up, and kissed her cheek with gentle affection. 'How are you?'

'Fancy asking that when here I am plumper and rosier than ever,' she chided fondly. 'But I'm never better than when you boys are home. The house wakes up during the holidays.'

He smiled. 'Even a house can't sleep when Rex is in it.' Looking round to old Minks and shaking him firmly by the hand, he added, 'I saw Miss Deacon on the way up, and she said my brother went out in 'Princess' earlier and hasn't yet returned.'

'That's right, sir,' wheezed Minks. 'Break his neck one of these days, he will, with those noisy dirty machines of his.' Then he softened his remark with, 'Do you think he's all right, Mr Roland?'

'Oh, yes. He's probably got his head inside the engine and forgotten where he is and what time it is. Better hold dinner until he gets back.'

'Meantime, I'll send up a nice tray of tea and some rock cakes,' said Priddy. 'You must be parched after your journey.'

'Mr Roland is a fully-grown gentleman, Mrs Prideaux,' reprimanded Minks in his haughtiest manner, 'not a schoolboy like Mr Christopher. I shall take up a decanter and glasses.'

'At this early hour!' exclaimed the plump woman, registering horror. 'You certainly will *not!* I'm sure there's enough temptation in London and other places he has to visit, without putting it in his way at home.'

'I could certainly go a cup of tea . . . and perhaps you'd bring up the decanter later on, when Rex arrives,' said Roland, the eternal peacelover, knowing the pair squabbled all the time over their areas of responsibility for their master's sons.

'Very well,' said Minks, slightly mollified. 'Do you wish to see Mr Jeffries tonight, sir?'

'No, no. Tomorrow will do. He's been managing the estate without my interference since I was last at home. I'm sure another day will make no difference.' He caught sight of the great open fireplace which always contained flaming logs in winter, and walked across to it with interest. 'Ah, I see you got Forbes in from the village to replace some of that crumbling stonework.'

' 'Course, Mr Roland,' Priddy told him indignantly. 'And he swept the chimney at the same time.'

'Good.' Spotting the refectory table at the far end of the hall, he moved to it. 'My word, you've got a lovely shine on that now. Did the new polish I brought from London do the trick?'

'No, sir,' Minks told him with aged disdain. 'Almost took the surface off, that stuff did. *That* shine was achieved by using Ted Peach's dubbin and a lot of elbow grease.'

Suitably chastened Roland moved on to comment on other things about the house that had been changed or improved upon according to his instructions at Easter. Then he stood for a while at the large recessed window-nook to admire the gardens at the rear, now in their full beauty.

So it was fully half an hour after his arrival that he finally went up to his room to take off the fawn formal suit in which he had made the journey from London. Priddy's tea was soon drunk, but the decanter remained full. Roland was not a drinking man. As a boy, he had seen a rider, drunk as a lord, take a thoroughbred over a difficult jump and break the poor creature's back. He had never forgotten the sight, nor the lesson it had taught him. Rex hardly touched drink because he said it impaired his judgment in machines, and Chris was too young, at eighteen, to consider the matter. Besides, the boy had been known to let entire meals cool and congeal, forgotten by him as he studied a book. He was only likely to get drunk on words.

Before dressing for dinner Roland made his way downstairs again and round to the stables—his home-from-home when at Tarrant Hall. The Sheridan stables were extensive, the old buildings now only used for storage and tack with new stables added to house the large number of horses. All the Sheridans rode, of course, and each brother had been given two mounts by his father. Rex had improved on his two more recently, but Chris still rode his ageing geldings on those occasions when the other two dragged him forcibly from his books.

But Roland had bought three thoroughbreds for himself, and they were housed in luxurious stalls designed to prevent any possible danger of the highly-strung stallions injuring themselves. In addition, there were Branwell's horses and several for the use of guests. This meant employing a staff of grooms and stable-hands as great as that in the house itself—all for a family only there for a matter of a few weeks at a time.

Ned Peabody, the Head Groom, greeted Roland with genuine pleasure as he walked in. 'Seen you arrive, sir. Now these varmints'll get some *real* exercise.'

Immediately absorbed in inspecting the gleaming flanks of the roan he had named after the village, Roland murmured, 'I'm sure you give them all the fuss and appreciation they deserve. How is the strained fetlock now? Did it respond to treatment?'

'Nary a sign of it since you went back, but there's trouble, guvnor. That mare down the end is givin' 'im 'ow's yer father these past few days. I tried all sorts to keep 'er smell from 'is nostrils, but weren't no good. 'E's right randy, an' no mistake. You'd best send 'im to stud, or 'e'll 'ave this lot down and mount that old granny when I aren't looking. I'm sure as you don't want no hack foals all weak in the joints—cos that's what you'll get.'

'Mmm, he does look restless,' agreed Roland, watching the shifting hooves of the animal thoughtfully. 'All right. Freddy Cambourne wants a thoroughbred for his mare. Surrey is about as far as I'm prepared to send him. I'll fix it up and let you know the arrangements for getting there.'

A whinny greeted him as he passed to the next, a grey with

15

strong shoulders, and he stroked the creature's nose whilst whispering endearments in the pricked ears. It did not embarrass him, in front of Ned, for the little man with the creased brown face did the same, in rougher manner. In the warmth of the stables with the familiar smell of horses inciting his senses, Roland lost all track of time as he walked around looking at the animals, discussing their health and diet, and outlining his plans for the holiday stretching ahead of him when he could devote most of his time to the love of his life.

He was just telling Ned that Miss Deacon was going to ride Shuba for the next few mornings, when he was brought from his equestrian world by a growing roar overhead that set all the horses fidgeting and snorting with unease. He looked ruefully at the other man.

'When my brother has qualified as an engineer, his first task, at my request, is to invent a *silent* aeroplane.' They began walking together to the stable door. 'But I suspect he'd claim there'd be no excitement in that. It's the volume of noise that provides the thrill.'

The brothers discussed that, and many other things dear to their hearts during dinner, but it was not until they were strolling in the garden afterward that Rex said, 'I take it Father doesn't intend paying us a visit while we're all at home.'

Roland shook his head. 'I called in at the office before I left London, as I usually do, and Peterson had just returned from Madeira. He told me Father was not too well again.' He gave his brother a candid look. 'You know what that means!'

Rex sighed and stretched out his hand to pluck a red carnation, which he fixed in his buttonhole with detached movements. 'Mother has been dead for fifteen years, and he is still suffering.'

'Only because he indulges his grief,' Roland said angrily.

'Oh, I don't know,' Rex mused, as they turned onto the path that led to the sunken garden overlooking the village below. 'Maybe he really can't forget her. Throughout history men have been known to love a woman to destruction.'

'Don't you mean "distraction"?'

'No, I don't. Incomprehensible though it seems to me, it happens. And men are ruined by it. I don't know why Father hasn't killed himself long ago.'

Roland was shocked and halted on the path, where the perfume of night-scented stock was almost overpowering. 'That's a terrible thing to say!'

'Is it?' Rex halted, too, and turned his thin mobile face toward him in the fading light. 'I'm sure I'd rather not live at all, if I had to live in darkness, as he seems to do.'

'But what about us?' protested Roland strongly.

'What about us? We've seen him so seldom, it would have made no difference if we'd never have seen him at all. Be honest, old chap.'

'All right, if honesty is what you want,' came his angry response. 'This house and estate could be going to rack and ruin, the staff of the London office could be forging the accounts, the wholesalers could be robbing him, and his three sons could be going to the dogs while he sits out there in Madeira in a chateau he has turned into a shrine. He has no sense of responsibility, no feeling of duty, no affection for anyone but a ghost. It's morbid, in my opinion. Do you truly think that's what Mother would have wanted?'

'I don't know,' came the gentle response. 'I was only five when she died. I hardly remember what she looked like, much less judge what she would have wanted.'

Roland turned away and walked on to the end of the path. From there, it was possible to see the glow of lamps within the cottages down in the village, dotted about the haze-filled valley with welcoming familiarity. Rising up was the damp, dewy scent of lush meadows full of buttercups and bright dandelions. Crickets were beginning to shrill from all over the darkening hills, and from the spinney above the church came the bark of a dog-fox. It was taken up by several domestic dogs lying on their front-doorsteps in the blessed cool of approaching night, but their exchange was short-lived. It had been a working day for most of them, and weary heads were heavy on weary paws. The door of the George and Dragon opened and shut as another thirsty man entered, allowing a snatch of piano music to escape. Young Bill Bishop was home on leave and trying to persuade the yarning yokels to break into song. He would not succeed. Men who had been working their bodies hard since sun-up, worked their tongues even harder when they got together of an evening with a pipe and a drink.

Roland felt his anger almost as a pain in his throat. These people were the salt of the earth; the village a monument to a way of life. From where he stood he surveyed half a county. Men had stood in that same spot centuries ago to defend it from invaders; others had watched the plough and the grazing sheep, knowing the land was rich and productive. Squires and yeomen had taken pride in this land, putting the sweat of toil or the gold of wealth into it making it what it was now. How dare his father turn his back on it, to live in some primitive Portuguese island whose volcanic soil had swallowed the bones of his wife a decade and a half ago?

A hand fell on his shoulder as Rex halted beside him to look down on Tarrant Royal. 'What you feel for all this, is probably what he felt for her. Who knows? But you more than compensate for his neglect. They are all aware of that.'

'I hope so,' he said reflectively, taking a last look at the bewitching sight below before turning to face his brother in the dusk. 'But I can't compensate for his paternal neglect. Young Chris has just walked off with the classics prize, the senior languages award, the Fairley scholarship for Greek and Latin, and the highest marks for English and French medieval literature ever gained by a pupil of the school, and Father was not there to see him receive them. I had important exams on that date, and couldn't deputize on that occasion,' he finished bitterly.

'I went along.'

Roland was surprised. '*You* went? Don't tell me Chris actually sat down and wrote you a letter about it.'

'Of course not. A friend of mine at Caius has a younger brother at Charterhouse, too. He told me the details . . . and I couldn't let the poor blighter have honours showered on him with no one there to applaud his hour of glory.'

Warm affection banished his earlier anger. 'Trust you not to let him down.'

Rex grinned. 'It gave all the matrons in flowered hats a hell of a shock when I roared into the quad on my machine. It was worth the day out just to see their faces.'

Roland laughed. 'I bet all the other boys would have preferred an oil-smeared brother in stained breeches and a leather jacket to their immaculately-dressed parents. Still, good thing Chris has now left the school. Manners would have thought your arrival frightfully infra dig, and favoured our brother with his opinions of his family.'

'A fat lot Chris would have cared. His head is constantly in the clouds.'

They began walking back to the house. 'We'll have to get him outdoors as much as possible this holiday,' Roland said. 'Once he gets to Cambridge in September, he'll have as much studying as even he could wish. He ought to relax and enjoy himself.'

'All right. I'll drag him out by his ear for a short spin now and again, if you'll tie him on a horse occasionally,' agreed Rex good-humouredly. 'But it won't make an atom of difference. I'll wager he's walking around the Greek Islands thinking of Aristotle and not even noticing the sultry peasant maidens with their inviting eyes.'

But Christopher Sheridan was not on the Greek Islands.

2

ONLY AS the train pulled into the little country station with its white-painted fence and beautifully tended rose beds did it occur to Chris that he had not let anyone know he was coming. It was a nuisance, for he would now have to walk the six miles to the village, leaving his baggage to be picked up by Dawkins the following day.

'Ahternoon, Mr Christopher,' greeted old Carter, waving his green flag and holding out the other hand for tickets. 'Surprised to see *you*, I be. Mr Roland come through day before lahst, and said you be off to forrin' parts like til nex month. Din you go then?'

'Apparently not,' said Chris, used to the old man's quaint way of reasoning. 'This looks very much like Greater Tarrant station, and you appear to be speaking English.'

The station-master, remarkably like a shorter version of Edward the Seventh with his moustache, full beard, and heavy stomach, gazed at Chris in bewilderment for a moment or two. Then he laughed.

'Oh . . . ar. You be 'ome, all right, sir.' He followed Chris to the exit gate, carrying one of the heavy battered suitcases. 'Dawkins baint be 'ere yet, else I'd've knowd you be comin'.'

'No one knows I'm coming.'

'Eh? 'Ow's that then?'

'I forgot to tell them.' Chris humped the case he was carrying onto the rack alongside several milk-churns and a square parcel covered in sacking. 'I'll have to leave my stuff to be collected. The trunk is coming freight, so Dawkins can pick them all up when it arrives.'

Shutting the gate behind him in dutiful fashion, Carter walked across the station forecourt beside the youthful passenger until they reached the road. There would not be another train through for two and a half hours, so he could take time off for a gossip.

'What you could do with is for Mr Rex to go pahst on that there motor-bicycle. He could be up to the house before you could say "mangle-wurzels" and send Dawkins down.' He leant on the sturdy gate-post, also painted white. 'Ted Caddywould was in two days pahst, and said close on all Tarrant Royal turned out to see 'im go by on that danged thing. Course, 'e doan go by 'ere, so I din see it, like. But nex day, there goes that arioplane right over my 'ead and off into the distance with no end of a danged racket. Break 'is neck one of these days, mark my words!'

Chris shook his head. 'There's no more likelihood of that than of Roland breaking his on a horse. They both know what they're doing. But you'll have to get used to aeroplanes, you know. This is the mechanical age. Before too long, everyone will be travelling about the country in their own motor cars, and going abroad in passenger aircraft. Locomotives will become obsolete.'

Carter wagged his head. 'Baint no use using them Greek words to me, Mr Christopher.'

Chris patiently explained that the railway system would gradually be used less and less as other forms of transport improved.

Carter wagged his head again. 'No, no, sir, that's never likely. Without trains we'd be back to them stage-coaches, and such. Can't never see that 'appening, not in a month of Sundays. Stands to reason.'

'Railways are not the ideal system, even you must see that,' went on Chris seriously. 'It's entirely dependent on a complex network of tracks with intersections built in areas where the ter-

20

rain allows it, not where it is desirable. It's colossally expensive to build, involves spoiling the countryside and filling it with smoke, and has a limited convenience. On the other hand, the motor car takes one from door to door and runs along roads already laid; the aeroplane needs no tracks or roads, and can land anywhere there is a piece of flat land. Either one of those systems would have taken me to Tarrant Hall, and I wouldn't now be faced with a six-mile walk.'

Carter, by now completely out of his depth, decided it was impossible to *gossip* with the youngest Sheridan boy. Everyone around knew he was a walking brain-box. Carter felt uncomfortable having to show he did not understand one word the lad said. He straightened up from his pose against the gate-post and began moving back to his beloved station.

'If you takes my advice, Mr Christopher, you'll jest pop in the Punch and Judy for a cup o' tea and a nice buttered bun afore you sets out. A young gentleman like you 'oos bin journeying needs a bit o' summat to keep 'im going. You'm fully as big as they brothers o' yours, and you still at school.'

'Not any longer, Carter. I go up to Cambridge in September.'

'My, my! That's one o' they uneeversities, baint it?'

Chris nodded. 'The same one Rex attended. But it was quite wrong for him. He's come down and fixed up a quasi-apprenticeship with an engineering firm that will fulfil his potential much better.'

'Will it now?' marvelled Carter, having no idea what the boy meant. 'Well, I'll see to them bags and the trunk, never fear.' Then, as he began turning away again, a thought struck him. 'If 'tweren't for trains, that trunk o'yourn wouldn't be arriving, now would it?'

Chris laughed. 'I see I'll never convert you to the superior economics of alternative transportation.'

'Aye, that you won't,' mumbled Carter to himself as he shuffled back across the courtyard, 'whatever in tarnation *that* is.' He re-entered his little kingdom through the swing-gate and sniffed his prize roses appreciatively. 'Arioplanes and motor cars,' he grumbled to himself. 'Noisy, unreliable danged things! You gets a train now, crossing the fields in a long line o' smart carridges, with a great green and black engine at front sending smoke flying out like a maid's dark hair. Now, that's a sight, that is. And 'er

21

arrives on time and leaves on time, no matter if it's Greater Tarrant ter Dorchester, or it's Land's End ter John o' Groats.' He turned to gaze at the track running away into the distance, seeming to shimmer in the afternoon heat. 'Ar, and she carries a danged sight more passengers than that there motor-bicycle or an arioplane,' he concluded with satisfaction. Then he cast a look at the tall well-built figure in grey flannels and striped blazer walking straight past the Punch and Judy Tea Rooms. ' 'Ansome lad like you ought ter be rolling maids in the 'ay on a lovely day such as this, stead o' talking a lot o' Greek nonsense nobbut another brain-box would understand.'

Christopher Sheridan would have had no difficulty finding maids to roll in the hay, had he wanted to. Already six feet tall, like his brothers, his outstanding good looks were completed by fair springy hair, a fresh-complexioned sensitive face, a firm mouth, and a build that suggested a sportsman rather than a scholar. But it was his eyes that made him the handsomest of the three Sheridans. Dark-lashed, almost violet-blue, they were wickedly attractive in a man. But the muscular frame was more often than not hunched over a desk or table, and those striking eyes were covered by tortoiseshell-rimmed spectacles that enabled them to see those things in which he was intensely interested. Maids in haystacks did not come into that category.

Two miles along the road Chris remembered the Punch and Judy and wished he had gone in for some tea. He had no money to pay for it—he had spent his last half-crown on a book at Waterloo—but Betty Perkins, who served in the tea-rooms, would have let him have it 'on tick'. She always did. But he had been engrossed in extending his theory on the future of public transport and had walked right down the High Street, through the alley beside the Plough and Wheatsheaf, and onto the road to Tarrant Royal without being aware of having done so. He consoled himself with the thought that Priddy would soon produce a large and satisfying tea, despite his unexpected arrival.

Another mile on he came to the lower stretch of the river that ran through Tarrant Royal, and left the lane by the bridge to scramble down to the water. With the temperature in the high seventies, the three-mile walk had made him uncomfortably hot and thirsty. But the river was always low in mid-summer and he had to go almost under the bridge to find a pool of any depth. He took off his blazer, unknotted his tie and rolled it up to tuck neatly into one pocket, then knelt down, put his spectacles carefully on the ground beside him, and cupped the clear refreshing water in his hands to drink.

He was bending over for the third time when he heard splashing and a small cry of surprise. Looking around too quickly, he over-balanced and fell sideways, half into the water and half on the grass of the river-bank. There was more splashing, nearer this time, and he pushed himself back onto his knees, reaching auto-matically for his spectacles. They were not where he expected them to be, so he groped on the damp grass while he tried to make out the features of what appeared to be a girl wearing a blue bell. Kneeling there, he peered up at the blur of a face against a blur of trees. But it would all remain a blur until lenses put it all into perspective for him.

'Are my spectacles anywhere around?' he asked her. 'I can't see much without them, I'm afraid.'

A few small splashes, and she was holding them out toward his hand. He must have knocked them into the water as he fell, for they were wet.

'Thanks awfully,' he said, pulling his handkerchief out to wipe them as he got to his feet. 'You jolly well startled me, you know. I didn't expect anyone else to be here.'

'Neither did I,' said the girl breathlessly. 'Least of all you.'

It was not a blue bell that she wore, but a blue cotton dress she held bunched around her knees while she paddled in the river. She still clutched it there as she gazed at him in the strangest way, as if she had seen something startling. He could not think why. They had known each other all their lives.

'Oh, it's you, Marion.'

'You're wet through, Chris,' she said, still breathless, for some unaccountable reason.

'I fell in the river, if you remember,' he pointed out. 'That's what comes of prancing about like a naiad.'

'Like a what?'

'A Greek nymph—a sort of water-creature. Except that naiads don't end up panting like you are. How long have you been here?'

'Your shirt is sticking to you. Why don't you take it off?'

'So are my trousers. I can't take them off, can I?' he said with rough impatience.

'What are you doing here, Chris?'

He pulled the blazer up from the ground and began brushing grass from his damp knees. 'The same as you. Trying to get cool.'

'I meant what are you doing at home. Roland said you'd gone away with a friend to some islands.'

'Milos, Paros and Naxos, actually. The trip fell through due to this Balkans scare.'

'What's that?'

He looked at her in surprise. 'Don't you really know?'

'If it doesn't concern housekeeping, medical knowledge or Tarrant Royal, I don't.'

'Well, for years the Austrians have been looking for expansion in the Balkans, but have been hampered by the growing revolt of the enormous number of Slavs living unwillingly in Austria-Hungary. Many people suspect the Mayerling affair was not just a *crime passionel,* but political murder. So of course, with Hungary agitating for self-government and . . .' he broke off, realising she was gazing at him in such a faraway manner she could not possibly be taking in what he was saying, and finished, in an abrupt manner, with, 'Codrington's father is with the Foreign Office and naturally could not leave the country when Serbia is sending Russia an SOS for help against an imminent Austrian attack. War in the Balkans now could prove calamitous.'

Marion was quiet for a moment, then said in a strange kind of voice, 'You look awfully different without your spectacles, Chris.'

He thought it a remarkably silly comment to make in the middle of a conversation about the European struggle for dominance, and wondered what on earth had come over her. She was usually quite sensible. Despite the heat of the afternoon he now found it chilly in his wet clothes beneath the shade of the trees. Deciding he had had enough of her company, he turned away up the bank by the bridge.

'I'd better go,' he said over his shoulder. 'These things'll probably dry out during the walk home.'

'Chris . . . wait,' she cried, scrambling up the bank after him. 'The pony-and-trap is on the far side of the bridge. I'm on my way back to the village.'

'Good-oh,' he said in relief, then looked pointedly at her bare feet and legs. 'You haven't been driving around like that, have you?'

She let the long skirt fall swiftly, and he was surprised to see her cheeks grow pink. 'My shoes and stockings are back there on the bank.'

He held out his blazer. 'Hang on to this while I go and get them. You'll take too long.'

Jogging energetically helped keep the chill at bay, and he jumped tree-trunks that had fallen, and dodged bushes with the nonchalance of someone used to long, testing cross-country runs around Charterhouse School. After a while, he came out of his thoughts of the Greek islands he had hoped to visit and remembered what he was supposed to be doing. She could not have left her things this far from the road, surely? Coming to a halt in an empty clearing, he frowned. Although his thoughts had been miles away, he would have seen shoes and stockings on the path if he had passed them. Sighing he turned back. He could have been well on his way to the village, by now.

Then she was there, running toward him, her hair falling from its pins and her face pinker than ever.

'Are you certain you left them along here?' he asked.

Arriving before him she panted, 'You ran off before I had time to tell you.'

'Tell me what?'

'They're on the other bank.'

'So that's why I didn't see them,' he commented mildly, pleased that his habitual forgetfulness had not played tricks on him, this time. 'I thought this was a jolly long way to come just to cool your feet in the water.'

'You do run fast,' she said, impressed.

'Well, I'm not running all the way back to the bridge and then down the other side, I can tell you,' he said firmly. 'There's a tree overhanging the water just back there. I'll swing across on it.'

'You'll fall in.'

'No, I won't.'

'Yes, you will.'

He moved off to where the sturdy limb of a tree stretched out almost to the other bank, then turned to find her behind him. 'When I'm across, trot along level with me until we reach your shoes. I'll toss them over to you.'

'They'll drop into the water.'

In the act of preparing to jump for a handhold on the branch, he looked down at her impatiently. 'You don't have much faith in my ability, do you?'

Her cheeks really flamed then. 'It's just that I . . . I've never seen you do . . . well, you've always been the quiet one.'

'I'll do it quietly, then. Will that give you more confidence?'

Jumping up he grasped the limb and began swinging his way out over the river, thinking to himself that the ancient crossings of the River Styx would have been far more dramatic than this. He could have waded to the far bank, of course, but that would have made him wetter than he already was. So he moved along, hand-over-hand, to the edge of the branch several yards from the bank. Then he swung back and forth in increasing arcs to give himself the momentum to jump onto dry land. Once there, he trotted back toward the road, finally coming upon the shoes and discarded white stockings. Stuffing them into the toes of the shoes, he glanced across to where Marion was just arriving on the opposite bank. One after the other he tossed them across to her, then sauntered back to the road, where he found Dr Deacon's pony-and-trap beneath the shade of the trees.

He leant against the little cart while he took off his spectacles that had steamed up, and was in the middle of polishing them with his handkerchief when Marion materialised mistily before him.

'You were absolutely splendid,' she gasped, out of breath.

He peered at her shaking his head. 'No one achieves anything with a negative attitude like yours, Marion. Positive thinking has been behind every great personality through the ages. Where would Caesar or Alexander have been if they had feared failure all the time? Would Hannibal ever have crossed the Alps? What about Stephenson and Blériot? They set their minds on what they wanted, then went out and got it. And I can tell you Franz Josef is certainly thinking positive, right at the moment. And in case you don't know who he is,' he added thinking of her earlier remarks on the Balkans, as he put his spectacles back on, 'he is the Emperor of Austria-Hungary, who is set on taking Serbia to add to his Empire.'

But she was looking at him in an almost trance-like manner, and he doubted if she had heard a word he said. He climbed into the trap ready to leave. If the man had his way, she would certainly know the name of Franz Josef before long. The whole world would.

The inhabitants of Tarrant Royal were not worrying about an Austrian Emperor, or his possible invasion of Serbia. It was the day of the annual cricket-match against Tarrant Maundle, their arch rivals. This year's event was extra-special, it being the twenty-fifth occasion that the two villages had hammered it out with bat-and-ball.

Admittedly, the first few meetings had been ramshackle affairs with their own rules and incomplete teams. On one famous occasion, the blacksmith's dog had been put in the outfield against Tarrant Maundle, and the fact that he had caught one man out still rankled between the two villages, who argued incessantly over the validity of it. But the last ten years had seen the event grow into a match of skill with strict adherence to M.C.C. rules, both sides stretching their village boundaries to the limit in order to obtain the best players.

Tarrant Maundle was out for blood this year, having been soundly beaten three times running mainly due to the inclusion in the Tarrant Royal team of Rex Sheridan, a player whose reckless style had rival captains perplexed as to how best to place their field when he was batting. Rumours had filtered through to Tarrant Royal that their rivals had a new star player, not only capable of bowling balls even Rex Sheridan could not hit, but who could knock up a high score quicker than any man in Dorset. Spies had been sent to the village fifteen miles away, but they had reported failure. Tarrant Maundle's lips were sealed, but their smiles were triumphant.

Up at Tarrant Hall there had been as much speculation as anywhere. Roland, who was to present the cup, was a steady reliable player himself, but believed one Sheridan on the team was enough. He felt villagers should represent the village, not the sons of the Squire *en masse*—Chris could wield a bat when forced to —and genuinely hoped to be able to present the trophy to Ted Peach, their own captain.

Rex took the match as it came, like everything else he did. He was not so fiercely intent on home victory as his older brother; it was the fun, the general comradeship, and the sheer enjoyment of whacking a cricket-ball into all the most inaccessible places that made it a good day for him. He laughed at the subterfuge of the opposing 'star' player, good-naturedly allowed himself to be bullied into putting in a bit of practice during the week leading up to the match, smiled saucily at all the girls who gathered to watch him, and bought the whole team a round in the George and Dragon afterward.

Chris was pressured by his brothers into helping erect the marquees, protesting mildly that he might be sound in wind and limb, as they claimed, but that he really had other things to do in his room. However, he dutifully held stay-lines and thumped wooden pegs with wooden mallets for half an hour on the evening before the match, then felt he had earned his escape back to the Hall. But he would not have missed the match for anything, because Rex was playing in it. So he was there promptly at eleven that morning, sprawled in a deck-chair, with a book of French poems in his pocket for when his brother was not on the field.

But it was not until well into the afternoon that he was able to delve into it. Tarrant Maundle were all out, and the home team had just begun batting with Ted Peach and young Bill Bishop. Knowing Rex usually came in at number four, Chris abandoned his chair for a while and flopped onto his stomach on the sun-warmed grass, opened the book, and rested his chin on his hands as he translated the beautiful stanzas.

'Hallo, Chris.'

He squinted sideways at the girl who had seated herself on the grass beside him. 'I thought you were helping with the luncheons.'

'We've finished. Everything's washed up and stacked away ready for tonight.'

'Good-oh,' he murmured turning back to his book.

'You can't do that.'

'Can't do what?' He was finding it difficult to think of suitable phraseology for two of the verses, and wished she would keep quiet while he grappled with it.

'You can't read while the match is on.'

'Negative attitude again, Marion?' he taunted without looking at her.

'What is it, anyway?'

'Take a look?' he invited, settling his chin more comfortably on his hands as he frowned over the literal translation versus the poetic one.

There was a waft of some kind of perfume as she leant closer, and her smooth brown arm was suddenly warm against his own

28

covered in thick fair hairs. The contact made him turn his face up to find she was not looking at the book, at all. It disturbed him, such scrutiny. It was as if she was intruding into his thoughts. Yet he suddenly found the translation of the difficult passage so simple, it seemed incredible that he had been puzzled by it.

'Tell me what the book is about,' she prompted softly.

'You wouldn't understand it.'

'Negative attitude, Chris?'

Her teasing words were accompanied by a startling look which made her eyes shine with something that was stronger than mere intrusion into his thoughts. It suggested she was capable of taking them over.

'They're French poems.'

'What kind of poems?'

'About love,' he admitted with ridiculous reluctance.

'Read me one.'

'I can't do that while the match is on,' he retaliated, sitting up. 'You just said so.'

'Is it because you don't know French well enough?'

'Of course not. I just don't know enough about . . .' He broke off feeling foolish. How could he explain that in order to translate works of passion and sexual desire well, one had to be able to understand the mind and emotions of the writer? In English, it was clear enough, in a foreign language the symbolism of certain words was prone to be elusive.

A burst of applause heralded the dismissal of Ted Peach, and Chris looked across to see his brother in cream shirt and flannels, his auburn hair glowing, walk out of the tiny pavilion with pads strapped to his calves, and a bat in his hand.

'There's Rex coming in as number three,' he exclaimed with enthusiasm. 'That must be because Phil Meakins hurt his hand earlier on.' He linked his arms round his bent knees, all set to enjoy the game once more. 'Just watch him show Maundle the stuff he's made of! That new prep-school sports master they boasted of so loudly might have scored a correct and unimaginative sixty-six, but Rex'll have them all chasing about like a pack of hounds faced with two dozen foxes all at once.'

'You think a lot of Rex, don't you?'

He turned in surprise. 'Doesn't everyone? He's one of the best people I know.'

'Daddy says he'll break his neck one of these days.'

Laughing he turned back just in time to see his brother's muscular arms swing the bat at the first ball and thump it way over the top of the George and Dragon. A great cheer went up from Tarrant Royal spectators, and it was the start of forty-five minutes of fun, excitement and thrills, as Rex cavaliered his way to a score of eighty-one, grinning with pleasure and winking at the girls who shrieked his name in worshipping encouragement.

Meanwhile, the sun had vanished behind ominous clouds, and Chris reflected that it was almost as if Thor had been waiting for the right moment, when the storm broke only moments after Rex had been caught out and walked from the field. The rain began suddenly and heavily, catching everyone unprepared and scattering them in all directions seeking shelter.

Chris got to his feet hurriedly, unbuttoning the front of his shirt to put the leather-bound book inside for protection. Then, his arm was seized as Marion said, 'Come on! Home's nearest for us.'

They ran the few yards to the edge of the green, across the narrow road, and up the long front path to the Doctor's house, heads bent against the beating rain as they ran. Marion flung open the door of the tiny waiting-room, and they both tumbled in.

'Ooh,' gasped Marion in laughing manner. 'Why is rain always so wet?' Pushing back her wet hair, she threw him a look. 'Don't answer that, Chris, *please.*'

'I wasn't going to,' he said in surprise.

'That would have been very unusual, then.' She swung round, shaking the skirt of her pretty green and white dress. 'I'll fetch us some towels.'

He carefully took the book from inside his shirt and wiped the leather lovingly with his handkerchief. Then she was back with a soft yellow towel for him.

'Thanks.' He put the book on the window-seat, then took off his spectacles to lay beside it while he rubbed at his wet face and hair.

'What an end to the day,' said Marion from a few feet away. 'I shouldn't think it'll clear in time for it to continue. What will Roland do—give them half a cup each?' She laughed in a high, unusual manner. 'All that fuss for nothing!'

He looked up in her vague direction and said, 'I should think they'll finish it some other time—tomorrow evening, perhaps. It's too important an occasion to leave it like this.' He reached out to the window-seat. 'But it won't stop tonight's bean-feast and the concert from going ahead, as planned.' The book was there, but nothing else. 'I say, Marion, have you seen my spectacles?'

There was a curious silence, then she said, 'Yes, here they are.'

He put out his hand. 'Thanks.'

Another silence, then a soft teasing, 'Come and get them.'

As sudden as a lightning strike outside that storm-battered house, a feeling of immense excitement rushed through him and was gone as quickly as it had come. But it left him intensely aware of the fact that, without those lenses, he could see no more of her than an indistinct pale shape ahead. How far ahead he could not even estimate . . . nor whether she really did have them.

'This isn't much of a joke,' he said angrily. 'Everything is just a blur.'

'You really ought to have them, in that case.'

'Well, then!' He held out his hand again.

'You come here!'

That suggestion of command, the strange breathless note in her voice, the knowledge that they were the only ones in the house and that all the time she withheld his aid to clear sight he was somehow in her power, sent the heady painful excitement rushing through him again, this time to stay. He began to move cautiously forward to where she stood, avoiding the outlines of chairs or the table containing magazines. But she was either further away than he thought, or she was backing as he advanced. The thought angered him, yet increased the excitement until his heartbeat raced and his thighs felt weak.

The darkness of a storm in full rage outside gave the room a secretive dimness that was no help to him whatever and, after a few moments, he knew she must be deliberately evading him the minute he drew near. Swallowing he tried to control his erratic breathing before moving off again towards the pale outline of her dress. It had developed into a game of pursuit and escape that was unbelievably thrilling the longer it continued. He now walked with his arms outstretched, feeling for her, impatient to catch and imprison her. Then what would he do? His heartbeat was now a heavy thud, and he felt hot all over.

She had cut off her own retreat by backing into a corner when his hand finally came into contact with her warm arm. A gasp betrayed her own heightened excitement and, as he slid his trembling fingers along her smooth skin, she pressed against him to touch her mouth against his.

It was such a soft, moist, warm touch, such an alien shock experience, he lost his head. Trapping her against the wall with the whole of his body, he embarked on something he had not known he could do so very easily. But kissing her only once like that was not enough, so he did it several times, his head pounding more with her every gasp. Then, obeying an instinct stronger than clear thought, his hand moved down to the soft mounds pressing against his chest bared by the open shirt, and his palm circled on them until their centres became hard and thrusting against the thin cotton.

By then, his own condition had become so unbearably painful he could stand it no longer. Breaking away from her he stumbled through the furniture toward the door, knowing his peace and isolation had been shattered by something he would be unable to ignore from that moment on.

Once in the garden, he stood in the deluge growing more and more saturated, while the fire inside him was gradually doused.

With the outcome of the match in suspension, the atmosphere during the massive supper and subsequent concert was high-spirited and relaxed, each side boasting unmaliciously of certain victory once the battle was rejoined. Outside the Village Hall the rain still pelted down, but nobody inside cared any longer. Everyone was tucking into meat pies, faggots, corned-pork, thick slices of pink juicy ham, crusty rolls and doorsteps of thickly buttered bread, hard-boiled eggs, plum-cake, batches of golden scones spread with strawberry-jam, apple-pies, and great bowls of trifle with cream.

The men and boys were loudly boisterous; the women and girls tried to hide their delight behind virtuous disapproval, but failed. Many females would be sorry in the morning; many a husband would be chastised by an indignant spouse. But it was wonderful while it lasted, and the harder it rained the more convivial grew those sheltering from it.

Rex was enjoying himself. He ate heartily, drank more than he really wanted in order to be sociable, and smacked as many female bottoms as the other men. And if he took advantage of those throwing their bonnets over the windmill for the evening by responding to their adulation with a lusty kiss, or a bear-like hug around their plump waists, he did it often and openly enough to show it was all innocent fun.

He felt sorry for Roland, who was so often obliged to stand in for their father. At only twenty-three he was far too young and occupied with his future career to take on the duties of the leading gentleman of the village. But the people of Tarrant Royal were yeomen, and demanded a substitute for the absent Branwell Sheridan. Who better than the eldest son, even though he was little more than a youngster? So Roland obliged. He was too polite and idealistic to refuse—idealistic in his attitude to English country life, that was. Rex thought it a mistake. Idealists were often cruelly disillusioned; his brother did not deserve that fate. As for this evening, Roland would probably have no wish to tickle a plump giggling matron with her hands full of plates, or enjoy sending the colour flooding a plain face with a few saucy words, anyway.

Chris was nowhere in sight, which was strange. Although he invariably managed to remain aloof in the midst of any group working hard to draw him out, and would certainly find the forthcoming concert completely inexplicable and tedious, he was always hungry. Rex was certain his young brother had intended making inroads into the supper, yet had not spotted him in the hall. He had been there on the green during the match, because he had seen the lad applauding wildly during his innings.

While the tables were being cleared away to allow chairs to be placed in rows for the concert, Rex laughingly escaped some of the Tarrant Maundle team bent on making him drunk, and pushed his way through the confusion of too many generals and not enough troops to where the Doctor's daughter stood helping to fold the long tablecloths.

'Marion, have you seen young Chris about?' he asked. 'You were sitting beside him at the match, weren't you?'

To his astonishment, the girl flushed scarlet and seemed unusually intent on the tablecloths. She had never been one of his conquests; she was a reserved level-headed youngster who had more responsibility than she should, at her age, in keeping her father's house and acting as his nurse at surgery. She had never really responded to flirting, and he had given up. What had he done to change things?

'When it rained, everyone ran. I don't know where he went.'

'Well, I'm surprised he didn't come for the supper. He has an appetite like a horse.' Still watching her blushing confusion, he went on, lightheartedly, 'I don't know how that expression grew so popular. Roland's thoroughbreds are so finicky they have to be tempted to take even the best money can buy.'

When she said nothing, he took the ends of the cloth from her and teased, 'Mrs Furness has been waiting for you to fold this in half for the last few minutes. It's not like you to be so dreamy.'

Folding the cloth with more panache than expertise, he walked to Mrs Furness with a wink, boasting that he was one of the world's fastest tablecloth-folders, then turned back to find Marion gazing at him with a strained expression.

'Could he find his way around without his spectacles? He wouldn't get lost or fall down, would he?'

'Who—Chris? Why do you ask?'

'I . . . oh, I just wondered.'

'He's as blind as a bat, almost,' he told her, wondering what the conversation was really all about. 'Too much reading. I've never found an effective way of stopping him. Take tonight, for instance.' He turned toward the jostling crowd. 'Here are all these lovely young girls waiting for someone to hold their hands during the concert, and he's probably cut along home to read some dry old stuff about Greeks or Romans.' He turned back to her. 'I don't understand the lad.'

But she had gone. He shook his head wonderingly. Even *he* failed to understand girls, sometimes. The opportunity to try, in this case, was denied him by the Rector who approached begging him to make his way to the back of the stage so that the concert could begin. Together with the young vet from Tarrant Maundle, and the twin sons of one of the other landowners in the district, Rex was due to perform a song-and-dance number in which saucy words had been put to well-known English folk-songs. None of them could dance, but had worked out a step routine that would pass for it. The twins were baritone choristers, the vet could not sing in tune, and Rex had a pleasant uninhibited tenor, so the sound was unusual, to say the least. But the accompaniment was splendid. The vet played the piano with gusto, and Rex used the same technique on a banjo he had picked up in a pawnshop in Cambridge. Although he could not read a note of music, he was one of those fortunate people who found they could sit down and play any simple tune on whatever instrument was handy.

The quartet opened and closed the concert with such success they were consequently mobbed the minute they left the stage. Abandoning all hope of remaining sober, Rex ruefully surrendered to the inevitable. The annual event would not be complete for the villagers if they did not deliver the young 'gentlemen' of the district noisily back to their mansions as drunk as their proverbial ancestors. It had happened for the past three years, and Rex always felt ill the following day. But, along with his musical colleagues, he resignedly drank the concoctions mixed amid winks and nudges by the yokels, and slipped very gradually under the table.

It was not surprising that he could hardly stand when they finally dragged him up to Tarrant Hall on a hay-cart and tipped him onto his front doorstep. He waved a cheery farewell to what appeared to be several hundred people, and clutched the long iron handle beside the door to prevent himself from falling down. There seemed to be a lot of bells ringing somewhere, and he shook his head to get rid of the sound. But they continued until the door opened, and three old men stood there.

He smiled fatuously. 'Hallo, Minks. Hallo, Minks. Hallo, Minks,' he recited to the trio, doffing the straw-boater he still miraculously had on his head. 'Can you hear those damned bells?'

'Can you walk, sir?' asked a dignified voice from one of them.

'Er . . . not very well.'

'I'll fetch Frank to assist you.'

Several other people appeared from nowhere. An arm was put around his waist, and a shoulder came up beneath his own left arm before they all set off. But the group did not take him toward the stairs where there was a wonderful bed awaiting him in a room up above. He protested, but was told gravely that Mr Roland was awaiting him in the study.

At first glance, his brother seemed to be sitting in every chair in the room, but as Rex was lowered onto a soft cushion Roland came to rest practically opposite him. He looked rather strange— almost doubled-up. Rex was puzzled. He could not be drunk, too, because he had left as soon as the concert finished. But there was definitcly something wrong with him. Rex leant forward with unsteady caution, but still his head spun like a top.

'S'matter, old chap?'

It seemed a long while before he got an answer, then Roland said, 'There was a telegram here when I got in. Can you read it?'

Rex wagged his head, which set the whole room whirling. 'Not a hope.'

Another long while, then, 'Father's killed himself.'

Rex felt himself slipping away, but managed to say before passing out, 'I'm surprised he waited this long.' He did not hear the full tragedy until the next day.

The drama of Branwell Sheridan's suicide in far-off Madeira after losing practically all he owned on the turn of one card, was of much more tragic significance to Tarrant Royal than the death of an Austrian archduke at the hands of a Serbian student in equally far-off Bosnia, although both had taken place on the same late-June day. The villagers had no access to the full details, of course, but rumours ran rife. They were somewhere near the truth.

The vineyards and wine-importing business had been inherited by Branwell's beautiful half-Portuguese wife, who had hated England's climate and was happiest in the sunny blossom-filled island off the coast of Africa. Madly in love, Branwell had abandoned his dignified political career for the wine trade, living in the Madeiran manor with her. When she died tragically young, he could not bear to leave the place where they had been so happy together, and sent his three sons to schools in England, with a motherly housekeeper and reliable staff to watch over them during their school holidays at the family home in Dorset. But he could never come to terms with his loss, even as the years passed, and he had grown eccentric and bitter, resenting the few demands parenthood made upon him and increasingly hating the vineyards surrounding the home where she had lived and died.

Terrible destructive grief, plus his growing dependence on the heavy wine that had made his fortune, led to the compulsive gambling that lost him all his Madeiran property, the contents of the Sheridan cellars, and the distributing company in London. Fortunately, he appeared to have forgotten Tarrant Hall and the estate surrounding it. He also appeared to have forgotten his three sons. The day after that fatal gamble, when he realised he had thrown away all his wife had held dear, he had jumped into the sea that foamed over the rocks around the coast.

The Sheridan brothers were stunned. They still had not received the full details, nor would they until their meeting with the family solicitor, the board of directors of the company that must now change hands, and their banker. But they all knew life would never be the same again. In his careless way, Branwell had allotted each of his sons allowances based on percentages, little considering that as the principal doubled, trebled, and quadrupled, so the percentages would produce corresponding increases to make each of them exceedingly wealthy. What Rex would soon earn as general handyman at the engineering works was no more than a pittance, but it would make him richer than his brothers by twelve and sixpence a week.

Of the three, he was probably the least surprised by the tragedy. It could not be that he understood grief, desperation and consuming devotion better than his brothers, for his was the sunniest and most adaptable of natures. But perhaps he felt, more than the other two, that each man had a driving force in his life and, when that was taken away, there might seem to be no reason to go on. Branwell had been a near-stranger, so grief for his father did not come into it, and he accepted the sudden plunge into poverty with philosophical resignation.

But he felt very sorry for Roland. Shattered beyond belief by what had happened, his older brother seemed unable to think or come to terms with the future. At the ridiculously early age of twenty-three he had inherited a mansion set in a large estate, but no income with which to maintain it. It was a situation he could never have envisaged in his plans for his life. Wealth had governed them all.

Three days after receipt of the telegram, Rex accompanied his brother to London for a series of painful interviews that would put the facts before them and help them plan their lives in their new straitened circumstances. It did not occur to either of them to take Chris: they were men, he was still a boy.

Chris had no wish to go with them. He was trying to cope with a greater upheaval than either Roland or Rex. Being the youngest, he had seen even less of his parents than his brothers, regarding Priddy and Minks as kindly bumbling chaperones, but Rex as his mentor. It was his red-haired brother who was always willing to listen, who was always prepared to slip him half-a-crown when he needed it. Rex, it was, who had seized him by the shoulders and marched him, laughing, out of the house for some fresh air when he had been too long with his beloved books. Chris was very fond of Roland, of course, but it was his middle brother who aroused immense devotion in his breast. Rex was always laughing. When he was in the house it seemed to smile, also. He was strong and athletic, recklessly daring, warm-hearted and versatile. He could pick out a tune on anything from a banjo to a comb-and-paper, put up a bravado performance on any field of sport, he could sing with spontaneous gusto and make everyone want to join in. He never let anyone down, and never made impossible demands on anyone but himself. To Chris, Rex had been father and brother and friend rolled into one.

Yet Chris could not tell even Rex what ailed him now. It was like a fever that confused his thoughts and drove him from the house by day; had him sleepless and burning with fantasies by night. When his school colleagues had followed behind girls in Godalming and teased them with comments and invitations to meet them after dark, he had thought it all rather boring. When they had told him of how they had put their hands inside girls' blouses during their holidays, he had thought the stories probably exaggerated, and the details of the girls' anatomies even more so. At public school it was impossible to escape being made aware of every aspect of male sexuality, and he had had the usual peculiar dreams that had produced evidence of virility. But desire had never touched him.

Now, it would not leave him alone. He was obsessed with his own awareness, and ashamed that it even overrode the tragedy that had hit the family on the evening of the day he could not forget. In the middle of a conversation, he would remember how his palms had circled on those soft mounds while the centres had risen up hard to meet them, and he would feel almost sick with excitement. Whilst trying to read, he would hear her voice again commanding him softly to pursue her. He would have to put the book down and go out into the grounds where the hot sun and teasing caressing breeze almost repeated that feeling of seduction he had experienced.

But the nights were worst. When darkness obliterated all but his thoughts, they ran riot until he again reached that agonising condition he could no longer ignore. He gloried in it, yet was ashamed. He had known Marion Deacon all his life; she was a girl from a good family. Yet he desperately longed to take off all her clothes, then his own, and lie on top of her.

The day his brothers went to London was the first of July, the traditional date for the Tarrant Royal carnival, and Chris waited with growing restlessness for the evening to come. In view of the fact that the Sheridans were officially in mourning, there would be gossip if he was seen there. Yet he planned to go and watch the floats go past from the little copse just beyond the forge, in the hope of seeing her. Perhaps it would end his fever; perhaps he would see her through the same eyes as 'before'. But, in his heart, he knew he did not want the fever to end just yet. It was the most exciting experience of his life.

The staff were all leaving early that day, aside from Mrs Prideaux and Minks, who felt attendance at the carnival would be a sign of disrespect to the dead, even though Branwell Sheridan had committed the sin of taking his own life. So it was easy enough for Chris to slip from the house after dinner when the old retainers believed he was reading in his room. The mid-evening air was heavy and still, bringing winged insects out in large numbers and beading his face with perspiration as he loped sideways down the wooded slope that gave a short cut to the forge. The sound of shouting and music told him that the procession was already under way and, by the time he broke through to the trees bordering the road, it was already level with the forge and Ted Peach's cottage.

Breathing hard after the exertion on such a close evening, he leant on one arm outstretched against a tree, and watched the floats pass one by one. Since the villagers planned the next as soon as one was over, a great deal of care, thought and attention to detail had gone into this year's depiction of scenes from history. But Chris appreciated none of it. He was looking for just one person.

It was dusk before the last float passed him, and he saw her. The subject was the suffragette movement. Ted Peach's daughter Violet was lying beneath the hooves of a cardboard racehorse wearing the colours of Edward the Seventh, Janey Banks was being forcibly fed by a muscular wardress who looked remarkably like her brother in a grey dress, and Marion, along with the Jessop girls, was chained to artificial railings with placards demanding the vote at their feet. He swallowed painfully. The symbolism of female

39

aggression combined with physical bondage set his sophisticated mind in a whirl with remembered prose and verse on the subject of sexual passions. Delilah, Cleopatra, Helen of Troy, Diana the Huntress, La Belle Dame sans Merci . . . and all the time his gaze was on her breasts outthrust by the fastening of her arms behind her back.

Night fell, and he made his way through the milling crowd to where the floats had completed their circular way around the village, and were being dismantled. Everyone's destination now was the fair in Lower Meadow, and Chris passed unheeded through those eager for the bawdy lurid fun of peepshows, coconut-shies, and roundabouts. Yet she found him first.

'Chris!' came her voice vibrant with excitement. 'What are you doing here?'

With heart thudding against his ribs, he swung round to see her in the tight sophisticated costume and hat of a militant aristocrat, cheeks dark with a blush, and eyes luminous in the lamplight from the George and Dragon.

'I thought you'd gone to London,' she said with sustained excitement.

'The others went. I stayed at the house.'

They stood looking at each other, unsure how to handle the meeting now they were face to face. Then, she said, 'I'm sorry about your father and . . . and everything.'

He ran his hand through his springy hair. 'Roland and Rex are frightfully worried, but I expect it won't turn out to be as bad as they think. As for my father, he was practically a stranger.'

'Poor Chris,' she said softly. Then, after a quick indrawn breath, added, 'I'm sorry about . . . well, you know what I mean.'

'You're being sorry about a lot of things tonight.'

She avoided his eyes. 'Rex said you really can't see much without your spectacles.'

'Didn't you believe me?'

'I . . . suppose not.'

The last stragglers appeared to have vanished toward Lower Meadow, and they found themselves momentarily alone in the lane. An owl began hooting in the churchyard, and from inside the George and Dragon came a burst of laughter to make their isolation seem more apparent.

'I worried about it, but didn't like to come up to the house when

40

you had just received such bad news. I thought you wouldn't be able to see, at all. Silly, I didn't realise you'd have another pair.'

'I have to, in case I break them.' The crickets were starting up all over the sides of the ditch, and a bat had started its silent oscillating flight in the courtyard of the inn. The stars were coming out in hundreds, and he felt he could not hold back from touching her much longer. 'I had a frightful job finding my way home that day.'

'I'm sorry,' she began, then laughed breathlessly. 'There I go again.'

'Yes.'

'Well . . . you'd better come indoors and collect them.' She began edging away. 'In case you break the ones you're wearing.'

'Right-o,' he agreed quickly, striding along beside her to the gate beneath the trellis arch. The scent of honeysuckle was overwhelming as he followed her into the garden and round the side of the house to the attached waiting-room where they had gone to shelter from the rain.

It was hot and dark inside that room, and she had made no attempt to light the lamp. But the pale wash of the rising moon allowed him to see her outline quite well.

'I think I left them in here,' she said in almost a whisper. 'Daddy's out. He was called to old Mr Wiseman, who's dying. I don't suppose he'll be back for a long time.'

Almost dizzy with the heat inside the room, and his own arousing desire for her, he stepped forward to catch her round the waist. With a gasp, she put her mouth up eagerly to meet his as he bent his head. Almost immediately, those remembered mounds were pushing against his shirt, and his palms went down to circle them. She gasped again, and trembled with delight. He was growing hotter by the minute, and his erotic fantasies were fast becoming reality. Fumbling with the buttons of the suffragette costume, he feverishly thrust his hand inside the opening in the bodice, until his fingers came into contact with bare warm skin curving up into a dome of unbelievable satiny firmness that rose to a small rigid knob at the tip.

'Oh, Chris!'

'Oh, God! It's beautiful!'

She made no attempt to stop him unbuttoning the rest and tugging it from her shoulders to bare the whole of her upper body.

The moonlight shining on twin breasts that quivered as she breathed hard, signalled the end of restraint on his part. He was in agony for relief, and had no intention of walking away this time.

At first, she showed the same eager, sighing submissiveness. Then, when his hands slid her lower garments right to the floor, she began to struggle.

'No, Chris. Oh, no, *no!*'

But the fight soon went out of her on the examination-couch behind the floral curtain. When it was over, they both had tears on their faces—he because it was the most thrilling, elating thing he had ever done. He supposed she was crying for the same reason.

3

ROLAND FELT as if he had been living through a nightmare for the past month. Every morning when he awoke, the weight of his problems had grown no lighter and the steps he was being forced to take were still unavoidable. Outwardly competent, he was still inwardly stunned. He bore the guilt of his father's weakness as if he had been responsible for it.

The mess had been mainly straightened out by the family solicitor to reveal a situation even worse than suspected. With the source of Sheridan income gone overnight, all that was left were properties, assets and a bank balance to assess. There was no London house, Branwell having sold that soon after his marriage, using his club during his infrequent visits to England. So that disposed of 'properties'. The assets were Tarrant Hall, its estate and contents. The bank balance was modest, and there was some jewellery belonging to both families of the marriage. That, apart from the small income derived from the Dorset estate, was all there was. By the time outstanding debts, legal costs in Madeira, and bequests from Branwell's will had been paid, there was frighteningly little left.

Due to the circumstances of his death, Branwell's bloated body, fished from the sea, had been hastily buried on a private hillside in Madeira, and Roland had arranged a small memorial service in Tarrant Royal church for those few distant relatives and friends who deigned to attend. But he had been overcome to find the tiny church packed with the villagers, and the grassy bank behind the seventeenth-century building covered with bunches of flowers bearing no names or messages. He was very moved. He knew the gesture was really for the three sons of the man they were supposed to be mourning, and it had brought the feeling of sadness the death of his father had failed to arouse.

His days were now burdened with the obligation to assume his new responsibility as head of the family, and make decisions about his brothers' futures. Still a student himself, it was not an easy task. With so many questions to be settled, one thing seemed indisputable. Tarrant Hall had to be retained as the family home; a base for them all whatever else had to change. Since the estate now had to pay for itself, the income had to exceed expenditure and that could only be achieved by cutting staff and upkeep costs. With great regret he pared down the staff to a minimum, and listened to plans offered by Jeffries, the estate-manager, for putting more of the land under the plough, to increase the milk-yield, add to the numbers of sheep, and embark on timber production from the section of forest owned by the Sheridans. It was all foreign to him, but he went around with Jeffries and tried to listen diligently to all the man recommended. In the end, he decided to be wise and put his trust in someone who knew his job inside out.

Although Rex, at twenty, was officially still a minor like Chris, Roland always thought of his middle brother as around the same age. Together, they had agreed without reservations that Chris must be allowed to go to Cambridge and on to become a Don. The boy's brilliant brain must be allowed to absorb knowledge and teach others; his predestined course was the only one he could possibly follow. His intelligence was such that any attempt to deny it fulfilment would be tantamount to destroying the boy, they both felt. Whereas they could adapt, Chris would find it impossible to do so.

Knowing he had no alternative, Roland faced the blow of having to abandon his medical studies and his dream of becoming a surgeon. It took him several anguished days to accept the truth of

43

that decision, and his heart was heavy enough as it was, without another sacrifice that was almost akin to cutting off his right arm. Reserved and outwardly stoical though he appeared, he could not bring himself to watch his valuable thoroughbreds being taken away on a gorgeous July morning, that cried out to him to canter across Longbarrow Hill on one of the creatures who were almost a part of him. He sat in his austere bedroom, with his head down and shoulders heaving, as the sound of their hooves clattered on the gravel beneath his window, then down the lane that would eventually take them to the station. His brothers tactfully left him alone to come to terms with his loss.

Similarly, they left Rex to himself on the day he returned from delivering 'Princess' to her new owner. The narrow sun-tanned face normally so alive, was distressingly bleak as he left the house in breeches and flying-jacket for the last time. When he returned by train and pony-trap, it looked as if the sunshine had left him for good. If Chris was aware of what it had cost them both to ensure his academic future, they did not know.

Roland discussed their young brother with Rex as the latter packed for his departure to the northern town, where he was due to take up his odd appointment in the engineering firm.

'Chris is going to miss you, Rex. With so many things to attend to I find I've hardly seen him since Father died.'

His brother looked up from stacking a pile of shirts into a suitcase. 'Neither have I, as it happens. I know I've been busy, but not that much so. Several times I've been up to his bedroom to drag him outside for some air, but he seems to have been out in the grounds already, sketching.' He straightened up with his hands on his hips. 'Strangely he shows signs of being more affected by all this than I expected. When it happened, my first thought was "Thank God his lofty intellect will allow him to float above such human frailties as suicide, scandal, and straitened circumstances." But he moons around Longbarrow Hill with pencils and block, doing innumerable sketches of everything in sight, and won't go anywhere near the village. It's so unnecessary. They've all been marvellous, with no suggestion of nudges, or whispers behind their hands when we pass. But he plainly feels he can't face them now. Strange, isn't it?'

Roland leant back in the chintz-covered chair. 'Oh, I don't

know. He's never been as close to them as we have, never really absorbed or felt attuned to rural life, in any aspect. And he's at that age between boyhood and maturity when he is easily wounded by the attitude of others. I remember getting frightfully upset because a schoolfriend's sister said I had large ears.' He smiled faintly. 'I went around feeling like a bull elephant, for a while.'

Rex shook his head with affectionate impatience. 'You take everything too much to heart. You always have.' He resumed his packing. 'I'm sure no one has ever said such a thing to young Chris. He's so good-looking, the only flaw is his inability or disinclination to recognise it. If I were in his shoes, I'd make merry hay while the sun shone!'

Roland looked at his bent red head and wondered if his brother's many flirtations had ever produced a serious attachment on his part. Probably not. The great love of his life had just been sold.

'You really are under no obligation to take Jake up north with you, Rex. Just because "Princess" has gone, you're not responsible for his future.'

'I know I'm not. But since I don't intend doing any of the handywork for which the firm was prepared to pay me, he might as well take the job in my place.'

Roland was taken aback. 'I don't understand.'

Rex walked to his chest of drawers for his underwear, and gave him a frank look. 'The money I got for the aeroplane is still there to be used for Chris, don't worry. But things have changed since I fixed that job, haven't they? Twelve and sixpence a week isn't enough. If I'm to become a qualified engineer, I'll need to buy a great many books and live in reasonable lodgings while I'm waiting to pass all those exams. I'll also need freedom to do all the practical work I want.'

'And?' prompted Roland.

'One of the directors who interviewed me mentioned that he was looking for a well-spoken reliable chauffeur for his fleet of motor cars. If he hasn't already found one, here I am.'

'Chauffeur! Rex, you can't,' cried Roland shocked.

'Why not?' came the calm reply. 'The wages might not be high, but I'll have a decent room over the garage and the same food as the other members of staff. The cars will be there for me to take to pieces as often as I like.' He gave a grin that was almost as audacious as before that telegram had arrived. 'Admit it, brother dear, I shall look extremely fetching in livery.'

'Fetching or not, you'll still be no more than a *servant.*'

'We don't regard ours with the contempt you put into that remark.'

'They are not Sheridans! In any case, you don't know how to drive a motor car.'

'Oh, I expect it's much the same as a motor cycle.'

But Roland had no chance to comment on that sweeping statement, because the door burst open, and Chris rushed in brimming with urgency.

'Minks has just brought up the newspaper. Austria has gone to war with Serbia over the assassination of their archduke, and Russia is mobilising! If Germany comes in, so will France. I don't see how we could possibly stay out of it then. It's absolute madness!'

Roland exchanged glances with Rex that spoke volumes about their young brother's informative opinion on something he appeared to find easier to understand than the domestic problems they had been trying to face during the past month.

'You're theorising, Chris. It'll never happen,' Rex told him, shutting the drawer noisily.

'In any case,' said Roland, 'it wouldn't come to that. We've no intention of going to war with anyone.'

But, a few days later, Britain mobilised her forces against the most formidable enemies she had ever faced. It was August the fourth.

During the following six weeks Roland sunk himself deeper and deeper into learning how to manage his estate as a full-time landowner—a somewhat impoverished landowner. With only Mrs Prideaux, Minks, Dawkins, and the minimum of general staff, he ran Tarrant Hall in a penny-pinching manner that distressed him. With reluctance, he agreed to steps suggested by Jeffries which he felt diminished the status of the estate and turned it into no more than a very large working farm. But it had to pay for itself, and meadows that presented a picture of serene landscaping now had to be made to yield. With so many young farmhands and labourers flocking to the colours, produce from the land would lessen at a time when it would most be needed.

But Roland did not forget his obligations to Tarrant Royal, and attended meetings of the Parish Council, opened fêtes, and generally showed that his personal disaster would not be allowed to affect the village. As Rex had said, the people of the district had been marvellous. There had been gossip, naturally, but the viciousness, if any, had been directed toward Branwell Sheridan, not his three sons who had made themselves so much part of the village it now embraced them with similar comradeship. At church each Sunday, Roland was greeted with as much respect and pleasure as he had always been, and the village chose to ignore the fact that their chosen Squire was now poorer than many of the area's 'gentlemen' farmers and, possibly, even than Dr Deacon who, although he had chosen to remain with the tiny country practice all his working life, had inherited a sizable sum on the death of his high-born wife.

It was to this fact that Roland was forced to attribute Marion's attitude whenever they came face to face. He had been shocked and hurt to discover she was the only person in the village who was uncomfortable in his presence now. It was true their regular morning rides had ceased abruptly after receipt of that telegram, with no apology from him for having left her waiting with no word of what had detained him. But when he had spoken to her about it and asked her forgiveness, she had turned aside with a few stammered sentences and moved away with high colour in her cheeks.

He felt deeply disillusioned by this treatment from someone who had been part of his life since they had all been children. Admittedly, the Sheridans had seen less of her during more recent years, due to her commitments to her father, but she was a very old friend . . . and the only person to let their straitened circumstances affect her.

In consequence, when Minks came to him just before lunch on the day before Chris was due to depart for Cambridge, and said that Dr and Miss Deacon had called on an urgent matter, Roland left his desk with unusual reluctance. The Doctor had been as genuinely friendly as ever, and had tried to persuade him to finish his medical studies at home so that he would, at least, be able to pass his finals, even offering to let him sit in at his surgeries to gain practical experience. So Dr Deacon he would have seen gladly. In company with his disdainful daughter, the old friend and medical colleague was not so welcome.

Minks had shown them into the drawing room, where the sherry decanter and glasses stood ready for any visitors, and Roland squared his shoulders before walking into the large elegant room whose many deep-windowed alcoves allowed sunshine in at any time of the day. But even as he spoke his rather self-conscious greeting, he realised this was not a purely social call. Both of them looked pale and strained—almost ill—and both pairs of eyes now fixed on him held expressions he found impossible to fathom.

That they had come with some bad news was obvious. His heart lurched, fear for Rex sweeping over him. His brother claimed his life was charmed. Had the charm run out? Yet, even as he thought of a road accident, or even a plunge to earth in an aeroplane he had somehow persuaded the owner to let him fly, his common-sense told him there was no reason why the Deacons should hear the news before him.

To cover his sudden apprehension he walked straight to the table holding the decanter and offered them each a glass of sherry in as normal a tone as he could muster.

'We haven't come to be sociable, Sheridan,' said the Doctor, the fact that he addressed a young man he had brought into the world and treated as a friend in cold tones and using his surname bringing fear back to Roland.

'You've brought bad news?' he asked, looking from the stout balding man in baggy tweeds to the slender girl, so white-faced and red around the eyes.

'As a father, I can't think of any worse. As a doctor, I have to accept the results of my tests.' Dr Deacon stepped forward and gripped the back of the huge settee with hands that were shaking. 'As God's my witness, I swear I'll thrash him raw when I get my hands on your brother.'

Reeling with the implication of words that could mean only one thing—incredible though it seemed—Roland gazed at Marion with the pain of twin betrayals filling him.

'I'm . . . I'm not sure I understand all this,' he stammered.

'Oh, *don't* you!' came the vicious taunt. 'My daughter's innocence has been outraged: she is nine weeks advanced into pregnancy, to put it in medical terms you might understand. Even if I hadn't recognised certain outward signs, my tests have proved positive. This morning, I discovered from her who was responsible. It's your bloody brother!'

Roland could only take so much. After all he had been through over the past two and a half months, this was more than he could handle.

'I admit Rex has a reputation for . . .' He hesitated, thinking of his brother's happy-go-lucky approach to girls. 'But I can't believe he'd . . .'

'*Rex!*' cried the outraged father. 'It isn't Rex but that young lecher Christopher. When I get my hands on him I'll . . .'

'That's out of the question,' cried Roland, fully as angry as Reginald Deacon. 'I never took you for a fool. Chris is no more than a *schoolboy!*'

'He's eighteen, and perfectly capable of fertilising female ova. So capable,' Dr Deacon went on in increased rage, 'he did it in a mere five minutes under my own roof whilst I was attending a dying man. Well, he'll pay for his pleasure, by God, he will . . . and he'll go on paying for the rest of his days!'

Roland was in the grips of an emotion he had never before experienced. A childhood friend stood before him bearing a bastard embryo, and his brilliant, studious, adolescent brother was being named as the father. The whole thing was preposterous, insulting and dangerous.

He looked only at Marion's father. 'Has she any proof of who is responsible?'

Reginald Deacon stepped toward him. 'You bloody insufferable . . .'

'Dr Deacon,' said Roland in loud tones that halted him. 'I have to remind you that we are both supposed to be gentlemen, and that you are in my house. You have just levelled a very serious charge against my brother, who is a minor. You can't expect me to accept it without hearing his defence. Just as you believe your daughter's veracity, so I believe in his integrity. I know there is some mistake. But, in the unlikely event of this being true, I will take full responsibility for his part in this. I trust you will do the same for your daughter. Since you have not mentioned the word 'rape' I take it you accept that she was a willing partner.'

Barely controlling himself, the older man said in an unsteady voice, 'My daughter, Sheridan, was a virgin . . . and is also a minor. If you are after the cut of your two brothers, you'll know from experience who is the aggressive partner in a case of seduction. You dare to insult her again and, your house or not, I'll knock you down.'

Without another word Roland rang for Minks, and asked him to request Mr Christopher to come down to the study immediately. He felt icily angry, and filled with a new contempt for the dark-haired pretty girl he had regarded with friendship and respect for so long. She was cheap and worthless. Not only had she been wantonly intimate with a man, she now attempted to blame someone else. The culprit was probably married, but her protection of him could hardly be more ill-contrived. Of all the people to choose, she had hit upon a schoolboy whose thoughts were so full of intellectual, high-minded considerations, he never even looked at girls, much less bedded them. It was that which hurt the most, he realised. The families had been close for years. How could she use such betrayal against them now?

Chris came in warily, and his gaze flew straight to Marion. Roland was irritated. Surely Minks had not overheard and warned Chris what was afoot! But his brother looked the picture of guilt coming in like that.

Reginald Deacon looked at the boy with near-murder in his eyes, but stayed where he was on the hearth rug. Roland went across to his brother and put a hand on his shoulder by way of support.

'Sorry to disturb you, old fellow, but I'm afraid something rather disagreeable has arisen, and I can't avoid bringing you into it.' He looked his brother in the eye and added, in lower tones, 'Please believe that I am only putting you through this charade because I have no choice. I want you to know that I have, and always will have, total faith in your sense of honour.'

Chris seemed to be extremely pale, and his eyes behind the tortoiseshell-rimmed spectacles kept darting glances at Marion. But Roland knew he had been overdoing the studying these last weeks prior to going up to Cambridge, and probably felt that whatever was coming should not be in the presence of a girl.

Wanting to get it over as quickly as possible, Roland said, 'I think we can settle the matter with just one question, Chris. Have you . . . have you ever been alone with Marion in her father's house . . . in . . . in compromising circumstances?'

'Chris, I wouldn't have said anything,' came Marion's broken voice for the first time. 'But I had to.'

The boy looked across at her like a trapped hare, then back at Roland. 'What's all this about?'

'Don't try to lie your way out of it, you young whelp!' roared the Doctor. 'My girl is carrying your child, and it's going to have a legal father if I have to force you to the church at the end of a rifle! You'll marry her and save her reputation, or I'll hound you and your family to their graves. Your father was a blackguard, and you're all tarred with the same brush.'

'That's enough,' shouted Roland, shaken by his brother's delay in answering with a negative. 'If you can't behave in a civilised manner, I'll refuse to continue this ridiculous confrontation and tell you to leave—*you and your daughter.*'

But Chris was looking at them all with something approaching panic. 'I can't do that. I can't *marry* her. I'm going up to Cambridge tomorrow.'

Roland gripped his arm and swung him round sharply. 'You're not . . . you're not saying that you *did* . . . that you could possibly be the father of a child—*her* child!'

Chris offered no defence whatever; his expression said it all. A physical blow would have been easier to take. Roland's ideals, his deep belief in family bonds that tied men close in brotherhood, mocked him as he stared at the handsome boyish face. A terrible coldness began to creep up inside him to mercifully freeze his emotions. From somewhere he found the ability to turn from his brother, and ask Marion in a voice that sounded hollow, 'Forgive me, but I have to ask if . . . if there is any chance of alternative paternity.'

She shook her head numbly.

Dr Deacon came up to where he stood with Chris, and said, 'You'll marry her as quickly as we can get the banns read. Even then, it'll be cutting it fine.'

The boy looked completely bewildered. 'I *can't.* I'm going to Cambridge tomorrow.'

Roland turned on him. 'You bloody little fool,' he said with quiet savagery. 'You threw away your whole life when you let your body rule your head.'

'What do you mean?' cried Chris desperately.

'You can forget Cambridge and a brilliant scholastic career. I'm the head of this family now, and I won't have any bastards bearing our name. You'll do the decent thing and give your child the heritage it deserves . . . and *I'll* get you to church at the end of a rifle, if I have to.'

The wedding was fixed for 30 September, and the very haste to marry two youngsters under age—the bridegroom a mere school-boy until three months before—gave rise to speculations that could not be avoided. If the child arrived late, they might get away with the claim of a seven-month baby and brazen it out, but the premature arrival of a child in wedlock was better than no wedlock at all. Talk would be shortlived, in any case, and the child would be a legal Sheridan with the advantages of that name to help him over the details of his conception.

The young couple were to live at Tarrant Hall after their marriage, so contact with the villagers would be minimal until Marion had passed the embarrassment of having her swelling figure scrutinised as the weeks passed.

Chris lived in a vacuum of misery until his wedding day, pray-ing that something would happen to save him from it. He could not begin to accept that the payment for no more than a few minutes of exquisite pleasure could be so total and destructive; could not begin to accept that the golden promise of academic laurels had vanished in an instant. One moment, he had been packing to embark on the second stage of a life that gave him aesthetic satisfaction, intellectual pleasure, and personal delight. The next, he was facing sixty years locked in a cage of domesticity with someone who had no understanding of all he gloried in, and who was getting all she wanted for her share of the guilt.

He did not see why he should pay so dearly, when it had been she who had deliberately awoken feelings in him that would satisfy her vanity. She had known all too well when inviting him into the darkened house that evening that, what had begun several days earlier, could only have one ending. Yet he was regarded as the villain.

Roland's attitude toward him had softened slightly, but nothing would change his stand that Chris had no alternative than to do the honourable thing. Even so, he had said several times that he prayed night and day that the girl would miscarry and remove the obligation to marry her.

No answer had been received from Rex to the letter Roland had written him explaining what had happened, and Chris's wretchedness increased further in the belief that his beloved brother was so disgusted he could not bring himself to write anything on the subject.

The money set aside for his education now had to be used to pay for the things a husband was expected to provide, and Chris was to become the estate-manager after working in harness with Jeffries for a year. To the young victim, it seemed too absurd to even consider. But even more absurd was the frantic planning for the wedding itself.

To minimise gossip, it was to be as grand and conventional as if circumstances were normal. Roland and Dr Deacon organised the whole thing with a thoroughness that was not allowed to suffer because of enmity between them, but Chris realised Roland had taken the whole business so hard, he would never forgive the man, or his daughter, for taking away the hopes of a third Sheridan.

In his moments of deepest despair, Chris thought of slipping away, leaving the country, and setting up as a teacher somewhere abroad. There were three things preventing him: the whole of Europe was locked in war, he no longer had the money to travel anywhere, and that damned baby would still be born and claim him as its father. With his head in his hands, he sat for long periods cursing Fate, who had decreed that his first carnal adventure with a female should prove fertile, while many men went through life bedding every girl they met and getting off scot free.

The thirtieth of September dawned azure and russet, a perfect autumn day in which the whole of nature rejoiced. The bridegroom and his best man did not. There had been no miscarriage, no last minute reprieve. The brothers dressed in their grey morning-suits ready to set off for the church, trying to ignore the preparations for the lavish reception on the lower floor of Tarrant Hall. They did not speak during the short drive down to the village. Chris knew Roland would never forgive him for landing himself in such a position, and he wondered how his brother had managed never to impregnate a girl, assuming that he had the normal desires of a man. Rex had never made any secret of his, yet apparently luck had run with him all the time.

At the thought of Rex, his heart sank even further. There had been no response to the wedding-invitation, and even a telegram had remained unanswered. Roland's condemnation he could just stand, but abandonment by someone he loved and admired so very much was almost more than he could take.

Yet, as the organ inside the packed church began the bridal music that signified that Marion was being led in by her father, the serenity of the moment was broken by a distant roar that grew louder and louder until it rose to a crescendo outside the church. Chris heard it above the strident music and his own heart-thump, and swung his head round in a rush of relief so great it put moisture in his eyes. Because of it, he saw only a blurred figure outlined in the arched doorway as he looked past the veiled figure in white on the arm of a man whose face was ashen and set in rigid lines.

His relief turned to disconcerting speculation, however, as the blur of unshed tears cleared and he saw Rex clearly, walking down the aisle behind Marion and her father. His red-haired brother was attracting more attention than the bride, for he was dressed in a smart uniform that fitted like a glove on his well-built figure. But it was not the chauffeur's uniform in which he had claimed he would look so fetching. This consisted of polished brown high boots, khaki breeches, a khaki tunic in double-breasted style with a high collar, and a narrow jaunty cap he whipped from his head as he came further into the church.

Realisation rushed in. His brother had volunteered and was going to war! Pride and excitement vied with each other as his gaze met Rex's over Marion's head, and he smiled when he saw the usual warm affection in those merry green eyes. Slowly one closed and opened in a message of understanding, and the terrible day became a little lighter. A swift glance at Roland showed he was also staring at Rex, but pride was tinged with alarm, in his case.

The marriage ceremony was tedious and lengthy, but Chris remembered all he had to say despite his eagerness for it to end, so that he could question Rex and find out all the details of his patriotic gesture. Somewhere in the midst of marital vows he realised his brother was offering his *life* along with his services to his country. But fear did not linger. He would not be killed—not Rex.

Throughout the signing of the register, the walk back down the aisle with Marion's hand tucked through his arm, and the dash to the churchyard gate to avoid the hail of rice from laughing guests, his mind raced with all he knew of the war situation. For the past three weeks he had been so immersed in misery he had not studied the progress of world affairs. The Germans had followed their declaration of war on France by attacking through neutral Belgium, and British troops had been rushed across the Channel to aid the French army. Paris had been prevented from falling, and the Germans had been halted. With Russia attacking from the East, the Austro-Germanic hopes of a quick total conquest of Europe had gone. What had happened since then? Why had Rex felt the need to volunteer?

When he heard the motor cycle coming up behind the carriage as they set out for the house, he looked round and said, 'Trust Rex not to let me down, after all. Doesn't he look splendid in his uniform?'

He hardly noticed that the girl beside him made no reply, so busy was he waving enthusiastically as Rex passed, grinning, and rode ahead of the carriage like an advance-guard, announcing their arrival with the rubber horn fixed to his handlebars. But when he came into the house where they stood greeting the arriving guests, he merely gripped Chris's arm and said, 'I'll see you later, old fellow.' Then he turned to Marion. 'As your brother-in-law, I am perfectly entitled to kiss you,' he said with his irresistible smile. 'I've always wanted to, but I've never had an excuse before.'

The kiss was somewhat warmer than it should have been, but it brought a little colour into the bride's cheeks. She smiled up at him a trifle wanly as she said, 'I've never known you to need an excuse before.'

'Ah well, new rules now I'm an officer and gentleman,' he told her lightly. 'A servant of the King has to behave with the dignity befitting the post.' He took her hands in his and squeezed them. 'Welcome to the family, Marion. We're proud of our new member. If you ever want help or advice . . .' he gave a saucy smile in Chris's direction '. . . or if this lad here ever ill-treats you, come to Uncle Rex.' Then he became quickly serious as he added, 'But try to remember you have a husband with a brilliant mind, and try to understand that there are only so many limits one can put on it before it breaks.'

The afternoon seemed to fly past, and it was not until Marion went upstairs to change into her going-away outfit that Chris was able to seek out his middle brother and step into the garden with him for a private talk. But he found himself tongue-tied, for once, all the import of that day returning in full measure to remind him that things would never be the same again.

Rex seemed to sense this, for he put a hand on his shoulder as they strolled down toward the sunken garden.

'There's always something nostalgic about late autumn days like this, isn't there?' he said. 'That clear blue sky holds a hint of summer passing in its coldness, and the smell of the sun on the fallen leaves makes me think of our childhood when we used to rush through them with the dogs, scattering them into the wind.' They reached the low wall, and Rex put one booted foot up on it as he turned to face him. 'They were marvellous days, Chris, and we were marvellous companions. But we've grown up.'

Chris nodded, looking out over the golden-bronze of the forested valley below.

'I suppose I should have had a word with you,' his brother went on, 'but you were always so uninterested in girls, I let it slide. Even so, you should have learnt the golden rule by now, that ensures one never gets into this predicament.'

Chris turned angrily. 'It's so damned unfair!'

'I expect Marion thinks that, too.'

His cheeks flamed. 'You *can't* be on her side. She asked for it.'

'They all do. A chap can't go around looking like you do without exciting girls. Good God, you read enough Greek and French odes to passion to be aware of that.'

'Oh yes,' he agreed bitterly. 'But none of them mentions babies and forced marriages.'

Rex frowned. 'Would it have stopped you, if they had?'

'No . . . probably not,' he reluctantly admitted, realising how different it was discussing the subject with Rex rather than Roland. 'Oh God, Rex, I just don't know how I'm going to face the next sixty years.'

Rex gripped his shoulder and shook it gently. 'You poor old chap! No one can take on sixty years in one go. Try taking them one at a time. Regrets never get a fellow anywhere. What you have to do now is turn what you have to good account and forget what might have been.'

Chris looked up into the face so seldom as serious as it was now. 'Got any ideas?'

His brother nodded. 'Marion is a jolly nice girl from a good family. What's more, she's very pretty. You're lucky. She'll be a credit to you, and knows how to run a home already. For a start to married life, you'll be living in your own home with all its comfort and space. The library is still complete, thank God, and yours to use. With a brain like yours you can teach yourself enough to obtain a post as a tutor somewhere after this child is born. Then, when the war ends, try for something similar abroad. There are plenty of Diplomatic families who would employ someone like you for their children.' He cocked an eyebrow. 'Will that do to be getting on with?'

It sounded like a ray of hope; it was infinitely more worth considering than becoming an estate-manager. Why was it things never seemed so bad when Rex was around?

He sat on the wall looking up at his brother. 'You're a bloody marvel!'

Rex grinned and cuffed him gently round the head. 'That's just what the recruiting officer said when I told him what I could do.'

Chris leant forward eagerly, forgetting everything else. 'When did you volunteer? What regiment are you in?'

'The Royal Flying Corps, muttonhead. What other regiment would a pilot join? I went up to their headquarters a fortnight ago, which is why Roland's letter and telegram never reached me. Thank God I went back to my old lodgings to say goodbye to Jake and found them, or I'd never have come today.'

'What made you do it, Rex? I thought the Germans had been stopped.'

'Only temporarily, you can bet. But it had nothing to do with that.' He let his foot slip from the wall and stood looking toward Longbarrow Hill. 'I wanted an aeroplane, and they wanted men. It was as simple as that.' He cast Chris a rueful glance. 'I was lost without the "Princess". I've just got to fly . . . and the R.F.C. is going to pay me to do it. That's what I call a real bargain. And even if the war is over before I'm ready to go over to France, they still want pilots. If I have to earn my own living, this is the only way to do it.'

Chris sighed heavily, his problem returning. 'If it hadn't been for the cost of my supposed university career, you needn't have sold "Princess" . . . and Roland needn't have sold his horses. Now I've chucked it all away. You must hate me.'

Sitting on the wall beside him Rex said, 'Great Scott, you really are sunk into the depths of despondency to think that of me. Here I am about to fly off into the unknown, and that sort of thing is liable to make me head for the sun and keep going. Where would the R.F.C. be then?'

Unaccountably emotional, Chris forced a smile. 'Idiot!'

'That makes two of us. Come on, that lovely girl of yours will soon be ready to leave. You'd better get out of that fancy outfit and into something more suited to a private tutor to the children of the Diplomatic Corps, or you'll miss the train.'

But Roland and Dr Deacon made sure he did not.

They reached their honeymoon hotel in Bournemouth too late for dinner, so they had a tray brought to the room. Conversation during the short train journey had been stilted and limited to essentials, Chris finding his gloom deepening once more on leaving his home and saying goodbye to Rex, with all that that farewell signified. He had hardly looked at Marion, just being vaguely aware that his wife was dressed in a blue wool costume, with a matching hat.

His wife! Oh God, how he hated her for what she had done to him! He had hunched in the first-class compartment, staring from the window at his own reflection as they chugged through the dark countryside. If Austria had not moved an army toward the Serbian border, Codrington's father would not have been called to the Foreign Office, the trip to the Greek Islands would have gone ahead, he would not have been there at the cricket match, and *his wife* would not have enticed him to physically wrest his spectacles from her. His present predicament could be laid at the door of Emperor Franz Josef of Austria-Hungary, he had then realised.

Once that had occurred to him, his brain had begun reviewing the sequence of events which had led to Austria's coveting of Serbia, and the fascinating occupation of tracing back through the annals of history to find the real original source of guilt for the fact that he was now sitting in a train to Bournemouth instead of reading in some cosy rooms in Cambridge, had so absorbed him,

Marion had had to tell him that they had arrived at their destination.

But, left alone in the large hotel bedroom with the hands of the clock pointing at ten-fifteen, the mind that could grapple with advanced mathematics, ancient pedantic languages, and the most obscure prose, could not cope with the problem of one bed for two people, when he wanted two beds, one for each person.

While he was still nonplussed, Marion, who had disappeared into the small dressing-room, now emerged in a long voluminous white nightgown with frills all around the top and silly blue bows all over it. She climbed into the brocade-covered four-poster and sat looking at him, her long hair down over her shoulders, and her eyes huge with something he had seen in them before on the night of the procession.

'Aren't you coming to bed, Chris?' she asked in the same soft persuasive tones as she had used in her father's waiting-room.

It caught him on the raw, and sent him forward to clutch one of the oak posts. 'You little hypocrite! For the past three weeks you've been going around like a wronged virgin, letting your father insult and vilify me, and wringing demands from my brother that I pay for my sin against you. They've never once been allowed to see what you're really like, never once suspected that you are fast and completely shameless. Now you're at it again! You *asked* me to undress you that night, and enjoyed every moment of it as much as I did.'

She looked slightly shaken, but remained composed. 'I didn't ask you to give me a child.'

Clutching the post tighter, he said hoarsely, 'Do you think I wanted to? Rex said I should have known the golden rule that saves a man from this predicament. Well, I didn't . . . and I still don't. But I've got one of my own now. You might have dragged me into this by using your body very cleverly, but you'll never confuse me with it a second time. I don't want to touch you or see you naked ever again. You've made my life a travesty of that of the villagers, and I'll never forgive you. *Never!*'

'Oh, *Chris!*' She was out of the bed and round to him before he guessed her intention. Clutching the post, also, she said desperately, 'I didn't want it this way, truly I didn't. What do you think it has been like for me all these weeks? Daddy has been completely broken by it.'

'Then why the hell didn't he get rid of it for you? He's a doctor, isn't he?'

Colour receding she said, 'He's not only a doctor, he's a strong Christian. The ethics of both are that life must be preserved at all costs. Roland upheld that, without question, as you know. In any case, abortion is a crime—even more so when performed on a member of the doctor's own family.'

'Damn that! No one but you and your father would have known, and it would have got us out of this marriage,' he said harshly.

'I didn't want to get out of it.'

He stared at her, accepting, once more, that she had deliberately trapped him. 'You will, when you find out what it's going to be like. I hate you, Marion.'

Slowly her eyes filled with tears. 'I love you, Chris.'

Feeling sick he went to sit on the chaise longue with his head in his hands. Then she was beside him, sinking down onto the floor with her nightdress billowing around her as she tried to look up into his face.

'When we were children, I admired you for your superior knowledge on every subject under the sun. When you began to develop, I found the combination of physical strength and disdain of it very endearing. When I . . . when I came upon you suddenly that day by the river, you seemed bigger, more muscular than ever. I hadn't seen you since Christmas, and my feelings suddenly took on another aspect. When I saw you without your spectacles that hide those wonderful eyes and with your wet shirt outlining your body, I knew I wanted to make you notice me in the same way.' Her hand crept up onto his knee, but he moved his leg quickly, and it dropped to the ground again. Her head hung down as if she were studying the rejected hand. 'But you still saw me as an unimportant childhood friend, so I had to make you realise I was a pretty girl. You responded too swiftly and violently. It took me by storm.'

'So you admit you wanted me to do that that night?' he said getting to his feet.

She looked up, tears now rolling onto her cheeks. 'I didn't intend to ruin your life. I did it for love.'

'Well, *I* didn't. I did it for lust . . . and lust has now grown cold.'

'But love can grow instead. I'll make it, I swear I will,' she said, brushing her cheeks with the back of her hands. 'Chris, *please* don't hate me. You've been brutal since you found out about the baby, but I took it because I knew you were upset about university.'

'*Upset,*' he cried. 'You have no comprehension of how I feel. You'll never make love grow in me.'

'You'll never kill it in me,' she whispered.

'More fool you!'

Getting wearily to her feet she said, 'Love is never foolish—it's just human. That's something you find it difficult to be, Chris.' She stood before him with all her pride at her feet. 'During the coming months I have to face my father's deep disillusionment in me, Roland's cold civility, and the gossip of everyone in the village. I'm willing to pay that price for you. You claim to have already paid a higher one. Perhaps you have, but I became your legal wife today in a ceremony you mocked by your complete indifference, and it will last until one of us dies. Please, *please,* help me, Chris. I'll be the perfect wife; I'll make you proud of your child. I'll follow you wherever you want to go, and I'll try to learn more so that you won't find me dull company. All I ask in return is that you accept this marriage and me as your wife.'

He looked at her in numb resignation. 'I don't have much choice with that gold ring on your finger, do I? But the sole reason for all this was merely to give a child a name. Well, I've given it one by going through that ceremony today. As far as I'm concerned, my honourable duty is now done. I'll sleep in the dressing-room tonight. In the morning, I'll ask to be moved to a room with two beds. That's how it will continue when we go home . . . except that the beds will be in separate rooms, also.'

He walked into the dressing-room and locked the door behind him.

The next morning Marion was sick in the wash-bowl as soon as she got out of bed, and continued vomiting for half an hour. The same thing happened every morning that week. When they returned to Tarrant Hall at the end of their seven-day honeymoon, Chris thankfully reclaimed his own bedroom. During the weeks that followed, he saw her only at mealtimes and subdued her into silence by ignoring her questions of the success of his day. Mistakenly he believed he could remain immune from her claims on him.

4

THE REPUTATION that was destined to make Second-Lieutenant Rex Sheridan's name familiar all over the world, began at the Central Flying School at Upavon on Salisbury Plain on Christmas Eve, 1914.

Much to his disgust, the fact that he was already an experienced pilot when he joined the Royal Flying Corps got him a home posting as an instructor as soon as he had finished his basic military training, and he had to watch those he taught go off to France and the great adventure of war, while he buzzed round and around the airfield with one novice after another in the rear seat.

Because of the urgent need for pilots, training was very basic and done on a hit-and-miss concept. The blame lay with the machines rather than the men. Unprepared for war, the Corps had a motley selection of aircraft at its disposal, each with its own peculiarities of performance. Often, a pupil would have two lessons in a Farman, then his instructor would find only a B.E. available the next day, or an Avro. This meant that 'flips', as they were called, could turn into a series of hair-raising stunts as the pupil copied what he had learnt and found the machine responding in an unexpected way.

In Rex's case, it was the other way around. He and his pupil got off to a bad start. The R.F.C., having derived from the Royal Engineers, was very much an army corps. But, in the way of offshoots, soon set about developing unique facets that distinguished it from its earthbound counterparts. Fliers being somewhat reckless and individual men, one of the first aspects to be discarded was the rigid discipline and military etiquette practised by the hidebound regiments dating back to Cromwell, and so on. This suited Rex admirably, having joined straight from university. But a number of regular soldiers applied for transfer into the Corps, and these men turned up at Upavon to be taught how to fly, fully expecting the School to be run like a military academy.

Some adapted to the more free and easy atmosphere with pleasure. Captain James Ashmore did not.

On arrival at the shed, Rex found this moustached gentleman looking at his watch with a frowning expression. The flight had been scheduled for 9 A.M.. It was now five minutes past.

'Captain Ashmore?' asked Rex pleasantly.

'You're late!' –

'Yes, I was late for breakfast.'

'That's no excuse.'

'It is when you've been practising night-flying,' he said in firm tones. 'Are you all set to go?'

'*Sir.*'

Rex paused in the act of pulling on his flying-helmet. 'I beg your pardon?'

'Don't you respect rank?' snapped the Captain.

'I respect the man with superior knowledge . . . which is me, at the moment.' He pointed heavenward. 'Up there, there's no time for vanities. While a man is saying "sir" he could be thrown into a spin. The object of flying is to get safely down again, whether you're a late fishmonger, or a smart captain of cavalry. We all look the same when in the midst of a pile of wreckage.' He jammed the soft leather helmet onto his red hair and fastened the strap under his chin. 'If you'd like to climb in, Captain Ashmore, we'll waste no more time. I have six more men booked before lunch and I don't want to be late for *that.*'

Rex immediately forgot the exchange as he took the aircraft up to two hundred feet and began demonstrating the more advanced manoeuvring his pupil needed after three earlier lessons with another instructor. Then, with his feet still resting on the rudder-bar, and his gloved hands lightly on the shaped grips of the cross-bar on the control-lever, he allowed his pupil to take over.

It was a cold raw morning with the frost still not dispelled from the more exposed areas of Salisbury Plain below them. Thinking wistfully of the lucky ones he had sent on their way to France, he shouted instructions automatically and wondered how soon he could get a posting over there. There was no excitement in this, just circling round and around at a few hundred feet, staring down at Stonehenge. Chris would doubtless find the circle of stone slabs of intense fascination. But he was heartily sick of the sight of them.

The lesson went well, Ashmore's pedantic attitude helping him through his paces with textbook correctness. But how would he be under attack, when a man had to think fast and inventively, Rex wondered.

No sooner had that thought occurred when Ashmore committed the cardinal sin of letting the nose drop whilst in the middle of a turn. But even as Rex bellowed the instructions that would correct the spin, he knew the man had 'frozen' at the controls with fear—something all learners did at some time or other. Taking over quickly, Rex did all that was necessary to pull out of the dive. But, for the moment, he had forgotten which aircraft he was flying and found the response to his actions sluggish and slightly different from what he expected. Rushing earthward with the icy wind whistling past his face, he tried to think what was wrong. By the time he did, it was too late to come out of the situation cleanly.

Flattening out dangerously close to the ground and just in front of a large shed, he banked to avoid it. But the ancient machine could not cope with such treatment. It dropped heavily, bounded with a sickening jolt that broke the wheel struts, then rose slightly to glide just above the ground until it reached a large haystack on the airfield's perimeter.

Rex spent Christmas and New Year in the next hospital bed to Captain James Ashmore . . . and that was how he gained his wish to give up instructing and go to France.

When a pilot went out to join a squadron already in France, he took an aircraft with him. Machines were lost as frequently as men, and a second-lieutenant in a nice clean uniform, straight from the peace and tranquillity of England, who turned up looking healthy and well-fed, was definitely unwelcome if he *walked* into the midst of his new comrades.

Rex flew in, but he had not expected such a reception committee waiting on the ground, such a collection of pale faces gazing up as he came in to land on a rough field that had been part of a farm until the R.F.C. had taken it over, along with some outbuildings. Looking down, he thought the entire squadron must be out to watch his arrival. Were they *that* desperate for men? Overflying the field prior to turning to land, he gave them a cheery wave to boost their morale. But no one waved back, each man still staring upward as though he had never seen an aviator before.

When he landed, he noted that the muddy surface had been well and truly churned up by aircraft wheels, and a spurt of excitement rushed through him. He was now 'on active service'. He could really claim to be part of the war now, and he would be flying the way he most enjoyed, free and individually.

He taxied toward the aircraft-sheds and noted, with some surprise, that even the mechanics were all lined up watching his approach. Had they no other work to do? He was being waved toward the end shed, so he swung the aircraft round to come to a halt in front of it, so that it could easily be wheeled in. Then he switched off and climbed over the wires around his feet to scramble rather stiffly to the ground. It had been a long cold journey, all told, and he was glad to arrive.

A mechanic with a poker-face came up to him. 'Mr Sheridan, sir? We was expecting you. P'raps you'd like to see your machine safely away, like most of the other gentlemen here.' He put out an arm to indicate the shed. 'We've reserved that one for you, sir.'

Rex peered inside the shed, frowned, then took a closer look. He found the answer to his comprehensive reception. At the end of the shed was a farm-wagon containing a veritable haystack.

He stood looking at it for a moment, then turned back to the mechanic and demanded to know his name.

The man's face grew even longer. 'Foxstead, sir.'

'Very well, Foxstead, let's get one thing straight from the start, shall we?'

Blue eyes began hardening slightly, and he snapped out, 'Yes-sir.'

'You find me a nice French wench, and I'll show you what else I can do with a haystack,' he promised with a broad wink.

Slowly the plain honest face broke into a smile that curled from ear to ear. 'There's some dainty little mademoyselles in the next village.' He signalled to his assistants to come forward. 'Leave this to us, Mr Sheridan. We'll put her away all right. You go off and settle in. She'll be ready any time you want her in the morning.'

'Are you referring to the machine, or the village wench?' asked Rex.

The smile broadened even further. 'Seems to me you won't have no trouble finding one of them for yourself.'

Laughing Rex pulled his two suitcases and spare flying boots and jacket from the other cockpit, and began walking across the grass to where a group of young officers were standing like a reception committee. Reaching them, he dumped his baggage on the steps of the hut, and looked at them all frankly.

'I'm Rex Sheridan. I knew you'd be pleased to see me, but I didn't expect you to go to the trouble of moving all the bloody haystacks in the area under cover, just to make me feel more at ease. I appreciate the gesture, however, and you must be thankful it wasn't a church I hit.'

There was general laughter, and he was invited into the hut that served as an Officers' Mess for the squadron. They all seemed to be around his own age, and had spent some weeks overseas flying patrols, doing reconnaissance work, and shooting down German observation balloons. There were not many of them, as yet, and they had a lot of sky to cover. They looked tired and pale, their natural youthful buoyancy bumped up to exaggerated proportions. The need to laugh made them go to any lengths to do so.

Rex soon saw why. The 'quarters' he was given turned out to be a bell-tent he could pitch anywhere he liked, so long as it was not on the airfield. The Mess was a wooden outbuilding that had belonged to the farm, and it still smelled of the beets and potatoes that had been stored in it, despite the scrubbing with antiseptic and several coats of whitewash. The Squadron Offices were similar. Even the Commanding Officer, a Major Crookhorn, occupied one 'stall' in what everyone proclaimed had been the farm piggery until the advance-party of 2F Squadron arrived on the scene and foolishly allowed itself to accept what the French farmer had slyly called 'spacious outbuildings' far from the farmyard and its smells. Small wonder the C.O. was nicknamed 'Porky'.

Apart from this collection of insalubrious sheds, there was a tiny village called Grissons several miles down the road, and a canal two fields away, along which barges passed regularly. For the rest, the countryside was green, hilly, and divided into farms, much like the area around Tarrant Royal. In summer, it would probably be very pleasant; in that early February of 1915 it looked desolate, depressing and icy. With only a tinny piano and a temperamental gramophone with half-a-dozen scratchy records to provide entertainment, the men of the squadron, particularly the pilots and observers who constantly risked their lives, indulged in boisterous sing-songs and games every evening.

Rex practically froze to death that first evening in his tent.

There were two other pilots in similar accommodation, and he had been informed by a drunken lieutenant, called 'Daddy' because he was the oldest at twenty-four, that when someone was killed they all moved up one in the sleeping order, so he might very soon be occupying a bed in the hut. Unfortunately for the 'Bedouins' as the tent-dwellers were dubbed, the last casualty had not even reached the hut. It was his tent Rex was now occupying. So, all in all, Rex did not get much sleep that first night on active service.

In the morning, he was allotted a batman called Jessop, who brought him a mug of khaki tea and a jug of lukewarm water much the same colour. The man was cheerful and friendly and, once Rex discovered that he hailed from Dorset, that unique relationship between a soldier-servant and his officer was assured. Lathering his face and opening his razor, Rex asked the man about the day-to-day life of the squadron. It was something of a shock to hear that barely two or three days passed without a crash of some kind. They were not always fatal, and often the fliers walked away unharmed. But the main enemy, it appeared, was not the Hun but the aeroplane. Engines constantly failed, struts and wires broke, controls responded too sluggishly (something Rex knew only too well), pilots froze to their control-columns in the open cockpits. The second worst enemy was the weather. Fog prevented navigation; freezing, pelting rain blinded men with the same results. The Hun was seemingly benign, in comparison. When encountering an aircraft bearing the black Maltese cross of Germany, the odds were even. He had a gun, and so did you. Providing yours did not jam—a regular occurrence—it was one aviator's skill against another. A good clean contest between gentlemen who respected each other, was Jessop's conclusion.

'Take young Mr 'Aines, now,' he went on. 'Already 'is tally is a D.F.W. and two balloons, and from each of these flights 'e comes back safe and sound like. Then yesdee 'e goes out on ordinary patrol, 'is engine gives up the ghost, and down 'e comes like a kestrel on a fieldmouse. Ends up climbing from a pile o' sticks, all cuts and bruises, ten miles inside our own lines. Praise be for that! The C.O. gets a message that the army's picked 'im up and sending 'im back. But they danged engines is responsible! If them that makes them 'ad to fly the machines they're in, there'd be a different story, make no mistake.'

Rex wiped the blade of his razor and tested the smoothness of his chin. 'You forget, Jessop, that only a few years ago men were jumping off buildings in the hope that two wings of feathers glued onto brown paper would allow them to imitate the birds.' He turned to waggle the razor at the plump indignant man. 'Your kestrel has perfected his plummet over the centuries. Aero-engine designers are still experimenting in the miracle of flight.' Then he grinned. 'Besides, if they had to fly the damned things they invented, there'd be none of them left to make the improvements.'

Lieutenant Mallory Haines, called Mal by his fellows, arrived back in the sidecar of an army motor cycle just as they were finishing their breakfast. Rex was the only one left sitting at the table as the rest scrambled up to go out and raise a cheer at his return. Then they 'chaired' him in, in schoolboy fashion and let him drop rather heavily into the chair at the head of the table, which was always left empty until occupied by a lost 'dove' safely returned. As the Germans termed themselves 'eagles of the air' 2F Squadron called themselves the 'doves of peace' that flew to combat aggression. Any man brought down who escaped death or capture was presented with an emblem made from doves' feathers, which he wore in his cap until one or the other finally overtook him.

In a noisy ceremony the recent arrival was questioned about his descent, the nature and precise situation of his cuts and bruises, then was presented with the dove emblem, which he proudly pinned into the front of his forage-cap. At that point, he noticed the silent spectator and asked to be introduced.

Rex shook hands with him, and Mal Haines regarded him thoughtfully before saying, 'Sheridan? Know that name from somewhere. Don't happen to have a brother who rides a horse as if he was born on one, do you?'

'Yes, do you know Roland?' Rex asked with a smile.

'Met him at a weekend-party. Never forget a name—especially when the fellow rides like that,' the youngster with a black eye and a cut on the chin told him. 'Right at the moment, I prefer horses to aircraft. Not so bloody far to fall.' He frowned and pursed his lips before venturing, 'I say, didn't your father . . .'

'Commit suicide? Yes, last July,' Rex agreed equably. 'Roland was left with the house and estate to run on very little money. He's had to sell his horses, I'm afraid.'

'He ought to be all right for some relaxation. Cavalry regiments are usually very keen to show off their crack riders.'

'He's not in the cavalry. I told you, he has a large estate to run.'

'You mean he hasn't volunteered?' came the astonished question. 'What's he hanging back for when they're crying out for men?'

Rex got to his feet. 'Perhaps he's determined there'll be a few left when madmen like us have finished killing ourselves and anyone else we can find, just as an excuse to do what we most enjoy —fly!'

The other man looked at him consideringly. 'I thought it was haystacks you met head-on.'

'Oh, I don't place restrictions on myself. I'm game to try any obstacle that looks soft in the middle.'

After a moment or two, Mal began to smile. 'Now that's out of our systems, we can carry on where we left off. The man you have replaced used to be my partner on patrols. I'll be glad to have you with me and teach you the ropes. Shall I tell the C.O. to fix it?'

'Of course,' agreed Rex, relaxing.

So, for the next week, Rex was introduced to the routine of patrolling the Allied lines in case stray Huns tried a bit of sharp-shooting on those in the trenches. Apart from the appalling weather during those seven days, when rain fell almost constantly and he returned weary, red-eyed, cold and saturated, it was a strange experience to fly over miles and miles of ditches running with mud and know that some poor devils were living day-in, day-out in them. Occasionally, something pale would flutter at the end of a bayonet in comradely salute, and Rex would wave enthusiastically back. But nothing seemed to be happening: the war had stopped in two lines of trenches facing each other across a few miles of mud, apparently for no other gain than killing anyone who looked over the rims. What had happened to the grand Teutonic sweep to conquer Europe, and the glorious defence of freedom to counter it?

The death-toll in the trenches seemed particularly poignant when a letter reached Rex after going from Upavon to the hospital where he had spent Christmas, back to Salisbury Plain, and finally out to Grissons via the army post office. It was from Roland to say that Chris had a son, born prematurely two days after New

Year, and that mother and child were doing well. He did not say how the father was, but went on to write of village matters and all he was doing with the estate. The news made Rex unusually thoughtful, and Mal commented on the fact as they walked across to their machines for their usual patrol, under pale bluish skies, for once.

'I've just heard that I'm an uncle,' he said. 'My brother had a son in December.'

'Good lord, I didn't know he was married.'

'This is my younger brother, not Roland.'

Mal laughed as he pulled on his flying-helmet. 'If he's younger than you he must still be in sailor-suits. I've heard of child-brides, but not many child-bridegrooms.'

'Poor little devil! I feel sorry for him,' murmured Rex.

'He seems to be doing very nicely, with a son already.'

'I meant the baby.' They reached their aircraft to find their observers waiting for them, and Rex called out to Mal as he climbed in, carefully stepping over the piano-wires around the seat, 'Don't you agree it's the wrong time to come into the world? Who knows what a mess we might make of it for him?'

Mal called back, 'Who needs a messy world when he's got an uncle like you? That's why *I* feel sorry for the poor little blighter.'

The patrol followed the usual pattern for the first hour and Rex, growing colder and colder in his open seat, was lost in thoughts of Chris as he flew steadily along the route he now knew by heart. His young brother had written no letter since his wedding—he had always been a poor correspondent—so he had no indication of how the boy was adapting to the marriage that had broken his life apart. Rex was worried whenever he thought about it. Brilliance could soon go 'over the top'. Everyone was familiar with the caricature of the 'mad professor', but there was a lot of truth in it. Since Roland characteristically chose to ignore something he could neither accept nor forgive, Rex was left to speculate on what might become of his young brother.

He was brought suddenly from his thoughts by a bang as his observer thumped the side of the aircraft—the usual method of attracting his attention. But he had no need to turn his head for enlightenment. Some distance ahead, an aircraft was flying low along the line of intersecting trenches held by the French and British troops. It looked like a bright yellow moth with black

70

markings as it glided along, a dark shadow cast by the watery sun moving along the earth with it. But it was a moth that spat death at those beneath it.

Rex gave a quick glance at Mal flying alongside, and encountered a broad smile beneath the goggles, and a gauntleted hand jabbing downward. He nodded agreement to Mal's signal to go down and sandwich the yellow-painted D.F.W. while they peppered it from both sides.

Excitement suddenly leapt through him as he put the nose down, first ensuring that the man behind him had translated the signals the same way and was ready with his gun.

It was heady, that first attack he had ever made on another flier and, strangely, the thought that he was attempting to kill two men was obliterated by the thrill of matching his skill against another's. Like fox-hunting, it was the chase that mattered; the tearing to pieces of one furry creature by a pack of others was an anti-climax.

As he dived on the unsuspecting German fliers, Rex realised the troops below were being raked with bullets whilst the blinding angle of the sun prevented their retaliation, and the lowness of the aeroplane precluded attack by the heavier guns. So busy were the Germans with their gleeful sport, they only became aware of the pair diving on them a short while before Rex and Mal began to flatten out and draw alongside. The faces inside that yellow aircraft were full of alarm as they turned toward Rex. Their best avoiding tactic—that of diving—was denied them because they were already so low. The alternative was to climb, but the enemy airmen would know they would be immediately dogged by two pilots ready for the move.

For a moment or two, all three flew along in formation, firing at each other all the while. Rex thought only of handling his aircraft to the best advantage for his observer with the light machine-gun, and so that he could get in a few shots at the yellow machines with his own service revolver on the cord around his shoulder. Although he heard German bullets ripping through the fabric just ahead of where he sat, he kept doggedly on the course that held the other in a sandwich with Mal on the other side.

Next minute, it seemed the enemy's gun had jammed, for the dark-faced German stopped firing as his pilot began to climb, leaving the yellow bi-plane completely at their mercy. But the grin left Rex's face very swiftly as their victim soared upward, and he pulled up the nose of his own aircraft to look straight at three other machines with the black cross on their wings, which were now diving onto himself and Mal Haines. Caught in their own trap, Mal signalled Rex to break away in an inward turn so that they would cross each other's paths with inches to spare and reverse their direction, thus fooling the men diving in the expectation of following outward climbing turns.

It was a splendid idea of Mal's, Rex thought as he went into the tightest right-hand turn his machine could manage, except that it damned near killed them all. It did more than confuse the enemy fliers. Aircraft criss-crossed in a desperate mêlée of machines that almost touched wing-tips, only a hundred feet above the ground. Further cooperation with his partner was impossible, under the circumstances, because they did not have the time to signal to each other in the midst of a group of two-to-one against them. So, fastening onto the tail of one of the D.F.W.'s he chased it determinedly as it flew close above the ground. But he knew his observer was not in the best position for firing, and he thought quickly. His quarry was shooting straight back at them and was plainly counting on superior speed to take him back over his own lines, luring Rex onto enemy territory. He knew he had to make his kill swiftly, or lose all hope of advantage in the one-sided scrap.

He acted without hesitation. Dipping the nose, he took his own aircraft down to a mere sixty feet and directly in line with the enemy machine, thus restricting the firing capacity of the other gunner, who would run the risk of shooting off his own tail, and improving the chances of his own, who would now be firing upward. The enemy pilot, who could not now see where Rex was, flung his machine into some uneasy manoeuvres to remedy it. But Rex was watching the D.F.W. like a hawk and matched turn for turn, swing for swing as he continued his crazy height just above the ground. All the time, his observer was firing up into yellow fabric and tearing it apart. Then, the enemy gunner slumped lifeless over the side, and the whole thing was over shortly after that. Half a wing suddenly fell from the D.F.W. and it turned onto its side, belching smoke, before dropping into some trees.

Flying over the spot a second or two later, his wheels not much above the tops of the trees, Rex saw the pilot struggling to get out, and waved to him. Then, as he turned, he spotted a whole crowd of French and English soldiers waving madly at him in jubilation.

He grinned at his observer, who looked surprisingly pale, and flew across to waggle his wings at the cheering troops.

But joy was shortlived. Another bang on the side by his back-seat flier brought his head round swiftly to see Mal, hot in pursuit of one enemy, unaware that another was flying very low and about to come up right beneath him. Instantly Rex made a difficult right turn over a farm, frightening all the cows in the fields, and put himself on a course that would take him head-on toward the yellow machine. The ruse worked. The German pilot's attention was taken by the new adversary, and he forgot about attacking Mal.

Later, Rex was to wonder when his intention to veer to port had turned into a calm decision to keep straight on and force the other man to veer in panic. At the time, all he felt was tremendous inner excitement as his collision course took him nearer and nearer the other flier, and he knew his enemy was going to call his bluff. He thought he heard a shout from behind, but he needed all his concentration to keep on the course that took him straight at the nose of the other aircraft. As he did so, he knew he had never experienced anything to compare with this thrill.

The German flier was young with a fair moustache, and was smiling as he fired his revolver at Rex, until the moment his nerve broke. Apparently forgetting how low he was, he tried to dive beneath Rex and hit the ground at full speed, smashing his machine beyond recognition.

Full of immediate elation, Rex found his glee turning to consternation as oil started squirting from his engine to cover his goggles with a thick black layer. Pushing them up quickly, he then received the jet in his eyes. Fighting to wipe it away, he twisted to appeal to his observer and discovered that the man was hanging over the side, apparently lifeless. Turning back swiftly he realised the aircraft was losing height much too fast. At the same time, the engine began spluttering and coughing ominously. Doing all he could to keep the machine up, and desperately dashing the oil from his eyes, his vision cleared just as the engine stopped altogether. It was then impossible to do anything.

'Oh no,' he groaned. 'Not another of the bloody things!'

His wheels caught the top of the huge haystack and, next minute, he was dangling upside down from an aircraft that was on its back. Somewhat stiffly he unfastened his belt and dropped to the ground. Apart from giddiness he was all in one piece, so he made his way along to his co-flier swinging head-downward. The man was still alive, but with a nasty wound in his shoulder that was bleeding a lot.

Leaving him dangling for a moment, Rex dragged some hay from the stack to make a rough bed for the injured man. Then, supporting the dead weight as best he could, he released the belt holding the observer in and eased him to the ground. As he did so, he heard a roar overhead and looked up. Mal was flying past looking down at the crashed machine.

Rex walked a few feet into the open and waved to let his friend know he was all right. Mal signalled accordingly, then headed off toward Grissons waggling his wings. There was no sign of enemy aircraft now. They had either shared the fate of the other two, or decided retreat was advisable. Going back to the wounded man, Rex took off his own long scarf and bound it tightly around the wound with inexpert concentration, wishing it had been in a more convenient part of the body. He had just finished the task when the man opened his eyes.

Rex grinned at him. 'I was just beginning to feel lonely with no one to talk to.'

The man's eyes swivelled to take in the wrecked aircraft above him. 'You mean, we're still alive?'

'I am . . . but you gave me a hell of a fright for a moment or two.'

The other stared at him as if looking at a lunatic. '*I* gave *you* a fright! You're mad! Suppose that Hun hadn't dived.'

'We'd be on the ground, just the same,' was Rex's cool answer.

'In fifty flaming pieces! Don't ever do that again when I'm flying with you.'

'Close your eyes next time.'

'I did. I think I fainted with fright.' He winced as he looked around again. 'How did we get down here?'

Rex made an apologetic face. 'A haystack, I'm afraid.'

There was no response to the admission, and the man's eyes seemed to be focusing on a point just above Rex's right shoulder. He turned to see two hefty men in rough clothes standing there staring at them, their expressions showing caution and curiosity.

'*Bonjour messieurs,* ' he greeted, walking toward them with hand outstretched.

'*Monsieur L'Aviateur, êtes-vous sain et sauf?*'

'*Oui, merci.*' He shook their hands firmly. '*Mais mon camarade est blessé.*'

They moved closer to see the wounded man, telling Rex they were from a barge on the nearby canal and had seen the whole aerial fight. Full of admiration for their English allies, they offered the spartan comforts of their boat, a rough bed, and simple hot meals until they passed Grissons two days later. Rex thanked them for their offer, but was doubtful about accepting it. His observer really should get expert medical treatment, he felt.

But before he was forced to make a decision, a rider appeared from behind the haystack. This was a young French cavalry officer, who had come across the field from the trenches, where he was attached as a courier to a unit holding the front line just ahead of the village. He immediately offered to fetch a stretcher-party for the injured man, and transport back to Grissons for Rex.

On the point of agreeing to this, Rex caught sight of movement behind the bargees. A girl of no more than eighteen, dressed in a brown homespun dress with an overtight bodice, and a shawl that did nothing to cover what the bodice revealed, was looking at him with petulant sultry invitation.

'*La nièce de ma femme,*' explained one of the bargees.

'Ah,' said Rex, revising his plans immediately, and telling the cavalryman that he would be glad of a stretcher and medical attention for his friend, but that he would return to his squadron on the barge, adding that he did not want to use military transport when it was urgently needed at the Front.

'Ah-ha,' smiled the French officer, a man after Rex's own style. '*C'est la guerre—vive l'amour!*'

When he walked across the dusk-filled fields after leaving the barge at a point on the canal nearest to the airfield, Rex had two-day red stubble on his chin, a satisfying lethargy in his limbs, and a bubbling happiness in his heart. Spring was on the way, women were soft and responsive anywhere in the world, and he had brought down two enemy aircraft with the help of his observer. Best of all, he was flying—flying every day and in the most exciting fashion. There was surely nothing more a man of twenty could want than what he had right now!

The sight of the silhouetted aircraft standing on the grass waiting to be put away into their sheds lifted his heart further. Mechanics would be flown to his capsized machine, and it would be brought back. Meanwhile, he would beg, borrow or steal another so that he could go up again right away.

News of his arrival spread like wildfire, and the presentation of the dove emblem to wear in his cap began an evening of celebration that went on into the small hours. Dinner was followed by an impromptu concert that allowed them all to relieve youthful verve that could not be done in more pleasurable ways. Rex was dragged to the piano to start them off on a sing-song that quickly degenerated to vigorous bawling of lewd verses to popular music-hall songs. He sang as lustily as the rest but, since everyone insisted on buying their new hero a drink, his performance grew more and more erratic until he could no longer see the keyboard clearly. At that point he was hauled from the piano-stool and dumped onto the floor to make way for a more sober entertainer.

It was while he was sitting there wondering whether or not it was worth the effort of trying to stand up, that Mal dropped heavily to the floor beside him and began fumbling inside his own unbuttoned tunic.

'Found something to show you,' he mumbled drunkenly. 'Been looking everywhere for it since you first arrived. Knew I had it. Now I've found it,' he finished with a fatuous grin. 'There you are!'

Rex had to look at it for a long time before it really jumped into focus. Then he could think of nothing to say. The photograph of a group of young men at a house-party showed Roland at his best. Laughing, windswept, dressed in breeches and silk shirt, he looked the epitome of wealthy upper-class youth. But when Rex had last seen him, his brother had worn a haunted worried expression and seemed to have aged tremendously in only a few months.

Suddenly maudlin, he turned his gaze from the picture. How things had changed since the days of that photograph! He had recovered his own lost hopes by joining the R.F.C. Chris had thrown his away by his own folly. But Roland was still paying for what their father had done, and would go on paying. He was that sort of person. For the first time, Rex wondered if he should have stayed and shared the burden. Had Roland looked on his going away to war as betrayal, he wondered?

'Ought to be in the cavalry,' murmured Mal. 'Don't understand it. Great patriot . . . at least, I *thought* he was.'

Rex got to his feet clumsily. 'Don't tell me that's why you volunteered. It was for the same bloody reason I did. *To fly!* We're selfish, Mal. My brother isn't. He's the most unselfish person I know, and it will destroy him, in the end.'

'Silly sod!' proclaimed Mal without malice.

'What's all this talk of selfishness and destruction?' came a voice behind Rex.

He turned to see a stranger around his own height, very dark-complexioned, with black hair and curiously pale, almost silvery, eyes.

'We were having a private conversation,' Rex admonished with the dignity of the inebriated.

'Then stop shouting at each other.' He smiled and held out his hand. 'You were away when I flew in to join the squadron. I'm Mike Manning, from Narraburra.'

'Where?'

'Awstralia,' supplied Mal getting to his feet beside Rex.

'How often did you refuel on the way over?' Rex asked him with a straight face.

'Oh, I've got a machine invented by the aborigines,' came the equally straightfaced answer. 'It doesn't need refuelling, just takes a rest in a haystack every so often.'

Rex shook his head sadly. 'Just my luck! I think I've invented something original, then some wild colonial boy comes along to tell me the natives thought of it first.'

All three sat in a corner with another whisky each, and Mike told them a little about himself. His father had been sent to Australia to 'make good' after he had got into bad company and been involved in a scandal concerning a lady in the Prince of Wales' circle. Joining the gold prospectors he had struck lucky and made enough money to buy a large property and raise sheep. Mike and his sister had gone to school in the city, and it was whilst travelling home for the holidays that Mike had been struck by the great stretches of land that cut people off from each other. At seventeen, he had begun building a flying-machine to remedy it. It had been completed six months ago, on his nineteenth birthday.

'The only thing was, it didn't have an engine in it,' he confessed disarmingly. 'I couldn't afford that. So, when I heard there was a war going on over here, I got on the first ship leaving for England. I guess I'd outgrown the excitement of just sitting in the damn thing on the ground, and I hoped the R.F.C. would have engines in theirs.'

'Only just,' warned Rex solemnly. 'How is it I don't remember you at the Central Flying School?'

'You were in hospital when I joined. But Captain James Ashmore told me all about you when he resumed his lessons. I hope, for your sake, you never come across him again.'

'He only broke an ankle,' protested Rex. 'Whereas I dislocated a shoulder, ripped off half an ear, and damn near made a eunuch of myself.'

'Must have been painful!'

Rex grinned at him across the top of his whisky glass. 'But the treatment more than compensates—especially if the nurses are pretty. Can you imagine having your . . .'

His fascinating question was never completed, because the C.O. entered at that moment to tell everyone that Rex's observer had arrived back from the French field-hospital.

'How on earth does a nurse put a bandage on *that?*' asked Mal as he got to his feet to join the others all intent on bestowing a dove emblem on the returning hero. But he never got an answer.

A different observer was detailed to fly with Rex on the following morning. A hangover from the night's hilarity, and the fact that he was flying a different machine with a different man behind him, made Rex approach the patrol cautiously. He ran through the range of hand-signals he used to make certain the other man understood what they meant, and he checked his control-lever and engine more thoroughly than usual before signalling the men on the ground to pull away the chocks. As he opened the throttle, he glanced at Mal preparing to take off beside him. They grinned at each other as both machines began bumping forward over the field, gaining speed with every yard.

'See you on the nearest haystack,' yelled Mal boisterously.

The tail went up, then Rex's B.E. lifted into the air at the same instant as the other machine. Caution fell away, and he felt the usual tremendous elation as he rose up, borne on the air like a bird, alongside a man whose blood, he knew, would be tingling like his own. They were a good pair. They understood each other. There was an even greater thrill when flying practically in harness, because the comradeship of the air was like no other.

They had just cleared the trees at the end of the field, and Rex turned to check that Mal was about to make a right-bank, as usual. At that moment, the engine of the other machine began to cough, cut-out, spluttered for a moment or two, then cut out again. The right bank turned into a complete loop only feet above the ground, and the machine plunged into a shallow quarry, the nose completely disintegrating on impact.

Stunned, Rex had to continue his manoeuvre before he could make an attempt to land in the small clearing beside the quarry but, all the time, his eyes were focusing on the wreck below for signs of life. Then he was horrified to see a lick of flame appear from beneath the body of the machine, and start to spread.

He returned to earth with such haste and urgency, the landing was violent enough to snap one of the wheel struts. But the others held as he brought his aircraft to a halt and leapt from it to run to the edge of the quarry and start slithering down the sides to where the B.E. was now blazing quite fiercely.

'Oh God!' he breathed, pulling up instinctively.

But it was only for a moment. Throwing off his gauntlets, he pulled the goggles back over his eyes to protect them, then rushed forward to where he thought he spotted movement beneath the observer's position. The heat burned his skin as if the flames were already touching it. The man had managed to release his restraining-belt and drop to the ground, but he was bleeding from the head and seemed unable to think for himself.

Coughing painfully in the smoke, Rex grabbed the man's arm and began pulling him clear of the wreckage, where he handed him over to his own observer, just arriving on the scene. But his thoughts were fixed on Mal up in the pilot's seat and, despite the flames that were now roaring along the fabric of the machine, he tried to crawl beneath it to where the front part had been so badly crushed. In his heart he knew he was attempting the impossible, and knew the fact would not stop him from trying. Fire was the Devil's strongest weapon, and the man had not yet been born who could walk unharmed through it. But he could not turn his back on Mal, and just walk away.

Knowing the whole thing could collapse on him at any moment, he forced himself to go forward to the pilot's cockpit. He never reached it. Flaming debris lay on the ground to burn his hands and knees as he moved slowly forward, and the pain of it grew so great he had to pause and consider giving up. Then he saw Mal through

79

the smoke and flame, dangling upside-down, imprisoned by his belt and too badly hurt to release himself.

'*Oh God,*' Rex rasped again, feeling desperate and helpless.

But, as he braced himself to a new attempt to penetrate fire that seemed to be taking the skin from his own body in the most agonising fashion, the wreck shifted and began to collapse onto him. Instinct led him to throw himself sideways and roll away before the whole flaming pile buried him along with the man who had been his first comrade-in-arms. He escaped incineration, but the fire continued to burn him for a week.

In the small sick-bay—another former vegetable-store—he lay in physical and mental pain. It was the first time he had witnessed death, and it had been in one of its most horrifying forms. He suddenly felt a lot older. His friendship with Mal Haines had lasted less than two weeks, but its very nature had made it special. Yet, as he was to learn over the next few years, there was soon another to fill the vacancy. Mike Manning seemed to sense that their destinies would run along the same course and, by the time Rex was walking around again, grounded until the bandages were off his hands, a friendship had been cemented between himself and the young Australian that was to totally change his life.

Two months later, Rex learned he was to be decorated for bringing down two enemy aircraft that had been machine-gunning troops in the trenches, and for his rescue of Mal's observer from a burning wreck. 2F Squadron had acquired its hero, and the living legend of 'Sherry' Sheridan had begun.

—————————— 5 ——————————

CHRIS STOOD on the hump-backed stone bridge and gazed down at the river, swollen now due to the January rains. His overcoat-collar was turned up against the biting wind that blew between the hills in which nestled the various villages around Greater Tarrant, and his tweed cap was pulled well onto his unruly fair hair. His shoulders were hunched as he leant on the ancient stone of the bridge, and the tears of a youngster not yet able to counter misery with the opiates of manhood stood on his cheeks. He had been desperate on the outward journey. Now he was going home again, more than desperate.

His forced marriage had become unendurable. He did not know what to do, which way to turn. Days had turned into endless hours of tramping around in mud and cow-dung, standing in gaunt freezing forest to inspect trees and decide which should be cut for much-needed timber, squatting in smelly barns to look at grain and root vegetables. Or they consisted of long boring discussions on yield, sheep-pest, and forestry, or even more boring study of pamphlets, farming publications, and costing lists. This was what an estate-manager did.

Then there were the evenings. The girl who had made herself his wife seemed to be constantly sick, or aching in some part of her swollen body. She did not keep it to herself, but expected him to somehow share it with her. She was always coming to his room as he was about to turn in, with pathetic tales of backache or pains in her groin, and asking him to ease them. Once, before he had realised her intention, she had seized his hand and placed it on her stomach where the baby was kicking. He had been completely repulsed by the moving bumpy flesh, and had shouted at her to get out and leave him alone.

Another time they had had a worse quarrel. On a day when he had been particularly tired and longing for the solace of his books, she had come to him with a woolly shawl she had just finished making. When he had shown no interest, she had violently up-braided him, accusing him tearfully of caring nothing for the child who was a result of his lust. At the end of his tether, he had replied that she had been so eager for it how could he be certain he really was the father of the child. She had slapped him around the face and run off crying. That night she had gone into premature labour.

The events that had followed were imprinted on Chris's memory so strongly he knew they would always be there. The frantic activity in the house, the snow that piled higher and higher, Roland's strained expression, and the frightened cries of the girl going through the mysterious process of giving birth. After a whole night and half a morning, the boy was born—delivered by

Roland in that house cut off by snowdrifts. But, although his brother added his request to Marion's, Chris would not go in to see his wife and son. The whole business had seemed like a nightmare to him, and he tried to shut it from his mind with Greek prose.

Rex's suggestion that he should study at home and try for a post as a tutor once the child was born was not working. He could not study. At the end of the day he was too physically tired, and those few times he had gone to bed with a book had been spoilt by a visit from Marion. Now, there was a baby crying night and day. It never seemed to stop. For something so small, it had a wail that managed to reach whichever room in the house he was in.

Dr Deacon had arrived at the house as soon as the drifts were passable, and had been so impressed and grateful for the difficult delivery and after-care carried out by the young man who had once intended to become a surgeon, he had offered a hand of renewed friendship. Roland had ignored it. He did not forgive and forget easily, and he had made it clear that the child he had brought into the world had already demanded too high a price for his existence than any man should be expected to pay, and no hand of friendship would ever remove that. The enmity continued.

The snow had given way to rain, and Chris's sense of desperation had mounted until he felt like an animal in a cage with bars closing in until he was crushed between the unyielding iron pillars. Then a letter had arrived from Rex, telling them that he was finally in France on active service, and how glad they had all been to see him because the war was turning into a long-term struggle and men were so desperately needed.

That letter had shown Chris his escape route, and he knew Rex had come up trumps once more. He had paid his debt to Marion —if he had ever owed one—and given his child a legitimate name. Babies were the responsibility of the mother, not the father. He was free to go. There was one place whence she could not possibly follow him, and whence no one would condemn him for going.

That morning he had walked from the house early and caught the first train to Dorchester, where there was a recruiting-office. Now he was on his way back to Tarrant Hall, and the bars of the cage had moved so close he could feel the pressure all around him. It made him terribly afraid.

He took off his spectacles to wipe the tears from his eyes, then threw the things to the ground in despair. They ruled his life; they dictated his actions at all times. He was totally dependent on those two lenses enclosed in tortoiseshell!

It was here, at this very spot, that he had come across a girl splashing in the water seven months ago. Half-blind without those lenses, he had fallen into the water and somehow aroused sexual desire in someone he had known all his life. She had withheld those same lenses from him in the midst of a storm, and offered a body that was all the more exciting because he could feel and not see it. Those circles of glass had trapped him. Now, they kept him in the trap. The Army had turned him down the minute they had tested his sight without them. Desperate for volunteers, they had nevertheless rejected a man who could not read a card bearing big black letters. He was young, fit and eager . . . but he wore thick spectacles, and they did not want him!

As he stood on that bridge it was as if his head were about to burst, as if his body would explode into a million pieces and disintegrate into dust. He was shaking from head to foot, and his heart was pounding with the fear of annihilation. Having reached that bridge, he seemed incapable of walking another step toward something from which he had been so certain escape was near. The greyness of the river was blurred into the greyness of the bare trees and the greyness of the stone bridge, as he stared at the scene before him with defective eyes.

Then he thought of all the great heroes who had achieved despite physical shortcomings—men with hunchbacks, withered hands, one eye, one arm, tiny stature, huge bulk. Physically he was sound. It was just that he could not see without aid. Would Caesar have given up for lack of lenses? Would Alexander have failed to conquer because the world was a blur? No, it was brains and determination that won through.

Suddenly, he remembered himself saying, in this very spot, 'No one achieves anything with a negative attitude, Marion.'

Bending with the swiftness of hope reborn, he groped for the spectacles he had thrown down. Polishing them with his handkerchief, he brought from his pocket the crumpled form he had filled in before going into the room where the simple medical tests had taken place. The doctor had smiled until he had tried to read the chart without aid. Then he had shaken his head and handed back the form unsigned.

Chris now smoothed it out and looked it over. There would be no problem memorising everything on it. It would be like a photograph in his mind. All he needed now was to look at all the eye-charts in Dr Deacon's surgery, and memorise those. With excitement mounting, the cage bars seemed to retreat. He would go to Bournemouth recruiting-office where they would not know him, and he would leave his spectacles off throughout the process. With all that information stored in his head, his only risk of failure would be if he fell over a door-step as he entered.

Roland always went through the post as soon as he could after Minks brought it in on the silver tray kept in the hall for the purpose. On that mid-February morning he stopped going through a draft Jeffries had drawn up for rotation of crops, and picked up the pile of letters immediately. He had spotted one from Rex, with all the stamps of the Army Post Office covering the creased envelope, and tore it open eagerly. It told him how his brother had brought down two enemy aircraft, and then landed in another haystack. Roland shook his head with fond exasperation as he read of that, followed by the return journey with the bargee's wife's niece. Rex wrote as he spoke, full of enthusiasm, warmth and humour, and the letter brought his vital presence very near.

Roland sighed. He badly missed his red-haired brother. There had been a closeness between them he had never reached with Chris. Admittedly, one was a man, the other a boy—he never thought of Rex as still a minor, although he was only twenty— but Chris was such an introvert, it was impossible to reach the inner personality. Life had not been the same since Rex went off to war: if he were killed it would remain less bright forever. Yet he wondered what a born flier without an aeroplane would have done if the war had not come.

He read on about the friendship that had been made with another youngster called Mal Haines. *We are looking forward to downing more Huns on our future patrols together,* Rex had written. *We make a good partnership, which is essential when danger looms.* Roland was glad his brother had someone he liked and trusted to pair with. He hoped this Mal Haines would be a restricting influence on some of Rex's more hare-brained schemes, but he thought it more likely Rex would talk the other man into them.

With the details of an alien bizarre life in France still in his head, he sifted through the rest of his post rather absently. Then he came across an envelope at the bottom of the pile that bore no stamp and just his Christian name in Chris's thick scrawl. Frowning, he tore it open and took out the simple message inside. Never in his life had he felt quite as he did then, and the weight of his emotion seemed suddenly too much to take.

Getting to his feet he went to the decanter and poured himself a sherry, before going to the fireplace to sink into a hide chair and stare into the blaze of logs. They had been real brothers, all three. Each, in his own way, would have defended the others to the hilt, put his trust in them, done anything for them. As small boys they had squabbled but, let any outsider attack, they would close ranks. Adolescence had taken them physically further apart, but spiritually closer. What was happening to them now? A selfish unbalanced father had been responsible for driving Rex to the only course that would fulfil the longing now denied him; a selfish wanton girl had taken Chris's hope for fulfilment, and had now driven him to certain death.

Rage filled him as he thought of the young dreamy boy who had arrived home for the holidays last June, and pictured that same boy stumbling through mud-filled trenches amidst blaspheming 'old sweats' who would instantly sense that he was what *they* would call effeminate. Although Chris was tall and well-built, he had hardly begun to shave yet, and was so exceptionally good-looking with long curling lashes over near-violet eyes, his withdrawn manner and obsession with poetry would suggest all manner of things to brutish men. Roland's fists clenched at the thought of how the boy could suffer, especially at the Front, where men grew desperate and violent. Chris's worst enemies might be amongst his own ranks!

But there was nothing he could do, except regret that he had not recognised the great despair that would have driven the boy to do something for which he was totally unsuited both in character and mind. He closed his eyes on the vision of Chris faced with the necessity to thrust a bayonet into someone; of his pale face staring across barren desolate land covered with wire entanglements, waiting in knee-high mud for the enemy to appear through the smoke of heavy gun-fire. Such experiences would surely break his spirit. Yet he must have felt his present life was doing worse —breaking his heart!

For a long time Roland sat cursing his failure to recognise his brother's state and help him. Keeping the house and estate going took all his time, and a bad winter like this could set things back drastically. They were living on a tight budget, as it was, and a girl with a child added to their expenses no end. He had been worried and preoccupied with other things, and thought he had done all he could to make things easier for Chris. Yet, in his heart, he knew Rex would have seen the lad's point of no return, whatever else he had on his mind, and done something about it. Would Rex lay the blame for their young brother's folly at his door, he wondered.

It was a while before Roland could bring himself to go to Marion's room attached to another fitted out as a nursery. She spent most of her time there, apparently devoted to her son. When he entered in response to her invitation, he found her at the writing-desk. There was a little colour in her cheeks that were so pale these days. She even managed a faint smile.

'I was just writing to Rex.'

'Why?' It was blunt and hostile, the only thing he could think of to say, with the other thing on his mind.

Her smile faded. 'Minks brought me one from him an hour ago. It was to congratulate me on the safe arrival of the baby, and saying how proud he was to be an uncle. I thought it was very sweet of him.'

'Rex is like that.'

'Yes. He always was the odd one out,' she said with undisguised bitterness. 'And he couldn't even write it himself because his hands were bandaged. A nurse had to do it for him.'

'I don't understand,' said Roland, having just read his own letter from Rex. 'Hands were bandaged?'

'He tried to save his friend from a burning wreck and got scorched, he says. I was tremendously moved by his writing that it helped him to accept Mal's death by knowing a boy had just come into the world to replace him.'

'Mal?'

'Mal Haines, that was the name of his friend. They flew patrols together, apparently.'

He passed a hand over his forehead, unable to take it in. 'I've

. . . I've just read a letter from Rex telling me he and this Haines fellow are looking forward to flying more patrols together. In the time I've taken to come upstairs, the man is dead. When were those letters written—a week, ten days ago? Rex could be dead by now.'

She came toward him. 'There would have been a telegram. Roland, you have been working too hard since your father died. No one can go on and on the way you have without feeling the strain. You don't look at all well. You never take a horse out purely for the pleasure of riding any more. It's as if you have turned your back on the creatures since you had to sell your thoroughbreds. I know it's small compensation, but a quiet hack across Longbarrow Hill would do you good.'

He looked her straight in the eye. 'Chris has gone.'

'Gone where?' she asked in lacklustre tones.

'Volunteered. He went into Bournemouth on the last train yesterday. He isn't coming back.'

He thought she was going to faint, but she just stood there swaying as she clasped her stomach with both hands.

'How long have you known?' she whispered accusingly.

'About half an hour. I have just found the note in which he asks me to tell you.'

'How cruel!' Her eyes filled with tears that ran unchecked down her cheeks. 'How cruel he can be! Not a word to me. Not a goodbye . . . or a regret.'

'Regret?' he snapped. 'What has he to regret? Only that you drove him to this madness.'

She gasped. '*I* drove him? I have done everything in my power to keep him here, to make the marriage work, to make him happy.'

'You've done everything save leave him alone. It wouldn't have made him happy, but it would have saved him from growing desperate enough to commit suicide like his father.'

'Roland . . . *don't,*' she cried, her hands to her temples.

'Can you truly see him rushing through ruined villages with a machine-gun, drinking himself into rash courage with rough wine filched from cellars, raping filthy peasant-girls just to escape from the terrible reality of death-on-the-morrow? Can you? That's what war is, Marion, and he's going out to meet it just to escape from something he regards as far worse here. He can't possibly survive, and he knows it.'

The girl sank onto a chair, totally distraught. 'He hates me. He told me he always would. But I thought the baby would . . . every man wants a son. How could he desert a helpless little creature who has done him no harm?'

'No harm?' repeated Roland savagely. 'From the moment that child was conceived it harmed Chris. It robbed him of his rightful future, and nearly all the things in life he held dear. And what that child didn't do to him, you did.'

'No, no,' she implored tearfully. '*Please,* don't say that to me. I loved him and tried to help him accept his new life.'

'By thrusting your pregnancy at him at every opportunity, and talking of nothing but booties and shawls! The average boy of eighteen is bored to tears by babies, and acutely embarrassed by pregnancy. When they are thrust upon him as an alternative to university, scholastic accolades, and a glittering career, he is revolted by them.' The full force of his young brother's disastrous past six months took hold of him and put emotional huskiness in his voice. 'All you ever saw of Chris was an attractive body and a dreamy manner, I should imagine. Well, you've destroyed him now, and this family will never forgive you. I'd be glad if you'd move out of this house as soon as you can arrange it, and take with you the child who will now never know the father whose name he bears. Chris has more than paid for those five minutes in your father's surgery. Neither he nor I owe you anything more.'

For the first two weeks Chris believed he had exchanged one form of total misery for another. His years at Charterhouse had inured him to strenuous physical activities which he had performed with ease, but lack of enthusiasm. So he was fit and muscular enough to cope with army 'physical jerks'. But military life seemed to consist of little else. When he was not jumping 'arms out, feet astride' in the company of forty-nine others, he was running around a field with a full pack on his back. When he was not doing either of those he was crawling across mud, scrambling through vicious barbed-wire, or climbing over walls and hillocks with a rifle and full equipment, then attacking bags of hay hanging from poles to stick them with his bayonet. That was the part that most frightened him. Never sure which was the sack, he would approach cautiously and peer at the khaki-coloured object in front of him. If it did not answer when he spoke to it and he was fully satisfied it was not one of his fellow-recruits, he half-heartedly jabbed with his bayonet, then ran on relieved that he had passed that obstacle safely.

The sergeant, a regular soldier with a great scar across his cheek from the Boer War, actually ran out of words to describe a recruit who looked smart and handsome in the uniform, was in prime physical condition, and was plainly a member of the intelligent upper-classes, yet who blundered through his training in a manner that would have made a village idiot appear quite normal. If the lad had not volunteered, he would have suspected that he was trying for a quick discharge.

That was, in fact, the one thing Chris feared the whole time. Much as he hated army life, however deep his misery over such mindless activity, the thought of having to return to a wife he detested, a child that did nothing but wail, and a daily study of lumbering bovine creatures made him struggle to cover up his inadequacies. But that same fear prevented him from putting on the spectacles that would have enabled him to do as well as his fellows. For two weeks, he had stumbled around in a world of blurs, having no idea who he was speaking to, what he was eating, or where he was walking. His survival was due to his cleaning his buttons in the latrines where he could put on the spectacles, and using his rest periods for solitary reconnaissance wearing those lenses on which he depended so heavily, and memorising the lay-out of barracks and training-areas, or making swift sketches which he studied in the latrines or beneath his blankets with a torch after lights out. But he survived by the skin of his teeth, because he was in constant trouble for ignoring officers who passed, for walking on the barrack-square—that most heinous of military crimes—and for making supposed frontal assaults on the enemy in a hesitant walking-pace which zig-zagged in front of the others almost tripping them up.

But his pretence was put to its severest test when they were all sent to the rifle-range for long-distance target-practice. Lying on his stomach he gazed miserably ahead unable to see more than a few yards of fuzzy grass. The targets lay somewhere in the grey blank beyond that. He was near the end of the line and sprawled there with his rifle, knowing that if he fired it he could very well kill someone. Yet, if he did not, it would be the final grounds for throwing him out as unfit. As the men further up the line began to fire he grew more and more desperate. What was he to do? He felt sick at the thought of either alternative, and his hands started shaking. He could not go back to Tarrant Hall now. It would be more than he could take to see the way she looked at him.

'Right then, Sheridan. Look lively, it's your turn!' bellowed a voice that made him jump. 'Load and fire—that's if you can tear yourself away from whatever it was you was thinking of. It's the same principle—you puts it in and you shoots it off. Isn't that right, lads?' he bawled with a dirty laugh that was augmented by others nearby.

With heart hammering against his ribs, Chris felt for the breech, put the bullet in, and closed it ready to fire. Nothing happened when he pulled the trigger, and the sergeant's voice roared that he 'had the bloody safety-catch on'. His hand ran along the barrel to find it, released it, then he fired praying fervently that he was not aiming directly at one of the target-men.

The sergeant moved on and Chris put his face down on the grass, sweating heavily and feeling ready to vomit. A minute later, he was told by a blur beside him that he was to stop rifle-practice and report to his company-commander.

'You'll go with Corporal Meaker,' continued the sergeant, '. . . and for gawd's sake leave that bloody rifle here where it's safe.'

His legs nearly buckled under him at that. He *must* have shot someone. Dear God, he should have made any excuse—pretended to faint—anything rather than fire into greyness that hid people from him. What would he do if he had killed someone? What would *they* do? On active service they would have no hesitation in shooting him. Would the same rule apply in training? As he followed the vague khaki shape that was called Corporal Meaker he felt more and more ill. Yet, despite his terrible fears, he knew immediately when they branched onto a path leading away from his company-office. The plan of the barracks was imprinted on his mind: they were going toward the sick-bay. A new fear arose. They thought he was mad and planned to lock him up! But he knew it was pointless trying to run away. He would only fall over someone or something and make matters worse.

The smell of antiseptic told him he was right, and he walked up the three steps he knew would be there and into a building bright with lights. The shape with him knocked on a door and opened it.

'Private Sheridan, sir,' he announced. 'In yer go,' he added, giving Chris a small push.

There was a man standing behind what must be a desk. Shaking and giddy Chris went forward and saluted him. 'Good morning, sir,' he managed to say. 'I was told you wished to see me.'

'Just as I thought,' came a voice behind him. 'Blind as a bat!'

Chris turned round so swiftly he almost lost his balance, and a hand came out to steady him. 'Take it easy, son. You'd better sit down while we get to the bottom of all this.'

He was grateful for the chair, but sat heavily realising his escape had lasted barely two weeks.

'That was my greatcoat on the tallboy you just saluted,' said the voice, moving round behind the desk. 'I put it there before you came in, to test my theory.'

He had to ask it. 'I didn't kill anyone, did I?'

'Sergeant Racer gave you a blank, just to be on the safe side.'

He put his head in his hands. 'Oh, thank God for that!'

There was a short silence, then the man said, 'You must have felt very desperate indeed to have taken that risk. I think you had better tell me what you felt justified such a dangerous decision.'

Since he now had nothing to lose, Chris told him how he had been turned down because of his eyesight at Dorchester, and how he had memorised the application form and eye-charts to be accepted at Bournemouth. Then he went on to describe how he had gone out with his spectacles in order to memorise the layout of barracks and training area, and made detailed sketches to study in the latrines or under his blanket at night—the two places he felt were safe to wear them.

'Incredible,' said the voice. 'Where are the spectacles now?'

'In the locker beside my bed.'

'Right. I'll send someone to fetch them.' The blur rose. 'Would you like a cup of tea?'

'I don't think I could keep it down, sir.'

'Mmm, bad as that, is it? Better have something stronger.'

A minute or so later he was given a glass of something smelling like aniseed to drink but, by then, he was strangely numb and resigned to his fears.

'How long has your sight been defective, Sheridan?' asked the man who must be a doctor.

'Most of my life, I suppose. Certainly since I first went to school.'

'Where was that?'

'Prep-school. Then Charterhouse.'

'Tell me about it.'

He began hesitantly but, as he related the years at Charterhouse enthusiasm warmed his voice more and more. It was wonderful to talk of those things he loved and thrilled to, so the details of his awards, scholarships and prizes came out without any suggestion of bragging, but more as an eagerness to share his great passion with a faceless blur who offered to listen. It might have been the aniseed drink or the relief of spending a few minutes with the glories of yesterday, but the nausea passed and he felt more confident than he had for some months.

Someone arrived with the spectacles, and the gift of clear sight they gave him after so long in a shimmering world doubled his sense of well-being. The man at the desk turned out to be a colonel in his forties, with a shrewd face and clipped black moustache.

Chris smiled at him. 'You look a lot better now, sir.'

'How did I look before?'

'Much the same as those sacks of hay we bayonet, I'm afraid.'

'Hmm. Good job Sergeant Racer took your rifle off you before you came here.'

Then Chris asked quietly, 'What's going to happen now?'

The doctor shook his head. 'I want a few more answers first. With your academic propensity why aren't you at university?'

Chris told his first lie. 'There was no money. My father lost everything at cards.'

The thin face registered surprise. 'Good lord, are you one of Branwell Sheridan's sons?'

'Yes, sir.'

'You have two older brothers, haven't you?'

'That's right. One's had to abandon his medical career.'

'That's a great shame. But not nearly such a disaster as your wasting your specialised kind of brain. Surely there was something else you could have done that would have given you a living, yet used your knowledge. Why were you so dangerously set on going to war?'

He told his second lie. 'My middle brother is in the Royal Flying

Corps, and already in France doing his bit for his country. He's
... well, he's something of a hero to me, and I suppose I wanted
to show him I could match up.'

'Yes, I see,' came the thoughtful response. 'You have no ambitions to become a flier?'

'Oh, no. Rex was a qualified pilot before he joined. Besides, I
didn't think I'd get away with crashing aircraft as easily as stabbing the wrong sack of hay with my bayonet.'

The doctor's smile was vague as he got to his feet. 'Now I want
to see just how bad your sight is. Come over here for a moment
... and I warn you, these charts I'm going to show you are not
the same as those you memorised.'

The test completed, the medical man shook his head. 'Amazing!
You got away with it for five days before Sergeant Racer came to
me with his suspicions. We've both been watching you ever since,
and I still wasn't absolutely convinced until you came in and
saluted my greatcoat.'

Gloom returned as Chris remembered the situation. 'Are you
going to kick me out, sir?'

'No, not just yet. You're a very interesting case. I want to try
some experiments with you.'

For the next week Chris was excused all other duties, moved to
a small room on his own, and allowed no visitors. During that time
he was given all kinds of tasks ranging from simple patterns to
make from coloured wooden blocks, to involved numerical conundrums. He was asked to translate difficult passages of prose in
Greek, Latin, French and Italian, which he did with ease and
speed. He was then given a long extract in German—a language
he did not know—and a standard German grammar. It was fault-
lessly translated by the end of the day.

Then, he was given pages of meaningless English words and told
to make sense of them. He did that even quicker than the German.
The next page was more difficult, but he had done it before he went
to bed. On the Thursday of that week he was handed another,
which he had until the end of the week to solve. He handed it back
on Friday afternoon saying it had taken him so long because the
typist had made several errors that had thrown him until he had
picked them up. It was the happiest week he had spent since

leaving Charterhouse and, at the end of it, he was told he would be attached for Intelligence work with the rank of second-lieutenant.

It was a measure of his delight that he actually wrote to Rex to tell him of all that had happened, and how thrilled he was with his new life. He did not write to Roland for fear of betraying to Marion where he was, but he asked Rex to pass on the news that he was happy and well.

The primroses had bloomed and gone from the shady banks alongside the river that flowed through Tarrant Royal. Now, the hedgerows were scattered with pinkish-white briar roses, and filled with the nests of birds which sang as sweetly and joyously as they had last June. Mrs Hobley's delphiniums were a riot of blues and mauves again, and small boys were scrambling amongst the branches of the oaks beside the village green. A start was being made on the erection of a marquee for the cricket-match against Tarrant Maundle on Saturday, but the usual enthusiasm seemed to be lacking. It was only at the Rector's entreaty, backed by Roland, that the event was taking place at all. The teams would be mostly old men. The Churchman's intention was to keep up morale, but several staunch villagers maintained it would do the reverse and upset those whose sons or husbands would never play again.

Tarrant Royal had made sacrifices, like every other village in England. Young Bill Bishop had fallen at Mons, Ted Peach had lost an eye and an arm at Picardy, the twins who had sung so rowdily with Rex at last year's concert were both blown up at Neuve-Chapelle in March, and Janey Banks' young brother who had dressed as a prison wardress on the carnival float had gone down with his ship somewhere in the North Sea. The only son of the landlord of the George and Dragon had been a victim of the terrible poison gas used so inhumanely only a month before, and had just arrived home, a shattered invalid, to face the sympathy of the outraged villagers. Violent patriotism had flared up over the past few months, and men were flocking to volunteer, deserting the land at a time when so much work had to be done. But even more violently patriotic were the women, who were rolling up their sleeves, taking their babies and children with them into the fields, and doing the jobs their menfolk usually did . . . and doing them very well.

As Roland drove through the village on that glorious late-June day, he reflected sadly on all that had happened since he had come straight from medical-school on his holidays last June. The stone post-office and general-store, the old inn, the forge where Ted Peach would never hammer out horseshoes again, the village green, the ancient slumbering church all looked the same, but the village seemed empty and unfriendly. Women no longer stood chatting at their doors, or struggled against a stiff breeze to peg out rows of sheets, pillowcases, or woollen combinations on lines strung across their gardens. Those few who were about took no notice of his passing, or hurried indoors before the pony-and-trap drew level.

He could no longer ignore the truth. Tarrant Royal had turned against him. After the years of growing up with them, after taking such a lively interest in their lives, after becoming a generous and caring Squire, the villagers, with the exception of the Rector, treated him with hostility. It had been growing over the past few weeks and he had turned a blind eye to salve his pride. From a few veiled comments at a committee meeting, it had mushroomed into open hostility from those families whose menfolk had already gone to war—some never to return. Then, at church last Sunday, the congregation had fallen silent when he had entered to walk to the family pew, and no one lingered afterward so that he could chat to them, as he usually did. Now, today, the turned backs and empty gardens said it too plainly to ignore any longer.

With his back stiff as a ramrod and his face set, he passed Dr Deacon's house and surgery, seeing the pram in the garden from the corner of his eye. Then he turned the small cart into the lane leading to Tarrant Hall, asking himself bitterly what more they expected from him. The Sheridans were more than contributing to the war-effort. Rex had been in France nearly six months now, risking his life every time he took off. Already, he had been twice decorated, and his list of enemy 'kills' plus his apparently fearless daring had aroused the interest of the Press, who were fast turning him into a hero for the people of England to cheer in the face of other losses and setbacks. 'Sherry' Sheridan, they called him, and reporters accompanied by cameramen had invaded Tarrant Hall

95

for pictures of the home and background of the celebrated flier. Tarrant Royal claimed their hero joyously, and photographs of Rex in the cricket-team had appeared in London newspapers besides, so it was said, in some Berlin publications. Roland found his pride in his brother swamped by fear that his charmed life might not last throughout what looked like becoming a long tragic war. He wanted a live brother and friend, rather than a dead Sheridan hero.

Then there was poor young Chris also in khaki. If that was not a family sacrifice, he did not know what was. The only news he received of his youngest brother was through Rex, and that was how he sent messages, too. Thankfully, the boy was still in England and likely to stay there, because of his poor sight that kept him from active service. Roland knew Chris would not come home when he had leave, and he spent a lot of time wondering what would happen when his brother had no patriotic excuse to stay away from his wife and child. Would he just vanish, and send an occasional cryptic postcard with a foreign stamp?

All in all, Roland's heart and spirits were heavy enough without the incredible hurt of hostility from those with whom he had been forced to share his future. Was it not enough that he daily expected to hear that Rex had challenged the Devil once too often, that he faced the prospect of never seeing Chris again, that he must see that ill-conceived child grow up to claim his rightful heritage from the family whose name he bore? Was it not enough that he was struggling to produce food in the form of grain, sheep and cattle, precious timber from his forest, and had just offered one wing of Tarrant Hall as a convalescent home for officers? Was that really not enough?

How could he go off to war? Who would run the estate? Who would produce the things so urgently needed by those who were fighting? There were more ways of serving than by standing in mud-filled trenches day-in, day-out. Did the people down there in his village really not appreciate that it was of equal importance to make the land as productive as possible for when the war was over, to keep England running, and to keep up the morale of those at home for when the dispirited men came on leave? The mere fact of seeing their homes and country unchanged would ease the strain of what they had been through and show them that their sacrifice to keep England free was not in vain.

No, two out of three Sheridans in uniform were enough! His plain duty was to use the land they owned to produce food, and to do all he could there in England. If every man just dashed off to France, there would be no society in which to return when it was all over. Life had to go on, and he had to be part of it. It was easy to rally to the colours and receive the adoration of a sentimental public. It was much harder to sacrifice one's brothers and obey one's obvious duty to be a man behind a man behind a gun. No medals would be handed to men like him, no plaudits given by grateful countrymen, no worship from susceptible women to someone in unglamorous civilian garb. But he would have given his all as much as any man when it was all over . . . and he would have borne the hostility of people whose simplicity prevented their seeing beneath the bravado of war to the solid substance that would ensure their children had a life as good, free and satisfying as theirs had been.

But his back was still stiff and his face just as set when he walked indoors to greet Minks and go straight to his study. Jeffries had joined the Dorset regiment a month ago, and Roland now had twice as much to do. The day's post was on the desk, and a letter from Rex lay on the top. Minks always gave it pride of place when one arrived, and Roland tore it open rather savagely, due to his present mood. His brother appeared to be having a splendid time at Grissons. His promotion to full lieutenant had come through, and he had celebrated the fact with his Australian friend, Mike Manning, in a small town they had reached in a 'borrowed' motor cycle combination.

The girls there were very friendly, Rex wrote, *but too friendly for a couple of French artillery officers, who wanted to fight a duel over the girls' honour with their gallant English allies. They chose the venue, and gave us choice of hour and weapons. After a quick consultation, Mike and I told them 'lavatory-brushes at dawn'. They walked out in high dudgeon, feeling insulted, and abandoning the girls' honour to us. Since it had already been sullied, we were glad the duel had come to nothing. A chap can get a nasty wound from a lavatory-brush in the groin!*

For once, Roland was not amused by his brother's banter, and he read on about the details of the terrible stalemate between opposing armies who staged major assaults and gained no more than a few yards at the cost of ten thousand lives, only to yield the ground again a week later at the cost of another ten thousand. Then came a brief sentence that assured him Chris was all right and very happy in whatever it was he was doing.

I just wonder what he will do when this is over, the letter ran on. *The poor little blighter must have been at a mental Rubicon when he ran off to be a soldier, but peace will face him with it again. I wonder if old Deacon ever wonders if he did the wrong thing by forcing Chris into that fatal marriage—or you, for that matter. It hasn't made anyone happy, and it wouldn't have mattered about the child being a bastard. There'll be hundreds of them after this ends.*

Roland crushed the letter and flung it into his waste-paper basket. Damn Rex! Criticism from his brother was too much on top of all else. War made people lose all sense of proportion. They allowed themselves to be swept along on tides of emotion and a temporary set of values. But, when life returned to normal, it would be the old standards that maintained it.

He reached for another letter, this time from the Army accepting his kind offer of a wing of Tarrant Hall for use as a convalescent home, and saying that someone would come to inspect the premises on the following Monday. It pleased him tremendously. Perhaps that would stop backs being so firmly turned the next time he drove through the village!

But whatever warmth had crept into him froze again when he saw the next envelope on the tray. He swallowed painfully as he stared at it. They came regularly once a week, but never on the same day so that he would not know when to expect them. Knowing what this one would contain, he nevertheless had to open it, to confront the contents. It fluttered out and lay on the carpet by his booted feet. A white feather plucked from a duck!

There was no written message, just a symbol that said more than words. He sat looking at it, feeling the pain of its symbolism filling him once again. What did she hope to gain? It would not bring Chris back to her; it would not give that child a devoted father. Had she any idea what it did to him; how much it added to the cost of having been forced to abandon his hopes of a career in order to work his land—something he was now determined to do in the face of opinions inflamed by patriotism?

Slowly he bent to pick it up and add it to the small pile in his drawer. He knew they would continue to come, but all the time he could face them and keep them near, his resolution would remain. Once he burnt them, threw them out, or refused to open the envelopes she would have won.

The staff at the small department to which he was sent were a strange assortment of men much older than Chris. But, for the first time in his life, his relationship with others was not dominated by the uneasy feeling that he was unusual. Having found his own level Chris forgot his misery, his married status, almost his identity in the delight of what he was doing. So avid was he to put his brain to work, he had to be forcibly ejected from his office at the end of the day. But, although he translated foreign dispatches with vital and dramatic content, and dabbled with inventing codes, he saw what he was doing only as enormous pleasurable *fun*. During his first two weeks he was given concentrated lessons in German and Russian. At the end of the fortnight German was like a native tongue to him. Russian took a little longer to master, but he could soon translate any message that came in only a little less perfectly than the man who had taught him.

The true nature of Chris's potential had been discovered by a man who had studied the human mind in Austria under a tutor who was a follower of Freud. Normal schooling had shown Chris to be brilliant. Extensive tests proved he was one of those very rare people who have total recall and a photographic mind—but only for those things that were of interest to him. Like those similar to him, he could forget what he had gone into a shop to buy, the names of people he found boring, the day of the week, and whether or not he had just cleaned his teeth. He was a psychological phenomenon; in plain language, a freak. Such people usually found life very difficult. But Chris had now found the perfect outlet, and forgot all else but his colleagues and what he did within those walls. It was total release.

But that same release brought the breakdown in health that had threatened him since his marriage. The concentration of his mind to the detriment of his body heralded a collapse that put him on his back with a fever for over three weeks. Doctors warned the head of the department that what might suit a scholarly middle-aged man was dangerous for a healthy young boy of eighteen and that, unless he was given a break from mental concentration, they would not answer for the consequences.

He was given leave, but stayed in his quarters, mooning around sketching everything he could see from his window. In the end, it was this talent for drawing that brought a solution to the problem he had become. Two staff-officers discussed their proposal with his senior.

'It meets most of the doctor's recommendations—plenty of fresh air, sunshine, change of surroundings, companionship of others his age . . . and no end of exercise.'

The man stared at them. 'You're mad!'

'We have had an urgent request for someone who can read messages from the enemy, translate during interrogation of prisoners, solve simple codes, and provide maps of the terrain. Young Sheridan is the very man they need, according to his report. It's an incredible stroke of luck that he's also a first-class Greek scholar, to boot.'

'The enemy are *Turks,*' put in the Head of Department sourly.

'It's much the same,' came the airy answer. 'They all come from the same area, don't they?'

'But Sheridan is classed as a non-combatant, because he has very defective sight.'

'He wears spectacles, doesn't he? Besides, there's no question of his *fighting.* He'll be drawing his maps and questioning prisoners safely behind the lines at Headquarters.'

'Well, I don't know . . . ' hesitated the man.

'There isn't anyone else,' came the firm decision. 'He sails with the rest at the end of the week.'

When Chris heard he was to board a ship for the Aegean his heart leapt with unbelievable excitement. He would be finally visiting the Greek Islands he had missed a year ago. To be there working on sketches and translations was his idea of heaven. No one told him his final destination was Gallipoli, where British and Commonwealth troops were dying in thousands on barren cliffs from Turkish bullets, dysentery, sunstroke, thirst, and military blundering.

6

CHRIS SAW the islands of Milos, Paros and Naxos almost a year from the day when he should have visited them with his school-friend. But he saw them only from the rail of a troopship as it steamed past on its way to Gallipoli at the start of August.

He was fortunate in being, perhaps, the only person on that overcrowded ship who was wholly absorbed and charmed by the emerald and gold islands in a sea of vivid cobalt blue, whose shores had witnessed scenes of greatness, disaster and romance. All the myths and legends of Greece, the history of conquest and great learning, the romance and beauty witnessed by poets filled Chris's mind as his eyes feasted on the actuality of those places he had lived in spiritually.

He remained for hours at the ship's side, sweating profusely as the fierce sun beat down on his pith-helmet, lost to all but visions of gods, beautiful white temples, men of superb wisdom, and gifted orators. He only ate dinner because another subaltern fetched him and broke the charm of his communion with the past. But he went back to his vigil throughout the long high-summer evenings that died so slowly. It was only when pale lights began to twinkle in the mauve haze, he realised it was close on midnight.

Yes, he was fortunate in his absorption, because those others with him on the ship could think only of what lay ahead and tried to cover their fear by drinking, singing brave songs, and by making friends with everyone so they would not feel so alone when the terrible moment came. They knew it would be terrible, because they had heard what had happened to those who had landed there earlier in the year. The drastic failure of the sea bombardment of the Dardanelles, with its loss of ships, the tragedy of the bungled landings into a hail of bullets that had turned the sea red with blood, and the present predicament of insufficient troops pinned down on sheer cliffs because of lack of cover and darkness to allow them to withdraw, had all caused a public outcry in England and helped to bring down a government.

The in-going one had been left with little alternative. The situation on the Western Front was appalling, and growing worse. Casualty figures like sixty thousand in one day were being received too often, and the dead had bought no more than a half-mile of devastated farmland, or a flattened village. A glorious victory was needed somewhere—*anywhere*—to boost morale and silence critics.

The original reason for mounting a campaign against the Turks on the Gallipoli peninsula—that of drawing Turkish concentration from hard-pressed Russian troops in the north—no longer existed. In addition, resistance from a nation not renowned for organised efficient armies had grown under the command of Mustapha Kemal, an ambitious nationalistic colonel who knew how to inspire troops into suicidal bravery. However, since the British and Commonwealth troops could not be withdrawn without wholesale slaughter, the only thing left to do was throw in enormous numbers of reinforcements who could not fail to capture the heights and overrun the Turks, thus providing the much-needed triumph that would focus attention on the Balkans and ease the deadlock in France and Belgium. A resounding victory would not only put fresh heart into the Allies, it would further damage the low morale of the Austrians and Germans who also needed a sign of hope for their decimated armies.

So reinforcements were embarked for the Aegean. Most of them had come straight from their brief training as the latest batch of volunteers. Most of them were young and under the command of boys. Most of them had never left the shores of England before. This, then, was the army that was to turn the tide, change the whole course of the war, cheer the might of the British Empire and confound the Germanic one.

As the fleet of ships steamed between the islands, those few officers and NCO's who had experienced battle, or life abroad, tried to educate their men on what to expect when they arrived at their destination, although none of them guessed the truth.

Chris, being a non-combatant on detachment to the headquarters already established on the peninsula, had no duties and was regarded by the senior officer aboard as something of a nuisance. This meant he had all his time to himself, and he dreamed away the time practically undisturbed, not hearing the comments of those who passed.

'Is 'e some kind of privileged bastard, Bert? 'E goes round doing eff-all.'

'One of them odd-sods from Intelligence. Got a lot upstairs, so they say.'

'Got a lot downstairs, too. Pity 'e's a bloke. I could 'ave fancied 'im.'

But, as usual, people sought him out from his willing detachment. One who seemed more persistent than the others was a subaltern of twenty, who had also been educated at Charterhouse, joined his university officer corps, then volunteered with half a dozen others after one of their friends had won a posthumous V.C. in Flanders.

'What difference did that make?' Chris had asked.

The youngster, called Rochford-Clarke, had looked at him in surprise. 'Well . . . you know. He'd lost his life in the most tremendously courageous way.'

'So it was too late to go and help him.'

'I . . . but you surely must see how we felt.'

'The war has been going on a long time, and thousands of men have lost their lives in the most tremendously courageous way,' he reasoned calmly. 'I don't see why, just because you knew this one, you should throw up your studies and enlist.'

Rochford-Clarke had flushed. 'I thought you were supposed to be brainy. Even an idiot could see that we had to go after that.'

'What if he hadn't won the V.C.?' Chris had asked with genuine interest.

But his companion turned the tables on him. 'What made you enlist, knowing you couldn't fight with eyesight like that?'

He trotted out the lie he had used so often he had almost come to believe it. 'My brother Rex joined the R.F.C. right at the start of the war, and has been in France for eight months. He's already downed more Huns than any other Allied pilot. I had to show him I could do my bit, too.'

'Good lord, your brother isn't "Sherry" Sheridan, is he?' came the expected awed question, followed by the enthusiasm which conveniently changed the subject.

After that revelation Chris found himself surrounded by his youthful fellow-officers whenever they gathered together. But he invariably slipped away at the first opportunity to stand at the rail gazing at the land in the distance, or into the cabin he had to share with three others to read in peace before they tumbled in half-cut and exchanging inanities in loud voices. They never gave up trying to reach him, however.

The heights of Gallipoli looked formidable in the sunset that put a satanic red glow on the stony cliffs rising from the narrow beaches. The troops on the ship had fallen silent at the first sight of their destination far away and glaringly white against the deep blue of the sea washing it. But, as the fleet had steamed steadily towards it, the sun had dipped, leaving the mesmeric stifling dusk that made men from the temperate green island uneasy for a reason they could not understand.

Chris understood and revelled in it. The ages were calling to him from over the sea, and he heard the siren voices with a heart that almost burst with longing. It was so strong, he was probably the only man in that entire fleet who trembled with excitement rather than apprehension when the distant rumble of sound clarified itself into heavy gun-fire, and the small grey clouds that floated spasmodically in the mauve sky became identified as smoke and dust from exploding shells that peppered the opposing forces who had been lambasting each other since April. In Chris's ears, the sound of modern warfare changed to the tumult of voices as phalanx after phalanx of Hoplites fell upon their enemies with spear and shield, and horses whinnied as they thundered toward each other carrying the officers of ancient armies into headlong conflict. Then, as the brief darkness covered the area, the cliffs became tiers of flickering lights as men heated their rations and made tea to enjoy during the night lull. But Chris saw only the dancing flames of long-ago camp-fires as bronzed warriors lay to rest on their shields while they spoke of the day's victories.

He came from his thoughts when Rochford-Clarke shook his arm and said, 'For God's sake, Sheridan, we're going ashore any minute. Where's your kit?'

'What?' The centuries rushed back to their hidden aeons, escaping him once more, and Chris felt bereft as he stared at the young face reddened by sunburn.

'Your kit, man! I thought we agreed you'd go ashore with me and my platoon.'

'Oh . . . yes. It's in my cabin.'

His companion looked out of patience with him. 'Well, get a bloody spurt on! I can't hang around for you once we're called.'

Chris made for his cabin, trying to push frantically against a tide of men coming up the companionways onto the deck.

'It's all right, dearie,' called one rough character. 'You don't need to run away until they start firing.'

There was a great deal of laughter, then a coarse voice carolled, 'Give us a kiss, darlin'. It might be your last chance.'

Breathless he reached his cabin, snatched up his heavy pack, clipped his Sam Browne on and slipped his arm through the retaining-cord of his revolver, before jamming his pith-helmet back onto his springy hair and going out again into the files of soldiers passing by. A minute later, he was struggling back again to his cabin to fetch the book he had been reading. He had reached a very interesting chapter on ancient ceramics.

Rochford-Clarke seemed very relieved when Chris reached him, but greeted him with the news that his platoon had been detailed for the last boat.

'So there was no panic, after all!' he exclaimed. 'And I almost didn't go back for my book.'

'*Book!*' repeated the other in stupefied tones.

'But I calculated how long it would take for each boat to make the two-way trip, and how many men would be carried at one time, and realised the last wouldn't go for another two hours. So I knew I had plenty of time,' he concluded mildly.

'You didn't know we'd be on the last boat.'

'I knew *I* would be. That was what ruled my decision to go back for it.' He hoisted himself up onto a box containing lifebelts, and stood his pack beside him. 'We've got another hour and a half to wait now. If they had worked all this out several days ago and given each boatload a whistle-blast for identification, we could all have stayed calmly in our cabins until we heard the appropriate signal. Getting everyone worked up like this is not going to help their frame of mind one bit. Now, when Caesar planned his attack on . . .'

'Damn Caesar . . . and damn you, Sheridan. If you're so blasted clever, why didn't they put *you* in charge of this whole operation?'

'Because I wear spectacles,' Chris explained patiently. 'The military rule-book says it is more important for a man to see than to think. The French don't seem to make so much of it, otherwise Napoleon wouldn't have conquered half Europe as he did.'

'Ohhh . . . damn you, Sheridan!'

'You've already said that,' he pointed out.

'I . . . well, I feel responsible for you,' admitted the boy two years his senior, with slight embarrassment.

'Whatever for?' asked Chris astonished.

'Someone has to be. You don't belong to a company or platoon. You don't have any defined duties. You don't even have a batman to sort out your kit. And . . . and your mind always seems to be elsewhere.' He pointed shorewards. 'Those are real enemies out there, firing real bullets. I don't think that fact has hit you yet.'

'Yes, it has. But I shall be safely behind the lines at Headquarters with my spectacles. It's you and the others I feel sorry for.'

'Oh . . . we'll be all right,' came the self-conscious answer.

'I do advise you to relax until they call us,' he said, taking up his book and finding the chapter on ceramics. 'Standing around like this for another ninety minutes is going to make you exceedingly twitchy.'

It was a good thing the beach at Suvla Bay was wider than most and overlooked by only a few Turkish defence-posts, because everyone was 'exceedingly twitchy' by the time the last boats made their way from the fleet to the hostile shore. As a result, orders were changed, reaffirmed, then countermanded again. Those in command could not agree on the next step to take, the exact translation of their orders, or the disposition of stores. Messages from the force already established three miles south failed to arrive; those sent by the new arrivals were never delivered because the runners did not know how to find the army that had been living in burrows dug in cliff-sides for four months.

Dawn arrived, and the sun came out to beat down on men waiting spread out across the sandy beach that provided no shade whatever. And they waited while those in command laid their plans, made further attempts to link up with the Anzac troops in the south, who were to attack simultaneously from their positions in order to allow the newcomers to storm the cliffs unopposed and join up with them to overrun the main Turkish defences.

It all took time, and the August sun blazed mercilessly down on pale-faced men in thick khaki serge, unused to such heat. They tried to make tents by draping greatcoats across their rifles stuck into the sand, but the outbreak of gunfire from the Turks at the top of the cliffs forced them to snatch up their rifles in readiness for an attack. But they had a greater enemy than the Turks.

They had each come ashore with a full canteen of water, but the further supply lay in tankers offshore. Between the blundering of the Commissariat and the regular shelling by the enemy of the stretch between shore and fleet, that is where it remained throughout that day and the following night.

Chris felt he would remember that nightmare of thirst and heat for the rest of his life. He sat on sand that burnt one's hands if they were placed on it, and sweat ran down his face like rain. His uniform was as saturated with it as if he had just walked out of the sea, and his whole body burned unbearably. The glare of sun on sea reflected on the lenses of his spectacles, blinding him and making his eyes ache. Despite the pith-helmet, his head throbbed with pain. But it was the desperate craving for a drink that was the biggest torment. His tongue felt swollen to choking proportions, his lips were dry and cracked, his throat was so painful he could not forget it no matter how hard he tried to concentrate on something else.

Concentration was virtually impossible and, as the day wore on, so was movement and communication. The entire contingent of troops was trapped in misery, with the means of relief floating just off the shore. Some keeled over with heat-stroke, some grew phobic and worsened their own plight by their agitation. A few ran into the sea determined to swim out to the tankers, but were picked off by the Turks the minute they left the beach that was safe from the range of the enemies' guns. Some survived to drink sea-water that increased their thirst to the point of madness. Doctors sedated those who ran amok. An officer shot one of his own men who attacked him with a bayonet. But the majority bore their misery in apathetic silence.

Lack of water meant they did not eat, either. No man could swallow food, and their rations lay on the sand, more often than not, to be covered with the mass of flies that added extra torment by swarming all over the men's sweating faces. Night brought relief from the sun, but that was all. Chris dragged himself from his torpor to go with Rochford-Clarke to immerse himself in the sea. It cooled his burning skin and freshened his sweat-soaked clothes, but the desire to drink it had to be fought with resolution greatly diminished by the past twelve hours. He then lay in his heavy wet uniform beside his young companion to sleep heavily and feverishly until the short night ended with blinding sunlight again.

Although water now became available, the men were sluggish, demoralised and depressed. A number were running fevers from heat-stroke, a lot more were suffering agonies from severe sunburn on their pale skins, still others were in the debilitating grips of dysentery. But word arrived that the attack was on for the following dawn, and the pandemonium of conflicting orders and lack of organisation began again. Ammunition was slow being brought ashore, medical supplies had been mislaid, rations were inadvertently spilled onto the sand.

Chris, feeling depressed and doubled up with pains in his stomach, several times asked those in command how he could get to Headquarters, where he was needed. But he was told his problems were of no importance at such a time, and he should make himself useful or clear out of the way. So he spent another day on the sweltering sands of that beach, feeling utterly useless while men dashed about in the mistaken belief that preparations for battle had to be hectic. He felt too unwell even to read. By evening, he was beset by an attack of dysentery that kept him awake all night.

Rochford-Clarke, who had fortunately escaped the worst of the stomach-cramps, told Chris he had better keep with him and his platoon during the assault, since he could hardly stay on the beach alone.

'Still feel responsible for me?' he teased weakly.

'Cut that out,' came the bluff rejoinder. 'You shouldn't be in this at all. If anything happens to you, they've lost their translator.'

'They've managed without me all this time, I don't suppose a few extra days will make all that difference. But I feel jolly surplus, I can tell you.'

'You won't, once the attack starts.'

But he did. With no men of his own to lead, he moved off with the other young subaltern, feeling his presence there might confuse the soldiers, and knowing little of the battle plan apart from what Rochford-Clarke had briefly told him.

They were among the last to leave the beach in the hour before dawn, and stumbled along in the wake of the first assault wave, weakened, demoralised by the heat, and racked with sickness. An hour of strenuous and difficult climbing faced them, and the sky was already a luminous tinted blue before they were halfway to the top. The positions of the Turkish guns were known, and the plan was to put them out of action before breasting the ridge and forging inland to meet up with the Anzacs working their way north.

Chris was sweating profusely again as he climbed, and battling against pains that knotted his stomach. The cliff was steep and stony and, when he looked over his shoulder, the sea looked serene and a great distance below him now. It was clear enough to see the lighters plying back and forth to the fleet anchored a short way offshore, bringing stores and supplies—so peaceful a scene it seemed incredible that they were clawing their way up the cliffs to kill whoever might be waiting at the top.

His illusions were savagely shattered when all hell suddenly let loose. The stillness of dawn was rent by cracks of ear-splitting sound as the guns at the top opened fire, and the air around him was filled with the scream of shells flying overhead to explode amongst the busy small boats several hundred feet below. One carrying ammunition went up with a tremendous thunder of sound that rocked the earth. At the same time, the unmistakable chatter of rifle-fire broke out ahead and just over the rim they were approaching. The sheer volume of it, plus the chorus of screams, shouts and whistle-blasts appalled him. They had been told there would be only slight resistance from the few Turks defending that particular area. That was why Suvla Bay had been chosen for the attack. But just up there ahead of him, there had to be a full-scale battle being waged.

The line of men ahead checked, surged forward again, then checked again when bodies began slithering from the crest to plunge down onto the beach. A red-faced captain obviously used to cliff-climbing, came over the top at suicide speed and began scrambling past them all, yelling, 'There's a whole bloody army up there! Orders are to go forward in waves and don't break ranks, whatever happens. Use bayonets, if possible. Ammunition is being blown up as it comes ashore.'

If Chris had imagined battle at all, it certainly was not like this. Reaching the crest, he scrambled over beside Rochford-Clarke, clutching his revolver which had a limited amount of ammunition. Ahead lay sunbaked stony ground stretching for several hundred

109

yards before dropping into a ravine, from where murderous fire was being directed by a force that was definitely far stronger than they had been led to expect. British troops were staggering across the open area in anything but organised waves, and half of them appeared to have no idea what they were doing. Some had come to a standstill at the first sight of the bodies of their fallen comrades, especially since most of the front-rank officers were dead amongst them. It was a scene of total confusion, fear, pain and death, all going on to a background of unnerving noise.

But Chris could be an onlooker no longer. Rochford-Clarke was running forward and shouting to his men to follow, so Chris had no option but to run with him, ill though he felt. Not once did he fire his revolver, however, because he would only have hit another Englishman ahead. For as far as he could see, the ground rose and fell in a series of shallow ravines, and the push forward was being accomplished by moving from the shelter of one, and rushing across open ground to the shelter of another. The dead and wounded were left where they fell beneath the feet of their comrades, for the stretcher-bearers to pick up later. As he ran, Chris vaguely registered the horror of the bloody wounds of war but, mercifully, the need to run on made them fragments of a sleeping nightmare that could not possibly touch him.

That nightmare lasted all day, and he no longer thought of anything but his own body. War was for brutes, not intellectuals, he realised, because his usually fertile mind seemed to close itself against reason and register only the anguish of trunk, and limbs, and intestines. At the end of that day, he and a horde of other khaki-clad brutes had slaughtered and agonised their way across some miles of barren wretched land that was of no use to anybody. When night fell, and they all stopped, his own thirst, hunger and exhaustion was all he cared about. It was the same for every other brute around him. They guzzled the contents of their canteens, stuffed rations into their mouths with frantic speed, obeyed all the calls of nature, seized the best area of ground, and went to sleep in total self-interest at still being alive.

But it all began again the minute there was a faint paling of the sky. Only, this time, it was even worse. The Turks came out of the greyness with such strength and ferocity, men fell around Chris as they tried to get to their feet, and soon formed a human carpet of broken bodies that heaved and moaned. He stared with unbelieving eyes at what he saw, then scrambled to his feet with the fuzziness of sleep still on him. Tugging his revolver clumsily from its holster, he began firing at men who ran at him with rifles—men with black moustaches and dark eyes flashing hatred. He killed some—he *must* have killed some. The line hesitated, dropped to the ground, and let forth volley after volley that thickened the carpet around him.

The noise was inhuman, deafening. There was a terrible scream beside him, and he turned. Rochford-Clarke had only half a face. Oh Christ! He pushed fresh bullets into his gun with fingers that would not keep still. He killed some more men, shot out an eye, covered limbs with blood.

Then they were coming with bayonets. He remembered those sacks of hay dangling from poles. It was the same thing, really. Except that hay did not scream and gush forth a crimson mess. *Retreat to the next ravine!* They all moved back and fired again. He ran out of bullets, so picked up a dead man's rifle. That was soon useless, too. He stared at the bayonet flashing in the sun. Just a bag of hay, that was all. If only it did not scream! *Retreat to the next ravine!* They went back again, and there were a lot less of them now. The heat pounded in his body, the blood pounded in his head, the breath pounded in his chest. He would sell his soul for a drink of water. He would sell the khaki brute next to him for a drink of anything.

Retreat to the next ravine! Retreat! Retreat! The ground shimmered and burned. Black moustaches and dark eyes flashing hatred. Where had they come from? There *was* a whole bloody army of them. They were only bags of hay. *Retreat!* His tongue was a strip of fur, his face a burning dripping mess. Everything was blurred. The lenses kept misting over, but he was afraid to take them off. He just did what everyone else did.

Retreat! He ran feeling desperately sick. Where had the other half of Rochford-Clarke's face gone? Falling into a hollow, he vomited. He did not think he could get to his feet again. But he had to when they rushed again with bayonets. They were only bags of hay. Why did they scream so loudly? He fell, climbed to his feet to run with the others, and collapsed into the next hollow, doubled up by the pains in his stomach. There was no time to nurse pain. Up again with the vague shapes running with him. *Retreat!*

Then it was night, and they were all back on the beach where they had landed from the boats. The khaki brutes ate, drank, and went to sleep—those who were left.

The grand August assault had failed. Massive Turkish reinforcements had been rushed in unknown to the attackers. The Anzacs had been driven back to their original positions on beach and cliffs. The force at Suvla Bay had suffered the same fate, and now proceeded to dig in and hold the narrow strip along the coast. Gallipoli was now a bigger embarrassment than ever to the British government, and the problem it posed was shelved in the hope it would solve itself. Those trapped on a peninsula from which it would be suicide to attempt to leave, yet who could only live a life similar to the mountain-goat, felt betrayed, forgotten and doomed.

Five days after landing Chris finally joined the Headquarters further down the peninsula. To reach it he had to wait for a runner who would guide him back through the warren of trenches, safe areas and ravines necessary to allow communication between them all without being picked off by Turkish machine-gunners.

The runner was an Australian trooper, who chatted nonstop all along the five mile up-and-down route. Chris hardly understood a word the man said, except that every other one was a profanity and had something to do with joining the bloody cavalry because he was a bloody stockman, only to be sent to this bloody hell-on-earth without any bloody horses. There was a little more about the bloody English, but Chris tramped along behind him sweating as usual, and thinking yet again about Rochford-Clarke losing half his head for the sake of someone's posthumous V.C.

The young subaltern had gone off to one of the hospital-ships on the start of his journey home, but Chris did not believe he would ever reach it. How could a person live with one eye, one ear, half a jaw, and half a brain? Would a man want to live like that, even if it were possible? He could not walk around like that. What would they do? Would he have a wax half fused to the real half? Or would he be like the Man in the Iron Mask, soldered for life into a grotesque metal helmet that would hide the bloody pulp inside from the eyes of the world—and his own one when he looked into a mirror? All he would then see was an expressionless effigy and know it was as much part of him as a foot or a hand, now. How would he eat, how would he sleep, how would he wash half a head of hair? Would it grow longer and longer inside that stifling mask until it grew matted and saturated with all that blood and brains, and choke him?

Chris could feel that mask going over his own face forever; feel the closing in of dark metal that would hide his deathly features and imprison him. He could feel the terror of being unable to read, to hear, to speak ever again, yet have to go on living for a lifetime with his hair growing longer and longer until it wound round his throat tighter and tighter to choke him. He was choking now.

Stopping abruptly on a path that wound through the spiky undergrowth in a ravine, he was violently sick into a bush. He had been doing that, on and off, for the past three days, every time he thought of that half a head.

'Take your time, sunshine,' growled the burly Australian not unkindly. 'We're all the same out here. If we're not bloody vomiting, we're bloody . . .'

But Chris was heaving again, and trying to forget Rochford-Clarke. When he had exhausted himself, he looked up to see his companion squatting on his haunches in the middle of the rough path, his wide hat that was tipped up on one side pushed forward over his eyes, rolling a cigarette with stained fingers.

'Better now?' he asked, offering the cigarette to Chris, who shook his head. 'Not got around to it yet?' he asked, putting it in his mouth and striking a match on a stone. 'I began when I was ten . . . and I was a late starter. I was a late bloody starter at most things. There aren't that many girls in the Outback.' He squinted across and grinned. 'I'll wager you've got around to that, mate, with looks like that.' He nodded at the ground. 'Sit down a mo. There's nothing to rush back for. We're here till the end of the bloody war.'

Chris sank down wearily onto the path, knees bent up and his arms draping over them as he gazed through misted lenses at the heartbreaking blue of the untroubled innocent sea.

'How old are you?' came the next question.

He continued to gaze at the blurred sea. 'I was nineteen some weeks before we landed here.'

'Quite a kiddo! Wonder how old you'll be when you leave.' He drew on the cigarette musingly. 'Any brothers in this bloody mess?'

'One in the Royal Flying Corps. He's an ace pilot.' He could not now picture Rex's face and it worried him dreadfully.

113

'Lucky bastard! The air's the only bloody place to be.'

'My other brother is running the estate and farm. Our house has been turned into a convalescent home,' he went on, hoping he would get a clear vision of Roland and Tarrant Hall. But all he could see was Rochford-Clarke with half a face.

'No sisters?'

'No.'

'Pity. If they'd looked like you I'd have taken me bedroll and billy-can over for a decko when this is all over.' He flipped the foul-smelling cigarette into some bushes and got to his feet stretching lazily. 'Life's bloody funny! There's you and me from opposite sides of the world sitting here talking like a coupla mates. But, when they finally call it a bloody day, you'll go off to some high-brow estate and marry Lady bloody Cynthia, and I'll go back to working the Outback circuit.' His bronzed lean face surveyed the barren cliffside and seascape before turning back to Chris. 'But on some flaming hot day when I'm riding around the herd keeping them on the move with me stockwhip, I might suddenly think of this spot, and a youngster from a different bloody world who sat with me for a smoko. And I'll never know if you might be thinking of it just at the same time.'

'I shouldn't think that's likely,' Chris told him, scrambling up. 'Because of the time differential, when you're riding with your cows, I shall be asleep.'

The man stared at him for a moment, then turned away muttering, 'Bloody Intelligence bloke! No flaming imagination!'

Headquarters consisted of a cave that housed half a dozen men —a British colonel in charge of the eastern sector, a New Zealand major commanding the Commonwealth contingent, a Welsh lieutenant of signals, a Scottish corporal who operated the crude ancient transmitter, an Australian ex-jockey who had turned clerk and cartographer, and a young lad from the Isle of Man, who made tea, cocoa, snacks and bromides for them all.

Chris's arrival was unexpected and put Colonel Petworth in a temper. 'I knew nothing about this. I never asked for any damned translator—especially a boy still wet behind the ears!'

'I understand it was a Colonel Partridge who put in the request,' stammered Chris, at the opposition.

'Partridge died two months ago, leading an ill-advised attack he launched on his own initiative. He was half-mad, you know. Trust him to do something like this.'

Chris listed his other qualifications, conscious that the others in that cave were regarding him with curiosity. He felt terrible.

'I see; an expert, are you?' countered the Colonel. 'How can you be an expert at anything at your age? What the hell do they think we do out here? Coded messages? We never get any damned coded messages—not even from our own side! Do they seriously think we have an espionage system at work on these confounded cliffs? A Greek scholar, you say? Do they think Gallipoli is a suburb of Athens? These Intelligence wallahs are always the same. So busy being damned geniuses, they can't tell a donkey's head from his arse.'

Chris wanted a drink, a change of clothes, and a shady place to lie down until his sickness passed, but he stood there aware that he was being made to look a fool in front of the others in that cave, and explained that he had taught himself a fair bit of Turkish on the voyage out.

'Really?' sneered the Colonel. 'Well, if you haven't taught yourself the Turkish for "bugger off" you've been wasting your time. And what's this about sketching? We're not here on an Edwardian picnic, Mr Sheridan.' He turned to the tall, deeply-tanned major of around thirty-five, with prematurely silver hair. 'God Almighty, Neil, save me from the Intelligence Branch!'

The Major smiled faintly at Chris and said to his irate superior, 'It's not young Sheridan's fault, sir. He had to obey orders. No doubt, this was the last place on earth he wanted to visit.'

'You're wrong, sir,' said Chris, warming to a softer tone. 'I should have visited Paros, Naxos and Milos last year, and it was cancelled. When I was told I was coming out here, I couldn't wait to arrive. I . . . well, I wasn't told what the true situation was. It came as a bit of a shock.'

'I bet it did.' The New Zealander held out his hand. 'I'm Neil Frencham, and I couldn't wait to get here, either. In better times, I'm a history teacher.'

Chris shook his hand, feeling slightly more human. 'How do you do, sir. Ancient history, I take it?'

'Most emphatically.' He smiled, his eyes crinkling at the corners. 'Now you're here, I'll have someone to share my interest.

These other gentlemen are naturally somewhat biased against anything concerning the inhabitants of these areas. Present inconveniences cancel out past glories.'

Colonel Petworth heaved a long sigh. 'All right, Mr Sheridan, I shall have to keep you since it's impossible to send you back. But God knows what I'm to give you to do. Graded as a non-combatant, you'll not even come in useful in an emergency. A blight on all those who, in their superabundance of grey matter, decide that one of their number is all we need to save the day.' He looked Chris over with resignation, then added in rough sympathy, 'You ought to be sitting at a school desk, boy, not out here learning how to ask a Turk "Have you any melons for my sick grandmother?".' He turned to the lieutenant sitting at a rough table covered with files and message pads. 'Find him a place to sleep, Tom, and if he's hungry sort him out with a meal.' Looking back at Neil Frencham, he said again, 'God knows what I'm going to do with him . . . and if he breaks those great magnifying lenses he's wearing, he'll be worse than useless; he'll be a bloody liability.'

After that dispiriting start life for Chris became a meaningless routine of incredible heat, discomfort and idleness. His 'quarters' were an embrasure off the main trench, about seven feet wide, ten feet long, and just high enough to allow his six-foot height to remain unstooped. The sides of the embrasure were of stony earth and so was the floor, but the roof was a tarpaulin from stores that had been landed amidst heavy gunfire. Beneath it, the atmosphere was stifling, but it kept the blaze of the sun from the sparse contents. And they *were* sparse. A straw-filled palliasse to sleep on, a tea-chest for a table, an ammunition-box for a stool, a primitive oil-lamp for which there never seemed to be any oil, a tin bowl to wash in, a piece of broken mirror. Together with his own kit, those things made up his home.

He took his meals in the cave with the others, and two batmen looked after them all with regard to washing their clothes, ironing them with flat-irons heated on field-stoves, and cleaning their leather. Living conditions being so primitive, they had little household cleaning to do, but they collected fresh straw for the palliasses once a fortnight, and put out the thin blankets to air. Toilet facilities were the open cliffside.

Chris knew that, as an officer, he was lucky. The troops lived in hollows they scratched for themselves alongside the trenches, and their way of life was not a lot different from the early cavemen. They ate basic rations designed for emergency periods only, and augmented them with anything they could borrow or steal from the sailors on the supply ships. The refinements of social living had vanished long ago; manners were non-existent. A feeling of abandonment by the rest of the world bred a mood that made each man feel he had nothing to lose. Danger had become almost a friend: bullets whistled past their nonchalance as an accepted part of each day.

Those stretches of trenches that were exposed to Turk gunfire because there was no overhanging protection were now traversed with almost uncaring lack of speed. Indeed, some of the more red-blooded had turned them into places of entertainment, holding their own lives to ransom by seeing how often they could cross from one side to the other without being hit. As a sport, it had an edge of madness to it. So did the water games, when men would deliberately swim out beyond the markers defining the safe-limit just to test whether the machine-gunners at the top of the cliffs were awake and on the job. Sometimes, their enemies just shouted and waved. At other times, they raked the water with bullets, and there was a great splashing race to get back beyond the markers. Some made it, some stayed where they were, shouting vituperation and shaking their fists until the sea reddened with their blood. Those were the men whose minds could take no more of what they had been forced to become, or those who saw no end but death and preferred to make their own decision on when it should be. The rest of that huge force endured their misery for one more day, one more week. And so did Chris as he tried to forget Rochford-Clarke with only half a face.

It was having nothing to do that became the most destructive element in his life. In no time at all, he had mastered basic Turkish from the book he had in his pack, then fretted because he could go no further with the language. Denied books, he took to writing. A diary he compiled of day-to-day life, he then translated into every language he knew. Then he wrote down every poem he could recollect, and did the same with those. When that palled, he took to inventing codes, trying for the ultimate, an unbreakable one. He worked out as many statistics as he could, even down to how many pairs of socks would have been worn out by the men on Gallipoli by the time they had been there for twenty years, how many would have died of old-age, and how many would need spectacles as strong as his before the time was up. On one particularly stifling stinking day, he even worked out how long it would be before the entire peninsula became a cesspit.

When he was not writing, he was sketching—his other love. As the subject matter was so limited, he found less and less satisfaction in it. Occasionally, he was sent by Colonel Petworth to climb through the scrub to a dangerous vantage-point with binoculars, to sketch the inland terrain and mark in the present positions of the enemy normally hidden from them. On those times, he would sit and swelter behind the cover of some scrub while he drew to his heart's content, page after page of distant views of the islands he still had not visited. On the first of these occasions he had returned without the information required, so absorbed had he been in his own thoughts. The Colonel's reprimand had been so stinging and humiliating, delivered in front of the others, that he never forgot again.

Periodic assaults were made up the cliffs in an effort to gain ground, establish a better foothold, get away from the terrible existence of the mountain-goat. But they were always beaten back with savage loss of life on both sides, and the mood of the men grew uglier. During these attacks, Turkish prisoners were sometimes taken, and Chris was called to interrogate them. It was seldom productive, because the enemy soldiers were mostly of the peasant class who spoke the patois of different villages. When Chris suggested to Colonel Petworth that he compile a dictionary of peasant phrases, he was told not to bother because the Turks were 'a parcel of damned sly buggers who would lie their heads off anyway'.

All in all, during those four months leading up to Christmas there was only one element in Chris's life that kept him going. That was his friendship with the New Zealander, Neil Frencham. Despite the difference in age and rank, they had a common interest in learning. Although it was a case of the pupil far outstripping the tutor, Chris's desperate need for an outlet for his knowledge and a use for his brain rather than his body made him accept Neil's approaches with eager gratitude. Together, they discussed everything under the sun, escaped their present existence by entering those of centuries before. They argued frequently, Chris expounding theories slightly beyond the older man's range and thereby annoying him. But, for all the knowledge Chris imparted on Greek and Roman beliefs, reasonings and attitudes, Neil responded with a profound and intelligent understanding of the Maori peoples and culture. Chris was fascinated. He could not get enough knowledge on a subject entirely new to him, and he seized every opportunity to be with the one person who showed him any sort of normal kindness and for whom he felt the slightest rapport. He sensed that the others discussed and resented their friendship, but he did not let it bother him.

Their difference in rank meant he could only enjoy the friendship when they were both off-duty but, on several occasions when Chris had climbed up to a lone and risky position at the cliff-top, Neil had arrived to sit with him for a while as they discussed and studied the view normally denied to them. It was only natural that talk should go beyond military installations to the distant islands, and they both enjoyed the peace and solitude that allowed them to forget what lay below for when they climbed down again. On one such day Neil had admired a sketch Chris had done of the wild terrain, a patch of flowering grasses, and distant hazy islands.

On sudden uncharacteristic impulse, Chris had held it out to him and said he could have it, if he wished. Neil had no sooner taken it from him, than there had been an explosion of gunfire aimed at them by a machine-gunner, who must have seen movement and was taking no chances. Quick as lightning, Neil had pushed Chris flat, then thrown himself over him as protection until the firing stopped. Later, Chris realised the man had been prepared to save his life by risking his own, and the feeling of friendship grew. If Neil had been younger and a little more carefree, Chris might have begun to feel he had found a temporary replacement for Rex.

Shortly after the machine-gunning episode, Neil told Chris he had found a wonderful safe place where it was possible to bathe out of range of the Turkish guns, but which was completely free of troops, boxes of stores, and small boats. Seizing the right moment, they both slipped away to scramble down a trackless slope and arrive, sweating and breathless, at the base of a narrow fault that ran up through the rock, and which overhung the sea in a convenient slab.

Chris was charmed with the peace and solitude which allowed a person to forget the 'mountain-goats' further up, and with the pleasurable contrast of white sun-baked rock, cobalt sea, and no sound but that of the water slapping against the sides of the minute inlet.

'How jolly clever of you to have found this without anyone knowing,' he said turning to Neil with a delighted smile. 'Did you use Maori water-divining techniques, or kick out some of your Kiwis who found it first?'

Neil laughed and ruffled Chris's hair with rough affection, much as Rex used to do. 'Cheeky young devil! Go on, get in there and wash away the lice! Think yourself lucky I condescended to share the place with you.' As they took their shirts off, Neil added, 'We can go in in the buff here. No dignity to lose in front of the troops.'

'Good-oh,' enthused Chris, longing for the pleasure of total immersion in the cold cleansing salt water, as he tugged off the rest of his uniform and carefully placed his spectacles on top of the pile. Then, naked, he looked at the blur of the other man.

'Come on, Demosthenes, I'll race you in.'

Neil did not answer immediately, and when he did it was in a strange intent tone. 'My God, you're only a boy, really, underneath all that wisdom. Petworth is right. You *should* be behind a school-desk, not out here staring death in the eye.'

Chris grinned, filled with the normality of that quiet bathing place. 'Hardly that, Major Frencham, sir. *We* are halfway down the bally cliff; *death* is up at the top of it.'

To his surprise a hand slapped him very hard across the bare buttocks, and Neil said, 'A whacking for impudence, boy. Now jump in there before I feel disposed to administer another.'

They swam and dived for fifteen minutes or so, until they were both breathless. Then they climbed out onto the flat rock to dry themselves in the heat of the sun, Chris feeling unusually contented. Groping for his spectacles, he began to polish the lenses that had splashes on them.

Suddenly, from close behind him, Neil said softly, 'You know, you have the most wonderful eyes of any boy I've seen.'

Something inside Chris began to curl up, and his feeling of well-being vanished instantly. He wished Neil had not said that. It brought back, out of the blue, something that the past four months had pushed to the far recesses of his mind to be forgotten. Now, like one of those murderous whistling shells, it zoomed out of nowhere to remind him that he had a wife and son at home—

a baby that did nothing but wail, and a girl who had been seduced by his eyes.

'So wonderful they can't see a bloody thing,' he said with ferocity, fighting a losing battle with the old feeling of hopelessness and despair. Hooking the tortoiseshell frames around his ears, he snatched up his clothes and began pulling them on. All pleasure had gone now. Neil had ruined everything with that one sentence.

'What's the matter?' his companion asked sharply.

He buttoned his trousers, head bent. 'Nothing. We ought to get back.'

A hand gripped his shoulder. 'Have I upset you? Forgive me. I intended quite the reverse.'

But Chris was no longer concerned with his companion, and began scrambling up the rocky cliff-face with scant care for safety. If he ever left this barren peninsula, if he ever abandoned his primitive home, if he ever found relief from constant blistering sun, it would be to return to something that would destroy him as certainly as Gallipoli would. A girl and a child who both bore his name would hang around his neck forever. They were inescapable, totally inescapable all the time he lived.

With sweat streaming down his face he clawed his way upward, knowing he had lost the illusion of freedom from them now. Suddenly, he was halted by hands that gripped his shoulders from behind, and he was swung round to face the man he had forgotten.

'Chris, *don't*. Don't run off like this,' Neil panted. 'I could bite my tongue out now. I unintentionally touched your Achilles heel, and you must have thought me cruel. But I couldn't help it, my dear. You looked so beautiful standing there naked, and those eyes with the long lashes curling over them were more than I could stand.'

'Wha . . . what?' he stammered, lost in memories of a village in Dorset that he dared not see again.

'It happened almost without my knowing,' said the other man in a voice husky with emotion. 'I was on the edge of self-destruction when you walked through the lines and into our midst. But these days we've spent together have been some of the most wonderful of my life, the hours we have had to ourselves in a way that shut out everything and everyone else, gave me a new reason for living. Then, down there in the water, it was like happiness rushing in from the past. You were so playful and provocative, I knew I

121

couldn't hide my feelings from you any longer. But my overture was the one thing that could hurt you. Please forgive me, Chris. I've grown to love you so much you have the power to hurt me, too.'

Like a charge of electricity hitting his brain, the import of Neil's words was a shock that brought him instantly back to the present. He stared in horror at the intent suntanned face of the man to whom he had given more of himself than he had ever given to anyone else, in the delight and release of finding a mind in accord with his own. He had looked upon this man as a fellow-enthusiast, aesthete like himself, a loyal friend, a substitute for Rex. He had spoken to this man of things very dear to him, of thoughts so long unconfided for want of a trusted, respected listener, of emotional responses to poetry and beauty of landscape. This man had also been *his* salvation in the midst of desperation, and he had grown to love him as an older brother. Now, stunned, revolted, cruelly disillusioned, he faced the latest betrayal in his short life, and it was the last one he could take.

'*Christ!*' he cried in sick anguish. 'Is that all people ever see when they look at me—a beautiful body? You filthy devil! You've made a mockery of everything I care about, everything that meant anything to me. I gave you my eager friendship: I even compared you with my brother. I believed that learning really meant something to you, that you loved all those things as deeply and passion-ately as I do.' His voice began to break with fervour. 'You've destroyed it all with your obscene perverted confession. You've destroyed all I had left!'

He turned away and scrambled up the rugged slope, driven by a desperation that could no longer be contained and caught in the fear of lost human identity. Up there, at the top of the cliffs, he could find freedom from it. He had seen others do it and shud-dered. Now, he wanted it beyond reason.

He had crossed the line of trenches and was halfway toward the crest, before he was seized from behind. Fighting desperately, he tried to shake off the older man who was clinging to his shirt with a grip that he could not break. For several minutes they struggled fiercely together, their boots slipping on the loose shale.

'Chris, for God's sake come down!' panted Neil, his face wild and frightened. 'This is madness.'

'Madness! *You* can speak of madness!' he accused, rasping with effort and desperation as he tried to break free.

Then his boot slipped, and he fell, pulling Neil down with him. Together, they rolled and slithered down the steep slope, thudding against small rocks and being torn by coarse bushes in their path, until they dropped into one of the trenches and lay winded. But Chris was soon on his feet again and scrambling up onto the slope, his urgent desire to get as far from the other man as possible.

'Chris, *don't!* For Christ's sake, don't!' came Neil's voice after him. 'That's no way out for you. You're worth far more than that. Suicide is for the unintelligent.'

He scrambled a little further.

'If you go up there, you are admitting that there is no more to you than a body. Let that brain of yours work now. There's never been a greater need for it.'

He moved up another yard, more slowly.

'A few feet from the top you'll realise I'm right.'

He stopped.

'Come down, Chris! That's an order from a superior officer.' Then the voice seemed to thicken with emotion as it went on. 'I see now that I made a terrible misjudgment. Don't worry, it's all over and will never be referred to again. You'll soon find I've destroyed nothing for you. It's my self-respect that has been demolished.'

Lying face-downward against the scree Chris heard the sound of the other man's boots as he walked away, and he could no longer hold back the sobs that racked his body. He sprawled there feeling lost, degraded, and terrified by his own loneliness. But he did not climb to the top of the cliff. When it grew dark he dragged himself wearily back to his hole in the rock for yet one more night.

An hour before dawn the Turks made one of their fierce frenzied attacks designed to shake them from their tenacious hold and drive them into the sea for good. Those manning the outposts sent runners with a warning, and men were shaken or kicked awake all along the maze of trenches to stand ready for a counter-attack. Nothing was ever gained in these suicidal clashes, and the death-toll was always high. But the Allies knew they dare not be driven from their precarious positions, and the Turks grew more and more enraged by their continuing presence, like a thorn that could not be plucked from their sides. Hatred flared strongly on these occasions, and men were prepared to do anything to vent it. Only when it was over and the cost was counted, did they wonder what it had all been for.

Chris stumbled from his straw bed, struggled into his tunic and breeches, and strapped on his gun-belt with automatic movements that overcame his terrible lethargy. When he left the shelter of his dug-out, the sky was already silver-blue and peppered with puffs of black gunsmoke. Machine-guns were chattering with vicious nonstop sound, and rifle-fire was rending the air around him with sharp volleys ordered by officers used to conventional warfare. Then, as he hurried the few yards to the cave headquarters past Neil's New Zealand troops occupying that stretch of the cliff, the thunderous salvos of the huge guns on the ships standing offshore made the morning a total travesty of the beauty that surrounded him.

He ran the last few yards to the cave from where Colonel Petworth commanded all operations. The Signals Lieutenant was busily scribbling messages and giving them to runners, the corporal was trying to make contact on the radio that was always failing when they most wanted it, and the young Manx private was handing round strong cups of tea. There was no sign of Neil. He would be out with his men directing the attack.

The usual pandemonium reigned, and Chris felt out of it, as usual. The Colonel regarded him as a liability and treated him as such. Yet, if he had not reported for duty, there would have been all hell to pay. As it was, Chris took a cup of tea and drank it down gratefully, trying not to think of the events of the day before. They had all been part of that unreality named war. Had the centurions, the legionaries, the hoplites felt such hopelessness, such degradation, such perverted desire for affection? The glories of ancient conquests were somehow tarnished by thoughts of such human failings. He had once told a girl nothing was achieved by a negative attitude, but he had it now with a vengeance.

The battle followed the usual pattern. Waves of men were sent 'over the top' to charge uphill with the object of capturing the machine-guns that raked them all so continuously. It was against all commonsense, but their positions halfway down the cliffs left them no alternative than to stay where they were and be killed, just the same. There was always the hope that one wave might be successful. The whistles blew, and the first wave clambered from their trenches and onto the exposed slopes.

Chris watched through binoculars from the entrance to the cave. The men ran as if they knew their last moments had come and were resigned to certain death. Within minutes, nothing moved on that cliff apart from the occasional inert body slowly sliding downward on the loose shale. Another whistle blast; another wave of men who fell alongside the others dotting the white stony surface halfway to the top. More bombardment from the sea; more frantic messages from Colonel Petworth. Another blast on the whistle!

Chris marvelled that the men obeyed the order to go, but over they went and began to scramble desperately toward the crest. Suddenly, the machine-gun fell silent. Chris could see the gunners still moving against the skyline, so the thing must have jammed. The mishap allowed the wave of troops to continue climbing beyond the line of their comrades' bodies and, with only inaccurate rifle-fire to face, they crept nearer and nearer the top. A new noise began. All around Chris men were cheering, shouting encouragement, flinging their wide hats in the air. Another whistle-blast, and these same men were climbing from the trenches that were home, highway and shelter to them.

The two lines of men were roughly a hundred yards apart—one only feet from the crest, the other advancing steadily behind—when Chris's attention was taken by the racing arrival of Neil through the lines of those waiting to go next. His face was worried and angry.

'They're going to take that gun,' he panted to the Colonel. 'My Kiwis are going to get that gun, at last, but I want better support from your troops on that other cliff to cover them when they reach it. There may be a whole Turkish division up there.'

Colonel Petworth swung around. 'I've given you what support I can rustle up already. They've suffered ninety per cent casualties over there, and there are no officers left to lead them. They won't go on their own, because they're too demoralised now. All I can offer is covering fire from the trenches.'

'That's no use,' snapped Neil. 'At this range, they won't hit anything at the top. I've got to have men on the slope to draw fire while mine take the gun.' He gripped the back of a chair angrily.

'This is the nearest we've ever come to taking one of their guns. We can't let them down now, or they'll give up completely. Sir, we *need* that success.'

'I know. I know! Send one of your subalterns across there to persuade them that someone believes in their chances of getting up that slope alive.'

Neil swallowed. 'I haven't a subaltern left. They all went down in the first three waves. That's why we've got to have that gun. These men will have to have died for a purpose, or those left will never be prepared to die in the future.'

Colonel Petworth did not like being spoken to like that, and he thumped the rickety table with his fist. 'Then give me an officer, damn you!'

Neil's mouth tightened. 'I've a captain with one leg in plaster, a lieutenant laid out with chronic dysentery, and myself. Take your choice. But if we lose that gun now we're so close to capturing it, I'll hold you responsible for the mutiny we'll have on our hands.'

The Colonel glared at him, red in the face, and at the end of his tether, like everyone else. Then, as Chris shifted his feet noisily, the glare was fastened onto him.

'Very well, Major Frencham, I'll give you support on the eastern flank. Young Sheridan can lead the attack.'

'*No,*' came the cry that betrayed much more than military protest. 'You can't send him.'

'He's a subaltern.'

'He's a non-combatant.'

'He's any port in a storm. We desperately need an officer: he is an officer.'

'I'll go myself,' came the desperate response.

Colonel Petworth flung him a contemptuous look. 'Don't make a sentimental fool of yourself, man. Sheridan is expendable. You are not. All we need is a figurehead, someone in officer's uniform out there in front to inspire confidence. You say we'll have a mutiny on our hands if we don't carry that gun. Mr Sheridan will be only too willing to save us from that. Won't you, boy?' demanded the commander who had gone beyond humanity or emotions.

Chris felt weak with fright, but he nodded. 'I don't know much about battle-tactics, though, sir.'

'You run like a mule with a bee under his tail and hope to hell they miss you. The others behind you will do the same. It's the only battle-tactic you need to know. If you feel up to it, you can shout a few obscenities in Turkish at the enemy when you get near enough.' He drew his bushy brows together and almost smiled. 'Have you learnt the Turkish for *bugger off* yet?'

Swallowing hard Chris managed to say, 'Not exactly. But I daresay I can think of something sufficiently vulgar to upset them.'

The Colonel put a hand on his shoulder—a rare gesture. 'Good lad! Scoot off, then, and find Lance-Corporal Green along the eastern transverse trench. He's got the whistle. When you get there, tell him to give two blasts to let us know. Then count to twenty and go.'

Chris moved away from his corner and, as he passed, Neil made an impulsive move toward him. But he did not even spare the man a glance, simply went out into the long winding trench knowing he would never see any of them again.

As he walked he was not thinking of the glory of dying for his country, the honour of leading a vital charge, or any such uplifting but false idealism. He was filled with anguish of knowing a man's mind and senses counted for nothing. It was his body that was valued—by girls who longed for physical conquest, by men whose desires were perverted, by war leaders who wanted a figurehead for doomed men. For nineteen years he had revelled in the philosophies of wisdom, the refinements of culture, the language of beauty, and the infinite complexity of profundity. Yet, in the end, it seemed all he was was a bag of hay.

7

THE PATIENT in bed 9 lay for a long while gazing from the window, finding escape from pain in the scene outside. Snow lay everywhere, clean, dazzling, sharply beautiful in the pale cold sunlight. It undulated in drifts blown by the blizzard that had raged the night before, but now the air was still, and it looked incredibly peaceful outside. There was a large open stretch which must be lawn, then an extensive shrubbery behind which rose a row of dark cypresses. The trees were dappled green and white, but the shrubs were weighted down by snow that sparkled and turned them into the fantasy foliage in the kingdom of The Snow Queen.

As he watched, birds alighted and flew off the branches, sending little powdery falls to the ground. Squirrels taking a holiday from winter slumber loped lethargically along the limbs of a giant oak just outside the window, then sat back on their tails to clean their whiskers with busy paws. Now and again, they looked in at him, and the contact of those bright beady eyes warmed him.

Only yesterday his bed had been wheeled to this corner, where two right-angled windows gave him a panorama of the extensive grounds. He felt a great deal happier in semi-privacy. Up by the door he had felt on view to anyone who entered: down here he was in his own world. It was a world that could well be Hades for the torment he was in. The whole of his body burnt as if he were roasting over the fires of the Devil, there were knives stabbing mercilessly into his stomach and neck, his head thundered with pain that never entirely vanished, his throat was constantly parched, and his hands were two throbbing areas of anguish to add to the rest. What was more, he appeared to be blind until someone put a contraption across his face that made everything spring into focus.

He had been born ten days ago, and the terror of it had not yet left him. When the torture grew too great to withstand he cried out. Then they rushed at him, enclosed him with dark-green screens and stuck needles in him. This bed was his prison. He was trussed up in a manner that made movement impossible. From beneath his arms to the tops of his thighs he was tightly bound, and his arms looked like two wooden spoons with huge ovals of white gauze at the ends. One leg was rigidly immobilised and fixed to the bed with metal rings. Utterly helpless, he could only turn when they turned him, had to lie flat when they lowered the backrest, had to sit up only when they decided he should.

There was the additional humiliation of being touched by them all, the privacy of his sex revealed to anyone who arrived at his bedside. The men and women who came seemed to enjoy his helplessness as they stripped off the bedclothes and began handling him, knowing he was powerless to stop them. They chatted all the time, calling him Christopher, or Mr Sheridan, and pretended there was nothing sinister in what they were doing to him. Then, as if to highlight their power over him, they took away the lenses and left him in a world of blurs until they chose to restore his sight.

Unable to withdraw from them physically, he withdrew verbally. Their greetings and questions remained unanswered; their silly casual chatter received no response from him. He had not spoken a word to any of them, and sat in his agonising world knowing they were angered by his silence.

He did not trust any one of those around him. They told him things he did not believe; said he was someone he knew nothing about. Who was Christopher Wesley Sheridan? They told him he was nineteen years old and came from a Dorset village called Tarrant Royal. There were two brothers called Roland and Rex, but no parents. Very convenient, he thought. They could easily produce two young men—there were dozens all around him—but not an elderly couple who would join in the deception. There was a war in progress, and he had been seriously wounded by an exploding shell as he had led a charge on a machine-gun post. He was now in a hospital for officers in Somerset.

He believed no word of their story. If there was a war in progress it was his against them. He was suspicious of their smiles, frightened of their power over him, and suffering deeply from the agony of what they had done to him. But pain would not break him, as they would soon discover. They had tried to break his silence with slyness, bringing to the bed on three occasions a blond young man in tweeds, with a dependable good-looking face, and saying he was the brother called Roland. The visits had not fooled him for a second. This 'Roland' was one of their own number and would get no more from him than they did, however hard they tried. He knew secrets he must never tell.

But they held one trump card that threatened his resistance. By day, it was a living nightmare; at night it became too real to accept and they put the needle in him again. His head was bandaged like an Egyptian mummy, with a slit for eyes, nose and mouth. Under those bandages he had only half a head. When they spoke of taking off those bandages soon so that he could see what he looked like, he broke out in a sweat of real terror. Those were the moments when he doubted his determination. If they began unwinding the white cloth to reveal one eye, one ear, and a bloody mess of brains, he would be totally lost.

At that thought, he realised the true reason why he had been moved to this quiet corner away from the others. They did not want anyone walking through the door to see a man with half a head. It was the most appalling gruesome sight. Now he was well away from the main part of the room, they would come and unwind the bandages, forcing him to watch in a mirror, until he told them what they wanted to know. Terror rushed through him, and the knowledge that he was powerless to move, to escape from them, brought cries of despair from the mouth that could only just move beneath the tight bindings. They were beside him immediately. He screamed at them, 'Don't do it; don't do it.' But they put a needle in his arm, and he began to sink into the familiar well of blackness.

It was dim when he opened his eyes. To his right was a blur of shimmery overhead lights, but he was lying in a pool of semi-darkness. Overriding the usual pain was a dreadful thirst. But he would not ask for a drink, neither would he ask for the lenses that helped him to see, because they could use his weakness to make him speak to them. So he lay fighting the craving for water. The sensation did not seem new to him.

Suddenly, a dark blur appeared beside him, and his heart lurched. What was about to happen? The blur remained, but he felt no hands touching him, no tampering with the bandages. Was this some new test? Did they hope to break him by keeping him in fear? When something did finally touch him, he almost cried out in fright. But it was merely the pince-nez being slipped onto the bridge of his nose.

Everything leapt into sharp clarity and looked reassuringly normal. Outside the windows there was an even more enchanting scene. Lights from further up the room were shining out onto the snow that was glistening with new frost, and lazy flakes were drifting down to nestle on the carpet already there. In his dim corner he felt part of the clean beautiful freedom that stretched before him outside. Pleasure as sharp as pain stabbed him as he gazed out into a world that was a total mystery to him. The vista increased as he was raised by the back-rest being wound behind him. The sight of that coldness made him forget his thirst. The beauty calmed his heartbeat.

Someone moved beside him, and he turned his mummified head suspiciously. She was wearing a starched cap and apron like those calling themselves nurses, but her long dress was pink instead of blue. He had not seen this girl before, and was instantly on his guard. She would get no more out of him than the others. Gazing warily at her, he found her gazing back, eyes full of some deep sadness, face very pale, body strangely stiff. They remained looking at each other for what seemed a very long time, then she turned away without saying a word. From the corner of his eye he saw her reach the senior nurse, shake her downbent head, then run out through the swing-doors. He was puzzled. What did they hope to gain by playing him at his own silent game?

But his change of glance brought the water-carafe into view, and thirst returned in double strength. It was so near, and he wanted it desperately. Stretching out one arm carefully he found he could reach it. Slowly he pushed the neck toward him until the vessel fell, spilling the contents onto the top of the locker. As it ran over the rim to cascade onto the floor, he moved his head painfully toward the tiny waterfall and opened his mouth. Barely near enough, only a few precious drops ran onto his dry lips, and he put out his tongue to take them in.

Someone was suddenly beside him, holding out a glass. 'Here you are, son. Why didn't you ask for a drink?'

The man was tall and slender, with silvery hair. Although he slept in one of the neighbouring beds, he knew he could not be trusted. He kept his lips closed as the man put the glass to them and tipped it. The water ran onto his pyjama-jacket and the sheet. It was almost worth the continuing thirst to know they would be angry about the wet sheet.

The man went away again, and the girl in the pink dress returned looking paler than ever and strangely red around the eyes, as though she had been crying. But she was silent as she mopped up the water, then went to fetch his dinner-tray. He always made a point of eating meals, because he needed food to keep up his strength for the day he escaped from this place.

The broth was good, but the girl's hand was so unsteady as she spooned it into his mouth a lot of it spilled on the sheet. She was not a lot better with the steamed fish, but they somehow got through it. There was the usual egg-custard afterward, and he thought anyone could have managed that easily enough. But she slopped it everywhere, and ended up knocking the bowl onto the floor and smashing it. There was a good deal of fuss from the plump nurse who hurried down the room to sort out the situation, and he was pleased that whatever they had been trying to achieve with the girl had been unsuccessful. She went off in tears, and one of the usual ones came to give him the intimate attentions to prepare him for the night.

It took three of them to change his sheets, which they did amongst constant chatter about how much better he was getting and, if he was good, they might take the bandages off his hands before too long. He ignored them, thinking of the girl who had made such a mess of their plans she had been his unintentional ally.

They got him clean and straight, let him look at the snow for a little longer, then whipped off the pince-nez, tipped some foul-smelling stuff into his mouth, lowered the back-rest and went off leaving him in his misty world. Unfortunately, they had tipped him back the minute after giving him the potion, and he had been forced to swallow it. He grew drowsy very quickly but, just before oblivion, it dawned on him that the girl in the pink dress had not been clumsy, just even more frightened than he was.

Later on, they unbandaged his head and there was only half a face underneath, all smeared with blood and bound round with long, long hair that filled his mouth to choke him. He struggled to look away from the ghastly sight, screamed at them to cover it up again, sobbed with the anguish of it all. They came and put a needle in his arm, and the mirror vanished leaving him unable to see anything more.

The girl in the pink dress came a lot during the next three days. She never said anything to him, just did the tasks she was given and went away again. But the others seemed to leave him alone when she was there, which quite pleased him. She was still clumsy, and he sensed that she was terribly afraid. He began to wonder if they were treating her like they treated him, although it seemed likely that she could get away if she wanted to. But her pale sad face bothered him.

His concern for her grew, and every time she was clumsy and was reprimanded by the plump bossy woman who ran the long room they were in, he felt sympathetic toward her. If he were not trussed up and so helpless, he would feed himself and save her from the sharp tongues of others. She seemed so alone in her sadness, and he knew, to his cost, what isolation meant. Why did she stay, when she was not tied and bound as he was?

Proof that she left the building and returned came on the fifth morning, when she arrived at his bedside after being absent the day before, and put a small vase of snowdrops on the locker where he could see them. He knew she must have travelled some distance to get them, because there was deep snow as far as he could see from the windows, and the flowers must have been picked at a place where the gardens were green. The small white hanging bells were so fragile and innocent, the sight of them put a pain in his breast that had nothing to do with that which had been with him over the length of his short life. The flowers were like a breath of the freedom that was waiting for him outside.

He shifted his gaze to her face, and their glances interlocked for a long moment as he tried to understand the sorrow in her brown eyes and decide why she had brought him the snowdrops. Was this a particularly subtle way of undermining his resolution? But there seemed to be a droop to her shoulders as she turned away to fetch his breakfast-tray, and he felt very sorry for her. If she was there to deceive him it was because she was being forced into it by them. What possible hold could they have on her to make her do something that caused her distress?

She sat on the chair near his head to give him his breakfast, as she usually did. But her hands shook as she spooned porridge into his mouth. And she made such a bad job of cutting the toast that was so crisp, it flew off the plate, nicking the top of her finger to bring a blob of blood. She automatically put the finger into her mouth to suck it, and he saw from the corner of his eye, the plump woman hurrying toward them with an expression like thunder. Anger touched him quickly.

'Don't let her frighten you,' he advised swiftly. 'Refuse to speak. They can't do anything about that.'

She looked up at him, her face turning ashen, her eyes darkening with shock, as her whole body grew frighteningly still. The plump woman stopped, then turned back, but the girl still sat like a statue, seemingly petrified. Then his spirits plummeted as he realised it was not them she was afraid of, but *him*.

When he could, he made himself ask, 'It's my face, isn't it?'

'Your . . . your face?' she whispered, as if she did not know.

'Only one eye, one ear, and . . . and . . .' He could not go on.

Her hands were so tightly intertwined the fingers had turned white, and the brown of her eyes was now shimmery with tears.

'Chris, why haven't you . . . ?'

'Don't call me that,' he said sharply, afraid now that she was one of them, after all.

'What shall I call you, then?' she asked so strangely full of emotion her voice was now thick and muffled.

He gazed at her through the slit in the bandages, suddenly as full of emotion as she, because she had brought it into the open and he was forced to put it into words he did not want to hear.

'I don't know,' he said helplessly. 'I don't know who I am . . . or what I'm doing here. But I know I can never leave, because I've only got half a head.'

To his horror, he felt tears well up in his own eyes and overflow into the bandages surrounding them. When she got up from beside him and fled down the length of the room, he understood why. But he lay there powerless to stop the tears, feeling that he had glimpsed a friendly hand reaching out into his darkness, and now it had gone. It was intolerably lonely.

They had to put the needle in his arm again that night, when he saw what he looked like in the mirror.

Rex was given a whole month's leave prior to Easter. He had spent previous shorter spells of leave either in Paris or another of the French cities where it was possible to forget or ease the strain of war. He could hardly believe it was a year and a half since it had begun; that he had been out there flying for fifteen months and was still alive. But he found it all too easy to believe it would go on for a great deal longer, and his chances of being alive when it finally ended were extremely remote.

His belief in possessing a charmed life had died long ago. He had seen too many confident skilled fliers plunge to the ground like a brand. That he had not yet done so was decided by Fate. The conviction that he would join Mal Haines and the others only when his time had come put a strange calmness inside him, and was responsible for his reputation as one of the top flying aces amongst the Allies. But it was not the old carefree recklessness which had led to his battle successes that were now publicised to the world. He had grown more calculating and coldly efficient. Those days of flying into haystacks were past. He valued his machine as greatly as his life, and brought it back behind his own lines even if it was breaking up around him. 'Fun' flying was finished. His life was bound up with aeroplanes in a far deeper way than it had been in the past, and he was the only pilot at Grissons who knew as much about the engine and structure of his machine as the engineers who serviced it. That knowledge had saved him on several occasions when forced to land behind enemy lines, and he had grown to respect the aircraft as a friend rather than a source of risky amusement.

The feeling that his time in the world would be up before too long might have sobered him as a flier, but it put an even greater reckless urgency into his social activities. Every girl who put up no more than token resistance, he took to bed and enjoyed as if she were the last. He strummed and carolled his way through evenings with his fellow-pilots in case he never did it again. He laughed fear in the face, indulged in pranks more suited to a schoolboy, defied rules and regulations.

But one aspect of his life had not changed. He drank very little. When those around him found it the only means of escape and relaxation, he was resolute in his limitations on himself. Drink impaired a man's judgment; his life might be lost on a glass of whisky. His friends and colleagues now accepted and respected his feelings, and had long ago given up trying to persuade or trick him into getting drunk—even on bad nights when members of the squadron had been lost that day.

The new single-seat biplane fighters had arrived in France in an attempt to break the German air superiority gained by the Fokker, and the pilots now had to navigate, reconnoitre, and operate the machine-gun while they were flying. Rex preferred being alone. It meant he held responsibility only for his own life. But it also needed the greatest clarity of thought a man could attain to co-ordinate all those skills when enemy aircraft were buzzing around him emptying their guns. So far, he had been phenomenally successful, to the extent that his name was high on the list of 'prizes' sought by the German squadrons operating in his area. Every young Hun pilot longed to claim he had shot down Lieutenant 'Sherry' Sheridan, and if he could be captured alive it would be the complete triumph.

Rex knew all this, and had many times exchanged signals of respect and understanding with German fliers he constantly encountered, who all wore special symbols of identification in the spirit of deadly sportsmanship that governed air battles. Rex, himself, would never take off without wearing his dove emblem in his flying helmet, and a cerise silk scarf around his throat, ends flying. His famous scarf was, in fact, the silk nightdress of a French countess who had realised her contribution to the war effort was to keep airmen in good spirits. Although the truth was widely known in flying circles, it was one fact the Press decided to keep from the British public, and their hero's talisman had been dignified into a silk shawl owned by a noblewoman of the distant French branch of the Sheridan family. Rex had been highly amused at this attempt to turn him into a Victorian ideal of God-fearing celibate hero much given to honouring distant French noblewomen, and had wondered what Roland would think of acquiring a foreign branch of the family he regarded so proudly. But he continued to wear his 'scarf' on every flight, acknowledging the attention and respect it earned from all those who tried to shoot him down.

The first few months of that year had been exhausting and depressing. The R.F.C. lost too many boy pilots, and desperately needed a machine that would outfly, outmanoeuvre, and outgun the successful Fokkers. Rex, nearing twenty-two, was regarded as a grandad in years and experience, but so many were coming straight from flying-school to be shot down before they could gain the experience needed to fly a new aircraft—even were one produced. However, Rex had one long-standing partner and friend in Mike Manning, who seemed to be overlooked by Fate, also. With the Australian, he made a steady and inspiring nucleus to 2F Squadron, that had earned him the respect of his own hard-pushed superiors. His example, both in the air and on the ground, was what kept men's morale high when defeat stared them in the face, as it surely did during those early days of 1916.

But even heroes reached a point when they had to rest, and it was wisely decided to give a month off to a man they could not allow to crack-up, especially when his young brother had just been returned from Gallipoli broken in mind and limb. Rex's request for leave to visit his brother in the hope of helping his condition had immediately been approved, and permission had been also granted to Lieutenant Manning to go to England to see his sister, who had come from Australia to do war work.

Rex's spirits were subdued during the tiresome journey back to England, and Mike wisely respected his mood. The news of Chris had come as a terrible shock, all the more so because Roland's letter had been uncharacteristically emotional about the tragedy, and disturbingly vague about just how ill their brother was. It had left Rex with the impression that Chris was no more than a mindless shell hanging on to life by a thread. If this were so, he hoped the boy would die, and soon. He had been deeply angry to discover he had been sent to Gallipoli to be sacrificed in a doomed campaign. They had all followed the details—those that had been released by the Press—and had read, with bitter irony, of the successful withdrawal that had been carried out with brilliant tactical efficiency without the loss of a single life. Rex had read of it without having the slightest idea Chris was in any way connected with the humiliating defeat at the hands of the Turks. Although he had received no letters from his brother for a long time, he had assumed he was absorbed with the secret Intelligence work he was doing and had forgotten everything else, as he often did. What could possibly have demanded the sending of a youngster with a superb brain and terrible eyesight to a war zone that clung to a cliff?

Rex's intention to go straight to the hospital in Somerset was thwarted by trains and cross-Channel services that were overcrowded, spasmodic and slow. He and Mike eventually reached London at six pm, so he decided to book into the hotel with his friend for that night, and go the following day, which was Sunday. While Mike went round to meet his sister, who shared some rooms with an actress, Rex had a bath, which he extended to an hour's duration by topping it up with hot water every ten minutes, then dressed rather unwillingly for dinner. He would rather have eaten it relaxing in his room, but Mike had been very keen to introduce his sister, and Rex had had to agree to the plan of dining *à trois* in the restaurant.

He stood for a while in the best room the hotel could provide, just looking with pleasure at the trappings of normal living he had not seen for a while. But London was not the city he had left behind. The streets were full of men in uniform on leave, and others with the wounds of war too plainly evident. There was the strange sight of women dressed as postmen and tram-conductors and dozens in the V.A.D. nursing uniform. There was an uneasy air of waiting about the civilians who went about their business with drawn faces. Zeppelins had begun raiding the coastal towns, and Londoners felt it would not be long before bombs were raining down on them and Britain's capital. Yet Rex could not imagine this proud city being flattened as some he had seen in France. It was unthinkable.

However, this room with its illusion of peace and comfort was his for the night and he stretched out on the bed to wait. He fell asleep. A hand shook him awake and he frowned at Mike in bewilderment. Standing beside his friend was an attractive slender girl in a yellow dress, smiling down at him with merry understanding in her eyes that were the same curious silvery-green as Mike's. That was the only similarity. Her shape was definitely more exciting than Mike's, her mouth was fuller and touched with pink, her face was smoother, softer, and golden from the sunshine of Australia, her hair was longer and put up in a pair of shining coils beneath the feathery hair ornament she wore.

Putting his arms up behind his head, Rex studied her in appreciation for a moment or two, smiling back.

'The dreams they provide in this hotel are better than any I had at Grissons,' he said. 'Hard luck, Mike.'

Her smile widened. 'Why do you say that?'

'Fancy a girl like you being a fellow's *sister*. What a disappointment for him . . . but jolly nice for his best friend.'

She stood looking him over as he lay on the bed quite relaxed. Then she held out her hand. 'Don't we get introduced?'

'Of course,' he said. 'But I only shake hands with men. I usually get a kiss from girls.'

The merriment flared again in her eyes, and she swooped quickly to kiss him on the mouth. Straightening up, she told him, 'I only did that to become famous. I shall be known as "the girl who has kissed 'Sherry' Sheridan", and my future will be assured. I shall receive proposals from dukes and earls now.'

'Make certain they're proposals of *marriage*, Sis,' put in Mike earnestly. 'I've heard a lot about English dukes and earls, and most of it is damned ropey—especially concerning innocent girls from the colonies who only know about farming and sheep.'

'Lucky old sheep,' murmured Rex, swinging his booted feet to the floor as he studied her slender waist. To think he had almost ducked out of meeting Mike's sister! 'The dukes and earls will have to take a back seat tonight, Tessa, and Mike's filial ties render him harmless. So the field is mine.' He put his arms lightly around her and kissed her again in teasing manner. 'Just to assure your fame, that's all. Now, shall we go and eat? I'm famished.'

It was like Christmas and the past rolled into one as he worked his way through seven courses the like of which he had long ago forgotten, and flirted with a lovely suntanned girl untouched by the tragedy of France, who spoke of her life on a vast farm in Australia which would cover most of an English county. Her voice with its foreign inflection charmed him, her pretty face highlighted by such unusual eyes soothed him, the freshness of her open-air personality was something his exhausted spirits badly needed. Between brother and sister there was obvious close affection, and Rex was immediately drawn in to make the complete triangle. It seemed he had known Tessa Manning as long as he had known her brother.

The night was still young when they finished their meal, and Tessa suggested they all go to the last show at the theatre where her actress-friend was performing.

'There's a box reserved for her friends every night, and I only have to show the ticket to get in,' she told Rex. 'Do let's go . . . please.'

Rex succumbed. 'Your brother hasn't got such winning ways.'

'Yes, I have,' argued Mike. 'But I don't waste them on *you*.'

They all jumped into a taxi and laughed over silly nonsense all the way to the theatre.

'Woe betide you if this ticket doesn't work the "open sesame",' warned Rex.

'The what?' she asked, intrigued.

He winked. 'Arabic, my girl. Stop here in the taxi with me and I'll teach you some more.'

Mike seized his sister's arm. 'It won't be Arabic. I know him too well. Come on!'

They were shown to one of the numerous boxes on the second

tier, and sat on the red-plush seats in semi-darkness because the second-house had already started. Even so, glances were drawn to the pretty girl escorted by two officers in the dashing uniform of the R.F.C., whose youthful faces looked weary and strained. Men from the 'Front' were always objects of sympathy, pride, and interest to those who soldiered on in England.

Rex hardly saw what happened on stage as a pair of dancing girls were followed by a comedian in a loud checked suit, then by a troupe of performing dogs. The large meal with wine, the darkness and warmth of the theatre, the long journey from Grissons, and the months of concentrated flying now caught up with him. Terrible tiredness began to creep over him, and he had to fight to keep awake. Thoughts of Chris returned. He reached for Tessa's hand and held it tightly, as if to hold on to the sweetness and normality of her and keep war at bay. She turned to smile at him in the darkness, but he felt suddenly choked at her youth. All the young men of the world were dying. Soon, there would be none left for her, not even dukes and earls.

Then she leant toward him and whispered, 'This is her now. Watch and listen carefully. She's good.'

'I'd rather watch you,' he whispered back.

'Shh!' admonished Mike. 'If you two want to spoon do it quietly. I don't want to miss this.'

Tessa's friend turned out to be a male impersonator, and Rex immediately lost interest. He did not want to see girls in men's clothes. He much preferred them in dresses or, better still, out of them. Laurie Pagett, as the girl was billed, wore immaculate top-hat and tails while she sang a saucy ditty in a surprisingly deep voice, about a young man-about-town who could not distinguish champagne from lemonade and was always offending hostesses. Rex heard it in the background of his mind, but his sleepy gaze was on Tessa's profile the whole time. There was a wholesome open-air quality about her face that reminded him of the girls of Tarrant Royal.

His thoughts wandered to other years and the securely peaceful atmosphere in which he had been brought up. They had been good times, only now appreciated because they had ended. He wondered what it would be like when the war ended. The Allies would win—the alternative was unthinkable—but would Europe be populated by women? How splendid for those few men who survived, he mused sleepily.

There was a sharp kick on his boot, and Mike leant across his sister to whisper, 'What do you think of *that* for a bit of nerve?'

Rex straightened up in his chair and glanced in the direction of Mike's nod. The entertainer on stage had changed from top-hat and tails, and was now prancing about dressed as a flier, with her arms outstretched like wings as she pretended to zoom up and down. But she had just reached the chorus of her song, and it was that that took Rex's attention.

> *When he flies oh-so-high*
> *All the mam'selles cry*
> *Chéri! Chéri!*
> *He can't love them all,*
> *But still they all call,*
> *Chéri! Chéri!*

There was another verse so blatantly, heroically patriotic it made him cringe, then back to the chorus which was repeated twice with the whole audience joining in. Rex then realised the figure on the stage had a cerise scarf around her neck, and a feather emblem in the flying helmet. For a moment he was nonplussed, as applause persuaded her to reprise the chorus again so that it could be sung with gusto all over the house. At the end, the girl walked to the front of the stage and treated her audience to an exaggerated saucy wink before 'flying' off into the wings.

'What a damned cheek!' exclaimed Rex, finding the situation hard to believe. She could only have been impersonating him with that scarf and the chorus of 'Chéri' which sounded like 'Sherry'. But how could he possibly have become the subject of a music-hall song? Then he thought he had the answer.

Looking hard at Tessa, he said, 'You had a hand in this, didn't you?'

She smiled with wicked delight at the success of her surprise. 'Mike always writes such a lot about you that doesn't appear in the newspapers, and I just passed it on to her when she said she wanted to do a number about "Sherry" Sheridan.' She hesitated a moment. 'You're not angry, are you?'

'Extremely. I could sue for defamation of character,' he told her, looking stern. 'That song states I can't love them all . . . but I do,' he concluded with a copy of Laurie Pagett's broad wink. 'You'll have to compensate for what you've done to me this evening.'

'I will?' she asked.

'Definitely! For a start, we'll take Mike back to the hotel. Then I will see you home. You'll invite me in for a nightcap, and I'll accept. Leave it to me from then on.'

'We'll *both* see her home and go in for a nightcap,' put in Mike firmly. 'I'm not leaving anything to you where my sister is concerned.'

So they all went back to Tessa's rooms in a boarding-house. It meant tip-toeing up the stairs and past the landlady's door, because her rules forbade male guests to go beyond the downstair parlour. Stealth won the day and they arrived undetected. But Tessa then broke the news that their 'nightcap' would have to be a cup of tea, because alcohol in the rooms was also forbidden.

'Good lord, she sounds like one of the sergeant-major instructors at Central Flying School,' grumbled Rex, sinking into what he judged would be the more comfortable of the two shabby chairs. 'Doesn't she care about cheering the boys from the Front?'

Tessa laughed. 'She'd be only too willing to cheer you. She's not so keen on her boarders doing it.'

With the tea made and the tray at their knees, Rex asked Tessa about the war-work she did in London.

She made a face. 'It's in a munitions factory. There's noise, dirt and stone floors, and the work is most awfully boring. The other girls are all right, but they're mostly from the East End, and I don't understand half they say—and certainly not their humour. I suppose I'll have to stick it out, but after a South Australian sheep station it takes some getting used to.' She poured the tea. 'I'd much rather be in the open air. I thought of driving an ambulance, but I know nothing of London and would surely get lost.' Handing Rex a cup she said, 'I long for space, and the peace of the country. But so must all of you—so much more. I'm just being a selfish little cat.'

Rex sipped his tea. 'While I'm on leave, you must come down

to my home in Dorset. There's plenty of peace and open space there. Come for the weekend—you and Mike.'

Her eyes sparkled silver. 'Oh, I'd love that, I really would.'

The door crashed open, and a figure carrying a pile of boxes practically fell into the room. Gloved hands grabbed at the sliding boxes, to no avail. They toppled one after the other onto the floor with resounding thumps. A voice that was low and husky said, 'That's torn it! If old Blisterbag doesn't rush up here thinking we're holding an orgy, I'll eat my hat.' Then it paused and added, 'Great Scott, we *are* holding an orgy!'

The girl just inside the doorway took the whole of Rex's attention, and it was as if his pulse had stopped beating due to a blow in the region of the stomach. She was tall, voluptuously built, with a pointed face full of dynamic, vivid beauty, and hair as red as his own, cut very short in curls that covered her head. Her eyes, green, upturned, and as wicked as they come, were fastened on him in a glance that seemed to still the blood in his veins.

'Do shut the door,' begged Tessa. 'She will be up if she hears you shouting about an orgy.'

The newcomer kicked the door closed with one high-heeled scarlet shoe, then let her black fur-trimmed coat slip from her shoulders to reveal a scarlet dress that clung to her splendid body like a skin. Rex continued to stare at her, feeling punch-drunk. A scarlet dress with red hair was a fascinating combination on this girl, who seemed to defy everything.

'So introduce me,' came the sultry voice.

'This is my brother Mike,' Tessa told her warmly. 'He's on four weeks' leave. I did tell you he was coming, but you never listen to anything I tell you.'

'Hallo, Mike,' said the girl, with enthusiasm, shaking his hand.

'And this is his friend, Lieutenant Sheridan!' Tessa grinned at Rex. 'My room-mate, Laura Pagett.'

He got to his feet without being aware of doing so. *This* beautiful, vital, feminine creature was the male impersonator he had just seen? But she was staring back at him with her hand to her throat, eyes full of alarm.

'Lieutenant *Sheridan!* Oh, hell!'

'He doesn't shake hands with girls. He usually gets a kiss,' advised Tessa with great enjoyment. 'And he saw your performance tonight.'

'Oh, hell,' said Laura again. 'So that's the end of that!'

'I can't believe it was you I saw,' Rex heard himself say. 'But why a song about me?'

'You give them all something to cheer. They get dreadfully depressed, you know, reading the casualty lists every morning. "Sherry" Sheridan has become a legend, a hero. It doesn't matter if it isn't all true. They believe it, and that's all that matters. They feel an inward pride in what you represent. I give them the opportunity to express what they feel too inhibited to do normally. Roaring out the chorus with me does them the world of good, and they go home feeling a little closer to their own sons and husbands because you are over there with them.'

'Good lord!' he said, astonished at her sensitivity.

'Aren't you furious with me?' she asked tentatively.

He shook his head. 'I thought that wink was a bit much.'

A smile touched her mouth and spread its brightness over the whole of her face. 'Don't you really shake hands with girls?'

'No.'

'Dare I kiss you, now you know who I am?'

His heart thudded ridiculously. 'I think you owe me that much, don't you?'

She moved closer and reached up to touch her mouth gently against his, but his arms went round her, and the kiss turned into something that startled them both by the time it finished. They stood looking at each other in acute awareness of danger, the other pair in the room totally forgotten. But he knew he was already lost. There had never been a girl like this before: there never would be again.

She recovered first, and stepped away, saying, 'Is it true that your famous scarf is really a silk nightdress given to you by a French countess?'

'How in the world did you hear that?' he murmured.

'Not from the newspapers. I meet lots of boys from France— especially fliers. They talk about themselves and what it's like out there. Is it true?'

'That's right,' he said, hating the thought of the boys from France who met and talked to her. 'But you shouldn't believe everything they tell you.'

'About you?'

'About anything. We're all terrible liars.'

'Speak for yourself,' put in Mike, reminding Rex that there were other people in the room aside from Laura Pagett. 'Hey, this tea is getting cold. Aren't you two going to avail yourselves of it? It's the only liquid refreshment "Old Blisterbag" allows.'

The spell was partially broken by Mike's intervention, and Rex abandoned his chair to Laura before sitting on a low stool beside her, while they all had another cup of tea. It was like being in a daze of unreality. That shabby rented room seemed luxurious after the farm outbuilding he occupied at Grissons—he had long ago moved up from being a tent-dweller—and there was a relaxed unhectic flavour about being there with his friend and two pretty girls. They laughed a lot and drank gallons of tea. But, the whole time, he was conscious of every movement, every word spoken in that husky voice, every expression on the mobile face of the girl beside him. He had four weeks in England. He wanted to spend every minute of every one of them with her. And he would not think about having to go back at the end of them.

At one point he asked her, 'Why do you dress up in men's clothes when you're such a success as a girl?'

She looked at him frankly. 'I suppose it's a form of defence . . . against men like you. In the theatre a girl is very vulnerable, you know. She either has to be tough, or pretend she is. I was brought up in a country vicarage in Staffordshire. My father was horrified when I made it clear I wanted to go on the stage. He forbade me to do it, predicting hell and eternal damnation if I did. I left home whilst he was conducting a marriage service, and I haven't been back since. But I found there was a lot of truth in what he prophesied. My upbringing had hardly made me tough, just determined. But when I pretended to be hard-boiled and experienced, men just took one look at me and decided I was fair game.' Her smile suggested she knew he was thinking along the same lines. 'Dressing as a man somehow floors them. Besides, it gives me much wider scope for my act than just tripping around the stage with a basket of paper flowers, looking "divine". It's much more fun being "Sherry" Sheridan.'

'I could see that,' he said, then took the plunge. 'I have to go to Somerset tomorrow to visit a hospital. My young brother was pretty well broken up at Gallipoli, and has no idea who he is now. Would you come with me?'

She looked at him steadily for a moment or two, as if her

145

decision was going to be an all-important one. 'Poor little devil!' Then she nodded gently. 'All right, if you'd like me to.'

He relaxed after that and let happiness engulf him. He would see her tomorrow; he would see her every day for a month! Soon, the scarlet of her dress seemed too bright for his eyes, the mesmeric huskiness of her voice too much for his mind. The room was warm, the hour was late. Everything began to grow more distant, and even more unreal.

When he awoke, he was lying on the floor, covered with a white blanket and with a cushion under his head. The luxurious suite in the best hotel had not been his for the night, after all. It took him a moment or two to assess where he was, then he got stiffly to his feet, almost falling over Mike stretched out beside him.

There was a wonderful smell of eggs and bacon, and Rex followed it to its source in a tiny alcove where there was an oil-stove to boil a kettle on. Beside the stove were two plates. Tessa was there in a blue-and-white-spotted dress with a wide blue silk sash around her tiny waist. She looked fresh and clean, and incredibly good to see after so many mornings of waking to an atmosphere of sweat, snores and stale smoke in a primitive stone building.

She turned, smiling widely. 'Hallo. So food has done what all three of us failed to do last night. You were absolutely dead to the world. Sorry you missed your wonderful soft bed at the hotel you'd been waiting for for so long.'

'What shocking bad manners I have! You should turn me out without giving me any of that breakfast you've got there . . . but I hope you won't.'

With a shake of her head she laughed. 'I shall be even more famous now. If it weren't for our landlady, I could put a plaque outside my door saying "Sherry" Sheridan slept here. They have things like that all over England concerning Queen Elizabeth.' She indicated the plates. 'I sneaked these up here for you and Mike. Luckily, Mrs Beamish leaves breakfast on the sideboard on a Sunday morning so that we can take it whenever we decide to go down.'

He looked at her suntanned face, her neat tidy figure, and the shining dark hair in a chignon. 'You're a very nice girl, Tessa.'

'And you're a very nice man. I would hate you to be hurt.'

He moved further into the alcove with its distant view through the chimney-pots of Green Park. 'What does that mean?'

'Exactly what it says.' She looked up at him very seriously. 'Take care, Rex.'

'I always do,' he promised, and kissed her on the cheek.

'Hallo, hallo, hallo, what's all this,' said Mike's voice through a yawn. 'Don't you even call a halt for breakfast, Rex?'

He grinned. 'Go away, you're cramping my style.'

'Phoo! Who cramped *my* style last night? Sis offered to go off to bed, but my headway with the delectable Laura was completely ruined with your inert snoring body at our feet.'

Rex did not like the inference, even in joking form. He hoped Mike did not regard Laura as *his* partner in the foursome.

'Where is she?' he asked.

'In bed, as she is every other morning,' supplied Tessa matter-of-factly. 'You won't see her until midday.'

'But she's coming to Somerset with me to visit my brother.'

'Well, you certainly won't start out until after lunch. I'm surprised she agreed to go on a Sunday. It's her one night off, and she likes to indulge in pure laziness for the whole day.'

Rex was dismayed. They would not get down to Somerset and back if their start was delayed until mid-afternoon. They would have to stay overnight somewhere, and he could not see Laura viewing that idea in any but a suspicious light. Then he had an idea.

'Suppose we all go! After visiting the hospital we could go on to my home and stay overnight. I could easily get Laura back in time on Monday.'

'Oh, lovely!' cried Tessa. 'I'll play truant from the factory to-morrow. After all, it's just as much help to the war-effort to keep the boys of the R.F.C. happy, isn't it?'

'That's settled,' pronounced Mike. 'I'll go and dash some water over my face, then can we *please* eat those eggs before they go solid?'

He went off surreptitiously along the corridor to the bathroom, hoping to evade the landlady or any other boarders who might betray his presence there. Before following him, Rex lingered.

'Does Laura really meet all that number of men on leave?'

Tessa cast him a look that was sufficient answer, and he chided himself for even asking. But he would have her for four weeks, at least.

They ate breakfast with some tea Tessa made, then they crept down the iron fire-escape to the road and made their way back to the hotel. There, they bathed, changed, and ate another breakfast while they discussed their plans with the help of a railway timetable. When Mike went up to pack his things, Rex sent a telegram to Tarrant Hall so that they would be met by Dawkins at Greater Tarrant station, and settled the bill. As he went upstairs again he felt quite jaunty. The company of the others would help him face the coming meeting with Chris that he dreaded.

Mike looked remarkably long-faced when he walked into their room, and Rex feared he had received a message from the girls cancelling the trip. But his friend held out a Sunday newspaper open at an inner page.

'I might as well draw your attention to this,' he said quietly. 'If we are going to stay there for the night, it's as well for you to be primed up.'

In curiosity Rex took the newspaper. But it was the last thing he expected to read.

VILLAGE DISOWNS SUICIDE'S SON read the headline. Then, in smaller letters underneath: *Brother of Flying Ace Branded as Coward.*

With heartbeat slowing Rex read an article telling how the entire village of Tarrant Royal had turned their backs on a man who refused to volunteer to fight for his country. Gradually, they had thrown him off village committees and councils, rejected his financial assistance for community events, refused to work for him, and erased his name from honorary posts. Much was made of the heroism of his younger brothers—one being the famous 'Sherry' Sheridan who was attacking Hun aircraft so tirelessly and bravely, the other being a patient in a hospital for seriously wounded officers after leading a courageous charge in Gallipoli. Where was the eldest Sheridan's courage, the article asked. Once known as one of Britain's finest huntsmen, he now appeared unwilling to jump the highest fence and prove his worth.

There was a lot about Branwell Sheridan's suicide, and hints that his eldest son had inherited his weakness of character. The article finished with a description of how the villagers had formed a human barrier to prevent their former squire from entering the

148

seventeenth-century church where there was a family pew, because they felt he did not earn a place in it, as his two gallant brothers did. They planned to do the same this Sunday, if their victim dared to leave the country estate that he prized above the defence of his country.

Rex was filled with painful sadness as he read to the end, and he looked up at Mike with an echo of it in his eyes.

'Oh God, poor Roland. This will have completely broken him!'

8

'I'M AFRAID there is little chance your brother will know you,' said the doctor gravely. 'Although I understand there was a very close relationship between you, his amnesia would appear to be total.'

Rex pounced on that. 'Why do you say "appear" in that somewhat sceptical manner? Don't you believe he has forgotten everything?'

'Yes, certainly, Mr Sheridan. There seems no doubt that life only began for him on the day he first emerged into full consciousness in this hospital.' His dark brows narrowed together as he frowned. 'But this is a dangerously complex case, and I confess it worries me a great deal. Like your other brother, you have probably always accepted Christopher to be academically brilliant, and thought no further. True, he is . . . but there is much, much more to it than that. Specialists in Military Intelligence discovered an intelligence of exceptional rarity, and medical investigation of such minds is only in its infancy. This terrible war is producing more wounds of a nervous and mental nature than battle has ever incurred before. We are feeling our way, Mr Sheridan, still feeling our way.' He fiddled with a pencil he held between his fingers. 'For most cases there is a standard course of treatment. Some can be helped; others will be mindless invalids for the rest of their days. But young Christopher is hovering . . . yes, *hovering* in a dangerous vacuum between recovery and insanity.' He sighed. 'I'm sorry, Mr Sheridan, I see by your face that my bluntness has upset you. I'm sure you are under enough personal strain as it is.' A brief smile flashed. 'We are all aware of your tremendous efforts in the air. But, in order to do my best for this unfortunate boy, I must make the position quite clear to you and ask for any help you can give me.'

'Yes, of course,' said Rex, alarmed and horrified by what the man was suggesting. 'But if Roland has not been able to help, it seems unlikely that I can. We were all three very close.'

'Mmm, so I have been told by your elder brother. But . . . well, he is a man of very strong unyielding emotions, and that is not the best type of personality for this problem. His anger and bitterness over Christopher's plight is most understandable—I share it, to a less personal degree. The boy was sent to Gallipoli through a gross administrative error, and ordered into battle by a desperate, over-tired, war-weary commander. It was inexcusable and deeply tragic. But such things are happening all over the world in this present madness, and young men are being robbed, not only of their minds, but half their bodies—if not their lives.' He looked frankly at Rex. 'I have no need to tell you this, Mr Sheridan, but your brother Roland is a little out of touch.'

Rex said nothing, but felt again what he had felt on reading that newspaper article. Roland might be out of touch with war, but he had no time for incompetence and foolishness—especially when it resulted in what Chris had apparently become. He would also defend his kin and what they stood for with all the strength of character he possessed. It was the Rolands of the world who brought sanity back when the madness ended, but such men were always underestimated and undervalued.

'To get back to this very complex case,' said the medical man. 'We have established, without doubt, that the boy's mind has shut out nineteen years of life so totally he has no recollection of anything before January the ninth of this year. This condition could be permanent, although it is not unknown for a blow on the head or some dramatic shocking event to operate a figurative switch in the brain that will reverse the condition, in an instant. That is not our problem; we have to leave that to the Almighty. What we have to do is help the boy to adjust to this terrifying situation.

'A brilliant mind might have shut out nineteen years of self-identification, but it continues to work at full power. Your brother is exceptionally brilliant, but only in certain directions. He is, and always has been, unable to cope with basics. This kind of brain crosses the fine line into eccentricity, and then insanity, far more quickly than the average . . . even without war and wounds to bring it about. In young Christopher's case the danger is very much heightened, and our main concern is to stop him crossing that fine line from whence he would never return. The treatment is still experimental, and has to be backed up by a few prayers.' He dropped the pencil he had been playing with and bent to pick it up, looking Rex full in the face as he straightened up. 'So far, we have had to rely on prayers alone. Your young brother is playing us at our own game, Mr Sheridan.'

Rex stared in complete confusion. 'You mean, he's pretending all this?'

'No . . . not exactly. But he's one jump ahead of us all the time. Already, the craftiness of the madman governs his behaviour. No, please don't be alarmed,' he put in quickly, 'he is still perfectly sane, at present. But he is full of suspicion, distrust and fear. For the first ten days we believed he found it impossible to communicate, until he suddenly confided to his nurse that he was remaining silent to hit back at us—*the enemy*. During those ten days he would have been in constant severe pain, but would not break that silence to ask for relief from it. Even now, after two months, he will only speak to that one nurse. Apart from that, he is filled with strange revulsion of both male and female nurses when they tend him, literally shrinking from their touch. But most distressing of all for us is his total refusal to take part in our tests. If it didn't sound altogether ridiculous, I'd say it was as if he had decided to hide his intelligence from the world. We have given him all kinds of things to do, from simple games with coloured wooden blocks, to conundrums, to metal rings that have to be twisted certain ways to part them. He ignores them all. We have given him books; he doesn't even open the covers. We even dressed a linguist as a male nurse and had him speak unexpectedly in Greek and Latin. Your brother looked through him as though he were not there.'

'Poor little devil!' exclaimed Rex, very upset. 'They were his greatest passions.'

'So I was told. Now, with medical examination telling us that, apart from the amnesia, there is no damage whatever to his brain, it suggests he is involuntarily withholding evidence of his intelligence. In time, we could probably get over that, if he wanted us to. Unfortunately, Christopher has no more idea of why he is doing it than we do. That is where the danger lies.

'Something happened to that boy before he was involved in battle—something so overwhelming it is ruling his behaviour even though he has forgotten what it was. We have gone into his history, and have decided it must have been after he left England. It's unlikely to have been on the troopship, because we have traced several young officers who went out to Gallipoli with him, and he would seem to have been his usual self then. But he left the Suvla Bay force after it landed, and went over to a Headquarters that had been established on the peninsula for some months.'

'What did they say about him?' asked Rex sharply.

The doctor shook his head. 'There were no survivors. The British commander and his staff were killed when a shell exploded on headquarters, and the New Zealander who led the Kiwis was killed on the field the same day as Christopher was wounded.'

'I should have thought that enough,' said Rex harshly. 'I've seen violent death and destruction. It affects every man. A boy with Chris's sensitivity and immense intelligence must have been completely shattered by these experiences.'

'I agree—but it shouldn't have left him repulsed by human contact—I would venture to narrow it down to *physical* contact. Neither would it have led him to abandon those things that had given him such aesthetic and intellectual delight. No, Mr Sheridan, until we can find the cause for this need to withdraw from the world, we can do little for him. The danger is that he will withdraw too far before we get to the root of his hell—for that is where he must be, poor fellow.'

Prepared for bad news, Rex still found it all very hard to take. Terrible wounds he had seen and acknowledged as something to be faced. But this was beyond him. Feeling choked he got up and went to look from the window, where other patients were being led or wheeled around the grounds in the sunshine. Daffodils bloomed everywhere, and a large pink magnolia was in bloom in the corner, yet men with broken minds were the only ones there to see them.

He felt so helpless. He knew Chris was lucky to be alive, and lucky that the war could no longer touch him. But someone must reach through to the boy before it was too late. What could possibly have happened to him at Gallipoli that had not happened to the other thousands there with him? Perhaps nothing significant, in itself. But, together with the loss of his academic future and a marriage he could not accept, it became the final straw.

It was then he realised no mention had been made of Chris's married state and the fact that he had a son of over a year old. As he swung round to speak of it, a door opened near him, and a girl in a pink dress and starched apron walked in.

'Marion!' he exclaimed in surprise. '*You* here?'

'I thought it was time I told you about the one nurse your brother appears to trust,' said the doctor. 'Unhappily, it is only because he believes she is a fellow victim of ours.'

'I don't understand,' said Rex, completely undermined by now.

'I'll leave you alone with Nurse Deacon,' the medical man said, with a smile, going to the door. 'She'll fill you in on the other details before you go in to see Christopher.' He looked back encouragingly. 'Try not to be upset by his lack of recognition. It doesn't mean your former bond was not valued by him. Let's hope we can all forge a new one, before long.'

He went out, and Rex took Marion's hands. They were cold, despite the spring warmth of the day.

'My dear girl, whatever is all this? The uniform, and "Nurse Deacon"? Roland said nothing about it in the letter.'

'He wouldn't,' she said quietly. 'He tried to stop it, but didn't succeed. To his mind, I am to blame for Chris being here.'

'No, that's nonsense,' he protested.

She shook her head. 'He hates me, but he's right, of course. Chris would never have volunteered if he had not been so desperate to get away from a wife and baby he found it impossible to own.' She looked at him with sadness filling her dark eyes. 'I *am* to blame—for everything. I seduced him, you know.'

'He was extremely seduceable,' Rex replied gently. 'I was surprised no girl did it before you.'

To his distress, she suddenly leant against him for comfort as she indulged in a fit of sobbing she had obviously been holding back for a long time. With his arms around her, he tried to calm her, despite his own unhappiness and bewilderment. Then he

153

coaxed her across to a settee, where he sat her down and settled beside her.

'Suppose you tell me everything. I always told you to come to Uncle Rex if you had problems.'

She scrubbed at her eyes with her handkerchief, sniffing and apologising for greeting him like a waterfall. 'My problems can't be compared with yours,' she stated, with a watery smile. 'You're a hero, you know. The papers are full of how you risk death every day and . . .'

'How about concentrating on that husband of yours,' he interrupted firmly. 'He's the one with the problem we have to solve.'

Her smile grew warmer. 'Oh, Rex, it *is* good to see you again. I've missed you.'

'That's what all the girls say,' he told her briskly. 'Now, tell me it all from the beginning.'

She began by revealing that Chris had kept his married state a secret from the army authorities. 'So the telegram went to Roland,' she said. 'But Mrs Rogers told me what it contained, of course, and I waited for it to be sent down from Tarrant Hall. When no message arrived, I realised Roland had no intention of telling me what had happened to the father of my child. Daddy was all set to storm up to the house, but I stopped him. I knew Roland would hold me responsible for the tragedy, and I understood why. There was nothing to be gained by confronting him and causing us both further pain.

'After several terrible days while I couldn't decide what I should do, I came here and saw Dr Stevens, whom you've just seen.' She sighed. 'I told him the full truth about our marriage and Chris's feelings toward me and, if he had told me to go away and stay away, I would have done so, truly I would. But he suggested I use my slight medical knowledge by becoming a probationer-nurse here. That way, I would be with Chris in a way he would accept, and be helping them, as well. We decided to use my maiden name, and leave things like that.'

He looked at her in compassion. 'It must be a dreadful strain on you, seeing him day after day like that.'

'It's better now than it was at the beginning. I went to pieces when he suddenly spoke to me as I was feeding him. Until then, apart from those unmistakable eyes, I felt I was tending an anonymous figure. With his head entirely covered in bandages, it could have been anyone in there. But the voice was Chris's, and it said awful things—mad things. I was horrified, and ran away from him.' She almost broke down again. 'I haven't courage, like you, Rex. I let him down when he finally turned to someone. Thankfully, he tried again. But I don't give him confidence; he thinks he is giving it to me. That's the basis of our relationship. It's ironical, isn't it,' she said sadly, 'that the only person he now trusts is the one he hates most?'

'Why was his head all covered in bandages?' asked Rex getting more anxious every moment.

'It still is. Don't you know what happened to him?'

'Not really. I suspect Roland was very upset when he wrote to tell me the news.'

She let that pass without comment, and went on to tell him things he found all too familiar listening. 'Chris was caught in a shell bombardment that blew off two of his fingers, smashed the bones in his left leg, and gave him wounds to the stomach and neck. He was left under blistering sun for several hours, during which time he was under machine-gun fire that entered his shoulder and right thigh. When it was safe for stretcher-parties to go for the wounded, he was given emergency dressings and assigned to one of the hospital-ships. But, as the small boat made the journey from shore to the vessel out of range of Turkish guns, a lighter carrying ammunition was hit and exploded nearby. Oil that had spilled into the sea caught alight, and the fire surrounded the boat carrying the wounded. By the time they got the men to safety, Chris had been badly burned. No one thought he would survive the pain of that on top of the shock and severity of his wounds. But he did, and was rushed home as an urgent case. No one realised that he had no idea who he was until he recovered enough to remain conscious. If it hadn't been for the fact that he shouts at them during his bad times, they would have thought him dumb. And he shouts the most awful things, using language that is vile and filthy.'

Rex managed a faint smile. 'He's been with Anzac troops.'

'But, oh Rex, the most terrible thing is he thinks . . . he thinks he has only half a head under those bandages. He has the most distressing nightmares about it.' She seemed even more overcome. 'He grows dreadfully violent when they approach him, and screams at them not to unbind it. You have no idea what it is like to hear him begging them to spare him; crying like a small child over something that is only in his imagination. They have to sedate him completely when they change the dressings.'

'So he hasn't seen himself without them?'

She shook her head. 'The burns are not particularly pleasant to look at, although the thick dressings already around his head kept the worst of the fire from disfiguring his face. His body will be permanently scarred, however. In his present state the staff think it would be better to wait until he looks more like his usual self before forcing him to look in a mirror. Once he can, it should make him a lot happier, and he should no longer regard everyone as his enemy.'

'Save you.'

'Yes . . . save me. He tries to protect me from them. Isn't it hopelessly sad?' she finished, tears brightening her eyes once more.

He took her hands and gripped them tightly. 'No, it's rather wonderful. He's showing the first signs of adult responsibility, and the first signs of caring for another person rather than things. He's actually reaching out to someone of his own accord. Marion, you have the chance to start all over again with him, knowing he can't hold against you things he can't remember. This time, I'm sure you'll make it work . . . if you want it to, that is.'

'Of course I do,' she cried. 'I want little David to have a father.'

'Yes, what's happening to my nephew while you're here?'

She smiled. 'He's fine. I see him every five days. Young Nellie Marchant from next door goes in every day and, although Daddy doesn't approve of my being here, he's wonderful with the baby. I don't have to worry . . . although I miss him a lot. Rex, you will come and see him while you're home, won't you?'

'Try and stop me! I've been waiting a long time to see the little bruiser for the first time. I've even brought him a present, although I'm not sure you'll approve. It's a rather naughty French doll.'

'Oh . . . *Rex!*' She laughed for the first time.

'That's what uncles are for—to introduce young lads to the things their fathers keep from them.' He got to his feet. 'Come on, let's go and see young David's father. Afterwards, I want you to meet my best friend, his pretty sister, and a rather special girl I can't wait to introduce to everyone. They've been waiting outside for me all this time.'

'Oh, bring them in,' she cried immediately, getting to her feet.

'If there are two pretty girls, it'll do the patients so much good to see them. They rarely see a girl out of nurse's uniform.'

'I should jolly well hope not,' he said sternly. 'It would set back their recovery no end.'

Her gaze searched his face closely. 'You're still the same nice man I've always known. Do you really do all they say you do in the newspapers?'

He took her arm. 'It's what they *don't* mention I do that you have to be concerned about, my girl. I'm not a nice man, and never have been.' Smiling down at her, he added, 'But you can persuade Laura I am.'

'Is she the special girl?'

'I'll say. After I've seen Chris, you're coming to have tea with us all. I'll fix it with Dr Stevens. He won't refuse a hero one request.'

But the lightheartedness was all an act. As they walked toward the ward, his heart was hammering against his ribs. He had seen fellow-officers dreadfully knocked-about; he had seen friends burn to death. But facing a silent bandaged effigy everyone said was his beloved brother was going to take a lot of nerve to carry off successfully.

He could not describe how he felt when Marion stopped at the end of the long ward, and smiled at a figure propped against pillows. One leg was in plaster, the left hand lying on the coverlet was deformed by the loss of two fingers. What could be seen of his body was covered in bindings. There was a kind of helmet on his head, padded at the back, low over his brow, and up to his nostrils, with a hole for the mouth. But there was no doubting it was Chris. The large violet-blue eyes could belong to no one else. They gazed ahead blankly.

Marion picked up a pince-nez from the locker beside the bed to fix on the bridge of his nose, and Rex marvelled at her calmness.

'I told you your brother was coming to see you,' she said quietly. 'Why did you take these off?'

There was no response, although Rex could see intelligence in the eyes now that they could see properly. Chris stared at him as if at an unlikable stranger. It was more than he could take, for a moment or two, and he understood why Roland had been so emotional in his letter.

'Hallo, old son,' he managed eventually. 'This is a bit much for both of us, isn't it? They've told you I'm your disreputable brother Rex, and they've told me you're my brainy brother Chris. With all those bandages over your face, I'll have to take their word for it . . . and so will you.' He sat beside the bed knowing the meeting was a failure. The boy sitting there had no idea he had spent nineteen years growing up in his company. 'I've brought you something to do while you're getting well,' he persevered, unbuttoning his pocket. 'It's a book of French poems that I would call risqué, and you would call aesthetic.' He put the leather-bound book on the coverlet, but Chris made no attempt to pick it up. His gaze was on Marion, and it held a flavour of accusation.

She smiled at him reassuringly. 'It's all right. He isn't a doctor. I checked when no one was looking. I like him, and I think he wants to help.'

Silence.

Rex felt he was achieving nothing, and just putting unnecessary strain on himself and Chris. So he got to his feet again and smiled at the shell of his brother as best he could.

'She's right . . . I do want to help. And it's my guess you need as much of it as you can get. You trust Marion. Think it over about whether you want to trust me, and I'll come again soon to find out what you've decided.' On the point of leaving, he had to say, 'There was a time when you would have put your life in my hands. If you'd just put your trust in them now, it would be a giant step toward recovery. Don't give up, Chris. You're worth so much more than that.'

He walked away, throat constricting painfully. But, when he reached the end of the ward and looked back, the patient in bed 9 was gazing in the other direction from his window. The book of poems lay ignored on the coverlet.

They all had tea in a cafe decorated with copper-kettles and warming-pans. They ate fingers of toast, cucumber sandwiches, scones with honey, and a plate of madeleines. To the observer, it was a party of attractive young people in high spirits, despite the overtones of war created by the khaki of the men, and the nurse's uniform on the sad-eyed girl. But, although he laughed a lot and was saucy to the blushing waitress, Rex could not forget that lonely terrified parody of his brother back there in the hospital.

158

Marion made no attempt to hide her identity, and chatted about her small son with great animation to Mike, who had deliberately taken the seat beside her. Rex was grateful. He had told his friend about Chris, and the marriage that had been a disaster from the word go. But Mike was being especially gentle and attentive to the girl Roland regarded as a greater enemy of the Sheridans than the Turks. Not for the first time, Rex wished he had been at home when the crisis had occurred, and two proud impassioned men had forced a pair of youngsters into something that had brought tragedy and despair . . . and all for the sake of a child who was being brought up by the girl-next-door, after all. It took a war to change outlooks and values. He just prayed the devastating outcome of brief compulsive adolescent passion would give them another chance—however tentative.

The tea-party had to be curtailed because four of them had to catch another train. Marion said she would be at home on the following Thursday, and hoped they would all come to admire her son.

'He's really one of the most beautiful babies you'll ever have seen,' she said with quiet pride. Then she looked up at Rex. 'There's no doubt that Chris is his father.'

He walked with her the short distance to the lane leading to the hospital, while the others were putting on hats and coats.

'I don't think I'll be there on Thursday,' he told her. 'But I'll go and see your father and David tomorrow morning.' At her quizzing look, he added, 'Laura has performances every night except Sunday. If I want to see her, I'll have to be in London.'

Marion's face, given some colour by the jolly company, turned to give him a considering glance. 'That's not like you, Rex. She must be really special.'

He smiled. 'Didn't I tell you that right away?'

They walked a few more steps, then stopped beneath some overhanging horsechestnut branches at the foot of the lane.

'Roland will be disappointed. He'll be expecting you to spend your leave at home.'

He frowned. 'I know. But he'll understand when I explain . . . and when he meets Laura.'

She passed no comment on that except, 'She's a very unusual girl.'

'Isn't she just!' he enthused. 'See how quickly she came up with

159

the idea of organising a concert at the hospital. The medical staff will approve, won't they?'

'Certain to,' she assured him. 'It's a splendid idea. She really did seem very upset over the patients.'

'Yes. You see them every day and have grown used to such sights. I have grown used to them. But Laura lives in a world of glitter and lights. The only troops she sees are laughing and happy.'

'Mmm,' mused Marion. 'I hope she realises what your life is like over there.'

'Oh, I shouldn't think she does for a moment,' he replied cheerfully. 'And I don't intend to enlighten her. I've only got four weeks, and there's much more that I want to say to her than that.' He looked at his watch. 'I do have to go, you know. I'll be down to see Chris as often as I can . . . and if you feel you'd like me here at any time, I'll give you the name of my hotel where I can be contacted.' He put his hand under her chin and smiled gently. 'Take care of him for us all. I'm sure his recovery lies in your hands alone, my dear, and that's exactly how it should be.'

Swiftly she stood on tiptoe and kissed him.

'Hey!' he exclaimed lightly, 'how is it I only get kisses from you now I'm your brother-in-law? I tried jolly hard and never got anywhere with you before.'

She smiled mistily. 'Dear Rex! Don't let yourself be hurt, will you . . . by anyone? One wounded Sheridan is more than enough.'

It was dark by the time they reached Greater Tarrant, but old Carter was there to take their tickets and lock up his beloved station after their train—the last to stop there that night—had pulled out. He made a most tremendous fuss of Rex, pumping his hand energetically up and down and saying how splendid he looked in his uniform.

'You'm quite famous now, sir, with they arioplanes you flies. I never thought—well now, *none* of us ever thought—that you was goin' to be in them there daily papers for all the world to read about.' He chuckled. 'Truth tell, we all sweared you'd break your danged neck in they contraptions, like.'

Rex managed to free his hand as the old man ran on. 'They come down 'ere with they photograph machines, you know. Tarrant Royal baint bin the same since. All lined up for the pictures, they was, so Ted Caddywould said. Then, the photyographer makes a flash and a puff o' smoke with a danged thing in 'is 'and, and Ted says little Gerry Phipps starts a'cryin' and a'bawlin' fit to kill. So they all looks at the little varmint, like, and all the photyographer gets is the sides of their 'eads. Give me a real larf, I tells you,' he declared, chuckling heartily at the thought of it.

They all stood there beneath the old lamp on the corner of the station-building, while Rex introduced Mike and the girls. Carter seemed tickled pink over the two pretty females, and gave Rex a wink so knowing it was worthy of being one of his own.

'I might 'ave knowed you'd be in the company of a young lady or two, Mr Rex. You'm not changed one groat, for all this y'ere war and nastiness. Course, Tarrant Royal baint like you remembers, sir. There's a good few lads gone as won't never be a'comin' back. I don't know what an' all! I means, it can't go on much longer, when all's said an' done! There won't be no young lads left, ceptin' some 'oo . . . well, now, best left unsaid, maybe. I always 'ad a great respect for you, sir . . . ar, and a strong likin', what's more. Same with that young brother o' your'n, ceptin' I never did understand arf what 'e said, like, 'im bein' such a brain box. Now that pore little shaver 'as lost 'is wits, an' doan know 'oo 'e is, like. That's terrible cruel, nobbut some folks say it's the Lord's punishment for sinners. But I looks at it more compassionate, like. See, there's young lads and maids fashioned by the Lord to tempt each other, an' sometimes the temptation gets too strong for 'em. Can they be punished fer that? I arsks meself. It's that little'un that'll suffer, in the end. "The sins of the fathers" is a very wise parable. You finds the truth o' it in many instances. Take Betty Gilbert, now . . ."

Rex decided it was time to get on, and interrupted him. 'Betty Gilbert is a granny now, and the Lord has long since forgotten what she got up to when temptation grew too strong for her. Has Dawkins arrived with the trap for us?'

Old Carter's face grew strangely expressionless. 'I looks after the station, sir. What others choose to do is their own affair.'

Completely in the dark as to what the old man meant, and anxious now to get home, Rex said briskly, 'You'd have heard Dainty's hooves on the cobbles, surely?'

'My hearin' baint good, these days,' was the vague reply. 'I'd best get on with lockin'-up an' gettin' 'ome to my supper. Nice bit o' 'am tonight, with carrots from garden, an' pease-puddin'. Doan want it spoilin', do I? I 'opes I'll be seein' you again, sir . . . an' it'll be a pleasure every time.'

He shuffled away jangling a great bunch of keys, half of which he never used. Rex gave the others a look of comical apology and left them briefly to walk out and search for Dawkins. The trap was there waiting in the usual place, and the old family coachman was standing beside the pony, making no attempt to come across the yard to search for them. A broad welcoming smile broke across his weathered face as Rex approached.

'Hallo, Dawkins,' he greeted warmly, shaking the old man's hand. 'It's good to see you again.'

'And you, sir . . . and you,' came the wheezy reply. 'We're all so very proud of you, and so thankful you're still with us. But then, you always did seem to have the Almighty and the Devil both on your side.' His smile began to fade. 'I understand you've been to see poor Mr Christopher, sir. How did you find him?'

'Quite seriously ill, I'm afraid. He didn't know me at all. It was a very sad experience. How is my brother taking it, Dawkins?'

'Hard, sir. Very hard indeed. What with everything else . . .'

'Yes,' put in Rex quickly. 'I read today's newspaper. What occurred this morning?'

Dawkins' expression hardened. 'Rector tried to reason with them, but they won't listen to any word in support of Mr Sheridan, sir. In the end, Rector let us through the vestry door. But the congregation walked out, sir . . . just up and left, to a man. Mr Meader conducted the service, just the same, and there was just Mr Sheridan, Mrs Prideaux and myself there in the church.'

'Oh lord!' said Rex, in concern. 'It can't go on like that!'

'Well, it will, sir, just so long as Mr Sheridan is up at the Hall. At the start, I tried to put his side of it all when I went down to the George and Dragon of an evening. And Mrs Prideaux spoke up smartly when she went for the shopping. But they're a stubborn community, as you know, sir, and a lot like their own sheep. Landlord won't serve me now, and Mrs Prideaux has to get her supplies all the way up from Blandford. They've turned against anyone working up at the Hall. But they'll not make us leave, sir, no matter what they do.'

The familiar station-yard with its white-painted gate and old coaching-lamp, the springtime smell of the Dorset countryside, the quietness and peace broken only by the restless stamping of the pony's hooves, the mention of the ancient church, the George and Dragon Inn, and the villagers he knew so well, all banished thoughts of Grissons, the deadly Fokker, burning men in burning machines, and the muddy devastation of France. Tarrant Royal became the world, the villagers an entire race, and their battle against his brother a grievous, heartbreaking problem. Suddenly, it was all that mattered.

He gripped Dawkins' shoulder. 'You are very loyal friends—you and Priddy and Minks. Let's get up to the house. I can't wait to see my brother.'

The coachman greeted the others courteously and gave rugs to the two ladies to put across their knees. Rex made certain he sat with Laura and put his arm along the back of the seat behind her, cupping her upper arm with his hand to steady her in the swaying trap. The six-mile drive home made eighteen months of his life fade into the background, the past attacked him so strongly. Memories of his old motor cycle and the way its noise announced his arrival to the villagers flooded through him. In that summer of 1914 he had come home to a secure future as a wealthy land-owner's son, with a job in an engineering factory he had negotiated so that he could use the facilities for dabbling in aircraft experimentation. He had had a motor cycle to dash around on, and the 'Princess' to ride the sky with him. He had had a father in Madeira, and two good-looking successful brothers who were as happy as he.

Where had it all gone? He now had neither a motor cycle nor an aircraft of his own, and he had to live off his officers' pay. Half his home was a hospital, his young brother was physically broken and on the brink of insanity, his elder brother was hounded and despised by those he had faithfully served, because he had not offered himself on the same altar. Yet the lanes looked the same in the early moonlight, the primroses on the banks gave off the same damp fragrance as before, the dog-fox still barked in the copse as he went a'courting, and those lamplit cottages had stood unchanged for years. A lump rose in his throat for the sadness of men that did not touch the animals, the flowers, the bright moon, the sturdy old buildings.

A hand touched his, and he looked down into Laura's upturned face in the moonlight. The rest faded, and he was filled with the ache of finding her once more.

'You can't live your brothers' lives for them,' she said softly. 'There's enough danger in living your own.'

'How did you know what I was thinking?' he said into her ear.

'I understand faces. I see hundreds of them in rows in front of me every evening. Yours is too sad, at the moment.'

His arm tightened around her. 'Not when I look at you.'

She glanced across at the others and made an exaggerated gesture. 'I really don't know what I'm doing here. Sunday is the one day I get to myself, yet I allow this man to drag me to a hospital full of patients whose plight plucks my heart out, then to his home in the middle of a hostile village. I hate the country, too. Can you tell me why I agreed to do as he asked?'

'Oh dear,' said Mike in sad tones, 'the cry of many a young maid, I fear.'

'You're doing it to ease your conscience,' Rex pronounced firmly. 'After prancing about twice-nightly in terrible mockery of me, you haven't the nerve to refuse me anything.'

'Oh yes, I have,' she retaliated. 'You won't get a silk nightdress from me to wear round your neck as a trophy.'

'Shhh!' laughed Rex. 'You'll undermine my standing in front of Dawkins.'

'Could you possibly have agreed to come because you want to improve your act by studying your subject more closely?' asked Tessa in teasing tones.

Laura's tongue went out in dainty manner. 'Don't betray my professional secrets. He'll be on his guard against me now.'

'Not me,' he said with fervour.

'Well, you should be. I'll stop at nothing to get what I want from you.'

His grin held all the sauciness of past years. 'That makes a pair of us. I knew I was going to enjoy this trip.'

The great circular forecourt in front of Tarrant Hall's impressive front-entrance was full of vehicles—a couple of motor-ambulances, several motor cycle combinations, a staff-car or two, and a very modern delivery-van bearing the name of a Blandford provision-merchant. The house was ablaze with lights; the scenes inside the large rooms being similar to those they had left behind at the hospital in Somerset. Nurses moved amongst the beds; young men suffered beneath their bandages.

Rex saw it all with dismay. The war was there in Tarrant Royal, after all. It was there in those rooms where he had eaten and played, as a boy; it was there beneath the eaves where he and his brothers had slept and dreamed of all they would accomplish in adulthood. It trod across remembered gardens with a faltering step, and looked out across Longbarrow Hill with pain-clouded eyes. It entered through that great arched doorway on canvas stretchers, and sometimes silently departed in long pine boxes covered with a flag. He shivered suddenly. His childhood had departed with the advent of antiseptic and thermometers!

Dawkins pulled up at the side-entrance, explaining that they could not go through the wards. As Rex was trying to assess how much of his home was still being used as such, Roland came out to greet them. Standing in that lamplit doorway formerly only used when entering from the stables, he looked every inch the landowner and squire. His well-proportioned figure was impressive in immaculate dinner-jacket and trousers, and the stark contrast of white starched shirt against the black cloth emphasized his healthy good-looks and blond hair that gleamed golden in the artificial light.

In his eagerness, Rex vaulted over the side of the trap and strode forward to greet his brother. But it turned into an emotional moment, as they gripped both each other's hands and found themselves lost for words that would come anywhere near expressing their feelings, after all that had happened in the past eighteen months since they had met. It was then Rex realised Roland looked ill and strained to the limit.

'It's been longer than I realised,' he said, at last. 'But it's good to be home.' He turned to draw Laura forward, and said, 'I've brought some very special friends of mine that I want you to meet.' Smiling down at her, he made the first introduction. 'This is my brother Roland, who is a great deal nicer and much more respectable than I am.'

Laura's vivid face registered cautious appreciation. 'He's also a lot handsomer! Hallo, Roland. I'm Laura Pagett. Your brother has exaggerated. The extent of my friendship with him is that he spent the night in my digs and has somehow persuaded me to spend these two days with him.' She turned to the others. 'Mike and Tessa are his real friends.'

'Wait until you've spent the two days with me before you make comments like that,' he reprimanded. 'Who knows what you'll be by then? Roland, Laura is a male-impersonator and does a wicked song that just evades being eligible for a law-suit by me.'

Laura's wide inviting smile was turned onto Roland, and her eyes danced with merriment. 'Watch it while I'm here! I might do one about you next week.'

Rex realised she had not thought about her words before saying them, but Roland took the inference that was not in them and said stiffly, 'How do you do, Miss Pagett. I think a law-suit by either one of us would be undesirable.'

Hurriedly Rex introduced Tessa and Mike, then all four trooped into the small panelled hall where the boot-jack still stood beside the stand containing oil-skins, weather-coats, riding-crops, and walking-sticks. Rex sniffed appreciatively. It still smelt of lavender-wax from constant polishing.

'How's Priddy?' he asked as they walked together into the side-corridor.

'Older. You'll notice a difference,' came the uncompromising reply.

'And Minks?'

'I should have retired him, but he has nowhere else to go.'

'What about Cook?'

'She left six months ago.'

'Left!' he exclaimed incredulously. 'When the others stayed?'

Roland cast him a quick glance. 'Her widowed sister was taken ill, and the kitchens are now part of the convalescent-home. My meals are cooked in the butler's pantry, which I've had converted. Priddy does the small amount of cooking—I don't entertain, these days—and her great-niece from Sussex helps with the vegetables and serves. It's a very convenient arrangement for everyone concerned.'

'Yes . . . I see.' He halted as his brother made to open the door that had once led into a morning-room. 'Roland, just how much of this house has *not* been taken over by the army?'

With one hand on the door, Roland halted, too. 'I have retained three bedrooms in the South Wing, two servants' rooms, my study, which I also use as a drawing-room, this morning-room where I now eat, and the outer hall which has been turned into the estate-office. It's far more economical, and quite big enough for me.' He smiled with the echo of former brotherhood. 'But the place will come alive now you're here, Rex. A whole month, isn't it? I should jolly well think you deserve it.'

'Er . . . yes. I want to talk to you about that later.'

'About so many things,' enthused Roland, leading the way to the study-turned-drawing-room. 'But there's plenty of time. Firstly, I want to know how you found Chris . . . although I expect I can guess the answer.'

The next hour or so passed in near-unreality as Rex sat in a familiar room that was in unfamiliar guise, in the company of a brother who represented his past, a fellow-pilot who shared his strange present, and two girls who were the hope for the future. Priddy had greeted him like a tearful mother, and eyed the girls like a possessive one. Minks had also broken down, embarrassing everyone including himself. Roland was being the polite host to three complete strangers as if he were still Squire of Tarrant Royal and the wealthiest man in the district. Yet, in the background could be clearly heard the noise and bustle of a military hospital that was only a door's-width away from them. Gradually, weariness began to wash over him as it had the night before. He needed sleep and more sleep. But, if he closed his eyes, he would miss the delight of watching Laura, and the even greater delight of catching her watching him.

It was Tessa who broke up the evening after they had been served with sandwiches and coffee. 'It must be the country air,' she said with a smile at Roland, who had got to his feet the minute she declared that she would like to retire. 'I'd forgotten how relaxing it can be. Will you please forgive me?'

'Of course,' he said, smiling back with his reserved charm. 'You'll be able to see the estate properly in the morning. You're in for a delightful surprise, Miss Manning.'

'I can't wait . . . and I do wish you'd call me Tessa. We Australians get rather overwhelmed by English formality in country houses.'

'So do we actresses,' put in Laura, rising to stand beside her and giving Roland an outrageously innocent look. 'I'm not sure whether I should shake hands with you on retiring, or pull my forelock respectfully. I have my doubts whether you always expect a kiss from girls, like your brother.'

'No, he doesn't,' put in Rex quickly, seeing Roland's expression. 'I told you he was far more respectable than I am.'

'You are also a very nice person,' she said to Roland with genuine warmth. 'After so long, I'm sure you have been wanting to talk to Rex about family matters and poor Chris, yet you have welcomed us all into your home at very little notice. Respectable, or not, I'm going to show my appreciation.' To Roland's complete surprise, she stood on tiptoe and kissed him lightly on the mouth, bringing a flush to his cheeks.

'What about the younger brother?' put in Rex, catching her around the waist and pulling her against him. '*He* gets the house and fortune. I'm left to get what I can.'

'The younger brother only gets a pull on the forelock,' she teased, tugging at one of her own red curls. Then, in perfect imitation of old Carter at Greater Tarrant station she said, 'I always 'ad a great respect for you, Mr Rex . . . ar, an' a strong likin', too.'

They all laughed, which woke Mike from his doze and set him on his feet apologising for his rudeness.

'This lad has been known to drop off at the controls of his machine and have to be flown home by his observer,' joked Rex with his arm along Mike's shoulder. 'But the last time he did it, he'd forgotten he was flying a one-seater and was halfway to Berlin before he woke up expecting his tea!'

'There's not a word of truth in it,' protested Mike laughing. 'Ask him about haystacks, if you want to hear something really amusing.'

After showing their guests to their rooms, the brothers went back downstairs and relaxed to the extent of unbuttoning their jackets and loosening their ties. They sat for a few moments just looking at each other in the quiet contentment of being together again. Then Roland sighed.

'You look older, Rex . . . much older.'

'So do you. Roland, you didn't mind my bringing them, I hope.'

'This is your home, whatever else it might be, at the moment. You bring whoever you like here.'

He shook his head. 'I relinquished that when I joined the R.F.C.

This house is yours by right of inheritance, and you're the one who is working flat out to maintain it. But I brought Mike and his sister, because I thought they'd appreciate it. They're both an awful long way from home.'

'Of course. Is Miss Pagett a long way from home, too?'

He trod carefully. 'Metaphorically, not physically. I'll talk to you about her later on.'

'Yes, perhaps you should,' was the slightly caustic comment. 'Now tell me about your visit to Chris.'

Rex leant back in his chair and looked frankly at his brother. 'You know there isn't anything to tell. He's there. That's all I can say.'

'No suggestion of recognition?'

He shook his head. 'God, it's an awful feeling, isn't it? I even took him a book of erotic French poetry he would have thrilled over before, but it might well have been a block of wood, for all he cared. Although you had told me how serious it was in your letter, I wasn't prepared for the actuality. What the hell do you think happened to him in Gallipoli?'

'You'd have more idea of that than I. What do men do in battle?'

'Usually something quite extraordinarily heroic. It's before and afterward that they go to pieces.' He decided to confront Roland right away. 'Marion was there with him.'

'She's always damned well there with him. As his next-of-kin I tried to stop it. They overruled me.'

'You're not his next-of-kin, though. She is . . . and she has every right to be there. If anyone can help him, it will be her. I know it's ironical, but he trusts her.'

Roland got to his feet. 'And what happens when he starts to remember? You weren't here, Rex. You didn't see what she did to him during those months; how she pestered and taunted him, how she thrust her pregnancy at him and talked non-stop domestic nonsense at every meal. She had absolutely no understanding of his mind, his approach to life, his desperate disappointment over Cambridge. She hung herself and her damned baby around his neck like two millstones, and expected him to stay afloat. My God, man, you must see that she is responsible for destroying him.'

'Now, she needs the chance to build him up again.'

'*She* needs!' cried Roland. 'To hell with what she needs. All I care about is what Chris needs . . . *and so should you!*'

Rex got to his feet knowing all this had to be said, and feeling sorry that it had. 'What Chris needs is someone to stop him from crossing the border into permanent insanity. Neither you nor I could do that, it seems. But Marion might and, whatever she has done in the past, I would forgive ten times over if she saved Chris's mind now.' He took a deep breath and let it out slowly. 'I think no one has ever considered her side of this—not even her father. He was set on saving his daughter's honour, but her heart seems to have counted a very poor second in his considerations. She's not a Scarlet Woman, or a wicked practised seductress, Roland. Old Carter put it into perspective just an hour or so ago when he said, "There are young lads and maids fashioned by the Lord to tempt each other, and sometimes the temptation is too strong for them." You have to agree Chris was more than enough to tempt any girl, and Marion is very shapely and pretty. If you haven't experienced times when the temptation is too strong you're not the man I thought you. Chris only did what we've both done a lot more often than once . . . except that he was so totally inexperienced he didn't stop when he should have done.

'It's my guess Marion thought she loved him, at the time. But the romantic dream must have fast faded when morning-sickness came along. Yes, she ruined Chris's chances and drove him to volunteer. But he ruined hers, too, don't forget. The past eighteen months must have been damned difficult for her. Pregnancy, husbandly neglect, hostility from her brother-in-law, and sneers from the villagers—apart from condemnation from a father she has loved and cared for for many years.'

'But *she* is not bodily smashed and a mental wreck, is she?' put in Roland savagely. 'That's what she has done to Chris—*your brother!*'

'I haven't forgotten he's my brother—a very dear one—and I'd give my own mind if it would save his,' Rex said, trying to stay calm. 'But you can't blame Marion for his wounds. They are the result of military blundering—*totally* the result of military blundering, Roland. Chris desperately needs that girl now, and she just as desperately needs to do what she is doing. Try to be generous and understanding toward her in this situation.'

Roland walked over to the desk in the curtained window-alcove. 'Come here a minute,' he said coldly.

Rex joined him, puzzled. His puzzlement increased when his brother opened a drawer filled with what looked like the pluckings from a farmyard duck.

Picking up one feather and holding it between finger and thumb, Roland said, 'Marion has sent me one of these every week since Chris volunteered, and is still doing so. There are others who have begun sending them, but hers are always in the same kind of high-quality envelope with the writing unmistakable. Generous and understanding toward her, did you ask me to be?'

Rex looked at the mass of white feathers, appalled. He knew what they must have done to his brother, and he closed his eyes momentarily in anger against the senders.

'There won't be many more,' continued Roland. 'As soon as I appoint a bailiff, I'm going into the army.'

'No,' protested Rex immediately. 'You're doing more than enough here. Don't let their lack of intelligence break you.'

Roland stared at him. 'Good God, it isn't because of the feathers —or the attitude of the people down there in the village. You should know me better than that, Rex. It's because of Chris. What has been done to him is so unacceptable, so tragic, so inhuman, I have to offer my limited knowledge to the Medical Corps so that I can try to help others, in his name. They're desperately short of doctors and nurses, I can't hold back any longer. That's why I'm glad you're here just at the right time. I want to discuss with you the terms of our wills.'

'Our *wills?*' repeated Rex, unable to think clearly, by now.

'Once I don khaki, there's no doubt I'll be sent to France. You are well aware how long men are lasting out there. It probably won't have occurred to you, but if you and I are both killed, and Chris is declared insane, Marion will get this house and the estate in trust for that ill-begotten damned child of hers. Now you see why I don't want her at that hospital where she can drive Chris over the edge the moment he starts to recall the past. I'd rather will Tarrant Hall and the estate to the army as a permanent hospital than let her and her father lord it up here. We've got to prevent that, at all costs!'

9

ROLAND HAD lain awake for long troubled periods during the night, and felt even more than usually worried as he drank the tea Minks had brought to his bedroom. Every awakening, these days, brought the sad remembrance of his shattered younger brother and his own impotence in that situation. His thoughts then usually moved to Rex and the terrible risks of his life in France.

This morning, he thought of Chris, as usual, then all that Rex had said the evening before about Marion. He could not agree, of course. If the loss of an entire battle could be attributed to lack of one horse, then the loss of young Chris's sanity could be blamed on a promiscuous girl. Nothing would ever change his feelings on that.

He had so looked forward to having Rex at Tarrant Hall for a full four weeks. They had last met eighteen months ago, and he had a feeling of terrible premonition that they would never meet again once they parted this time. However, his brother had breezed in with his friends, looking very tired and more mature, but banishing all overtones of drama and sadness with his lighthearted manner. It did not seem possible that Rex had done all he must have done since going to France; had seen some men die at his side and others by his hand. Apart from lines of strain on his face, the experiences seemed to have had no effect on him.

Yet, even as he thought that, Roland realised he was wrong. Beneath the surface an awareness of the sands of time running out must be strong, or his brother would never be acting the way he was over the actress he had known only twenty-four hours. It was completely out of character, and immensely disappointing. It was also very worrying. Rex appeared infatuated beyond reason with the most impossible girl. Although Laura Pagett apparently came from a respectable upper middle-class family, she had abandoned her background to make a living in the sleazy artificial world of the music-hall—as a male impersonator, of all things! That meant she must sing coarse songs with unattractive verve, dress in trousers, and generally ape the male sex in gestures and manners.

To be honest, Roland could not believe she could be very successful, as such. Although he would describe her as statuesque rather than dainty, her figure was guaranteed to push up any man's pulse-rate, and her face was so vividly, wickedly female it seemed unlikely she could ever pose as a male. True, her voice was unusually low for a woman, and her red hair was as short as a boy's, but the husky voice was excitingly seductive rather than masculine, and her hair that sprang up in a mass of bright curls asked to be caressingly ruffled by a male hand.

At that point, Roland brought himself up short and unwillingly acknowledged that Laura Pagett aroused his basic responses very strongly, which was why he was very wary of her. She was the kind of girl who could pull a loving husband away from his wife; a man away from the true and loyal woman who kept his home for him and brought up his children with love and devotion. A girl like Tessa Manning, for instance. There was a young woman who appeared to have all the qualities he had once believed could be found in Marion Deacon. If Rex had to spend his leave with a female, why not a nice girl like Tessa? He knew the answer, of course. Rex would never get what he was seeking from his friend's sister.

Roland had long ago realised his middle brother needed sexual release far more often than himself, but he wished Rex could have sought it nearer home for the next four weeks, rather than fixing that desire on a girl in London, who was likely to play him for all she could get before he went back to France. Having seen Tarrant Hall Laura Pagett was probably under the impression that Rex was a man of means instead of a junior officer living entirely on his salary as such.

He sighed as he finished dressing, and turned his thoughts to his more pressing problem—that of finding a bailiff to run the estate for him. All the able-bodied men had taken up arms. An old man would be too cautious, too set in his ways to cope with the changing demands of a country at war. He could not leave all he owned in the hands of someone from the city, who knew nothing of running a farm, or a large house, come to that. There was the possibility of also leasing the land to the army, but that would only be a last resort. He felt they had enough with the larger part of his home. But nothing would weaken his determination to offer his medical knowledge in order to help young boys like Chris, who had been robbed of their rightful futures. Deep conviction that this was even more his personal duty than supplying food and timber for a hard-pressed country made him resolved on volunteering for the army as soon as Rex went back to his squadron at the end of the month. That left him with very little time to put everything satisfactorily in order.

The problem was still occupying him when he left the house and walked briskly across to the stables, intending to ride down and check some fencing that had been brought down by a recent storm. Sheep had soon found the gap and streamed into the lane. He had had no end of a job getting them back with the aid of the dogs, and he had then been forced to repair it himself. But he was no expert fencer, and thought it would be as well to see how it was standing up.

It was a fine exhilarating morning. Cockerels in the village below were announcing that it was time everyone stirred from bed. He breathed the fresh country air with its mixed scents of dewy grass, baking bread, rich newly-turned earth, and wild violets. Deep regret sliced painfully through him. He did not want to leave all this; it was England, free and peaceful and productive. His heart would remain here when he went to war. He had tried so hard, withstood so much in his desperation to keep it unchanged for afterward; to save his beloved country from becoming barren and devastated as Europe would surely be. He knew he had lost that battle. When he left this house, this estate, this village, he knew he would never see them again as they had always been. Whatever lay ahead of him would change both man and outlook, so his dream of rural peace and fulfilment would die forever. Could he replace it with a new dream, or would the time for dreams have irrevocably passed by then?

Entering the stable, his reflexes jumped at the sight of someone standing by his horse. She was just as startled, for she gasped as she spun round to face him, hand going to her throat nervously.

'Good morning,' he said, avoiding addressing her by any name. 'You're about very early. Couldn't you sleep?'

'Oh yes, but this heavenly morning awoke me, and I couldn't possibly ignore it any longer,' she said enthusiastically. 'Once I came outside, I just had to see your horses.'

'They're only hacks,' he said dismissively.

'They're very sound . . . and in top condition,' came her slightly reproachful response. 'It's nice to find someone who really looks after his animals. Some of the dray-horses in London break my heart with pity for them. At home, our lives depend on our horses, you know, and they get better treatment than the men.'

'How many do you have?' he asked politely.

'About thirty or forty.'

He stared at her. *Thirty or forty?*

It was plain she was amused at his astonishment. 'With two hundred and fifty thousand head of sheep to control we need quite a few stockmen, and each man needs a spare horse. They are mostly whalers—good sturdy beasts who can stand long hours in the sun. We use them ourselves, for working. But we have some thoroughbreds, as well. Daddy races them.'

He walked to her fascinated by what she was saying. It sounded quite incongruous coming from a tiny-waisted brunette with laughing silvery-green eyes, who was dressed in a modest skirt and blouse in burnt-orange with cream trimming. Yet she had the golden bloom of health on her skin, and the honest steadfast gaze of a girl from the country, he realised with sudden pleasure.

'You must forgive me, Tessa,' he said with a smile, finding no awkwardness now in using her first name. 'Last night was a little confusing, and I didn't really absorb all that was said. Rex simply mentioned that your father had a farm.'

She laughed up at him. 'And you thought it was similar to this? My word, no. We call them stations in Australia, you know, and some of the really big ones cover an area as large as Scotland or Wales. The cattle stations in the north are so immense it can take a man a month or more to ride right round them. It's real wild country up there. But Woollumgeela is beautiful—green rolling land with the tributaries of the river cutting through it like diamond ribbons.'

Fascinated further, he said, 'Woollum-geela?'

'That's the name of Daddy's station.' Her teeth were very white as her smile widened. 'It sounds really weird after the dignity of Tarrant Royal, Tarrant Maundle, and Greater Tarrant, doesn't it?'

'It docs, rather.'

'But you should see it!' She reached up absently to stroke the nose of the horse nuzzling her for attention. 'A man of your type would lose his heart in Australia. On a station there are only sheep or cattle, stockmen born to the land, dogs and horses. There are few—if any—women, and they know their place.'

A pin-prick of awareness stabbed him. 'What makes you think I'm that type of man?'

His question was ignored. 'Of course, it's nothing like the picturesque beauty of English country villages, and patchwork fields lying on the slopes of gentle hills. But you'd be captivated by the peace and grandeur of such land. The only method of getting from place to place is to ride. You've no idea of the exhilaration of a dawn gallop after sleeping under the stars, and then to eat breakfast cooked in a billy over an open fire,' she told him with bubbling enthusiasm in her voice. 'Now I must "come clean" as the stockmen say, and confess that I would give anything to be allowed to ride one of your horses.'

'Anything?' he repeated, what she had said about sheep-stations and sleeping under the stars beginning to add up to something stimulating in his mind.

She grinned. 'How about going down on one knee and pulling my forelock?'

The use of Laura Pagett's words put him on his guard slightly. 'There's no need to go that far,' he heard himself say. 'You only have to ask politely.'

Her laugh was a delightful sound in the early morning quiet. 'You have the most perfect manners of anyone I have come across. Do you ever do anything that isn't perfectly *polite?*'

It almost brought a smile from him. 'Quite frequently. If you had ever hunted in my company, you would be shocked!' His glance went to the saddles on the wall. 'There are several there for ladies.'

She came up to him. 'I ride astride. It's more comfortable when in the saddle all day.'

'You're a good rider?'

'Of course. Do you doubt my ability?'

Another pin-prick stabbed him at her frank challenge. 'I'm far too polite for that,' he countered. 'I'll give you ten minutes in which to change.'

'No need.' She laughed, and stood astride to reveal that her skirt was a culotte.

'So you came to the stables this morning determined on this,' he accused, still a little out of his depth.

'I confess it. Oh, Roland, after all those weeks on the ship coming over, and six months in that awful factory, you must see that my first encounter with horses would be irresistible. May I ride one without delay, sir? There, is that polite enough?'

The pin-pricks of awareness were coming so fast now he found himself laughing lightly as he gazed down into her eager face.

'Absolutely,' he told her, unbolting the door of one of the stables. 'So polite I'm letting you choose your mount.'

They rode gently up to Longbarrow Hill until they reached the barn where Rex had kept 'Princess'. Roland felt memories of the past take hold of him as he thought of his brother returning after selling his precious machine, and his own last gallop up here on the horse that had been the perfect partner in triumph and success. On his own, he might have turned back, but Tessa was urgently eager beside him, and her words were still in his ears against his will.

But all regret and reluctance fled when they began to canter across the sweet green hilltop with the sound of thundering hooves filling his ears, and the sight of her slender graceful figure delighting his senses. She was a natural rider, not a trained one: her body moved with the horse in one wonderful flow of partnership. The canter turned into a gallop and he knew then that he had beside him a girl who could be his match if she ever hunted. But Tessa Manning would not be happy with the restrictions of that type of horsemanship. She was free, uninhibited, and joyful on the back of a horse, and asked no more than the blessing of open space and a wide sky above her.

They raced side-by-side along Longbarrow Hill, and he had no hesitation in taking her down through Windyleaf Copse, across Middle Meadow slashed by the river, up along Hawthorn Slopes, past the old saw-mill, and back through the long avenue of beeches that led to the West Wing of Tarrant Hall. It was a gruelling route, but she took it with perfect ease, bending low over the saddle and handling the strange gelding with the confidence of an old friend. She took the gates with inches to spare, jumped the river with perfect judgment of distance, and never flagged once during the entire distance.

A mile from the house he reined-in and turned to congratulate her. But she was looking at him, her unusual silvery eyes full of elation, and spoke before he could.

'I knew it would be wonderful, but didn't guess just *how* wonderful,' she told him breathlessly. 'Our stockmen ride more easily than they walk, but you make a horse *fly*, Roland. With you in the saddle even a hack turns into a thoroughbred.' Coming alongside, she added, 'I teased you earlier. Will you please forgive me?'

'I . . . of course,' he stammered, struck by the lovely picture she made against the background of his distant home. It occurred to him how right she looked in this country setting, and a quick flicker of regret that she must work in a London factory touched him unexpectedly. How could she bear to do it?

Unwilling to return to the house yet, he explained about checking his fencing and asked if she would like to accompany him. They rode slowly, cooling their mounts off, and discussing sheep. It appeared she was an expert on the subject. When they inspected the Sheridan flock she was slightly critical over the state of some of the lambs, suggesting implements to the ewes' feed during the winter months that would improve their milk. Roland excused himself on the grounds of insufficient farm labour, but left the subject quickly since he did not want to admit the reason why he could not get people to work on the estate. Instead, he issued her a challenge.

'I thought you said earlier that the few women on Australian stations knew their place. You appear to have done much as you liked out there.'

She gave him a sideways glance. 'I said they *knew* their place. That didn't necessarily mean they kept to it.'

He smiled. 'I see.'

'No, perhaps you don't . . . at least, not all of it,' she said frankly. 'As things were going it seemed fairly certain that I would become the wife of another sheep-farmer, and a woman has to be knowledgeable and capable out there. If her husband falls ill, has an accident, or gets bitten by a snake, she has to be able to take over and run the place alone.' She shrugged and looked over the rolling hills of Dorset. 'I suppose it's different now.'

'Everything is different now,' he said heavily, thinking again of how he must leave all this at the end of the month.

The idea came to him like a bolt from the blue, and he studied the girl covertly as they took their horses slowly uphill back to the stables. She knew more about sheep than he did, she rode like a man, she understood the paperwork of running a farm, she was a woman who could also tackle household affairs, and she was unhappy in a factory. Tessa Manning had trained all her life for this, and would be the ideal bailiff for Tarrant Hall and the estate. She was young and imaginative, she would not be fired with patriotism and go to war, she did not come from the village and, therefore, did not share their antagonism of him.

Sighing deeply she said suddenly, 'This is all so beautiful after London.'

'Why don't you stay for a while—you and your brother,' he said with careful persuasion. 'Just because Rex is hell-bent on going back this afternoon, you two don't have to go, surely?'

She turned to him with a disturbingly intent glance. 'There's my job at the factory.'

He made a dismissive gesture. 'I'm sure they'll understand if you take the rest of the week off. After all, your brother is here only a short while, and who knows when he'll get leave again?'

The intensity of her gaze increased. 'You really want me to stay?'

'Yes . . . very much.'

'I . . . oh yes, of course I would! There's nothing I'd like more.'

'That's settled then,' he declared, well-satisfied. 'Come on, let's have a final canter back to the house.'

Having overcome one obstacle—that of coaxing Laura from her bed by mid-morning—Rex was faced with another. She stood beside him on the sun-washed gravel of the forecourt, looking totally stunning in a cream fine-wool dress trimmed with black velvet and jet beading, and regarded him with horror.

'Walk down to the village! You must be mad! I never walk further than the nearest tram-stop. I'm a city girl, not one of your country wenches.'

He gazed at her in fascination, still unable to believe she was real and he had found her. 'You told me you had been brought up in a country vicarage.'

'The *civilised* country. Trains ran directly to our village, and there was even a tram from the city that came as far as the outskirts. It used to be a great treat for the children to be taken to see the trams being pulled around on the turn-table. This place isn't anything like it, or I'd have left long before I did.' She smiled up at him. 'It's very pretty, but it's the back of beyond. No wonder you took to the air when you lived here.'

He grinned. 'Do you ride?'

'Not if I can help it. Horses and I made a pact to keep out of each other's way some years ago. I mean to stick to my side of the bargain.'

Thinking quickly he said, 'Wait here a moment. What's the use of being a hero if one doesn't take advantage of the reputation once in a while?'

It took very little time, a bit of outrageous play on the doomed flier trying to make his last days happy, and slight blackmail as the second son of the house they had been loaned to persuade the military to close their eyes while he 'borrowed' one of their motor-cycle combinations for an hour or two.

It was worth the effort, if only for the pleasure of lifting Laura into it and making her comfortable with cushions. They set off down the drive with a roar, and Rex tried not to think of the old days when he had raced uphill to his home with no more on his mind than getting out to 'Princess'. It seemed too many years ago to dwell on, so he concentrated on scaring the wits out of his passenger with his daredevil brand of driving, and enjoying every minute of her nearness.

They were catching the afternoon train to London so that she could be at the theatre in time. Roland was very disappointed, Rex knew, and had been reproachful toward Laura a short while ago, when she had come downstairs. But it made no difference to his plans. These four weeks were his alone, and he intended to spend them with this girl who made the world seem sane in the midst of madness. Having Laura beside him as he rattled through the familiar lanes eased the regret of noticing faces that had gone; the beloved features that were there no longer. The heartbeat of Tarrant Royal seemed to have slowed to the point where it was in danger of stopping. There was a new careless face to the village. Fences had been clumsily repaired with odd planks that had not been painted, thatch was growing untidy and wispy, gardens that had been a riot of colour looked uncompromising with their stark regimental rows of vegetables, and the old rustic seat around the base of the huge oak outside the George and Dragon was covered in bird-droppings that had always been scrupulously scrubbed away each morning, in the past.

But warmth of feeling for him was unchanged, he discovered. His progress was soon halted as the old stalwarts of the village spotted him, and clustered around the popping machine to clap him on the shoulder or pump his hand up and down. Such lavish acclaim on his exploits and personal courage were unwelcome in the face of their treatment of Roland, but he responded with his usual good nature, sensing that he represented, to them, some sunshine in the gloom of lost village youth.

Laura was welcomed just as warmly (although the male impersonator Laurie Pagett was completely unknown to them) and she was regaled with stories of his cricketing success, harebrained exploits in 'Princess', and even some of his childhood scrapes. She laughed and delighted them all with her beauty and breezy personality. City girl though she claimed to be, she knew how to win the hearts of people whose entire world lay within village boundaries. With her winks, knowing nudges, and disconcertingly free way of speaking, she soon had old gaffers chuckling and the rosy-faced women holding their ample bosoms to ease their shaking laughter. As for the youngsters of the village, it was almost too much for them to behold, in person, the red-haired heroic aviator they regarded as second only to God, and the equally red-haired creature with him, the like of whom they had never seen.

The laughter slowly died away when Rex explained that he had very little time and must move on if he wished to see his little nephew for the first time. Some of the group moved away then, but those who stayed asked sympathetically after Chris. A little of the sunshine Rex and Laura had brought faded as reality stepped in again with a heavy tread, and farewells were tinged with sadness as they wished Rex Godspeed, and begged him to take care of himself.

But he was not prepared to let reality and sadness touch him yet, and grinned down at the lovely girl in the sidecar as he headed off toward the doctor's house.

'You knocked them for six . . . and I know just what that's like,' he told her.

Her hand waved nonchalantly in the air. 'It was an audience and I responded. I can't resist playing to a crowd.'

'You mean, it was all an act?'

'Of course.' Her eyes narrowed wickedly. 'There were some marvellous old characters there that I can work into my routine. I studied their words and mannerisms the whole time. What do you think of this?'

In an instant, she had whipped off his cap and placed it tilting forward over her face, which she screwed up into a fair imitation of an elderly wizened expression, with her eyes half-closed.

'Oh ar,' she quoted in her low husky voice that had caught the Dorset inflection perfectly, 'you'm got a roight young lady there, Mister Rex, an' no mistake!'

It was clever, it was funny, and it was devastating to the way he felt about her. Gazing down into that vivid upturned face he found himself longing for something that had never bothered him before—to keep this girl for himself alone.

'I don't know what that would do to an audience,' he said, taking in every detail of her with eyes that seemed dazzled, 'but it makes me crazy to kiss you. If I were not on this . . .'

'Rex,' she cried swiftly. *'Look out!'*

Too late he turned to discover he had forgotten the bend in the lane just before Dr Deacon's house. The motor cycle had gone straight through the open gate into Ben Browning's field, and was just about to hit the soft remains of a haystack.

'Oh no!' he groaned, squeezing the brake hard.

They came to a halt surrounded by loose flying hay, and Laura dissolved into helpless laughter, as she brushed wisps from her bright hair and the neck of her dress. But the smell of the warm hay surrounding them, which brought disturbing recollections of his present profession, and the reminiscent mood brought on by meeting old friends, all combined with the seduction of warm springtime England to fill Rex with the urgency to live as fully as possible. Climbing from the saddle he strode round to lift her from the sidecar, but the kiss she accepted in laughing understanding turned into something far more physical than a teasing salute as he surrendered the whole of his heart to a woman for the first time.

She struggled free and gazed up at him, her eyes dilated with some kind of shock. 'That was a little more than I'm prepared to take from you,' she said breathlessly.

He swallowed, fighting the desire to do it again. 'I've hardly begun.'

'Then I suggest you stop right there.' She turned away from him and looked out across the field, her body trembling with reaction. 'I should have listened to the voice of reason and stayed in London. It was madness to allow you to persuade me to come away with you like this.'

He moved up behind her, his hands cupping her upper arms to draw her back against his chest as he said against her springing curls, 'Half my first week has already gone. I have to go back at the end of the month.'

'Which is why this is so ridiculous,' she told him in an unsteady voice. 'Four weeks is nothing. When you get back there all this will seem unreal.'

He lowered his head until his mouth rested against the warm curve of her neck. 'Don't treat me like an adolescent boy,' he murmured.

She turned quickly in his arms, and it was plain she was under stress. 'An adolescent boy would be easy to handle in this situation. I could make him forget war for four weeks, then send him back with a scented handkerchief to dream over until they killed him.' She took a quick trembling breath. 'But a man of your calibre is vastly different. I don't know where it would lead, where it would end. Yes, I do,' she contradicted quickly and passionately. 'It would be easy to send a boy back, with no regrets. But *you* . . . I don't want your kind of four weeks! I have a career to build. I love my work: I love the theatre and the excitement it creates. I love the thrills and disappointments, the lights and the crowds. I love holding a theatreful of people enthralled, making them sing along with me, *wielding* them. I love applause and admiration. I want to top the bill, become a household name, get myself announced in lights. I don't want your kind of four weeks,' she repeated emotionally. 'Put me on that train this afternoon, then go home, Rex.'

'I can't,' he confessed quietly. 'I love you, Laura.'

'Oh no . . . *no,*' she told him vehemently. 'You mustn't.'

'It's too late. I already do.'

Pulling free she walked to the far side of the haystack and leant against it, head averted from him to gaze in the direction of Ben

Browning's duck-pond, where snowy ducks were noisily waddling back and forth, or plucking loose pieces of down from their plumage with their flat yellow bills, in a frenzy of springtime preening.

The small country scene beneath skies free of gunsmoke and battling, spiralling aircraft broke away the protective layers of pretence Rex had built up, to expose the fear, desperation and horror of what he had left behind in France knowing he had to return. In that moment, courage disintegrated, fortitude fled. He was afraid of dying, burning like a living torch as he plunged to the ground. He dreaded ever climbing into a cockpit again and taking off wondering if he would return this time. His stomach turned as he thought of the odour of petrol, the stench of heated gun-grease, the strong smell of his own fear-sweat as he flew back to the airfield. How would he bring himself to go back to all that and leave all this when the end of the month came? How would he get through the coming days without being haunted by the thought of it?

Go home, she had told him. But his home was now full of broken men to remind him that the odds against his becoming one of them were growing dangerously short. In the few rooms that were left, Roland was obsessedly arranging to leave and offer himself on the same altar of slaughter, and in Somerset his other brother had already sacrificed his mind to the senseless cause. Sick and suddenly swept by a feeling of doom, he realised he had reached a point where, if he did not hold on to something, he could go under. 'Sherry' was no hero now.

Laura turned at his clumsy approach, and her cheeks paled further as she saw what must be written on his face.

'How do you know you don't want my kind of four weeks?' he challenged gruffly.

'Please, Rex,' she whispered. 'You are only making things worse.'

'You can't say you don't want something until you know what it is,' he persisted with desperation. 'And I haven't told you yet.'

'You'll end up being hurt!'

'That's my affair.'

'It's mine too. I'll be doing the hurting.'

'That's easily solved. Be nice to me instead.'

As she began to turn away again he seized her shoulders to prevent her. 'I won't ask much of you, I swear,' he promised, making his last bid. 'I know you have to be at the theatre every evening. I just want you to spend the days with me.'

'*Every* day . . . for four weeks?' she challenged uncertainly. 'That sounds like a hell of a lot to ask.'

'Compared with what I usually expect from a girl, it isn't,' he retaliated, realising she might respond more favourably to a light-hearted approach. 'And think how much good it would do your career to be seen around with "Sherry" Sheridan.'

Surrender was already more than a possibility when she asked, 'How did you come by that name? Everyone here calls you Rex.'

'The "Sherry" bit is the invention of hero-worshipping young-sters. Government propaganda encourages that. But anyone who really matters calls me by my name.'

'How do you know I'm not a hero-worshipping youngster?' she said softly.

'Are you?' he managed through a constriction of his throat.

'Why do you think I sing a song about you every night?'

The green glow in her eyes made a mockery of all she had said a moment ago, and he pulled her gently against him, the world now blessedly containing only a peaceful village, quacking ducks, and a girl he would never forget.

'Does that mean you will accept my kind of four weeks?'

'I suppose so,' she conceded with a soft sigh against his tunic. 'But I still worry over what they'll contain.'

'Don't,' he advised. 'You'll love every minute. We start off like this.' The kiss was comprehensive, but containable. 'Then, because half the first week has already gone by, we make up for lost time,' he told her, kissing her again several times.

'That's quite enough lost time,' she protested eventually, push-ing him firmly back against the hay. 'If this is the start, I dread to think how the four weeks will end.'

'How you do worry,' he chided with a touch of his old self. 'There are twenty-four days to go yet, and you'll be far too busy to think.'

But he dreaded to think how the four weeks would end.

The first week passed too quickly for him, and was a mixture of delight and impatience. Laura was a dedicated and true profes-sional who would let nothing hamper her performance. This meant that she insisted on arriving at the theatre each evening an hour before the time her act was due to go on. Since there were two houses, this made afternoons very short and restrictive. Rex was hard put to devise things to do that would please and entertain her, besides giving them the chance to be comparatively alone.

He spent his evenings at the theatre in the box set aside for any of her friends but, although he watched her and marvelled that he had been so dismissive of her that first time, he soon found the rest of the programme repetitively boring. He had tried sitting in her dressing-room before she went on, but it was clear to him that he was in the way and distracted her. Between houses they slipped around to a little restaurant for some supper together, although she was always nervy and keyed up for the second house. Rex understood, to a certain degree, because he was the same before each patrol. But it did not help his growing desperation at time passing.

Away from the theatre Laura appeared to have forgotten her fears over their relationship. He found her a very passionate girl who allowed him more leeway than he had expected. But they were playing a dangerous game which grew more and more inflammable as the days went by. Yet she had enough caution to refuse to go to his hotel room after the performance, and it was the cause of some trouble between them. At the witching-hour he naturally wanted to take her somewhere where he could do more than hold her hand and kiss her restrainedly. But it was still too cold to head for a park or the embankment, and the back seat of a taxi had its limitations with the driver sitting a few feet away. Despite all his pleas and promises of good behaviour she stubbornly refused to go back to his hotel. Mike and Tessa were still at Tarrant Hall, or he might have persuaded her she would be perfectly safe with his friend in the adjoining room. As it was, he fell more and more helplessly in love with her, and watched the figures on the calendar change with growing urgency.

Twice he forced himself to journey down to visit Chris, and returned dispirited and upset because the boy had again ignored him, appearing to be still hanging on the cliff-edge of total insanity. His admiration for Marion grew each time, all the more so since he had seen the child sired so disastrously by his young brother. David Sheridan was a beautiful boy so like his father it was almost heartbreaking. Rex knew it must cost Marion dear to leave her baby for others to bring up, and also face the fact that his father might never know or see him.

Rex had been apprehensive about his meeting with Dr Deacon that day, since the elderly man was so full of enmity against both his brothers. But, while Laura had played with the toddler, the men had talked and Rex discovered the medic was sad rather than angry concerning Roland.

'I understand why he is staying up at the Hall,' he had said. 'We are very much alike, your brother and I—stubborn and proud, with a determination to do what we think is right, come what may. He would have made a good doctor . . . but, there, Fate decided otherwise.' He had frowned. 'Ironic, isn't it? I'm probably the only man in this village who would speak to him, but he won't speak to me. In one respect we differ. He's young and hasn't yet learned to forget things said in anger. I know that life is too short, sometimes, and pride can lead to regret when it is too late.'

But on the subject of Chris, his attitude had been a contradiction of all that. 'It has been a long, sad and sorry affair, and I think young David is the one we should concentrate on now. His mother should be here with him, which is her rightful place. As for the boy's father, I pray the Almighty, in his compassion and wisdom, will end the chapter cleanly and mercifully as soon as possible.'

Picking his words carefully, Rex had replied, 'Perhaps the Almighty senses an opportunity to start a new, more successful, chapter.'

'My girl has been hurt enough,' had been the terse verdict. 'God forbid that she should go through it all again.'

Rex had been surprised to hear that Mike had been across to the hospital on several occasions, and surprise had turned to speculation on hearing from Marion that his friend had also been to see young David on the days that she had been at home in Tarrant Royal. Feeling he should have a word with his friend on the subject of his brother's wife, and guessing Roland was forging ahead with his plan to settle the estate and join the Medical Corps, Rex asked Laura to go home with him for the third weekend of his leave.

'I know you regard it as the back of beyond,' he teased softly, 'but I might get you to myself in a haystack.'

'Your brother doesn't approve of me,' she murmured, as she

leant against his shoulder on the park-bench where they sat feeding the ducks.

'He doesn't know you the way I do.'

The wicked eyes turned up to look at him. 'No one knows me the way you do.'

'That's the way it should be. But I'd like to know you a lot better.'

'Forbidden subject,' she reminded crisply. Then, after a moment or two asked, 'Are you going to call and see Chris on the way?'

He shook his head. 'It doesn't help either of us.' Playing with the fingers of her hand he held, he confessed suddenly, 'When my turn comes, I hope I'm killed outright. It's . . . well, it's degrading for the poor devil to sit there like that day after day, after what he used to be.'

She turned to him, full of surprising distress. 'Rex, don't say things like that. Don't even think them.'

Taken aback at her near-tears, he said quickly, 'I'm sorry, I didn't mean to upset you.'

Taking him further aback, she entwined her fingers with his and looked down at them, saying with emotion, 'I can't get him out of my mind. I even dream about him at night. Yes, I do,' she confirmed, looking up quickly. 'I've never come across . . . well, you know what my life is like. Laugh, Clown, laugh . . . and forget the real world and its sorrows. But, sometimes, even in the middle of my song, I suddenly see that silent mass of bandages that is actually living and breathing and terrified. Then, out there beyond the footlights, there is suddenly a whole audience of silent, white, lost people.' She gripped his fingers even tighter. 'Rex, I don't know what Chris looked like, but those magnificent eyes peering through that mask haunt me.'

Choked himself, he said, 'The rest of him is also magnificent . . . *was* magnificent.'

'Oh God, I can't bear it!'

She got to her feet abruptly and walked away to stand by a tree at the water's edge. He went after her in swift consternation, and found the tears spilling onto her cheeks.

'Laura . . . *darling* . . . what has brought this on?'

She turned to face him, full of wild accusation, and cried, 'See what you've done? I knew what your kind of four weeks would be like, but you talked me into it, didn't you? Now, I love you so much, I'm terrified. If you came back like . . . like *that,* I couldn't face it. I know I couldn't. I don't know how Marion stays there with him day after day. It's brave and very wonderful.' Her tear-bright eyes moved restlessly in their passionate search of his face. 'But I'm not a bit brave. It would break me up, and I'd never recover.'

He held her close in his arms while she cried, both of them oblivious of passers-by, because he was going back to war, and she had just told him she loved him.

They spent the rest of the day until it was time to go to the theatre the way young lovers do, and Rex surrendered her at the stage-door, feeling elated yet even more conscious of the sands of time running out. Throughout the first performance he sat fighting the overwhelming desire to make her totally his before he went back to France and faced what lay awaiting him.

The battle for the air was hotting up; the Allies were losing pilots as soon as they arrived from basic training. Boys like Chris were taking off on their first patrol and vanishing forever. Those who survived were going out three or four times a day, then cracking up under the strain—experienced fliers like himself and Mike. Machines were few, and so were the men to fly them. The stalemate in the trenches continued, and the war looked like being won only when one side ran completely out of men. It could be years before that happened, and Rex knew he would not get leave again for a very long time—if ever. As casualty figures rose, so those who could still fight would be forced to do so. As the well-known acts continued, he reached the conclusion that his whole life consisted of the next two weeks. After that, the count-down would begin.

When the second house began, he went off to a place he had used during his Cambridge days, and reserved a private room with supper and champagne laid on. Returning in time to see Laura do her song about him with even more verve than usual, he felt heady with anticipation. But she seemed perfectly happy with the ar-rangements when he told her, because it was pouring with rain and blowing a gale outside.

When they entered the room he felt uneasy, however. He had not remembered the decor was so garishly, overwhelmingly crude.

189

It was not what he had wanted for her, at all. But the supper was very good, and plenty of champagne helped make the surroundings assume a beauty they did not have.

He tried to be patient, to approach her slowly and in a way she would willingly accept. But she looked so beautiful in a dress of emerald-green shot-silk with a coffee-coloured chiffon fichu at the neck, he lost his head the minute she finished eating and leant back in her corner, smiling invitingly at him across her champagne-glass.

Sliding along the seat to trap her in her corner, he said, 'I thought that damned show would never end tonight.'

'You shouldn't sit there night after night,' she chided. 'You must know all the acts by heart now.'

'Oh yes,' he agreed softly. 'I know them all by heart—including this one.'

Taken completely by surprise, she nevertheless put up no initial resistance as he went into action with the skill and finesse of a practised seducer, easing her gently but firmly down onto the velvet-covered seat as his mouth touched lingeringly on all the locations guaranteed to set a woman trembling with involuntary sighs of pleasure. She responded ecstatically, her fingers moving against his shoulders and in his hair as she tried to contain her need to give him what he wanted.

But his past successes did nothing to help him now. Deep love for this particular woman made him too eager, too passionate to take time to play delightful preliminary games. Desire ruled him completely. His love-words tumbled from him in desperate sentences; his hands moved instinctively with no heed for his lessons in experience. For the first time in his life he failed to charm his partner into submissiveness before attempting to take her, and he paid the penalty.

Struggling desperately from beneath him, Laura stood up, clutching her dress to her breasts with one hand, and smacked him extremely hard across the face with the other.

'I knew bloody well what you wanted when you suggested four weeks with me,' she cried, shaking with anger, 'but I fell for it, hook, line, and sinker, didn't I? Despite what I seem to be, I'm very soft inside. You really got to me with your hero-flier pose. You worked damned hard on me, and nearly succeeded. But I'll tell you what I tell every other bastard who tries it on with me.' She backed into the middle of the room, her face white and shocked. 'Just because I work the halls and live an independent life compared with most females, it doesn't mean I'm fair game for any man with a roving eye. I'm a virgin . . . and that's the way I intend to stay.' As he got to his feet she shouted, 'If you take one step toward me before I get out of the door, I'll kick you where it hurts most. That'll keep some other silly susceptible bitches safe until you go back to France.'

The door closed behind her with a crash that rocked the room, and sent a small crude gilt cherub sliding from the wall to disintegrate on the floor in a tiny pile of cheap plaster.

He walked the streets of London for the rest of the night, and ended up in Covent Garden as the flower-sellers were collecting their fragrant wares. He bought a huge bunch of roses, then took an early taxi to Laura's lodgings. Mrs Beamish answered the door in her dressing-gown and muslin cap only after he had been hammering for a full ten minutes. But, strangely, her waspish words faded away when she saw his face and the great bunch of pink roses still with the dew on them.

Laura came down to the parlour in a Chinese-style wrap, and her arrival was far too quick for her to have been asleep. She looked red-eyed and miserable, as he faced her with eyes that were bleary from lack of sleep.

With Mrs Beamish standing by to see fair play, he asked, 'Will you marry me before I go back to France?'

'Yes,' she said, as if in shock.

'All right. I'll go and see about a licence,' he told her.

Out on the pavement he realised he still had the roses. But it did not matter now.

10

'FOR GOD'S sake, have you taken leave of your senses?' stormed
Roland. 'This is utter madness!'

'We are living in a mad world,' Rex told him quietly, having
expected a reaction something like this from his brother.

'But to *marry* the girl!' Roland's good-looking face expressed
outrage. 'A *Sheridan* marrying a cheap little music-hall per-
former!'

'I trust your adjective refers to the music-hall and not the per-
former. I realise this is something of a shock to you, but restrict
your criticism to me and leave Laura out of it, or we are likely to
come to blows,' he said tersely.

'How can I leave her out of it when she is the cause? You can't
possibly go through with this. The whole thing is out of the
question, you must see that.'

'All I see is a girl I love.'

'Love!' cried Roland contemptuously. '*You*, in love! Almost
since puberty you have been tumbling girls wherever you go or
happen to be sent. It's an enjoyable game, as far as you are concerned, and you know enough never to be caught in the same
trap as Chris. How could you let this one take you for a ride?'
He strode about the hotel-room which Mike had sagely left for
the sanctity of the downstairs lounge, and let his anger run riot.
'I saw through her when you brought her down to Tarrant Hall.
My dear deluded brother, she believes you are a man of wealth
and property—which you should have been if our parent had
not also lost his head over a woman. All she has in mind is
getting her hands on what she falsely believes will come to your
wife, on marriage.'

Rex sighed as he studied his older brother, handsome and impressive in a suit of top-quality tweed that proclaimed him as the
upper-class landowner.

'Roland, I sometimes think you never see beyond the boundaries of that damned estate of yours. Laura hates the country—

thinks Tarrant Royal is the back of beyond—and her sole ambition is to top the bill with her name in lights.'

The statement halted Roland in his tracks, and his anger seemed to increase. 'In your own words, you have just presented my case perfectly. She doesn't give a damn for the family background, and is already married to her career as an actress—no, that's too grand a term for what she does. Cancel this wedding before you sacrifice all you are and could be, and tumble her as you have all the others.'

'She's not that kind of girl.'

'*Ha!*' was his brother's contemptuous expression of disbelief.

Rex was losing patience. He resented the way Roland was treating him. It might have been effective where Chris had been concerned—albeit with disastrous results—but he was a man of almost twenty-two who had lived half a lifetime in the past two years. The 'head of the family' attitude was out of place in this situation.

'I warned you just now to watch what you said about Laura,' he began in firm tones. 'The last thing I want to do is quarrel with you for the first time in our lives. There's too much affection between us to throw it all away on futile words. I'm being generous enough to understand the way you feel: be generous enough to do the same for me. I'm getting married because I love her—very deeply.'

'You discovered it in three weeks?' It was more subdued, but still contemptuous.

'In three minutes.'

'Oh God, you've lost your head like an adolescent boy! Believe me, you'll go back to France and forget all about her with half a dozen others.'

'No, I shall never forget her.'

Roland looked at him closely for a few moments, then asked, 'You really feel that strongly?'

He gave a faint smile. 'Haven't I been trying to impress that on you for the last fifteen minutes?'

'If it's true, I don't know how you can subject her to this. No man has the right to ask a woman to become his wife, when there's every possibility she'll be a widow within the year.'

Rex walked across to him and gripped his arm. 'Now you have just presented my case perfectly, in your own words. I have a strong feeling of time running out. Statistics suggest it, even if you don't believe in presentiment. I desperately want this week with Laura. Without it, I don't know whether I can go back.'

He stared in disbelief. 'You're not suggesting that you . . .'

His hand dropped back to his sides. 'Yes, I am. You have no idea what it is like. Ideals fly on the wind, moral standards take a beating, patriotism and glory are second in line to self-preservation . . . and a man's better nature listens eagerly to Satan. They shoot deserters, you know—in their backs as they run. But every man standing by as a witness knows that there, but for the grace of God . . .' He swallowed. 'You shouldn't believe all that government propaganda in the press about England's young heroes. I need this week with Laura to make dying acceptable.'

Visibly moved Roland said, 'You're cracking-up under the strain, Rex. They'd keep you here on medical grounds, if you explained.'

'Oh, my God,' he cried in exasperation, 'don't you understand *anything?* Every man in uniform could do that. Instead, he finds some other means of carrying on. What you're going to encounter in France is going to break your mind, unless you can make it more flexible. It's *hell* over there, Roland, and I want my week of heaven before returning to it.'

His brother walked away to stand with his back to the room, looking from the window. 'I looked forward to these four weeks so much. With the tragedy of Chris hanging over me, the pleasure of your company seemed even more attractive than usual. But I feel I no longer know you.'

Rex took hold of the back of the chair. 'I'm sorry. It wasn't the way I had planned my leave, you must know that. But Laura walked in through a door, and I knew my love for her mattered more than anything else in the world. War changes us all, makes us selfish, greedy for life. I feel I should have done more for Chris, tried to help him in every way possible. But each day of these four weeks has been like a weight on a pair of scales, tipping inexorably against me. My passion for Laura needed fulfilment, and marriage was the only answer.'

Roland turned to face him slowly. 'What if there's a child from this . . . fulfilment?'

'I'll make certain there isn't.'

'So, for the sake of sexual satisfaction you are going to give this girl who has taken you by storm your name and all you own?'

'Which amounts to nothing,' he reminded coldly.

'Unless I'm killed before you when I get out there. Under the terms of my will, everything goes to you as next in line.'

'Change your damned will,' he suggested savagely. 'I don't want it—any of it.'

'And let Marion get Tarrant Hall in trust for that child? I already told you I was prepared to do anything to prevent that.'

'All right, leave the bloody place and all that goes with it to some charity—and leave me to lead my own life,' he said in a rare burst of deep anger. 'One day soon you'll discover how little any of it matters, and grow more human. Integrity has been your god, but the time has come to put away false gods and acknowledge that you are more than liable to meet the real one sooner than you expected. He might give you a rough time of it if all you can claim to have done is worship a pile of bricks in the middle of some fields.'

Roland's face had grown pale and set. 'You think it's more worthy to marry a girl for the sole purpose of possessing her body for one week?'

Regret for his outburst, and what was happening between them made his voice husky. 'Not more worthy; more typical of human frailty. But I've given you a false impression, apparently. Yes, I'm marrying her at this eleventh hour because I want her and conditions aren't normal. If there was no war, however, I'd still marry her. I shall love her until I die, *whenever* that might be. It's something beyond my control.'

They stood looking at each other for a long while, each in his own way trying to reach out to the brotherhood that had always been there. Finally, Roland said with weariness, 'Where has it all gone, Rex? That summer of 1914 when we all came home for the long holidays, life was rich and good and golden. Now, all our hopes and ambitions have come to nothing. Chris, who had a brilliant mind, has had it broken. You, who had the lightest and gayest of hearts, have lost it forever.' He put out his hands in a gesture of helplessness, then let them drop again. 'You saw what obsessive passion did to Father. Don't let it do the same to you.'

Rex shook his head, saddened by his words. 'It was grief that destroyed Father, not passion, of any kind. And in my case, it is not likely to be me who is left behind alone to mourn . . . and Laura

195

is a born survivor.' He held out his hand. 'Come to my wedding this afternoon and let me pop champagne corks for one week with your blessing.'

After slight hesitation Roland gripped the hand. 'You'll pop them for a lot longer than that, you rascal. You know you have a charmed life.'

Greatly relieved Rex gave him one of his broadest winks. 'Tessa is counting on you being there today. She has really fallen for you.'

'Good lord, whatever makes you say that?' came the startled question.

'I haven't abandoned *all* my wicked ways. I still recognise a willing wench when I see one—even when she is willing for it to be some man other than me. I suggest you pop a few corks yourself before you don uniform. Don't hurt her any more than you have to,' he asked. 'She's a nice girl.'

But his words must have fallen on deaf ears as his brother was apparently lost in thought. There was little time for contemplation, however, because the door opened and Mike walked in holding a newspaper, his expression brimming with amusement. Something had persuaded him to interrupt a meeting that had promised to be slightly stormy, and risk the consequences.

'Wow, are you in for a surprise, old mate,' he greeted Rex with a deliberately broad Australian accent. 'Take a dekko at this!'

Rex took the newspaper in curiosity, having no idea what could be so important. The headlines were an inch high. *FLYING ACE TO WED ACTRESS*. Then, half-inch high words announced *R.F.C. hero 'Sherry' Sheridan today marries girl who sang his praises.*

Completely nonplussed Rex read the column which informed its readers of his meeting with the celebrated Laurie Pagett, after seeing her impersonation of himself on stage during the first night of his leave. This was followed by a highly-coloured account of how he had 'swept her off her feet' and down to the family estate in Dorset to meet his two brothers, one of whom was hanging between life and death after courageously leading an attack in Gallipoli, the other fighting a battle against an entire hostile village over his strong reluctance to emulate the heroic younger Sheridans.

It was love at first sight for the vivacious male-impersonator and the handsome daredevil young aviator, the article claimed, and then gave full details of time and place of the marriage, finishing with the information that Laurie Pagett would be giving her usual performance at the second house that evening then spending a week's honeymoon with her new husband before he returned to keep the skies above France free from German aircraft.

'What is it?' asked Roland, walking across to take the newspaper from his hand.

Rex looked at Mike, filled with a mixture of disappointment and confusion. 'She couldn't have done this, surely?'

'Oh yes, she could,' his friend said vigorously. 'It's the best publicity she could ever hope for. She's made no secret of her wish to be billed in lights, and this is just as good.'

'Christ Almighty!' swore Roland with vehemence. 'This won't be a wedding, it'll be a theatrical performance.'

The taxi taking Rex, Roland, and Mike to the venue was halted a quarter of a mile from its destination by the throng of people and traffic. It inched its way along until rounding the final corner, when all three occupants stared in disbelief. A crowd of some thousands surrounded the building they were heading for, blocking the road completely as people shifted and swayed, waving Union Jacks, strings of bunting, and bunches of flowers above their heads in celebration. Then, on the zephyr that blessed that mild March day, came the faint sound of voices in ragged unison singing Laura's song. *Ché-ri! Ché-ri!*

'Oh no!' groaned Rex as the implication of the scene hit him.

But Mike began laughing loudly, and expressed his enjoyment with a 'Yah-hoo' in roustabout fashion as he leant from the window to shout, 'Stand back! Here comes the bridegroom!'

'I can't get through this mob, guv'nor,' complained the taxi-driver looking round at his passengers.

'I'll get you through,' cried Mike having the time of his life. 'If I can sort out a mob of half a million sheep, I can control this lot.'

Next minute, he was on the running-board and heaving himself onto the roof, where he began to make a series of curious calls and shouts in his throat plainly intended to get animals on the move.

'He'll start a stampede,' groaned Rex again.

'I don't think I can stomach this,' said Roland, from beside him. 'It's making a mockery of the whole thing . . . including *you!*'

'Stand back and let us through,' called Mike's voice from the roof. 'Here he is. The man of the moment, "Sherry" Sheridan.'

Entering into the spirit of fun, the driver began chuckling unrestrainedly as Mike's words got through to the people. Then, as they recognised the uniform of the man on the roof, the cry of 'here he comes!' began to ripple through the pressing throng ahead. Next instant, those nearest to them spotted Rex inside and descended on the taxi, pulling open the doors to drag him out and hoist him up onto the roof beside Mike, before clambering up with them to wave their flags in triumphant frenzy.

In a state of unreality Rex sat on the front of that taxi roof surrounded by total strangers who had been joined by others clinging to the sides, the bonnet and the rear of the vehicle, and witnessed the patriotic hysteria of a British public starved of hope or a victory for too long. It was frightening, it was daunting, but it was irresistible. Cheer upon cheer began to rise for him alone, as he realised that he represented to these strangers what he had also represented to his old friends at Tarrant Royal. At that moment, he was every parent's son, every woman's husband, every child's father or older brother, every patriot's hero, and the responsibility of being so weighed heavily on him.

In something of a daze he began to acknowledge the eager waves of those surrounding him as the car moved slowly forward. Then, he caught himself smiling back at the fervent shining faces upturned to form a sea of admiration and delight for something that had brought a brightness to their lives when everything else looked so black. Suddenly, he remembered Laura saying to him, 'I understand faces. I see hundreds of them in rows in front of me every evening.' His bewildered disappointment in her began to evaporate. Whatever her reasons for sharing their love with the entire country, these people who had gathered here this afternoon were an audience longing to live a pretence for a while, to be young and in love again, to lose themselves in what might have been, to find an embryo which would turn into a memory one could tell future generations when the holocaust was over. He understood her statement that she loved holding people enthralled and making them sing along with her.

A strange sensation of power swept over him as he realised he had only to get to his feet, as Mike still was, and he could mesmerise this crowd into doing almost anything he asked. But power had never been an ambition of his. Instead, he stayed where he was, laughing and waving his understanding of their hero-worship in the same way he had done during the annual cricket-matches against Tarrant Maundle. He bent to shake the hands of elderly or disabled men, gave gay throwaway salutes to war-wounded in their blue hospital suits, and winked saucily at all the females, old or young. For a while, he forgot chattering machine-guns, the sound of a German Fokker diving on him, the smell of overheating engines, the sight of a colleague burning in his cockpit as he plunged to the ground, and was again the carefree young man who had fetched out a whole village in welcome as he had come home on his motor cycle for the long holidays that summer of 1914.

By the time the car was almost at the building, the euphoria had grown to proportions that would no longer allow him to remain out of their reach. The crush increased to halt them, and Rex was pulled unceremoniously from his perch to be immediately surrounded by people whose enthusiasm took small account of the comfort of their hero. With Mike beside him, he had to battle his way into the building through an almost solid wall of men who thumped him heartily on the back, and women determined to kiss him or strip him—sometimes both. Those who failed to do either took Mike as a substitute, and both men lost their caps and most of the buttons from their tunics before they practically fell through the doors shut firmly behind them by two uniformed officials.

Breathless and more than a little daunted, Rex leant against the wall and regarded his friend with concern. 'I hope to God I don't look the way you do.'

'Worse . . . much worse,' proclaimed Mike with a devilish grin. 'She'll turn right round and go home again when she sees what you've been up to, my lad. You look positively indecent,' was his verdict as he flicked at Rex's breeches. 'Which wench pulled *those* buttons off, I wonder?'

'Oh lord!' exclaimed Rex in dismay, looking at the gap left by two missing fly-buttons. 'I can't stand up to be married like this! Have you got a pin?'

'More to the point, have I still got the *ring!*'

Mike hurriedly went through his pockets, while Rex experienced an anti-climax that had him longing for a quiet little ceremony such as he had planned. This was not what he had wanted, at all, and some of his disappointment returned.

The ring was still safely in its box, and Rex was walking across

199

to a large mirror fronted by a massed flower arrangement so that he could comb his dishevelled hair and do what he could to his ravaged uniform, when Roland, whom he had completely forgotten, walked in looking immaculate in his dark-grey suit and bowler hat.

'However did you manage to escape their clutches?' asked Rex in astonishment.

'They have all rushed off to wait for the bride.' His glance flicked over Rex. 'In case you were too busy to notice, there were newspaper cameramen busily taking pictures of that scene just now, and they certainly won't let you leave without posing with your wife on the step outside,' he said calmly. 'It might be a good idea to leave by a back entrance when the time comes . . . and an even better idea to find somewhere in this building where you can wash all that lip-salve from your face and pull your clothing into something approaching decency before the ceremony takes place. You can't possibly get married in your present state.'

Rex then went to the mirror and saw the extent of the public enthusiasm for him. His cheeks were smothered with the pink grease women were more and more using to emphasize their mouths, his hair was completely tumbled over his flushed brow, the top part of his double-breasted tunic was flopping down through lack of buttons, and the wings stitched to the breast of it were hanging by only a thread or two.

'Oh no!' he groaned. Then he turned to accuse Mike. 'This is your doing—you and your damned sheep-station technique!'

'Not guilty,' retaliated Mike, his own disreputable appearance worrying him not a jot. 'The person to blame is your beloved, old mate . . . and here she comes, by the sound of it.'

Judging by the commotion growing outside, he was right, and Rex forgot all else in concern for her treatment by an adoring public. But he had no need to worry. A bride was practically hallowed by onlookers, and Laura walked through the door, followed by Tessa, looking stunning in a blush-cream lace dress, large deep-pink hat with a cream chiffon water-lily on the dipping brim, and carrying a spray of pink roses with cream camellias. Rex gazed at her with the pain of knowing she was about to become his. But emotion was short-lived as she caught sight of him and burst into peals of laughter.

'Oh darling, you didn't hit *another* haystack, surely!' she gurgled in the most un-bridelike fashion.

The actual ceremony took place with the bridegroom and his best friend looking decidedly the worse for wear, and the two witnesses uncomfortably aware of the fact. The party managed to slip away through a side entrance, and the taxis stopped at the hotel to allow the two fliers an opportunity to change into their spare uniforms, before going on to the celebration meal at the Savoy Grill, which Rex had planned. It was in the foyer that they posed for the photographs that should have been taken earlier, before going in to eat.

Rex had sent an invitation to Marion, saying how very much he hoped she would be able to come. But a congratulatory telegram had arrived from her, instead, indicating that a letter followed. Her presence would somehow have represented young Chris, and Rex found time in the midst of his turbulent happiness to recall sadly his young brother's forced wedding eighteen months before. But it was not a day for sadness, and even Roland fell beneath the spell of Laura's gaiety as they sat around the flower-decked table eating the best money could buy, those days, and drinking pink champagne. More vividly beautiful than usual, she set Rex on fire with the promise of the night to come as the minutes ticked past too slowly for him.

But they had first to go to the theatre, where his wife was committed to a Saturday-night performance. Rex had protested strongly when told, but she had explained that her contract could not be broken, and had won him over with kisses and a bargain that, if he waited patiently whilst she did her ten-minute act after the wedding, she would do anything he wanted for the following week.

'Anything?' he had queried ardently. 'That's a dangerous promise, I warn you.'

She had laughed with husky seduction, and kissed him on the tip of his nose. 'I thrive on danger, darling. You'll find out.'

With the other three in a following taxi so that they could watch the show from the usual box, Rex and his new wife set out for the theatre, he kissing her all the way, until she cried for a truce in order to get her breath back.

But it was not her plea that stopped him, it was the sight of the mass of people milling outside the stage-door.

'Oh no, I'm not going through all that again,' he said firmly, leaning forward to tap the driver on the shoulder. 'Keep going, and head for Richmond.'

Laura caught his arm. 'Darling, don't be silly. I *have* to go.'

'I don't,' he retaliated, 'and as you're now my wife, you are obliged to go where I go.'

'No, I'm not!' She leant forward. 'Turn around, driver!'

He took her by the shoulders and turned her to face him, worried by her attitude. 'Laura, this is our wedding-day, and it's being ruined by sharing it with the whole of London. What happened earlier was something I couldn't avoid, because it was on me before I knew. But I have no intention of presenting myself as a plaything to an uncontrollable crowd for a second time. Next Saturday afternoon I shall be saying goodbye to you at Victoria Station, and I want you to myself until I have to let you go. So far, I've taken your unwelcome publicity stunt with good grace. Don't push me too far.'

'It wasn't my idea to give all that information to the Press,' she said indignantly. 'At least . . . not at first. It was while we were discussing the problem of getting next week off and adding it to the end of my run at this particular theatre, that Ben realised what an opportunity there was for a little publicity.'

'A *little!*' he exclaimed, remembering the seething mass of hands reaching for him.

Her face in the pale lamplight from the street outside looked full of concern. 'When I agreed it would be worth doing, I had no idea it would turn out like this.'

'Who is Ben?' he challenged.

'My agent—Ben Schumacher. He's very good.'

'So I discovered to my cost. Well, he'll have one less client after this.'

She kissed him, stroked his cheek, implored him with her eyes, whispered erotic promises in his ears until he agreed to go back to the theatre and sneak in by the loading-doors, so that she could fulfil her agreement and not be sued for breach of contract. But, even as they drove there, he knew Roland had been right. This had not been a marriage, but a theatrical performance. Yet he loved her so much it was difficult to be angry, and he had every minute of every day after this until he had to leave her. All she really asked was his patience for an hour or so longer.

By the time they got back to the theatre by a roundabout route to avoid the waiting crowd, Laura was worrying about the time. But, when they finally entered the backstage area of the theatre that was totally strange to Rex, the stage-manager came swiftly across to tell her, low-voiced, that her act had been rearranged to close the show for that one night. She was still agitated, nervous, and totally oblivious of her new husband beside her as she had a long whispered conversation with the man.

Rex felt awkward and in the way there in the wings, with a juggler standing out in the vivid lights of centre-stage, no more than a few yards from him. The stale heat, the dimness, the smell of greasepaint and sweat, the raucous music from a third-rate orchestra out-front, and Laura in her lace dress, so near yet mentally so far from him, made the moment unreal, and the airfield at Grissons his normal world.

Then, the juggler had finished, and Laura was walking hesitantly into the limelight from the wings, still in the dress and hat she had worn to pledge her life and love to him, and still carrying the flowers that had been a bridal bouquet. Something inside him cried a protest, but such thoughts were swept away as the whole theatre exploded into applause, and cheer upon cheer rang around the auditorium. Laura looked almost dazed, but nowhere near as dazed as Rex felt. It seemed to him that he stood there for an eternity as the whole place went wild, and he watched with pride but a sinking heart as she slowly recovered her composure, began to respond, then took advantage of that very power he had earlier sensed and declined to use.

She became a different person entirely. Gone was Laurie Pagett, the dapper man-about-town in top-hat and tails. Instead, there was a vivid, breathtakingly lovely, voluptuous girl, who glowed with life and vitality as she nodded to the leader of the orchestra and cast her eager, all-embracing glance at those rows of faces she loved so well.

Rex was filled with the hurt of knowing she had not looked at him with such ecstatic happiness, even when vowing to keep herself unto him until death parted them. It was then he realised he would never make her totally his, even with physical possession of her body. The theatre would continue to hold her until she decided to let it go.

She began to sing. It was not her usual programme, but a sentimental song of the war. The low husky voice that had so suited the saucy numbers of the male-impersonator, now became seductive, totally feminine, and full of emotion as she went through *Keep the Home Fires Burning*. Rex found his throat constricting, but it was not the sentiment of the song that caused his reaction. She was superb, she was stunning . . . and she was his wife!

When the song ended there was a moment of total silence before the audience went wild again. All around Rex there was a growing number of artistes crowding into the wings to watch, and applauding with the audience. They all knew something exciting was happening that night. And Laura knew it, too. With the sense of power plainly filling her more every minute, she had a quick word with the ageing maestro, then suddenly threw off the beautiful hat, dropped the bouquet beside it onto the boards, and went into a fast-paced song usually performed by two ancient peroxided sisters well laced into spangled costumes that revealed puffy bosoms and over-plump legs.

But Laura turned that number into a sensation as she strutted back and forth, her gorgeous red curls flaming in the spotlights, winking and using her wicked eyes to emphasize the words to the greatest advantage. But, if she had not already captured every heart in the building by then, a daring high-kick with skirts pulled to the tops of her thighs on the last line, completed the mass capitulation. She knew it, everyone in the wings knew it, and so did Rex as his love for her plunged helplessly even deeper.

As the roar of acclaim slowly subsided, she nodded again at the lead conductor and began the song he would never forget.

> *When he flies oh-so-high*
> *All the mam'selles cry*
> *Chéri! Chéri!*

But the chorus got no further than that. Applause rose to a crescendo again, accompanied this time by shouts and cries that were indistinct in the tumult. Then flowers began showering down onto the stage—everything from single blooms to posies of violets to expensive sheafs of roses tied with bridal ribbons—as the sentimental British public went wild with enthusiasm. Laura had to stop, because she could no longer be heard. Then, as if she had had it all planned, she turned to the wings and began walking toward him, hands outstretched.

'Oh no,' he muttered, backing. 'You won't get me out *there!*'

But she had allies. Those around him practically lifted him off his feet as they 'helped' him to make his stage début. Blinded by the lights, dazed by what was happening that day, and deafened by the noise, Laura had seized his hands before he realised and dragged him to the centre of the narrow space left by a front-cloth. Once there, afire with excitement, she stood on tip-toe and kissed him lightly on the mouth. He was vaguely aware of lights flashing down in the auditorium, but straight thought was impossible with that roar in his ears, that strange darkness hiding row upon row of pale dim faces, flowers raining down all around them, and the girl he desired above all other holding his hand and laughing up into his face with the knowledge of power over him as much as her rapturous audience. He acknowledged it unconditionally as he gazed back at her.

Then, the wild romantic fervour of the watching unseen hundreds took hold of him, too. His old daredevil carelessness returned, and he drew her into his arms for a kiss more lingering and expert than any she could give before saying softly for her ears alone, 'Try anything like this again, and you'll get far more than you bargained for.'

But the hysterical delight of the crowd was now channelled into one desire as the shouts and roars became a concerted chorus of 'Chéri! Chéri!' until it thundered around the walls and bounced off the ceiling.

Laura, seemingly composed now, lifted her right hand to silence them, pulling Rex forward with her as the band struck up her song. But her voice was unsteady as she put over the first verse, and tears glistened on her lashes as a multitude of voices roared out the chorus.

> *When he flies oh-so-high*
> *All the mam'selles cry*
> *Chéri! Chéri!*

He can't love them all
But still they all call
Chéri! Chéri!

Caught up in the emotional unreality of it all himself, Rex was not surprised when her voice broke completely during the second verse, and she was plainly too overcome to go on any longer. Thinking quickly, he bent to pick up her wedding-flowers and took the one step to the footlights before flinging the lucky bouquet out for some eager lovelorn girl to catch. Then, as the chorus was taken up again with gusto, he swept his wife up in his arms in a theatrical romantic gesture he knew she would love, and carried her through the wings and straight out to the street to the taxi he had paid to wait for them.

'*Now* we'll go to Richmond,' he told the driver as he put Laura onto the seat and sank down beside her. 'Make it a quick getaway or we'll have half London after us.'

He pulled the tearful exhausted girl into his arms so that his cheek rested against her bright hair. 'You have more than kept to your agreement, my darling,' he told her softly. 'This is where you start doing anything I want for the next week.'

For two days they remained in their hotel-room, so intense and all-consuming was their passion. They popped champagne-corks literally and metaphorically, unable to believe the incredible delight of finding a sexual partnership where selfishness proved to be generosity. Each could arouse the other within seconds, and neither had restrictive attitudes toward their own or each other's body. The outcome was a passionate, erotic, and possessive relationship that flourished in the atmosphere of time running out.

Rex forgot the world and everyone in it during those first two days. 'Who taught you to do things like that?' he demanded ardently after one mid-morning hour.

'You did—just then,' she responded with dreamy submissiveness as she lay on her stomach. 'You're a randy bastard, darling.'

'And you're a wanton little devil,' he breathed.

She rolled over to give him a wicked smile. 'Always wanton more!'

So he gave her more.

Another time she pranced from the bathroom dressed only in one of his shirts and with her silk nightdress tied around her neck like a scarf, to sing some extremely vulgar words to her song about him. The performance had him delightedly outraged at such sentiments being expressed by a girl. Seizing a hairbrush, he chased her around the suite of rooms, threatening to give her a thrashing for such behaviour. But she was quick and nimble as she leapt over the beds and all around the chairs in the sitting-room, knocking things over as she went to impede his pursuit. The final spanking was enjoyed by them both, and led to a more than usually hectic expression of love as they rolled about the wreck of the room extending the mood for as long as they could.

Afterward, as they both lay exhausted on the floor, entwined in pale-yellow sheets, Rex murmured, 'When did you make up those damned bawdy words?'

'I didn't.' She rolled her head sideways to look at him through half-closed eyes. 'One of the stage-hands sang them to me when we went for pease-pudding and faggots between houses one night.'

'Oh?' He felt violently and inexplicably annoyed. 'He had no right to force you to listen to something that is more suited to a soldiers' barrack-room.'

'He didn't *force* me . . . and I thought it was very funny.'

'Did you?' He tried to sound casual. 'How often did you have supper with him?'

Rolling to lean over him, she teased him with her eyes and fingers. 'Jealous, darling?'

Stilling her fingers with the strong grip of his own, he said, 'Don't ever make me, Laura. That's one thing I won't take.'

Her lightheartedness faded. 'I can't become a nun when you go.'

It was the first mention of their coming parting and what would follow it. It brought the careless idyll to an end immediately. Rex sat up and ran a hand through his hair restlessly as he recognised the broken pieces of the past two days could not be put back together without cracks between them now.

'We'll have to go into the business of getting you an apartment,' he said, leaning on his forearms against his upbent knees. 'There's not much time, but you can't stay with Mrs Beamish.'

'Why ever not?' came her voice from the floor. 'It's cheap, and I get on well with Tessa.'

He turned to look down at her. 'You're my wife now. The situation is different.'

'Once you go back it won't be.'

It touched him on the raw, because he did not want to think of that. 'I don't want my wife living in cheap lodgings,' he said irritably.

'You won't be there to see them.'

'Stop that!' he cried. 'What are you trying to do?'

She sat up beside him. 'I'm trying to be practical. What do I want a grand *apartment* for when I'm quite happy sharing a room with Tessa? Besides, it's very convenient for Ben Schumacher's office. It's useful being close to one's agent because when anything unexpected crops up, he contacts those nearest him first.'

'You won't need Ben once this present engagement ends,' he pointed out.

'Of course I'll need him. How else am I to get work?'

He frowned. 'You won't need to work with a husband to support you.'

'What?' She stared at him in incomprehension. 'You surely don't mean you expect me to give up the theatre.'

'Naturally. You're my wife, now.'

'What difference does that make?'

'A hell of a lot,' he cried. 'I don't want you having faggots with foul-mouthed scene-shifters night after night.'

After a moment or two, she went into peals of laughter. 'You are jealous! Oh, my darling darling, don't look so ridiculously outraged. He only sang some dirty words to me once when he had had one too many. He didn't ravish me over the pease-pudding, *night after night.*'

She tried to push him back onto the floor with provocative playfulness, but he caught her wrists and held them as he said unsteadily, 'I love you, Laura. Don't ever treat my love as a joke.'

'I love you, too, don't forget,' she snapped, scrambling to her feet to look down at him. 'I wish to God I didn't.'

It hit him like a slap across the face, and he got to his feet beside her. 'It's two days too late to make a statement like that,' he said hoarsely. 'I thought you were happy.'

'I am happy . . . and I'm terrified,' she admitted, pleading with her eyes for his understanding. 'Rex, I don't know what I'm doing here with you. I never wanted this. I don't know how it happened.

My career meant everything to me; I had ambitions. The last thing I wanted was to get married.'

To his distress she walked across to gaze from the window in a dramatic change of mood. 'You walked into my life and wrecked all my plans. In five days' time you're going to walk out again, and leave me sitting in the middle of the wreck.'

He went across to her swiftly, pulling her back against him and burying his face in her curls. 'Don't you think the same thing happened to me, my darling? You walked into my life and took it away from me altogether. You *are* my life now, totally and unconditionally. I'm not thinking of what comes later. We have five days yet.'

She turned to reveal tears on her cheeks, and cried wildly, *'Five days!* What arc five days out of a lifetime? This is all your doing. I didn't want to get married like this.'

'Neither did I . . . and it's all *your* doing,' he insisted roughly. 'If you hadn't been so damned virtuous you could have been here with me like this without getting married.'

Collapsing into his arms she poured out all her fears and doubts over the hasty marriage. He tried to soothe her, convince her that the war would be over soon and they would have much more than five days together, then ended up agreeing to her plea that continuing her theatrical work would occupy her days so that she would not worry herself into illness over him.

'I promise to keep away from scene-shifters,' she whispered against his neck as he finally carried her back to the bed. 'And if I have a slack period, I'll get started on organising the concert I promised for the patients in your brother's hospital.'

But the prospect of her having a slack period vanished when they descended to the hotel-lounge for the first time the following midday. The newspapers there were full of pictures of their kiss on stage, and of Laura's high-kick that revealed very shapely legs.

THE NEW DARLING OF LONDON read one headline. FAREWELL TO LAURIE PAGETT AND HALLO MADAME SHERRY, stated another. HERO'S BRIDE TAKES THEATRE-LAND BY STORM, proclaimed a third.

Whichever angle they took, every one of them predicted a glittering future for a male-impersonator who had revealed herself to be the most ravishing, alluring, vivacious red-head ever to grace a stage when she abandoned male garb and stepped from the wings as herself. 'Madame Sherry' was a phrase widely used, and there was no doubt that was how Laura would now be known in theatrical circles.

The next five days were nothing like the first two they had so blissfully spent. Ben Schumacher, who had ill-contained his impatience until Laura emerged from connubial hideaway, pounced on her with details of offers that had poured in from sources that would have been undreamt of before her marriage. Rex dragged her away stating that she would have plenty of time to discuss business the following week. But, wherever they went they were spotted and recognised. Rex popped champagne-corks, true enough, but in company with members of an adoring public. He tried desperately to retain the solitude they had enjoyed earlier, but they were followed whether strolling through Richmond Park, lunching beside the river, boating on it, or dancing in romantic fashion beneath the moon. Perfect strangers found everything they did intensely exciting to watch, and apparently felt the couple owed them the privilege of sharing their honeymoon with them all.

To compensate him, Laura was even more expressive and abandoned in her love-making when they finally went to bed, and he was practically stunned by an eroticism he had never before found in a female partner. She never referred to her fears over their marriage again, but he was forced to admit that it would be asking the impossible to expect her to give up the theatre now. He did insist that she move to a reasonable apartment that he could regard as home, and this time she made no objections. What had suited Laurie Pagett plainly was not right for Madame Sherry.

On the day before his last, he spirited her away down to Somerset and left her in a quiet little hotel while he visited Chris one more time. The outcome was heartbreakingly the same, but he left his brother some fine pencils and a sketch-block in the hope that he might one day recall his artistic skill and use them.

Saying goodbye to Marion was the overture to the terrible inevitability of the following day, and his farewell of Roland who had arranged to visit the hospital at the same time, put the seal on sadness he found impossible to contain, for a while. Before returning to Laura, he walked alone on a dusk-filled hillside until he felt able to face her.

The scent of that early evening in a county of gentle landscapes and rich productive land threatened to increase his unhappiness with its reminiscent qualities, and he wandered in his self-imposed solitude thinking of the unpredictability of life. He thought of Tarrant Hall and three boys who had been very close in brother-hood. An hour ago, grown into manhood, those same boys had tried to reach each other and failed, through no real fault of their own. How had it happened?

He walked on, hands thrust deep into the pockets of his breeches as the occasional twinkle of light began to appear in the haze of near-night, where women who were now alone in their cottages or farms lit the lamps and prepared for another evening of dreams and fears. The thought made him feel guilty. He had not been back to his home since leaving it with Laura. Priddy, who had been almost a mother to them all, would be hurt by his neglect. The things he had planned to do there, the friends he had wanted to visit, the places that had called to him whilst in France, had all been forgotten with the advent of Laura. Time ruled him just when life called out with its most vigorous voice. It rendered him helpless, this love for a girl with hair as red as his own, and wicked eyes that promised and teased at the same time. He had wanted a week; now he craved much much more. Greed for her made him cry 'shame' on something that took mud-splattered millions from their womenfolk.

Swallowing hard he found tears blurring his vision of the dark-ening landscape. This was how helpless she had rendered him! He had feared returning without making her his. Now, he feared it because she was.

Reaching a cluster of trees he leant against one as rabbits scam-pered around his feet, and stared over the dew-damp fields while he came to terms with the past four weeks of his life and what he must do on the following afternoon. Then, he dropped down the hill into the lane, and strode back to the glow of the tiny hotel, glad the death of the day was finally over and night was uncom-promisingly offering solace.

It was a night he could take back to warm the coldness of separation. They loved and languished the hours away until Laura finally fell asleep in his arms. But he lay awake until dawn, just watching her. He might never see her again after that day. But he had loved her, and had lived through a champagne-time that many men found elusive from birth to old age.

211

She roused, and they made love again. But it was desperate, and overshadowed by the thought of a train that was due to leave Victoria Station at 4.15 pm.

Then they were there on the platform on a cold, wet and blustery day, and their bleak expressions told each other that the champagne had run out; the corks had stopped popping. The station was full of men in khaki, and white-faced women. It looked grey and dismal in the gathering dusk, as the smoke from waiting engines darkened the sky.

Mike was facing the need to say farewell to a beloved sister, but Rex was oblivious of anyone but Laura as he held her in his arms and searched for things to say that were of great significance. But, as always on such occasions, the flying minutes were filled with jerky inanities that would have been better left unsaid.

Soon, the guard called for passengers to climb aboard and close the doors ready for departure.

Rex swallowed hard. 'Take care of yourself, darling.'

She clung to his hand, pale and tearful. 'You, too.'

'You will write?'

'Of course.'

'I gave you the address, didn't I?'

'Yes . . . yes.'

There was a blast on a whistle to signify departure.

'Oh God, I can't bear it,' she cried, looking at him like a frightened trapped animal. 'This is why I didn't want your kind of four weeks. Why didn't you put me on a train and go home that very first day?'

Holding her still, although the train was starting to move, he studied her face for one last time. 'I asked for a month, and you gave me the world. Don't have regrets, or you'll snatch it away from me again.'

Kissing her fiercely, he let her go and ran for the door Mike was holding open for him. Behind him he heard running feet, and her husky voice crying, 'I don't regret it. I don't . . . oh, I *don't.*'

But when he looked back through the open window in the door, smoke had swirled beneath the overhead canopy to obscure the platform and all those on it. She seemed to have gone from his life as dramatically as she had entered it.

11

THEY CLIMBED stiffly from the back of a truck around midday. The airfield looked abandoned; the squadron was out on patrol. Despite the pale sunshine, it was depressing, as if they had been cast out by their colleagues and need not have made the tedious, danger-ridden journey back to Grissons. Neither of them said anything as they picked up the bags dumped on the ground beside them by a soldier with a sallow, haunted look, before he climbed back into the passenger-seat and the truck drove off again.

Rex raised his hand in half-hearted salute of thanks as he and Mike began to trudge across to the building they used as quarters. The tents were still there for those who were the newest arrivals, or who preferred a Spartan life. It could be pleasant in the summer, but Rex had experienced a winter in one and had no desire to be Spartan again. The old stone out-house echoed with the sound of their boots, and was ghostly with the voices of those who had passed beyond those four walls but left behind a whisper of laughter and conversation that could be almost heard again when the airfield was quiet and deserted.

Rex threw his bag onto the bed he had occupied before going on leave. 'The blighter can go elsewhere now,' he pronounced, indicating another man's personal belongings on the locker. Then, he sat on the edge of the bed, still wearing his greatcoat, and stared round listlessly. 'This is just like being the first boy back at prep-school after the holidays. You've got to be there, yet there's nothing to do and no one to bloody well talk to.'

Mike kicked moodily at the bed. 'You could talk to me, for a start. You've hardly said a damned word since we left England.'

Deep in depression he could not shake off, Rex took a moment before saying, 'All right, I'll say something to you. What game are you playing with my brother's wife?'

Growing warily alert Mike said slowly, 'Come again, old mate.'

'What are you up to with Marion?'

'Is it another of your quaint Anglo-Saxon customs to defend the family name from all comers?'

'No, that is one of Roland's quaint customs. I'd just like to know how things stand. After all, the poor devil is smothered in bandages and at the worst possible disadvantage to protect the mother of his son. I know you saw her a lot, because she told me so.'

Mike strolled to the open door, which allowed an elongated triangle of sunlight to warm the stone floor and gild the brown army blankets on the nearby bed. He looked out over the airfield that could have been just a springtime meadow with buttercups trembling in the light breeze, quiet and deserted as it now was. With hands in his breeches pockets, he leant against the door jamb and confronted Rex.

'I've fallen for her. I think she's got a hell of a terrible life, at the moment, and I don't think he deserves what she's doing for his sake. I know he's your brother and I do feel bloody sorry for him—for any man in that state—but I just wonder if it wouldn't be better for all concerned if the One Above finished what He began in Gallipoli. If Chris goes over the edge, life will be a living hell for him, and she'll never bring herself to cut free of him. If he recovers, life will be a living hell for them both, because they'll be back where they started and there'll be no escape to the war this time.'

Rex knew all he said was basically true, but he said, 'That's brutally honest, Mike.'

'We're living in a brutally honest age. Tell me, Rex, would you want to submit *your* wife to that?'

'Laura wouldn't do what Marion is doing. She'd throw herself into her career to try to forget, and end up breaking her own mind.'

Mike stared at him. 'I thought you worshipped the ground she walked on.'

'So I do . . . but we agreed to be brutally honest, didn't we?' He looked at his friend penetratingly. 'I either return from this war whole, or I don't return at all, Mike. If I ever crash and get trapped in a burning cockpit, don't rush over and drag me out.'

The dark Australian returned his penetrating glance, then said laconically, 'I preferred it when you weren't speaking to me.' Then he straightened up, cocking his ear to the door. 'Hallo, that sounds like them returning. I wonder how many there are?'

Only two-thirds of the squadron came back, and half the dead were boys the two returning pilots had never had the chance to meet. There were strange faces amongst the survivors, too, young, pale and shocked. Rex felt like an old man against their extreme youth. One turned out to be a boy straight from Charterhouse, who had been a junior during Rex's last year there. He blushed scarlet when the legendary 'Sherry' Sheridan recognised and spoke to him briefly as he walked wearily from his battered B.E. with the others.

There was a new air of desperation amongst those pilots who had been with the squadron for some months and, as they spilled into their sleeping-quarters, they gave their reasons for it to the pair who had been away. The new Fokker was proving deadly against the antiquated machines owned by the Allies, and the Huns were systematically knocking them all from the skies. German morale was high, naturally, with heroes like Max Immelmann, known as The Eagle of Lille, and Oswald Boelke each receiving the 'Blue Max'—most coveted medal for flying 'kills' against their enemies. Correspondingly, the spirits of English and French fliers were low. They needed more pilots and, more importantly, a new aircraft to give them parity with their opponents. They were determined and they had plenty of courage, but it made them helplessly angry to see their colleagues dying needlessly because the odds were so heavily against them in machine-performance.

Of course, they had their own aces, like the one who took pride of place in their own squadron, but even 'Sherry' Sheridan's brilliance must be hampered by out-of-date aircraft. Rumour had it that a big land offensive was planned for mid-summer, yet the R.F.C. and French Air Corps would be unable to give effective air cover with exhausted pilots in slow, cumbersome, patched-up machines.

Listening to all this, Rex found he slipped back into the old routine without really being aware of it, and he discussed the problems lengthily, and with some heat. But, once in the Mess that evening, it was flatteringly obvious that his return was like an injection of hope into a flagging spirit.

Despite the depressing number of empty chairs, the excitement of men returning from leave with news of home, the air of confidence they exuded because they were the mainstay of the squadron and proved it was possible to stay alive in the skies over France, plus the opportunity for celebration and horseplay over the celebrated marriage of their hero, turned the evening into one 2F Squadron would never forget.

Drink flowed freely, and the recent bridegroom was dragged to the piano to start off a sing-song. He began with *They didn't believe me,* which was in praise of the wife he had left behind him, and his colleagues were quick to respond with a roared out version of *Hold your hand out naughty boy.* Wisely changing his tactics, he turned to more bawdy songs of the war, and they were soon all intoxicatingly happy. All except Rex.

The teasing and ribbing over his marriage was inevitable and had to be taken in good part, especially when he was treated to a small charade, which had plainly been rehearsed for the occasion. A youngster wearing a red woolly wig walked up and down singing Laura's song about a lemonade-drinking man-about-town, in a deep baritone voice. Then, he opened his tunic to reveal a pair of female 'breasts' made from the thin rubber appliances issued to soldiers stationed in French villages, which he suddenly inflated with the help of a bulb and rubber tube filched or borrowed from the M.O.'s surgery. With the swelling of his 'breasts' his voice grew higher and higher, and the laughter grew louder and louder. Well away by then, several of the eighteen year olds were then submitted to the indignity of being stripped in case they were really beautiful girls under their masculine clothes. One of these victims was Giles Otterbourne, the boy Rex had recalled being at Charterhouse.

As the lad was dressing himself again, Rex walked across, bringing another scarlet flush to the fair-skinned face.

'Sorry about that,' he said easily, ignoring the other's obvious hero-worship. 'They did things like that to me when I first came. How long have you been with the squadron?'

'A week, sir.'

'Mmm. Haven't had time to settle in yet, then. I suppose they've sent you out all over the place.'

The youngster nodded. 'It's been a bit hectic, yes.' Then he ventured, 'Congratulations on your marriage. I read about it in all the newspapers just before I left England . . . and saw the photographs. Your wife is a pretty stunning girl.'

'Yes, she is.'

'Still, I expect you're glad to get back and have another crack at the Hun,' came the ingenuous comment as the boy buttoned his tunic and pulled it straight. 'You've got thirty-one already, haven't you, sir?'

'Are you counting aircraft, or dead men?' Rex asked with sudden inexplicable venom.

Red flooded his face again. 'I . . . well I heard your score was thirty-one,' stammered the boy. 'No one said . . . I mean . . . I thought . . .'

'You must have known my brother Chris,' he said to put an end to the subject, and soften his own approach to a boy who reminded him too strongly of what his young brother had once been like.

'Oh, yes,' came the response augmented by relief at passing what had plainly been a *faux-pas*. 'He was a couple of years ahead of me, and streets ahead in brains.' He grinned with disarming candour. 'I'm a bit of a duffer, actually.'

'So is anyone compared with Chris,' Rex told him dryly. 'I never understood half he was on about.'

'I heard he's most frightfully wounded after Gallipoli. Before I left Blighty I met some of the chaps from my year who haven't yet been sent to France, and they were all talking about the Old Boys. Gaynor, who was in the year below yours, won a posthumous V.C. only two weeks after he arrived out here. I expect you knew about that.'

'Yes, I did hear the news.'

'And there was another of our chaps at Gallipoli with your brother. One of Gaynor's friends called Rochford-Clarke. We heard he was most awfully knocked about during the initial landing to attempt a link-up with the Anzacs. He actually died in a hospital in Cairo, but none of us can imagine how he survived so long. Someone said he was left with only half a head.'

'Half a head?' repeated Rex slowly, something Marion had told him coming back to him at those words.

'Pretty terrible thought, isn't it? But it won him an M.C.'

'Yet it didn't win him Gallipoli, did it?' murmured Rex, still lost in the significance of coming across what he thought might be the key to one of Chris's problems.

Unaware that Giles Otterbourne was visibly taken aback by his hero's apparent lack of enthusiasm for medals won posthumously, Rex walked away with only one object in view. To write immediately to Marion with the information.

The dawn patrol was always the best of any, for Rex. Sleep had refreshed him, and the losses of the day before had been laid to rest with an evening of rowdy determination not to mourn. But, that first morning back at Grissons, Rex had not recovered from his own personal loss. Nights without Laura were hours of restless longing. A virile man, at the best of times, he now suffered the torment of being deprived of a passion that matched his own. And the teasing of the night before had left its legacy. He was wondering who was kissing her now.

So his heart was like lead as he walked to the waiting aircraft lined up in the chill of early morning. Mike seemed to be in a similar frame of mind as he walked beside him, swinging his flying-helmet from his left hand and gazing round at the clearing cloud that promised a fine day. Foxstead, who had become Rex's unofficial personal mechanic, greeted him with a smile as the pair approached.

'I knew you was back, Mr Sheridan, so I picked out the best one for you.'

'So I should hope,' he responded, summoning up his old cheery manner. 'How are you, Foxstead?'

'Nicely, thanks, sir. Been a bit busy while you been away, but we'll soon have them on the run again now.' His smile broadened to reach the tips of his ears. 'Mr Jordan and Mr Netherfield dropped notes to the Huns yesterday telling them you was back, just to put the wind up their Fokkers, so to speak.'

'The devil, they did!' exclaimed Rex, laughing. 'No one let that secret out last night.'

'We were too busy celebrating, that's why,' put in Mike heavily, not yet able to come to grips with morning frivolity after the night's heavy drinking.

'Oh yes, many congratulations, Mr Sheridan. I suppose you won't be so interested in haystacks now,' gibed Foxstead.

'Only as soft landing-places,' Rex replied with a wink, and subconsciously slipping into the old routine as if he had never left it.

While he was checking the guns he was approached by the

Commanding Officer, who had been dining with a cavalry regiment temporarily bivouacked on the other side of Grissons, and so had missed the return of his two longest-standing squadron members. He greeted them both, and said all the usual things about Rex's marriage.

He smiled and added, 'I heard a rumour that the Berlin newspapers can't agree on the outcome. Some say you'll be far more cautious now you have a wife awaiting your safe return, others that you'll be doing even greater deeds of daring to lay at the feet of your lady. The Teutonic notion of chivalry,' he explained apologetically, the elaborate words sounding wrong on his lips. 'Which will it be, Rex?'

'I shall settle their argument for them, of course.'

The other man gripped his shoulder. 'You two came back just at the right time. We've taken some terrible losses, and they're all dog-tired. You inspire them, because you've been here so long. It proves to them that it is possible to survive and to be the victor, even in these machines.' He nodded at Rex's neck. 'Why aren't you wearing your scarf?'

Feeling foolish, Rex murmured, 'It seemed inappropriate now.'

A slight frown creased the senior officer's brow. 'From what I have heard of "Madame Sherry" she wouldn't object to something that has become your talisman. However, I want you two to take some of the youngsters under your wings, this morning. They're plucky boys, but their confidence has been undermined by some unpleasantly dramatic losses this past week. Take three each, and restore some of their earlier cockiness, will you?'

After a brief discussion with the rest of the squadron, they took off in formations of four, an experienced pilot leading three others, and headed for the front-line, which had not moved its position since Rex had been away. It seemed strange, at first, to be back in the cockpit, checking the guns, watching for landmarks, and signalling to the three in formation with him, one of whom was Giles Otterbourne. In each pilot's pockets were two bombs, with another two tucked into the fronts of their flying-jackets. Their objective was to bomb and machine-gun a moving column reported by balloonists to be coming up as reinforcements just north of the Somme.

Rex was never happy with bombing or strafing. He preferred aerial attacks, where one flier matched his skill against another.

It seemed a different thing altogether to blow men apart as they walked along, unable to get away. Despite all that, he found the old excitement returning as he climbed into the blue dawn and felt the cold air rushing past his face. The weather had improved during the month he had been away, and he saw, with pleasure, that the orchards that had been rows of bare trees had now become a sea of pink and white blossoms. He waved to Mike, some distance away, and pointed them out to him. But his friend seemed unimpressed by the sight.

'I suppose you'd rather see a hundred thousand head of bloody sheep,' he muttered to himself. 'Or the same number of people all determined to strip me naked for my wedding.'

Thoughts of that experience flitted in and out of his mind as he studied the ground below, made signals to his protégés, and kept a look-out for Fokkers. It was as if the marriage and Laura had been part of a dream, so quickly had it passed and been replaced by war again.

The column did not exist or, if it did, was not where reports had indicated. Signalling that they should split up into fours and go in search of it until they reached the limit fuel would allow before they must turn back for Grissons, Rex took his own formation in a tight right-hand turn and began to fly toward the rising sun. As senior pilot he felt obliged to take the most difficult sector, and pushed the goggles up to avoid the dazzle on the lenses. Checking that the others had followed and knew what to do, he flew on searching for movement below and gazing often at the sky for enemy aircraft.

When they came it was out of the sun, as he had feared. Nine Fokkers in immaculate formation, their pilots undoubtedly congratulating themselves on their find. Rex signalled them all to spread out and climb, but a youngster called Phipps had already been singled out and had three enemy aircraft on his tail. Leaving the others to do as he ordered, Rex made a tight turn to come up behind the Germans, firing his guns at the tail of the nearest one. But another dived out of the sun practically on top of him, and he was forced to pull away to avoid the bullets ripping into his own tail. In that moment he saw flames leaping from Phipps' engine as the B.E. went out of control. The boy jumped to his death rather than burn, but his clothes were already on fire and he dropped like a smaller torch beside the spiralling aircraft.

Outmanoeuvring his attackers, Rex climbed up beneath a Fokker that was practically glued to Giles Otterbourne's tail, and kept on climbing, firing his guns until it started to belch smoke and lose altitude. It was a move Rex used a lot, despite the risk of hitting the belly of the other machine head-on, or of the wreckage falling on him.

Pulling out of that climb he turned to see Otterbourne chasing two of the enemy with fearless skill. Rex was impressed. There, if he was not mistaken, was another ace flier in the making. Sure enough, as Rex turned his attention to two others who were coming up after their destruction of Phipps, the boy accounted for both his quarries by killing the pilots. *Are you counting aircraft or dead men?* This boy made no distinction between the two, apparently. Gone were those days of downing a machine and flying over to wave good luck to the enemy pilot clambering from it!

Now the odds were only two to one against them. Rex motioned Giles to circle and come alongside him so that they could make a dual attack on five of the enemy who were pursuing their other pilot, a young lad called Brent. He was all too plainly in a corner with so many after him, and Rex guessed he had 'frozen' from the fact that he was making no evasive tactics. He was an easy target flying in a straight line, unable to let go the control bar to fire his guns.

Indicating to his companion to attack from the rear, Rex made a fast climb, angled his machine in a turn until he was ahead of Brent, then went into a shallow dive that would take him headlong toward the group, using their own tactic of coming out of the sun. With perfect sight of them, he emptied round after round into the enemy machines, forcing them to scatter from the sandwich they found themselves in.

Rex accounted for two that broke apart and fell in flaming pieces. Another, he sent off with smoke pouring from it and plainly crippled. Giles accounted for a fourth, which was extremely creditable with the sun half-blinding him. The fifth decided to cut his losses and was a speck in the distance when Rex remembered the last of them, who had carefully stayed out of the general mêlée.

It was as well he did remember it, for it was coming up behind him fast when he scanned the sky for a sight of it. It was then he recognised the aircraft markings of an old adversary he had tangled with on more than one occasion. Smiling grimly Rex suddenly looped and tricked the Fokker into passing him. Then, he was able to shoot at will into the other machine, whose tail took a great number of the bullets.

It curved into a climb and began to circle. Rex signalled Giles to join young Brent, recovered but badly wounded, and escort his comrade back to Grissons while he settled accounts with the remaining enemy. More confident when he had only himself to worry about, Rex climbed after his adversary, trying to assess the other's next move. But the German seemed content to circle, watching Rex like a hawk and hesitating to make the first move. But Rex was not to be drawn, and circled patiently hoping to break the other man's nerve.

Suddenly, the Fokker climbed into the sun, taking advantage of the blinding light to confuse Rex, then hurtled down guns chattering before he knew it. Bullets ripped into the fabric all around him, then a burning pain in his left temple led to a rush of blood that blinded that eye. Rex put up a gauntlet to wipe it clear and saw the Fokker had dived past him, flattened out, and was about to come up under him for the kill.

Quick as lightning, Rex pushed down the nose of his own machine and challenged his opponent in the manoeuvre for which he was famed. On a collision course, he dived as the other climbed, daring his opponent to keep coming and not veer. Both had guns blazing as they grew nearer and nearer, and Rex's heart was thudding as he raced downward knowing he intended going through with his challenge.

When it was almost too late, the German broke under the strain, and they passed with wing-tips almost touching. It should have been the end of the fight, because Rex was ready for that moment. But, incredibly, his gun jammed leaving him to dive impotently on, knowing he was the one wide open for the kill now.

But the acceptance of certain death lasted no more than a few seconds. As the Fokker turned and screamed down on him, another aircraft came in from the west, guns chattering loudly in deadly aim. It was flown by Giles Otterbourne, who should have been on his way back to Grissons.

It was all over before Rex could really take it in. The German pilot, wily as they come, made a brilliant diving veer to attack the reckless inexperienced boy. The body jerked as it was raked with bullets, then Giles Otterbourne exploded as the bombs he was carrying in his coat were activated. The blast caught the German plane, and it was blown into the path of the severed B.E. The two machines went down together, the enemy aviator falling like a stone toward the earth. Then there was only Rex in his aircraft, and the whole empty sky.

He brought in the wounded Brent, coaxing him every mile of the way and every foot of his descent, until the lad landed, taxied to a standstill, then practically fell from his machine to vomit on the grass beside it. Rex landed a few minutes later, fighting a pull to starboard caused by damage and unable to see through his left eye for blood.

The others were already back, apparently unsuccessful in their mission, and the pilots were keeping vigil for their return.

Mike came up quickly as Rex began to climb from his cockpit.

'You've been hit!'

'Not as badly as the machine. Foxstead, get her patched-up right away,' he told the mechanic sharply. 'Let me know the minute she's ready.'

'You're not going out again!' exclaimed Mike. 'That's a nasty wound on your temple.'

Rex jumped to the ground and began striding toward the shed that housed the Medical Officer. 'I'm going to find that bloody convoy . . . and you're coming with me,' he told Mike, who had fallen in beside him. 'If our balloonists saw it, it's there somewhere. We're going to get it.'

'What happened to Phipps and Otterbourne?'

Rex halted in the doorway of the improvised surgery and leant on an arm outstretched against the wall, realising how dizzy he felt.

'They came out of the sun and got Phipps before we had a chance to do much.'

'And Otterbourne?'

'He disobeyed my order to return. In doing so he saved my life. I expect he'll get a posthumous medal for it to add to all those boys he told me about last night. He admitted he was something of a duffer, but he was really a bloody little fool. He thought medals were all that mattered. But what's the use of them if they don't know which fragment of you to pin them on?'

He walked into the surgery unaware of the strange look Mike was giving him.

It was the start of a new phase in the career of 'Sherry' Sheridan —a phase that was more daring, more spectacular, more ruthless than ever. The British public, the Royal Flying Corps, and 2F Squadron particularly, lionised him. But those who knew him well grew worried.

No matter how many times Roland told himself he was doing it because it was his duty, he knew deep inside that it was a lie. Outwardly, it was easy to feel he had an obligation to see his brother's bride, check that she was all right; that it was the least he could do for Rex, who had had only a brief week of marriage before returning to the war. But he felt a twinge of conscience when he collected Laura from her new apartment, and an uncomfortable stirring of guilt when glances strayed to their table or followed them when they got up to dance at the exclusive night-spot he had chosen for the occasion.

Rather shamefacedly he acknowledged to himself that he had thought to overwhelm the girl from the music-hall with the upper-class sophistication the Sheridan family accepted as normal. But he had forgotten Laura was an actress, and she had checkmated him well and truly. Wearing a chiffon dress in three layers of shaded blues from indigo to hyacinth, with a daringly low back and trimmed with silver bugle-beads, she looked so stunning there was no doubt she stole the evening. Who, amongst the other guests, would imagine he was in company with his sister-in-law? Laura was the epitome of a high-class mistress, not a wife.

He felt that very strongly as they returned to their table after a foxtrot, and she flashed him a smile as he held her chair for her.

'Rex dances the same way he does everything else,' she told him in her low husky voice. 'But a girl feels safe with you.'

For a brief moment he felt ridiculed, then told himself a girl *should* feel safe with her husband's brother.

'I am glad I came, Roland,' she confessed as he sat opposite her. 'I very nearly didn't.'

'Oh . . . why?'

'I thought I might have been in for a wigging.'

'A what?'

'I know you don't approve of me.'

The truth of it threw him. 'That's utter nonsense.'

Her laugh was seductive and fascinating. It suggested an intimacy their short acquaintance did not earn, and she studied his face in disconcerting manner before saying, 'You are the most well-behaved man I have ever come across. It's just too good to be true. What are you hiding?'

He poured more wine into her glass to cover his embarrassment. 'Good manners don't necessarily hide anything.'

'They do when people say what they don't mean.'

'Perhaps the people you normally mix with aren't well-behaved.'

'There . . . you see! I knew you didn't approve of me.'

He countered that with, 'I hardly know you well enough to approve or otherwise.'

'Rex hardly knew me well enough to marry me . . . but he did.'

'That was only two weeks ago,' he mused. 'So much seems to have happened since then.'

Her vivid provocative face shadowed slightly. 'For the first three days I sat in my posh apartment, screwed into a wet weeping ball of misery, missing him like hell, missing Tessa, missing my old digs with the strict motherly landlady, and wondering how I was going to get through each day knowing he could be suffering agony, dying, or already dead. Then I found I couldn't even remember what he looked alike. All I could picture was that poor mummified boy in Somerset.' She looked across at him in disconcerting helplessness. 'Roland, I'm not a bit like Marion, you know. I think I'd *die* if Rex returned to me like that.'

He felt his mouth twist. "Don't compare yourself with Marion. You don't know the facts behind that marriage. Chris wouldn't be there if it weren't for her.'

'I do know the facts,' she said quietly. 'Rex told me everything . . . including your feelings on the subject. I think you are being rather hard on the girl.'

'What you think doesn't really come into it,' he said, resenting the fact that Rex had told a comparative stranger private family business, and also that she should choose to criticise him at a time like this when the other revellers were all so happy.

She switched directions disconcertingly to ask, 'Have you ever been in love, Roland? *Really* in love—madly, irresponsibly, unwisely, yet totally?'

The music had struck up again and her voice rose accordingly. He felt those at neighbouring tables must have heard, and grew angry at her nerve in asking him such personal questions in such a public place. What right had she to question him, anyway?

'Are you trying to tell me that was what was behind Chris's marriage?' he asked coolly, leaning back and sipping his wine. 'He was a mere schoolboy. His head was full of Greek and Latin.'

'But Marion's wasn't,' she pointed out.

'On that point we are in total agreement. Now, do you mind if we leave that subject?'

Her slanted green eyes glowed at him across the table. 'I think you have given me the answer to the question you would not acknowledge just now.'

He remained silent, feeling curiously exposed in that dim sophisticated club with a background of tango music so suited to Laura's startling personality. He now wished he had not arranged the meeting. She was not the brash impressionable flirt he had imagined. She was getting under his skin in the most disturbing way, and taking the evening out of his hands. It was not a situation he had before experienced, and it made him feel vulnerable—as if she were peeling away the protective layers with which he had surrounded his emotions for years.

'I tried very hard not to marry Rex, you know,' she said above the compulsive beat of the tango.

'Then why did you?' he demanded.

'Because he turned up at my digs at six o'clock in the morning with an armful of pink roses and looking as if his whole life was in my hands.'

He frowned. 'Marrying him only made it worse, surely.'

She put her hand out across the table to touch his, and he felt a stirring of excitement at the contact. 'You know him better than I do. Have I made it worse?'

When he did not reply she challenged him. 'You think I should have become his mistress instead, don't you?'

The music had stopped, and the question sounded embarrassingly loud. 'It's not my affair,' he said in a low voice.

'But you are making it so by asking me out in his absence,' she told him with a warm smile. 'I'm very grateful for your kindness. You're a very nice person when you give yourself a chance to be human.' She squeezed his hand. 'You won't guess, but I was

226

growing desperate when your letter arrived. I felt as if I had been cleaved in two and one half taken away when Rex left. It's terrible at that station, seeing all those white-faced women, and the men who already look haunted before the train pulls out. The track looks so desolately empty when there's nothing left but the remnants of smoke hanging in the vacuum. It took Tessa half an hour to persuade me to turn away and go home, wondering if Rex and our happiness had ever been real. The other women looked equally wretched . . . and I realised I was about to join their desperation of looking through the casualty-lists each day. That was when I knew I'd never survive that way. I *have* to throw myself into my career, in case he never comes back. I *have* to pretend he was never here for those four weeks; that I don't love him so much my heart is almost breaking. If I don't . . .' She broke off as the music began again, and said thickly, *'Please,* can we dance? I'm getting far too sentimental.'

'Of course.' He got to his feet, unexpectedly moved by her description of saying goodbye to a troop-train. When he went it would be with no one to wave, or smile through her tears, or wish him Godspeed.

The waltz was dreamy, the lights were low, and she seemed happy to be held close in his arms. Neither of them spoke, just moved together to the music in that curious unreality that pervades a night-club dance floor. It was about halfway through the dance that Roland could no longer hide from himself that he would give anything to be able to ask this girl to see him off when he left. But he knew he could not. It would be opening the cracks in her heart, to go through it all again. With swift clarity he understood then why Rex had done what he had. It had not been merely to possess her lovely young body, but to know she was his alone. That knowledge had been enough to sustain him when he had been forced to leave, perhaps never to see her again. Unconsciously he tightened his hold on her, and rested his cheek against the top of her red curls. It was meant as an apology and, in a small way, compensation for her absence when his own train pulled out on its way to France. It was also because his brother had found her first.

They returned to their table, and Roland was disturbed to find tears on Laura's lashes as she sat down. But after drinking most of the wine in her glass she smiled brightly and said, 'I told you

227

I haven't half the courage Marion has. So, if it wasn't to give me a wigging, why did you ask me out, Roland?'

'To say goodbye. I'm joining the Medical Corps at the end of the week.'

She was visibly upset. 'Oh, no! Roland, *why?* All the other men are sacrificing themselves, and I thought you were so confident and sure in what you were doing. I know what has been happening in the village, but I thought you strong enough to ride them out. Why are you doing this?'

The intimacy of that place, the strange feeling of closeness to this unusual girl, and the thought of that empty track at Victoria Station made him say something he could not have said to anyone else save, perhaps, Rex. He only told her his feelings now because he was about to abandon them.

'Laura, heroism traditionally wears gold epaulettes and brave colours. But, sometimes, quieter men see things the world forgets when flags wave. Here's an example. At school, two small boys fight over ownership of a kite. As their fists start flailing, their friends first cheer them on, then join in, until *ten* small boys are fighting each other. At the end of the scrummage, it is still only one of the original small boys who walks off with the kite. But ten of them have bloody noses and black eyes. That's when they need the one boy who has been standing by with ointment and a damp sponge. If he had joined in, there would have been *eleven* injured small boys—and still only one would have walked off with the kite. A war is exactly the same, except that whole nations lie dead at the end of it. I was just afraid there'd be no one with ointment and a damp sponge left at the end of this one.'

She was quiet for a moment or two, studying his face with eyes grown deep green with feeling. 'You didn't have to explain all that to me. I knew why you were doing it, and admired you for sticking to your convictions, no matter what. I don't understand what has changed, why you are giving in.'

'Because of Chris,' he admitted. 'Seeing him like that made me realise that holding the ointment was no longer enough. I have to start using it.'

She still looked upset. 'What is going to happen to your home, to the estate?'

'I've asked Tessa Manning to be my bailiff and look after the place while I'm away. She's perfectly capable of doing so.'

'My God,' she exclaimed, 'what did she say to that?'

'Agreed with pleasure. That factory didn't suit her at all, and the thought of living at Tarrant Hall for the duration of the war was so attractive she jumped at the chance.'

Laura looked at him consideringly. 'You do realise she'd also jump at the chance of falling in love with you, don't you?'

It shook him. 'Good lord, no. Whatever makes you think that?'

The orchestra striking up the next dance brought an interruption to their conversation. Then, as dancers got to their feet, there was a minor scuffle around a table where a group of young naval officers had been rowdily entertaining two under-dressed and over-painted young women. One of the girls could not decide which of three prospective partners to accept, and was swaying on her feet as she loudly declared she would dance with all three and tried to embrace them with inebriated generosity.

As she half-turned Roland saw, with surprise, that he knew her. Rosalind Tierney was an acquaintance from the county set, who was an avid horsewoman and dedicated racegoer. The daughter of an eminent admiral, she was wealthy, well-bred, and darkly beautiful. But, right now she looked more like a harlot, and was behaving in a way she certainly never had on the few occasions Roland had been one of her escorts.

He turned back to Laura with a frown. 'Would you care to dance?'

'I'd much rather hear about your plans. Does Rex know you intend to volunteer?'

He nodded. 'I told him I would as soon as I found a bailiff. I shall be leaving Tarrant Hall at the end of the week to go to a general training camp. After that I shall be classed as a medical-orderly and sent to France, I suppose.' He sighed slightly. 'Ever since Chris was wounded I've wanted to do this. But finding the right person to take over hasn't been easy. The estate was rather thrust on me at a time I least wanted it, but I've grown proud of what I inherited far earlier than I'd imagined and therefore loath to leave it in any but capable hands. Tessa knows more about sheep than I do, and understands the running of a place fifty times the size. It couldn't have been more fortuitous when Rex brought her down.'

'He also brought me down,' she reminded him softly. 'And I spoiled your plans to spend his leave there together.'

He shrugged. 'I thought it might be some time before we met up again, that's all.'

'No wonder you disapprove of me.'

'No,' he protested. 'I don't. I never did. At least . . .'

Their table was suddenly jerked as passing dancers bumped into it, and he looked up in annoyance at their clumsiness. It was Rosalind Tierney still insisting on trying to dance with three men at once.

'Whoops!' she mumbled drunkenly, peering at them both through her collapsing coiffure. 'Beg pardon, I'm sure.' Then she bent forward to push her face almost against Roland's, and he could see her breasts swinging free of any supporting garment as her daringly-cut dress sagged at the neckline. 'My God, it's Roly Sheridan! You look different without a thoroughbred under you.'

She straightened up and stood swaying dangerously as she studied him through narrowed eyes. 'Oh no,' she corrected herself, 'it isn't the horse that's missing—it's the uniform. I remember now,' she proclaimed, turning to her companions. 'He's a coward! Listen everyone, this man's a cow . . . *coward.* Yes, he is.' Her voice rose higher. 'You've read about him. He'll jump fences bravely enough, but if there's a . . . there's a *Hun* behind them, he hides away at home.'

Swinging round so fast she almost lost her balance, she half-fell across the table, hair tumbling down, mouth scarlet with sticky reddener, and her sagging neckline revealing her naked body beneath right down to her hips.

'You *bastard,*' she swore. 'You lily-white bastard!' Then she began to cry, and the tears put dirty lines down her cheeks as her mascara ran. 'They stuck a bayonet through Reggie. My *darling* Reggie. They ki . . . killed him. He's *gone,*' she whimpered with grief so acute it turned her into a demented creature. 'And my brother went down with the old ship. He's out there somewhere in the ocean flo . . . floating along with all the others, and I'll never find him again.' Her face twisted grotesquely as her companions tried to pull her upright. 'Leave me 'lone! But Daddy'll find him,' she flung at Roland. 'He's out there floating along too. But there's no one . . . no one to find my Reggie,' she ended, on a pathetic wail.

The naval officers succeeded in getting her back on her feet and held her steady as she looked at them, overcome with emotion her drunken state was intended to deaden.

'Throw him out!' she ordered wildly. 'He's sitting there like a smug fat worm. Throw him out of here!'

One of the youngsters tried to persuade her to move away, while another apologised to Roland, saying that she was really not responsible for what she said. But, seeing her orders were not about to be carried out, she turned back to the table, jerked one arm free, and picked up Roland's glass to fling the contents right in his face.

He got to his feet as dark red wine ran down his chin and onto the immaculate starched shirt-front. Not all Marion's white feathers, or the enmity of the villagers had affected him like this did. Marion had done it from spite; the village people from ignorance. But Rosalind Tierney was one of his set, a fleeting girlfriend, someone who should have thought the way he did. She had done it because her menfolk had fought, and she did not have the kite. She vindicated him even as she accused him.

Her companions took her away sobbing and beyond straight thought, but people were looking across with animosity now, particularly the women. Some began to hiss softly. One said, in a voice that carried clearly, 'His two brothers are heroes, so I suppose he thinks that excuses him.'

Holding on to his self-control with difficulty, he looked down to find Laura ashen-faced with anger. 'I'm very sorry about that,' he said through a tight throat. 'I'll see about getting your coat.'

'I've no wish to leave, unless you prefer to,' she said. 'I'm quite happy to remain and continue our conversation.'

He tried to smile. 'Thanks, but I think we might as well go.'

He took her arm as they crossed the floor, and diners began a soft insistent knocking with their cutlery handles against the tables. But Laura walked like an aristocrat going to the tumbrils, and he found her composure helped him to ignore the knife-and-fork suggestion of being drummed out in disgrace.

It was a while before he could get a taxi, and neither of them said a word until they were sitting together in the back seat dimness.

'Don't take it to heart,' Laura said softly. 'Rex wouldn't, but I have a feeling you will.' Her hand took his. 'Listen to the words of an old-stager who has even had a rotten tomato thrown at her as an expression of public disapproval. One day they hate you; the next they love you. They're as fickle as a young flirt, and just as unable to control their feelings. But the important thing is to make them feel *something*. It's when they walk past as if you're not there that you have to worry. No one will ever do that, because you are true to yourself, my dear. And it won't surprise me if your name is up in lights one of these days.'

Because he was going away with no one to wave him goodbye, because he knew he had been wrong about her, and because there would never be another girl like her, he leant forward and kissed her briefly on the lips.

'That was for Rex,' he told her. 'Because he would want to thank you for just being you.'

The primroses were out all along the banks that lined the lanes of Tarrant Royal, and 1916 had produced some outsize flowers as if in defiance of the rows of vegetables that now filled the village gardens. There also seemed to be more lambs than ever before, bucking around the meadows from the sheer joy of being alive, and filling the air with a chorus of baas that echoed around the tiny village.

Up on Longbarrow Hill Roland was saying goodbye. Like a courtesan tempting her lover to stay, Tarrant Royal had produced a soft enticing spring day that gave clear-cut outlines to the washed stone walls of the beautiful thatched cottages in higgledy-piggledy pattern just below him. Even a stranger could have traced where the road through the village twisted and turned between the cottages, but Roland knew every foot of the dusty way, and the shape and size of every home beside it. His heart ached as he thought of old friends within them who now turned their backs as he passed, and others who had died with their friendship still intact.

His gaze rested on the church spire for a moment. Symbol of England's past, and witness to its future. Last week, Janey Banks had married Bill Bishop's young brother before he, too, went off to face death. And yesterday, there had been the christening of Ted Peach's latest offspring. Losing an arm had not impaired the blacksmith's creative prowess, and the whole village had been glad to welcome a little mite into the community to compensate for the numbers being lost. Roland had not been present at either event —the Rector came to Tarrant Hall to hold Sunday service for patients and medical staff, so Roland and his small household also attended—but he had been as pleased by the two happy events in a long series of memorial services as the rest. He hoped, like everyone else, that Jimmy Bishop had done his duty before going to war, and left his bride with a child inside her. Thoughts of that nature led to a fervent hope that Rex had not left his bride in that state, despite his confident assurances. One Sheridan child with an uncertain future was enough.

Roland had thought for a very long time about his young nephew, David, whom he never saw apart from distant views when passing the Deacons' gate, and what might become of the estate in the event of his own death. During his leave Rex had declined the offer to inherit a country gentleman's life, and his marriage to Laura certainly suggested he would never be at Tarrant Hall if he owned it. For a pair such as they, a distant rustic retreat was senseless. So Roland had bypassed his middle brother and left the place to Chris in his new will, with the proviso that he was declared mentally fit to handle his own affairs. If not, or if he died before that time, his son David was to inherit on reaching the age of twenty-one. Until then, the property would continue under the trusteeship of Rex, and Tessa Manning. That clause ensured that Marion would never reign at Tarrant Hall or get a penny of Sheridan money without Chris at her side.

He squared his shoulders as he gazed further afield, and saw the pale green of new crops shading the reddish-brown of ploughed fields. He had grown to love this charge that had been thrust onto his unwilling back, and the wrench of leaving it now was severe. Would his own sons one day share this, or would it lie neglected until a small boy became twenty-one?

He had been to the recruiting-office and signed the necessary papers. The officer who had interviewed him had tried to persuade him to take a commission in the cavalry, saying that officers in the Medical Corps were qualified doctors, so he would not be eligible. But Roland's strength of purpose could not be shaken, and he had enrolled as an orderly. However, the man had suggested the N.C.O. rank would probably come early to someone who had completed all but his final year of medical studies.

He was due to report the following morning for his basic military training and, in his heart, Roland knew he could not have entered the cavalry even had he possessed no other skills. His deep passionate love for horses would not have allowed him to take the creatures into battle, where they would be blown or torn apart, terrified, and betrayed in their trust for man.

Today, he intended to leave for Somerset to pay a last visit to Chris. Then he would stay overnight in the hotel used by Laura and Rex on his brother's last night in England, before going on to the training-camp the following morning. Knowing he was not likely to leave for France for some weeks yet, he nevertheless said his farewells standing there on that mid-morning. If he ever saw it all again, it would be as a free man in a free world. Until then, he would keep away.

His luggage was already in the trap when he returned to the house, to take leave of it and those who had served him well. Poor Priddy found the occasion too much for her, and sobbed as she said goodbye to the third of her 'boys' going to war. Minks was not a lot braver as he shook Roland's hand, and managed to say in his quaking voice, 'Good luck, sir, and come back safely. I'll try to be still here when you do.'

'Of course you will, old fellow,' Roland assured him, fighting emotion himself. 'Look after each other, and Miss Manning. Oh, and don't forget that split panel in the Long Room, will you?'

'As if I would, Mr Sheridan,' came the reproach from an old man with tears in his eyes. 'We'll look after the place while you're away, never fear. Why, we've been here all our lives and love it like you do.'

Tessa walked with him to where Dawkins was sitting in the trap waiting. She seemed wrought up, too. They stopped beside the vehicle, and he held out his hand.

'Goodbye, Tessa. Thank you for being here. We'll keep in touch wherever I am.'

She put her hand in his. 'Goodbye, Roland. God watch over you.' Then she reached up and kissed him on the mouth. 'Courage comes in many forms, my dear,' she whispered, 'and I love you for yours.'

Shaken by her demonstration of something he had not been prepared for yet, he climbed into the trap, and Dawkins told the pony to walk on. But the gentle progression down the hill between the horsechestnut trees seemed as painful as having a limb slowly torn off, and the drive through the village stabbed him with a myriad barbs of memories. In the garden of Dr Deacon's house, young David Sheridan was tottering unsteadily over the grass, full of chuckles over a tiny black kitten playing with a screw of paper tied to a string by the girl who acted as his nanny. The toddler's hair was as fair as his father's in the sunshine, and the child's innocence of shattered minds and broken bodies was more than Roland could take.

'Can't you go any faster?' he rasped.

But Dawkins either could not hear, or could not answer.

So the six miles to Greater Tarrant became an endurance test for man and master, as the ageing pony Dainty trotted the familiar distance, unaware of the significance of this particular journey. When the outskirts of the tiny town were reached, Roland knew that from that day onward, he would be less of a man. Part of him would always remain here, whether he returned, or not.

Old Carter at the station touched his cap and said, 'G'day, sir.' But inborn civility for a landowner he had known all the man's life allowed just that and no more. There was no smile, no long gossipy diatribe, no personal interest on where he was going and for what reason. The general factotum at Greater Tarrant station had no word or recognition for Dawkins at all. The old coachman similarly ignored the other as he carried his master's luggage onto the platform. Roland bought his ticket to Somerset from Carter, now manning the tiny ticket-office, then walked back to his old retainer with hand outstretched.

'Well, goodbye, Dawkins. Look after that cough of yours, and don't forget to ask that pretty nurse for a dose or two of the aniseed syrup if it comes on worse again this winter.'

Unashamedly crying, Dawkins gripped the outstretched hand with both of his own. 'Mr Roland, sir, you don't have to do this terrible thing. We'll all stand by you, no matter what others think.'

'Yes, I know, old friend. But I'm doing it for Mr Christopher. People are giving up what they love in order to help him: I must give this up in order to help some other man's brother.' He put a hand on the old man's shoulder. 'Don't leave Dainty standing too long, there's a good fellow.'

Then Roland was left alone on the small platform overlooking meadows and distant rolling hills, with the sound of carolling skylarks high above. The gentle breeze lifted his hair as it fell across his brow, and fanned his cheeks. And there were tears in his own eyes now.

*   *   *

A few weeks later, the atrocious and appalling losses on the Western Front forced the British government to introduce conscription. Every able-bodied man within the age limits had to don uniform and leave everything to go to war. Ownership of the kite had still not been determined.

12

THE PATIENT in bed nine could not decide whether it was more beautiful with the snow bringing enchanting silence and a wonderful cold cleanness to a vista of white-coated trees and virgin stretches, or with this present pale-green beauty of new life, with fat yellow catkins dangling in a gentle breeze, brown flower-beds overshadowed by proud ranks of rainbow lupins, and the lawns turned into a Piccadilly Circus by industrious nest-building birds.

He knew about Piccadilly Circus; could have described it in detail, had he wanted to. Why he knew about it was part of the continuing nightmare. He had been having strange grotesque dreams lately, dreams that were so disturbing he preferred the problems of being awake. During the days there were long periods of peace—like this present one—and he could, to a certain extent, control what they tried to do to him. When the dreams came, he was at their mercy. And the girl called Marion was never there at night-time.

He lay now against the back-rest and gazed at the gardens through his windows, which they had opened today because it was so warm. He could smell the springtime, feel the gentle air, hear the twittering as birds courted each other. He very much wanted Marion to share those things with him, but she would not be coming until the afternoon. She had told him she was going home for a day's rest and would not be back until two o'clock on Wednesday. The time had gone so very slowly without her. It always did when she went home, and he was always afraid she would not come back.

If she really did go home during those absences, why *did* she return? Did they have so great a hold on her? Perhaps they made her tell him lies, then kept her away just to punish him for not speaking to them. If he ever got the chance to leave, he certainly would not come back. But then, where would he go? Besides, he could not go and leave her here. She would be unhappy without him. Why he was so sure of that he could not fathom. But he *was* sure of it.

Today was Wednesday, and she would be here at two o'clock. Although he never ticked off the days on the calendar hanging on the side of his locker, he knew. There was a great number of things he knew, but some of them puzzled and frightened him. Sometimes, in the middle of a day-dream a mental picture of pages of figures or disconnected words flashed across his mind. They never stayed long enough for him to make any sense of them, but he felt sure that if he wrote them down immediately afterward and studied them, they would tell him something vital. He never did write them down, because they were all part of the things he must not reveal to those around him.

But he pushed aside unpleasant thoughts and lay enjoying the living panorama a few feet away outside the window. They said he was Christopher Wesley Sheridan, who had been born and raised on a Dorset country estate. He felt sure country life was not unknown to him because of the pleasure he derived from the sights and sounds of nature, but that did not mean they spoke the truth. He could be anyone from anywhere.

He trusted them no more now than he had at the beginning. They still delighted in touching his body whenever they could, and still tormented him by trying to take the bandages off his head. They had to put a needle in his arm because he fought them, and the bandages were always back in place when he woke up. Pain was still with him night and day, but it was very gradually diminishing. He was still unable to move of his own accord, but his arms no longer looked like outsize wooden spoons. With the removal of bandages from his hands he had discovered there were only two fingers and a thumb on his left one, and both were very red and painful to bend.

It meant he could now feed himself, although he was so clumsy

237

they put a long rubber bib on him. He had felt so humiliated in front of Marion, he had refused all food for a day and a half. Now, she put the tray across the bed and left him in isolation until his plate was empty. It took him painful ages to accomplish it without leaving a mark on the bib, and the food had turned cold before he was halfway through it. But it was one small triumph against them that somehow kept him going in the midst of terror, despair, and the feeling of crossing an abyss on a tightrope. Without Marion he might have let himself fall. But he had to retain his precarious balance for her sake.

He thought again of her return, and wished it was afternoon now. Out on the oak there was a jay, bright and perky, pleased with his courting plumage which was heightened attractively in the sun, as he posed first this way and that to catch the eye of any female in the grounds. How he would like to point out that bird to Marion, so that she could also enjoy the picture of confidence and well-being it presented.

Once again, his gaze strayed to the sketch-block and pencils on the locker, that the red-haired man called Rex had brought. Feeling that it had all been part of the plot against him, he had resisted the urge to use them for over a month. But, all at once, the desire to capture for Marion something he so much wanted her to see overcame his distrust.

The instinct that had told him many times that he could draw proved to be right. But his fingers were stiff, making it difficult to hold the pencil with the authority needed to make a good reproduction of what lay outside the window. He fretted over his inability to draw as well as he was certain he could, and he forgot all else as he painstakingly concentrated on the bird that he was sure would fly off too soon. He could fill in the background afterward, but it was the symbolic jay he first wanted to capture.

He was not happy with his efforts when it spread its wings and departed, the bright-blue flash vivid against the pinky-grey body. But the clumsy sketches were sufficient to capture the bird's cock-sure posture, and the artist put that page aside so that he could begin the background on another. Since it was impossible to draw detail with fingers as stiff as they were, he decided on a hazy impression of the scene, as if it were early morning with the remnants of mists blurring outlines.

There were other difficulties besides stiff fingers. The holes in the bandages that allowed him to see were more confining than he had previously realised, when he wanted to take in an entire panorama. He was propped up at an angle that was insufficient to make sketching comfortable, and his immobilised leg formed a white plaster barrier between himself and the window. But desire was stronger than opposition, and he slowly and carefully covered the page with something that turned into a totally absorbing task. Finally, unaware that the others in the room had been served with their lunches, emptied their plates, and settled for an afternoon nap, he looked at the finished drawing with a surprising sense of gratification.

It was not what he had set out to do, but the overall indistinct effect was strangely attractive. It was somewhere, yet anywhere. It was there, but only in a dream. It beckoned irresistibly, yet to walk across that lawn and through the trees would make them disappear. It appealed to him very strongly, with its ethereal anonymity.

He realised it was now impossible to add the bird. That jay had been real, full of confidence and strength. The scene was a fantasy. Put one within the other and it would all fall apart. He reached across for the page containing the sketches of the jay, intending to destroy it, but it slipped to the floor as he moved. It lay a few feet from his bed, taunting him with his helplessness to reach it. He felt violently that he wanted no one to see that bird he had drawn just for Marion. What was he to do? Swivelling his eyes to see what was on his locker, he noted a jug of water, a glass, some red flowers in a vase, a bowl of fruit. He decided to use them all. One might not achieve it; all the lot would create such a mess on top of that piece of paper it would be ruined.

Turning his head carefully he saw that the men in the other beds seemed to be asleep, and two women dressed as nurses were talking quietly together at the far end of the room. Despite the pain such movement brought, he slowly reached out and put his right arm along the back of the locker, then swept it forward as fast as he could, sending everything on it to the floor. It made a most tremendous crash in the still atmosphere. Some of the other men sat up in bed and began shouting loudly. The nurses came hurrying down the length of the room with urgency written all over them. But the piece of paper was sopping wet now, and covered with a mixture of broken glass, squashed banana, and red petals that had given the flower-water a red dye.

He found the whole thing intensely amusing. Bound and tied though he was, he had scored one over them. He increased his victory by hiding his picture beneath the sheet under his normal leg, and by taking off the pince-nez to put with it. They knew he could not see them clearly without it, so their angry looks and tight mouths would all be wasted. It was agony to smile, so he had to do it inwardly as he closed his eyes and pretended to be asleep.

Marion was there when he woke up. He knew it was her because she was always a pink blur instead of a blue one. Besides, he knew her outline well by now. Thankfulness welled up in him, and he said the first thing that came into his head.

'I thought they might have locked you up.'

Marion's voice said, 'Why ever should they do that?'

'You weren't here.'

Her hands reached beneath the bedclothes for the pince-nez. She always knew where he put it. 'Why are you hiding?'

'I'm not hiding.'

She placed the lenses on his nose, and her grave face leapt into perspective. 'When you take this off it means you're hiding.'

She looked nice, and he was extremely pleased that she was there, at last. 'You really are very illogical,' he told her. 'I'm the one who can't see without them. They can still see me . . . so how can I be hiding?'

She shook her head in gentle confusion. 'I'm not clever enough to explain it, I only know you are.'

'Why didn't you come at two o'clock?'

She sat beside the bed. 'I did. But I was speaking to the doctor for rather a long time. You were asleep until just now.'

'No, I wasn't. They just thought I was,' he lied, not wanting her to know they had forced him to drink their potion. 'Did you really go to your home?'

'Yes, of course.'

'Why do you always come back?'

'Because I want to.'

His heart sank. What threat did they hold over her to make her say that? 'You can tell the truth to *me*,' he whispered. 'I can be trusted not to say anything to them. I haven't told them about the numbers, have I? That's proof enough.'

240

'What numbers?'

He clamped his lips, knowing he should not have mentioned them even to her.

'What numbers?' she probed quietly.

'I didn't have any lunch,' he said. 'I'm most frightfully hungry.'

Sighing she stood up and began folding back the screens around the bed. 'I've brought your tea.'

'What is it?'

'Bread and butter with syrup, a piece of fruit cake, and strawberry blancmange.'

'How do you know it's strawberry? Have you tasted it?'

'No, but it's pink.'

'What has that got to do with it? Flavour is a taste, not a colour. Why can't strawberry blancmange be yellow?'

She smiled. He always liked it when he made her smile. 'What a funny thing to say.'

'Is it?' He teased her some more. 'You haven't answered.'

'Yellow blancmange would be lemon flavoured. It couldn't be strawberry.'

'Why?'

'Strawberries are *pink*.'

'So is your dress, but I bet it doesn't taste of strawberries.'

The smile developed further into a laugh. 'More like boiled linen and starch, I should think. Trust you to be prosaic, Chris.'

The warmth inside him began to chill. 'I thought you agreed not to call me that.'

She was turning away from him to get his tray, so he did not see her face. 'That's your name.'

'I don't like syrup,' he said harshly.

'I'll get some jam instead,' she offered, putting the tray across the bed.

'No!' He ignored the tray. 'I don't really want any tea, anyway.'

'You said you were hungry just now.'

He looked down at the bedclothes. 'Did I?'

She sat down beside the bed again and looked up at him with a crease on her brow. 'Why did you push everything off your locker this afternoon?'

'Why did they have to tell you about that?' he asked, wishing they had not.

'It upsets them when you suddenly do things like that.'

'Good.'

She put the plate containing the piece of fruit cake down on the coverlet where he could reach it easily. 'Why did you do it?'

'I had a reason—a very good reason,' he said in a voice that was low enough for only her to hear. 'I had done something special just for you, but it dropped onto the floor. I didn't want them to see it. It's not very nice being here like this,' he said awkwardly. 'I feel so helpless, sometimes. I couldn't pick it up, so all I could do was knock everything over onto it and spoil it.'

'What was it?' she asked in a funny voice.

'A bird.'

She looked strangely upset, so he tried to impress upon her how important it had been. 'It was a jay. It had been out there on that oak-tree, so full of life and colour in the sunshine. Then I realised it was too real for the garden. When it fell on the floor, I had to tip things over it, or they would have had it.'

She looked at him in silence for some moments, and he sensed she was distressed by what he had said. It was all turning out wrong. It was always the same. People never understood what he was trying to say.

She suddenly put on the bright smile and hearty tones of those dressed as nurses. 'Why don't you eat some blancmange? Just because it's pink, it doesn't have to be strawberry.'

'Don't change,' he begged, through a tight throat. 'You sound like them now. I didn't mean to upset you.'

Her pose collapsed immediately. 'I'm sorry. I was being silly.'

'Was it the jay?'

'I suppose so.'

He reached beneath his normal leg for his drawing. 'This isn't really very good. That's why I decided to leave the jay out. It seemed much too positive a creature for the mood of this.' He offered her the page. 'It looked so lovely this morning, I wanted you to see it. This was the only way I could think of achieving it.'

She took the piece of paper as if in a trance, and sat looking at it for long anxious moments. He did not know what he would feel if she did not like it.

'It's not one of my best, I'm afraid,' he said, to soften the blow should she reject what he had produced.

But she looked up, eyes shining with rapture. 'It's *marvellous!* Ever since Rex brought the pencils and block I've been hoping against hope it would do the trick. How could I have guessed you were talking about a *drawing* of a jay?'

'You didn't think I threw things onto a real bird!' he exclaimed in indignation, delighted with *her* delight. 'How extremely silly of you!' He reached for the dish of blancmange, realising he was hungry enough to eat it, after all. 'A real bird would have flown away, now wouldn't it?' Putting the first spoonful carefully to his mouth, he noticed with astonishment that there were tears on her cheeks. The spoon went back abruptly to the dish. 'What's the matter?'

'It's coming back! You remembered how to draw.'

'I always knew I could,' he told her slowly, caught up in the significance of her words. 'But with my arms like spoons it was impossible. That one still isn't all that good.'

'But it is!' she cried. 'It's absolutely marvellous, Chris.'

'Stop calling me that,' he said sharply.

'Why? You know it's your name.'

'I don't know who I am.'

'Yes, you do . . . or you wouldn't have put this on your drawing.'

He stared at the paper she held out. There, in the right-hand corner, he had written C. W. Sheridan. A dreadful coldness began to spread right up through his body, setting him shaking. He started to feel extremely ill—sick and giddy, as if he was falling into that abyss. She was on her feet, silently mouthing at him. But he was now running from the one person he had trusted. She had forced him to be Christopher Wesley Sheridan, and he was terrified of that truth. Because of it, he began to retreat further into the comfort of oblivion.

Out on the Western Front, one of the most hideous battles ever known was being waged between the French and Germans for possession of Verdun. Begun toward the end of February as a desperate attempt by the Germans to break the deadlock of trench warfare, and gain the strategic and morale-boosting victory that was so vitally needed, it turned into an extended massacre of proportions too great for the human mind to accept.

The area around Verdun was reduced to a scene of horror as unending hills of crater-scarred mud stretched into the far distance, broken only by charred, spike-tipped stumps that had once been trees. Beneath, above, and scattered across this vista of hell were the bodies of *seven hundred thousand* soldiers. As the year advanced and the weather grew warmer, the decaying corpses spread disease like wildfire. The wounded were dying of gangrene, pollution, and lack of medicines. The survivors, the whole in mind and limb, were going mad from the strain on their minds, or turning into old men with bowed shoulders and the shadow of death in their shocked eyes.

Yet the battle for Verdun could not be ended: no one could win it. The French, drowning in liquid mud and reduced to drinking their own urine, would not loosen their skeletal hold. The Germans, decimated, sick, and demoralised, could not triumph yet dared not lose face by withdrawing. The British were entreated to launch their offensive on the Somme as soon as possible, to end the misery of Verdun and tip the scales. Preparations that had already begun were stepped up and, as details of the grimness of Verdun trickled through to the British lines, the mood of the men grew tenser and hatred of the Germans increased. Official military publications made no mention of bombing attacks on English towns by the successful German bombers and the sinister Zeppelins. But the men heard it all in letters from home, and vowed revenge of a particularly savage kind.

All this while, the men who patrolled the skies over France were also being driven to the edge of endurance. By the start of June, the life expectation for a new pilot was two weeks. They fell from the blue through inexperience, faulty aircraft, overwhelming opposition, or just sheer exhaustion. With battles at critical stages, reinforcement columns on the march, enemy raids on the trenches, observation-balloons spying on troop movements, the waves of Gotha bombers en route to England, the R.F.C. had not the manpower to cope. Since cope it must, the weary men in their patched-up machines had to go out again and again with scarcely any rest in between. The boys straight from school never matured; the wily experienced aces were broken old men at twenty-two and twenty-three.

Rex and Mike were in that last category. By that mid-June of 1916 they were flying three missions a day, often taking the dangerous and unpopular night-patrol, and daily watching their colleagues slowly incinerate in the summer skies over the holocaust below. Their faces had grown thin and taut, their eyes contained a strange wildness that suggested they saw things that were no longer there, they spoke in quiet clipped tones, and their tempers were shorter. Yet they were still a source of inspiration to those around them. Mike now had a score of thirty successes to his credit. Rex had forty-four, with at least another half-dozen brought down over German territory that could not be confirmed. The renowned 'Sherry' Sheridan, with his cerise silk scarf flowing out in the slip-stream, was a figure sought desperately by all the German fliers in the area. To send this daring, apparently nerveless, aviator hurtling from the sky was the aim of novices and experts alike, and his continued presence in the sector around Grissons was a barb in the morale of the German Flying Corps.

But there was a barb in the morale of the celebrated red-haired flier that had nothing to do with war. It was jabbing him painfully as he eased himself from his cockpit after a balloon-bursting trip with a youngster called Robin Caversham. Short, blond, and fresh-faced, the boy looked as if he should still be wearing short trousers and a school cap.

For all his lack of inches, he was bumptious, and fell in beside Rex, saying, 'Well, that's another blimp gone! The Hun in that bally basket went down a lot quicker than he went up.'

'And a lot hotter,' said Rex sharply. 'I doubt if they found much of him left when he had burnt out.'

He handed his spare rounds to the armourer standing by, and veered off towards the Mess, leaving the boy staring. But there was only one thought in Rex's mind, and it had been there on both the flights he had made that day. In consequence, his stomach was tight with tension, and a pulse jerked at the base of his throat as he strode through the open door and over to the rack where any letters that had arrived that day through the Army Field Post Office were pigeon-holed under pilots' names. His heart leapt at the sight of white envelopes in his box, and he snatched the two up with a surge of excitement. They must have been held up all this time!

Then sick disappointment filled him as he studied the handwriting. One was from Roland, the other from Marion. He walked out into the sunshine and along to the corner of the outbuilding. There, he could contain himself no longer. With a burst of savage frustration, he hurled his helmet and goggles as far as he could, then leant back against the wall, hands thrust deep into his breeches pockets, gazing up at the sky in silent protest at his situation. He had been back at Grissons nearly three months, and there had been only two letters from Laura, the last six weeks ago.

He stood there fighting back the disappointment and fears that raged through him. What was wrong? What had happened? He wrote long, long letters to her several times a week. Why were there no replies? London was being bombed. Could she be dead; lying in a hospital maimed? No, surely he would have been informed of anything like that. Her letters must have got tangled up in the labyrinth of the Army Post Office. Yet here were two from other people that had reached him from England within the week. Convoys were being bombed; ships in the Channel were being sunk. Sacks of letters must have been lost in that way. But not *every one* she had posted!

He closed his eyes in a rush of painful jealousy. Was there another man? What about all those others on leave that she had admitted meeting—especially fliers, who had told her the truth about his scarf? What of the stage-hand who took her to supper between houses and sang vulgar songs to her? He saw her again clearly, clad only in his shirt that revealed her marvellous long legs, prancing with devastating provocation from the bathroom, the most outrageous verse coming from a mouth so sweetly sensuous, and challenging him to retaliate. Her silence was breaking him apart. He lived from day to day in the hope that there would be a letter on the morrow. Six weeks! In God's name, what did it mean?

There was little more time to wonder. An orderly found him there and said the Commanding Officer wanted him. Half an hour later, he was airborne again with four of the more experienced members of 2F Squadron, heading toward the front line to intercept a group of Fokkers reportedly harrying a convoy containing vital food supplies. They passed Mike returning from a solo observation flight, and headed for a position far enough away to make a return after dark probable. No one liked night-flying. Navigation was difficult, and landing was hazardous even with guiding lights on the airfield. That was why Rex was being pushed into yet another flight that day. He knew the area so well, even in darkness, he would bring them all back like a homing-pigeon.

They destroyed one and damaged two others before the Germans decided to call it a day. The sight of the cerise scarf was enough to daunt one or two immediately, and an example of

'Sherry' Sheridan's technique of the head-on collision challenge, made the rest soon join their fainter-hearted comrades. The five members of 2F Squadron returned safely, although one overtired pilot made a careless landing in the semi-darkness and broke the wheel-struts of his machine, sending the ancient B.E. onto its nose, and hardly finding the energy to climb out from the wreck.

Dinner had already been served to the rest of the squadron, so the five tramped wearily in to sit at the long table for a meal that had gone dry from being kept hot too long. But it all went down with automatic trenchermanship, and they then joined their companions in a room that was heavy with dispirited gloom.

Rex did no more than nod in response to Mike's languid greeting, and flopped into a well-worn chair to read his letters with lacklustre interest. The pain of Laura's neglect was eating into him more and more, and he read his brother's account of his transfer to a hospital on completion of his basic training, with a feeling amounting to petulance. Roland should have stayed where he was at Tarrant Hall, where he belonged. He had been doing something really worthwhile there. Now, he was just another fool in khaki to be drowned in mud or blown to pieces and scattered over the landscape of France. What had he been so noble for? Being killed with a bandage in his hand would not help Chris. Roland was a high-minded idiot. Chris had volunteered to escape a life he could not face; he, himself, had done it merely to indulge his passion for flying. But Roland had donned khaki for the sake of an ideal—and he was the Sheridan whom everyone had dubbed a coward! None of it made sense, and Rex was sick to his heart of being a hero.

In that same mood he slit open Marion's letter. It began with the heartening news that Chris had been unable to resist the lure of the sketching-block. He had used it voluntarily and with pleasure, despite his hands that had still not completely recovered from the burns. Rex read, with some excitement, how his young brother had signed the sketch, as he always had in the past, without being aware of what he had done. Then came the blow! This involuntary act of self-recognition had brought about a relapse into the silent unreachable man he had been on arrival at the hospital. Marion feared he had remembered everything, and hated her more than ever. But the doctors assured her it was not the case. Their opinion was that he could not face his own unconscious

247

admission of identity, and had retreated from it to anonymity. Whether it would be permanent or not depended on his strength of character, but he would not emerge again until his subconscious mind was ready to accept himself as Christopher Wesley Sheridan.

She went on to write that she had been low-spirited since then, and wondered whether she should stay at home with her child, as her father vowed she should.

If I thought I was really helping, there's nothing I wouldn't do for him, Rex, she wrote. *But I sometimes wonder if I'm somehow destroying his pride even more by being there to witness his helplessness to accuse and banish me.*

Feeling his own depression deepen, Rex was about to put the rest of the letter aside for a while when Laura's name leapt up at him from further down the page. He read eagerly.

The staff at the hospital are delighted, of course, because the boys here have so little to cheer their sterile lives. It's so good of Laura to remember her promise and arrange for the concert in the midst of her frantically busy career. They are coming for the last weekend in June. She's such a wonderful person, Rex. You must be as proud of her as she is of you. She freely admits that wonderful tour of the Midlands' halls, and this new show she is rehearsing would never have come her way if she hadn't married 'Sherry' Sheridan. She has promised free seats for Tessa and me when the show opens next month. I'll write then and tell you all about it—as if you won't have heard it all already from your wife.

Rex read no more of the letter, which then went on about news of Tarrant Royal. It was like sitting in the cockpit during a steep uncontrollable dive—his breath being snatched away, enormous pressure in his temples, and cramp-like pain deep in his stomach.

'What's the matter, old mate?' asked a voice beside him. 'Bad news about one of your brothers?'

He lifted his gaze slowly to meet Mike's, and knew he had to pull out of that dive somehow. 'I'm going to get drunk tonight,' he proclaimed.

And he did—totally and paralytically. In the process he strummed the piano, sang with more than the usual gusto, told jokes of unparalleled vulgarity, organised wild and risky contests of skill and manhood, and spent his entire month's salary buying drinks for everyone in sight. It raised morale and eased tension:

it made him more popular and revered than ever. But, when he came to the next morning, he was still diving.

The challenge was Teutonically theatrical and quite ridiculous in the present savage stage of the war. But it had been issued and could not be ignored.

Since his return from leave, Rex had three times encountered a budding, youthful German ace flier who had reputedly been sent to one of the squadrons in the sector to boost morale and prove that 'Sherry' Sheridan was not invincible by shooting him down. His name was Heinz Von Heldermann, an aristocrat from a proud line of military heroes. He had begun his career as a cavalry officer, then transferred to the German Flying Corps when it became apparent to him that trench warfare gave him no opportunity for dash and glory on his expensive horses. Flying had become his passion, and he had notched up a reputation for daring against all odds in a very short time, distinguishing himself from the rest of his fellows by going into action wearing his gaudy, gold-splashed cavalry jacket beneath his open flying-coat.

The most recent encounter between the two aviators had been in the midst of their own squadrons, and the personal scrap had lasted fifteen minutes before Von Heldermann had made a dash for home, signalling that he was out of ammunition. Then, last night just before dark, a lone Fokker had flown low over Grissons to drop a message weighted by a stone, that was an invitation to Lieutenant Sheridan to meet Count Von Heldermann in single combat to finish what had proved inconclusive the previous day. It was, in effect, an old-fashioned challenge to a duel, a Germanic attempt to defend his honour, an almost Wagnerian insistence on conquest or death.

2F Squadron was roused to the typically British urge to 'teach the arrogant bastard a lesson he would not live long enough to heed', and waited confidently for their champion to do it. But the Commanding Officer made it officially known that he would, under no circumstances, condone such whimsical challenges. The war was at a desperate stage, and the members of his squadron were there to support the army grimly hanging on against terrible depravity, not to indulge in egotistical solo combat that would put a valuable machine at risk.

But the C.O. knew, 2F Squadron knew, and Rex knew the challenge had to be met. In his present mood of madness, it was just what he wanted. Pride was at stake, and Rex had to acknowledge it was more than his own. The colleagues of the man who did not return from the encounter would be demoralised. Rex was determined they would not be his own.

Despite the official ban on accepting such a challenge, every member of 2F Squadron, including Mike Manning, was at a window or open door when Rex walked across, just before dawn, to the aircraft that Foxstead had somehow managed to have ready with its engine running. The C.O.'s door was firmly shut.

Rex took off and circled Grissons before heading for the rendezvous. The prospect of what awaited him left him strangely calm, but he thought of the Berlin newspapers that had argued over whether marriage would make him more cautious, or more anxious for laurels to lay at the feet of his bride. Unashamedly he acknowledged that today was for Laura, first and foremost. It would not be laurels, but Von Heldermann's life he laid at her feet, if he were the victor. The fact that the thought should have appalled him and did not, indicated the state of his mind as he approached the rendezvous in the first light of morning, and scanned the sky for his opponent.

The blond German was there, and they circled each other several times, smiling and nodding their agreement on the rules. Only one of them would return that morning. Then, with a mutual salute that was a symbolic raising of swords, they both acknowledged that the duel had begun.

They started making wider, more watchful circles in the silver sky, like swordsmen walking around each other awaiting the right moment to lunge. Rex sat in the cockpit, content to watch the other aircraft's performance for a while. Like all Fokkers it was superior in nearly all respects to his own B.E., but he was familiar enough with these machines to have devised his own tactics based on their few weaknesses.

In this case, there was another point in his favour. Von Heldermann had issued the challenge, and was fanatically dependent on being the victor. He was unsure of himself beneath that arrogance, and needed recognition as a hero. It meant he would put impetuosity before caution. Daring, skill, and even recklessness were fine in a pilot, but hot-headedness was dangerous. For all the risks

Rex took, he was always cool and calm when making decisions. So, he veered away, unwilling to make the first move, common-sense telling him that the longer he could prolong the affair, the more rattled Von Heldermann would grow. With luck, the man would bring about his own downfall.

At first, they were evenly matched in guile and flying skill, each clever enough to anticipate the other's actions, and getting a lot of shots on target. By unspoken agreement, they aimed for the machines rather than each other in a return to the early days of chivalry between airmen. Rex worried about the number of holes appearing in the fabric all round him, and hoped the old B.E. would not let him down before he stood a chance of victory.

They dived and turned in fierce battle for some minutes, each aircraft sustaining heavy damage. Then Rex saw a chance to make one of his unorthodox climbing attacks, and achieved the first real blow by holing the other's fuel tank. Rolling over in a desperate turn, Von Heldermann wiped the spurting oil from his eyes and climbed before making a shallow dive on Rex, guns blazing as he passed dangerously close. Despite the great jagged tears in the wings caused by this, Rex felt a surge of triumph. His opponent was growing angry, and the chance of his rushing into a thought-less manoeuvre was increased.

However, just as Rex was telling himself he must watch the other man like a hawk so that he was ready for the impetuous move when it came, there was a crack behind him. He glanced swiftly round to see a gaping hole in the fuselage near the tail, where Von Heldermann had put so many bullets the fabric would no longer hold together. Cursing beneath his breath, and knowing he would have to make adjustments to all his manoeuvres to allow for the imbalance of the tail, Rex looked back to find his opponent screaming up at him, using his own daring nose-to-nose challenge.

Instinct told him Von Heldermann meant to stay on course, even if it meant he died along with his victim. But Rex had no intention of being caught with his own trick, and veered away well before the German could fill the nose of the B.E. with bullets. As Rex guessed, the other pilot took the veer as a sign of lost nerve, and a smile of contempt appeared on his face as he flashed past in a tight turn from his original course.

Rex's smile was slightly grimmer. Overconfidence added to anger had been the cause of many a man's downfall. So he continued to counter aggression with caution, driving the other man to greater impetuosity in the desire to gain his kill. The sky changed from silver to lemon-yellow as the sun began to come up and, for Rex, it became a matter of judgment more than aerial skill. The waiting was definitely telling on Von Heldermann but, once the sun came high, the Fokker's superior climbing and turning performance would allow its pilot to use the blinding light to put Rex at a disadvantage.

By now, both aircraft were riddled with holes and hard to handle. Von Heldermann was losing fuel fast; Rex feared a violent movement would rip off his own tail altogether. They had both fired a great number of rounds, and the guns were hot. That was when they often jammed. If that happened to either one of them it would presage his death. Chivalry had reached its limits in this contest. It was now 'death at any price'.

With the sun rising higher, Rex abandoned the cautious tactics he had been employing. Von Heldermann's expression showed clearly that he thought 'Sherry' Sheridan's reputation had been grossly exaggerated, and that evidence of the man's condescension fanned the ember of Laura's neglect into a glowing determination to confront her with something she could not ignore.

With a suddenness that took the German by surprise, Rex began to attack in earnest rather than parry, and swooped in a dive to come up under the Fokker with the sun still low enough to blind the other man as he looked down. He put a long accurate burst into the belly of the enemy machine, then found his climb slowing until the B.E. faltered and began to fall away in a spin, unable to take the strain put upon it.

Before he knew it, Von Heldermann came up behind him fast, firing all the time, and showered the cockpit with bullets. There was a burst of sharp agony that burnt into his shoulder, and he gasped, bending forward instinctively with his hand over the wound. Then, as Von Heldermann flashed past recklessly, presenting a perfect target of his port wing, Rex realised why. His own gun was hanging from its mounting, completely useless, and the German knew the game was over. Withdrawal was impossible and death was imminent. It was clear that the Count determined to make victory as slow and humiliating as possible now he had his victim at his mercy.

But this was where an old fox was slyer than a brash cub.

Slumped forward in pain and feeling his aircraft go into a dive Rex still kept his head. He could not go out like this. He *would* not. Then he realised his weakness could be turned into strength in the face of the other's cocksureness and confidence.

Still slumped over the controls, Rex adopted a 'falling leaf' dive, the air rushing past his face to clear the giddiness brought on by his injury. As he guessed, Von Heldermann followed him down, ready to fire a finishing burst at the first sign of recovery. But the avid German was so busy watching his adversary's floating and diving technique, he forgot to watch his own height. When Rex suddenly pulled out of his plunge with very few feet to spare, it was too late for Von Heldermann, who could not pull up over the tops of some trees and went into them, the Fokker exploding in a mushroom of black smoke and flame.

Rex had hardly had time to feel a sense of triumph when he realised his own aircraft had performed its last manoeuvre. Nothing would coax it to climb above the few feet it now maintained, and the tail, after the strain of that deliberate spiralling dive, suddenly snapped and hung by just one tough piece of fabric. Weak from exhaustion and loss of blood, Rex just had time to unclip his restraining belt when the machine somersaulted, throwing him out some yards clear of it.

Fighting unconsciousness, Rex tried to crawl as far as he could. Behind him, the B.E. burst into flames, which fed on the fabric until there was nothing left but a charred mess in the middle of a field.

When Rex came to he was surrounded by men in mud-caked khaki.

'Are you English?' he asked weakly.

'Not 'arf, mate . . . and bloody proud of it with blokes like you on our side,' pronounced one with a grin. 'There's only one flier 'oo wears a silk nightie rahnd 'is neck, and I'm going to write 'ome that I've shaken the 'and of "Sherry" Sheridan.'

He grabbed Rex's hand and pumped it up and down enthusiastically but, as it was the one attached to his wounded shoulder, he passed out again.

His return to Grissons was greeted with lunatic pride and excitement. But his greatest reward for what he had done was to find Mike waving a letter from Laura at him.

Darling, Darling, Darling, it began, *please, please forgive me. Whatever must you think of my dreadful treatment of you? I deserve your most bitter words and a vow to have nothing more to do with me. I returned to the apartment only yesterday to find a huge pile of letters from you on the mat. How you must hate me for not answering them, but my dearest darling, I had no idea they were there, or that you would write so many. I deserve to be thrashed except, my virile stallion, I suspect I should enjoy it so much it would not really be a punishment. So much has happened to me lately. I have been working till I drop into bed with exhaustion. But you have no idea how I long for you, how empty my triumph is without you here to share it. I love you, love you, love you.*

The rest of the letter was as vivid as Laura herself, as she told of her concentrated tour of the Midlands, and the offers received by her agent, Ben Schumacher, since she had appeared on their wedding-night as the girl she really was. It went on to give details of the concert-party she had organised for the patients in Chris's hospital, and of how well she and Marion got on together over the arrangements. The long rambling letter ended with some marvellous intimate passages that made his toes curl, and set him wondering how much of it the censor had passed on to all his pals.

In consequence of that letter, Rex was in a daze of delight and longing for her throughout the party his colleagues held in his honour that night, and he longed to be alone so that he could write to her about Von Heldermann so that she would know he had done it for her.

The following morning he discovered he would not need to write to Laura. The Commanding Officer called him into the office to pass on the contents of a communiqué just received. Rex had been promoted to captain and given command of a new squadron being set up in readiness for the great military offensive the following month. This squadron was to be equipped with the new Nieuport fighter, and consist of experienced men who would fly them to the best advantage.

'While I see the point of not risking our best aircraft on boys who have just arrived out here, it also means, Rex, that 2F Squadron is going to consist of inexperienced fliers in worn-out machines. It will do morale no good whatever . . . and just when you have put such heart into them with that damned quixotic affair with Von Heldermann, that I know nothing whatever about.' He grinned. 'You're a bloody fool, but I've never been so sorry to see a man leave my command. Trouble is, you've become more than just a mere aviator, and this country needs all the skill and flair a man possesses, in the areas where it will do the most harm to the enemy. The aircraft are in England, at the moment. These orders are for you, Mike Manning, Cedric Meader and Gerry Keane to go over there and fly them back, along with some men already in England following injuries. You leave today.' He held out his hand. 'Good luck! I'm afraid there'll be no leave granted any of you. In the five days before you fly back, you have to learn how to handle these new machines, teach the new boys how to survive in battle, and organise your squadron. No second honeymoon, old chap. Sorry!'

But Rex was not listening. In two days he would see Laura, hold her in his arms, make love to her. Five whole days and five whole nights! He would have killed *five* Von Heldermanns for that!

13

THE NEW aircraft were very exciting. The greater manoeuvrability, the more modern design, and the fact that each machine was brand new, filled the pilots with the confidence of meeting the deadly Fokker on equal terms, at last. That, together with the respite and pleasure of being in England where there were no sudden calls to take to the air, no utility farm-buildings for quarters, and no empty chairs round the table each day, was like a tonic to the battle-weary men from Grissons.

They lost no time after arriving on Salisbury Plain at midmorning after a night-crossing in taking the Nieuport up to try it out, and each man enjoyed the luxury of flying for the pleasure of it, knowing he had not to continually scan the distance for enemies, or fly with his head practically back-to-front on constant alert for the Fokker coming up fast behind him. Midsummer in

England had never seemed so wonderful before; the sun had never shone like this, the Wiltshire landscape had never looked so green, the birds had never sung so sweetly. And each one of them had never felt so avid for living life to the full before it ran out.

The introduction to the new aircraft, the lecture on its virtues and peculiarities, the test flight, the get-together of all those who would form the new squadron, took the whole of that first day until late in the evening. Then, despite the fact that no leave had been granted for the five-day period, the men who had come over from France all mysteriously vanished into the lavender haze of the late-June dusk.

Rex had not exactly stolen the motor cycle, because he had ridden off on it under the bemused eyes of the lance-corporal guarding the vehicle compound, using his new rank of captain to assure the youngster breezily that he had to visit his dying grandmother, who would leave her fortune to a cats' home if he did not get there in time. The first thing he had done on arrival at Upavon had been to study a railway timetable, which had soon shown him some other means of getting to London would have to be found.

As soon as he drove out into the country roads his heart almost burst with elation within him, and he pushed the motor cycle to its limits as he raced toward his girl who had no idea he was so close to her at that moment. The machine was intended for dispatch-riders and was the fastest available vehicle with a powerful engine that shattered the peace of the towns and villages settling to sleep as he passed through.

Even with this dream of a motor cycle beneath him, it was a long journey that taxed him mentally and physically far more than his exultant spirits realised. By the time he reached the outskirts of London, it was one a.m. and the streets were deserted save for the occasional policeman patrolling his beat. These men gave him a friendly wave, used to seeing dispatch-riders dashing headlong carrying vital documents, and Rex grinned as he waved back. The only vital thing about his journey was the impatience to take his wife in his arms and satisfy himself of her continuing love.

He swung his leg stiffly over the saddle as he pulled up outside the apartment he had never lived in, and wheeled the machine into a shadowed corner of the building. But weariness fled as he mounted the stairs leading to the door bearing number twenty-three, thinking of the incredulous delight that would appear on

256

Laura's face when she opened it in response to his knock. But he had forgotten her ability to fall into bed after a performance and sleep through anything—even a visit from her husband who should have been in France.

When soft knocking brought no results, he resorted to loud knocking. As his impatience increased, he began thumping with his fists and calling her name. Such extreme measures were successful only in that they aroused every occupant on that floor to come to the rectangle of doors around the landing to complain of the disturbance to their peaceful night.

Rex looked at their angry dressing-gowned figures, and turned on all the charm he could muster as he confessed his identity, explained how he had ridden through the night to see his wife, and how he had no key to get in.

'It takes little short of an earthquake to wake her,' he continued appealingly. 'I'm cold, hungry, and tired, and very likely to have to spend the night outside my own front-door unless I can wake her to let me in.'

It did the trick almost too well. Two or three came to add their fist-power to the door, the neighbouring pair hurried into their own apartments offering to knock on the connecting walls, and one quaking old gentleman, declaring himself to be a former mountaineer, scoffed at feeble raps on walls, and proposed climbing from his outside balcony across two others to Laura's, and waking her from there. Afraid the old boy would never make it, Rex volunteered for the feat himself, convinced it was the only solution.

Fortunately for him, as he was standing on his host's balcony looking down at the sixty-foot drop, two ladies in silk wrappers, with their iron-grey hair in curling-rags, came rushing in to say Mrs Sheridan had answered the door, and would not believe he was there.

They met in the middle of the elderly mountaineer's sitting-room, and he was stunned anew. He had forgotten how breathtakingly sensuous she looked in the middle of the night, when her wicked eyes were luminous with sudden awakening, and her red-gold curls flamed around her head in a tumbled mass. But it was her mouth, full and soft with deceptive innocence, that made restraint impossible.

Surrounded by sympathetic and fascinated strangers, they stood looking at each other as if the past three months had been three years, before Rex pulled her against him in a kiss that rewarded those watching with a delightful romantic reminder of what it was like to be young and desperately in love.

He did not remember walking into their own apartment and kicking the door shut behind him, because his arms were around Laura, and she was gazing up at him in rapturous disbelief. The next kiss, in the darkness of a room he had only seen once before, lengthened into an overture to possession as his hands ran feverishly over the warm lines of her body in the satin nightgown beneath her wrapper.

But she arched away from him, her hands against his chest, to whisper, 'Why didn't you let me know you were here?'

'There wasn't time.' His gaze searched her face hungrily.

Her eyes glowed brightly in the light coming from the adjoining bedroom. 'Is this another of your damned four weeks?'

He shook his head. 'Five days, that's all.'

'Oh my darling, my hopeless impossible darling!' She pulled his head down to hers, tormenting his lips with her own as she alternated her words with swift kisses that were wet with her tears. 'What a hell of a way to arrive! You looked . . . so wonderful standing there . . . surrounded by old ladies with rags in their hair . . . and a dear old windbag talking about . . . climbing over balconies.' Her fingers began unbuttoning his tunic, and her body was trembling in his arms. 'Would you really have climbed out there?'

'Yes. I thought it was the only way to get to you.' He picked her up in his arms and headed for the bedroom, adding thickly, 'All the way from Grissons I've been thinking of the moment I'd do this, and I've waited too long already.'

She matched his heedless impatience as they lay on the sheets warmed by her earlier sleep, and it seemed their love and desire had been heightened even further by separation, as they lost themselves in a passion that could never ignore the running of the sands of time.

But three months had passed since their last union—three exhausting, nerve-wracking, fear-filled months—and Rex lost the battle with virility to fall heavily asleep across Laura's body in the midst of a lull between spasms of desire.

When he roused it was to find the low sun blinding him, and

he lay with his eyes closed in a half-doze, his mind and body reluctant to come out of it. All he wished to acknowledge was the fact that there was a naked female body next to his, and instinct suggested what he should do about it. He rolled over sluggishly and began to fondle the silk-smooth breasts. When he followed that with an attempt to turn the girl to face him, he realised the body was inert and unresponsive. Squinting sleepily through one eye he saw a cloud of red curls on the pillow beside him, and he remembered it was his wife in bed with him. Fighting somnolence he went further in thought to wonder where he was and how he had got there. Then it all rushed back, and he hauled himself upright, to put his head in his hands.

'Oh, *Christ!*' he swore savagely, then looked around for a clock.

When he caught sight of one he swore again, and turned to shake Laura awake. But that was a task to daunt all but the most determined, and he abandoned it for the time it took him to stumble into the bathroom to wash. He had no razor with him, so the rough red stubble had to remain. Then he traced his clothes to the places he had dropped them a few hours before, and began frantically pulling them on while he shook Laura again, and said loudly in her ear, 'For God's sake wake up! I've got to go.'

But it was not until he dragged the bedclothes off her and began slapping her bottom quite briskly that she came out of her deep sleep to protest in very unladylike fashion at the assault on her.

Buttoning his tunic with one hand and stroking the red marks he had raised on her with the other, he said, 'Darling, I should have left an hour ago. Get me a cup of tea, and something quick to eat while I tell you the plan. Laura, *please,*' he groaned, sensing that she was drifting away again. 'I shall be hellish late, as it is, but I must get something inside me before I set off.'

'Go to hell,' came the angry mumble as she groped for the bedclothes.

But he tugged them right off and onto the floor, then grabbed her ankles and pulled her to the edge of the bed. 'I'll have you off there and bouncing on the floor if you don't wake up this minute,' he threatened. '*Now,* Laura.'

The urgency in his voice must have got through to her then, for she opened her eyes and dreamily recognised him. Next minute, she was up on her knees, arms clasped round his neck to pull his head down for a rush of frantic, apologetic and deeply provocative kisses.

'Rex . . . oh *darling,* have I been ages waking up?' Her tongue was busy against his mouth, and her body was moving sinuously as he lost his balance under her onslaught and fell onto the bed, where she immediately climbed on top of him to lie like a warm, sleepy, wriggling puppy, covering his face with wet kisses, nibbling his ears, and nuzzling his neck.

'Don't be cross with me,' she murmured, sinking her teeth gently into his shoulder she had reached by pulling open his tunic again. 'I'll put you off to sleep again like I did last night.'

'I've got to leave,' he said desperately, when his mouth was free of hers and his hands were trying to keep hers still. 'Oh God, you foxy red bitch,' came his gasp of pleasure-pain. *'Stop that!'*

Her low husky laugh was right in his ear, and he had to fight to resist her. But he knew it was then or never, so he rolled over to hold her immobilised while he told her breathlessly that he could be court-martialled for taking a motor cycle without permission, for leaving the airfield without informing anyone of his whereabouts, and for driving to London with petrol reserved for carrying vital dispatches.

'On top of that, I shall be late back. There's a formation-flying exercise at nine. God knows how Mike will explain my absence, but he will. Darling, I'd give half my life to stay with you now.' He kissed her swiftly and fiercely. 'But *I can't.* Do you understand?'

She nodded, fully awake and familiar with the true situation now. Her eyes had lost their playful wickedness as he slowly released her.

'Is that all there is, then?' she asked quietly as she lay looking up at him. 'A few hours in the middle of one night, then goodbye again.'

'No! No, of course not.' He pulled her against him and held her as he explained his plan. 'I'm at the Flying School until Monday. We go back with the aircraft that morning. It means we have four more nights together. There's a nice quiet hotel near the airfield which will be ideal for us. After I've left, pack a small bag and catch the train to Salisbury. I'll book a room for you as I go past.' He put her away from him and gave her another swift kiss. 'Now, please make me a cup of tea, and a sandwich I

260

can eat on the way. I shan't get anything to eat until lunchtime.'

She stayed where she was, the milky whiteness of her body sharply contrasting with the vivid red of her hair. 'I can't.'

On his feet again and re-buttoning his uniform, he said, 'Every woman can make tea and a sandwich, even if she can't cook.'

'I meant, I can't come to Salisbury.'

His fingers stilled as he looked at her over the hands at his high collar. 'What do you mean?'

'I have a performance every evening at seven-thirty.'

He continued hooking the collar. 'Not when I'm in England. You're coming down to Salisbury to be with me for the next four days.'

She waited a while before saying, 'Darling, please try to understand. The show only opened last week. The whole thing has been planned around me. I'm the star . . . at least, I will be by the end of the run. I'm trying to prove myself. People are used to seeing me as Laurie Pagett. It'll take a while to really create Madame Sherry. I'm still experimenting, finding out what goes over well and what doesn't. Besides, two men have risked a lot of money on this show, and they'd never agree to my having a week off at this stage.'

'Then have it without their agreement.'

'They'd kick me out and put an end to my future career.'

'I risked that to come to you.'

'They wouldn't court-martial a popular hero.'

'They wouldn't kick out the star of the show,' he retaliated, angrily. 'Star, be damned! You're my wife, Laura, not a working-girl. I only agreed to your carrying on at the theatre because you pleaded that you'd be bored while I was away. Well, I'm here now, and I want you with me.'

Her cheeks flamed, and her temper took wings. 'And I want *you* with *me* . . , but I can't have you because you have to go to war. I knew and accepted that when I married you . . . and you knew my commitment to the theatre.'

He gripped her shoulders hard. 'I married a little male impersonator, not some star called Madame Sherry. If I hadn't been turned into an impossible hero by the British public would you have married me, I wonder?'

'And would you have married me if I had been the kind of obliging whore you normally escorted around?' she flung at him.

'If I had given you what you wanted in the tawdry surroundings of that club, you would never have made me your wife. I'm a person, not a talking body, Rex. That's what I tried to tell you that night.'

'I know what you tried to tell me that night,' he said heatedly. 'And you might remember that I'm not just a talking body, either, and find time to write me a few letters in the middle of your stardom when I go back to France.' He turned away, sick and disappointed. 'Goodbye, Laura.'

He was almost at the door when she practically leapt onto his back, and clung there with desperate arms around him, her tears soaking into his collar.

'Forgive me! Oh darling, darling, please forgive me. I love you so much I have to hurt you.'

He stopped and turned round wearily, drawing her against his chest with all the helpless love she aroused. 'It's not even four weeks, this time, but four *days,*' he said huskily, stroking the curls beneath his chin. 'I've been almost crazy without you over there. You're my life, my everything.'

She arched back and studied his face with tear-stained unhappiness. 'I wish to God I'd never met you. This terrible separation tears me apart. I want you, sometimes, so much that I feel I'll die of it. I've been almost crazy without you, too, and every time there's a knock on the door I think it's a telegram saying you . . . you . . . The only way I get through the days is by concentrating on this show. *Understand,* oh my darling, please understand.'

Conscious of time flying past, he tried a bewildered compromise. 'You could travel up for the performance each day, then come back afterward.'

'There'd be no train at that hour,' she pointed out. 'And what would be the use of my staying at this quiet hotel all day, when you are at the airfield flying?'

'Four nights, that's all it would be.' He returned to his original theme in desperation. 'Surely there's an understudy.'

'I'm not taking a stage-role, Rex, I'm doing my own act.'

'What happens if you're ill?'

'A substitute act goes on in my place.'

'Then let her go on for the next four nights.'

'And risk letting her take over for good?'

Worn out, hungry, loving her, and feeling betrayed, he found himself saying tautly, 'Perhaps she'd take over for you at the quiet hotel with me.'

Face tightening, Laura said, 'I'll ask her. In the darkness you probably won't be able to tell the difference.'

'Yes, I would,' came his savage retaliation. 'She'd have a heart under her left breast.'

'And another man's hand-print, no doubt,' she flashed back. 'She stops at nothing to further her career.'

'I must remember to look under yours next time we meet, in that case.'

'You *bastard!*' Her hand caught his left cheek squarely and very hard, making it sting. 'You arrive in the middle of the night without any warning, ravish me until I collapse, then expect me to throw up my career to dash down to a plain the Druids discovered, so that you can ravish me again between flights.' She was fighting back the tears again. 'I'm so damned exhausted and overwhelmed I can't think straight. But I know I can't be like all the other wives and sweethearts—desperate broken women who read the casualty-lists every morning to find out if they can live for another day, or if their world has come to an end. The only way I can carry on is in my cottonwool unreality. I'm not going to lose that for four nights in your arms that will only break my heart again.' She put her hands to her temples in distress. 'Don't ever accuse me of adultery again. I'm so totally yours, I'd die rather than let another man take me.' She faced him with pain all over her striking features. 'I thought I had shown you that. I thought . . . you knew.'

Rex could not trust either himself or her to touch again, so he said, with some difficulty, 'All right, I'll get back here tonight, somehow. Leave the door unlocked, or I'll have the old biddies out in force again.'

Then he left quickly, and went down the stairs to the motor cycle he had hidden for the long journey back.

For the next three days, Rex worked flat out at getting the men under his command into an efficient team that knew the Nieuport's potential, limitations, and weaknesses, and each other in those same respects. He, and the other three experienced fliers from Grissons, taught the new men all they knew about battle-tactics, the characteristics of the average German aviator, and the qualities of the Fokker. They practised tight formation-flying, and rehearsed manoeuvres involving two or three of them together that would confuse the enemy in a general mêlée. They worked out signals they would all use and understand in the air, they sharpened their marksmanship by firing at the targets. They studied maps of the area around the Somme, where the new offensive was to be centred, and they were provided with information on the latest enemy strengths and positions, some of it being what they themselves had gleaned only a week before.

Knowing what they were returning to, most of them tried to relax during the peaceful late-June nights. Mike spent them with Tessa, who had left Tarrant Hall to stay in the quiet hotel while her brother was there. But Rex risked military discipline to help himself to a motor cycle and speed up to London the minute he was free, signing requisition notes with breezy bravado.

Laura left the door on the latch, and was there waiting for him with a meal on a tray and a bath ready. They would sit close together while he ate, talking of all that happened to them both that day. Then, they would make love, lie quietly in each other's arms to speak of things that could only be said after such complete union, make love again, then sleep until the alarm-clock told Rex he had to leave. After that first quarrel, they were wildly, madly happy. There seemed to be no end to the development of their ability to make each other sexually fulfilled, and Laura became so skilled in the refinements of arousal, Rex fell ever deeper into the well of a passion that ruled him. When he left her before each dawn, he lived only for the moment when he would push open the door to see her curled up on the sofa waiting for him that night.

On his fourth evening, while they were relaxing in that quiet period after passion, Rex found himself telling her about Heinz Von Heldermann. Yet there, in the normality of that room and after the delirium of her sensuality, he found he could not offer the man's life as a token to her. The whole affair now seemed unreal, bizarre; the pride he had felt, the acclaim from his fellows, the congratulations of his Commanding Officer, seemed rather sickening, in retrospect. He could clearly remember the man's face— broad, arrogant, handsome. A man who could have his pick of women; a man who would live life to the full. Then he remembered pulling out of the dive and seeing the other man plummet into the trees, explode, and burn.

To try to erase that picture, he pulled Laura close and laid his cheek against her bright head, to murmur against the curls, 'When I'm here with you, I wonder how I can do such things day after day.'

Her fingers trailed lazily up his thigh. 'You do them because it's them or you, darling. Anyway, that one asked for it, didn't he? What a sauce, flying over and dropping a challenge addressed to you personally. You had no choice but to go out and finish him off.'

She had chosen the wrong phrase, and he had the sudden conviction that what he did seemed as unreal to her as the theatre did to him.

'But you don't understand, Laura. I took a man's life just to prove I was a better flier than he was,' he said with emphasis, feeling the enormity of what he had done for the first time.

Her fingers reached the top of his thigh and began to explore further. 'You're a better flier than anyone. They all know that.'

Trying to resist her, he hung on to his theme. 'That's not the point I'm trying to make. I've never been like that over things I can do—proving I can go one better. War turns men into beasts.'

She rolled onto her stomach across his legs, and began to nibble delicately. 'Long live beasts, if they all have what you have, darling.'

Her sultry chuckle, combined with what she was doing, was more than he could stand. Heinz Von Heldermann and all he represented was forgotten, as he tried to prove to her that he was also a better lover than anyone else.

The windows beside his bed at the end of that long room were pushed right back, and the grounds outside slumbered beneath the heat. Although there was only a sheet covering him, his body felt damp and uncomfortably hot, especially the one leg that was tightly bound and immobilised.

Longing swept over him—longing for the deep blue ocean where he could swim naked, longing for a breeze-kissed hillside where he could sprawl with his head pillowed on his arms while he dreamed, longing for freedom! He lay gazing at the sloping lawns, clustering trees, paths leading who-knew-where, and was filled with unbearable longing for the freedom to walk out there, and move on and on until he found the answers he needed. Tied, bound, and helplessly weak, he found his chest nearly bursting with the pain of that longing, and tears welled involuntarily in his eyes. When would it end?

It was the sight of the jay, of course. That bird was a symbol of something, but he felt too tired to work out what it was. Brushing away the tears he put his spectacles back on, then lay for a while watching the jay until it flew off, leaving the garden a deserted enchanted place that had no identity. Strange fantasies began to wander through his mind as he gazed out there; figures of ancient warriors, and women in draped garments half-materialised and vanished again before he could study them. Meaningless words came and went; columns of numbers blurred against visions of white temples. What did it all mean? What could such things signify?

Gradually the garden began to come alive, as men in wheeled chairs were taken across the grass to form companionable groups beneath the shade of trees, and others walked with the aid of sticks and crutches, enjoying the beauty surrounding them. Now and again, a nurse in the familiar blue dress would walk past to pause for a while in laughter and conversation with the men.

Shortly afterward, the visitors began to arrive—ladies in pale floating dresses and beautiful shady hats with ribbons and artificial flowers on the brims, and men in light summer suits, or blazers and straw hats, with cream flannels. Just like Henley Regatta! There were other men, in uniform, who spoilt the scene completely. So he shut his eyes to picture the riverside scene again, as he remembered it. Everyone in that mind-picture seemed at least ten feet tall, so he must have been a small boy when last there. Someone very important was rowing in one of the races—important to him, that was. Funny how he could see it all so clearly, except for that small boy and the shadowy figure in the boat.

It frustrated him, so he opened his eyes again. The garden was quite full of people now. He could even hear their eager voices floating to him on the still air. A pretty young woman standing by a bed of deep-red roses laughed at something said by a man with crutches.

He frowned, as he looked at her. Deep-red roses! Where had the lupins gone? There had been masses of rainbow lupins in that bed. How could there be roses now? June was the month for roses, and it was only early spring. Still frowning, he looked for the catkins hanging fatly from bare branches; the birds gathering nesting material. But the trees were a mass of leaves, and the fledglings were on the wing, being fed with garden grubs.

Breaking into a sweat, he turned to look at the calendar on the side of his locker. The black printing leapt up at him. JUNE 1916. He clutched the sides of his bed, because he felt giddy. Dear God, where had April and May gone? The jay swooped past the window again, and he had to believe that two months had passed since he last saw that bird on the oak outside. The calendar could not be one of their tricks, because Nature revealed the truth. Frightened and bewildered, he clung to the bed, trying to come to terms with what had happened. Was he in Bedlam; was none of it real? Was he still a small boy at Henley, having a nightmare because he had eaten too much strawberries and cream? Who were all these people outside his window? Were none of them anything but phantoms?

Sweat beaded on his forehead and began to roll down his temples and onto his cheeks as he fought back terror. But that was only its beginning, as he realised there were no bandages over his face to soak up that running sweat. He began to scream as he thought of the mask they would soon put over his head, so that the hair would grow longer and longer inside it and choke him. With strength born of terror, he clawed at the locker in an attempt to get off that bed and run. Then, his screams were born of agony in his leg that became so overwhelming, the sound of his own voice grew fainter and fainter in the onset of night.

When he opened his eyes everything was a blur, and the fuzzy pink outline of the girl called Marion was beside the bed. There was a strong smell of antiseptic, starch, and laudanum. His pyjamas and bedding were fresh, he was lying flat, and the dark-green screens were around him. He felt incredibly weak—so weak and lifeless he sensed he would slip away altogether if he did not cling to something.

'Help me . . . for God's sake, help me,' he whispered through dry lips. 'Don't let me go.'

A hand took his in a tight clasp, and the pink blur hung over him. 'Chris?' came her familiar voice, thick with tension. 'Chris, can you hear me?'

He tried to nod, but it was a terrible effort.

'Don't be afraid, I'm right here,' she told him. 'Do you understand what I'm saying?'

It was more like a sigh than an affirmation, but he was gripping her hand as hard as he could and as long as he was doing that he knew he could not slip away.

'You fell over the side of the bed. They had to give you an anaesthetic to re-set your leg. That's why you feel the way you do. You've only just come round.'

Next minute, spectacles were put on him, and he saw her face clearly, only a few feet away from his. Behind her stood a man in a white coat. Then he remembered, and felt the terror rise again.

'It's all right,' she said quickly. 'Everything's all right.'

'My *face*,' he croaked.

'There's nothing wrong with your face, Chris. It's all there.'

'No . . . oh no!'

'*Think*,' she urged. 'Haven't I just hooked your spectacles over *both* ears? And aren't you looking through *both* lenses? Now don't get frightened again, *please*. I promise it's all right.' She half-turned. 'Have a look in this mirror.'

It was what he had dreaded all this time, and she was going to make him look. He had seen it before, all bloody with a mess of brains and hair. He could not face the sight again—he knew he could not. His scream was a mere whimper, but it made her put the mirror down on the bed and start running her hands over his face with the lightest of touches, saying quietly as she did so, 'You had severe burns and a deep wound in your neck, that's all. We had to keep it all covered until the new skin was ready to stand the light-rays. Your face is complete . . . and it's a very nice face, Chris. Here, feel for yourself.'

Before he guessed her intention she lifted his hand to move it carefully over features that felt rough, but complete and normal.

'Now will you look in the mirror?' she asked gently.

For answer he just looked at her in bewildered gratitude. When she held the mirror up over his bed, he gazed up at a face that was bright pink, very youthful, and topped with thick springy blond hair. The eyes that gazed at him were large, violet-blue and dark-lashed, with thick spectacles emphasizing them even further. It was not the horrific half-head he had imagined . . . but it was the face of a complete stranger.

His gaze swung back to Marion's. 'I did see it,' he said weakly. 'There was only half of it left.'

She shook her head, putting the mirror back. 'That was some-one else. Rex wrote to me about it. That terrible battle you were in did many things like that. He thinks it was a friend of yours who lost half his face, and that you saw him like it. That's why you couldn't forget it.'

He lay thinking it all over, hardly noticing that the man in the white coat nodded at Marion, then departed. That face he had seen just now belonged to someone called Christopher Wesley Sheri-dan. He had written that name on the corner of his drawing, so he had to accept that they had told him the truth about that. It did not make him happy, for some reason, but he accepted it because his intellect told him that signature had come quite natu-rally. Now there was the face that had merely been badly burned, not blown half away. Had he been wrong about them, all along? Was this really an army hospital; were these people around him really doctors and nurses, as they had always maintained? Could those two men truly be his brothers? Was he not a prisoner, after all—or Marion? Could there have been a war, and a battle in which he had been seriously wounded? Would he really be able to go out, one day, and walk along one of those garden paths into the cobwebby mysterious beyond?

Such thoughts exhausted him into wanting to sleep. But there was something he must know first. He looked up at Marion, knowing she would tell him the truth.

'What happened to April and May?'

She smiled, and drew nearer to take his hand again. 'They had so much to do, they couldn't wait for you, I'm afraid.'

His eyelids began to close. Had he been somewhere, then? But it was all right. He would see them next year . . . and the deep-red roses did look marvellous against the summer green of the trees. Soon, he was so soundly asleep he knew nothing of Marion lifting his hand gently to her mouth before she put it carefully back onto the white coverlet, and slipped through the screens.

That last Sunday in June was another lovely day, but the patients were not receiving visitors in the shady garden that afternoon, because there was to be a concert for them all. As the weather was so perfect, the entertainers who had come from London agreed to use the broad flagged terrace for their performance, and a piano had been carried out there for their use. The men who could walk, and those in wheeled chairs, were seated on the lawn under an awning that hung down the sides of that terrace. Others considered well enough to see the concert had their beds wheeled into the ward off which the terrace lay.

Chris did not really care about the concert, but he cared very much about being considered well enough to see it. He knew he would be immobile for a long time yet, because he had further damaged his leg by trying to climb from his bed a week ago. But his passionate desire to pass along one of those garden paths to see what lay beyond, made him welcome any advance toward that day, however small. From this other ward, he glimpsed a different view of the hospital grounds and, grouped around the folded-back doors as the beds were, it was almost like being out there on the terrace.

He lay propped up against the back-rest, lost in his own thoughts. Although he now answered nurses and doctors when they spoke to him, he had little to do with the other people. Some of those in his ward did not like him, he knew. Others liked him too much, he felt, and aroused his suspicion. So he kept to himself . . . and he had Marion. She was coming to the concert, and had promised to sit by him to watch it. But she had not come yet because she was helping the performers to get ready.

Chris was a little curious. Marion said that the girl who had organised it was married to his brother Rex. That was the red-haired man who had brought him the sketching-block and pencils. They had talked a lot lately about his brothers. Rex was with the Royal Flying Corps in France, and Roland had apparently just gone across there to join a field-hospital. Chris realised he must have spent a large section of his past with those two, yet he would feel nothing whatever if they should be killed in the war that was apparently continuing. It was a fact he could not deny, and he supposed they must feel upset about it.

To tell the truth, he could remember little about them now. He thought the one called Roland had been a large blond man dressed in tweeds, and betraying subdued anger when he had visited. The red hair of the other had been a striking feature, and he had been wearing a uniform of some kind. But the main impression of that man had been one of gentleness, despite his large build.

It seemed to Chris that he was having another of his puzzling visions when he saw the subject of his thoughts walking toward him right then. Yet Marion was walking with him and looking up at him with such radiance on her face, he sensed they knew more of each other than they revealed. There was a secret they shared —one that shut him out completely. All his old suspicions rose up again. Who was Marion, if she was not a fellow-prisoner, as he had thought?

They weaved their way through the cluster of beds to reach his, and Marion said gaily, 'Here's a lovely surprise! Rex is in England to collect some new aircraft, and has been given permission to visit you and see his wife's concert.'

The red-haired man looked much older than Chris remembered, but he had a very attractive smile that reached his eyes.

'This is a delightful bonus,' he explained. 'We came over for five days to pick up some aircraft, and I never guessed I'd round off the trip with a visit to you and a concert both on the same day.' He sat on the chair beside the bed and looked at him critically. 'They've done wonders with your face, Chris.' He reached into his pocket. 'I'm afraid I'm one up on you now. Before, we had to take each other on trust. Now, I know you're my brother, and this might help your side of the business.' He brought out a notecase and took from it a rather battered photograph, which he held out. 'Summer 1913. Roland and I had to physically drag you outside for that to be taken.'

Chris looked at the photograph. The sepia colour was somewhat faded, but the faces of the three young men were clear enough. He recognised Roland, carefree and laughing, in silk shirt and riding-breeches, one booted foot up on a fallen tree-trunk. Rex was lying on the grass, propping his head up on one bent arm, and winking saucily at the person taking the picture. Astraddle a branch above Rex's head was an extremely handsome boy wearing spectacles. The youngster's face was remarkably like the one he had seen in the mirror. He looked from the picture to the aviator beside him, unable to think of anything to say.

'Bit of a shock?' asked Rex gently.

'Yes.'

'You can hang on to it, if you like.'

He shook his head, and handed the photograph back. 'It means a lot to you.'

'And nothing to you?'

Looking frankly into those tired eyes, he said, 'I'm afraid not. Sorry.'

Rex began putting the notecase back in his pocket. 'We were all a great deal younger and ridiculously innocent then. Perhaps it shouldn't mean so much to me, either.'

'Oh yes, for God's sake hang on to all that,' he said vehemently and without thought. 'You've no idea how terrible it is when . . .' He broke off feeling that, like his face, his inner despair was not yet ready to face the light. He must keep it covered up.

Rex ignored the outburst, saying easily, 'Marion tells me you've been drawing again.' His attractive smile broke out readily. 'It's about the only thing you *can* do, all bound and bandaged like that, isn't it, old son?'

Marion had gone away again, and Chris could see her through the doors leading to the corridor, talking to a man with very dark hair in R.F.C. uniform, standing with a girl as dark as he. Something about the way Marion was looking up at this man suggested there was a secret between them, also. He felt unbearably deserted as he watched her.

'. . . possible to pick up original sketches by French artists,' Rex was saying as Chris turned his face away from the sight of a man and a girl looking at each other with such pleasure. 'I'll try to get hold of one or two and post them over to you.'

'You don't have to do that,' he said gruffly.

'I know . . . but it's one of the few things I can decide for myself, these days.' He gave a quick sigh. 'If you ever feel like writing back —just as one chap to another—I'd enjoy hearing from you. Being on an airfield is very much like being here, you know. It's very restricting, and one soon loses touch with what's going on outside.' He smiled faintly. 'Your life is all chloroform, starch and bedpans —mine is engine-oil, piano-wires, and forced landings in hay-stacks. And I don't have pretty nurses around all day to compensate.'

'How well do you know Marion?' he challenged.

'Oh . . . not quite as well as you do, I should think,' came the easy answer.

'Yet you wrote her a letter.'

'That's right. I'd heard about a chap who'd gone out to Gallipoli with you and received bad head injuries. I thought it might have something to do with your unfounded fears on those lines. It seemed a significant coincidence that I should hear it from a young lad who had been a pupil at our old school. Giles Otterbourne. He remembered you well.'

'I'm surprised. He was a frightful duffer.'

'Was he?' came the slow comment. 'How do you know that?'

Chris looked at the other man for a long time, frowning. 'I just did.'

'Do you remember what he looked like?'

He shook his head, 'I don't know why I said that. It often happens. I see things that don't mean anything, too. Like the numbers. I'm always seeing *them*.'

'What numbers?'

He felt stricken then, knowing he should not have mentioned them. 'Look, they're going to start,' he said, nodding toward the terrace where the pianist had taken his seat.

The concert was a tremendous success for players and audience alike. Chris quite enjoyed it, after all, even though he had spotted the dark-haired man and girl being seated outside by Marion before she hurried in to sit beside Rex. Chris pretended not to notice that she had come back, and kept his gaze on the terrace, where a man was encouraging little black dogs to jump through paper-hoops and do very funny tricks. Everyone laughed, except one patient from Chris's ward, who began to sob uncontrollably. He was always doing it. They wheeled his bed away quickly.

Then a girl came and began to sing a song with rather saucy words. The red-haired man beside the bed grew tense, and leant forward watching her intently. Chris could understand why. The girl was more beautiful than anyone he had ever seen. She was tall, with vivid red-gold hair and an unbelievable shape. Her waist was small enough to hold with both hands, yet above and below it she curved out to almost twice the measurement. But it was her face, pale, pointed, with slanting eyes in a dark colour he could not identify at that distance, and a smile that made a person feel it was solely for him, despite all the others around. That face held him spellbound as it changed from smiles, to impudence, to mock innocence, while fooling no one that it was not hiding something much more exciting.

She went, and a clown with enormous feet that kept tripping him up had everyone laughing again. Yet Chris knew that, like

273

him, they were all waiting for the girl to come back. When she did, it was like something hitting him hard in the chest so that he could hardly breathe. She was one of his mysterious figures that came and went so quickly, yet this one stayed and was real. In a beautiful white draped dress with a garland around her curls, she stood incredibly still and intent to sing a song with a tune so haunting he found the tears welling up and blurring the lenses until she seemed as ethereal as his phantoms. Afraid they would wheel him away like the other man, he swallowed hard and had to let the spectacles remain blurred while he realised she must be Diana, the Huntress. Vague visions of distant islands, deep blue sea, white cliffs and temples wavered in the blur caused by his tears. *Naxos, Milos, Paros.* The words came into his mind, but they were not from the pages that made no sense. They were places, he was certain, and this girl's music had originated from them.

Suddenly aware of the total silence around him, he took off the spectacles and wiped them so that he could see what was happening. The men were all sitting spellbound, gazing at the girl who seemed to be pouring her heart out with those sweet, low, husky stanzas. Then his moving gaze reached his brother, and he was startled at the naked pain of his expression as he watched the girl who must be his wife. There was no pride in it, just near-agony. What had happened to the laughing young man in the photograph, who had been winking so light-heartedly?

Two men with banjos filled in before the interval and coaxed many of them to sing along in the choruses of well-known songs. Then, while the players took a quick rest, some of the doctors did a chorus from *Floradora,* with others dressed as nurses. By this time, some of the laughter was growing a little wild, and several other beds were wheeled away. Chris had lost the impulse to laugh, and was feeling very tired. But he dreaded being wheeled away, so lay back quietly through the performances of a juggler, two girls who practically turned themselves inside-out in acrobatics, and a black-faced man who played tunes on anything from a beer-cask to a thimble.

The girl returned to end the concert, and there was a gasp as she marched smartly onto the terrace dressed as a grenadier guard —at least, her top half. Below the tightly-fitting jacket and tall bearskin she wore nothing but flesh-coloured tights. Her legs were long, beautiful and devastating to look at. She sang patriotic songs in that husky voice that would rouse even the most sluggish to fervour. Totally entranced Chris watched her marching sensuously back and forth, pausing by some of those flanking the terrace to flash her leg high in the air in a kick that revealed the brief black satin garment beneath the tunic.

They all loved it; the faces of the men glowed as they watched her. Then she picked up the crutch of one patient and hobbled comically around on it while she sang in funny bass tones like an inebriated man. When she returned it to its owner, she took off the bearskin and put it on the man's head, dancing away with her bright curls shining in the sunlight, a saucy smile in response to cheers from those surrounding her.

Next minute, she was tripping inside straight toward him, and Chris felt his heart bump. But she seized Rex's hand and dragged him unwillingly and rather set-faced, Chris thought, out onto the terrace, where his appearance was greeted with another rousing cheer and crutches waved in salute. It fell very quiet, however, when the girl signalled Rex to lift her onto the piano, where she sat to sing the lovely and sentimental *Every Little While*. But this song was for one man only, and they all knew it. The pair looked at each other as if there would never be another time or place, and the sadness of those two figures so poignantly posed filled Chris with longing to draw it, write it, or set it to poetry. He knew about passion and its hopelessness. He knew of lovers who had stood like that, who had loved and lost, who had endured silent and unfulfilled adoration. Over the ages, there had been hundreds, and he knew them all. Yet he could remember none of their names or faces, although he was sure he had once been so familiar with them. He felt he would burst with sadness over it all.

Then the concert was over. There were several speeches of thanks, and one of the patients in a wheeled chair came forward to give the girl a lovely sheaf of apricot and cream roses. She stooped and kissed him on the cheek, to everyone's noisy delight. Then the nurses began to wheel everyone away for tea.

A tray was brought to Chris, but he could eat nothing of what was on it. He felt too dazed and confused by all that had happened that day, and sleep was coming up fast. But Rex appeared with the girl, holding her arm as he led her down the long ward. She was now wearing a dress of soft floating yellow material caught around the hips with satin ribbon. Close to him, she looked more beautiful than ever, and he could see now that her eyes were a deep glowing green.

'They've only allowed us a minute, because you must be tired,' said Rex. 'But I wanted you to meet Laura—your sister-in-law. And she very much wanted to meet you.'

'Hallo, Chris,' she greeted in the low voice that made even that exciting. 'I'm so glad they've taken off your head bandages. It must be so much more comfortable for you.' She smiled up at her husband. 'My God, you Sheridans are a handsome breed! I thought Roland was splendid enough, but young Chris goes one better still. Those eyes! No wonder the nurses all refer to him as "the Greek god".' She turned back and winked at him. 'You're not supposed to know that, so don't give me away, will you? Did you enjoy the concert?'

He nodded, unable to speak.

'I'll try to organise another one later on.'

Rex squeezed her arm. 'I think we'd better leave the lad alone now. He does look rather tired.' A hand dropped on his shoulder, and his brother's voice sounded rather thick as he said, 'I'll come and see you on my next leave, old son. Keep up the good work. You're winning through, you know. And I can't tell you how good it's been to talk to you again. Chin, chin!'

'Goodbye, Chris,' said Laura softly. 'Don't worry. Everything is going to work out fine.'

They walked away. Behind them he could see Marion talking to the dark-haired man again. He pushed the tea-tray away, then took off his spectacles so that everything would be a blur. He did not want to see any of them any more.

Marion came eventually and grumbled about his uneaten tea while she straightened the bed. Then, struck by his silence, she asked, 'Chris, why are you hiding?'

It always annoyed him when she accused him of that, so he retaliated by asking, 'What are you really doing at this hospital?'

A small pause. 'I'm a probationer nurse.'

'Why do you always do everything for me?'

'Because you're a patient here.'

'The others don't have the same person all the time. Why do I?'

A longer pause this time. 'You're angry with me, for some reason. What have I done?'

'I don't need you here all the time. You must have other things to do.'

'All right, Chris. I'll ask to be put on general duties, if you'd rather.'

'Yes.'

The pink blur moved away, and he closed his eyes as he turned his face into the pillow. When Laura Sheridan had stood there a few feet away from his bed, he had been shaken by a sudden violent desire to take off all her clothes and lie on top of her. Now, he felt so deeply ashamed of the thought and the physical outcome, he could not bear Marion to find out.

They flew back to France on a stormy morning that put an end to the summer idyll of the past few days. The problems began straight away, when one man had to turn back on the brink of crossing the Channel because of engine-trouble. Another had to land in a field at Calais, then realised he did not know how to get to Saint-Brioche, the new squadron's base. He did not arrive until twenty-four hours after the others, and then with a broken wheel-strut.

The new airfield could have been Grissons. There were the same old farm buildings and tents. But it was nearer the front line, and the guns could be heard constantly, like thunder rumbling in the distance. The Somme offensive had begun, and they were rushed into action immediately.

Normal routine became a frantic programme of patrols, interceptions, and balloon-bursting, all with the deadly addition of anti-aircraft barrage from the Germans trying desperately to hold ground against an equally desperate attempt to take it. The Battle of the Somme was turning into another Verdun, with even greater slaughter, as another vast area of France became a horrific landscape of muddy craters and charred wood.

'Sheridan's Skuas,' as the squadron was soon nicknamed, lost men and machines on every flight. The Nieuport was good, but could not work miracles. The superiority of the Fokker was losing ground and, had there been enough pilots and aircraft, the Allies might have gained dominance of the skies. But the new pilots were boys straight from school, with less than fifteen flying hours to give them confidence when in a tight corner. They survived for no more than two weeks, and Rex now had the hard task of writing to their families, sending back their personal effects.

But he was a man suffering his own personal torment. His last day in England had affected him disastrously. Delight that Chris now looked like a person rather than a mummy, and was plainly improving, had been overset by the distress of his non-recognition. It had been worse now that he looked and spoke like the beloved brother he had always been. It had been difficult to accept that the boy had no feelings for him whatever, after the close understanding of nineteen years.

Then there had been the concert. It had been a shock to discover how Laura had changed her act. Used to the Laurie Pagett routine he had seen over and over again in that music-hall box, Madame Sherry had seemed like a betrayal. The male-impersonator he could share; the sensuous, beautiful girl who was his wife, he could not. He had seen the way all those men had looked at her; enjoying her body, loving her glances, her smiles, the invitation in her eyes that she skilfully managed to suggest was for each man alone. She had deliberately played on her powers of attraction, deliberately excited with her body.

As he had watched her perform, had watched those watching her, he had known she *was* a star. The theatre would never release her now. Yet, he had allowed her to drag him out there, as she had done on their wedding-night, and peel back the layers to expose his ruling passion for her for all to see. At the time, he had been captivated, rendered immobile before her by the poignancy of the song, the sweet huskiness of her voice that seemed to sing only for him, the fire in her eyes that told him anything he wanted to know. And when it had ended, there had been the bewilderment of finding they were surrounded by applauding people. In those first moments of emergence from captivation, he had wondered whether she had been as lost to everything as he had believed, or whether she had used him as part of the act.

Yet he had been angry over such thoughts almost immediately, when he had found her in a quiet corner of the garden, away from the celebrating actors, overcome by tears.

'They're all so wonderful, yet so physically broken, I can't bear it,' she had cried, turning into his arms. 'You didn't see their faces, as I did. And the mental patients, like young Chris, were like children around a Christmas tree. At one stage, I really thought

278

I couldn't go on. Then I saw you sitting there with Marion and knew I must.' She had looked up at him with immense sadness on her lovely face. 'I'm weak, Rex, and very ashamed of the fact that I'm not doing something more worthwhile, like Marion and Tessa. But, for a while, I made them happy, didn't I? Just for a while.'

'Of course you did, darling,' he had assured her, drying her tears. 'And happiness is *very* worthwhile.'

They had strolled together through the shrubbery-paths, arms entwined, each very conscious of their coming parting on the following morning. They rested for a while beneath a shady tree and there, lying with his head resting on her lap, he had told her of his new certainty of surviving, no matter how long the war continued.

'When I went back to Grissons after our marriage, I felt that death was very near,' he had confessed, looking up into her frightened face. 'A short time afterward, you remember, I was locked in single combat with a man as experienced and determined as I was. At the vital moment, when my guns jammed, I knew this was my time. I looked Death in the face and acknowledged that it was the end. But a boy called Giles Otterbourne died in my place, against orders and quite needlessly. Because of him, my name has now been wiped off Death's list, and it won't appear again until I'm old and grey.'

She had stroked his face dry of her tears that had started again, and sworn she would never let him grow old and grey while she had a body and a pair of hands to keep him as her king of beasts. Yet, that night at the hotel near the hospital, he had been no lion, but a lamb.

The appalling humiliation of that night's impotency weighed him down all the way back to France, and in the following weeks. His failure on the very night of their greatest need to pledge their love, the stigma of physical weakness, the shame of lost virility beside the naked body of a woman who was the queen of arousal, nearly broke him apart. He grew bad-tempered and anti-social, retiring more and more into the isolation of command which brought extra duties to tie him to a desk when he was not flying.

But, as the holocaust of the Somme continued, he began going out on solo missions between the others, ranging the skies looking for victims, and taking on impossible odds in the almost insane need to push his tally of 'kills' higher than any other pilot on either side. He succeeded. His score crept up toward fifty as he returned day after day with the wild look still in his eyes, his aircraft riddled with holes and breaking up around him. And he was now drinking heavily night after night.

14

SEPTEMBER, and the Battle of the Somme had still not been won. That great new weapon designed to defeat trenches, crater-devastated landscapes, and any amount of gunfire, had been launched against the Germans. Except that the marvellous armoured vehicle that ran on caterpillar-tracks had not been so much *launched* as *lurched,* and old soldiers sniffed derisively, claiming the tank would never last. The Germans had retaliated with their terror-weapon, the flame-thrower, to initial effect until it was plain the operators of them were such perfect targets against the vivid light, they were picked off before they could do much damage. So, the long hot summer had dragged by, and the battle had deteriorated into the familiar trench-warfare, with periodic attacks 'over the top' which slaughtered men wholesale and gained nothing.

Kitchener had been lost at sea just before the great offensive had begun in that July. Haig had taken over, but the troops felt no cheer at the thought of a new leader with new ideas. If he had any, they certainly were not apparent as week succeeded week and another winter loomed like a khaki spectre. The cream of British youth, who had volunteered with such patriotic fervour and had unhesitatingly climbed from their trenches time and time again in answer to the call, were now tired, decimated, and ill. Trench-fever, shell-shock, dysentery, malnutrition, and foot-rot were all too common amongst those who had sailed away almost two years ago to finish it off before Christmas. But, more often than not, those sick men stayed on duty, because the field hospitals were full of wounded and dying.

On the first day of the Somme offensive there had been 57,000 casualties. Three months later, the toll was too horrific for the mind to contemplate. There was no end to it in sight . . . and it had begun to rain, day after day, to turn the surface of France into a sea of mud, once more.

As Roland sat hunched into his great-coat in the back of the ambulance, gazing out at the long ribbon of mire across which they had already travelled, and at the endless snake of plodding men, heads bowed against the driving rain, his thoughts travelled back seven months to Rex's wedding day, when his brother had so ardently defended his right to 'a week of heaven before returning to hell'. He saw quite clearly the athletic devil-may-care figure in a uniform that typified all Rex gloried in, and heard again his brother saying, *What you're going to encounter in France is going to break your mind, unless you can make it more flexible.*

After three months, it had not. It had broken his heart, instead. On the road like this, in emergency dressing-stations set up near the trenches, in field hospitals behind the lines, the evidence of the Empire's finest young men being systematically wiped out caused him such anguish he wanted to shout it for all the world to hear. No such release being possible, he bottled it up inside and withdrew into the quiet stoicism that had dominated his personality ever since hearing of the suicide of his father two years earlier. But, as he tended the bloody victims of battle, he saw his fears being realised. These fine young men from cities and villages were the backbone of Britain; the bronzed youngsters with far-off visions in their eyes were the new pioneers of Australia, New Zealand, and South Africa. The tough rangy giants with a laconic way of speaking were the future generation of Canada. They were all vanishing from the face of the earth. What would become of the factories and mills, the gentle productive farmland like that around Tarrant Royal; who would tame the vast wild areas in Africa and the Antipodes; would the backwoods of Canada, the great frozen lakes, and the glorious craggy mountains be abandoned to nature from lack of young men with courage?

Casting his vision further, he also realised that France would suffer even more, with the land as well as the people being destroyed. And what of Russia with its starving millions, and the rural peasant states like Hungary, Poland, and Serbia? Finally, before the war could be terminated, Germany would have to be brought to industrial and pastoral ruin. Surely, if commonsense and rational attitudes could only be adopted by all concerned, the warring nations would see that it had to stop now if there was to be anything left at the end.

This was what broke his heart. His mind was not in danger ... *yet.* It was, in fact, working very well. Although there had been a two-year lapse in his medical studies, he had found it very fresh in his memory after enlistment. In consequence, he had been given lance-rank on leaving for France, and was now a full corporal with responsibility for drugs—when there were any—and the daily running of the small field-unit beneath the command of a French-Canadian doctor called Matthew Rideaux.

The two had struck up a cautious friendship, and the curious character of a field ambulance unit managed to dispense with the restrictions of rank that would normally hamper such a relationship. The two men had much in common. They were both unmarried landowners, spoke French fluently, had a passionate love of country and heritage, and never demanded the inner thoughts of the other or intruded too far into the private life of someone met in the false state of war, which threw people together then wrenched them ruthlessly apart. Both Roland and Matt Rideaux protected their emotions jealously.

They were moving on now towards a village with the odd name of Croix Des Anges—not the happiest association, under the circumstances. A push forward by a Canadian battalion had gained some ground, and the troops were reputedly fortifying the village which was little more than a ruin. The snake of British soldiers they were accompanying were to reinforce the Canadians in a desperate attempt to hold on to an area of devastated farmland, which the Germans seemed just as desperate to have back. It was all part of the madness.

As Roland gazed at that scene of unrelieved mud, he wondered if they would even know when they reached the village where, they had heard, the casualties of that forward push were piled up under scant shelter from the rain.

'Oh my gawd, Corp,' said a voice behind him, bringing him from his reverie, 'here comes the bloody Fokkers!'

True enough, a glance at the sky to their rear showed the group of black specks approaching low and fast, sighting the column as their target. Roland's heart bumped. He felt desperately sorry for the marching men, who had no real shelter from air attack and no real chance of retaliation. In this kind of aerial bombardment, the machines zoomed down and raked the road with machine-gun fire, besides tossing grenades and bombs on all sides with devastating effect. Then they flew off to do the same on another road, leaving death and mayhem behind.

There was a scramble to leave the ambulance, and the men of the unit dropped to the road to scatter in every direction. Although the red cross was clearly marked on the roof, they were in the middle of a column of troops and were no more immune than they.

But Roland did not slither and slide to the verge and throw himself face-down in the barren field, as did the rest of the team. With the aircraft black, noisy, and deadly only two hundred yards off, he dragged his booted feet through the mire to reach the horses pulling the ambulance. They had been halted by the driver, and stood drooping in the shafts, exhausted, caked with mud, and broken-spirited. They knew his voice; they drew comfort from his hands on their bridles. But they still stood numbly, harnessed to the heavy truck, as if resigned to dying before they even reached journey's end.

It seemed they might. So low the pilots' faces could be clearly seen as they smiled, the Fokkers raced the length of that road three or four times, turning the slow, silent plodding khaki snake into a writhing, bleeding serpent that had been severed along its whole length, each section continuing to wriggle. The stutter of machine-guns, the crack of grenades exploding, the deep crunch of bombs that tore great chunks from the road, the screams and shouts of men, the shrieks of terrified beasts, the roar of flames from burning trucks, and the din of diving aircraft made the afternoon a discordant symphony of war.

The ambulance horses were as terrified as any on that road. Despite their emaciated condition, they found the strength to plunge and rear in an attempt to escape from something they could not understand. Roland was hard-pressed to hold them: calming words were no antidote to the sounds around them. Grimly holding the leathers, he fought to keep his footing in the mud, fell full length, struggled up again, then was dragged twenty or thirty yards by the runaway beasts, finally slithering to a stop as an aircraft buzzed overhead and sent a whistling hail of bullets in an unerring line down the centre of the road. He heard them rip through the canvas hood of the ambulance, then something thudded against his steel-helmet a fraction of a second before the mud ahead began leaping up into little brown spurts as if frogs were jumping in glee. One of the horses staggered, hesitated, then slid sideways in the shafts to hang screaming in agony against its partner.

The Fokkers were distant specks in the sky again, but that section of road was now a scene of burning vehicles, men in flames, broken bodies, bolting horses, filthy mud-covered troops struggling to regroup, mounted officers turning helpless circles on stunned horses that would not obey commands. Everywhere, thick smoke drifted over upturned lorries, deep watery pits in the road, dead animals, and boxes of supplies, broken and blown over a wide area. Tea, sugar, jam, flour, cocoa, suet, custard-powder, rice and bars of yellow soap were all settling into the mud over the road and bordering fields. Blankets lay everywhere like dark saturated blobs, and boots were severed from their pairings, gradually filling with the rain that still pelted down on everything.

It was only a fractional impression as Roland, choked and shaken, unslung his rifle and lifted it with unsteady hands to take aim. But his arm was grabbed, and a sharp voice said, 'God dammit, there are *men* in agony out there. Get to them!'

With the horse's screams filling his ears, Roland looked at Matt with heated defiance. 'One bullet and one second, that's all it takes. I can't do the same for a man.'

'Then you should have joined the Veterinary Corps! Get going with those stretcher-bearers. I mean it!'

Feeling the betrayal of man toward animal sticking in his throat, he ran to where his men were tugging the stretchers from the back of the ambulance. The canvas was full of holes. Had there been patients in the ambulance, they would surely have been dead now.

They did what they could, but it was never enough. Dangerous open wounds were full of liquid mud so that it was impossible to see their full extent. Bandaging and cleansing could not be done in the pouring rain in the middle of a mire, yet there was no room in the ambulance for the large number of casualties. Some needed immediate urgent surgery to save their lives, others should be totally immobilised if they were not to bleed to death. There were broken limbs, loss of sight through bomb-blast, and stomach wounds that promised a slow agonising death. One man had half his face blown away, and Roland well understood why Chris should be so haunted by the sight.

As he worked on those who could be bandaged or splinted well enough to be taken on in the supply-trucks to Croix des Anges, Matt was dealing with the more serious cases. Roland worked quickly and expertly, in command of what he was doing despite the anguish he felt over the horse still hanging over the shafts. He sighed with relief when a passing cavalry officer put a bullet in it. After supervising the dispatch of the walking wounded and those fit to travel in the remaining trucks, he went to join Matt, who was administering morphia to those so seriously ill the pain was unbearable. Even so, he was forced to let many suffer, due to the shortage of the drug. A few aspirin had to suffice, in most cases.

'That's the last of the hopefuls on their way,' he told the Canadian. 'I've sent Mercer with them in case of unexpected complications, and told him to send out ambulances from the unit already at the village.'

But there were no ambulances or supplies at Croix des Anges. The Canadians they were supposed to be joining had advanced further. But the British commander wisely settled where he was in a place that was no more than a map reference and a pile of rubble. He knew from experience that rapid advances were usually followed by equally rapid retreats to a well-fortified standpoint. The Canadians would be back, he was certain, so he set his men to digging in. In no time there were trenches, fortifications, subterranean cookhouses and stores, and an underground hospital ward in the cellars of what had been a village inn.

The makeshift hospital was necessary due to a message that reached the new arrivals soon after they dragged into Croix des Anges. The road along which they had travelled was now cut across by advancing Germans, and the only other route to link up with British units was also in the hands of the enemy—for the time being. No one doubted that the normal ebb and flow pattern would continue, and movement would again be possible. But it meant that the sick and wounded could not be moved out to base hospitals, leaving the ambulance unit with the responsibility of doing what they could for an impossible number of victims. The cellar hospital was the best solution, until such time as traffic could get through once more.

When the Field Ambulance Unit finally made its way into the devastated village to hear this crushing news, two-thirds of those in the vehicle were already corpses. As Roland had said, one could not put a man out of his agony with a single bullet, like a horse, and patients had endured all the tormented stages of dying as the ambulance had been laboriously pulled for miles along the pitted muddy road by the remaining horse and members of the unit, in shifts, in the middle of a wet, bitterly-cold European autumn.

After three months' experience of battle casualties, the last few days had affected Roland strongly. It was the first time he had ever doubted his plain duty. His upbringing, and four years of medical training, had instilled and maintained in him the belief that life must be preserved, at all costs. That belief had governed his reactions to his father's suicide, and his brother's schoolboy impregnation of a girl for whom he cared nothing. Those feelings remained unaltered, but the dedication of a doctor to keeping patients alive as long as possible now seemed, to him, to need qualification. His years at medical school had concerned civilian peacetime medicine, and the hypothetical cases that were part of the training had always died their lingering deaths in the sterile tranquillity of a well-equipped modern hospital, or in their own beds, surrounded by loving tender relatives. There had been nothing in the curriculum or textbooks about watching and hearing the drawn out death-throes of men on a foreign wind-swept roadside, beneath an awning open to rain and night-frosts, with no beds, no drugs, and no loved ones to hear their last confessions that would send them to their Maker absolved from the mistakes or sins of their short lives.

Roland's own deep faith had stirred to ask a question. Medical knowledge was intended to heal. If it could not heal, it was to help the doomed die with comfort and dignity. There had been no dignity in the past few days, had there?

As he helped to carry stretchers into the comparative warmth and shelter of that ruined cellar, he was more than usually quiet, preoccupied with this tiny crack in the convictions of a lifetime. But it did not diminish his appreciation of what had been done by those who had gone ahead. The sparse straw that had packed the bottles and barrels had been spread beneath blankets to make a reasonably soft surface for the patients, the floor had been swept and doused with spirits from one of the unbroken kegs—as good a disinfectant as they could get—rough sleeping-platforms had been made for the medical-staff, and fires were maintained to sterilise instruments, cook rations, and dry soiled blankets.

Roland saw every patient from the ambulance well settled, then went across to Mercer, a tow-haired former cow-hand.

'You've made a frightfully good job of this place,' he said warmly. 'It's pure luxury after that roadside, I can tell you.'

'Thank you, sir . . . I mean, Corporal.' The man broke into a grin. 'There I go calling you "sir" again. It still don't seem right not to.'

'So you've said before,' put in Roland quickly. 'Have you made records of the Canadian casualties left behind here? Captain Rideaux will want a brief idea of what we have on our hands.'

'Aye, I have that. Two's already gone afore you got here. The others is much the same as always—head wounds, broken guts, bad gouging from falling on t'wire.'

'Any hope of recovery?'

The tow head wagged. 'Tha's guess is as good as mine. 'Tis prayers, not us'll do it.'

While Matt had a quick look at the men left behind at the Canadian advance and cheered them all by revealing that he was Canadian, too, Roland stacked what medicines they had in the most protected corner he could find, sorted out with the cook what sort of meal he could produce in the quickest time from the rations he had, then walked wearily across to the bed-platform he had reserved for himself. Arranging his personal kit along with his rifle, tin helmet, water-bottle, gas mask, and blanket-roll, his thoughts returned to the niggling doubt that, once it had arisen, could not be placated by reason or convictions. Branwell Sheridan had made death disgusting and ugly by his own will. But these men deserved better than this in return for their courage.

'You look like a polecat who has the heat on and finds it's not the mating season,' said a warm rich voice beside him.

Roland straightened up from his task and gave a faint smile. 'I'm continually amazed at the wide variety of your similes. I haven't heard that one before.'

'You're not likely to again,' said Matt. 'It wasn't very good, was it?'

'I have heard better pearls from your lips.'

The Canadian shook his head. 'You're the darndest corporal I ever came across, you know that? Why don't you take that last examination and become what you're cut out to be?'

'You know why.'

'The saints save me from a "noble" man!' he ejaculated. 'You think old Saint Peter will give you a better reception at the Golden Gates if you kneel in the mud as a corporal, rather than take a year off in the safety of a British hospital to learn the rest of your trade?'

Roland gave another faint smile. 'Saint Peter doesn't influence me one way or the other. In another year, the war might be all over.'

'It sure as hell won't be.' The dark-complexioned face that rarely betrayed what went on inside the man, studied Roland with a resigned expression. 'The longer it goes on now, the longer it's likely to. All the best men will be dead, and the dregs that are left won't have the heart or courage to make a bid for victory. We should have finished this off in the first three months. Now, it's too late.' He sighed heavily. 'Generals rarely win wars, in my opinion. More often than not they prolong them with their idiot decisions until poor bastards like these in here take matters into their own hands.' He lowered his voice slightly. 'Morale is putrid, at the moment. I tell you, pal, if we don't take the Somme, this war will go on long enough for you to qualify . . . and then some.'

Roland sat on his folded blanket on an upturned barrel, and looked up frankly. 'Is it any easier to watch men die with officer's rank than with stripes on your sleeve?'

Matt stared at him for a moment or two with a frown creasing his brow. 'So what's eating you now?'

'The virtues or vices of integrity.'

'Wow, that's some thought . . . but it's out of place here.'

'Why? It's scenes like these that make a man think.'

Putting his booted foot up onto the barrel beside him, Matt poked him in the shoulder with a gentle finger. 'You're not here to think, Corporal, but to help the afflicted.'

'What if I can't help them?'

'They die. It's a fact of life.'

'It's also a fact of life that we shoot animals to end their misery. Do we think so little of our fellow-men that we stand by and let them suffer beyond endurance?'

'You think we should play God?' came the harsh question.

'Aren't we already? If we believe a man's injuries are God's will, isn't it presumptuous of us to cure him? Should the limit of our purpose be to make the victim as comfortable as possible, feed him, give him a drink and a cigarette, then leave him to God's further will?'

'What's gotten into you, for Christ's sake?' The foot slid to the ground again with an angry thud. 'You're not turning conchie, are you?'

Roland shook his head. 'Is it likely?'

'Well, you took a darn long time to volunteer, I gather. Don't tell me it wasn't because of suffering mankind that you joined, but some girl's white feather.'

He let that pass. The difference in rank might be overlooked for social convenience between them, but it would rear its ugly head if a quarrel arose. The words touched a raw spot, nevertheless.

'Wouldn't I have done what you just now advocated and finished my studies safely in England to become the officer and gentleman my background demands? I received enough white feathers to clothe a flock of ducks . . . but you know very well why I joined.'

'Sure I do . . . your kid brother. Sorry, that was a rotten thing to say. I guess we're both tired and rock-bottom worked-out. If it's any comfort to you, it also tore my guts out watching those poor bastards in hell on that roadside.'

Roland looked him squarely in the eye. 'It was they who needed the comfort, not me. One quick bullet, one swift action, that's all it would have taken for each of them. If I had been there alone with them, I might have succumbed to their pleas.'

Matt stretched to his full height and stifled a yawn in exaggerated fashion. 'I didn't hear one goddamned word you said, or you'd be out of here and squatting in a trench with those poor sods of infantrymen for the remainder of the war. And those stripes would be off your sleeve for good.' He began to turn away. 'I'll leave you with another thought. Suppose some buddy like you had decided to give "comfort" to your kid brother when he was dragged out of the burning sea, all charred, with his guts hanging out, and his mind blown. Would you be grateful for *that* kindly act?'

It struck him very forcibly and he gave it a serious reply. 'No, of course not. But, if he becomes a permanent madman, my brother might have thanked him . . . and so might his infant son.'

Matt paused, then cuffed Roland gently on the shoulder. 'There goes another of my theories on Englishmen. They *are* emotional.'

'Me . . . emotional?' queried Roland in astonishment. 'I'm the most rational person out.'

'Sez you!' came the cynical comment. 'Be careful though, pal. It could get you in a hell of a lot of trouble.'

The Canadians returned to Croix Des Anges three days later. Less than one-third of the battalion had survived the advance and retreat. They, together with the British reinforcements, settled into the trench-network that had been dug in the village and began the usual routine of sniping, dawn and dusk rushes to put machine-gun posts out of action, night-time raids to cut the enemy's wire, assaults on the rats that fought for occupation of the trenches, invention of new artful ways to get extra helpings of the unappetising rations, invention of new ways to keep dry in a downpour, invention of new words to popular songs that gave vent to their feelings, and invention of new ways to win the war that gave even greater vent to their feelings.

There were always letters to write, of course. Some men never posted them. Some gave up after the first line or two, because what was there to tell that they had not already told? Others wrote long pages full of lies that suggested they were having the time of their lives in France. The intention was to cheer their loved ones; it never occurred to them that they might do the reverse with their suggestion of bordering insanity. Although at home people were protected from the full horror of the Western Front, they knew enough to recognise wild imaginings when they read them.

But there were brighter aspects to the subterranean life with a sky full of bullets. One supply got through to the village with food, clothing, medicines and cigarettes. Best of all, it brought the letters from home. The same trucks returned along the disintegrating road with red crosses marked on them, carrying the more serious patients needing protracted treatment, or to be sent home for good. However, it was anyone's guess whether the road was still open and traversable.

Roland and Matt welcomed the medicines and supplies, as well as the opportunity to send their bad cases to the rear. The numbers in that cellar had been increasing steadily with every raid and sneak assault, and two of their own team had been seriously wounded whilst out in No-Man's-Land picking up wounded.

Roland found that the most nerve-wracking of all his duties. After a dawn raid, the dead and wounded had to be left lying between the two stretches of wire all day, until darkness provided some cover. Even then, both sides were constantly sending up star-shells to illuminate the barren scene in case of silent creeping attackers. Stretcher-bearers were fired upon before being identified as such, and sometimes *after* being identified. Warfare had become a desperate business with no time for the niceties of respect for the wounded or those who tended them. The ideals that had dominated Roland's thinking and motivation for twenty-five years took another knock each time he crept out into the eerie darkness of that narrow stretch of sucking mud between the Anglo-Canadian lines and those of the Germans, then had to lie flat for hours on end or slowly slither backwards to safety because a machine-gunner had vengeance on his mind that night. Such attacks sometimes prevented help reaching the suffering victims who had been waiting twenty-four hours in the rain and wind for a friendly voice or a hand on theirs, and they became corpses to lie with all the others who had died alone out there. Roland's ideals took an even harder knock when his own side did the same to German stretcher-bearers.

Then there were the gas attacks. It seemed the most inhumane weapon of all, to Roland, and the most cowardly. But the success of such attacks was variable. All too often, the veering wind carried the gas back over the Germans who had released it, and use of that silent sinister weapon was decreasing.

Throughout those weeks at Croix Des Anges Roland kept going with thoughts of Tarrant Hall and his estate. Tessa wrote long letters twice each week, although they invariably arrived in batches with long gaps in between delivery. The letters told a success story which he had no reason to doubt and, more and more, he thanked heaven she had turned up at exactly the right time. She was very happy and managing farm and estate very well.

Roland wrote equally long letters in reply, but he mentioned little of his present life, concentrating on the home so dear to his heart. He missed it all with a quiet desperation he revealed to no one, least of all Tessa, and each one of her letters laid another layer of sadness on his soul as it brought so vividly to life the old house, the stately trees surrounding it, the view from Longbarrow Hill, the village church, the winding lanes of Tarrant Royal, the fields full of long-tailed lambs. In the six months since he had left it all behind he had realised doctoring was not his only vocation, as he had always imagined. His heart was in the land and its cultivation, so much so he yearned for the sight of a peaceful green field, grazing sheep, a graceful home set in formal gardens. Tessa's letters were the nearest he got to it.

She also wrote that she had visited Chris again since the day of Laura's concert. The fact that she concentrated on how well his face was recovering from the burns, how his stomach wound was progressing, and the burns on his back were giving him far less pain now, suggested that his mental condition had reached another hiatus, for some reason.

Roland wrote letters to the boy, of course, but he knew they were awkward stilted attempts to bridge the amnesiac gap, and there were never any replies. Still he prayed for the day when there would be. Letters from Rex had been fewer since he had joined the new squadron. Roland was not surprised. Command would give his brother extra duties, and the Somme offensive had kept the R.F.C. busy. Word was that the Germans still held the upper-hand in the air, claiming four Allied victories for the loss of one of their own. But the sorely-pressed aviators went up time and time again to combat the menace and show their enemies they were nowhere near despair or defeat, or ever would be so long as there was a machine left and a man to fly it.

From Croix Des Anges it was possible to watch the aerial battles when the weather cleared. But the continuous rain and low cloud had prevented any such clashes for some days. Roland was glad. It meant Rex would be safe for another week or two. They were all surprised, therefore, when the sound of a low-flying air-craft was heard on a morning during the first week of October, and a single machine of the R.F.C. appeared just below the rain-clouds, circled, then came in to land not far from the cellar hospital. The pilot climbed stiffly from it and began walking across the open area totally careless of the fact that the enemy was not much more than a mile away in hidden trenches.

'He's darn cool,' observed Matt, standing beside Roland in the entrance to their hospital, watching the visitor's arrival.

'He always was,' responded Roland. 'If I'm not mistaken, that's my brother. How he found out where I was and has the time to go on a family visiting jaunt, I can't guess.'

But he received a shock when Rex bowed his head beneath the low entrance and stepped down into the cellar, pulling the helmet from his bright hair. His brother's face was gaunt and hollow-eyed, his frame bony, his complexion yellow. He looked ill, haunted, as if the light had gone out of him completely. The comparison between the man Roland had last seen in Somerset on the final day of his honeymoon and the person now before him was frightening.

'Hallo,' greeted Rex with a curious taut smile as he held out his hand. 'God, I thought our squadron buildings were primitive enough, but this beats everything I've seen. How do you ever manage to cure anyone in this ruin?'

Roland found his hand clasped so tightly he had the absurd notion that there was a touch of desperation in the hold.

'However did you know I was here?' he asked, still shocked by his brother's appearance.

'Reconnaissance photographs, old lad. We know where *everyone* is.' There was a touch of his old bravado in the sweeping statement. 'It seemed too good a chance to miss when you were so near, and the weather doesn't permit flying.'

Roland smiled. 'Something of an ambiguous statement in view of your arrival, isn't it?'

That was passed over as Rex fastened his dull gaze on Matt. 'You must be the doc-in-charge. Canadian, aren't you?'

'Right first time.' Matt offered his hand. 'It's a real pleasure to meet you, Captain Sheridan. I mean that. We earthbound mortals practically light candles at your shrine.'

'Foolish waste of candles,' was the brief comment.

Roland touched his arm, still unable to believe he was really there. 'I find it socially tiring being the famous "Sherry" Sheridan's brother.'

'You want to try being Madame Sherry's husband.' It was curt and bitter in tone.

Thinking of that night with her, and the wine that had been flung in his face as she had sat beside him, Roland asked quietly, 'How is Laura?'

'Don't you read the newspapers?'

293

Matt turned away. 'I'll go fix us all a drink. There might be a medicinal something-or-other for an occasion like this.'

'Here,' called Rex, bringing from his flying-jacket a bottle of brandy. 'I come bearing gifts. There's some chocolate and cigarettes in the cockpit, and a large tin of fancy biscuits. I thought your lads might like them.'

'That's mighty good of you.'

'Don't thank *me*,' came the swift reply. 'Parcels arrive long after chaps are dead, and it'd be bloody stupid to send them back with their personal effects. We're sick of home-made fruit cake, chocolate, tins of cherries, and strawberry jam. Glad to get rid of some of the damned stuff. I'll bring over some woollen socks and long underwear next time. We're using them to clean the engines.'

Giving him a long considering look Matt said, 'Some of the guys at Croix Des Anges would give their souls for any of that.'

'The rightful owners already have,' was the terse reply. 'So your lads are welcome to it. I'll get the squadron to make a low level drop one day soon. If we pack it into boxes it should be all right.'

'It'll be difficult with the Huns so near.'

'We'll bring a few grenades to drop on them first.' He frowned. 'How about that drink, by the way.'

Matt moved off, and Roland took his brother across to the sleeping-platform he occupied out of sight of the patients. Rex threw down his helmet and goggles before sitting on the planks resting across two upturned barrels. His breeches and fur-lined jacket were wet through, but he seemed unconcerned about it as he looked up at Roland.

'So, how are you taking to a life of travel and adventure?'

'The same as any one of us, I should imagine.'

'You should have stayed where you belong. You gave up doctoring for the sake of that place; now you've done the reverse. Anyone could do what you're doing here.'

'You know I couldn't have stayed, anyway. Conscription would have caught up with me eventually.'

Rex nodded. 'I'd forgotten. Everything seems so long ago. Mike says Tessa is making a success of running the estate.'

'Her letters suggest so, and I'm certain she's telling the truth.'

'Are you going to make an honest woman of her when you get back?'

Roland scowled. 'Your choice of phrase is characteristically wild. Tessa is already an honest woman, as far as I know. No, I'm not thinking of marrying her—or anyone—when this is over. There'll be too much to do trying to put the country back on its feet.'

His brother gave a twisted smile. 'Doesn't love fit into your plans?'

Remembering Laura in her dress of shaded-blue chiffon, Roland said, 'Not your kind of love, Rex. It doesn't seem to make you happy, in any case.' After waiting for a response that did not come, he went on, 'You must realise we don't see many newspapers in an isolated spot like this. You'll have to elaborate on your earlier remark.'

The tired lined face was angled toward him. 'My wife is a budding star; the new darling of London. She's an even bigger attraction to the British public than I am. Soon, they won't be asking you if you're "Sherry" Sheridan's brother, but Madame Sherry's brother-in-law.'

'Her success bothers you?' Roland asked, thinking Rex was a fool not to have known his marriage would lead to this.

'Her success? Good lord, no! It's what she's always wanted.'

'So why are you so unhappy?'

Rex got to his feet and practically exploded with anger. 'God Almighty, what a bloody stupid question to ask! Why are we all unhappy? Christ, I would have thought even six months in this filthy senseless business would have stopped you being so typically damned pedantic.' He ran his hand through his hair nervously. 'Don't you long night and day to be back at Tarrant Hall—that's the nearest you seem to get to loving anything? That's how I feel about Laura.'

'So, I should imagine, do most married men about their wives at home. I have to write letters for those who aren't up to it, and their sentiments are about the same as yours, Rex. But they're not going to pieces over it.'

Matt came up with Rex's bottle of brandy and three tin mugs. 'A small tot three times a day, or one mugful once. Take your choice,' he greeted with raised eyebrows.

'Need you ask?' said Rex immediately. 'We might not be here for the second or third tot. Fill 'em up!'

As if to underline his sentiment, the sound of heavy firing rent the morning. The ground shook and trembled, sending showers of earth and dust down on them from the unstable layers above them. They all ducked instinctively, and Matt said, 'Right on time! Some poor bastards are about to go over in five minutes' time. We'll get 'em back in pieces about twelve hours from now.'

Roland was taken aback at how his brother tossed back the large tot in one gulp and held out his mug for a refill. This was the man who had always maintained that drink impaired a pilot's judgment!

'That's strong stuff, Rex,' he warned.

Rex grinned. 'I know; I brought it, remember? Have you any brothers, Doc?' he asked above the din of artillery outside.

'Not that I ever heard of. But my pa was a prospector and got around some before he bought up the ranch. Could be a few somewhere, I guess.'

'Let's drink to them.' Rex swallowed the next tot almost without letting it touch his lips, and took the bottle from Matt to pour again liberally into all three mugs. 'Let's drink to all bastards. We practically have one in our own family, don't we?' he added, looking quizzically at Roland.

'Not that I ever heard of,' he replied tightly, using Matt's words. 'What is the latest news of Chris? Our letters take absolute weeks to reach us here. I suspect Tessa is hiding news of a slight relapse in progress.'

Rex shook his head. 'Not really, from what I can glean. He's grown suspicious of Marion, for some reason. But that could be a good sign, because it means he's feeling more secure and able to cope with things on his own. It upset her, of course.'

'I can't think why,' was his response, the old anger against the girl still within him. 'She surely didn't think . . .'

'I don't know what she thought, but I can guess what she hoped, because I hope for the same thing. If that doesn't come off, they're back where they started . . . and they might as well have let him die instead of hauling him from that blazing sea.'

'Oh Jesus, not another advocate of euthanasia!' exploded Matt. 'Does it run in your family?'

Rex turned to him with a peculiar smile. 'Must do. Our papa leapt off a cliff, you know. Wise man knew when enough was enough!'

Roland could have hit his brother—something he had not

wanted to do for a very long time. Matt's face betrayed an interested perplexity over the history-book of the Sheridan family that Roland had carefully kept closed, and which Rex was now flippantly opening, page by page.

'How do you find the new aircraft?' he asked in a determined attempt to leave the subject of family matters.

'The same as it finds me—bloody marvellous, but outnumbered four to one. You know, of course, that they're calling this whole thing off shortly. It's been a whacking great failure. The Frogs have got a mutiny on their hands, and the Ruskies are planning a revolution. The Austrian army is finished; the Huns are starving.' He began to laugh. 'The only ones not cracking up are us. But the conscripts don't all share our willingness to die, apparently. That's why we've got to sit it out through another winter, while they are bullied into some kind of shape to join us. It'll go on for years yet . . . unless we mutiny, too.' He poured more brandy, then raised his mug. 'Here's to mutinies, God bless 'em. We could all go home and forget this.'

'I was hoping you'd have a word with some of the guys here,' put in Matt pointedly. 'You're something of a hero, as I said before. But if that's all you can come up with, we'd better forget it.'

Rex finished his drink. 'Oh, I can give them the speech I reserve for the schoolboys who arrive at my squadron in nice clean uniforms, still virgins and determined to "play the game chaps". I'm good at that. They go off inspired, and never live long enough to grow disillusioned.' He frowned. 'I don't know, of course, whether any of them realises what a bloody fraud and liar I am as he slowly burns away. Still, I should think he'd more than likely be concentrating more on the need for a bucket of water, shouldn't you?'

'Yeah, I suppose so,' said Matt slowly.

Roland was feeling more and more upset at the way Rex was behaving, and at the amount he was drinking. He felt helpless to do anything. Rex had always been so assured and independent. The qualities were still there, but in dangerous categories, he felt.

'If you had a piano, I could give your lads a tune or two. It's my guess they've had as many stirring speeches as they can take,' Rex was saying, suddenly serious. 'After what they've been through these past two years, I'd feel presumptuous playing the hero, anyway.'

'One of the lads has a mouth-organ,' drawled Matt. 'That any use to you?'

'I'll say.' There was enthusiasm in Rex's voice now, and he put the mug aside. 'Is it all right to get them going a bit?'

'Sure. Hell, just the sight of the great "Sherry" Sheridan conducting a sing-song will get their spirits up.'

'Save the compliments until you've heard me,' put in Rex, walking out into the open part of the cellar which formed the general 'ward'. 'I hope they sing loudly enough to cover my mistakes.'

Roland knew it was a scene he would never forget. A ruined cellar on a rainy October morning, gunfire shaking the foundations and ceiling, men with terrible wounds lying on blankets on the floor, and Rex in his old oil-stained uniform standing with one foot up on a box while he produced magic from a tiny silver-coloured instrument. He also produced personal magic as the old personality shone through the wreck he had become, and brought the response his warmth and gaiety had always coaxed from people. As he changed from the sweet haunting melodies that had lit lights in eyes dulled by pain, to lively music-hall tunes that had fingers and feet moving in rhythm beneath the blankets, Roland found himself tremendously moved.

The sadness of all that had happened since that summer of 1914 washed over him to constrict his throat and blur his vision. How would it all end? The possibilities ran through his mind in terrible procession, but one thing he knew for certain. It would never be the same again. Why had they been so careless of such bounty? Why had they not cherished it, hugged it to themselves with delight, made much more of it? Why had they imagined it would go on forever?

The owner of the mouth-organ took over, and Rex led them all, with his pleasant tenor voice, in songs that went from the vulgar to the degenerate, then to the unashamedly patriotic. By that time, the cellar and its many entrances were crowded by the men who were standing-down from the forward trenches for a few hours, and the swell of voices must have reached the German lines. That was when Roland realised his brother had spoken the truth. This war could be won by Christmas with enough men like this, inspired by men like him.

But the moment was broken when the musician began on Laura's now-popular song *Chéri, Chéri*, and a hundred voices roared out the chorus. Rex turned away, the visit over, and Roland saw the pain on his brother's face once more. Deep within his soul he knew it was women who had ruined both Rex and Chris.

A cheer went up as Rex fetched his goggles and helmet, and he gave an abstracted wave before shaking Matt by the hand prior to leaving. Then, Roland walked with him to the steps leading up to ground level where the Nieuport stood waiting.

'I'll need some help getting away, and several chaps to take the supplies I brought,' Rex told him in a return to the clipped tones he was using on arrival.

But a voice floated up to them from one of the patients. 'How many have you got now, sir?'

Turning on the steps, Rex said, 'Forty-nine . . . but I'll get the half-century on the way back, just for you, son.'

Another cheer rose up as they walked up into the open again and bent their heads against the beating rain. Roland felt even more deeply upset. Rex was just twenty-two, yet he was calling youngsters 'son' like an old man. They spent a moment or two looking over the machine while two soldiers took off the packages Rex had brought with him. Then they shook hands in farewell.

'I'll come again, if you stay here long enough,' said Rex. 'It was good to see you . . . you don't know how good.'

'Yes, I do,' he replied warmly, 'because I felt the same way. It was a marvellous surprise. I feel awfully cut off, sometimes, don't you? If you get any further news of Chris, let me know. We lose a lot of mail because our supply-columns keep getting strafed.'

A ghost of Rex's old grin appeared, as he climbed into the cockpit. 'I'll see what I can do about that situation.' Roland felt so inadequate, all of a sudden. The moment demanded wisdom, an unforgettable remark, a word of unbreakable brotherhood. All he said was, 'Take care!'

Rex put up his thumb to the soldiers who had volunteered to swing his propeller, then switched the engine to roaring life before leaning over the side to yell above the noise, 'Don't ever change. We'll need men like you to restore our sanity when this is all over.'

Then he was off, up into the leaden sky to vanish into the cloud. But, when Roland had reached the top of the steps where Matt and a crowd of troops had been watching the take-off, the Nieuport suddenly appeared again only a few feet from the ground above the position of the German trenches, racing across the area, guns blazing at those below and drawing a hail of fire from them in return. Then it finally vanished into the cloud, heading for Saint-Brioche.

Matt still stared at the spot where cloud had swallowed the aircraft. 'There goes a hell of a good guy who is as near to breaking his mind as anyone I've ever met.'

Roland walked slowly back down the steps into the cellar without saying anything. He knew it was true. Rex had asked him not to change, but would he be the third Sheridan with a touch of madness by the time they all went back?

15

THE VISIT to Roland affected Rex more than he had suspected it would. His brain was too tired, and muddled by brandy to form an analysis, but it was something to do with the youth-now-flown symbolism that surrounded Roland, the echoes of Tarrant Hall and the glorious sunshine peacefulness of Dorest, the painful dragging back to reality from the present nightmare, and the sadness of seeing a man like his brother, once so renowned a horseman, so beloved and respected a squire, so wholeheartedly a scion of England and Empire, in ill-fitting rough uniform, performing the menial medical tasks in a ruin that was under constant fire.

Rex acknowledged that there were thousands of men in similar conditions, but the difference in his brother's case was that they had appeared not to have changed him. Certainly, he had looked tired, but his blond hair had gleamed with cleanliness, his good-looking face had still expressed pride and confidence, his athletic frame made a mockery of the shapeless serge, and his bearing and manner proclaimed him the born gentleman. Roland *shone* through the mud and squalor. Ridiculous though it seemed, he had made Rex feel a sham. Worse, he had brought a longing to turn back the clock and start again at that summer of 1914. Yet, as he circled the airfield at Saint-Brioche, peering down at the waterlogged grass, he knew in his heart he would never obey Laura's advice to walk away from her on that first day, no matter how many times he might relive the moment.

Taxiing up to the sheds he was angered by the absence of any mechanic or maintenance staff. Although the weather was too bad for combat flying, they knew he had gone out and should have been waiting for his return. Switching off, he climbed from the cockpit and dropped heavily to the spongy ground that squelched around his boots, before striding toward the sheds where he guessed the men would be sitting around chatting.

The door crashed back beneath his hand, and eight startled faces turned his way.

'Just what the hell do you think this place is—a games centre for malingering numbskulls?' he roared. 'Which of you is supposed to be on duty?'

All eight jumped smartly to their feet, but only one found the courage to speak. 'We was standing-by, sir. But seeing as how the weather had grounded the squadron we . . .'

'It didn't ground me, and you bloody well knew it,' Rex continued in the same volume and tone. 'I have just circled the airfield, come in to land, and taxied right up to this shed without disturbing your intense concentration on a card-game. It could be Oswald Boelke standing here, or his young protégé, Von Richthofen. It could be an entire squadron of Huns!' He thumped his fist on the doorjamb. 'When you are on duty you watch that field every minute of every hour, do you understand? Whether the squadron is grounded, or not. On a day like this, enterprising men might decide to make a low-level bombing-raid to destroy machines that they know will be on the ground. The only good thing that would conceivably result from that would be that you would all be blown sky-high with the aircraft.' He turned to go. 'Some of you get my Nieuport in; the rest can take cloths and buckets out to mop up some of those puddles!'

Ignoring their expressions of total disbelief of his seriousness in giving such an order, he left the building and made his way to the squadron-office, filled with the futility of giving orders of any kind. They seemed to make no difference to the progress of the war. Inside the damp chilly room he threw down gauntlets and goggles as he pulled off the leather helmet with a weary hand. Damn Roland for making him think of England!

He poured a drink and downed it defiantly as he slumped into the wooden armchair, shivering in clothes that had been twice saturated in an open cockpit. The fur collar of his flying-jacket stuck wetly to his neck, his famous 'scarf' hung dripping across his shoulders, and the legs of his breeches had let rain through to the long woollen underwear they all wore for warmth, and thence through to his skin. It did not seem to matter whether he was wet or dry. Nothing seemed to matter any more.

On his desk he saw there was a letter addressed in Marion's handwriting, and another from Jake, still at the engineering factory in which Rex had once intended starting his career in aeroplane design. He opened that one and scanned through the two short pages. Physical disability kept Jake from conscription. Rex thanked God some had escaped.

Pouring another drink, he reached for Marion's letter resignedly. After the meeting with Roland he felt too close to his past brotherhood to hear about Chris. But he must read it in case there was something of importance . . . and he had promised Roland to pass on any news. The letter did not concern Chris.

Please believe that I thought long and seriously about this before writing to you, Rex. Daddy says you have a right to know; Tessa believes you should be kept in ignorance. But I have the pain of personal experience to sway my judgment, and your unfaltering friendship deserves mine now.

His heartbeat thumped agonisingly as he absorbed the opening lines and sensed that he was about to die slowly as he read on. But Laura's betrayal did not follow the course he had imagined; could ever have imagined. His glance flicked back and forth over the lines as he scanned them and took in the essence of what they told him.

. . . but she left it far too late . . . some terrible old woman in a back street . . . must have been total agony and she could have bled to death . . . pure chance that Tessa was in London and called to see her . . . friendly with one of the Sisters at Tarrant Hall . . . down to Dorset in one of those ambulances . . . all very discreet, for both your sakes . . . truly think Daddy saved her life . . . still desperately ill and her mental state is delaying recovery . . . you get compassionate leave . . . some difficulty hiding the truth if medical evidence

is needed . . . know you have more than enough to worry you . . . faced the truth about Chris, and feel you would want to do the same . . . very dear friend, Rex . . . I hope to God I've done the right thing.

They were putting the Nieuport away as he opened the door and began crossing the rain-swept area leading to the sheds. He knew nothing of his curt orders or their astonished questioning of them. He knew nothing of the propeller being swung, the preliminary run across the field in visibility fast deteriorating, or the take-off over the familiar line of trees. He knew nothing of the ghostly sensation of flying through a grey downpour that saturated him even further and beat into eyes unprotected by goggles that were useless in such rain.

He *was* dying slowly. Since that night three-and-a-half months ago, he had tortured himself with the memory of his failure in Laura's bed, and the forced inability to return to her to wipe out that humiliation with renewed virility. Yet, those five days in England had resulted in the indisputable proof of his manhood. Even as he had failed her, she had carried his seed within her. His son, perhaps a replica of the lusty gorgeous boy Chris had produced; or a sweet miniature of her mother, with red-gold hair and tiny petal hands. He had sired a child, and she had destroyed it. Carelessly, in a filthy room in some back street, she had given her beautiful body into the hands of a hag with a kitchen-knife and a bucket of lime in order to rid herself of the child of their love. The thought broke his mind.

He did not know how much time had elapsed when the cloud began to thin and watery sunshine dazzled him with white brightness. Breaking out into clear skies, he looked over the edge of the cockpit at the glittering ribbon of water below. Still on course! If he followed that river it would take him to the coast.

But he was so busy studying the river he forgot that others hunted in those same skies, and the familiar death-rattle of bullets ripping through fabric and wood was there behind him without warning. In the act of turning to look over his shoulder, an excruciating sensation of burning pain raced through his right arm and he folded forward instinctively. The movement saved his life. The next burst of fire travelled a mere inch over his head to tear into the struts supporting the upper wing, and splinter them badly.

Gasping with agony and conscious of a warm stickiness gather-

303

ing in his sleeve, Rex flung the Nieuport into a steep turn as a Fokker painted a defiant yellow flashed past unprepared for his manoeuvre. Trying to hold the control-handle with fast-numbing fingers, Rex fired several rounds into the side of the enemy machine as it tried to correct its over-shoot and turn on a sixpence. The pilot jerked and fell back, face covered in blood; the machine humped over into a spin, gathering more and more speed as it plunged to the fields below. The half-century had been notched-up.

But the death-rattle came from behind again, and Rex came out of his shock-suspense to take in the scene around him in the split second before he was hit again in the same arm, lower down and just as agonisingly. Above the burning fire of his wounds, he realised what he had done. His aircraft had emerged from beneath cloud right into the centre of an entire formation of enemy machines.

Instinct and experience took over from a mind hazed by pain, and he was only half aware of pulling back into a climb that put a terrible strain on the splintered wing-struts. But they were ready for such a move, and he was followed upward by three of the Fokkers while the remainder broke formation and began circling a short distance off to watch the certain end of 'Sherry' Sheridan, at last.

But his opponents were unaware that the R.F.C.'s most popular ace was ruled by even more than his usual conviction that Giles Otterbourne had died in his place to take him off Death's list. Hardly able to steer his machine with his shattered right arm, Rex had to manoeuvre and fire his guns with the left, which restricted his fighting-power. Pain and determination made up the balance, however. Swinging about the sky in a giddy succession of turns and dives, he evaded the worst of the deadly hail from his three adversaries, and then performed one of his celebrated climbing attacks to riddle the belly of one with bullets that punctured the oil-tank and caused a fiery explosion that broke the machine in two. Flying safely through the burning pieces he levelled out behind one of the other two and poured round after round into its tail, despite the desperate swinging evasive action of its pilot.

But blood was running from his arm now to form a pool by his feet, and there was no feeling left in it whatever. This meant he was limited in firing-ability when movement demanded use of the control-handle. Despite the damage he had inflicted on the aircraft ahead, it continued to fly. With its partner coming up fast behind him Rex discovered his ammunition-drum was empty, most of it having been used to fire at the trenches near Croix Des Anges. Unable to change drums in a sandwich as he was, and with one arm out of action, he realised it was an extremely dangerous situation. Remedying it by going into an immediate steep dive that was so suicidal the man behind had never envisaged such a move, Rex achieved the surprise he had intended. But there was a bonus. The long burst of fire intended for the Nieuport now brought down the crippled Fokker ahead, and the German zoomed furiously past the smoking wreckage of his comrade's machine as it began to spiral out of control.

Swooning from loss of blood and the suddenness of his dive, Rex gazed blearily at the ground that was coming up at him fast. But the rush of icy air pulled him back from a complete faint in time to drag on the control-handle and level out not more than a hundred feet from the ground.

The hornets were buzzing in vengeance now. Totally out-numbered though he was, Rex had already accounted for two of their number, and they were out for the kill. There were forty-nine more of their comrades to avenge where this man was concerned, and they were determined he would fight no more. Glancing up Rex saw the remains of the formation screaming down on him from every direction and knew that, collectively, they would stop him from reaching the coast. No one must be allowed to do that.

Dropping to fifty feet, he raced along the course of the river like a fox making a desperate bid to escape the howling pack of hounds out to tear him apart. But, also like the fox, he knew a sly trick or two and cast a quick look over his shoulder at the dark shapes homing in on him. True to national form, they were coming up behind him in orderly fashion in the absolute confidence of having him caught in a trap. They might well succeed, because their superior machines would overhaul his within a very few minutes. His life depended on their overlooking the fact that they were dealing with someone who had flown over northern France for the best part of two years now, and knew the terrain well. A few miles ahead a canal branched from the river, cutting through woodland. That was where the fox would go to earth!

It was touch and go whether he would reach the spot before

they overhauled him, and Rex dropped even lower in an attempt to gain on them and possibly scare off some of the more timid amongst his pursuers, whose nerves would not withstand the sudden hazards of bridges or clumps of tall trees when flying with their wheels trailing the grass. One or two certainly broke formation and veered off in panic climbs, but they were gaining on him enough now to bring the Nieuport within range of their guns. Several bursts hit his tail and tore the fabric badly. The machine began to waver and wobble just when he needed the greatest steadiness for what he proposed doing. His mouth tightened, and he tried to ignore the pool of spreading blood that was making his feet slip on the controls.

More gunfire; an ominous crack from the area of the tail. A frantic glance to the rear showed the leading Fokkers to be no more than yards behind him. Then he spotted the dark spread of the trees and knew the canal was almost upon him. It was there he would take the greatest chance of his short life. With no hope of using his own guns, he had to make a right turn that would take him right across the path of the oncoming enemy.

Then it was there, just ahead, and there was no longer any judgment left in him. Weak and giddy, his breeches and boots now covered in blood, too, it was the skill of the born flier that took him in a sudden right turn, dropping to a dangerous fifteen feet to pass beneath the oncoming enemies and straight into the narrow cutting through the trees that was the mere width of the canal, plus a few feet on either side. Once there, with the propeller making feather patterns on the cold steely-grey water, and dense pines almost touching each wing-tip, Rex knew he had to keep straight and true to the end of that watery avenue, or die.

His ruse worked. Unprepared for such a move, the Fokkers had flown on. It would take them a few minutes to work out what he had done, and search for the canal. To do that they would have to climb, because he was flying below tree level, and climbing would lengthen the gap between them. The wobble of his machine was worsening. He was finding it more and more difficult to maintain height and steadiness. The canal looked menacing below his feet; the trees seemed to be crowding in on him. But all he could think of was an old woman with a kitchen-knife and a bucket of lime, and there was wetness on his cheeks as his anguished inner-self conquered the weakness of mind and body to keep him going.

The German pilots found him and renewed their pursuit far too late. The old fox had led them to their own destruction in their heedless determination to bring about his. Where the canal burst from the trees, the French held a strongly-fortified castle, with a line of trenches equipped with ancient but effective heavy artillery.

Beyond rational thought Rex flew on across these lines at a height that had the French gunners ducking their heads. But they recognised Fokkers when they saw them, and the afternoon broke apart as the big guns opened on easy targets. Suddenly, the sky was full of floating black gun-smoke, wheeling aircraft, and flaming plunging wreckage. Just below his wheels Rex was vaguely conscious of upturned faces, arms waving, and the sound of cheering. But then, a youngster with a face of a near-child, pulled a trigger in his excitement, and machine-gun bullets smacked into the underside of the Nieuport.

Rex let out a cry of agony as his upper thigh seemed to split open, and the sky around him darkened to night. The impact as his machine hit the ground threw him forward hard, and he knew no more until tremendous heat brought him to semi-consciousness. Through blurred eyes he saw the orange fire of Hell surrounding him in reality now. The roar and crackle of it blotted out any other sound. Wood and fabric were eaten quickly by the ravenous licking flames as he lay helpless to move. Tears were fresh on his cheeks as he thought of her and faced the unbelievable end of something that had lasted so short a time, yet had ruled his life completely.

If I ever crash and get trapped in a burning cockpit, Mike, don't rush over and drag me out.

But they did and, at the first tug, Rex lapsed into unconsciousness so total he knew nothing more until he came to in a French hospital. They adopted 'Sherry' Sheridan as their own hero then, and he was told he was to be awarded the Croix de Guerre for his action that day. No one, at any time, asked what he had been doing so far from his squadron base and heading for England.

They flew him back to England as a passenger in a two-seater. The authorities, in their wisdom, decided a home-posting would be a timely move for their double hero. They did not share Captain Sheridan's confidence in Giles Otterbourne's substitution, and felt luck had run his way too long for prudence.

At such a depressing stage in the war—the Somme offensive had finally ground to a halt as an acknowledged failure—general morale could not afford to be dealt the blow of losing a man who had continually laughed in the face of the enemy and shown them they were completely vulnerable. In other words 'Sherry' Sheridan, and all he stood for, was indispensable in that bleak winter of 1916–17. The inspiration and pride he instilled could be put to better use touring cities and public schools on lecture tours, then training the recruits he had drummed up, than in leading 'Sheridan's Skuas' on further missions that endangered his life. England had more than enough dead heroes. A live one was desperately needed, at that moment.

In addition, the bizarre escapade that had reached the pages of the world's newspapers and earned him such a distinguished French decoration, had happened at the very time when public feeling at home was growing ugly over the horrendous loss of life over the Somme, with no victory to show for it. To put before the people of Britain a young man of considerable physical attraction, who symbolised courage, steadfastness, and patriotism even at the bleakest hour—and one who was wounded in romantic and respectable places—was an opportunity too good to be missed. On that day, his action had led to the destruction of eleven enemy aircraft—two of which he had claimed personally to take his score past the coveted fifty. Putting such a man on public show would persuade every mother her son, every widow her husband, every girl her sweetheart, had been as heroic and steadfast when he had laid down his life for his King and country on the battlefield of the Somme.

So it was, in the middle of November, Rex arrived at the airfield at Brooklands with his arm firmly held in plaster and still limping from the thigh wound, to find a battery of cameras and newsmen with notebooks to take down his every word and grossly exaggerate it in print. The senior R.F.C. and military officials who greeted him made him pose for photographs in and out of the cockpit, then ushered him into an office so that he could answer questions fired at him by the eager newsmen, amongst whom were now quite a sprinkling of emancipated, aggressive, bright-eyed young women who were filling vacancies left by young men conscripted for the Front.

Rex did his best to concentrate on what they were saying, but his answers were mainly based on what they, themselves, had written in previous editions, because he had little recollection of what he had done that day. All that had been in his mind, at the time, had been a crazed determination to fly until he reached Longbarrow Hill. The feeling was still in him now—though not as full of the strange insanity that it had been then—and he only schooled himself to do as his superiors demanded because they had promised an official car to drive him direct to Tarrant Hall if he was a good boy and played the hero for them. There was the added carrot of a month's leave before starting a tour of the country to tell propaganda lies and line up recruits.

So he played the hero. He told lies. He smiled and waved. He allowed them to sign his plaster-cast with their names and silly slogans. He wore his 'scarf', winked broadly, and suggested there was no greater proof of virility and manhood than to go to glorious war, all in front of Pathé newsreel cameras. But all through it his yearning grew greater and greater until he feared his performance would fall apart. Perhaps it was apparent to others, for a grey-haired colonel began to wind up proceedings, telling the pressmen they would be given a full itinerary of Captain Sheridan's tour, and asking that he now be accorded peace and privacy to visit his sick wife and convalesce at his country home, where he would be given further treatment for his wounds.

Then they began to leave the building for the waiting car. But Rex was nearing the door when a young woman carrying a camera rushed from the group to stand in his path, breathing hard, her pretty face flushed with emotion.

'How long are you going to go on killing?' she cried in a well-bred voice. 'How many lies are you prepared to tell? The world is deluded by men like you who glorify war. You're no hero—just a mass murderer!' She took a deep breath to steady her passion. 'I challenge you to look me in the eye and deny that it's a mortal sin to take a man's life . . . and another to go out urging boys who are mere children to do the same.'

Her provocative manner, her vivid lively face, her absurd inde-pendent spirit reminded him so strongly of Laura the last rem-nants of his poise almost vanished. But he had still not reached the car, and they were all watching his reactions. There was only one way of dealing with her. Pulling her to him with his uninjured arm, he kissed her very soundly on the lips before murmuring,

'Unite the women of Germany, my dear, and we'll all willingly stay at home.'

Then he went out to the car, leaving her with colour even further heightened and a bemused expression as she watched his departure with as much admiration as her colleagues.

It was a long journey down to Tarrant Royal, and the start was slowed by a huge crowd that had gathered outside Brooklands and stretched out to line the road leading from it to cheer and wave. The military propaganda department had done its job well!

The girl-reporter who had resembled Laura had rekindled the flame within him, and Rex began to burn with an echo of the madness that had governed his actions that day over France. News had reached him through official sources that his wife was recovering from her illness and was no longer in a critical condition. Through the same channels, a message had been sent to Laura telling her of his intended arrival that day. But, as he sat in the back of that car, it was as if he had just received Marion's letter. As the miles passed he began dying slowly all over again. The girl at Brooklands had been full of health and verve, so like the one who held his immortal soul in her hands, and had been prepared to destroy it along with the child he had given her by submitting to a crude, disgusting abortion that had almost destroyed her, also. How was he to face her now?

It grew dark long before they reached Dorset, and he was reminded of the journeys on that commandeered motor cycle that he had made during the summer to be with Laura because she could not—or would not—be with him. He had been so ardent, so eager. Small wonder passion had made a fool of caution on one of those nights. He had told Roland confidently that there would be no child-of-the-war, but he had made Chris's mistake, even with experience to guide him. Yet his young brother's unwanted lust-bastard had been brought lovingly into the world and given his rightful name. The legitimate child of his own true-love passion had been destroyed before he had known and wanted it with pride. Did she think so little of him?

By the time the car was travelling the lanes of Tarrant Royal he was practically in a fever. When it turned into the steep approach to his home he was deeply afraid, as he had never been before. Giles Otterbourne might have died physically for him, but it was still possible for his spirit to be extinguished. He would know the moment he faced her.

But first, there was old Minks, more stooped and even greyer, to give him a silent emotional greeting. And Priddy, who laughed and cried at the same time as she kissed him, scolding him for taking such risks and getting himself nearly killed.

Then Tessa was there, looking as fresh and glowingly healthy as ever to say, 'Welcome home, Rex. Thank God you're safe.' Giving a grave smile she added, 'As you don't shake hands with girls, I suppose you want a kiss.'

It was soft and sisterly, on his cheek not his mouth. He realised why when she whispered in his ear, 'She's up in your old room, and looks every bit as terrified as you do.'

He left them there forgotten as he walked slowly to the foot of the staircase previously used by the servants, and glanced up the tightly curving flight to the landing that would lead him to the room that had witnessed his childhood, his tumbling early youth, his happy reckless teens, and the carefree twentieth year in which he had so cavalierly used the war as a means to continue his passion for flying. How could he have known then what it would come to mean? A mass murderer? He had shot down fifty-one aircraft containing men. Some had died; some had not. But, yes, he was a mass murderer, he supposed. Was that how Laura saw him? Was that what had persuaded her he would not care about the loss of another—perhaps two?

He started up the stairs, and it seemed comparable with climbing Everest. At the top lay the unknown, the hazardous. Maybe he would never descend again. Maybe his life would end up there. The door to his room lay at the end of a corridor. A piece of thin wood now closed off the rest of the house; beyond it lay the familiar rooms in the guise of hospital wards. It all added to his sense of disorientation. At the door he hesitated for a moment, his heart thudding so strongly against his ribs it made him feel faint. Then he turned the handle and went in.

She was standing by the bed as if she had been waiting there for his footfall. The soft amber wool dress glowed with the light from the fire as it clung to her thin frame, her beautiful hair now hung to her shoulders in red-gold waves that gave her a feminine frailty her cheeky short curls had previously denied, and her face, even paler and more pointed, seemed dominated by eyes that had lost all wickedness to desperation as they gazed at him across the width of the room.

He found it impossible to move, to say anything. All that had ever happened between them hung suspended on that moment as they searched each other for a sign, for a foothold on a bridge that would link them, a bastion that would sustain their weakness. Yet, as he stood there locked in hesitancy between destruction or salvation, he knew he was as helplessly caught by her as ever—even now with this terrible deed like a barrier between them. But he remained unable to break his own silence or stillness. Instead, he broke her.

'*Don't!*' she whispered eventually in a kind of moan. 'Please don't look at me like that.' Taking a step toward him, then one or two more, she stopped and began to cry silently as she looked up into his face. 'Say . . . say you'll forgive me, or I'll *die.*'

The silence that followed was broken only by the spitting of a log on the fire. He was as diminished by her humiliation as he had been by his own on the last night they had been together.

'Why?' he asked in a cracked voice. 'Why, Laura? You could have killed us all.'

In reply, her hands went up to cover her face and her shoulders shook.

'I suppose it was the damn theatre. Well, you've destroyed your hopes with your own hand,' he said, hating himself with every word he uttered. 'Your career is over and finished with.'

Still she stood a few feet from him, weak with sobs and the emaciation of illness. The fire inside him was reaching explosion point as he went on.

'I'm in England for nine months. You'll go with me everywhere I go, is that understood? You'll keep house and cook. You'll be at my side at lectures, and you'll be charming to the poor bastards of boys who'll believe all I say. You'll forget Madame Sherry and be plain Laura Sheridan. You'll be my devoted wife, and we'll have a proper bloody marriage. You'll . . . oh, dear God in heaven!' He broke down, took two steps toward her and held her against him with his sound left arm. 'Don't cry like that, my darling . . . it tears me apart,' he murmured through his own gathering tears. 'Don't you know that if you had been lost, then so would I? Life *is* you. I thought I had shown you that.'

Every season seemed to bring its own delights. October had been a glory of coloured leaves, and Chris had concentrated on them rather than those around him. Summer had terminated in a visual symphony of yellow, russet and red, with mornings of glittering frosts, afternoons of wreathing mists to add to the mysterious enchantment of that garden he could not yet enter, and short periods of clear-skyed brilliance which highlighted the riot of scarlet berries, rich gleaming horse-chestnuts, and great shaggy chrysanthemums that showed that even the death of a year could be beautiful.

There was nothing beautiful about the death of men. All too often, those around him in the ward would be wheeled out with the sheet over their face during the night hours. Sometimes he saw them go out, yet they were back there in the morning, so he was never sure which was a dream and which reality. But there were others during the daytime, when he was definitely awake, who began screaming or sobbing and would not stop. One had jumped right through the closed windows and been carried back foaming at the mouth, whimpering, and covered in blood. Another had suddenly seized a nurse around the neck, accusing her of killing his brother. It had taken several white-coated orderlies to free her. Chris never knew what became of those patients. They were taken away and never came back. It always worried and upset him so much he began pretending there was no one else with him in that long ward, and concentrated on the garnering squirrels who buried nuts willy-nilly and ate their fill of the bounty of berries until their furry bibs were stained red with the juice.

His own condition had greatly improved. Although his leg was still trapped in the weighted apparatus, its repair having been set back by his fall from the bed, his torso was now free of the tight strapping and thick covering of foul-smelling jelly designed to ease the agony of the burns. His skin was still a vivid pink and covered in crinkles, but the pain it gave him now compared with earlier months was so little it could hardly be called pain. The deep scar across his stomach played him up badly, sometimes, and he was still only allowed certain things to eat because they said his tubes inside were still mangled up. He tried not to think of that whenever he swallowed anything, but sometimes could not escape visions of chicken soup, steamed fish, and jelly all seeking a tortuous route through blood and pulp. He had seen what men's stomachs looked like when they were open. Where he had seen it was not clear, but he knew he had. It was a sight no one could forget, once seen.

They had to do more to him now, so his periods of peace and solitude became more and more valued. But he hated what they did, stripping back the bedclothes to expose his body to all eyes, washing him, soothing ointment over his skin, bending and stretching his limbs in gentle exercise, massaging his shoulders and thighs—all to the accompaniment of smiles, eyes brimful of delight, and girlish references to the number of hearts he would break once they got him back on his feet. On two occasions he had suffered intense humiliation when the massage of his thighs had brought an uncontrollable response for them all to see. They had appeared to think nothing of it; just laughed, called him a saucy boy, and carried on with what they were doing. But he had retired into silence for the rest of the day each time, and thanked God it had not happened in front of Marion.

She took part in the washing and massage ritual sometimes as part of the general duties she had adopted at his suggestion, and he hated them even more on those days, finding himself unable to meet her gaze. He missed her very much and deeply regretted his outburst that had sent her away that day. He hoped constantly that she would leave what she was doing in other parts of the ward and come to talk to him as she had done before. But she never did, except when she had been told to do so, and then he was too shy to say any more than was necessary to her.

But he had other forms of comfort and companionship now. One afternoon he had taken up a leather-bound book that the man called Rex had brought on his very first visit, and a new world had opened up within its covers. He found he could read French with total ease, and the lyrical aesthetic beauty of the love verses within had filled him with excitement so intense it had set him aching for some outlet for what he felt. He had found it in the most stimulating yet guilty way—an obsession with the girl he could not forget. It was she who had awoken his sexual feelings so dramatically on the day of that concert, and she who then became the unknown object of passion in all the poems he read. Now, he knew the verses by heart and lay reciting them to himself in the darkness before he went to sleep, until one night he realised he was quoting poems that were not even in the book. They came and went in his mind, giving him tremendous pleasure when they materialised and a sense of loss when they went again.

Yet it was not long before he sensed there was a discordant note in his flights of fancy. For several days he was disconsolate, until there floated into his mind an ode to passion in an entirely different language. Immediately, a memory of Laura Sheridan in a white draped garment, wreath around her short flaming curls, matched up with the words, and a whole flood of Greek poetry then rushed in from the past to be greeted with aching gladness by his starved spirits. From then on, she became the goddess of temptation, of love and eroticism, of inspiration, of male worship, according to the meaning of the ancient ode that filled his mind and soul at the time.

Soon, he began writing verse himself, painstakingly translating it into Greek if the sentiments allowed it, or using French if the words and similes were too modern for the classic language. His sketching-block came into full use, either as pages onto which his verse was scribbled or for drawings that were as contrasted to what he could see from his window as anything could be. Temples, barren landscapes, strange villages, and warriors with ancient weapons and splendid physiques rioted over the pages. There was always a goddess featuring somewhere in them. But, although he knew the goddess was Laura, he could never put a face on the figure. His memory of that afternoon at the end of June was vivid in every respect. Except that, when he came to draw that exciting pointed face that had promised every man present anything he had ever wanted, the image always blurred and somehow became superimposed by Marion's features—or those of the other nurses who tended him. Sometimes, he would grow so frustrated tears would come unbidden, bringing with them a sense of desolation so great the day would blacken for a while. It was during those black periods that all the old fears would return, together with his sense of being nobody from nowhere—a prisoner in some strange limbo where he was being punished for something he could not remember doing.

Then, one afternoon toward the end of November, Marion walked deliberately down the length of the ward toward him, and smiled in her old way as she approached. He brightened up no end.

'Feel ready for a surprise?' she asked gaily.

'It depends,' was his cautious reply. 'Why does everybody use the word, assuming a happy context to it? Surprises can be exceedingly painful and unpleasant. I don't want one of those.'

Her smile grew warmer. 'Trust you to analyse everything. Tell me what would be a painful and unpleasant one.'

'A needle in the arm, a spoonful of cascara, or even Matron with an extra helping of that frightful tapioca pudding.'

She laughed, and her eyes twinkled at him in a way that pleased him. He liked her very much, really, and it was nice to be the centre of her attention again, without having to ask to be.

'What about a happy surprise?'

'To be told I could go,' he replied instantly.

'Where would you go, Chris?' It was quiet and strangely wistful.

That question spoilt everything, so he looked out of the window, ignoring her.

'Your brother and his wife are here to see you.'

Still he looked from the window, but excitement raced through him so fast he felt almost sick with it. 'Rex?' he asked, afraid there might be some mistake.

'Of course. Roland doesn't have a wife.'

He risked facing her. 'I thought he was back in France.'

'He was. But he was badly wounded in an encounter with a large number of enemy aircraft, and they brought him home for a rest. The French have given him a medal for what he did. He's now one of the most decorated pilots in the R.F.C.'

'She'll be pleased about that,' he said, burning with jealousy while knowing Rex would have done it all for her.

'Laura? Yes, I suppose so.'

It was said in such an odd tone, he felt he had to confront her. 'If you had a husband who was a hero, wouldn't you be pleased?'

She walked away without a word, and he stared after her in surprise. But it did not last long. He was more concerned with straightening the sheets and patting his unruly hair into some kind of order before she came back with his visitors.

In the first seconds he was incredibly disappointed, for they seemed like two strangers. The man in uniform had his arm in a sling and looked like an ageing nonentity as he limped down the ward. The girl with him was much thinner than he remembered, and hung on her husband's arm as if for support. When they reached his bed, however, he saw the row of coloured ribbons on the new khaki tunic, the lines of experience and pain on a face still young, and the warmth of a smile that could only be for someone dear to him. And in those green eyes was an enigmatic happiness that was an echo of the gaiety of the youngster who had been winking in the photograph he had been shown.

Then Chris realised that Laura Sheridan was even more beautiful than he remembered from four months ago, and that was why he had been unable to draw her face. Her hair was now longer and put back into a riot of curls and waves that left the narrow lines of her face beautifully outlined and enhanced her eyes further. The wicked promise in them had now softened into a glow of adoration when they were turned to her husband. Chris was immediately reminded of the cameo of this pair, she on the piano singing down into his rapt upturned face as they had forgotten the terrace and all those sitting around it. It did not lessen Chris's obsession that she indisputedly belonged to another man, neither did it lessen his feeling of guilt.

'You look absolutely splendid,' said Rex by way of greeting. 'Progressing by leaps and bounds, by the look of things.' He gripped Chris's shoulder. 'Keep it up, old lad, and you'll be back at home before I go back to France.'

'Oh Rex, that's months away, yet,' put in Marion quickly. 'Don't think about going back.'

'Hallo, Chris,' said Laura with soft gentleness. 'I'm sorry I couldn't get back here with another concert, as I promised. But I've often thought about you, and Marion told me of your progress each time she came home on her day off.'

Chris did not understand that. 'Do you both live in the same house?'

'Er . . . no.' Laura looked at her husband quickly.

'Since I got back from France we've both been at Tarrant Hall,' Rex explained. 'Marion's house is not far from there.'

'That's quite a coincidence.'

'Yes, isn't it? A happy one, in this instance, because it meant we have had progressive news of you.'

His brother said it very smoothly, but Chris felt they all had some kind of secret between them. He had had that feeling before where these three were concerned.

'Why haven't you ever spoken of that?' he asked Marion sharply.

She seemed unruffled. 'For a long time now you haven't wanted to talk to me. I probably would have told you a lot of things, if you'd been interested.'

It checkmated him very effectively, so he said, 'I've been very busy.'

'Reading and drawing,' Marion explained to the visitors.

'That book you gave me is splendid,' he told Rex. 'I don't think I really thanked you for it on the day you brought it.'

The warm smile broke out again making the face momentarily as young as it really was. 'I think we were both a bit scared of each other that first day, Chris. But I'm glad you like the poems. As I said at the time, they're what you call aesthetic, and I call pretty damn rude.'

Chris grinned. He could not help it. 'I'm most awfully glad you came today. I was feeling a bit lonely.'

'You don't have to be lonely,' put in Marion. 'You isolate yourself of your own free will.'

'Haven't you got duties to do?' he retaliated quickly.

'Yes, but I asked her to join us,' said Rex. 'Laura and I regard Marion as our friend—and so should you, young Chris. She's been very kind to you.'

'It's her job. She's a nurse.'

'So are the others. Have they done what Marion has done for you?'

'I think it's going to be a severe winter,' he announced calmly. 'When the holly bears so many berries it means there'll be snow at Christmas time. Old Ben Tarrow says it never fails.'

There was a peculiar alertness on all their faces, and he realised why. It irritated him, for some reason, and he said, 'Don't get excited. I have no idea why I said that. It's always happening, and doesn't mean a thing, you know.'

'What does Ben Tarrow look like?' asked Rex casually.

'Old . . . that's why I called him *Old* Ben Tarrow.' He was doing it deliberately, and they probably guessed as much. In fact, he had a vague picture in his mind of a bewhiskered face looking at him over a stile and saying those words. The stile and man seemed enormously tall. He must have been a small boy when the man had passed on that piece of country wisdom to him.

'I've brought you something, but I'm afraid it's not some more very rude French poetry,' Laura said into the silence, and gave him a small folder. 'I don't know much about your tastes and interests, but I thought you'd find these interesting.'

Because she had given it, he wanted to hide it under the bedclothes and look at it when he was alone. But she was plainly expecting him to open it there and then. Inside the folder were two or three dozen pages, in vibrant colours, of scenes and individual costumes for a stage production of Julius Caesar, marked with pencilled instructions by the designers.

'It's an original set dating back seventy-odd years,' she added casually. 'A friend gave them to me, but I thought you'd appreciate their worth more. Rex says you're a brilliant Latin and Greek scholar—and Julius Caesar is Latin, or something like that, isn't it?'

Delight amounting almost to ecstasy flooded over him. So that was what his dreams and visions meant! No wonder he was so taken with temples and goddesses, and could write things in Greek, at will. A brilliant scholar! The idea thrilled him. Why had they not told him before? It explained so very much. He leafed through the sketches finding each as precious as a crock of gold.

'Thanks most awfully,' he mumbled, too overcome to meet her glance or say anything more.

They left him looking at the pages for a while, then Rex said, 'I saw Roland before I left France. He's having a very rough time of it over there in a front-line field-hospital. In his own funny way, he's doing it for your sake, Chris. I wish you'd answer one of his letters. It'd mean such a lot to him.'

'I wouldn't know what to say,' he replied, far more interested in his present from Laura. 'And don't you think it'd do more harm than good to concoct a polite letter full of meaningless rot—like writing letters to horrible aunts, at prep-school? How I used to loathe that.'

'In that room at the back of the bathrooms, with a howling draught from the windows and a clock that used to miss one tick in five?'

'We used to sit there counting the ticks, and forgot all about our letters,' he said, smiling in remembrance.

'That's right.' The tired kind eyes looked at him with new brightness. 'And do you remember old Ford-Meakins, who used to crack his fingers as he walked amongst us to check that we really were writing letters?'

Chris recalled the man's beetle-brows clearly. 'He didn't like me.'

'He didn't like me, either. He used to call me Sheridan Minor, because of Roland. I hated it. It made me feel like a midget.'

Chris chuckled. 'He used to call me Demosthenes.'

As soon as that name was out it was as if a cloud had passed over the sun. He had no idea why, but he suddenly felt frighteningly alone and facing a hill he *had* to climb, yet which contained something unknown and terrible at the top.

'What's the matter, old son?'

Rex's face came into perspective, and Chris was relieved that it was not another face that he saw.

'I'm tired!' It was blunt to cover the way he felt. Marion had moved away to talk to the man four beds along, and he felt sorry he had said what he had to her. When Rex and Laura went, there would only be Marion left.

Rex got to his feet and helped Laura up beside him. 'Perhaps we've stayed too long. We'll leave you to have a quiet spell before they bring your tea. Is it still bread-and-butter and syrup?'

He nodded wearily. 'Mostly. And blancmange that has to be strawberry because it's pink.' He looked up at Rex. 'I don't like it frightfully much.'

Rex laughed and ruffled his hair affectionately. 'Good lad. Neither do I. We'll come again soon.'

'I'd like that. And . . . thanks for the Julius Caesar.'

'I'm glad you're pleased,' said Laura, looking so marvellous he was overcome with sadness almost too great to bear because she was going. 'Goodbye, Chris.'

She bent to kiss him very gently on the mouth, and he desperately wanted to put his head on her breast and cry all the sadness out of him. Instead, he turned his head away so that he would not see them go. Then he took off his spectacles so that he would not see anything. But he knew his tears would be seen by the nurses, if he was not careful, and his fears grew again. The men who kept crying and would not stop were wheeled away never to be seen again. If they did that to him, he would be lost.

For the next week he was completely happy and absorbed in the present Laura had brought him. He re-drew and elaborated on the scenes, writing Latin inscriptions and putting in figures of the

320

great orators and statesmen throughout the ages . . . in addition to a Laura goddess, of course. And he wrote page after page of everything that came flooding into his head. It came so fast he spent every minute he had putting it all on paper and revelling in the pleasure of all it said and represented.

He often thought of old Ford-Meakins, the prep-school master who always cracked his fingers, and vague memories of other men in black gowns and mortar-boards came and went, sometimes identified, sometimes not. Throughout it all shone his passion for Laura, who had told him he was a brilliant classics scholar. He knew it was the one thing in the world he wanted to be; the knowledge thrilled him. He might not be a hero like Rex, but he was *something* she could admire. So he wrote and wrote, covering large numbers of pages with words in French, Greek and Latin, as all the things he had ever known seemed to come into his mind like a ravening horde.

He wrote other pages in different languages that gave him little pleasure and seemed extremely mundane in text. Some of the things he wrote made no sense at all. But, after puzzling over them for a while, the juxtaposition of words dawned on him. The resulting prose must have been something to do with the Greek or Roman wars, because it was all about troop movements, the positions of guns, the dates of battles, and routes taken by ships. They did not interest him half as much as the rest. One page was in a language he could not even identify, and the passage seemed to concern melons for a sick grandmother. It seemed somehow familiar, but had a flavour of lunacy about it that he did not like.

The pleasure all this industriousness gave him had one reservation. He knew it must all be kept secret. People did not understand. They mocked his brain; they were derisive of learning. To reveal that he knew so many things would induce ridicule, scorn, and other more subtle dangers. His prowess must never be mentioned; a lot of knowledge was a dangerous thing. So he hid all his drawings and writing beneath the pillow whenever anyone approached and, at night, he put it all beneath the mattress. When they came to strip his bed and turn the mattress, he stuffed it all up his pyjama sleeve.

But he must have been careless one day toward the end of that week, because the elderly nurse who always took night duty gave him his medicine—which he proposed spitting out when she had gone—then stooped to pick something up from the floor. It was one of his sheets of paper.

"Hallo, what's this, Mr Sheridan?' she asked as of a child. 'Secret messages, is it? *Two battalions moving up on Wednesday, and cavalry to form a pincer on each flank.* Whatever does all that mean?'

He had always hated her, even more so now. 'Give it to me!' he demanded furiously. 'It's mine.'

'Now, now, now,' she admonished, in clucking manner. 'That's quite enough of that, young gentleman, or I'll give you another spoonful of bromide.'

He realised he had swallowed the first spoonful, after all, and made a lunge for the paper before he grew too sleepy. 'Give it to me!' She stood out of his reach, so he bombarded her with wild demands to hand over what was his, to stop stealing his things, and threatening her with dire punishment if she did not hand it back immediately.

Others came and held him restrainingly. He was afraid then that they would find the rest of the papers, and began scrambling for them feverishly, tugging at the mattress. Two men in white coats came to hold him while they put the needle in his arm, and that was when the elderly nurse discovered the remainder of his precious pages.

The screens went around him, and they held him down when he fought for possession of the secret documents now being shown to those standing around the bed. So great was his desperation, he began to scream curses at them, using all the most obscene words he knew. Soon, a man in khaki uniform appeared through the screens, listened to what had happened, took a look at the papers, then spoke low-voiced instructions.

By now, Chris was feeling leaden, unable to move his limbs, fighting the compulsion to close his eyes. It was the needle. It always did that. Next minute, they pulled back the screens and began to wheel his bed out toward the door. He could not believe it was happening, after all this time. He had been so good, so quiet, so careful . . . and in one short moment he had done what the others had done, and was being wheeled away never to return. He had stopped shouting; he had stopped struggling. Perhaps there would be a last-minute reprieve now he was silent and still. But they wheeled him out through the door, which swung closed behind him, and he knew it was the end for him. He looked up at them, crying helplessly because none of them would look his way, give him another chance; crying helplessly because Marion could have saved him except that she was never there during the night. Now, she would never know when and where he went; never know he was sorry about the way he had treated her lately. And there was Laura and Rex. Although he wanted his brother's wife, it did not stop him from liking him a great deal. It had been nice to have a brother who was a hero. He would probably be upset now . . . and Roland, who wanted a reply to his letters. He had not been nobody, after all. He had had a family, and a friend called Marion . . . and he wanted them all desperately. But the leadenness had reached every part of him now, and his lashes closed on the wetness within them.

When he opened his eyes he lay in a quiet terror knowing that the blur could be eternity. But his spectacles were immediately put on his nose, and he saw a man standing beside him. Rolling his eyes to look around him, he saw he was in a small room with bars over the window. He could see nothing of the grounds he loved, only a brick wall outside. He would never walk along those paths and see what lay outside now.

They came, one after the other, asking him about what he had written on the papers, what it all meant. But he stayed very still and silent, staring at them blankly. They told him that if he talked to them about it, everything would be all right. He was too clever to be taken in by that trick. That was all part of the training to test one's resistance to questioning by the enemy. A man must not break, no matter what they did to him, or promised him in return for information. He might even be shot . . . but he said nothing.

Time blurred. He had no idea how long he had been in that room. Nights had come and gone as frequently as his questioners. Then, one day, a new man came through the door, tall, prematurely grey, with a strange accent. Chris recoiled from him on sight. This one was not interested in his knowledge, but his body. His name was Neil, and he wanted to take him swimming, get him naked, then do something disgusting to him.

It was unbearably hot. They had had no water to drink since they had landed, and the Turks were just at the top of the cliff. The noise of gunfire hurt his ears, and men were falling all around him, screaming in their agony. There were blasts on a whistle, and they all had to run uphill. They were all dead, but they kept on running. He had come out of his little cave and gone along to Headquarters, as usual. There was no one left, and he had to climb up that cliff and die. They knew he would die, but they made him go. Neil tried to save him. *You looked so beautiful standing there naked, and those eyes with the long lashes curling over them were more than I could stand.* But that was why he knew he had to go. The moment of going over the top was almost nerveless, it was only when he was halfway across that murderous open stretch that he realised he might be left with half a head, like Rochford-Clarke. But it was too late then.

Captive in that bed, all Chris could do was hide from this man who had made him want to die. He took off the spectacles and threw them as hard as he could. But that was not enough, so he hid in the recesses of his own mind.

16

THE ANGLO-CANADIAN force retreated from Croix des Anges at Christmas. The troops had heard tales of the past two festive seasons, when apparently carols had been sung in unison across the trenches, and combatants had met in No-Man's-Land to shake hands and share chocolate or cigarettes. But that Christmas of 1916 inspired no warmth or goodwill in those who had been ruthlessly slaughtering each other for three months over the possession of a flattened village.

The Germans chose Christmas Eve to mount a desperate offensive, and the dispirited decimated companies that had held the position since September trudged from it under cover of darkness rather than be overrun. Some might willingly have become prisoners-of-war if it had not been well-known the German troops were starving. The alternative to capture was the prospect of endless muddy tracks through broken villages and razed farmland in icy rain and whistling winds, with another line of slime-and-corpse-filled trenches at the end of it. But there would be food and mugs of tea so, when one went, they all followed—a long stumbling column of mindless automatons who had forgotten any life but their present one.

The tiny medical unit remained in the cellar until the last possible moment with those of their patients who could not be moved, and with the new casualties of the present attack. It was worse now than it had ever been in that old cellar. There had never been any means of heating it, but the bitter December weather penetrated the sandbagged walls to add to the misery of the wounded men shivering under insufficient blankets.

For the past month, the staff had been unable to send patients back to base hospitals because bridges had been blown, roads bombed into non-existence, or ambulances destroyed. So the field unit was hopelessly overcrowded and understaffed. Supplies were low or used up. The serious patients would have to be left to the enemy when the area was taken. Until that happened, the medical staff would do all they could before they left with the rearguard, taking with them all those fit to travel in the one temperamental motor-ambulance.

To protect this precious vehicle from attack, it had been backed down the slope into the cellar amongst the patients, giving the staff even less room in which to work. There was no guarantee it would be safe there, of course. The German bombardment was desperate and indiscriminate as Matt Rideaux and his orderlies moved from patient to patient, feeling the urgency of time running out on their work. When the captain in charge of the rearguard left to cover the secret retreat gave the word, they would have to abandon most of the men lying helpless on straw scattered over the floor. The knowledge was already in the eyes of the victims and was more terrible than the pain there, also.

Roland found himself now immune to the sight, smell and sound of battle victims but, as he pushed his way through the mass of blanket-covered patients in that dimly-lit cellar, he found it impossible to look into the eyes that contained that condemnation. Suppose the men in those boats offshore at Gallipoli had left Chris to his fate? Each of these people before him was someone's son, brother, husband—even father, as Chris was.

'Compliments of the season,' said a voice in his ear, and he looked up to meet Matt's glance. 'It's just gone midnight,' came the explanation as the doctor edged past him to reach a man coughing up blood in the corner. 'I guess the bells are ringing out at home.'

Roland hardly saw what he was doing, hands working automatically as his mind winged to a Dorset village where he had spent every Christmas before this one. There was not often snow, for it was a benign county, but hoar-frosts decorated the bare hedgerows with glittering tinsel, the Christmas roses bloomed defiantly, and the holly trees glowed with shiny red berries. In the belfry of the ancient church the bells rang out across the whole valley, mingling musically with those from the church at Tarrant Maundle on still frosty days. The villagers flocked to morning service—except for one family of Catholics who drove to their own church in Greater Tarrant—and along the lanes the aroma of roasting goose wafted from tiny cottage windows.

The parish poor and elderly always received a goose or duck, a plum-pudding tied up in a cloth, and one article of warm clothing from Tarrant Hall, all taken round in the pony-trap by Dawkins the previous day, and the village children had always sung carols in the great hall of the house before going for cocoa and sweetmeats in the kitchen with Priddy on Christmas Eve.

There had been a tall tree by the staircase, decorated with lanterns and garlands. When they were boys, he and his brothers had raced downstairs on Christmas morning to find their presents at the foot of that tree. More recently, they had exchanged gifts in the morning-room after breakfast, thanking each other with affectionate smiles and a grip on the arm. Then there had been the Boxing Day Meet, when the surrounding hills had rung with the bay of hounds, the huntsman's horn, and the thunder of hooves. Afterward, they had all gathered for dinner in the long banqueting-hall to relive and celebrate the day's sport.

But clouds passed over the brightness of his visual memories as he thought of all those who would never hunt again; and they darkened further when he recalled how his parcels had been rejected, left unopened on the doorsteps where Dawkins had placed them last Christmas; how the children had struck Tarrant Hall from their list when carolling around the village; how he had been voted off the Hunt Committee and excluded from the brave attempt by the elderly members to maintain the Boxing Day tradition, taking their dinner at Dr Deacon's home, instead. He frowned. The villagers had dubbed him a coward for working his land to provide essential supplies for his country when they were most needed. Would they think him a hero, more of a man, when he turned his back on these dying men shortly and left them to the enemy?

The thud of shells seemed to be lessening. It always did halfway between dusk and dawn.

'Gawn nasty quiet, Corp,' wheezed the youngster enduring the rough-and-ready treatment Roland was forced to give him. 'D'yer fink they're comin' over the top?'

He shook his head and smiled automatically. 'Not yet. Our rearguard hasn't come in.'

'P'raps they're all dead now.'

'Not our lads.' Roland put the blanket back over the oozing chest wound. 'There you are, you'll find that more comfortable now, son.'

As he moved on he realised he was now doing what Rex had done—calling men just a few years younger 'son'. He felt as old as their fathers. The past six months had made him feel as old as even *their* fathers!

Introspection vanished next minute when his attention was taken from the mangled foot he was studying. Lying nearby was a middle-aged sergeant wearing the uniform of the Canadian regiment, and it was apparent that he was choking to death through asphyxia. Leaving the foot that would have to be amputated, Roland went swiftly to the man in paroxysm and saw there was no time for an operation to remove the obstruction in his throat. Death would occur long before then.

He looked up swiftly and called across to Matt, who was in the midst of taking a bullet from a lad's shoulder with a light but sure touch.

'Captain Rideaux, come quickly!'

'Damned impossible,' was the level reply.

'It's an emergency.'

'So are they all, Corporal.'

It was really a job for a qualified doctor with sterile instruments, in a hospital where emergencies could receive intensive after-care. But the man was about to die, and Roland knew what could save him . . . possibly! Feeling like an executioner he stood gazing down at the patient's distress.

The bullet now safely removed, Matt approached to assess the situation, then shook his head significantly. There were others with a better chance of survival. But Roland had made the mistake of letting himself look into the eyes of this Canadian, and it was his undoing.

Heart thudding against his ribs he took up the man's rifle, unclipped the bayonet, then cut across the blocked windpipe, making a deep gash. Quickly taking the patient's gas-whistle from his belt, he wrapped it in gauze and inserted it into the incision to keep it open. It had taken but a few moments, and the sergeant had slipped into semi-consciousness, but he was now breathing, and asphyxia had been averted. Only once during his years at medical school had Roland seen a tracheotomy performed, and he had just successfully achieved the same with only the rudest of instruments and very little confidence. He stood gazing down at his work in stunned astonishment, filled with an absurd pride and sense of satisfaction that overrode all else for that short moment.

'Christ, I spent the first year as a doctor praying I'd not be faced with one of those,' said a soft voice beside him. 'You deserve a medal.'

Reality returned swiftly as Roland looked up at his superior. 'I deserve nothing. He's certain to die, anyway.'

'Only because this is not a hospital.' Matt began moving away toward another orderly who was signalling him urgently. 'But I thought you advocated mercy killing. How come you acted like a true doctor in an emergency?'

There was no opportunity to make a reply to that. Figures materialised from the darkness of the various gaps in the sand-bagged walls, and Roland stared at the grey uniforms and bucket-shaped helmets of German troops. One of the soldiers shouted to an officer somewhere, and a middle-aged lieutenant appeared almost immediately to look around at the sombre scene.

'*Gott im Himmel!*' he exclaimed wearily. '*Was Unglück!*'

Roland thought the misfortunate was theirs rather than their captors', and said so in tense tones. Surprised to hear someone respond in the same language, the German stepped further into the cellar, peering across the dimness to see who it was.

'What has happened to our men?' Roland asked, still in the

limited phrases he had picked up from his student days. 'The ones in the trenches.'

'They are all dead,' was the toneless response. 'How did you expect to hold the line with so few?'

Conscious of Matt resuming his work on one of their patients as if there had been no interruption, he ignored that and countered with a question of his own. They were all prisoners; he needed to know.

'Have you any medical supplies with you?'

The man laughed harshly. 'Have *you* any food?'

'Haven't you?'

'We have not enough for ourselves, much less prisoners. We thought you had all gone.' It was blunt and tinged with exhaustion. 'What are you doing here?'

'We were to have gone with the rearguard,' he informed the man through a tight throat. 'In that ambulance.'

'You have no rearguard.'

Silence reigned for a while as the lieutenant took stock of the situation, watched by troops who wore the same look Roland had seen on all men living in trenches for month after month—gaunt and wild! He felt sudden apprehension. Desperate men did desperate things!

'What is the new position of your battalion?' came the next probing question.

'I cannot tell you that, sir, as you are well aware.'

It was almost as if he had never required an answer, because he went on. 'We need this place for our own wounded. You must clear these men out right away.'

'Clear them out!' cried Roland angrily. 'There's nowhere else to put them—and some of them are too ill to be moved, anyway. These men are wounded prisoners-of-war. You are obliged to take responsibility for them.'

With a sudden surprising switch to guttural English, the man said, 'Go! In that—go!' He waved a hand at the ambulance. 'Quickly go end I say notting.'

'What the hell are you talking about?' asked Matt laconically, now taking an interest in what had been an incomprehensible conversation until then. 'Go where? There's nothing in this damned God-forsaken area but this cellar. You're stuck with us, bud—and we were here first.'

'The Lieutenant has decided not to take us prisoners as we are a medical unit,' put in Roland quickly, having a terrible suspicion that the slightest hesitation by them would suggest only one other solution to a man at the limit of his endurance. 'He is allowing us to rejoin the main force.'

'Yes, yes,' came the urgent affirmative. 'All go. Now!'

Matt put his hands on his hips. 'Now just let's get this straight, Lootenant. There is no darned possibility of us *all* going. Some of these men . . .'

'. . . will take a while to shift,' put in Roland with heavy emphasis, praying Matt would understand what he was trying to get across to him. 'Once we catch up with our own troops *we* can ensure they take the road to recovery, can't we, Captain Rideaux? The course of treatment I once suggested wouldn't be the right one at all, I see that now. We had better take them with us.'

Matt gave him a long look that took in the implication of his words. 'Do you mean the treatment we give to horses?'

'Exactly,' agreed Roland fervently. 'I think we should accept the Lieutenant's honourable and humane gesture and set off as soon as possible.'

It was a sickening and heartrending business piling suffering men one on top of the other into an ambulance designed to take one-sixth the number. Even then, some had to be placed on the roof and lashed in position. They did not understand why it was being done, and cursed the medical staff through their agony. But Roland and Matt worked swiftly, conscious that the bulk of the German force would be entering Croix Des Anges before long and might not be as lenient as the advance-party commander.

Overloaded as it was, the ancient ambulance would not make the climb up from the cellar and had to be pushed by the German troops, who must have been as convinced of prevailing madness as the suffering passengers. After several attempts the canvas-topped vehicle sporting red crosses lurched up to level ground, and they set off after their retreating comrades.

They drove without stopping for a long period, until the cries and moans from within the ambulance became too much for Matt.

'Oh God, this is bloody inhuman!' he exploded. 'You sure as hell better be right, Sheridan.'

'I'm right,' Roland assured him, finding the terrible journey just as much of a strain.

'Just where did you learn that lingo? It was all kinda private between you and him.'

Keeping his voice as low as he could in the jolting noisy vehicle, Roland said, 'He told me they wanted no prisoners, and they needed that cellar for their own wounded. He said they had barely enough food for themselves. When he suddenly resorted to English, it struck me he didn't want his own men to know he was letting us go to our own people. That's when I got really worried. He was one of the old Officer Corps Germans, who still believe in the code of warfare. The rest might not have been so gentlemanly.'

'*Gentlemanly!*' exploded Matt. 'Christ, you upper-class bastards really get me! You call it gentlemanly to throw these poor sods in a heap and bump them over muddy roads in freezing weather? And a merry Christmas to you, too, buddy,' he finished bitterly.

Holding on to his temper Roland said in a fierce undertone, '*They wanted no prisoners!* You know what would have happened to them if we hadn't brought them with us.'

'Isn't that what you once advocated—a humane bullet to end their suffering?'

'It wouldn't have been a bullet,' he snapped, unable to control himself any longer. 'They're as short of ammunition as they are of food. Lend your imagination to *that,* for a moment.'

They went on for some time with silence between them, with only the plight of their patients to emphasize their separate thoughts. After a while, Matt shook his head in the darkness.

'This finally does it. If you hadn't understood that guy's language and passed me the tip, I'd have made one hell of a stand for suffering humanity. And we'd all now be dead. As I've said before, you're the darndest corporal I've ever come across. After the way you handled that situation, to say nothing of the neatest, most audacious tracheotomy job, I'm recommending that you be sent home to qualify as a doctor and officer . . . and to hell with your stupid aspirations to avenge your kid brother's insanity.'

Spring 1917, a time when land offensives should be made. But no one any longer had confidence in breaking the deadlock that was now in its third year. Each army had thrown its might into battle with increasing desperation, and nothing had ever been gained. Generals were bewildered and at their wits' end; armies

331

were on the verge of mutiny. So, while the entrenched troops noted the passing of time only because the eternal mud began to harden beneath their feet, warfare took to the air in earnest, the cocksure German pilots intending to knock the R.F.C. from the skies for good. But they had reckoned without a nation of people who traditionally fought best with their backs to the wall. From Britain and the Commonwealth came a succession of eager patriotic youngsters to replace those who were lost, and aircraft were patched up again and again until it was a miracle if any part of the original remained.

There was a dog-fight overhead as Roland climbed from the sidecar of the motor cycle that had brought him on the last leg of his journey to his new posting in the front-line sector near the town of Ypres—known to the British troops as Wipers. He had only been away two months, yet the return to the battle zone shocked him anew. How could he have so quickly forgotten the desolation of landscape, the colourlessness of everything, the stark reality of war in the ruined cottages, the tilting signposts bearing superimposed names daubed by soldiers with a sense of humour, and broken churchyards scarred now with lines of trenches cutting through the ancient gravestones? There was no respect for consecrated ground: the whole expanse of France was that now, with the graves of so many all across it.

'Welcome to Gillyhook, sir,' said the driver, using the British soldiers' cosy pronunciation of the name of the village of Guillehoek. 'It ain't much, but it's 'ome to those of us as 'ave never 'ad the chance of one of them big 'ouses in Wipers itself. There's plenty of nightlife, sir, and firework displays at least three times a week.' He pointed skyward with a grin. 'And if you find time dragging during the day, there's always the "circus" performers giving a display.'

The German air ace Von Richthofen, otherwise known as 'The Red Baron' because he flew a red-painted aircraft, had formed a 'flying circus' of skilled aviators which was having great success against the R.F.C., and enough of the old pioneer spirit remained for the man to be regarded with almost as much respect by the Allies as his own people.

But Roland gave only a faint smile in response, and thanked God Rex was safely in England for a while. His brother had done more than enough to counter German dominance of the air during the past years. Yet men like him were desperately needed against the growing legend of Von Richthofen's indomitable fliers.

Returning the man's salute, Roland picked up his bags and began scrambling across the rubble to where he had been told he would find Colonel Reeder. While he was doing so, one of the aircraft overhead fell like a spinning torch to the earth, the black crosses on its wings proclaiming it as one of the enemy. When it exploded on impact, Roland was startled to hear the earth around him ring with the sound of hundreds of cheering voices. Looking from side to side he then became aware that what looked like areas of muddy devastation were alive and moving. Whole regiments of men living underground were waving anything they could lay hands on to their comrades of the air.

It was strangely exciting, this overwhelming presence of healthy lively men. The post of Regimental Medical Officer was new to Roland, and vastly different from what he had been doing. As an orderly with a Field Ambulance Section, he had dealt only with battle casualties brought to the rear by stretcher-bearers—of which he had been one during his initial days as a soldier. Now, he would be living in the trenches with the same men day after day, dealing with such varying things as trench-fever, foot-rot, dysentery, rat-bites, influenza, corns and constipation. In other words, the equivalent of a civilian G.P. like Dr Deacon. Naturally, there would be battle casualties, but his responsibility would then be to decide whether on-the-spot treatment would suffice, or whether the wound was serious enough to send the man to a unit like Matt Rideaux's. He was in two minds about the appointment. To counterbalance the fact of not facing unrelieved blood, pus, and agony was the prospect of getting to know the men so well, their loss would mean too much.

As he neared his goal he felt he was entering a new phase of his life. He had not had to return to England to qualify, after all. Such was the need for doctors at this desperate stage of the war, the authorities had read Matt's report, questioned Roland on the extent of his medical training, then put him through a written and practical examination at one of the main hospitals in France. At the end, they had told him he was more knowledgeable than many men already serving as medical officers, given him the rank of lieutenant, and sent him out to replace a man who had been blown apart by a shell.

333

Roland was no fool. Medical officers in the field lasted no longer than infantrymen when posted to an area like Ypres, which had been bombarded by the Germans since the end of 1914 in an effort to capture it from the British. They were still shelling it daily, and the British were still there two and a half years later. If he survived for six months it would be a miracle; if he did not, they would promote another promising orderly to replace him.

Reaching the flight of reinforced steps leading down into a bunker somewhat ostentatiously labelled Regimental Headquarters, Roland descended into the earth telling himself there was no other smell in the world like that of a trench. On first entering, it was vile and overwhelming. Yet he knew that living with it day in, day out, rendered it almost unnoticeable. After two months in reasonably civilised conditions, however, it hit him anew as he dipped his head to enter the underground chamber. One sight of the men who looked up at his entry made him extremely conscious of his brand new jacket and breeches; the shining leather of his Sam Browne and boots.

He saluted a haggard yellow-faced lieutenant-colonel, and said briskly, 'Good morning, sir. I'm Sheridan, the new M.O.'

'Oh, is it morning?' came the query in a voice that seemed pitched too high for such a large man. 'I should have been relieved half an hour ago. Where the hell is Major Brookes?' The last was addressed to a lieutenant sitting at a table covered with such an array of papers they could not possibly have been in any order.

'Watching the scrap, I shouldn't be surprised,' came the laconic answer. 'His two sons are operating in this sector.'

'Yes . . . yes, so they are. Still, I don't know how he can tell which they are, unless they've got "Hallo Daddy" painted on the sides of their Nieuports. Glad to have you, Sheridan. The notice of your pending arrival will doubtless reach me sometime later this month,' he continued in the same conversational tone. 'Roberts bought it two weeks ago, and Corporal Trent has been having a whale of a time on his own. Just stopped him from operating on a poor bugger with belly-ache after eating a cake sent out by his girlfriend. Greedy sod ate it all himself, thank God, or we'd have had the whole of A Company ill.' Bushy eyebrows rose. 'You look very pretty in that damned new outfit. Life is somewhat raw in the trenches, you'll find.'

'Yes, sir, I've been in a trench before.'

The eyebrows waggled. 'Have you, by jove? Thought you'd come straight out from Blighty. Well, in that case, you should have known better than to arrive looking so bloody smart!' He stood up and held out his hand. 'Welcome to Gillyhook. *Sheridan*,' he mused. 'No relation to the R.F.C. wallah, are you?'

'Yes. I'm his brother Roland.'

'Are you really?' He mused further. '*Roland* Sheridan. I've heard that name before. Seen it in the newspaper, haven't I?'

Roland nodded, and said briefly. 'It's possible.'

Fortunately Major Brookes arrived to take over at that point, so the subject was dropped. There was no time for Roland to settle in, if such a thing was possible in trench living. He shared a bunker with two infantry subalterns called Tanker and Bream. He thought they sounded like a music-hall turn but were, in fact, a pair of youngsters who had been in the army only three months and still thought of the war as a 'jolly old lark'. No more than eighteen, they immediately dubbed Roland 'Methuselah'. He found little in common with them, unable to even make a comparison with Chris, who had always been such a serious introverted boy.

Their relationship could not be called homosexual since they made no physical advances toward each other, yet their interdependence irritated him. It took him a day or so to realise they were school-chums who had enlisted together, and only managed to survive the horrors surrounding them by pretending nothing had changed. No sooner had he formed that conclusion than Bream was beheaded by an exploding shell, and Tanker, into whose arms the head had descended, lost his reason and had to be sent to the mental wing of a base hospital.

After that, Roland had two others to share his quarters. Another eighteen year old called Bisset, who was constantly drinking absinthe, and a full-lieutenant by the name of Charles Barr-Leigh, who was immediately dubbed Charley Barley by the entire battalion. With Hilary Bisset furtively and silently drinking in the corner of their foul-smelling dug-out, Roland found himself forced into closer companionship than he normally experienced with the third inhabitant of what had been named, by the mysterious overnight appearance of a painted board over the entrance, *The Gillyhook Krankenhaus*.

Their sense of humour showed the spirit of the men he had

joined, and Roland's admiration for them knew no bounds during that first month of his duty as a regimental doctor. Day to day life, if it was not suddenly ended by a bullet or shell, was fairly predictable. At dawn and dusk there would be an artillery bombardment from both sides in anticipation of an attack. If one came, the men knew what to do. If it did not, they stood-to just the same and risked death from exploding shells, or burial alive when trenches caved-in. During the night they took watches while certain groups ventured out to mend the wire or bring in wounded who had been sniped at whilst on look-out duty. To hamper such work, the aggressor who was not engaged in it would send up star-shells to illuminate the area and fire at anything seen moving.

The daylight hours were spent in periods that only differed because the stood-to men were up on the firing ledges that allowed them to peer over the top, and the stood-down men sitting listlessly with their feet in the unspeakable muck that formed the very bottom of the trenches. The duty periods were often welcomed because they allowed an opportunity to see something other than mud walls a few feet apart stretching in every direction. Not that the scene on the surface was any better; it simply alleviated the shut-in feeling.

Every so often there were gas attacks, when a fearful noise generally described as 'milkmaids trying to get milk from a herd of bulls by mistake' warned everyone to don gas-masks. More often than not it was a false alarm, claimed by the raisers of it to have been genuine, except that the wind changed and blew it back over the Huns. When the gas really came silently stealing across the barren landscape, it always caught a few too slow or disbelieving. Roland always had plenty on his hands then, and found these cases very distressing. To a man of his nature, it seemed the basest type of warfare imaginable.

But after his work with Matt Rideaux's unit, he found the new life soul-destroying because of its stagnation. Each day seemed the same. Sick parade brought the usual maladies, and the usual malingerers; each bombardment meant broken bodies that needed to be sent on for treatment and others who were mentally broken by one shell too many. Those were the most difficult cases, because Roland had to judge whether it was a temporary breakdown of nerves or a final one. How could any but the most experienced specialist make that judgment?

336

Time passed almost unmarked between those high mud walls that allowed sight of nothing but the area of sky directly above. The occupants seemed to take on the colour of mud, food tasted of mud, and everything smelt like mud. After four weeks Roland felt he had lost his identity; his past years. But his admiration flourished for those who were approaching their third year of such living and still retained their sanity and sense of humour. Then he realised they were the men of English cities, and villages such as Tarrant Royal, whose stalwartness and worth he had always stoutly proclaimed. Suddenly, he knew he had been wrong. War would not destroy them all, as he had feared. They would not allow themselves to be destroyed. At the end of it, when ownership of the kite had been finally settled, they would return and take up where they had left off. England *would* survive.

The terrible pattern of trench life had to be borne somehow, and most of those enduring it had resorted to some way of blotting it from their minds whenever they could. Those with mercenary bent played cards for all manner of stakes, or invented new games from old cigarette-tins, empty 'Brasso' canisters, boot-polish containers, pieces of string, fragments of shell-casing, scraps of khaki serge taken from corpses lying around, and any other useful material. There were more vindictive personalities always inventing new ways of catching and executing the myriads of rats that shared the trenches with them; others which concocted patent liquids claiming to clear a man's body of lice quicker than it took a Minnie (trench-mortar) to do it.

Those with plenty to say wandered from group to group starting an argument on any subject with anyone who would rise to the bait; others with skilled hands spent innumerable hours fashioning any object that could be made from any others. There were always plenty of amateur entertainers—natural comedians, choristers, and wizards of the mouth-organ. But there were also those who were unskilled introverts, and these were the ones most likely to succumb to the strain.

As medical officer to a regiment, Roland's job was to prevent this and encourage every kind of hobby or pastime. To this end, liaison with the padre was usually very helpful. But Roland had a dreadful obstacle to overcome. He was an unskilled introvert himself, and was already finding it unbearably claustrophobic spending twenty-four hours a day contained within mud walls rearing up well above his head on both sides wherever he stood or walked. When resting in his own bunker, or walking to any other part of the extensive intersecting trench system, all he could see were those walls. With Matt Rideaux's unit they had moved from area to area. Even in the cellar hospital at Croix Des Anges, there had been space to move and the opportunity to go up to the surface.

Diagnosing his own malady, Roland tried desperately to prescribe treatment. If he had been Chris he could have sketched, or translated Greek, or created poetry; if he had been Rex he would have had any number of friends to roister away the hours with. Unfortunately, he was not in the least artistic, and had already finished the reading matter available until the next delivery of mail —even the lewd censorable stuff.

As for friends, the other officers were decent enough men with whom he was on good terms, yet none of them drew the same rapport he had shared with the Canadian doctor. In truth, he missed Matt's laconic friendship and lazy outlook on life, in general. In the bunker, young Bisset was fast going to the dogs over a faithless fiancée no older than himself. Seeing the boy's suffering, Roland had cause to be thankful he had not tied himself to any girl before leaving England. He remembered Rex asking, *Doesn't love fit into your plans?* And his own reply: *Not your kind of love.* What he had felt for Laura that evening before he left had been a wilder kind of emotion altogether, and it made him ashamed to think of it now, in retrospect. Perhaps he was incapable of real love. He hoped to God he was. It destroyed men, as it had done his father, and was doing so with Chris, Rex, and young Bisset.

The other occupant of the bunker, Barr-Leigh, was around twenty-two and the third son of the Earl of Milchester. His two older brothers had already been killed, so he was all set to inherit the title if he survived. If not, there were two younger brothers also in France, and three others still at school, he told Roland with the kind of breeziness that covered the first stages of shell-shock. He was dark-haired and moustached, well built and extremely handsome. Like many of his breed he had little understanding of the ordinary man and tended to treat his subordinates as he would his dogs—praised them when they were good, roared at them when they were not, and ignored them most of the time. He drank in proportion to most officers, smoked the usual number of cigars, and talked of girls, gambling, and gee-gees in a loud educated voice whenever he was in what passed for an Officers' Mess, or any other large group. Yet he showed a different face in the bunker, and Roland worried about the man's shaking hands and moods of savage anger sparked off by overly persistent rats, or damp candles that refused to light.

So, with Bisset uncommunicative and sullen, and Barr-Leigh beginning to crack under the strain of three years of war, Roland found little comfort in the earth dug-out that served as his home. The claustrophobia of trench life made him dream of the open spaces surrounding his real home, and his longing for Tarrant Royal had never been more acute. To ease it he began writing extremely long letters to Rex full of 'do you remember?' and 'can you recall?'; equally long ones to Chris saying the same thing in informative guise. He also wrote reams to Tessa. None of the letters told anything of his present life, they were full of recollections and descriptions of home.

After some days of this he realised the letters were merely pen-pictures to salve his own heartache for what he had left behind. Chris remembered none of it, Rex was too obsessed with his Laura to care about it, and Tessa did not need to read of things that were spread before her in all their glory. He tore up the letters. Depressed he further tortured himself by dwelling on how all the old familiar places would look now March was well advanced, yet found it impossible to express his thoughts to his fellows for fear of their uninterest or, worse, their ridicule.

A partial solution to his growing restlessness came within that week. Wherever soldiers are stationed in large numbers some enterprising man will start a newspaper or magazine full of prose and poetry significant only to those who would understand and appreciate their singular purpose. Word had gone around that *The Gillyhook Gazette* was about to be created, and entreaties for copy were hard on the heels of the announcement. The Editor, a major who had run a small-town paper in civilian life, asked Roland to do a piece about steeple-chasing. But he was reluctant, feeling that only a small number of the prospective readers would find it of interest. To contribute a medical article would almost be an insult, yet Roland knew he was not the type to pen a witty sparkling piece of prose such as Charles Barr-Leigh would dash off to delight jaded spirits.

Finally, at the end of three concentrated days of tending the sick and wounded who were as depressed and far from home as he, he sat in his bunker and wrote, by the light of his last candle, a detailed description of English country life in the month of March, signed it 'The Waysider', and sent it along to the editor of the publication.

He was unprepared for the thrill of pleasure it gave him to see his words in print, and even more unprepared for the reaction it brought. In the midst of all the comic verse, witty prose, cleverly disguised leg-pulling of well-known regimental characters, his un-sentimental but sincere account of home had reached the souls of even the toughest amongst them. They wanted more! An appeal was circulated for the mysterious 'Waysider' to write another column for the next issue.

Taken unawares Roland tossed the matter around in his mind for a few days, not sure he could repeat his success. It was one thing to dash off a little piece about the countryside in March because he felt he had to put it into words or burst; quite another to compose a pen-picture knowing hundreds of people were count-ing on it for momentary solace or escape.

He had not reached a conclusion when several days of concerted attacks by the Germans kept him busy all hours of the twenty-four and brought him a problem far more tricky than any other. A period of fine weather encouraged commanders to take advantage of it, but the enemy was quicker off the mark. Three days of heavy shelling, gas attacks, and nocturnal hell-fire to keep everyone from sleeping preceded an infantry assault on the trenches of the west flank. The men were on stand-to for the whole three days, sleeping as they stood for short periods at a time, and being sustained by soup and 'wads' which were distributed by men from the cook-house, who carried it through the miles of intersecting trenches. They often never reached their destination because shells exploded ahead of them, blocking the way; or because shells had exploded beside them, adding their bodies to those decomposed trunks and limbs that cascaded from the collapsing walls.

It was the first time Roland had experienced such sustained attack first-hand, and he worked automatically, his dazed brain unable to accept what was going on around him. The noise was a non-stop pressure on ear-drums and senses—the whine and crump of heavy shells, the whistle of mortar-mines, the constant rattle of machine-guns, the steady crack of rifle-fire, the clangour of the gas-gong, the tortured screams of men. Thick smoke everywhere, flying earth and other indescribable fragments, the silent choking killer that penetrated men's lungs and left them to die slowly and agonisingly. The excited commands in high boyish voices as subalterns prepared to repulse a bayonet attack; the gruffer roar of experienced N.C.O.'s as they repeated the commands. The oaths, the profanities, the careless bravado, the stifled fear, the cries for help, the sobbing over a slaughtered friend: all these were part of real battle, Roland discovered.

It went on and on. The clear skies were blotted out by smoke and dust, the familiar walkways collapsed, were fractured, or simply disappeared altogether, the usual order became chaos. Groups of men left without officers or N.C.O.'s let loose with their rifles in rash and useless bursts. Some merely crouched at the bottom of the trench amidst the carnage of their leaders and stared glazed-eyed at the bodies as if expecting them to speak, even then. Others, convinced they were the only men left alive, went over the top in suicidal madness and were immediately machine-gunned.

Roland began by dealing with casualties as they were brought in, but so many routes became blocked, he and the orderlies went out searching for wounded. With a bag slung over his shoulder he ran along duck-boards as fast as the congestion of desperate crouching men would allow, scrambled over piles of mud and filth from which the most gruesome things protruded, and flattened himself against the mud walls each time he heard the approaching whine of a shell. Wearing a gas-mask because the gong had sounded yet again, he was torn between trying to judge the extent of a man's wound through the eye-piece that had steamed up, or risking the chance of the warning being false and taking the mask off. He decided on the latter, had made a brief examination of a gaping expanse of raw flesh in the man's upper thigh, then smelt the unmistakable whiff of gas and had to put the mask on again.

The patient could not be moved under present conditions and was in terrible agony. So Roland put the man's gas-mask on him, then reached in the medical satchel for morphia. With his vision blurred by the mask he could not immediately see it. But a prolonged search proved fruitless. Unbelievable though it seemed, the supply that was always kept in the bag had gone. In a state of mind that could only accept what was presently happening around him,

Roland had to cover the wound with a dressing, then leave the victim to bear his pain until things had quietened enough to send people to bring him in.

He worked on for several hours, growing more exhausted and filthy, until he had to return for more bandages and dressings. He collected morphia and went out again, running in the direction of calls for help, frantically digging in piles of earth for men buried beneath, in case some might still be alive, and doing what he could to relieve the terror and loneliness of fatal injuries. During that time he forgot all else but what he had learnt in a London medical school a lifetime ago, and what Matt Rideaux had taught him about being a doctor.

The attack was repulsed on all sectors, and the Germans appeared to have exhausted themselves to the extent of offering no form of aggression whatever for a whole week. The weary shattered men had little rest, however, for they had to repair and strengthen the broken ramparts, bury the dead, and make detailed reports. Roland still worked flat out as more and more victims were discovered half-buried in slime and were brought to him. The orderlies on his staff were cheerful reliable men who knew enough about minor wounds to deal with them, and he was full of praise for their unflagging competence. The fact that he had expressed it seemed to embarrass them, but Roland knew they appreciated what he said and respected him for taking the time to even notice what they did.

It was fully a week before he had time for more than a sluice down and a cat-nap between duty. Then, he thankfully made his way to the officers' bath-house—a rather grandiose name for a dug-out containing two tin hip-baths which could be filled with hot water heated on a field-oven by batmen. Like every other man Roland was infested with body-lice which were impossible to banish entirely and, after a week during which he had never removed all his clothes, the prospect of doing so and immersing himself in water and disinfectant from head to toe was his present idea of paradise. Baths had to be booked in advance, and he was surprised to find his fellow bather was Charles Barr-Leigh, who confessed he had swapped with an artillery captain for the privilege of having a private conversation with Roland.

'You can do that any time you like, surely,' was Roland's casual comment as he stripped off his stained and filthy uniform. 'You

342

know, Colonel Reeder chastised me for turning up here in brand new togs that looked "too bloody smart". Whatever was he worried about?'

'I'll tell you what *I'm* worried about, Doc,' confided Charles lowering himself into the bath. 'Young Bisset.'

'He's a fool!' proclaimed Roland, trying not to scratch himself just as the lice were about to die. 'He's reaping the harvest of emotional short-sightedness.'

'Good God, you sound like the Padre. You haven't been getting too friendly with him, have you?'

The hot water and Lysol closed over Roland, and he shut his eyes in sheer bliss, wishing Charles to the Devil. An event such as this should be accompanied by complete peace and quiet.

'Shut up, there's a good chap,' he murmured.

'But I need your advice.'

'Come to morning sick-parade. I'm off-duty,' he murmured further.

The sound of splashing followed by a sigh suggested that his companion could not find the tablet of Lifebuoy. 'I think Bisset funked this last affair.'

Roland's lids flew up and he looked across the dug-out to the other bath faintly visible in the light from the sandbagged entrance. 'What do you mean?'

'I mean, I think he's turned yellow. I want your opinion on what I should do about it.'

The therapeutic relaxation of bath-time ruined, Roland gave the man his full attention. 'Ought to do about what? The boy is very young and immoderately agonising over some girl who should never have promised fidelity to him under these conditions. That doesn't make him a coward, does it?'

'Being absent from his post during an attack does.'

Totally unbelieving Roland stopped in the midst of soaping himself. 'Are you sure of that? There was such confusion, and it was impossible to get through to some sectors. I know from my own experience.'

'That's the excuse he used to his company commander,' said Charles still groping beneath his bent knees for the elusive soap. 'But I've asked around, and no one seems to have seen him for the whole three days.' His hand emerged from the water clutching his prize, which he waved at Roland. 'You can't tell me other men got through where he couldn't. I've suspected it before, but never been certain. Now I am. When I finally got back to our bunker after it was all over, I found him already there, clean as a new pin and fast asleep on his bunk. At least, I thought he was asleep until I smelt something overpowering wafting from him and realised he was completely blotto. I couldn't raise him at all, and he didn't surface for hours. Funny thing, though, it didn't smell like absinthe this time. It was something familiar which I couldn't quite place. But he was drunk all right—dead to the world and not a scratch on him. I swear he couldn't have left that bunker the whole three days.' There was a significant pause. 'Well, what do you think I should do?'

Roland did not reply. He was remembering the morphia that had been missing from his satchel—a bag that had been left in the bunker on several occasions when he had visited the latrines.

'Well?' demanded Charles irritably.

'I think we should leave things as they are,' he said slowly, 'until we have more proof . . . or until I have a talk with him.'

17

IT WAS not an easy task finding the right opportunity to speak to Hilary Bisset and, if Roland was honest, he did not relish it. What did one say to a love-sick boy? He could hardly call on past experience. Chris had been a person with his head in academic clouds and his one excursion into sexual temptation had been a momentary thing that had left him unenamoured with it. The talk that had resulted from it had been painful, practical and totally disastrous, as Chris's consequent actions had proved.

Roland had once tackled Rex on much the same subject. But his flame-haired brother had been no eighteen-year-old boy. At twenty Rex had seemed to close the three-year gap between them without difficulty. Admittedly, he had been entirely ruled by his passion for Laura when he decided to marry her, but Roland could not imagine Rex funking battle over her, much less stealing opiates in order to blot the girl from his mind.

Of course, he could not accuse Bisset without proof, and he had none. All he could reasonably hope to do was talk to the boy about his problems and try to decide whether he was a liability on active service, or not. It did not help that Roland had no patience with men who made such utter fools of themselves over a woman they ever reached such a stage. With the lesson of his father always before him, he knew what the end could be.

His opening came when they all heard they were being sent to the rear for a rest while other regiments that had been in reserve took over in the trenches. There was an additional rumour that home leave would be granted. But that turned out to be only a rumour. Even so, the prospect of a few weeks in the village of Guillehoek itself was pleasant enough to put everyone in an amiable mood.

'Pity they couldn't change the destination to Pop,' grumbled Charles, using the affectionate abbreviation for the town of Poperinghe, where trains regularly disgorged khaki-clad reinforcements for the Ypres sector. 'But we might be able to appropriate a staff-car or, at worst, a motor cycle and have an evening or two at Skindles. What do you say, Doc?'

'Rather,' Roland agreed. 'I had the bad luck to be picked up at the station when I came, and only saw the place as I drove through it. Is the hotel as good as its reputation?'

Charles closed one eye suggestively. 'When you've sampled Skindles, you'll never be the same man again.'

'Well, I shall be glad to get into Pop,' put in Hilary. 'My supply of the jolly old green stuff is napoo.'

As the boy was busily engaged in packing his kit, Roland nodded his head to suggest that Charles should vanish for a while, then said casually, 'Why don't you change to something that's easier to come by? All that absinthe will rot your boots.'

'I don't put it on my boots,' came the reply that was so like the kind of thing Chris would say, Roland suddenly found himself with the right words to hand.

'Hilary, wherever you plan to put it, it won't change things at home. If you're mature enough to fight, you're mature enough to accept defeat.' As the boy continued what he was doing, Roland added, 'Well, aren't you?'

There was still no evident response, but something about the youngster's humped shoulders as he stuffed things into a bag reminded him of Chris packing his things for a honeymoon he did not want. Following hard on that came a shaft of sadness for the brother who was a mental stranger now, and he realised that Chris must once have felt as lost and desolate as this boy thrown into something as terrible as war. Had anyone tried to help him, he wondered.

'I have another brother as well as the aviator, you know,' he said suddenly. 'I haven't spoken about him because the whole thing is frightfully sad . . . and because I feel partly responsible for it.' As he added those words he realised it was the first time he had admitted it to himself.

Having said that much, it seemed easy to relate the whole of a story he had always regarded as private family business. But the dimness of that hole in the earth, and the vulnerable attitude of the boy in khaki as he thrust things into his bag with scant regard for their condition, made him understand the desperation his brother must have felt to cheat the doctors into accepting him for *this*.

The minutes passed as he talked, and the whole sorry business came vividly to life again in his mind so that he forgot where he was and who he was with. It was only when he reached the heartbreaking fact that Chris was presently suffering a mental setback from which he might never emerge, that Roland again became aware that he was in a bunker near Ypres with a young lad who did not appear to be listening to one word of what he had said.

Feeling that he had betrayed Chris in some way by telling his story, Roland said wearily, 'But what is the tragedy of one young life amongst so many? I feel it strongly because he is my brother . . . but then all the others are brother to someone, I suppose.'

'I'm not,' came the somewhat muffled admission. 'My people were killed in China. I was brought up by various members of the Mission Society.'

Realising that he was getting through to his listener after all Roland asked quietly, 'Is your girl a missionary's daughter?'

Hilary shook his head, still with his back turned. 'Her father is an extremely successful barrister. He's frightfully wealthy and influential.'

'Then you did very well to get his permission to be engaged before you left for France.'

Hilary swung round, his face full of misery. 'We didn't,' he blurted out. 'Megan said he'd never agree to it, so I bought her a ring and she wears it on a thread round her neck—or, at least, she *did.*'

Roland should have thought it foolish. But somehow, in that vile-smelling bunker with the late afternoon twilight making it almost impossible to see across it, it sounded sincere and desperate.

'I'm sure she still does,' he said. 'And I'm sure she still feels the way she did about you. But people at home have no idea what it's like out here, how much things mean to us. How could they?' He suddenly remembered Rex saying almost the same thing to him in defence of his need to marry Laura before returning to France. 'Megan hasn't seen you for six months, and has no idea when you'll be back. She must be lonely, and there are lots of boys on leave who need cheering up. Hilary, a man can't expect a girl to give up her whole life to someone who can't promise her anything definite.'

The youngster sat on his bunk, now only a dim figure in the interior gloom. 'She knows I meant what I promised her.'

'That was six months ago. Do you still mean it now?'

There was a pause, then hesitantly, 'What an odd thing to say. Of course I do.'

'Are you certain?'

'I . . . well, a chap doesn't change his mind over something like that.'

'My brother Chris did. In his case it was too late. Now, a young girl of twenty is legally tied to a man who might become a permanent lunatic. And a young boy of two years faces the prospect of never seeing the father locked away within high walls.' Feeling ridiculously overcome by his own words, Roland added, 'For heaven's sake write and release the girl from her secret promise so that she can have the chance of happiness without feelings of guilt. Then, when you've done that, get into Gillyhook or Pop as fast as you can, and find a girl to have fun with yourself. You'll

347

find that much more satisfying and infinitely more pleasurable than absinthe . . . or any other form of escape from reality,' he put in pointedly.

After a short silence, the hesitant voice said, 'Is that your advice as a doctor?'

'No, it's my advice as an older brother. I wish to God I'd given it three years earlier.'

The village of Guillehoek comprised a group of typical Flemish cottages lying beside a cobblestone road, a small church, an *estaminet*, and a chateau that was now no more than a gutted reminder that anything large enough to be fixed by the sights of German gunners manning the long-distance artillery was a target for destruction. Several of the adjacent cottages had been reduced to rubble with the loss of several Belgian lives, but the remainder of the village was intact and bustling with life. The peasants continued their normal day-to-day routine; the bustling life was provided by the British Army.

Guillehoek was known throughout the sector as a rest-centre and a casualty-clearing-station. Motor and horse-drawn ambulances rumbled through the streets at all hours of the day and night; trucks, motor cycles and staff-cars dashed back and forth on urgent errands; regiments of cavalry clattered in for several weeks during which they exercised their horses, and held impromptu equestrian events which were immensely popular, before clattering out again. And troops from all parts of the British Empire and Commonwealth tramped in from the front-line trenches for a short respite from constant danger.

Guillehoek was popular with the troops because of the cavalry races where pay packets could be lost or exchanged on one race, because there were local girls and British nurses there, because there was the *estaminet* for liquor, and a charitable Forces Canteen where food, non-alcoholic drinks and entertainment were offered. There was also the river to swim in when the weather was warm enough. In the words of the troops 'a proper ruddy paradise'.

Roland was particularly interested in the place because it was to the casualty clearing-station that he sent men in need of treatment beyond his capabilities, and they were either patched up and returned to the trenches, or sent in ambulances to the railhead at

Poperinghe where hospital trains took them to base hospitals, or on to England for the rest of the war. It was his intention to make himself known to the staff and discover the similarities, if any, with Matt Rideaux's unit, for which he still pined, if he was honest with himself.

For a man who had never had close relationships with anyone save his brothers, Roland was surprised at how much he missed the cautious friendship of the Canadian. Charles Barr-Leigh was lively, witty, and generous with comradeship, but Roland could not help feeling it was all a pose to cover a different man underneath. Matt had not given as much of himself, but there had never been any doubts as to his true personality.

The officers were billeted in the cottages in Guillehoek, two to a building, and it surprised Charles almost as much as it surprised Roland himself when he elected to share a billet with Hilary rather than the more obvious choice of the older man. Hilary seemed very pleased. Their talk had done both of them some good. The boy had emerged from his maudlin uncommunicative state, and Roland experienced a strange affinity to the protectiveness he had always felt toward his brothers. With their father almost always absent, the boy Roland had tried to assume a rôle beyond his years of capability where Rex and Chris had been concerned. Rex had soon proved he needed no father-figure and, in retrospect, Roland believed Chris had not even missed it. With no other close friends, and with the constant fear of losing his brothers, Roland had been starved of a sense of responsibility. Hilary had placed it fairly and squarely back in his hands. Or rather, Charles had by confessing his suspicions of the boy's cowardice.

In Roland's mind, the theft of the morphia had been to dull the young subaltern's self-imposed misery over a romantic ideal, not to cover cowardice. That the boy had done it at the time of an unexpected attack had been a dangerous mistake that could have had monstrous consequences, if Charles could have proved it. Roland had reassured the man that he had dealt with the situation and felt confident there would never be a repeat of it, and the whole affair had been put to the back of their minds as the fortunate break in routine arrived.

The family hosting Roland and Hilary consisted of four members: Madame Cocteau, the matriach, Madame de Brouchard, her married daughter whose husband was a prisoner-of-war, her children, Lisette who was seventeen, and Emil who was fourteen. They were quiet peasant folk who made the series of foreign guests as comfortable and content as possible. But the young girl was strictly chaperoned, and the older women offered no more of themselves than polite housewifery. Only the boy seemed inclined to fraternise, and all he spoke of was hoping the war would last long enough for him to join in.

Lisette was very pretty, and Roland had hopes that Hilary might transfer his too-susceptible affections to her, despite the close protection of mother and grandmother. However, the first things they did were sleep for fifteen hours at a stretch, eat a large tasty meal, go for a brief walk around the village to get the lie of the land, then return for a further long comfortable sleep.

As some slight reciprocation of goodwill toward their obligatory hosts, they put on their trench-coats against the March chill and went out to collect wood. It was not exactly scavenging, but blasted trees, split and butchered trunks, broken limbs lying around were there for the taking, and manhandling them onto a push-cart was very heavy work for women. Roland and Hilary found it enjoyable and relaxing, returning to the cottage with a plentiful supply of logs from which they would also feel the benefit.

They sat that evening before a blazing fire and talked of home. Although the family spoke Flemish, they understood French when Roland or Hilary addressed them in that language, and a smattering of English. But they had all retired to the one bedroom they now appeared to share, leaving the two officers alone in the main room of the stone cottage. Hilary did most of the talking, telling Roland about his parents who had been murdered by Taipings, and his rather sombre upbringing by people who had taken on the responsibility of a mission orphan. He had been educated at a church school for the purpose of becoming a minister, but the prospect had never appealed to him and he had volunteered before his eighteenth birthday made him eligible for conscription. On being commissioned and given embarkation leave, the unsophisticated youngster had spent it in London with his fellow-officers. There he had met and been bowled over by a pretty young girl at an after-theatre party. Within the week they had promised each other everlasting devotion, and he had given her an amethyst ring to signify their secret engagement before he left to catch the boat-train.

Listening to all this Roland guessed the truth. Hilary was a well-built youngster with dark sad eyes and a past that would instil romantic Byronic notions in a young girl. Put him in a dashing uniform and order him to war, and her heart would go out to him. But there were thousands more like him, and her heart would go out to them all! On his part, Hilary had plainly broken away from a repressive lifestyle and had been on the brink of adventure, which had only needed a lovely face and soft cuddlesome body to complete it. Probably still a virgin, Hilary had been prevented by the trenches from finding other lovely faces and soft cuddlesome bodies to soften the intensity of his feelings. Here in Guillehoek he would.

In return for his own confidences, Hilary pressed Roland for more information about his family, especially Chris, who appeared to fascinate him. But there was little more to be told about a boy who had always lived in a world of his own, and did so with a vengeance now. Yet, even as he proclaimed this, Roland had the feeling Rex would have found quite a bit to say about their young brother. But then, Rex had always been a *chum* rather than a pseudo-father to Chris.

Had he tried too hard, Roland asked himself as he sat staring into the leaping flames of the fire in company with a boy who was now plainly looking to him for that very thing. Perhaps he should leave Hilary to his fate. The advice he had given both Chris and Rex had been useless. At the time, he had been ruled by standards and principles he had never doubted until now. No, he did not doubt them, exactly. It was simply that he was growing to recognise they often had to be tailored or bent to suit the circumstances. Human nature was vulnerable, men were all different . . . and life was too short. All at once, sitting in that Flemish cottage in a room lit only by the flickering reflections of the fire on plain walls, Roland felt an intense longing to be with his brothers again and somehow show them he understood more than he had done before.

Yet, when he sat in the rough truckle-bed with Hilary soundly asleep in the other one, and tried to write to Rex by the light of a guttering candle, there seemed no way of putting into words what he wanted to convey. Maybe it was too late, anyway. Laying aside pen and paper he settled down for sleep. But he stared at the ceiling long into the night, the pain of Chris's present plight again lowering his spirits along with memories of how it had been when they had all come home for the long summer holidays of 1914.

Charles fixed a trip into Poperinghe with his customary flair, and coerced Roland into taking the other seat in the staff-car. Hilary had been offered a lift in the sidecar of a motor cycle, so they all set off in high spirits for what Charles promised would be a night of fun and frolics. Roland remembered very little of it. An attack of trench-fever overtook him during the evening, and he passed out whilst dancing with a shy serious girl called Marie, finding himself in a bed in the Casualty Clearing Station when the fever broke. His intention to visit the place and investigate the way it operated had not been meant this way. But he got his wish, just the same.

When he returned to the de Brouchard cottage he discovered Hilary had taken his advice and found a girl to cuddle. But it was not a Belgian girl from Pop. Rosie was a volunteer helper in the canteen in Guillehoek, and Roland was pressed into going there the following evening to meet this 'angel'.

Hilary had reserved a table by the simple expedient of hiding the folding chairs behind the hessian curtains, and he brought them out with a flourish as they both sat at the utility table.

There was a gramophone to provide music. *If you were the only girl in the world* was being played over and over again by a maudlin soldier who resisted all attempts to drag him away from the machine. Since the song was very popular with everyone, especially those who had seen *The Bing Boys are Here* whilst on leave, no one was unduly averse to hearing it seven times in succession. But it created an atmosphere of nostalgia that got under a man's skin after a while, and Roland was no exception. This kind of evening was not really popular with him; did not suit his somewhat shy temperament. It also seemed likely he would be playing a very unwelcome third with the young lovebirds, which was even less suited to his temperament.

Hilary went up to the counter to order tea and toast for them, and Roland wished very heartily he had not allowed himself to be talked into the meeting. All the conviviality served to highlight that loneliness that lived with him, these days, and that damned tune going on and on reminded him of the nightclub and Laura looking across a table at him, accusing him of disapproving of her. Yes, he disapproved of her, all right—as a wife for his brother. She was the kind of girl who . . . but it was better not to think along those lines.

Hilary returned with the food, to say his girl was busy in the kitchen and would join them for a short while as soon as she could. But the moment came quicker than expected, for Roland was still in the process of spooning sugar into his tea when Hilary said enthusiastically, 'Good-oh, here's Rosie already.'

At first sight of the girl Roland had a surprise. She was no cuddly eighteen year old, but a woman around his own age, tall, very shapely despite the unflattering overall, with dark hair drawn back around a classic face that betrayed her good breeding. But as she neared their table his surprise turned to outright shock. The last time he had seen this girl was in that nightclub he had just recalled, and she had thrown a glass of red wine in his face while calling him a coward—had done it in front of Laura and the other diners. The humiliation of the incident flooded over him anew in that utility hut filled with smoke and blaspheming men, just a few miles from the trenches of Belgium.

Rosalind Tierney's smile was for Hilary alone during the first few moments. But it slowly faded leaving her face pale and intense when she turned as Roland got to his feet to be presented.

'Hallo, Rosalind,' he said quietly, remembering how drunk she had been that night and hoping it had passed from her memory.

But it had not. She stood looking him over from head to foot as her lip began to curl. 'My God,' she cried, 'so they finally caught up with you, did they? That means you didn't even have the guts to proclaim yourself a "conchie".' Spinning round to Hilary she went on, 'Is *this* the man you described as your friend, sweetie? Well, let me warn you right now. Watch him when the guns start firing . . . then see if you feel the same way.'

With that bitter advice she turned and walked off again, leaving the pair in the corner staring after her.

'What was all that about?' asked Hilary in puzzled tones. 'Do you know each other?'

But, unlike the previous occasion, Roland could not take it on the chin this time. He had been through too much lately. Seeing only her accusing face, hearing only her vicious words, he headed for the door and almost fell out through it in his effort to get away. Back in the hut, the soldier was playing *If you were the only girl in the world* for the eighth time. The melody rang in Roland's ears as he lurched through the darkness of the night, uncaring of which direction he followed, while the enclosing blackness was constantly broken by the vivid flash of heavy artillery, and the floating arching star-shells in the distance. Out there, some poor devils were being shot to pieces and leaving girls like Rosalind Tierney lost, terrified and angry.

For the next couple of days Roland kept much to himself. The start of April had brought a brief flush of very warm weather, so he took advantage of the freedom to walk in open spaces. Not that the flat countryside around the area held any charm for the eye of the beholder. The army boots of too many nations had churned up the fields and lanes, the bitter weather of winter had brought decimation of the poplars so profuse in the area, and the gutted chateau stood as a grim reminder that shells could easily reach the village if anyone considered it necessary.

But the sky was a clear light blue, and the sun shone down with welcome warmth, sparkling the river as it ran alongside the road on the outskirts of Guillehoek. That was enough to tempt a man like Roland to let it soothe his soul as he wandered with his thoughts for company. Certainly, he felt relief from claustrophobia, and pleasure from smelling sweet fresh air, but these two things did not soothe his soul.

For some while he was burdened with comparisons. The flat-featured Flemish landscape, even without the destruction of war, was a poor substitute for the beauty around Tarrant Royal, and the insidious seduction of the zephyr caressing his face with warm fingers made him long so much for what he had left behind, he found himself blinking back tears. Crying was totally out of character, yet he felt no surprise or dismay. Since he had left England it was as if he had been slowly bleeding.

He walked for a long while alongside the river, conscious of the bubbling, splashing water as it ran, yet lost in the lanes and meadows of the Dorset he had loved for twenty-six years. He travelled in memory along the way from Greater Tarrant to his home, seeing old Carter running the station single-handed with love and pride, and passing the Punch and Judy Tea Rooms where Chris always got away without paying, because he forgot to take any money with him, and the little waitress was sweet on him. Then it was on over the bridge, past the water-meadows and the duck-pond, with the snowy birds quacking happily. After that, one came to Ted Peach's forge, the village green where Rex played cricket with such cavalier merry gusto, Dr Deacon's house and surgery opposite the green, the George and Dragon with its spreading oak, and the old church with its beautiful stained-glass windows glowing like jewels in the sunshine.

Just past the church was the uphill turning to Tarrant Hall, and there were Priddy, Minks, and Dawkins smiling a greeting. Behind them in the panelled hall were Rex and Chris in flannels and school blazers, full of pleasure at all being together again.

Coming to a low bridge he stood with one booted foot on the cornerstone and gazed into the past as the tears swelled onto his cheeks. Had he been so *very* wrong to want to preserve all that? With Chris broken in mind as well as body at nineteen, and Rex facing death or mutilation every time he climbed into a cockpit, was it so incomprehensible to everyone else that he had wanted to keep *something* of them so that they could never be entirely destroyed?

Yet Charles Barr-Leigh had already lost two brothers, with two more at the front whose lives, along with his own, stood every risk of being lost, also. Three others at school would be drawn into it, if it went on long enough. An entire family sacrificed for England!

Only now he had witnessed such sacrifice at first-hand did he believe he must have seen things through eyes blinded by short-sightedness. England would have to be saved by a whole generation for the next one, so that children like David Sheridan would value and preserve all its traditions and beliefs.

At the thought of Chris's son, Roland bowed his head in regret. After he had turned Marion out of Tarrant Hall he had not seen the boy, except for glimpses as he had passed the doctor's garden. Yet David was a true Sheridan, his brother's child, who had every right of birth to be brought up at Tarrant Hall and run laughing through the estate. Instead, he was being reared by a village girl at his grandfather's house, while his mother acted nurse to a young man lost in the labyrinth of his own mind. The child's father did not know of his existence, his senior uncle had deplored it. Only

Rex had made him welcome, had represented the family to which he rightly belonged, despite the mistake of his conception. To this two-year-old boy and his like would fall the responsibility of preserving the spirit of England, and the spirit of those who had fought to save it.

With that strong in his mind, he sat there beside the river and began to write in his notebook all he wanted to say to his young nephew: It took the form of a letter, telling him the things about England that meant so much to him and asking the boy to regard them, in years to come, as a legacy of love from all those who had died so that he might have them.

When he had finished he realised he could never send it. David was too young to read, and Marion would find such words insincere from a man to whom she had sent so many white feathers. At that point, it struck him that he had just written the next offering by 'The Waysider' for the *Gillyhook Gazette*. Although it had come spontaneously from his longings, it must surely echo the thoughts of many.

Roland stayed out for most of that day, sitting beside the river to eat the bread and cheese given him, on request, by Madame de Brouchard. Most of the time he was in reverie and hardly noticed the time passing. It was only a growing chill that signified late afternoon that sent him back to the house.

Hilary had been out all day, also, and returned in time for supper in a strangely excited mood. At first, Roland thought he had been drinking heavily, and was disappointed that the boy had slipped back to his old ways. But after the Belgian family had left them alone before the fire, as usual after the meal, Hilary revealed the source of his restlessness. It came out hesitantly, however, after a lengthy chat about the concert to be staged in the canteen by a dozen members of an Australian regiment presently in Guillehoek.

'They vow it will beat anything yet put on at the Cloth Hall,' commented Roland with a smile, it being a popular joke about the famous old building in Ypres which was now no more than a shell amidst rubble. 'We daren't miss it.'

'I've already asked Rosie to go with me,' confessed Hilary shyly, irritating Roland with a diminutive of her name that did not suit her in the least. It made her sound like a barmaid.

Roland leant forward and tapped out the pipe he had taken to smoking since inhabiting the trenches. The aroma of the tobacco helped to disguise the smell of dank earth and other viler things always present.

'Hilary, you aren't making the same mistake, are you? My advice to find another girl to cuddle was meant in general terms. I trust you haven't any plans for buying Miss Tierney an amethyst ring to hang round her neck when you leave.'

The youngster shook his head as he gazed at the burning logs in the hearth. 'I'm not that much of a fool any longer. My feeling for Megan was frightfully immature.'

'I see,' said Roland faintly amused. 'Have you written to the girl about it?'

'No. I didn't think it was a very decent thing for a chap to do. To suggest he had other interests now, I mean. Not frightfully flattering for a girl, is it?'

'No, but it's honest.'

'Well, I'm not sure honesty is the right form, in this instance,' came the frank admission. 'In any case, she's probably realised it was all very shallow, as I have.'

'You were deadly serious when you first told me about it,' Roland reminded him.

'I know, and that's what I thought until . . . well, until I learnt about life.'

Putting the pipe on the corner of the rough scrubbed table, he studied the youthful face gilded by the firelight. It was sensitive, vulnerable, with a full generous mouth.

'That's a very profound remark.'

Hilary turned so that only one side of his face was illuminated. The other was shadowed by the evening darkness in that room.

'Doc, I don't know what I'd have done without your friendship. I've never had anyone to talk to about things . . . really important things. You've helped me no end.'

Roland felt strangely embarrassed. 'You'd have grown out of that infatuation, in time, anyway.'

'I didn't mean that, actually. Knowing you is sort of like having a brother of my own, although I feel frightful about it, in some ways. Because of Chris.'

'Because of Chris?' he repeated in surprise.

'I suppose it's that I hope he wouldn't feel I'm going behind his back and trying to take his place. I do feel most awfully sorry for him, you know.'

'Yes, I know you do.'

'I . . . I think about him a lot, and about all the things that have happened to him. When he was my age he already had a son, whereas I . . . well, I hadn't even . . . I mean I didn't know about girls. *Really* about them.'

Already suspecting what he was about to learn, Roland knew he would not stop the boy's confession.

'I suppose it must have been obvious,' Hilary said with self-conscious offhandedness. 'This afternoon she . . . Rosie, that is . . . she invited me to her quarters and let me *love* her. Isn't it absolutely marvellous? I had no idea. And Rosie was splendid. I was under the impression that girls weren't keen about it. I mean, I always thought a fellow had to talk them into it. You know, take them unawares.' He laughed nervously. 'Rosie was frightfully keen . . . and almost took *me* unawares. Well, not quite, you know. She really is the most ripping girl, Doc. I'm sure she wouldn't have said what she did the other night if she really knew you.'

His eager voice enthusing about how easy it had been and how wonderful loving a girl was faded to the background as Roland fought the anger sparked off by the thought of Rosalind Tierney, bright star of the County set, prostituting her body to anyone who wanted it—even an inexperienced boy.

Early the following morning Charles burst in from the neighbouring cottage with the news that they had been ordered back to the front-line.

'There's a big offensive at Arras underway, and the regiments that relieved us have been sent down there as reinforcements,' he told Roland and Hilary. 'There's a rumour the Canadians have taken Vimy Ridge and are holding on to it by the skin of their teeth. With a new push in support of them by Anzac troops, this could be the beginning of the end, Doc.'

'If it's all happening at Arras, why've *we* got to go back?' complained Hilary sitting up in the truckle bed, his hair rumpled from sleep, his young face full of dismay.

'Because if this is the big push through to Berlin, lad, we shall have to attack in our sector, as well,' came the breezy expansive reply. 'Come on, show a leg! We're moving out in two hours' time.'

'*No!*' It came out as almost an anguished cry from the youngster who looked no more than the schoolboy he really was.

Charles flung Roland a significant look and seemed on the verge of verbally attacking Hilary. But he was prevented by Roland getting out of bed, saying in lighthearted tones, 'The boy has just discovered the full extent of the delights of village maidens. Small wonder he views imminent departure with cries of protest.'

No one else gave cries of protest, but they were there in their set expressions as they fell in with all their kit to march back to the trenches they had left less than two weeks before. The march to Guillehoek had been accompanied by laughter and the songs beloved of soldiers. There was no singing on leaving the village; just silent men marching through the cobbled street watched by Flemish peasants full of renewed fear for what the move would mean for themselves and their homes.

A different trench, a different bunker. But they were all the same. The smell, the high enclosing walls, the sudden death. An hour after they arrived it was as if they had never left, except that it was curiously quiet as the men went about with tight lips and haunted faces. No one believed this was the final push to Berlin. After nearly three years, it would take a march down Unter den Linden with Berliners lining it on their knees for it to really sink in. But they all knew it would not be long before they would be ordered to make another all-out attack, which would gain them a few hundred yards and lose them a few thousand comrades.

Those not on stand-to wrote long letters to their families and friends, and some to people whom a stupid long-ago quarrel had alienated. These last were to be posted in the event of their loss in the coming battle. Friends exchanged packages of personal effects to be sent to designated addresses if one should survive the other. Notoriously quick tempers were now well controlled, cardsharps no longer cheated their comrades. Even the rats were spared their usual persecution in a mood of 'live and let live'.

This tense prelude to battle was unknown to Roland, who had never been involved in a planned concerted assault before, and the mood caught him, too. Literally burning his candles at both ends he sat well into the night writing letters to Rex, Chris and Tessa; to Priddy and Minks and Dawkins; to the Rector of Tarrant Royal; to his bank manager, solicitor and, finally, to

David Sheridan. The last three were only to be posted in the event of his death.

The other two occupants of the bunker were contrasts in examples of stress. Hilary was very quiet and drinking absinthe again. Charles was volubly restless, pacing the dug-out and smoking cigars one after the other.

Seeing Roland writing yet another letter, he said with his inimitable bravado, 'I have no need for instructions to the family solicitor. They've already done it twice when my older brothers were wiped out. It'll just be a question of handing it all on to Ralph, who's the next in line after me . . . until they find *him* on the wire, and are forced to change the name to Bertram. If the war goes on long enough young Rupert might even inherit. But if *he* goes on the final push to Berlin, he'll be able to imitate Lord Cardigan at the Charge of the Light Brigade and say, "Here goes the last of the Barr-Leighs!"'

'I don't think much of that, if it's meant to be a joke,' said Hilary thickly. 'There are times when you are most awfully unfunny, Charles.'

In one of the flash spates of anger that worried Roland, Charles turned on the young subaltern and grabbed him by the throat of his tunic.

'You damned impertinent blighter!' he roared. 'Just because you've finally dipped your wick it doesn't make you a *man*. You're still a lily-livered mission orphan, and don't forget it!'

Roland got to his feet and gripped Charles's shoulder. 'I think that's more than enough on the subject. The lad is feeling the strain, as we all are.'

Charles swung round, shaking Roland's hand off. 'Trust you to leap to his defence. Don't think I don't know what's going on. You made it pretty obvious when you insisted on sharing the little sap's quarters in Gillyhook.'

Furious, Roland grabbed him again, and all his inborn pride and defensive instincts led him to say, with quiet viciousness, 'You filthy-minded bastard! If you don't apologise I'll knock those words right down your throat.'

Since Charles was shorter and less weighty, the prospect seemed unattractive enough to cool his temper. 'All right, all right, take it easy, Doc,' he said with soothing sarcasm. 'It's immaterial to me what you two do, and let's not lose our heads *before* the Huns can knock them off.' With that he ducked beneath the low entrance and left the bunker.

Hilary was staring at Roland with a frightened look on his face. 'He didn't really mean that, did he? Is that what others think?'

Roland knew the reason for his fear. 'Of course he doesn't imagine we have that kind of relationship. And neither does anyone else. You've made it pretty obvious you've been mooning around over some girl ever since you've been here.' He ran his hand through his hair, still on the fringe of anger. 'Charles has been at the front for a lot longer than I have . . . or you, for that matter. We have to make allowances.'

Hilary let that sink in for a few minutes. Then he said, 'Why do people always seem to misunderstand you? I told Rosie what you told me about volunteering *before* you were conscripted.'

'Did she believe you?' he asked wearily.

The dark head shook. 'I don't think so. Why does she hate you so much?'

With a sigh he said, 'It's not me but the whole world that she hates. The man she loved very deeply was killed during the first weeks of the war. Then she lost her father and her brother at sea when their ships went down. Her grief for them turned me into a coward because I was still safely in England and not wearing a uniform.'

'Did you know the man she loved?'

'Yes. He was a very decent chap.'

Turning to pick up something from his bed Hilary looked at it as it lay in his hands. 'If I get killed, I'd like her to have this. Will you give it to her, Doc?'

'Not if it's an amethyst ring,' he said, to lighten the mood.

'It's my mother's cameo. It's all they found in the ruins of the mission after the Taiping attack. I wasn't supposed to have it until I was twenty-one, but the Head of the mission gave it to me on the night before I left for France.' He looked up at Roland. 'Promise me you'll give it to her in person, to make sure she gets it.'

'Of course,' Roland assured him, almost seeing Chris sitting there in his place. 'But you'll be able to hand it over yourself the next time we go to Gillyhook for a rest period.'

After initial advances the fighting around Arras deteriorated into the inevitable slaughter between forces entrenched within range of each other, and the Allies were forced to face the fact that the Germans must have brought up fresh troops without their knowledge. The R.F.C. was asked for more concentrated observation services, but they were pushed to their limit with exhausted pilots and faulty machines. In desperation they turned to the Royal Navy, who sent to France eight squadrons of pilots with their own aircraft who worked with their military counterparts.

Back on the ground, the faltering offensive continued, token attacks as diversionary measures being ordered all along the line. The Guillehoek contingent were engaged in one barely a week after their return.

Roland was busy with casualties soon after the attack began in the hour before dawn. The noise of it was now familiar, but none the less disturbing. Now the action had begun everyone seemed back to normal, and he realised it was the waiting for battle that was so destructive on men's nerves. Once they were in the thick of it, they became steady.

The same applied to himself. The growing number of men waiting for his attention did not throw him into a panic, and he worked methodically with hands that were skilful and sure. He was glad he had seen the clearing-station in Guillehoek, where most of the men would have to be sent. He chatted to some about it as he applied field-dressings or injected morphia to help their anguish. None of them really listened, he knew, but the sound of a calm confident voice against the moans and background gunfire gave them a sense of normality in the midst of Hell.

It seemed that he had been on the go for hours answering the constant call of 'Over here, Doc' and an orderly had just brought him a great tin mug of strong tea when a commotion outside heralded two stretcher-bearers holding by the arms a man who was doubled forward and sobbing uncontrollably.

'Mr Sheridan, can you take over quick?' called one as soon as he spotted Roland. 'It's a bit tricky, sir.'

Straightening up from applying a field-dressing to an ear that was half torn off, he frowned. The casualty was an officer, and however badly they were wounded they rarely made such an exhibition of their suffering.

'What's the problem?' he asked, nodding to an orderly to finish what he was doing, and starting to walk across to his men.

'It's Mr Barr-Leigh, sir. Run amok, he did, and shot Mr Bisset.'

The place seemed to spin momentarily. *'What?'*

The other man spoke up. 'We was told he shot Lieutenant Bisset, sir—*dead.*'

'I . . . I don't understand. Who told you this?' he demanded.

'Sergeant Crane. He came to fetch us. When we got there Lieutenant Barr-Leigh was crouching at the bottom of the trench in this state, sir. Mr Bisset was lying there dead beside him. Seems the order came to go over the top, and Mr Bisset was halfway up the rampart when his hold slipped and he fell down jamming his foot between the duck-boards. While he was struggling to free himself, Mr Barr-Leigh starts screaming about funking it. Then he shot him—in cold blood,' finished the man in shocked tones. 'Then he sort of collapsed. Major Tanner wanted him out of the way, and sent Sergeant Crane for someone to bring him to you.' The two men exchanged looks, then the same one went on, 'He's not violent any longer, Mr Sheridan. But he seems to have gone off his head.'

In a state of shock Roland nodded to them that he would take over, then put his arm under Charles's armpits to help him to a nearby upturned box. In the midst of his sorrow for young Hilary, Roland knew this man was a fellow sufferer of his young brother Chris. A man who could take no more.

Feeling sick at heart, he said, 'Come on, old fellow. It's all right now.'

The familiar face gazed up at him as tears flooded down it. 'I *had* to do it,' he pleaded hysterically. 'He was a coward. The order came, and he wouldn't go. All my brothers went, and they're all dead. I'm the last of the Brudenells,' he sobbed, identifying himself with Lord Cardigan at the Crimea. 'You have to shoot cowards in battle. It's laid down in orders. Shoot them in the back as they run. I knew he would funk it. I watched him and he tried to come back. I had to do it. I *had* to do it. You do see that, don't you?'

Once seated on the box Charles seemed to vanish out of himself. His eyes glazed and he slumped back against the wall, staring at some secret known only to himself and muttering unintelligibly. As Roland prepared a sedative, he blamed himself for not recognising who had really taken the morphia from his bag that day.

18

Dr Chandler came in at his usual time smiling a greeting. 'Hallo. Had a good night?'

'Yes. It was the first time I didn't wake up in a sweat of fear,' Chris told him.

'Good-oh. That's one bloody big step forward.'

'Your language gets worse.'

The doctor grinned. 'Put it down to my chequered career Down Under. We can't all be sons of some English country squire.'

Chris tried to shift to a more comfortable position. 'I wonder if my childhood was chequered.'

'Why don't you write and ask your brothers?'

He had heard that one before. 'It can't have been too exciting, if I've forgotten it.'

Settling on the chair beside the bed, the older man raised his eyebrows in a quizzical expression. 'You forgot Gallipoli. That was exciting enough for any bastard, I should have thought.'

As usual, he had an answer that effectively checkmated Chris's arguments. No longer afraid of Chandler because he was too similar to Neil Frencham, Chris had gradually established a wary relationship with the neurologist and trusted him enough to co-operate in the daily sessions together.

Christmas had come and gone without his knowing, and he was still frightened at the way entire series of months could be lost from his life without warning. One minute it had been autumn, the next minute spring again. Where had he been, meantime? Bill Chandler called it 'involuntary withdrawal' due to the returning memory of something Chris did not want to face. It made him seem a weakling, yet total recall of the hell of Gallipoli was something that took a bit of facing. Most of it had become reality now and, two days ago, he had finally confessed the disillusion of discovering Neil Frencham's true feelings for him. The doctor had pointed out that Chris was a young man with girl's eyes, and had been fortunate in that he had attracted a man who had plainly had deep respect for him as well as male passion.

'I've known of some youngsters like you being the victim of mass sodomy in the trenches. Poor bastards mostly commit battle suicide at the first opportunity. We've got one here, though, clean out of his mind.'

Chris had found the information sobering. Speaking more and more about his months in Gallipoli helped him to gain a feeling of identity; a personality of his own. He could now remember feelings he had had out there beneath the sun and the bullets; the shock of seeing Rochford-Clarke's mortal wound. He recalled how he had translated everything he could think of into all the languages he knew, written poetry, made sketches. He also vividly recalled that day Neil had swum naked with him, then confessed his love. He had climbed a cliff wanting to die, yet something told him there had been more than desperation to get away from Neil that had been behind his death-wish. *That* lay further back than Gallipoli; back in the part of his life that was still a mystery. Before Gallipoli there was no more than a blank, with a few disconnected memories of boyhood that told him little of importance. He was avid to learn what lay in that blank, yet strangely frightened of doing so.

At the moment, they were working on his uncontrollable spasmodic recollections of pages of figures and meaningless words. They told him he had worked on translating secret messages and inventing codes for the army prior to Gallipoli, and he guessed that was why he had been convinced he must hide what he had written of them, and why he must not mention them to anyone. Because he was ready to recall such things, his daily sessions with the neurologist were designed to hasten recollection so that he would not scribble classified information on any scrap of paper he could find.

But he hated his new room with no other view from the window than a brick wall, and repeatedly asked to be moved. The answer was always the same: a view of the grounds would distract him from concentrating. His habit of escaping reality in drawing or day-dreaming was well-known, and they felt he was recovering fast enough now to be able to face his past. Yet they had no intention of telling him the details of it. *He* had to tell *them;* and he could only do that by remembering.

His first request on coming out of his lost winter months had been to be allowed to see the nurse called Marion. They told him she had left the hospital. When he asked why, they avoided answering. He had then asked about his brothers. Roland was now a medical officer in Belgium; Rex was in the north of England drumming up recruits for the R.F.C. His wife was with him. That information had been supplied without request, and Chris realised he still felt the same about Laura Sheridan. It was one detail he did not tell Dr Chandler.

But he really quite enjoyed the daily sessions which demanded the full use of his brain, and that morning he took the pages handed him and set to studying them intently. Part of his pleasure in the task was watching the astonishment on the other man's face as he unravelled pages of apparent nonsense in a very short time. That morning was no exception—at least, until the very last page he was given. Staring in deep concentration, his first reaction was one of disappointment.

'This isn't a language I know,' he admitted.

'Yes, you do.'

His spirits lowered. 'Oh lord, I was doing so well until now.'

The Doctor stood up smiling. 'That one is a deliberate poser. To stop you getting too damned big-headed. Just look at it for a while until it comes to you. I can wait.'

While Chris puzzled over the odd-looking words, the other man went to the door and asked whoever was outside to bring a tray of tea and biscuits. Then he returned to sit beside the bed, silent and relaxed. The solution remained elusive until the mid-morning refreshment had arrived and almost been consumed. Then something stirred in Chris's brain to suggest understanding.

In the middle of eating a biscuit, he murmured, 'Well, I've no idea what it means, but I think the language could be Turkish. I only studied it briefly during the voyage to Gallipoli, you know. I'm hardly an expert.' He looked up at his questioner and smiled. 'Colonel Petworth once told me it was useless unless I knew the words for "bugger off".'

A big smile crossed the sunbrowned face. 'You didn't take his advice, then. In rather more refined manner, that is what that phrase means.'

It struck Chris as so crafty a move on their part, he said, 'You sly devil!'

'I have to be with blokes like you, who are even slyer.'

Chris finished his biscuit, lost in recollection of that time and place he had put from his memory for over a year. 'It seems awful that they are all dead now. When I left that Headquarters they were all so certain we had made a breakthrough by capturing that gun.' His hand dropped heavily to the coverlet. 'I wanted to die out there, you know. I tried to climb the cliff to the top so I would be seen and machine-gunned. I couldn't face the fact that a man's mind counted for nothing against the attraction of his body. Neil wasn't the first person to show me that. It had happened before.'

'Oh? Other men?' came the casual question.

But there came the grey mist that blocked the view into the past, once more, and he had no idea why he had said those words.

'I don't know . . . I mean, I don't remember them. But it *had* happened before.'

'At school, perhaps. A senior boy?'

'Perhaps.'

'Or maybe it was a girl?'

Thoughts of Laura filled him immediately. Did *she* find his body attractive? Hers made him long to touch it without clothes on.

'You like girls, don't you?' came the nudging question.

'If they're intelligent,' was his immediate reply.

Dr Chandler tilted his chair back on two legs and looked at him musingly. 'You set great store by intellect, don't you? Do you never get a thrill from looking at a girl's shape?'

He knew what the man was doing. 'Fat chance I get of seeing one in this room.'

Undaunted the neurologist went on, 'Suppose I sent in a young redhaired nurse and locked you both in. What would you do?'

Why a redhead? Did he know about the passion for Laura? 'Ask her to make my pillows more comfortable,' he said bluntly, knowing such an answer would annoy the man.

'A bit unimaginative, isn't it?' came the response.

'What would you do with a girl if you were lying here like me?'

Dr Chandler grinned. 'As much as she'd let me before smacking my face. Chris, why do you always retreat from me whenever I bring up the subject of sexual attraction?'

'I thought you were here to help me remember secret codes. Let's get on with that!'

367

The chair legs hit the ground with a sharp sound. 'I've also helped you remember many other things, including some damned erotic French poetry. You're so bloody proud of your mind! Why aren't you as proud of your body? It's a very fine one.' He held up his hand. 'All right, take that look off your face, young man, I'm not about to rape you. I prefer young female redheads.'

'Then lock *yourself* in a room with one, and leave me alone,' he flamed, in sudden inexplicable anger. 'It's always the same, this obsession with my body.'

'Is it any worse than your obsession with your brain? There are very few people who possess a mind the equal of yours, which will mean a very lonely life if that's all you're going to look for in people.'

'I can't look for anything, can I, shut in here like this?' he accused, really worked up. 'I already lead a lonely life. Haven't you any idea how lonely it is day after day staring at a damn brick wall and longing to get out into the sunshine with all the others? I wish to God I was back as I was last year. I might have been in worse pain and bandaged to the eyeballs, but I had two windows showing me a whole world outside, and all the other men in the ward.'

'But you shunned them, I understand. Hid yourself away by removing your spectacles so that you wouldn't have to admit they were there. Are you saying it would be different now?'

'And there were visits from my brothers,' he ranted on, 'as well as Marion there all the time.'

'You liked her, did you?'

'Yes,' he flung at the man. 'She didn't ask damn foolish questions all the time.'

'But I do, is that it?'

He chose not to answer and would not look his questioner's way.

'All right, Chris, I've put you through quite enough today, I think. But here's an answer, for a change—to a question you have asked many times. You're leaving this room tomorrow morning. We've decided it's time to transfer you to another hospital where you won't feel so lonely.'

So Chris never did walk through the shrubbery he had studied for a year, dreaming of what lay beyond it. He left the hospital in an ambulance with darkened windows, but he was lying almost flat so could not have seen much if they had been clear. A strange fear beset him. Despite his longing to get away, his fantasies of the world awaiting him, he was afraid and even more lonely than he had been in that last room. A fleeting return of his old suspicions had him believing he was the victim of some strange organisation which was using him for its own dreadful purposes, and he was presently being spirited away, as Marion had been, where his brother and beautiful wife would not find him. All the conversation about attractive bodies the day before must mean they knew now how he felt about Laura.

But Bill Chandler, who travelled in the ambulance with Chris and the nurse, seemed his normal friendly self, and Chris gradually drifted into relaxed sleep. The laboured sound of an engine tackling a steep hill roused him again a few minutes before they came to a halt.

Dr Chandler smiled at him. 'We're here . . . and you're not about to be thrown into a deep dungeon where your body will never be found.'

'How . . . how did you know what I was thinking?' he asked in astonishment.

'Sorry, Chris, but we cheated. You were given a sedative this morning to make the journey easier for you. You shout rather a lot in your sleep.'

He glared at the man, wondering what else he might have said. But the rear doors were now being opened, and several white-coated orderlies were there ready to carry him in. Curiosity grew uppermost. Through the open doors he could see grey stone walls covered by ivy, sunshine on a neat gravel drive, an impressive front entrance with heavily-studded door that stood open to reveal a polished wood floor covered with drugget to take the constant tread of army boots.

They began to slide the stretcher out carefully, taking the weight with practised ease, and the vista widened to reveal a very large crenellated house with trees surrounding it. For a brief moment he believed they had driven in a circle returning to the place they had just left, but when they finally carried him inside after a curiously long business in the open, he saw that the interior of this house was completely strange to him. A huge panelled hall with an open fireplace that would need a whole tree sawn into logs to fill it, a graceful panelled staircase leading to the upper floors, a glimpse right through the entrance hall to a room containing a lovingly polished refectory-table, and a recessed window-nook that revealed a hint of colourful gardens.

He looked up at Bill Chandler quickly. 'I want a window that lets me see something other than a brick wall.'

The man was studying him with surprising intentness. 'What would you most like to see, Chris?'

'I don't know . . . trees, flowers,' he extemporised. 'It will have to be a room on my own, I suppose, so I won't be able to see other people.'

The doctor nodded. 'I think you'll be happy when you get to it.'

Chris thought the man's tone hardly matched the optimism of his words, and said so.

'I had a feeling you were going to be more excited than this over the place, that's all,' came the comment.

'I might be when I've seen it all. But it's just like the other one, really, and it has the same kind of antiseptic smell. No doubt, there'll be strawberry blancmange here, too.'

With that pronouncement Chris concentrated on looking around as they carried him through the long panelled corridor, past the open doors of rooms turned into wards, until the end of the impressive passageway was reached and light burst in from all directions. His room was, in effect, a very large conservatory.

It would be like living in the middle of the garden, he thought joyously. There were blinds that could be pulled for shade, but he would have a panoramic view of graceful lawns, beds of roses and forget-me-nots, colourful mixed borders, a dove-cote, a distant sunken garden and, beyond that, an amphitheatre of green hills covered with grazing sheep. In addition, he could see through the inner glass to the men in the ward, despite physical isolation.

He turned to say something of his feelings to the neurologist, but he was no longer there. Just the nurse who had travelled with him, the orderlies preparing to transfer him to the bed, and a strange staff-nurse who was supervising the operation.

'Hallo, Mr Sheridan,' she greeted him briskly. 'I don't know what you've done to deserve the best room in the house, especially one of your own, but it must have been something very special. I shall expect you to be a model patient.'

'I haven't been up till now,' he told her frankly, 'so I shouldn't think there's much chance of it. Where is Dr Chandler, by the way?'

'He'll be back presently.'

Why did people in hospitals never answer questions, he thought irritably, the pain of being shifted from stretcher to bed temporarily blighting his sunny spirits. But he was not that way for long. The delight of this place after his last solitary confinement returned, despite the interruptions of being washed and put into clean pyjamas—which had already been done before he left the other place—and given a lunch-tray containing food of the usual boring quality. But he was hungry and ate it all, feeling an unusual bubble of happiness inside him.

The trays had all been cleared away before Bill Chandler came to see him and ask if he approved of his new quarters.

'I'll say,' he enthused. 'But I don't understand it, at all. Firstly, you keep me shut up in a place where I can't see a thing, because you say I'd be distracted. Now, I'm suddenly put here where there's so much going on and so much to sketch, I don't know what to concentrate on first. What's it all about? There's something behind all this, isn't there?'

The man who so strongly resembled Neil Frencham gave a faint smile. 'You're too intelligent, by half, boy. Well, we thought you were ready to go one stage further in your recovery. It seems we anticipated too much.'

'Why?' He was mystified by it all. 'I *am* ready. In this room I'll progress very quickly, you'll see. I love it here already.'

'You should, Chris. You were born and brought up here. Tarrant Hall is your home.'

The bubble of happiness vanished as the implication sank in. He sat silently trying to accept the setback in the way he had learnt to accept others. Then he took off the spectacles and laid them on the starched cover. He no longer wanted to look at childhood scenes that meant nothing whatever to him.

Another damned hotel-room, thought Rex as they were conducted to the first-floor of the Hare and Hounds. They seemed to have done nothing but pack suitcases in one country inn to unpack them some hours later in another for the past three months.

The room into which they were shown followed the usual pattern—large bed with lumpy feather mattress, chintz-covered chairs, marble-topped washstand, monoprints of The Hunt on the walls, casement window overlooking a forecourt of cobbles, where wooden benches and tables provided a convenient meeting-place for the men of the village. Except that there were few men of the villages left. The customers who sat at the rough-hewn tables now were troops on leave, farm-workers too old or infirm to be conscripted, and factory-girls on a day out—bold laughing creatures with bright lips, strident voices, and cigarettes in their hands, whose unusual freedom as substitute males had gone to their heads.

Rex found the 'new woman' unattractive, but Laura championed their liberal outlooks and attitudes. He often found her out there talking to them, her face alive, her laughter as spontaneous if not as loud as theirs, and was forced to admit that she had not looked as happy since giving up the theatre.

For the first month of his posting in England he had been recovering his own health and sanity, so hardly noticed the inner change in his wife. They had had so little time together, and even that had been dominated by the desperation of a forthcoming parting, perhaps forever. So Rex had had no standard by which to compare the new pattern of living they were forced to adopt. Never before had they lived as a day-to-day husband and wife, although their present mode was hardly usual, touring the country with a night or two in each place he gave a lecture, then several weeks in some small hotel such as this present one near an airfield where he trained new pilots to fly every model of aircraft they were likely to be forced to use in France.

At first, he had blamed the illness following Laura's dangerous abortion for her lack of vivacity. That their reunion had not been totally rapturous had been due to his own incapacity of a half-healed thigh wound and an arm in plaster, plus Laura's lingering internal sensitivity to any kind of sexual union during that first month's leave he had been given on arrival in England. Now, they could love each other as freely and imaginatively as they always had. Yet the fire seemed to have gone out of her.

The elderly porter put their cases on the rack, expressing his wish that they would be comfortable during their brief stay. But he refused the tip Rex offered.

'Oh no, Captain Sheridan. It's a privilege to do even such a small service for a gentleman like yourself. I've lost both my boys. One went down with his ship in the Dardanelles, the other in the North Sea. But all the time there are young men like you keeping the flag flying, I feel they won't be sacrificed in vain.'

The man went out quickly, and Rex pocketed the half-crown in some relief. Things were a bit tight until pay-day at the end of the week.

'I asked the girl to bring up some tea,' said Laura, unfastening the fox fur and throwing it onto the bed.

'I'd rather go down for it.'

She glanced at him quickly. 'You won't get served with a brandy at this hour.'

'When did I say anything about brandy?' he asked, irritated by her inference. 'It's a sunny day, and I noticed an attractive tea-garden round at the side. It would be nicer than sitting in here, surely.'

She came across the room to him, and he thought again that he would never tire of looking at her. Her illness had made her willowy; her beauty had taken on a fragility that increased his desire, yet heightened tenderness.

'Sorry, darling. I know you hate being shut in. It's just that the journey seemed so long, and I feel filthy. I don't think I'm up to facing the public.'

'I'm not asking you to do a song-and-dance act down there, Laura. You don't have to "face the public" to drink tea and eat a buttered muffin.'

He expected her to make a face at him, or show her tongue cheekily. Instead, she said with surprising bitterness, 'I know only too well, *you* are the last person to ask me to do a song-and-dance act!"

It touched him on the raw. 'I didn't put an end to your career. You did that yourself.'

She swung away and went to grip the windowsill as she gazed out at the rural scene. 'Go on with the rest of it, then. How Marion's letter made you so crazy you flew through the middle of the whole German Air Force, won the Croix de Guerre, and returned to England the wounded hero so that we could live happily together as normal man and wife.'

'But we're not, are we?' This mood always descended on her so suddenly he was never prepared for it. 'How long is it going to take you to adjust?'

She spun round to face him. 'Adjust to what? This nomadic life going from city-to-city, village-to-village, living in country inns that are all sickeningly rustic, and where old yokels pull their forelocks with reverence as they decline your half-crowns?'

'When you were doing it as Laurie Pagett or Madame Sherry you thought it the ideal life. I'm not a fool, Laura. I knew you weren't the normal wife and mother type when I married you.'

'Why *did* you marry me, Rex?'

'Because you slapped my face when I tried to love you without it.'

She stared at him for a moment or two in indecision. 'At least you've started being honest, instead of pretending it was all roses and romance.'

'It *was* all roses and romance,' he said quietly. 'Have you forgotten the occasion?'

'How can I remember something that happened while I was in a state of shock?' she cried.

'If I had proposed on the stage of Masters' Theatre, you'd have remembered every detail, no doubt.'

'When did I ever make a secret of how I feel about the theatre?'

'Never. But the reason you gave for continuing was that you couldn't bear to sit at home reading the daily casualty lists while I was away fighting. You would go to pieces, you said, if you couldn't lose yourself in acting. I'm here now, safe and well. The reason is invalid.'

She looked trapped standing with her hands behind her on the windowsill, and her beautiful eyes darkened by distress. 'I lied. You damn well know I lied! That wasn't the only reason. I wanted success so badly I would have done almost anything to get it.'

'You did.'

It came out harsh and accusing, and she seemed to physically crumble as she sank into a chintz-covered chair. 'Are you ever going to forgive me for that?'

'Are you ever going to forgive yourself?'

That seemed to revive her anger as she looked up at him with green fire in her eyes. 'Men always come out of these things like a damned phoenix rising from the ashes. *You* impregnated me;

you deserted the battlefield without permission. But you won a medal and emerged a greater hero than ever, while I was the one who suffered the agony of ridding myself of something neither of us wanted.'

He frowned. 'What made you think I didn't want it?'

It silenced her momentarily while her anger changed direction. 'Are you saying you deliberately made me pregnant?'

He shook his head. 'Not under these circumstances. I have more sense than that.'

'But under other circumstances you would?' she challenged hotly.

They were entering deeper water than he wished, so he went across to where she sat. 'Darling, it's pointless discussing such things now. When the war is over everything will be vastly different.'

Drawing her hand away from his she leant back in the chair to gaze up at him defiantly. 'Rex, you said just now that you knew I wasn't the normal wife and mother type. You're right, I'm not!'

'And?'

'And the advent of peace won't change that.'

He sat on the edge of the other chair while he sorted out in his tired mind what she was telling him. Then he reached out to take both her unwilling hands in his.

'Laura, for me there's something that won't ever change, and that's my love for you. I've been tempted by any number of girls, but this is something so great I can't even now begin to control it. I've tried desperately hard to understand why you did what you did, and come up with the conclusion that it's as impossible for me as it would be for you to understand that it was a symbol of my . . .' He hesitated for lack of a suitable word. Possession, ownership, conquest, virility? None of them was totally what he meant, and any one of them would make her hackles rise.

'What I'm trying to say is that you mustn't judge what we have now in terms of the future. I don't like this mode of life any more than you do, which is probably why I drink too much now. I was born to fly, not go around giving speeches, judging babies at fêtes, presenting academic prizes to boys I have to persuade to go off and kill. I want to get back there and do my job towards ending the war and getting back to normal living.'

He knelt on the floor to touch her bright hair with possessive tenderness. 'Don't fight your love for me; don't resent mine for you. What we have is one of the few good things to come out of all the horror and misery.'

She pulled his hand down to hold against her cheek, and he was surprised to feel wetness there. 'What a bitch I am,' she murmured. 'There are thousands of women across the world crying for the men they have lost, and I'm crying over the one I've found.' She gazed up at him with no denial of how she felt. 'Do you think I'm totally wicked?'

'Oh absolutely,' he said with a swift surge of pleasure that the storm had passed. 'What would I want with you otherwise?'

'*Rex!*' she protested a moment later against his shoulder. 'Stop that! The girl with the tea will be here at any moment.'

'She'll have to wait her turn in the chair,' he declared, nibbling her neck. 'I haven't finished with *you* yet.'

They had their tea and muffins in their room, after all, and Laura made certain Rex had no regrets about the garden at the side of the inn. Then it was time to prepare for the evening ahead of them, which they did in vastly different mood than the one of early afternoon.

Rex was due to speak to the pupils of Chapterdene School on the following morning as part of his drive to persuade senior boys that there was no more thrilling and enjoyable life than that of a pilot in the R.F.C. But the Dean of the school was an enterprising man, who hastened to enhance the academic boredom of the annual governors' dinner and evening concert by inviting one of Britain's leading air aces and his unusual wife to the function. Needing a weighty grant to extend the school's facilities, the wise Dean thought to soften up the elderly pompous governors with the help of Madame Sherry. Unfortunately, he did not take into account the effect her presence might have on the pupils of the school.

They were both in a somewhat reckless frame of mind when they arrived at the school to be greeted on the steps by the Dean.

'Good God, it's Friar Tuck!' exclaimed Laura in an undertone, making it difficult for Rex to return the little round man's greeting in level tones. But she positively glowed when their host went on to say, 'Your husband can take centre-stage in the morning, Mrs

Sheridan. Tonight, the spotlight will be on you, I feel certain. The school has never had a night like this before, and never will again. We are honoured and privileged that you consented to attend our rather dull gathering.'

'Not at all, Dean dear,' said Laura, laughter bubbling in her voice. 'Wild horses wouldn't have kept me away from a chance to cheer up the little chaps.'

Loving her madly in this mood, Rex felt his spirits rise. Perhaps they had reached a turning-point with their quarrel of the afternoon, and everything would go right from now on.

Their entrance into the Dean's sitting-room where the governors and their few ladies were already gathered to drink sherry, was all Laura could have wished. With the exception of one man in his early fifties, the governors were elderly glum-looking men in formal wear that was rusty with age. The women looked equally glum, and equally rusty. The effect on this group of people, of a pair of youngsters each with vivid red hair, one in flattering uniform, the other in an evening-gown of shimmering green silk that clung to a body of exciting proportions, was stunning.

With a leap of excitement Rex knew instinctively that his wife was going to behave with breathtaking unpredictability that evening, and he would be powerless to stop her; would be too enchanted to stop her. Madame Sherry had a captive unsuspecting audience, and she would play to them for all she was worth.

After the general introductions, she began by exclaiming in awed tones, 'All Old Boys of Chapterdene—how amazing!' Then, turning to the quartet of wives, 'And four Old Girls!'

'Dear me, no, Mrs Sheridan,' fussed the Dean, missing the double meaning. 'Chapterdene does not take female pupils. Never has taken them.'

'Oh, what do the boys do in their spare time?' she asked with sympathy.

'We have all manner of extra-curricular activities,' put in a grey-bearded churchman with all seriousness. 'Aside from the usual sporting pursuits there is an astronomical study group, a chess society, botany rambles to collect rare specimens, a drama section, madrigal society, and a chamber ensemble.'

'And very frequent cold showers, I suppose!' said Laura with a straight face.

'Most assuredly,' supplied the Dean earnestly. 'At Chapterdene we do not approve of coddling the boys. We aim to make men of them.'

'Do you really?' she commented, the flavour of astonishment lost on them all.

At least, all but one. Rex noticed the one younger man, who had been introduced as Colonel Winters, standing in the shadows and shaking with silent laughter. He walked across, curious about the man's identity and his presence there.

'Captain Sheridan, your wife is one of the most delightful women I have ever come across,' he greeted Rex, still smiling. 'You are a man to be envied.'

'Thank you, sir. Mrs Winters was unable to accompany you this evening?'

'I have never married. I went straight from the Frontier Wars in India to the one in South Africa. By the time I was in a position to take a wife I realised I was doing quite well without one, and dispensed with the idea.'

'But you are an ex-pupil of Chapterdene?'

'Oh, yes, I've enjoyed many a cold shower,' he said with another smile. 'I came onto the Board of Governors on the death of my father a few months ago. This is all quite new to me, seeing the school from this angle.'

'Tomorrow morning I've got to talk to the boys and persuade them that a career in the R.F.C. is the chance of a lifetime for them all. I'm afraid that will make them into men quicker than any cold shower.'

'You mean, it will make them into *dead* men, don't you?'

Rex was startled by the vehemence in the man's voice. Although the man was unmarried, it was possible he had a son involved!

'Within an average of two weeks, yes,' he agreed.

'It's criminal,' the other exploded. 'This whole war is a sign of madness. I've fought in battles all over the Empire, but they were never like this. Hundreds of thousands lost in *one day!* It's totally unacceptable. Before a year was out they should have been suspending hostilities and talking round a table. Is it their intention to go on until there is only one man left, and will he then declare *himself* the winner?'

Rex sipped his sherry. 'You'll find an ally in my elder brother.

Roland preaches the same sentiments. Unfortunately, no one of consequence appears to listen to him.'

'I thank my stars a Boer bayonet put an end to my soldiering, because I swear I'd not have the stomach to send youngsters like you to pointless sacrifice.' His gaze went beyond Rex to where Laura was still bemusing the elderly guests. 'Enjoy your lovely wife, Captain Sheridan, and make her happy while you can. Thank God there are still some women who have not become nurses, factory-hands, tram-conductors, or farm-workers. Long live beauty, and the ability to make people laugh! They are two qualities in danger of dying along with the nations.'

The man's unusual philosophy made Rex thoughtful during the dinner, which was eaten in company with the pupils who sat at long tables in the graceful arched Great Hall of the school. Laura had caused a sensation on entering, and Rex noted with amusement that the senior boys were neglecting their meals through optical worship of Laura, as much as the junior boys were over him. He almost choked over his soup when his wife gave one particularly dog-like sixth-former a broad saucy wink, which flooded his face with scarlet colour and had him loosening his high starched collar. A cold shower for *him* tonight, without doubt, Rex thought with an inner chuckle.

But he also noted his wife's animated conversation with Colonel Winters across the table, and the way her vivacity seemed reciprocated in the man's whole demeanour. Used to the admiration of other men for a girl who aroused it with a mere glance, he felt an uncomfortable stab of jealousy for this man old enough to be his own father. There was something different about the interest of Colonel Winters that made Rex unable to accept it with the usual confidence.

There were several long boring speeches from various governors after the meal, and Rex kept glancing at his watch, willing the hands to move faster toward the time he could take Laura back to the hotel. But there was a concert first. He knew all about school concerts; had performed in them himself. But he had grave doubts about the entertainment value of what would be considered suitable fare for this group of influential dignitaries. Possibly, even Gilbert and Sullivan would be considered too light!

The first three turns seemed to bear out Rex's pessimism. A

dramatic recitation, a piece by the chamber ensemble that was thankfully short, and a solo by a boy soprano who was so nervous he sang as if standing on the heaving deck of a ship. There was some comedy provided by an extract from *A Midsummer Night's Dream*, with a talented clown playing Bottom. This brightened the atmosphere enough to make bearable a piano duet by two very junior boys, a melodramatic monologue offered with unbelievable histrionics by a boy who gave every appearance of taking himself seriously, and a mime. Rex could not decide whether it was the murder of Julius Caesar, or the betrayal of Christ by Judas. Whichever it was, the mummers put all they had into their roles and earned the applause at the end.

Then, totally unexpected and out of keeping with the rest of the concert, the whole cast trooped onto the stage with one of their number taking over the piano-stool recently vacated by the music-master, to sing with uninhibited boyish enthusiasm a selection of songs popular with the troops. Rex was sorry they sang the respectable versions. It would have made the evening sensational if they had offered the words he knew to the governors and their ladies!

Catching Laura's eye, he grinned. She smiled back in happy conspiracy, knowing all too well what he was thinking. He then pointed covertly to his watch, and nodded toward the door to indicate that he was anxious to leave. The widening of her eyes told him all he wanted to know, and he prepared to get to his feet the minute the show was over. But he was thwarted in the most unexpected way.

The medley of songs ended with a thumping chord on the piano and, while polite applause greeted what had plainly been a surprise item, a good-looking senior boy appeared from the audience and produced a beribboned posy of flowers from behind his back. Completely assured, even though all eyes were on him, he presented them to Laura and said something that only she heard above the dying applause. A moment's hesitation, then she nodded and got to her feet.

The boy jumped onto the platform and held up his hands for silence. 'Ladies and gentlemen,' he began in confident manner, '. . . and those of you who are not yet of sufficient years to be regarded as gentlemen. You have stoically sat through our humble effort to be entertaining, but we have with us tonight a most beautiful and talented lady who makes us blush for our own temerity. The last item was our impromptu and inadequate tribute to Madame Sherry. But she has very graciously consented to end the evening by showing us how it really should be done.'

Heart thudding against his ribs Rex watched Laura step up onto the platform with the aid of the boy's hand and to a roar of cheers from the pupils of Chapterdene. The Dean and governors seemed totally frozen. Torn between the instinct to stop what was about to happen before it was too late, and the breathless anticipation shared by all who stared up at a stunningly sensuous woman in a vivid evening-gown so incongruous in an academic setting, Rex found himself as helpless as he had ever been before her magnetism.

After a brief consultation with the boy at the piano, she embarked on a ballad from *Chu Chin Chow,* currently the rage with all troops on leave in London. It was demure and very affecting, sung in her husky intimate tones, but something stirred warningly inside Rex as he sensed the spell that was being cast that evening, in an old mellowed-stone hall that had probably never rung with the sound of a lone female voice before.

But it was merely the calm before the storm. Hardly had she finished and the clapping begun, than she nodded to the young maestro who was evidently destined to become a dance-band leader, and the introduction to one of her most daring numbers thumped out to demand silence. Rex groaned inwardly even as he thrilled to the tantalising swing of her hips and the high kicks with her skirts pulled high over the legs that drove him crazy. Nothing would stop her now!

All around Rex boys began to clap in time to the rhythm, and he recognised the look in her eye as she stepped down from the platform and began an outrageous assault on the susceptibilities of the governors by tickling their chins, flicking their beards, or mussing their grey locks. She even perched on the lap of one and planted a kiss on his bald head, before moving on to pick up a very small boy who seemed paralysed with shock, and kiss *him* on the mouth, as she sang a paragraph about loving boys both old and young.

Back on the platform she ended with a curtsey so demure it made her words appear saucier than they were, and Chapterdene School went wild. But the inevitable happened. Amidst the cheers and shouts could be heard the piano chorus of Laura's famous song, and the neat rows of boys scattered into a milling cheering mass which disregarded order, formality and elderly governors, as several hundred voices began to sing:

> When he flies oh-so-high
> All the Mam'selles cry
> Chéri, Chéri.

Rex was surrounded and dragged onto the stage with his triumphant wife, deafened by the song that had become his own. She put her arms around his neck and kissed him, but he saw the look in her eyes and knew the fire was back in the girl he adored. Sadly, it was not he who had put it there.

That night, their passion resumed its old perfection and ferocity, with the wild surprise of the evening taking hold of them both. And this time, it was not tinged with the fear of imminent parting.

Rex went to talk to the boys next morning with a vigour and enthusiasm he had not been able to find since the start of the tour. For the first time in a long while he managed to make aviation sound as exciting and adventurous as it truly was, and injected into his words the feelings that had been within him during those early days with 'Princess'. His audience was eager, and he was elated with the joy of being young and alive. For once, he pushed aside thoughts of men plunging to the earth in burning machines, of bullets ripping through fabric to embed themselves in human flesh, of flying in desperation of one's life. He put aside the usual rehearsed speech that appealed to patriotism, a man's debt to King and country, and the chance to avenge their schoolfellows by killing the Hun. Instead, he found himself talking of flying in its pioneering guise, of the golden future for aviation, the incredible difference to world-wide communication the aeroplane would make, and the future importance of the men who knew how to fly them.

While he inspired the spirit of adventure and conquest in most young breasts before him, Laura sat beside the Dean at the back of the platform, dressed becomingly but demurely in a costume of blue wool trimmed with swansdown. The Dean was an unhappy man. The grant had not been forthcoming from the governors, who had felt discipline at the school had been neglected to the point of inviting anarchy from the pupils. But he had been offered a considerable sum from Colonel Winters, with which to build a real theatre so that the boys could mount full dramatic productions twice a year which would bring in the funds needed. The Dean knew it would be foolish to decline the offer, yet could not approve of the use to which it must be put. So his manner toward Laura, who must be regarded as the cause of his dilemma, was rather more offhand than it had been the previous evening.

When Rex departed with his wife, however, he made no secret of how he regarded her, and the Dean decided that heroes might very well earn the gratitude of a nation, but they left much to be desired in their personal attitudes and morals—especially in front of young impressionable boys!

The Sheridans laughed all the way to the hotel, where their mirth soon gave way to a more physical expression of their happiness.

Later, as Rex lay in drowsy satisfaction, Laura came across to the bed, dressed and tidy, to drop two envelopes onto his bare chest.

'The post has arrived, darling. It was brought across from Sunford Officers' Mess by the most divine courier. Tall, dark and handsome, with the bluest eyes imaginable.'

He sat up swiftly, seizing her and falling back to the pillows with her held close to him, struggling and laughing.

'And what else did he have, might I ask?'

Her hand ran over his body as she listed the masculine attributes in turn. 'Exactly what you have, sweetie,' she murmured, nibbling him in all the exciting places. 'But yours are far better.'

It was not difficult to ignore the letters for a while. He guessed one would be from his banker and, when he got around to opening them, he found he was right. He read it while Laura ran a bath for him, and it blighted the brightness of that early afternoon. He was overdrawn to a staggering sum, and even next month's salary would make little difference to it. For the first time since his father's suicide Rex knew the strain of living on a junior officer's pay alone. In France there had been little to spend money on, so his allowance to Laura had been easy to settle. Since he had been in England, however, he realised his wife had adopted a lifestyle prompted by her brief enjoyment of fame as Madame Sherry. Her clothes were expensive and numerous; she liked being escorted to smart places and travelling in style. Unpalatable though the truth might be, Rex had to accept that all he had done until last November was provide Laura with rent for the apartment and enough for the tradesmen's bills. The luxuries had been bought with her own earnings. Now that had stopped, his money did not stretch anywhere near far enough for them both. He kept the apartment they rarely managed to occupy and, although the army paid all his own travelling expenses and hotel bills, they most definitely did not provide for his wife. His own insistence on having her by his side all the time proved costly.

During the four months he had been in this situation he had said nothing to her, because he knew very well what her solution would be. Perhaps he could get a loan from Roland from the Tarrant Hall estate funds, just to tide him over until he returned to France. But, on reflection, he guessed his brother needed that even more himself, with only the rank of corporal until lately. The estate was already paying maintenance for Marion and little David—an arrangement started on Chris's marriage and obliged to continue when he joined the army and left them to fend for themselves. Roland might be determined to deprive the girl of the chance to be mistress of their home, but he was a stickler for doing the right thing and standing by his obligations to their wounded young brother.

Rex ran his hand through his hair several times as he sat in the bed. He would have to hope the family banker would be lenient for old times' sake, and the steadiness of the eldest Sheridan. Roland was like a rock when it came to honesty and integrity. A man could trust him with anything—even his wife!

Picking up the other letter, his heart quickened. It was an army notification. Orders to return to France? They had come on the wrong day. Where he had been frustrated, irritable, longing to get back into action with the men he knew and trusted, last night had bewitched him anew into wanting never to leave Laura's side again. But it was something quite different, and he looked up in swift gladness to tell her. She, however, was reading a letter of her own, and her face was flushed with suppressed excitement.

'Rex, listen! You'll never guess who this is from,' she murmured, her eyes still moving from side-to-side as she read the page.

'No, I won't. So tell me,' he invited.

384

'Colonel Winters.'

Immediate jealousy made him say, 'What the hell is he writing letters to you about? You hadn't met before last night, had you?'

'*Isn't* it incredible!' she cried, her attention on the letter.

He got to his feet and went to her. 'What's this all about?'

Resisting his attempt to take the page from her, she smiled at him vividly. 'Colonel Winters, my splendid naked husband, is an "angel". He's a financier who backs all kinds of enterprises, including theatrical shows. He wants me to go to his London office for a chat.'

'So do a lot of other fifty-five year old bachelors, no doubt. And *none* of them are angels,' he said tautly. 'The bloody nerve of the man!'

She put her arms round his neck and teased his mussed hair with her fingers. 'Think what it could lead to, darling.'

'I already have.' He pulled her hands down and held them safely imprisoned. 'I'll send his letter back with one from me.'

Unable to use her hands, she began covering his mouth with tiny kisses. 'Darling, this could be a wonderful chance for me.'

He drew his head back. 'To do what?'

'You know damn well,' she retorted crisply.

'And you know damn well what my opinion on that subject is. We had all that out four months ago.'

'And I've tried keeping to your rules . . . darling, I have tried, haven't I? she pleaded. 'But it doesn't work, you know it doesn't. This man has only asked to talk to me. It probably doesn't mean a thing. But if it did come to anything, I'd talk it over with you first. *Please*, darling.'

'No.'

She pulled away from him. 'You'll be back in France by September and I'll be left all alone again.'

'No, Laura!'

Looking at him with dark passion, she cried, 'Have you any idea what it's like for women in this war? Have you ever thought? I hate aeroplanes because you fly them. I hate living near airfields and always wondering if the wheels are going to fall off or the engine is going to fail. You love every minute in those machines, but I hate being married to a man who risks his life every time he climbs into one. And you're not going to stop doing it when this war ends. It's in your blood, Rex.' She paused to see his reaction to that, then went on, 'And the theatre is in mine. I was perfectly honest about that right from the start.'

He knew she was right, saw the force of her argument. But he wanted her beside him every minute until he had to go back and face the horrors once more. Maybe he did not know what this war was like for women, but she did not really know what it was like for the men. Despite his confidence in survival he needed her love to get him through the anguish of death for all those around him. He needed her love to get him through these present months of doing something that made him feel riddled with guilt. He needed her love to make him complete.

He told her all that as he held her close and buried his face in her perfumed hair. Then he murmured, 'I want you to come with me to Tarrant Hall to see Chris. I have a letter saying he has been transferred there, and is so much improved he's been asking to see us both. That's more important than some lecherous colonel who thinks actresses are fair game, isn't it?'

She showed him how important it was, and they were unaware of the bath overflowing until water began to lap around their feet.

19

TARRANT ROYAL seemed like an empty village, these days. The women were working in the fields, repairing fences, hedging and ditching, checking the lambs, sowing and planting. The young girls had gone to the cities to be nurses, or ambulance drivers, or canteen-workers. Violet Peach had surprised everyone by joining the Church Army, and was dispensing tea, hot pies, and bath buns to troops in transit at Charing Cross station. Bessie Peach, younger daughter of the crippled blacksmith, had shamed her father and the village by going to London to give comfort of quite another sort to troops in transit. That had been a harder blow for Ted Peach than the loss of his arm in battle.

The small children were left in the charge of grannies too old for farm-work, or pregnant women unfit to undertake heavy manual tasks. But the youngsters no longer played in the lanes as they once had, running laughingly from garden to garden, meadow to meadow. Ambulances and motor cycles with sidecars plied from Greater Tarrant station to Tarrant Hall through the village, and the leafy ways were no longer safe for small carefree children who did not yet understand the meaning of it all. Yet, to these latest members of the old Dorset village, ambulances, motor cycles roaring past, mothers up to their elbows in turnips, and fathers who were no more than photographs of men in uniform on the sideboard, their present life was the accepted normality. How it had been before 1914, the peace of those long summer holidays leading up to that fateful August, the tranquil village with its traditional cricket-match, baby-show, ploughing competition, and carnival; the sleepy lanes that were only awoken briefly by Rex Sheridan's motor cycle before slumbering again, lulled by the soft clip-clopping of horses' hooves: all this was unknown, and therefore not missed by them. A village had entirely changed its face. The children would now determine its future one.

Rex and Laura went through the familiar lane practically unnoticed, except for Ted Peach who waved his remaining arm as they passed the smithy. Laura still thought it 'the back of beyond' despite her recent tour of many such small villages. But Rex was saddened each time he visited his old home. Unlike Roland, he had breezily taken it all for granted, in the past. Now it was passing beyond recall he realised the true value of that rural way of life that had been such a source of enthusiasm and pride to his elder brother.

Tarrant Royal had forgiven its squire the moment he had donned uniform and had now forgotten white feathers, closed doors, and an empty church. But Rex guessed Roland would never forget, and certainly never forgive something that must have hurt him very deeply. When the war finally ended, would his brother be able to adapt to this new brasher community?

Coming into view of Tarrant Hall Rex also observed how his home had adopted the guise of hospital so well in the two years it had been functioning as such, he had difficulty in remembering it as it had been through his childhood and teens. Would *that* ever be the same again when the war was over?

The driver took them automatically to the front entrance, so Rex helped Laura out and picked up their cases to take round to the side door, thanking the driver for meeting them at the station.

'That's all right, sir,' came the cheery reply. 'Miss Manning told the C.O. when you were arriving, and I had to go in for supplies. But it's a pleasure to do anything for you, sir . . . and Madame Sherry.' His grin was for Laura alone.

Tessa was there to greet them as if she had been watching for the car to arrive. She looked fresher and prettier than ever, with the golden glow of early sunshine on her skin. Roland should have married her before he left, thought Rex as he gave her a smacking kiss. His brother had certainly chosen the right woman for this background, but he was too damned slow. With lusty doctors and susceptible patients around, a girl like Tessa was liable to be stolen away beneath his own roof.

'You look more luscious every time I see you,' he greeted her. 'That glow on your face is too good to be true. Name the dastardly devil who has put it there, and I'll ask if his intentions are honourable.'

Tessa laughed merrily. 'For a married man you're still impossibly saucy, Rex. I doubt if your intentions have *ever* been honourable.' She embraced Laura. 'No need to ask if normal married life suits you, my dear. You look marvellous.'

But Rex had just caught sight of someone standing on the far side of the hall, and cut short any further complimentary exchanges by walking in with his hand outstretched.

'*Mike!* You old rascal, what in God's name are you doing here?'

Tessa's brother was grinning with the delight of his surprise, and thumped Rex on the shoulder in rough greeting.

'I'm here to keep an eye on you, old mate,' was his Australian come-back. 'You're not the only flaming hero around. The Ones Above proclaimed that I was as much in need of a rest as you.'

The mere sight of his friend brought the other side of his life vividly to the forefront, and he was away in that world within an instant. 'How are George and Wally? Did Higgins ever get that old B.E. back on its feet? What's the squadron tally now? Are the Nieuports standing up to the job all right?'

Mike looked past him to the girls. 'Bloody marvellous, isn't it? I might be standing here on two tin legs, with my chest held together with bandages, yet all he wants to know is how the squadron is managing to survive without him.' He pushed Rex aside with an elaborate action, and advanced on Laura. 'Since I saw you making free with my sister just now, old mate, I shall make free with your delectable wife.'

So saying, he took Laura into a comprehensive embrace that took so long, Rex had to remind him of the time. Flushed and laughing, Laura released herself and said to Tessa, 'There's something about men who fly that makes them irresistible, isn't there? Oh, it's good to be back in a home again after all those village inns run by old men smelling of ale, and chambermaids who creak in the joints.'

'Do come inside,' begged Tessa. 'Priddy went off to make tea when I saw you arriving, and it'll be stewed by now. She's made some of her special treacle tarts for you, Rex.'

She led the way into the small sitting-room she used, and it struck Rex that it did not seem odd for this girl to be conducting him into his own home as if he were a guest. Tessa Manning looked so right at Tarrant Hall she ought to be its mistress in the future.

The next half-hour was a mixture of gladness and sorrow as Rex gave Priddy a bear-like hug, heard all her news, then sympathised with her sadness on being allowed to take Chris a meal, only to be treated as a stranger.

'I know, Priddy, it's the kind of blow that's difficult to describe. We've all been through it, and it has nothing to do with how Chris feels about us. He wouldn't hurt you for the world if he had any control over his illness, you know that.'

'Yes, I know, Mr Rex, but it's that awful with him sitting there just as he always was, and looking straight through me as if all those years had never happened.'

'But he *is* getting better. That's the most important thing.'

She went off then, leaving Tessa to give all the latest gossip of the village and the estate. Finally, she broke the news that Minks had died only two days before. Rex should have been immune to the loss of friends, yet it hit him hard. Perhaps he was hardened to burning men, smashed-up aircraft and mangled corpses. But Minks had been part of his old life, and it seemed too much to take on top of all else. Could nothing and no one survive?

Tessa went to him as he stood gazing from the window. 'I'm sorry, Rex. He had the best possible attention around the clock, but I think he had no wish to face the future. He held on after you and Chris left, but Roland's departure was more than he could face at his age. I know he could never bear the thought of the young man he practically revered crawling around in the mud carrying stretchers. After the way the village treated their squire, he felt it was the final degradation. No matter how often I impressed upon him that it was Roland's own wish to do what he was doing, he believed the people of Tarrant Royal had driven him to it.' She sighed. 'I didn't tell him Chris was here. He was already ill, and it seemed unnecessary to subject him to the distress Priddy experienced on not being recognised. I hope you feel I did the right thing.'

He nodded, still looking from the window. 'I suppose we're all finding it difficult to bend, and poor old Minks just snapped under the strain. He'd been with us for years and years, you know. We were his family. If he'd been faced with Chris as he is now, I think his heart would have snapped, too. Yes, of course you did the right thing.'

'The funeral is tomorrow. The Rector has agreed to hold it in the church at Tarrant Maundle. After Roland left, Minks vowed he would never enter the village again as long as he lived. I thought we should respect his wish, even now.'

Very moved Rex turned to her. 'What a wonderful person you are! Roland is a complete fool.'

She flushed, but remained matter-of-fact. 'I had a long letter from him yesterday. He was in a place he couldn't name for a long rest-period behind the lines.' She smiled. 'That's all he said about his own life. The rest of the letter was full of reminiscences and questions about this place. Typical, I thought.'

'I had a letter, too. It was much the same, I should imagine. But don't blame him for keeping quiet about things over there. Being a medical officer on the field is not an enviable job. It gets pretty hectic, even in places behind the lines.'

'In places behind the lines there are attractive nurses, Sis,' put in Mike pointedly. 'Just as there are good-looking doctors here. Being a man's bailiff means no more than just that. I think you should accept some invitations.'

'I do,' she told him serenely, 'and since I have never interfered in your affairs, *old mate,* I suggest you stop interfering in mine.'

'Well said,' cried Laura. 'It's time we women made a stand to our right to a life of our own, free from dictatorship by men. I'll join you in that.'

Rex decided it was time for male dictatorship. 'You'll join *me* in a visit to young Chris,' he said firmly. 'That will do far more good than a girls' revolution. Come on, the poor lad has been asking for us.'

Rex had not seen his brother since November, when Laura had given him the pictures of the stage-set of Julius Caesar. Soon after that Chris had suffered one of his periodic retreats from life, and visitors were forbidden then. Rex was not quite sure what the effect of this would be, and prepared himself for anything. But it was a delightful surprise to walk into the West Wing conservatory to find the patient sitting up with only pillows for support, his handsome face almost free of the pinkness of burns, his hair brushed and shining with health, talking animatedly to a uniformed doctor with prematurely grey hair, and an un-military way of sprawling in a chair tipped back on two legs.

Then Chris caught sight of them, and a bright blush swept over his face. Oh lord, thought Rex in dismay, I do believe the silly young fool has fallen for Laura! The blush did not go unnoticed by the doctor, who glanced keenly in their direction before getting to his feet with a look on his face that was almost as foolish as the one on Chris's. Rex was used to grown men looking at his wife that way, and it was a source of pride to him. But his young brother was different altogether.

'Hallo, young Chris,' he greeted. 'So you decided your family wasn't half bad, after all, and came home. I hear they had to throw out all the aspidistras so that you could have this place to yourself.'

'Hallo, Rex,' came the shy response. 'Thanks for coming. You look better than the last time I saw you. You had an arm in plaster, and a frightful limp.'

'You didn't look so hot yourself,' he answered flippantly, still finding it unnerving—even more so now the boy was so much more himself—to converse with a beloved brother who responded as no more than a recent acquaintance.

'Every time I visit you, you look more handsome,' Laura told him with her disconcerting candour. 'Small wonder the nurses exchanged the aspidistras for *you.*'

His blush deepened, and Rex touched her foot with his own

hoping she would soft-pedal with the compliments when he so blatantly reacted to them. But Chris was launching into something he had obviously been working on for a while, because pretty speeches had never been forthcoming from him before.

'I had been meaning to write you a letter about the Julius Caesar pictures, Laura, but I didn't know quite where to send it. And they wouldn't let me contact anyone for a bit. I hope you didn't think it frightfully rude of me.'

She put a hand on his shoulder and gave him one of her most stunning smiles. 'I knew when I gave them to you that you were pleased, my dear. I didn't require a letter to tell me so.'

His magnificent eyes were full of conflicting emotions as he gazed at her. 'All the same, I would have written.'

'I'm the miserable so . . . devil who stopped him,' put in the doctor, hastily correcting his language in front of a lady. 'The name is Chandler, Captain Sheridan, and I'm really glad to shake your hand. Any man who can snatch a girl like this from the clutches of everyone else, deserves my admiration.' His grin was as saucy as his words. 'Madame Sherry, I join the long line of those who can only admire you from afar. I wish I were the patient instead of the doctor. This young man is sure to be favoured with more of your attention than I shall get.'

'If there are any favours to be given, *I* shall get them, Major Chandler,' put in Rex lightly. 'There *is* a long line of admirers, and you are right at the back, sir. Chris gets special treatment because he's Laura's brother-in-law, not because he's a patient. I'm sure all the nurses fuss over him far too much, as it is.'

'Have you done any sketching lately, Chris?' asked Laura taking the seat offered her by Dr Chandler. 'You have a most wonderful view of the gardens from here.'

'I expect I did a lot when I lived in the house,' he answered with a touch of bravado. 'They're going to ask Rex to bring down some stuff from my old room—in case it helps, you know—and there are sure to be sketches that are better than any I could do now. I'm really not that good yet. My fingers stiffen up, sometimes. Anyway, I've been pretty well occupied with work for Dr Chandler. Do you know about the codes, and so on?'

'Rex told me.' She smiled. 'It's all highly secret, I understand. You must have a wonderful brain, Chris. Not like me. I'm a real duffer.'

'Brains aren't everything,' he responded quickly. 'You can make a whole crowd of people do anything you want them to do, just by singing and dancing. That's *really* clever.'

Rex was standing practically open-mouthed with surprise at all that when the doctor tapped him on the shoulder and nodded at the conservatory door to indicate that they should step into the garden and leave Laura with Chris.

It was a warm scented evening that was too nostalgic for Rex, with one brother still in war-torn France, and the other a too-familiar stranger who did not recognise his own home. The perfume of wallflowers massed in a bed along the stone wall of what used to be the library wafted across to him in that gathering dusk, and unreality closed in on him fast. Seeing Mike so unexpectedly, and going just now into that part of his home that was now filled with broken men, brought back the sombreness of war. For four months he had been free of constant gunfire, the strain and fear of daily combat, the peculiar swift comradeship that ended just as swiftly; and he had lost himself in the exciting uncertainty of life with Laura. He had pushed everything else from his mind, deluded himself that it could go on forever, refused to think beyond each day. Now, he was home, yet he was not. He was free and safe, but for how long? Laura adored him, but would it last forever? Maybe Chris was lucky to feel that he was nobody from nowhere!

'There's something about this country that gets at you,' said a voice beside him suddenly. 'On a night like this, in a place like this it's almost like the ages rolling back to the very beginning. I always thought Englishmen were arrogant prigs, but I have to admit I understand them now. If I had been brought up to live at the Hall, I'd probably be the same.' He lit a cigarette, spoiling the smell of the wallflowers. 'I'm sorry about all us bloody doctors making free with your home.'

Rex turned from contemplating Longbarrow Hill with all its memories. 'You don't have to be sorry. My brother Roland could be doing the same with a French chateau before long.'

Bill Chandler puffed on his cigarette. 'We hoped Chris would remember his home. He didn't. There's an area in his life he's still frightened to approach. I know the basics. I'd like you to tell me the details.'

Rex thrust his hands in his pocket. 'Don't you think it's time he was told he's a married man with a two-year-old son? It didn't escape your notice that he's growing infatuated with my wife.'

'No. As a matter of fact, I thought it a very good sign. It answers a puzzle over his response to my comments last week about red-heads. Captain Sheridan, let me tell you a little of what we are trying to do for your brother. Those rare few who have an intelligence so refined it makes even a university don appear a fool, find life very difficult. Their very rareness makes it impossible for them to form normal human relationships, either because—as in Chris's case—they are unaware of their tremendous mental superiority, or because they *are* aware of it and regard themselves as freaks. Which they are, of course. It might seem a strange thing to say but, if he survives, that shell in Gallipoli could be the best thing that has happened to him.'

Rex jumped on that immediately. '*If* he survives? What are you implying, Dr Chandler?'

'I'm not implying; I'm stating. That boy might look practically cured to you, but he's as close to the edge of insanity as he always was. It comes as a shock? I'm sorry. But the truth has to be faced. He could withdraw again at any time, and there is no guarantee that he would not remain that way this time. As I said earlier, people like your brother find relationships difficult. Chris has been exposed to the extremes life can offer in the space of one year. Many ordinary men have found that unacceptable and retreated to a pretence which makes them happy. In Chris's case it is far more dangerous.' He waved a hand. 'Let's walk, shall we?'

Shaken by what he was being told Rex set off beside him along the old stone path toward the sunken garden illuminated by no more than lights flooding from the windows now dusk had finally arrived.

'I have made great progress by establishing a contact amounting to friendship and trust with Chris,' his companion continued, 'and his helplessness due to the deep severity of his wounds has obliged him to depend on others in a way he has never needed before. He has actually reached the stage of wanting and asking for the company of others. That's marvellous; a real step forward. But there is this last hurdle for him to face, and I have to admit I'm apprehensive. Chris is a very unusual case indeed, which is why he was brought here when I was sent to take up a new post. It seemed an ideal arrangement for us both, since I had already made such headway with him. We also hoped that the unexpected sight of his home would be strong enough to put cracks in his last defences. But they are far stronger than we anticipated. He is involuntarily fighting it like mad, and the situation is too dangerous to rush. He has to face it of his own free will. To tell him he has a wife and child he hated so much he went to war to escape them would almost certainly condemn him to immense distress, if not worse.'

'What if he is never willing to face it?' asked Rex harshly.

'He still could recover physically and live a good life, with the first eighteen years of it a permanent blank. His wife would be granted a divorce without any difficulty.'

'But he has a son.'

'Yes. I've spoken at length to his wife. She is an otherwise sensible girl who ridiculously holds herself responsible for everything—including the war, it strikes me. When Chris withdrew last November, she left the hospital. There was nothing she could do when he was in that state, and she rightly decided her baby was of an age when she should be with him. Strangely, Chris has asked about her a lot, and seems to think we have some peculiar power over her. His intelligence tells him there is something special about that girl, but his memory won't let him in on the secret. Tell me about the affair.'

So Rex told him all he knew about the disastrous forced marriage and the sacrificed academic career, adding that he had not been present when it had all happened, and Roland could probably be of more help.

'One thing I am sure of is that he blames Marion every bit as much as she blames herself. There's no disputing she deliberately seduced him without giving any thought to the possible consequences which did, of course, destroy all Chris's hopes and ambitions; all he valued and held dear. It also destroyed her own future.' He frowned. 'In retrospect, I see that Roland and I did little to help. My brother is a stickler for doing the right thing, and forced the boy to stay here at Tarrant Hall with his pregnant wife, working on the estate as a trainee bailiff—a job that was totally incompatible with his nature. And I was too concerned with following my own career to do more than tell him he was a fool to have got caught, and to work out his own salvation with the brains he so plainly had. I suppose we both forgot that he was barely eighteen and no more than a schoolboy.'

'Mmm,' mused the other man. 'That was how he behaved for

a long time, I was told, but he's fast catching up the two-and-a-half years that have passed since his life first became unacceptable, and maturity is setting in. The biggest obstacle I still have to overcome is his reluctance to face sexual sensations. We knew from his wife's own confession why he flinched from the attentions of female nurses; now I also know why he was afraid of male orderlies touching him. He is ruled by the fear that his mind is ridiculed and his body coveted by everyone in sight. The poor lad suffers daily when he is washed. Good thing he is unaware that the nurses fight over the privilege, and that hearts are palpitating beneath starched pinafores in the ward beside his room, as they make all manner of excuses to peep in at him.'

Rex thought of Laura still in there beside Chris. 'There's nothing wrong with his sexual sensations when he's with my wife.'

Chandler grinned. 'To be impervious to your wife a man would have to be a monk . . . and then some! I hope she is in there doing what it would take me weeks to achieve.'

'Why not get his own wife up here and let her try?' was Rex's answer to that, not without some heat.

'She has been ill—a breakdown. I'm not surprised after all she has been through. As you said just now, she also ruined her own life. It takes a lot of guts to volunteer to nurse a husband who hated you enough to trick the recruiting-board in order to involve himself in something that was so catastrophic to his nature, and who then returns like a mummified stranger with fits of madness.'

'Don't you think it takes a lot of guts for a man to wake up one morning, as Chris did, and still have fits of sanity?' asked Rex quietly. 'I can't begin to imagine what it must have been like for him, but I'm not sure I could cope with it as well as he has done. I've seen some courageous men over the past months, but Chris has a special brand of courage—he and the others like him.'

'He tried to kill himself in Gallipoli.'

'Say that again.' Rex's mind was full of thoughts of his father's suicide.

'He admitted to me that he ran away from his would-be male lover and intended climbing up the cliff to commit battle suicide. The man stopped him. That was the day before they sent him to do the same thing under orders.'

Rex found that hard to take, and stopped to look out into the velvety darkness of a garden where he had played with his young brother, and dragged him from his books on so many occasions so that he would enjoy the sunshine and fresh air. He felt his throat tighten as he thought of that same boy feeling so alone and desperate he would rather face death than go on. Then, into his mind came the words of Colonel Winters two nights before: *Enjoy your lovely wife and keep her happy while you can. Long live beauty and the ability to make people laugh. They are two qualities in danger of dying along with the nations.*

When they returned to the conservatory to find Chris's head close to Laura's as they both laughed over a sketch she had tried to make of the Dean of Chapterdene School, Rex knew he was going to let her go to London, after all.

Chris felt immensely pleased with himself as he sat in the bed sorting through the things Rex and Laura had brought him that morning from his old room in their part of the house. He remembered none of them, of course, but they were all fascinating. He tried to form an impression of the boy he must have been; searched for an identity amongst scraps of Latin and Greek, sketches clipped together in bundles, newspaper cuttings about archaeological finds, and appallingly bad verse scribbled in his own handwriting, which made him blush with its immaturity. Everything supported the concept that he had been, as Laura had once told him, a brilliant scholar. And yet he felt he had never been a really small boy, or had begun collecting things in his teens, for there were none of the treasures of the very young.

There were well-thumbed books inscribed with fond messages from his brothers on various birthdays; others given by someone who had merely written: *To Christopher from Father.* He had been told that his parents were dead, and they had held no interest for him. Now they did. He scribbled a note for a nurse to pass through to Rex when he returned from a funeral that afternoon, asking him to come and talk to him about their mother and father. He suddenly wanted to know everything he could about his past. He could not bear to think Laura knew things about him that he did not know about himself.

He had spent a long time alone with her the previous evening, and every minute of it had been wonderful. She smelt of dark red roses, and her low husky laughter made him think of funny things to say that would promote it. Once or twice her fingers had

397

brushed his and he could still feel the sensation on his skin. Ashamed of the ugliness of his left hand with the two fingers missing, he had hidden it beneath the sheets at her approach. But her admission that she found him handsome had made him forget his disfigurement.

He was certain she liked him, but he felt very guilty about Rex. His brother was the sort of person everyone admired. He was a hero. The evidence in this box of boyhood things showed there had been great affection and friendship between them in the past. It was wrong to feel as he did about Rex's wife . . . but it was too strong to banish. Dreaming of her had helped him through those months of physical helplessness. But even that was coming to an end. The staff-nurse had just revealed that his leg fractures had finally healed well enough to allow him to spend periods sitting in a chair. After fifteen months in bed he must now begin to learn to walk again. She had warned him it would be painful and difficult, so he must not expect miracles. It would take time and courage. But the prospect filled him with delight. That was another reason why he was feeling pleased with himself that afternoon.

In an optimistic frame of mind he picked up another small book from the bottom of the box Rex had brought in. It was a leather-bound volume with gilt-edged pages, such as people used for keeping a journal or record of foreign travels. On each page was a beautifully-pressed and labelled wild-flower, with details of where and when it had been found. On the flyleaf was written: *To Christopher Wesley Sheridan from Marion Ann Deacon. 18th June 1909.*

He sat staring at it for a long time. A thirteenth birthday present from a girl who had known him well enough to go to immense trouble to produce something that was almost a work of art. He now recalled something he had forgotten over the past few months; a careless explanation to cover something he had not understood. Marion lived near Tarrant Hall! There *was* a mystery about that girl—he had sensed it from the start. That mystery belonged to that part of his past that was still a blank. Did she hold the key to something he still did not want to remember? Where was she now? Why had she left the hospital so suddenly, and why would no one tell him where she was? What had persuaded her to pretend to be a nurse, casting aside a childhood friendship so easily?

All those questions swum around in his head until his happiness of the earlier part of the day vanished under a blanket of helplessness. How would he ever find the answers to these questions until he could walk and go in search of them? But they had warned him it would take a great effort and a long time before he would be mobile. Could he wait until then? Then his helplessness increased further at the thought that he might never find the answers or, if he did, he might wish they had remained locked inside his subconscious.

He put aside the box of things and took off the spectacles while he roamed in unhappy realms of thought. When Rex came in answer to his note, he had fallen asleep, worn out with contemplating the unknown.

Rex and Mike walked down to the Deacons' house soon after breakfast on that second morning. Tessa was busy with accounts; Laura was still in bed. There had been a heavy shower just before they set off, and all down the lane from Tarrant Hall to the village the hedgerows shimmered with diamond drops illuminated by a pale sun fighting the clouds for domination, and spiders' webs hung like crystal veils between the branches of thorn bushes. On both sides of the narrow way small streams of rainwater ran down toward the ditches lining the main route through the village and, as the two men progressed, their boots grew muddier and muddier. All around them the air was filled with the song of thrushes announcing the end of the storm, and the distant bleating of lambs who did not like having their fleeces soaked the minute they awoke.

It all went unnoticed, because they were deep in a discussion they could not have in the presence of the two women. A new offensive had begun at Arras; and the Americans had finally come into the war as an ally. But the two fliers were battle-hardened and did not believe, as many now did, that the war would be over in a matter of weeks.

'It will take the Americans some months to prepare and train the numbers of men needed to tip the balance enough to bring the Huns to their knees,' said Mike shaking his head. 'The war has gone on too long for any kind of negotiated settlement. Too many men have died, and the hatred has gone too deep. They will have to be totally defeated now. The first of the American troops will arrive over here with the happy-go-lucky feeling of adventure we had at the start. It's only natural. They'll go into battle with gusto and a certain amount of chivalry. Only when they see their friends dying in thousands around them, when they've lived in mud holes for months on end, and they fully realise what is being done to the face and people of France will they fight with the ruthless determination that is needed, at this stage.'

Rex nodded in agreement. 'It takes a long time, or something drastic to make the average man abandon civilised behaviour. In addition, they won't have the distress of knowing their people are being bombed in their own homes while they are over there fighting, as we have. I'm thinking of giving up the London apartment. We're rarely there, and the damned Gothas are far more dangerous than the Zeppelins were. I'd rather use Tarrant Hall as a base between lecture trips.'

'What does Laura think of that idea?'

He grinned. 'I haven't put it to her yet. You'll know when I have. The air will be blue.'

They reached the bottom of the hill and turned left into the lane that led through the centre of the village. The ditches were full of water that bubbled along toward the main outflow into the stream, and small children were hanging over their garden gates, racing sticks on the water or dropping paper boats onto the moving tide and craning their necks to watch the vessels' progress as far as they could.

'Before I left France they were already building up for this Arras offensive,' Mike told him. 'We were flying as many as *four* missions a day against Fokker attacks on our convoys and ammunition dumps. The more experienced ones amongst our number had to take on the balloons. You know how I hate that.'

'Don't we all,' said Rex with feeling. 'The poor bastards in the baskets can't fire back in defence, and we both face death by frying when the bloody things burst. Still, all the time balloons are cheaper to lose than aircraft, we'll all go on using them for observation.'

'And balloonists don't have to be trained to fly,' pointed out Mike. 'How are you getting on with your recruiting drive?'

'Oh, it's money for old rope,' Rex told him with bitterness. 'I go round filling sixth-form boys with patriotism and daring with my lectures on the gallant life of a pilot, then I sit them in the cockpit at one of the flying-schools, teach them tactics that sound in their ears like the advice of a rugby coach before a vital but sporting contest, wave them goodbye in the full glory of my uniform with its row of medals, and go home to make love to my wife. There's nothing to it . . . except that I can't get their damned eager faces out of my mind unless I dull it with brandy. I wonder what they call me as their flesh begins to char, and their eyeballs are scorched from their sockets.'

Mike's steps slowed, and he turned to face Rex as they reached a gate leading to the water-meadow. 'I thought this posting in England was devised to *stop* you from cracking-up. You never said things like that over there.'

Rex leant on the gate facing out over the meadow, and felt immense relief at being able to speak of feelings he had suppressed too long.

'Over there you live with it, in it, *above* it. There's little time to think. Boys come and go so fast they all start to look alike. A chap called Brett Rope vanishes over Hun lines, but you don't mourn because the bastard will probably turn up a few days later. When he doesn't it's too late to be sorry.'

'He's a prisoner-of-war. We heard last month,' put in Mike quietly.

'Then he'll probably starve to death. Roland wrote about some *leutnant* who let them all get away from Croix Des Anges because the Huns haven't enough food for prisoners—even wounded ones. Brett would have done better burning after all. Bloody agony, but quicker than starving.'

'Rex, you've got to get this obsession with burning out of your system.'

'Can you?' he asked harshly. 'When I was with the squadron I could, at least, protect the immature idiots to some degree, or have a crack at getting the Hun who got them. I'm ashamed of what I'm doing here, Mike. I have to make it sound good and clean and noble, and their shining eyes and bloody stupid adoration twists my guts every time. Out there, they know only too well what you are asking them to do and see you doing it alongside them. For the past three months I've lied and cheated, accepted invitations to dinner afterward, then gone home to comfort and a decent night's sleep in a bed, knowing another batch of mothers is about to be destroyed through my day's work.'

'Do you think telling the truth would be better?' countered Mike with a touch of anger. 'They've all *got* to go to war. Let them start out believing what we believed when we joined. If some old man of twenty-two had told you what it was really going to be like, would you have given him your devoted thanks . . . and would you have wanted to believe him? Rex, you stand for something they have to hold on to or they'd never get as far as France. And it *is* still there, however much we all think we have lost sight of it, or we'd have arrested the King, as the Russians have just done with their Tsar, and our men would be killing us all off and leaving the trenches like the peasant-soldiers on the Eastern Front.'

Rex turned to his friend. 'You should be doing this tour instead of me. You sound far more convinced—or else you lie far better. Why are you in England, anyway?'

'Got the shakes, old sport. Can't keep my hands still. Haven't you noticed?'

He had, but made no comment other than, 'How many girls have I heard complain of the same thing? You haven't changed, Mike.'

'But you have.' He gave Rex a keen look. 'How is it with Laura?'

'Marvellous.'

'Have you told her all this?'

'Of course not.'

'You should.'

'Would you tell Tessa?'

'She's not my wife.'

Rex decided to change the subject. 'When are you going to get one, you lecherous devil?'

'The girl I want is already married to your young brother.'

Rex sighed and turned round to lean back on the gate with crooked arms. 'And Chris has got his eyes on Laura. I hope to God that doctor knows what he's doing by not telling him he has a wife and son.'

'Seems an eminently sane bloke to me. He's after Tessa.'

Rex gave an exasperated laugh. 'How on earth do we find time for emotional tangles in the midst of everything else?'

'It keeps us all sane.'

'Does it?' He thought of that flight to England that was only halted by a French machine-gunner's error. He straightened up. 'I hope Tessa finds happiness. She's a girl in a million, and Roland should have realised that. He's so damned controlled, I sometimes wonder if he knows what to do with a woman.'

Rex had a shock when he entered the Deacons' house. Marion looked far older than her twenty years; thin and tired. But her face lit up when she saw the visitors her father ushered into the parlour, where she sat with a patchwork-quilt tucked round her legs. Her lack of surprise at seeing Mike told him his friend had already called at the house since arriving at the village two days before. With Chris currently adoring Laura, how could he take a righteous stand against the boy's wife? She had plainly been very ill, although he had not known it was a total breakdown until told of it by Major Chandler the initial evening.

'It's far too long since we met,' he told her warmly. 'But you had gone away to your aunt when we came home for Christmas. How are you, Marion?'

'Oh, lots better,' she assured him. 'It's a great help having a doctor for a father.'

'You're keeping a stern eye on my young nephew, too, I hope,' he said lightly to Dr Deacon.

'Our boy is fine,' was the uncompromising reply from a man who avoided acknowledging any link with the Sheridan family for his grandson. 'In another week, Marion will be well enough to dispense with that girl Maisie, and he'll have his mother's care—which he should have had all along,' he finished gruffly before going out.

'I've brought young David a present,' he said to cover the moment. 'It's quite respectable, I promise.'

'Rex, you shouldn't.'

He grinned. 'I've also brought one for you . . . which isn't at all respectable.'

Faint colour entered the face that was too pale as she unwrapped the camisole of Nottingham lace.

'Laura was with me when I bought it,' he explained, 'so she won't be down here to tear out your hair over it. I had to buy her one to keep the peace.'

She smiled somewhat mistily at him. 'You are a dear, Rex.'

'I know.'

'I'm not going to be left out of this,' put in Mike. 'Don't you both agree that I'm a real old love?'

'No,' said Rex promptly. 'Go away and amuse young David for a few minutes while I talk to this gorgeous girl.'

'I know you, young Sheridan,' grumbled his friend. 'You just want to persuade her to put on that bit of lacy nonsense you brought. Do not trust him, gentle maiden.'

'I wouldn't dream of chasing after my brother's wife,' put in Rex in mock outrage.

'Why not? He's chasing after yours.'

With that piece of monumental tactlessness Mike went off to find David Sheridan, taking the musical drum Rex had brought and leaving behind a very telling silence.

'What was that all about?' Marion asked finally.

Rex tried to avoid it. 'Did you know Chris is up at the house?'

'Yes. They told me he was being moved. They also said he had emerged from his latest setback.' She fixed him with an intent gaze. 'What did Mike mean?'

'Nothing really. The lad is miles better than I ever hoped he'd be. He has remembered all about Gallipoli now—which was pretty horrific, Marion. It sent stronger men than Chris out of their minds, you know.'

Her hands folded and unfolded the lace in her lap. 'Has he fallen for Laura?'

'She's there, and you aren't,' he said awkwardly.

'I was, but he didn't want me any longer. I tried, Rex, you know I tried to atone for all I had done to him. I had already considered coming back to look after David when Chris told me he didn't want me always around him. Then he had another of those terrible spells of semi-madness—he gets very violent, you know—and they had to isolate him. I'd walk past the room and hear him screaming and yelling about the enemy, and I suddenly couldn't stand any more. I just wanted to come home and pretend none of it had ever happened.' Her eyes began to fill with unchecked tears. 'But David was here to remind me, night and day.'

Full of concern Rex leant forward in his chair and took her hands. 'All right, take it easy. It's all perfectly understandable.'

'No, Rex, don't be kind. Let me go on,' she pleaded on a rising tone. 'I haven't been able to tell any of this to Daddy, because he is already so angry, and I'm afraid of his bad heart. But I have to confess to *someone*.'

'How about Mike?' he suggested quietly.

The tears spilled onto her cheeks. '*Don't*, Rex. I feel treacherous enough as it is.'

So he found himself forced to listen to something that sounded to him the saddest thing on earth.

'I left the hospital and came home to forget, but I found myself . . . hating . . . my own child because he was there to remind me. I . . . I . . . at one stage I actually thought I might do the boy some harm.' She was clutching his hand so tightly her fingernails dug into his flesh. 'I began taking laudanum from Daddy's cupboard to keep myself calm, and the amounts got bigger and bigger as my fears grew. One day, I must have taken too much.'

Rex winced. He understood only too well what she was describing.

'I don't know how long I was ill,' she went on in a broken voice, 'but during that time I relived all Chris had done to me, in return, and realised that I . . . that whatever it was I had felt for him long ago had died on the day he walked away from me to join the army, and crushed me from his life as if I had never existed. He had wanted to die rather than face life with me: two months ago I wanted to do the same.' She loosed his hands and sank back against her cushions, looking at him with utter desperation. 'But neither of us died, and we are still tied together.'

Very moved and feeling totally inadequate, Rex said, 'But he'll be different. Dr Chandler says he's already forming relationships he couldn't manage before. When he remembers it all, he'll be different.'

Her tears began again, faster this time. 'But *I* shan't! I never want to set eyes on him again. I told Dr Chandler that.'

'You're still not well,' he soothed, wondering if he should call her father.

'I'm *perfectly* well,' she sobbed. 'And I love my baby again. I just want to live here with David in peace. But now I know *he's* there at the top of the hill, I can't. Why did they have to send him here, of all places?'

'Because it's his home,' he told her thickly, feeling desperately sorry for her.

'At first, he was just another helpless patient like all the others, and it was easy to forget all the things he had said and done. It didn't even look like him, that bandaged figure who had no idea who or what he was,' she went on through her floods of tears. 'But he looks like Chris now, and I'm not even sure he isn't doing it all deliberately just to be kept there . . . away from me. Well, I *want* him to stay there. I don't ever want to set eyes on him again, or hear his lunatic ravings. I wish they'd take him away . . . miles away from here. Oh, Rex . . . dear God,' she moaned in mental anguish, twisting her head from side to side on the cushion, 'forgive me, but I keep wishing he'd go permanently insane, and set me free!'

20

CHARLES BARR-LEIGH was sent to England to join the growing number of young men who would fill mental institutes for the rest of their lives. Hilary Bisset was officially listed as 'killed on active service', and the war continued swallowing ordinary peaceable people in its ravenous perverted jaws.

The offensive in the Ypres sector gathered in momentum as the series of diversionary attacks were linked into a concerted bid to break the German grip around the salient, once and for all. During the first days of June a massive British attack at Messines signalled the start of the Allies' intentions. It was a signal heard even by English people in coastal towns just across the Channel, when thousands of pounds of explosives were set off, followed by such an intense artillery bombardment the thunder of noise travelled for miles.

Messines was taken and held, the Germans being driven back across the canal running through the district and being too weakened and demoralised to attempt a counter-attack. Then, unbelievably, a temporary halt was called while plans and tactics were reviewed, revised or revoked. All along the Ypres front line men waited in the soul-destroying limbo of pre-battle, despairing of the lost chances and never knowing when the call would finally come. Where they had stood frozen and sodden in trenches knee-deep with water and liquid mud, they now sweltered between those high enclosing earth walls as summer temperatures soared and the sun beat down on their tin-hats and thick khaki serge uniforms.

More men's nerves broke under the unbearable strain of it all; more men's bodies succumbed to fevers and the ravages of insanitary living. Roland found his resources strained as an increasing number of patients appeared with dangerously high temperatures, internal disorders, persistent sickness, toothache, dysentery, headaches accompanied by temporary blindness, and multiple boils. Knowing what it would be like once the battle got seriously underway again, he worried over the general poor health of the men who would be asked to give their utmost at that time. He sent in requisition after requisition for drugs and stimulants which never came. He had frequent bad-tempered discussions with the Catering Corps on the subject of diet, knowing their requisitions also met with blanks and that they could not be blamed for the monotony and poor quality of the rations. He spoke at length with the Padre about maintaining the faith and trust of the men, and with regimental officers about keeping their troops occupied and interested so that their morale did not flag. With the exception of the Padre, they all looked at him askance and asked if he was feeling all right.

'At present, yes,' he replied sharply to them. 'But I shan't if the worst happens. These men are in such bad physical shape, it would only need an epidemic of something to break out, and the Huns would be able to saunter across here with their hands in their pockets.'

Ironically, when a minor epidemic did hit them, it was Roland who was the first victim. A couple of days of feeling off-colour had been followed by the discovery that his body was covered in scarlet spots which he had no difficulty in diagnosing as measles. Ordered by his C.O. into Guillehoek for isolation in one of the small rooms for officers at the casualty clearing-station, Roland's departure was accompanied by mocking cheers, lewd remarks about the side effects when adult males caught the children's complaint, and offers of ways to keep him occupied and interested so that his morale would not flag. He took the ribbing in good part, despite how ill he felt, and lay for some days in a room with the curtains drawn surrendering to the weakness assailing him and worrying badly about the risk of becoming impotent through catching the malady at his age.

When he began to convalesce, all his other worries returned, also. In the background of them all was the drama of Hilary Bisset, who had touched his life only momentarily yet who had somehow represented Chris and shown him things he had not seen before; and Charles Barr-Leigh, who had also represented Chris by shockingly demonstrating how a human being could be broken by an unbearable load without those living close to him being aware of it.

During those days when still in isolation but well enough to sit up, he spent many hours regretting things he could do nothing about. His commonsense told him depression was a normal result of high fevers such as he had had but, for the first time in his life, he admitted to a feeling of loneliness. His self-sufficient and reticent nature had never demanded more from others than he had been prepared to give them. But, all at once, he felt the need to speak to someone of all he felt—of his impressions, his experiences, his fears and sorrows. The ideal candidate for such confidences was Rex, but his brother was in England with his dangerously seductive wife. Fortunate devil! Rex would not be feeling lonely. Except, of course, one could not speak to a woman of the thoughts now seething in Roland's brain.

Several days passed, and his restlessness increased until he felt so full of emotions he wanted to express, there was only one outlet. The second contribution to the *Gillyhook Gazette* that he had written beside the river that day had been very well received, and he had become aware that he could put into the written word all those things he found so difficult to express verbally. Asking for paper and pencils from a nurse, he began writing a series of letters to his young nephew, in which he expressed with clarity and unsparing honesty the pulse-beat of war; the things it did to men and women, the horrors and strange joys of a soldier in the trenches, the courage and fears of the innocent civilians who watched armies marching back and forth through their towns and villages, destroying or using them for their own ends before being driven out again by the next invaders.

He wrote the full episode of Hilary and Charles with compassion, regret and dignity. He wrote of the German *leutnant* who had let them escape rather than obey ruthless orders that would force wounded men to die slowly and helplessly. He wrote of girls like Rosalind Tierney, who tried to hit back at a world gone black. Then, to his surprise, he wrote of girls like Marion, who could not hit back because their children demanded a life from them.

He read none of them through when he finished, feeling instinctively that spontaneity would have provided a vividness his natural reticence would deplore. In any case, he had no intention of sending the letters. The boy was a mere child. In years to come, the right moment would present itself, and Roland hoped the writings might help the boy understand his own father, whatever state Chris might then be in. On the other hand, the pencilled letters might never be read by anyone but himself as a reminder of his youth.

As soon as he was freed from isolation he wrote a note to Rosalind asking her to visit him on a personal matter. There was no reply, and she failed to turn up. He was angry. It would be simple to send Hilary's cameo up to the canteen by one of the orderlies, but the boy had asked him to give it in person and Roland felt he wanted to explain to the recipient just how much the gesture meant. So he had to wait until he could go himself.

It took him a few weeks to recover fully from what had been a severe attack, but thankfully appeared to have left no humiliating side-effects. He strolled up to the canteen on a late June evening that highlighted his sense of loneliness with its seductive heaviness of midsummer. Once again, his spirit travelled back to Tarrant Royal and past midsummers, and longing was added to loneliness as his boots rang on the cobbles of a Flemish village street. The physical weakness following his illness seemed pronounced as he pushed open the door of the canteen.

It was almost as if time had not passed since that previous evening, except that it was unbearably hot inside. The troops and officers were thronging a room full of smoke, and someone was playing *If you were the only girl in the world* on the gramophone. The full sadness of Hilary's death hit him as he remembered the boy bringing folded seats from where he had hidden them behind a curtain.

A burst of laughter broke his reverie, and he glanced across the counter to see Rosalind enjoying the flirtatious attentions of two R.E. officers. He stood for a moment unobserved by her, wishing he had never been burdened by this mission. Just because she had given a boy his manhood by letting him use the body she no longer valued, she did not deserve a token representing a Christian woman who had been murdered by Chinese whilst upholding her deep faith.

Looking at her now it was hard to believe she had once been so proud and dignified. True, she had always had a volatile temper which could flatten a man's ego with a few well-chosen words. But she had always been popular with the London and county set, with a coterie of admirers whether in the saddle or on the dance-floor. Although he had taken her to dinner on several occasions, Roland had never seriously considered himself one of her bevy of suitors. But they had common interests, which had made their brief interlude enjoyable on both sides. Then, Rosalind had met Captain Reginald Matravers, of the Royal Horse Artillery, and fallen headlong in love with him. They had become engaged two days before he had left for France. He had been amongst the first British casualties.

Looking at her again now Roland recalled her radiance in the photographs of the engagement party that had appeared in the society publications. Could this really be the same girl? Yet he realised the face of the Rosalind of the past had been haughtily beautiful with a touch of petulance to the mouth and features that had been untouched by experience. This young woman in white might be less striking, but she looked infinitely more human, he supposed. What would Reggie Matravers, her father and brother think if they could see her now? Surely they would not have wanted their loss to destroy what she had been!

The laughter faded from her face as he went forward, and she spotted him. Sensing that she was about to move away, his tone was sharper than he intended.

'Don't walk off! I have had to come here, since you wouldn't respond to my note.'

Her lip curled. 'I don't respond to anything of *yours,* especially that damned imperious attitude. Just because your serfs disowned you, it's useless trying to be Squire of Gillyhook now you've been forced into uniform.'

'Is there somewhere private we could go for a moment?' he asked, trying to remain controlled.

Her eyes blazed. 'I wouldn't go anywhere with you, private or otherwise.'

One of the R.E. officers got to his feet. 'Is he bothering you, Rosie girl?' he asked in an Irish accent.

'No, I'm not,' Roland snapped, aware that several of the nearest men were glancing round in curiosity. 'I am trying to deliver a message from one of her friends who was killed in action last month.' Looking back at the girl, he added, 'Young Hilary Bisset asked me to come. That's the only reason I'm here.'

Although she appeared to have abandoned her intention of walking away, she made no comment.

'He's dead,' Roland told her in quiet tones, thinking she could not have taken in what he had said.

'He's in good company, then.'

'Is that . . . all you can say?' he challenged.

'What did you have to say for two years?' she retaliated, in empty tones.

It was difficult to continue, but he forced himself to do what he came to do. 'Hilary gave me something he wanted you to have. I think you should know its history before I hand it over. Could we at least go outside for a moment?'

'Ah-ha, I've heard that one before,' put in the R.E. officer who had been eavesdropping on their conversation. 'Don't trust him, me darlin'.'

'I don't,' she assured her admirer, her gaze still on Roland. 'You can tell me about it here. I'm with friends.'

It touched him on the raw, and he lost his temper within a matter of seconds. 'I'm not going to discuss some poor bloody deluded boy's dying wishes while you pour cups of tea and sell your pride along with the jam doughnuts!'

He left the canteen in such a state of anger he could not bring himself to return to the hospital immediately, yet his lone walk along the river took him past the cottage he had shared with young Hilary. What must he do; what was his duty to the boy? Every instinct urged him not to hand over the cameo to a girl who would regard the gift with satirical ingratitude. Yet Hilary had wanted her to have it, and he had been charged with delivering it.

Walking to the river was a mistake. With the sun finally going down in misty rose-coloured splendour that turned the water an unusual silvery-pink, and the balmy air adding to the sense of another time, another place, the banks were already occupied by courting couples strolling arm in arm, or seated beneath trees in amorous isolation.

Roland had to return to the hospital, after all. He felt conspicuous and bereft walking alone amongst so many pairs. With sleep evading him and the uncharacteristic sense of loneliness now so strong it had become a torment, he took up a pencil and wrote another letter to David Sheridan. It was unlike all the others he had written. This was full of bitterness, pain and a sense of abandonment by the whole of mankind. Above all, it illustrated very vividly the isolation of the soldier in a foreign land when he had reached the point of no longer believing in himself, or what he was fighting for.

The following day was hotter than ever. Roland ate breakfast outside along with several other officers, who were recovering from injuries that would not prevent their return to the trenches. It was Tuesday, and he had been told he would be discharged as fit at the weekend. In truth, the beds were needed. Rumour was rife that the next big push would be during the following week or two, and high casualty figures were expected.

By ten, he was so restless he went out for a walk hoping the banks of the river would be free of lovers at that hour of the morning. It was clear and clean, and one could hardly believe there were guns, wire entanglements, and men living underground not so far away. He knew an alien fear of going back to it all, and now understood Rex's fierce determination to 'pop champagne corks' before returning. He wished he had popped a few himself, so that he could look back on something now. But not with Tessa Manning. She was the kind of person one dedicated one's life to. It needed a girl like Laura to give a man the kind of memories that made all this bearable, and Rex had had to marry her to get them.

Halfway through the village he was brought from his contemplations by the sound of an altercation ahead, where soldiers were grouped around an ambulance. Roland could see the red cross on the side of the vehicle which had halted short of the clearing-station, and seemed to be the subject of raised voices. He might have passed without further interest if the human voices had not been interrupted by the frightened whinnies of a horse, and a girl's imperious tones demanding action. Roland knew the voice, but it was not for Rosalind Tierney that he interceded. It was for the horse.

A pitiful scene greeted him when he pushed his way through the group. One of a pair of horses dragging an ambulance had succumbed to exhaustion and repeated terror. Half collapsed between the shafts, it was unable to get up again because the traces were hopelessly twisted around its legs. The driver, probably also suffering from exhaustion and repeated terror, was plainly at the end of his tether and anxious to reach the clearing-station where he would be able to rest for several days. From inside the ambulance, which must have been stifling in that heat, came demands to get on with it, and faint moans of men needing urgent attention.

Everyone was heated and irrational, too busy shouting at each other to do the obvious thing that would solve the situation. Rosalind was in a rare temper, cheeks flaming and eyes full of contemptuous anger as she faced the driver.

'If you hit that poor animal once more, I'll have you tied to a gun,' she cried. 'That creature is half dead.'

'So am I,' came the fierce reply, 'and I don't need no emotional bitch telling me what to do about it.'

With that, he swung at the horse with his whip, more in defiance of the girl than any desire to punish the animal. 'Get up, you bugger! Come on, get up!'

Rosalind snatched the whip from the unsuspecting man's hand and set about him with it so that he had to protect his head with his raised arms.

'See how *you* like being beaten and whipped,' she taunted in furious tones. 'You great bullying brute!'

Several of the troops standing by started to laugh at the spectacle of the soldier being subdued by a canteen girl, and the others were starting to join in when Roland said in a voice like thunder, 'Stop this charade and get that horse up immediately!'

Rosalind turned with the whip in her hand, halted by the command. Her victim lowered his arms, prepared to take on all and sundry.

'Who the hell are . . .?' His challenge tailed off and he stiffened to attention.

'God help us all in battle if you are an example of the British soldier's quick thinking,' snapped Roland. 'That horse is going to break a leg if it's not released soon.'

So saying, he snatched the bayonet from the belt of one of the bystanders no longer laughing, and began cutting through the traces holding the horse in its dangerous position. 'Hold its head, Rosalind,' he instructed over his shoulder. 'It's so terror-stricken by now it could bolt the moment I get it up.'

As he worked on the leather he was conscious of her taking the cheek-straps in her hands, and her soft confident words that she knew would calm the animal.

'Steady, steady,' he murmured as the creature's hooves scraped the cobbles in desperate premature attempts to rise. 'Watch him!' he called sharply to the girl, 'and for God's sake, someone, hold that other horse, or it'll also take fright and ruin everything.'

The last trace was severed, and Roland moved quickly to hold the cheek-straps beside Rosalind as the beast heaved to its feet with the energy inspired by fear. Together they struggled to hold it steady while still in close proximity to its partner in the shafts. For a few minutes the creature remained restive, its eyes wild, its hooves stamping. But the original exhaustion triumphed, and all the fight went from it as its head bowed and the whinneying ceased. Fear that it was about to expire made Roland speak lovingly and encouragingly in the manner of an experienced horseman as he led it gently from between the shafts and over to the side of the street. But it seemed able enough to walk, and he looked over to the group of people still clustered around the ambulance.

'Roz, take it on up to the clearing-station. The stables are at the rear. Go slowly and talk it every yard of the way. I don't have to tell you how.'

She walked across to him, her attention focused on the horse as she took over to allow him to go back to the others.

He confronted the driver with suppressed anger. 'You're not fit to be in charge of horses.'

The man's face was sullen. 'I'm tired, sir. I've come a long way with this ambulance.'

'*So has the horse!* But he has been pulling it, not sitting on his backside in the cab. If that creature survives, it'll be no thanks to you, and I'd rather shoot it than put it in your hands again. What's your name?'

'Hancock.'

'*Sir.*'

'Hancock, sir.'

'Right, Hancock, there are about five hundred yards to go to the clearing-station. Get in the shafts with that other tired horse and start pulling so that you get some idea of what it's like!'

Hancock was aghast. 'I can't do that, sir. I'm never strong enough to do that.'

Roland smiled grimly at the troops standing around. 'I'm sure your chums who thought Miss Tierney's defence of that beast so comical would be willing to share the experience with you. In other words, fall in all of you and pull this vehicle up the road! There are wounded men inside needing treatment.'

The stunned soldiers recognised an order from an officer who also happened to be a doctor, and did as they were told. With Roland leading the remaining horse, they progressed up the bumpy road, overtaking Rosalind when they were nearly at their destination. Probably for her benefit, the driver muttered something about officers always giving the orders and doing none of the work. But Roland overheard him and lashed out with continuing anger.

'I was a corporal orderly in this war until four months ago, Hancock. Up near Croix Des Anges I helped pull an ambulance a distance of four miles—and so did the captain in charge of the unit—because one of the horses had been killed in an aerial attack. *Four miles,* Hancock, and it rained all the way.'

There was not another single grumble until they reached the clearing-station, and the medical staff took over. Roland went straight round to the stables with the horse that had remained in the shafts, and handed it over to a stable-hand with the advice to give it a long rest before sending it out again. He knew he was wasting his time, as he would be to report Hancock. The man was tired. They were all tired. Horses were desperately scarce, and when they dropped dead someone benefited from the flesh.

Rosalind appeared then with the other one, talking gently to encourage it along the final few yards. But it looked beyond help now. He gave similar advice about resting it, just the same. Then he turned to the girl.

'Thanks for your help.'

She half nodded. 'Thanks for coming to my rescue.'

He looked at her steadily. 'I had to, didn't I? Old habits die hard.'

As he started to walk away she came up beside him. 'Roland, wait a minute. Please.'

Slowing he turned his head. 'Well?'

'Don't . . . don't just walk away like that.'

'Why not?'

His abruptness seemed to disconcert her for a moment or two. Then she gave a strained smile. 'Because old habits die hard, as you just said.'

To cover a sensation of longing to reach out to her in some way, he said out of the blue, 'They'd be holding the Harwich Trials at home . . . and I'd lay a tenner on the weather being atrocious, as usual.'

For a while he thought she would not respond, then she said in a curiously breathless tone, 'And I'd lay a tenner on Albatross beating Korki, this time.'

'You'd lose your money again.'

They stood gazing at each other for some moments, until he said, 'I'd buy you a cup of tea, but the *estaminet* isn't open yet and neither is your canteen. I might scrounge one from the nurses if you'd like to come in.'

She shook her head. 'Come to my quarters and I'll make one.'

'Is that allowed?'

'Of course not, but you did say you wanted somewhere private while you told me about Hilary.'

Her room was at one end of a long hut housing the other girls, and they both tiptoed in knowing it would mean a lecture for Rosalind if they were caught. But it put an exciting sense of guilt into what was only an occasion to carry out a dead boy's wishes. The spartan room was furnished in typical army style that made a bedroom look like an office. A bottle of scent on something that resembled a filing cabinet, and a lace-trimmed handkerchief sachet on a round-headed stool beside the bed, looked alien, yet strangely exciting in such masculine surroundings.

Roland's gaze reached a folding chair. Across the back hung a filmy camisole and petticoat trimmed with ribbons and embroidered with butterflies. Carelessly dropped on the seat was a pair of silk knickers, also embroidered with butterflies.

All Roland had seen of such articles since leaving England had been the erotic postcards pinned on the sides of dug-outs by subalterns who brought them back from leave, keeping the best for themselves and selling the rest at extortionate prices to their fellows. The new shorter skirts now revealed the ankles of girls daring enough to wear them, but the postcards showed what was under those skirts. Roland found himself longing to pick up the underwear, feel the softness of the material, enjoy their feminine daintiness.

'I thought you wanted tea,' said a soft voice.

He drew his gaze away to meet hers as she stood beside him with a cup and saucer. Did she wear such things beneath that starched uniform? What a waste that they could not be seen and admired!

'Thanks.' He took the cup and hastily reached into an inner pocket where he kept Hilary's cameo. 'I was asked to give you this in person, although I was not asked to tell you its history. But as I believe it to be quite valuable, I felt you should know the story behind it.'

He held out the little package of soft satin just as Hilary had given it to him. 'It's an antique cameo.'

'I really don't want it,' she told him wearily. 'I hardly knew the boy.'

'That's not what he told me.'

She had removed the starched cap that hid most of her lovely dark hair and, sitting sideways on the bed, her shape was outlined against light from the window. Roland could not take his gaze from it.

'He was a fool, like all the others,' she murmured.

'How many others, Roz?'

She sipped her tea. 'Does it matter?'

'Of course it damn well matters.'

'Why?'

Strongly aware of the frilly underwear on the chair beside him, he said, 'Because you used to have pride. Because you were intelligent and loyal. What's happened to you?'

She put her cup and saucer down with a bang. '*War*, my dear Roland. War has happened to me. I've been in it a damned sight longer than you have, don't forget.'

He put his own cup down with a bang. 'If you're back on that subject there seems little point in my staying. This was a mistake. There's no truce, after all.'

She scrambled from the bed to stand before him, her dark blue eyes candid, her breath, quickened from the swift movement, fanning his mouth.

'I'm sorry about the other night in the canteen. Hilary said you had volunteered before conscription.' The scent of honeysuckle growing in an English hedgerow reached him from the region of her throat. 'But you can't get away from the fact that it took you a long time to do it. I was suffering right from the beginning.'

'Do you think I wasn't?' he cried taking hold of her shoulders. 'Both my brothers joined at the outset. One is an acknowledged hero, but he didn't become what he is without facing death every day—not only from the enemy but faulty machines. Do you think I didn't suffer knowing I might never see him again? And the other one, no more than a schoolboy, was blown up at Gallipoli. For eighteen months he has been hovering between life and death, sanity and lunacy, with no idea of his identity or his past. Do you think I didn't suffer when I visited the hospital and each time he looked at me as if I were a stranger?' Worked up to top pitch now and gripping the soft flesh of her shoulders with fingers that shook, he went on, 'And do you think I didn't suffer when old friends shunned me, and when people I had tried to serve as Squire sent me white feathers . . . or when girls I had known and admired flung wine in my face? *You* were suffering from the beginning? So was I. In my own little way, so was I. But I stayed at home because I truly believed I was doing my best duty for my country and my brothers. All right, I was wrong. *I was wrong!*' he shouted huskily. 'But, for God's sake stop reminding me how wrong I was!'

Rosalind had paled, and there was something astonishingly like tears on her lashes as she stood there pliant in his grip.

'So you do have feelings, after all.'

It sounded crueller than anything she had said to him yet. Hardly aware of what he was doing, he forced himself to let go her shoulders, and turned to pick up his cap. Seeing the wrapped cameo, he put his finger on it and pushed it along the table-top toward her.

'You can't refuse this. It was his death-wish that you should have it.'

He never got as far as the door. She was there leaning back against it, looking at him with desolate misted eyes.

418

'Is that all you came here for, Roland? Is that *really* all you came here for?'

He stood there under bombardment. She was his past with its innocent triumphs, its harmless victories. She was a world he had been forced to leave but never forgotten. She was something he had shut from his heart rather than let it bleed. She was a way of life he would never find again.

Dropping the cap again he reached for her. 'You know damn well what I came for.'

Her body was a haven for his intolerable loneliness; her generosity was a joy he had almost forgotten existed. It did not matter that there had been others before him, or that there would be others in the future. For now, she was his release, his sanity, his means to continue for a little longer.

For the next four days Roland did not exactly pop champagne-corks, but he did the nearest thing to it, under the circumstances. He spent every possible minute with Rosalind, walking along the river banks to quiet places where he would lie with his head in her lap, as they talked of all those times before August 1914 when they had been so very young and full of optimism. They spoke of horses and all things connected with horses; they reminisced on racing and past championships; they argued the respective merits of famous hunt venues. But they never dwelt on the riders who were now gone, or the rôle of their beloved horses now. They shut out the present with mutual determination, and found something to temporarily neutralise it by dwelling in a wishful fantasy that had no beginning and could survive no end.

Those four days were a bubble floating above reality, in which they were completely enclosed within themselves. Because of that, Roland's natural reticence dropped away in the assurance that confessions and confidences would never go beyond the shining rainbow sphere surrounding that period with a girl who supplied all he needed.

They made love at every opportunity, she bringing out a passion hidden deep within him, and only once before suspected when he had been confronted with Laura. It was selfish and almost savage, dragged to the surface only by girls who suspected its existence and could reciprocate in kind. For Roland, it was total release. He abandoned himself to it without reservations.

When the weekend came they said goodbye like civilised people and never looked back to wave. Roland was welcomed back in the trenches with the usual gusto accorded those who had been hospitalised for a while then returned for further duty. Comments like, *'If they didn't want you any longer, why should they think we did?'* or *'What did you do to upset Matron?'* were augmented in Roland's case with very rude questions about the state of his manhood, and whether he had had the spots absolutely *everywhere.*

In his dug-out, shared now by two new subalterns, he found drawings pinned to the wall to illustrate the saga of an M.O. who worried too much about the religion, rations, and rheumatics of his men, and the terrible fate that overcame him. There was only a sly reference to his measles in the *Gillyhook Gazette,* with a drawing of a podgy baby dressed in napkin and peaked army cap, his body marked by oversized spots. The caption beneath was: *We knew they were taking recruits from the schoolroom, but this is getting ridiculous!*

Roland laughed at it all, and added his own witticisms to cover the claustrophobic return to high earth walls that shut out the rest of the world. But that tiny atom of the world that was left to him soon became such concentrated horror, claustrophobia was swamped by it.

The delay was over, and the third battle for total control of the Ypres sector was on again. For almost a fortnight the plain stretching before the Allied trenches was continuously bombarded by heavy guns with the intention of decimating and demoralising the enemy before the infantry advance. In addition, a massive air attack was mounted, and the skies above Ypres were black with every conceivable type of aircraft.

Those waiting days in the trenches became nerve-wracked hours of thundering guns, the scream and whistle of shells, the aerial stutter of machine-guns, and whining plunging aircraft. The nights were sleepless periods of pounding heavy artillery fire, blinding flashes of exploding shells, and the white brightness of star-shells overhead to illuminate everything with eerie clarity in the surrounding darkness. The tension was back in those earthen corridors, and if men noticed their friends' hands shaking uncontrollably, the corners of their mouths twitching, or their eyes beginning to stare from sunken sockets, they did not remark on it. They simply licked their lips nervously once more and prayed for the order to advance.

Then the weather broke, and torrential rain turned the plateau they must cross into a quagmire of cratered destruction. The battle order they had prayed for came, but it turned them all into victims of their own bombardment as, in a grey obliterating downpour, they scrambled over the top and entered a hell of mud and slime with unexpected shell-holes filled with water which looked no more than surface puddles, and broken splintered trunks reaching branchless into the greyness above. It was a windswept plain of desolation vanishing into the mists of the distance where the enemy waited. Were they still there in force? Had they retreated from the attack? Had they been substantially wiped out? The answer would only be apparent after slogging, struggling, squelching, slithering, *swimming* across miles of mud from which had emerged the bloated decomposing corpses from the two previous campaigns that had failed to push beyond the Ypres Salient.

They went, as they had always gone in response to orders, sinking waist-deep into ooze, clawing and swearing, filthy with the stinking ordure that coated boots and trousers, faces determinedly set, and pale beneath the ravages of sun and wind as they passed the horrors and mutilation of two and three years ago that had become disinterred. The Royal Engineers had gone ahead to make 'roads' of planks for the thousands of marching feet; the valiant horses drawing gun-limbers, ammunition-wagons, and supplies; the wheels of motor cycles, lorries and ambulances. But the driving rain that liquidised the mud soon made these slippery and practically unrecognisable. Men strayed from them and drowned in the sucking mire, unnoticed by the passing anguished army. The hooves of horses found no grip on them and the beasts fell, dragging guns and vehicles into the mud, too. The air was rent with their shrieks of pain and terror as their struggles took them deeper into the sticky mass holding them fast. Dispatch-riders found their vehicles skidding, and they were tossed headlong, often finding their machines too deeply engulfed to retrieve. Lorries and ambulances moved slowly, causing congestion and often inducing soldiers to move aside to allow them passage, the men forgetting there was no sure foothold beside the designated walkways.

So, while the khaki horde inched its way forward, shells continued to scream overhead and unexploded mines that had lain underground for months and resurfaced, went off to add to the graveyard of the god of war. The appalling weather prevented aerial attack, but death came through the air, just the same. Silent, merging with the mist, spreading out to every part of that plain and to the abandoned trenches beyond came the creeping yellow killer cloud. But this was new; even more terrible and agonising than before. The primitive masks helped men from inhaling it, but it clung to their bodies to burn their flesh and turn the skin into huge yellow blisters that would not heal. It invoked such terror, it was only an excess of national grit and the rigid training of one of the finest armies in the world, drawn from all parts of the Empire and Commonwealth, that ensured the advance continued.

In the rear, Roland's unit, along with the staff of all the other dressing-stations, was growing more and more appalled at the number and state of the casualties flooding in. Working in the most primitive manner in conditions that were well nigh impossible, the medical men stayed on their feet night and day in the fight to save as many lives as possible by their instant limited treatment. But they were sickened, and helpless to do much for the mustard-gas victims. It was a new and frightful weapon; so frightful it was hard to accept that human beings could use it against others.

Roland worked like an automaton. There was no time to think, to consider the wound, to rack his brains for the best treatment. He had to close his ears to agony, shut his mind to suffering. There was blood and more blood. His hands and clothes became saturated with it; the smell invaded his nostrils and stayed there, even when the gas-gong sounded and he had to work in the mask that hindered clear vision. It was worse than at any time with Matt Rideaux's unit—even those nights on the roadside—and it was more like butchery than doctoring!

The battle and the rain continued. As the regiments advanced, so did the field-doctors. Carrying their supplies and equipment mostly on their backs, they crossed the plain of Passchendaele behind the troops, struggling for a footing, wading through a porridge comprising mud, muck and men, facing clouds of thick yellow gas that threatened them as fatally as their patients.

It was a living hell of anguished unreality that had trapped them all, and the advance was merely pushing the treadwheel of horror around and around with no hope of escape from it. Roland passed the stage of feeling anything. The stubble on his face turned into a beard, his eyes grew red-rimmed and watery, the blood on his clothes dried and stiffened, the lice on his body bit unmercifully, his limbs grew sluggish, he smelt of sweat and the other odours of his profession. He was aware of none of it. The casualties became a series of lumps of grotesque broken flesh passing before his eyes. Drugs ran out. Bandages were inadequate. Field-dressings had to be used sparingly. The fresh supplies coming up from the rear often never arrived. The horses were dead or stuck in the muddy swamp-ground. The wagon had been blown up by a mine. The drivers had been gassed and were rolling in frenzied spasms in the mud to ease the burning obscene blisters rising up all over them.

The days passed, and the sun came out. So, too, did the Fokkers. Added to the cries for stretcher-bearers were cries for water, as wounded men lay helplessly gazing at the aircraft marked with black crosses that dived out of the sun to rake the ground around them with bullets. Then came the Nieuports and B.E.'s with roundels on their wings, to protect the army on the ground, and machines began falling from the sky, ally and enemy alike, to add to the burden of doctors.

The advance continued slowly but surely until the order came to halt and dig-in. Losses had been many thousands, and the Germans were now counter-attacking too fiercely. The Allies must go to ground again. Another line of trenches; a few miles gained. Passchendaele, the final objective, was still in the hands of the enemy. The regiments dug in and took up the life of sewer-rats once more. The medical staff continued to treat the casualties until the flood had reduced to a trickle. Then, and only then, they recollected that they were human, and began the process of returning to that state.

Roland worked out a sleeping-rota for his staff so that they could recoup their strength, yet remain able to deal with the aftermath casualties—the men who had kept going despite minor injuries and maladies, those to whom reality was returning and could not stop vomiting, those who had lost too many friends and found it intolerable to continue without them. And there was the usual string of patients suffering from boils, foot-rot, constipation, dysentery, trench-fever, infected rat-bites, and bronchitis.

Even after sleep, a bath, and fresh clothes, Roland found little relief. He felt old. Not merely double his age, but a thousand years old. What was more, he knew the capacity to feel young had gone forever. At twenty-six youth had ended. It seemed that nothing would ever touch his senses again. Even thoughts of home were like ghost pictures flitting through his mind, having no substance and no meaning. Outwardly he took up the brave pretence that was gradually reasserting itself in the new muddy alleyways not far from Passchendaele. But inwardly he was emotionless.

The irrepressible wits were already inventing lewd explanations for why any place should be named 'Passion Dale', and new general jokes on the subject replaced those on the Cloth Hall at Ypres. Soldiers had to chaff at fear, or go mad. Hatred was once more being vented on the eternal rats, games of cards were underway once more for strange stakes, new cruder words were being put to old tunes. The *Gillyhook Gazette* was re-named the *Passion Dale Post,* and began to be circulated. The first issue was full of jokes, comic stories, poems of satire and wit, and another piece by 'The Waysider' about a village midsummer carnival. No one would have guessed that contributors and readers alike *all* felt one thousand years old.

It was not until the anaesthetic horror began to wear off that Roland knew he had to hit out or crack up himself. Some kept going by doing unspeakable things to rats, some roared out filthy songs and guffawed at equally filthy jokes, some took boys like Hilary Bisset into a distant dug-out and broke them. Roland retired into a corner for several hours with pencil and paper. He did not read them through when he had completed the many sheets of writing, just put them with the other letters to David Sheridan, then went to sleep feeling drained and *two* thousand years old.

It was some weeks later that a medical lecture was to be given in Guillehoek, and all doctors were told to attend. In common with other regimental M.O.'s Roland felt lectures were a necessary evil of the military system. But this particular one was on the subject of gas-warfare, with information on the new mustard-gas, so they all felt it would be worthwhile.

It was a tedious business getting to the village now, and involved crossing the miles of cratered barren battlefield where the mud was beginning to harden in the late summer sunshine. They made the short harrowing journey on the previous day, the lecture being scheduled for 9 am and quarters were arranged for them in large tents, the cottages already being filled. Gillehoek was now busier than ever. Being so far behind the new front-line the clearing-station was in the process of being turned into a base-hospital, and the village was filled with vehicles, piles of boxes and equipment, engineers and pioneers expanding the site, and high-ranking officers strolling about looking at everything with critical eyes.

The canteen seemed more crowded than before when Roland walked up there an hour after settling into his tent. As he opened the door he almost expected to hear *If you were the only girl in the world*, but a new batch of recordings must have arrived from England. A female voice was singing

> *You called me baby doll a year ago,*
> *You told me I was very nice to know.*

Half a dozen men were joining in above the laughter and conversation surrounding them, and Roland had to raise his voice so that the girl behind the counter could hear his request to see Miss Tierney.

'Rosie?' she queried, busily pouring tea from a huge metal pot. 'She ought to be here by now. That'll be tuppence, thanks,' she informed the corporal she was serving. 'It's funny she hasn't turned up. I told her I didn't mind coping on my own for a while, but she knows it gets busy around now.'

Her smile was friendly but not inviting, and it was plain to any man of sense he would get nothing from her but what she served across the counter. Her blonde healthy prettiness reminded him of someone. Perhaps it was Tessa Manning, except that he could hardly remember the features of the girl he had appointed bailiff until his return to Tarrant Hall.

'Are you with the new hospital, Doctor?'

'Eh? Oh no, just passing through. I thought I'd look up Rosalind while I was here. We're very old friends.'

'Oh, well, you're sure to find her at her quarters, if you know where they are. Do tell her to hurry up, will you? It's getting too much for one person already, and we haven't reached the busiest time yet.'

It was a sultry evening with the hint of a storm in the offing, and it seemed strangely hushed without the sound of distant gunfire now as he reached the hut on the outskirts of Guillehoek. There was no response to his knock, or to his quiet call to identify himself. It was unlikely she could have passed him on her way to the canteen, so she could be anywhere in the village. He would have to wait until the following day to let her know he was there. On the point of turning away, he stopped. It might have been the need to satisfy himself she was not there with another man, or a desire to see the room where she had given him the fortitude to go back. Whichever it was, he went in uninvited.

Rosalind was lying on the bed, fully dressed and as still as death. He knew instinctively that he was too late, even as he observed that there was life left in her. The two empty aspirin bottles beside the bed, and the photograph of Reggie Matravers with his champion horse, Gunnar, that was lying by her slack right hand told him he should have come here as soon as he entered the village. Even so, he dashed to the door and ordered the nearest passing soldier to run like the wind for a stretcher-party, then returned to the unconscious girl and began what emergency treatment he could to save a life that did not wish to be saved.

After sinking into a coma, Rosalind Tierney died by her own hand at 2 am. A post-mortem examination revealed that she had been in the first stages of pregnancy.

Roland missed the lecture on gas-warfare. He went for a solitary walk along the river-banks until he had covered such a distance he was the only living thing in sight. For hours he sat leaning back against a tree as he gazed out over Flanders, and all he could hear was that record playing *If you were the only girl in the world*.

Finally, he took from his pocket a pencil and pad that had been intended for taking notes at the lecture, and he began to write about the fingers of war that reached out to touch everyone.

He walked slowly back to Guillehoek in the late afternoon, shaken by an overpowering thought. The embryo child might have been his; that embryo child might have been the second Sheridan bastard!

THE NEW show opened in mid-July and was an instant success. Colonel Winters was apparently not only an 'angel', he was a shrewd judge of the art of promotion. On his advice, the leading lady firmly refused to be billed as Madame Sherry, and appeared as Laura Sheridan, which banished lingering memories of the male impersonator, Laurie Paggett, but made no attempt to take advantage of the heroic reputation of her husband.

John Winters told her she must make a bid for a career in her own right, which would out-last the war and the short-lived adulation of the British public for brave men. He also told her she must use her talent in more sophisticated manner; take it up from the level of the music-hall to the serious theatre. Her presentation must concentrate on glamour, her sauciness must be subtle rather than broad, and she must aim at two things—to make every man in the audience fall in love with her, and every woman envious rather than jealous of the fact.

What the British public needed in that summer of 1917 was something to make them forget the war. They wanted laughter, catchy tunes, a look back on better, more leisurely times, and girls who were dressed in the most beautiful clothes imaginable. Given the title *Bows and Boaters,* the show had a turn-of-the-century theme, with scenes at Henley Regatta, Hyde Park, and Horse Guards Parade. Yes indeed, the military flavour crept in, but it was all scarlet jackets and feathery plumes with not a hint of khaki. As for the girls, they had never worn such spangles and satins. Laura had an outrageously daring set of costumes which revealed her beautiful body without suggesting vulgar burlesque. The songs that had been especially written for her suited the low husky pitch of her voice, and were seductive rather than suggestive. Her dances were intricate, graceful and tantalising, but the only high kick she performed was at the final curtain when the full-length glittering black skirt she wore parted to the waist to reveal her long shapely legs clad in black mesh tights, and a body-suit beneath that fitted like a second skin. It was sensational and just right. If the audience wanted more, it meant coming again.

On the opening night Rex had a box to himself where he could hide behind the curtains, and he had bribed the orchestra leader with more than he could really afford *not* to play *Chéri, Chéri* no matter who asked for it. He had no intention of being dragged onto the stage this time. He need not have worried. Laura had seen the wisdom of John Winters' advice and would not ruin everything by doing an impromptu finale with her famous husband. This was her real chance for stardom.

With that opening night their marriage entered a new phase. From that evening back in April when Rex had reluctantly told her to meet Winters, Laura had been so brilliantly happy he was forced to realise just how much a shadow of her true self she had been over the past months. Loving Rex with a generosity beyond words, she made every hour they spent together a joy he could scarcely believe.

Unfortunately, the time they spent together was very little. Laura lived in the London apartment all the time now, despite Rex's fears about the frequent German bombing of the capital, and he was obliged to move around the country, as before, doing his duty of promoting the R.F.C., boosting morale at fêtes and garden-parties, and trying to teach boys the skill and experience of a long-term pilot before they faced the enemy. He went home as often as he could, but they were back to the pattern of Laura having performances each evening and needing to sleep for most of the morning. There was little time left for togetherness.

But, like it or not, Rex had to accept that the theatre was as much in Laura's blood as flying was in his. He could never now ask her to give it up. The most he could achieve was to prevent it from becoming her entire life to the exclusion of him. But he knew in his heart that however successful she might become, the light inside her would die without him.

When away from her in lonely little country inns he drank more than he should to chase away the nightmares about burning men in burning aircraft. But there were now other nightmares. Those of jealousy. John Winters had told Laura she must make every man in the audience fall in love with her. She was succeeding too well. Bevies of admirers waited eagerly outside the stage-door every night for her, and when Rex was away she agreed to join parties for supper in the smart places. It was all good publicity, good for the show, she told him, and he was reasonable enough to see her point. She loved only him. He knew that. But he still felt jealous of all those who could be with her when he could not.

During those first weeks following the opening of Laura's show Rex was conscious of emotions pulling him in opposite directions. Much as September loomed like a black cloud over his passion for Laura, he yearned to be back at his real job. Tutoring and tea-parties were not in his line, really, and things were not going well for Allied airmen in that bleak year. One of the R.F.C.'s other aces, Captain Albert Ball, had been finally killed by Von Richthofen's squadron early in May, at the age of twenty, and the numbers sharing that hero's fate were frightening. Morale was taking some bad knocks.

The Germans now had a new aircraft to augment the Fokkers. Called the Albatross, it was being made in large numbers in an attempt to knock the Allies from the skies for good. But British designers had been busy, also, and produced an excellent aircraft called the Sopwith Pup, which had been a great favourite with pilots until superseded by the brand new Sopwith Camel. In addition, there was the S.E.5, an experimental prototype being tested by British squadrons. And there was the French Spad. With these machines and men of high courage flying them, there was no sign of the defeat the Germans hoped for. Yet still no sign of complete Allied domination of the air over the battlefields.

Rex had been to the Royal Aircraft Factory, and other design workshops to see the development of the new aircraft, and had flown the first models along with other seasoned pilots and instructors at the various flying-schools. His expert advice had been sought by designers and R.F.C. authorities alike, but he had upset several eminent men by suggesting they should try to fly what they had just designed.

'Not for the fun of it, you understand,' he had added, 'but imagining half a dozen Fokkers on your tail.'

Fortunately for his career, other pilots said much the same things. Even so, in some cases the fault was deemed too small and the demand for aircraft was great, so the machines were put into production and delivered with warning notes to all who flew them. Rex thought it was all very well to tell pilots in advance that the rear spar was liable to snap during a steep dive, or that a sharp turn could develop into a spin before they knew, but the men of the R.F.C. flew a wide variety of machines—whichever happened to be available—and in the midst of a scrap they had quite enough to do trying to kill the enemy whilst staying alive themselves without trying to remember what they must *not* do.

His point was proved in the most bizarre manner one day in August, all the more so since he had once applied to join one of the home-based squadrons that had been formed to combat the bombers and Zeppelins that were attacking London and coastal towns with growing frequency. His application had been unceremoniously turned down. With so many flying heroes being killed, 'Sherry' Sheridan was more valuable where he was, at the moment.

His frustration deepened when a spell at an East Coast flying school meant he also saw very little of Laura. On that particular day in August when the promenades along the coast were full of folk on a day out at the seaside, and the beaches below were dotted with children having donkey-rides, Punch and Judy tents, and elderly men easing their aching feet in the briny, Rex took up a boy on his first flight. The lad was sick after two circuits of the airfield, and Rex told himself he had in the rear cockpit a candidate for immediate cremation once he reached France. Yet he had been touchingly keen on the ground, and so overawed at finding Rex was to be his instructor he had eagerly affirmed that he would watch and listen and learn during every moment of the flight.

Acting and speaking mechanically Rex travelled mentally to France while his accumulated frustrations consumed him. Any experienced pilot could do what he was now doing, any man too old, too infirm, or too slow for further combat. If ace fliers were dying, they needed to be replaced by other aces, not boys like this one bringing up his breakfast. Over there, Rex could protect them, inspire them, infuriate the Huns, show them a new trick or two! He had been in England too long. They would think 'Sherry' Sheridan was finished. They would forget him, forget their fear of a man with the famous cerise scarf, forget that he had been the most sought after target of every ambitious or arrogant German pilot over the Western Front, at one time.

Then a terrible thought struck him. *Was* 'Sherry' Sheridan finished? Had marriage swamped his courage that day he had deserted the war intending to fly to England because Laura was ill following an abortion? Would these months of garden parties and school lectures and theatrical gossip have robbed him of his expertise in combat? Would he now be slow, cautious, unprepared? Would he have forgotten the terrain he used to know so well? The armies had moved since last November. Towns and villages had changed hands; some had vanished off the face of the earth. Could he now confidently lead a squadron across the front-line area? What was more, would they now follow him with the blind faith they used to have? Worst of all, would news of his return arouse the old German eagerness for his blood, or would Von Richthofen and friends merely shrug and continue drinking schnapps?

On the heels of his longing to prove they would be most unwise to dismiss him came a vision that suggested his thoughts had become reality. Floating out of a small fluffy cloud about two thousand feet above him, and rapidly losing height, came an aircraft bearing a black cross on its wings. Rex had never encountered one before, but he recognised it immediately from photographs. Unbelievable though it seemed, it was a Gotha bomber—a great long bi-plane with a fuselage that seemed to stretch out behind the propeller almost as long as the wing-span. It was a cumbersome thing that had nevertheless been successful over France and Belgium, and had recently been launched against England from bases just across the Channel, putting coastal residents in fear.

For a few moments Rex flew on toward it, still trying to accept that it was there, his experienced eye assessing the possible reasons for its presence at such a height. That it was in serious trouble was evident, but just how serious could only be gauged at close quarters. One fact was indisputable: the pilot would be determined to get as near to home as possible before coming down.

Rex was flying a patched-up old Nieuport two-seater suitable only for training purposes, but he headed for the Gotha, all that forgotten in the sight of his first enemy for months. Guessing that there must have been a bombing raid further down the coast at Southend or Folkestone, it seemed likely the machine had been hit by artillery, or a fighter of the Home Squadrons who had been unable to pursue it. With the big aircraft rapidly losing height, Rex gained on it quickly and saw the rear-gunner hanging lifeless over the side. That meant the tail of the machine would be undefended and present the best area of attack.

It was only when he was closing in on the enemy fast that Rex realised he was unarmed, that he was not in France with drums of ammunition at his feet, and that he had a pupil in the rear cockpit. But he was close enough now to see the pilot staring at him in apprehension, and the navigator lying back in agony with blood over one shoulder. They were sitting ducks for an armed fighter, and Rex knew he could not allow them to cross the beach below and head out to sea where they might conceivably land safely, or ditch in the water to be picked up by their own navy. Aircraft and engines were scarce. A captured Gotha, to say nothing of its crew, would be invaluable.

Shouting instructions to the boy in the rear to train his gun onto the enemy and keep it trained on them no matter what happened, Rex did the same with his own as he embarked on the most dangerous piece of bluff he had ever devised.

Working on the premise that a pilot in a damaged aircraft, with a dead rear-gunner, a badly wounded observer, and several hostile miles of sea to cross before reaching home territory, would never imagine an enemy would approach so boldly training two empty machine-guns on him, Rex flew as close as he could. Then he angled his gun for deadly aim and pointed forcefully in the direction from which the Gotha had just come. Then he waited, heart thudding against his ribs, to see what would happen.

For a minute or two, the German stared back apparently assessing his chances. His hand crept to the handle of his own gun, then he looked the Nieuport over as it clung like a limpet to his side, and must have decided that two uninjured men in an undamaged fighter with two guns pointing right at him were uneven odds. His hand dropped again. Sweating freely Rex swallowed in relief and pointed inland again, emphasizing the order by edging so close the wing-tips actually touched for a brief second. The German had to turn to avoid a collision.

Slowly but surely, Rex edged the larger aircraft round until they were on a course that would take them back to the flying-school. Each time the enemy pilot glanced his way he pointed to the green open space growing nearer and nearer dead ahead, and watched for any sign of deviation or sudden aggression. Then, when they were almost above the field, Rex pointed downward very force-

432

fully, receiving a nod of understanding in return. The great bomber, which had been gradually losing height all the way, dropped steeply toward the circle of grass. But the man had either misjudged the weight of his empty machine, or had not allowed for the damage to the underbelly of his aircraft. The descending glide turned into a dive as the nose dropped too far and, as Rex was accompanying his captive in, he saw it plunge into the ground and burst into flames that shot up and almost caught the fabric of his own wing as he rapidly throttled back and swung away to land fifty yards off.

With his own engine still running, Rex scrambled out and began to run back to the burning aircraft. But he had only gone a few yards when an explosion put an end to any hope of saving the occupants. Rex pulled up and stood looking at the funeral pyre, the truth of what he had done burning into him as if he were also in the flames.

'We did it, sir. *We did it!*' exclaimed a voice high with elation beside him. 'The blighter swallowed it hook, line and sinker!'

Shaking and sick Rex turned on his heel and began walking away over the grass as the fire-engine and ambulance raced toward the blazing pile, lost in a world of his own.

He went home for the weekend and, in the train, all he could see was that burning wreck mirrored there in the window as he gazed at the passing scene. The sickness was still mastering him; he had found it difficult to eat during the two days since the affair.

The Press had gone to town on an incident that was a wonderful morale-booster to a British public demanding better protection against German raiders; the R.F.C. had cheered an exploit they thought was colourful, daring, and full of the kind of panache with which they liked to be accredited. The authorities had severely reprimanded him for risking the life of a student-pilot.

It had all gone over Rex's head, diluted by the shocking truth he had to face. He had become an instinctive killer. The sight of a black cross on that machine had made him forget where he was and who he was with. If his guns had been loaded, Rex would have unhesitatingly shot them from the sky. In attempting to capture them he had killed them, anyway. There had not been a moment when he had stopped to consider, think what he was doing, tell himself he was holding the lives of two human beings in his hands.

Leaning his hot forehead against the cool glass of the train window he fought the sick feeling in his stomach as he closed his eyes against that roaring mass of aircraft fabric and human flesh he saw reflected. What had become of the young man who had flown 'Princess' so joyfully over Longbarrow Hill and dreamed of a future designing even more wonderful aeroplanes? Those dreams had not been of death-machines, but beautiful, sailing, engine-driven birds that would take a man wherever he wished, over water and mountains, to conquer the world of vast distances. Where had those dreams and aspirations gone? What had happened to the person he had been then, when life had been a playground for the kind of adventure and thrill that had harmed no one?

We did it, sir. We did it! The blighter swallowed it hook, line and sinker! He had tricked two men into dying. What had happened to the old spirit between aviators who respected each other's skill; who engaged in honourable combat until one acknowledged defeat and withdrew from the contest with a salute for the victor?

The questions piled in one after the other to torment his weary brain throughout the journey, and continued after he had reached his apartment to find Laura had already left for the theatre. He had not seen her for four weeks, and an evening without her now stretched ahead like another four weeks, he felt. The apartment seemed full of her scent, her laughter, her sanity. He felt unreasonably bereft as he dragged off his cap, tunic and boots, to pad across in his socks to pour himself a brandy, then prowl around the empty rooms with growing desperation at his enforced solitude.

One drink led to another as the answers to those questions bombarding him grew more and more elusive. Then he sat down with the bottle as a companion while he watched the hands of the clock move round bringing Laura's arrival nearer, but ticking his life away, he knew. Where would it all end; would anyone be left to find out?

He had drunk a considerable amount by the time Laura let herself into the apartment, so did not immediately jump up to greet her. Instead, he muttered thickly, 'At last! Come here and compensate your poor husband for his long wait!'

She remained where she was, occupied with removing her shawl and elaborate hair ornament. 'There was a reception on stage at the end of the performance for members of minor foreign royalty who had been in the audience.'

'Damn all minor foreign royalty!'

She began walking to the kitchen where her maid always left a supper-tray. 'I think I'll have some warm milk and go straight to bed.'

He got heavily to his feet. 'Damn the warm milk! Let's go straight to bed.'

Without looking at him she said, 'I'm tired, Rex.'

'So am I . . . but I want my wife first.'

Turning on him as she reached the kitchen door, she cried, 'To hell with what you want, for once.'

'For once!' he ejaculated. 'I haven't seen you for four weeks. A whole month, you might note! When I do I expect you to behave like a wife, not some glamorous nymph flitting about the stage for minor foreign royalty to admire.'

His words unleashed a tigress. '*You expect!* Have you ever considered what *I* expect? Well, I'll tell you. I expect a husband, not some glamorous hero soaring about the sky with a French whore's nightdress around his neck.'

His anger rose to meet hers. 'As you're so fond of telling me, you knew what I was when you married me. You didn't have to.'

'Yes, I did! You were desperate and going back to France.'

'Perhaps it's time I went back there again!'

'Why bother?' she raged. 'You can be a hero in England, apparently. "Sherry" Sheridan brings the war to him, if he can't get over there to it.'

Suddenly, her attitude made sense, and the deep hurt of her words sobered him a lot. 'You make what I did sound like an attempt at self-glorification.'

'Wasn't it? Won't September come quickly enough for you that you have to risk throwing your life away over England?' she cried on the edge of tears. 'It wasn't heroic, it was sheer stupidity. Suppose the bluff hadn't worked? Suppose he had riddled you with bullets—you and that boy in the back seat? *You'd* have been the ones on the ground in a great burning pile . . . and . . . and I'd have died, too.' She put her hands to her temples, and her voice almost broke as she continued. 'You once accused me of risking all we had for the sake of my career, and I'm not sure you have ever forgiven me. But you did the same thing up there two days ago . . . don't you see?'

'Oh God, Laura, I didn't do it for the sake of my career.' He was fighting to stay upright in a room that seemed to be spinning all around him. 'Do you want the truth? I did it because that black cross now tells me to kill, because the sight of an aircraft bearing that mark means I have to make them burn before they do it to me, because it's the unmistakable sign of death. It's instinct. I did it for all those poor devils who have turned into a screaming torch before my eyes, and for all those clean pink boys I've been sending out to do the same over these past months.' He stared at her and saw only that burning wreckage. 'I did it because that's what I've become. The only difference between Chris and me is that I have you to keep me marginally sane . . . except that . . . except that I even expect *you* to smoulder and blacken beneath my touch sometimes.'

In a moment she was there against him, stopping his words with her mouth, stilling his shaking with her hands, bathing his wet cheeks with her own tears.

'*Don't, oh darling, don't,*' she whispered. 'I didn't mean what I said. I was so afraid, so terrifyingly angry that even here you were risking your life. Why haven't you told me all this before? I've admitted I haven't Marion's courage, but I do have total love for you which overrides weakness.'

Somehow she got him to the bed, and he sank onto it sick and giddy, thanking God she was there with him to banish that vision of searing death. Then he felt her hand gently pushing his hair back from his forehead in a soothing gesture.

'Roland was right. When *all* the small boys are fighting over the kite, there's no one left to hold the ointment and damp sponge. That's left for the girls to do.'

On that Sunday there was to be a special event at Tarrant Royal. It so happened that several of the young cricketers of the two rival villages were home on leave at that time, and the Rector had had the idea of reviving the annual match that had lapsed since the start of the war. The occasion was intended to raise funds for war widows and their children. With village and national heroes in opposing sides, the event was expected to attract people from all over south-western England. Add the further thrill of seeing

Laura Sheridan, star of *Bows and Boaters,* and the Rector knew huge crowds would turn out on that summer Sunday. The only possible cause for failure would be the fickle English weather. But, on the evening before, the country sages looked at all the signs and predicted a beautiful day on the morrow.

For Chris it was a red-letter day. He felt excitement bubble inside him the minute he awoke that morning. Laura was coming! The hospital had an air of extra bustle about it as nurses hurried about their tasks, and patients exchanged gossip up and down the ward, the subject being the event everyone had been anticipating for days.

The match was due to begin at one-thirty, but the members of the two teams were arriving by eleven for a church service in dedication to the fallen of both villages. Afterward, they were due to join the organisers and local dignitaries for luncheon to be served in a marquee on the lawns of Tarrant Hall. In the village itself there would be stalls selling local produce, home-made jams and pickles, sheepskin, wood, and lambswool items made in the cottages, soft toys, and fresh flowers. There would also be displays of sheep-dog skills, country dancing by the village children, a fur and feather show, and a procession of decorated farm-carts. When the match ended it was to be followed by the traditional supper and concert.

Extra trains were running from the nearest big towns to Greater Tarrant, and all manner of transport had been loaned to bring passengers from the station to the venue along six miles of country lanes. The village green was not big enough to cope with vast numbers of spectators, so the gardens of all those cottages surrounding it were to be open for public use on that one day. Some enterprising villagers were putting chairs in their upstairs rooms for anyone willing to pay sixpence for an uninterrupted view. Others were opening hay-lofts and attics, provided they gave a sight of the green.

The patients at Tarrant Hall who were fit enough for such an occasion were to be allowed to watch the match from a special enclosure. Chris was included in this category but, as Tarrant Hall was his home and his famous brother was to play in the match, he was invited to join the luncheon party in the marquee. His fellows were green with envy—not because of the luncheon or his famous brother, but because Laura Sheridan was going to be there.

Chris felt sick with impatience as the morning passed too slowly. Although he had seen Laura several times since being transferred to Tarrant Hall, she had not been down since the launching of her show everyone was talking about. That meant she had no idea how well he had progressed lately, and would not know he could walk with the aid of two sticks. He was limited to short distances, and it was more like a crab-crawl than anything else. But it was still the most marvellous feeling after months and months in bed.

Learning to walk had been difficult, very painful and more than frustrating. But the impetus to keep trying, and trying with all his might, had been his overwhelming desire to see that show with Laura on stage with spotlights on her, and the dimness of the surrounding auditorium to give him the deceptive impression that he was there alone with her. To see that show he had to get to London. To get to London he had to be able to walk. So he had done all they had told him to do, eaten the awful meals—including the hated strawberry blancmange—in order to keep up his strength, and meekly swallowed their pills and potions so that he rested when they said he needed to. In fact, he had been a model patient.

This new Chris was the subject of some suspicion by Bill Chandler, who knew him of old. The older man still had frequent friendly chats between sessions with other patients, and was prone to throw in sudden comments about sexual reactions to girls, so Chris began chatting to the pretty nurses who flocked around him, just to allay suspicions. He wanted no one to guess how he felt about his brother's beautiful wife.

On that Sunday he was going to surprise and impress her. Not only would he be walking, he would be wearing uniform instead of the blue hospital suit. The other patients would be in that distinctive garb but, as he was attending the luncheon, they had handed over a subaltern's uniform for the first time.

As a nurse helped him to dress in it, his sense of anticipation increased. The smart cut of the khaki made him look rather dashing, he thought. Would Laura think so? Getting to his feet again had proved he was as tall as his brothers, and mirrors showed his face was quite a nice one, not marred by burns as his body was. Fortunately, they could be hidden by clothes. As for his mutilated hand, he could always keep that in his pocket when talking to her.

He went through to the house with Bill Chandler, who had been invited by Tessa to join the luncheon party. Bill said it was because the Australian girl was not immune to his considerable charms, but Chris had a feeling it was really so that a member of the hospital staff could keep an eye on him. He was not supposed to go anywhere alone—even to a marquee on the lawns of his own home. Once, he would have resented it, been as difficult as he could as a reprisal. But today was special and far too important to him for that. In any case, his attitude had changed a lot over the past summer months, and it seemed to be due to getting on his feet again. There was no doubt being bedridden and dependent on others for everything warped a person's views on life. Getting upright had made him conscious of his size and strength; realise he was a man, not the boy the staff had made him feel with their ministrations.

Mobility had given him the coveted independence he had tried to gain by precociousness. On this particular Sunday in August he was overwhelmed with well-being and happiness. He knew who he was and what he really looked like. The smart uniform gave him a sense of normality the blue hospital-suit did not, and he was joining a crowd of people who would see him as a son of the house, not as a patient for whom they must feel sympathy.

As Chris stood leaning on his sticks beside Bill in the marquee he found it difficult to concentrate on what those around him were saying. He was watching for Laura to come over from the house, and everything else was unimportant until then. A few people had approached to greet him with cautious friendliness, but none of them seemed familiar and he returned brief answers that soon had them turning away again.

After the latest incidence of it Bill turned on him. 'She was only trying to help, you know. They all are. You don't have to bite their heads off.'

'You try being faced with dozens of people who've known you all your life, yet you've never seen before. I don't suppose you'd exactly fall on their necks.'

'But do you have to be so bloody blunt?'

He shifted his weight on the sticks and grinned. 'It comes of spending so much time with you. Your appallingly bad manners are catching.'

The other man looked at him shrewdly. 'Cheeky sod! What's made you so sharp today, I wonder?'

'The prospect of a jolly decent luncheon, for once,' he lied quickly. 'I've already pumped Tessa for details of the menu.'

The dark-haired girl smiled in response. 'I tried to kid him there was strawberry blancmange for dessert, but he's nobody's fool, innocent though he looks.'

'Take note of that piece of widsom, Major Chandler, sir,' Chris advised.

But Bill was looking past him to the entrance of the marquee, and when Chris followed the direction of his gaze, excitement was almost a pain in his chest. Laura was in a stage costume, without doubt, and she drew all eyes as she entered on the arm of her attractive husband. An Edwardian dress of white lace with a bustle, and scarlet ribbons everywhere, fitted her voluptuous figure like a skin, and the sensational picture was completed with a huge white lace hat, trimmed with black ostrich-feathers, and a scarlet silk parasol. To war-weary people she was the escape they needed, and a round of spontaneous applause broke out within that great tent.

Dazed Chris hung on his sticks as he fought the sudden acceleration of his heartbeat caused by the appearance of this girl he had dreamed of while struggling through the pain and effort of learning to walk again. For this moment he had done it; the sight of this flame-haired girl was his reward.

'Isn't she absolutely marvellous!' he breathed.

'Absolutely . . . but she's also very much *his* wife,' came the pointed comment from the man beside him, as Laura looked up at Rex while they were momentarily halted by the applause, and smiled into his eyes as if there were no other person present.

Chris was riven by a shaft of jealousy. It would be a blind man who remained ignorant of their exclusive love for each other, and he was reminded of that concert at the hospital when she had sat on the piano and sung *Every little while* for Rex alone. Laura Sheridan might smile and charm her way into a person's heart, he realised, but hers was given unequivocally and forever to her husband.

It was inevitable that the glamorous star of *Bows and Boaters* should be immediately surrounded, and it was some time before Rex freed himself from the bevy of his own admirers to come over to his young brother. The cream flannels and tailored blazer gave him a raffish air that tended to detract from the lines of strain that should never have been on such a youthful face, and the haunted look in his green eyes. Chris had never seen this stranger-brother out of uniform before, and the sporting clothes looked so right on him, his greeting was unselfconsciously warm.

'Hello, Rex. You look so assured the other team ought to be trembling with fear already.'

Rex laughed. 'Fat chance of that. My word, young Chris, I'd forgotten what you looked like the right way up . . . and all that strawberry blancmange has given you some enviable muscles. Wouldn't you agree, Tessa?'

She smiled back at him. 'Don't mention that stuff, it's a sore point with Chris. Today, he's all set to make inroads into Charlotte Russe, Almond Chiffon, and Cherry Pie with cream.'

'What . . . all of them?' cried Rex in mock horror. 'The lad'll be sick and unable to watch me cover myself with glory at the wicket.'

'I'll be there,' put in Bill, 'and if you turn out to be better than any of the locals where I come from, I'll eat my hat.'

'Put some strawberry blancmange on it and it won't taste half as bad,' joked Chris.

Bill adopted a despairing expression. 'The boy is getting above himself now he's mobile. I preferred him when he was tied to the bed.'

Rex leaned against the tent-pole, hands in his pockets as he studied Chris. 'You really have made wonderful progress lately. It must feel good to get on the move again.'

'Yes, but I feel a bit like a crab trying to lose a race,' he confessed ruefully, 'and it's hard on the armpits to lean on these sticks for long.'

'At least you are back in the race,' said Tessa quietly. 'Poor Roland appears to be stuck in the mud somewhere in the vicinity of Passchendaele. I had a long letter from him this week and, from the hints he dropped, I imagine he's been in the thick of things out there.'

'Yes, I heard from him, too,' said Rex on a quieter note. 'He's all right, thank God.'

Remembering something that had slipped from his mind in the excitement, Chris spoke up. 'Rex, I wanted to ask your advice about something. It's a bit of a problem, actually.'

'Oh?' said Rex, 'why me and not Bill here?'

'Well, I suppose you'd call it family business.'

'Fire away then.'

'Come and show me those famous puddings, Tessa,' said Bill tactfully, and they moved off leaving the brothers alone.

Shifting his weight more comfortably again, Chris explained what was troubling him. 'Roland sent me a letter, too. It had something in it—a kind of antique cameo. He wrote that it had belonged to the mother of someone who had shared a dug-out with him back in the spring. The fellow was killed, and as there were no next-of-kin Roland felt he—this chap called Bisset—would want *me* to have it. The whole thing makes no sense to me, and Roland offered no explanation. He just asked me to take great care of it. I feel jolly awkward about the whole affair. What do you think I ought to do about it?'

'Exactly what he says,' came the immediate reply. 'Roland never does anything without good reason, take my word.'

'Yes . . . but a *brooch!* It's a funny thing to send a chap.'

'You can always give it to . . . er, to a girl, one of these days.' Rex gave a sigh. 'I do think you should write to him, Chris. I know you say it's difficult for you, but perhaps you've never given any real thought to how difficult it is for *him* to have you treat him like a stranger. Imagine how you might feel if Bill Chandler looked at you one day as if he had never seen you before, and refused to answer when you spoke to him.'

'I'd be glad. He's an infernal nuisance sometimes,' he mumbled because he did not know what else to say.

Rex gave a faint smile. 'It's been difficult for me, too, old lad. I don't mind admitting that first meeting in the hospital was too much even for my unshockable nature.'

Chris felt even more awkward and at a loss. 'I couldn't help it. I didn't ignore you deliberately.'

Rex straightened up. 'Of course you didn't. I know that. But you've progressed so far now it ought to be possible to make some approach to Roland. He's out there in Hell, believe me, and he's done no end for you, in the past. Give it a try, Chris, even if it's only a few words of rather rude Greek. Any kind of response will mean more than you can guess, to him.'

'I don't know him like I know you,' he protested. 'I've never even spoken to him. I thought . . . well, I thought he was a doctor pretending to be my brother.' Confessing that made him feel terrible now. Had he really been so near to madness?

'You never will get to know him if you ignore his letters,' pointed out Rex quietly. 'You always were inclined to give very little of yourself to others. Now's your chance to make up for it.'

That piece of advice coincided with the arrival of Laura at their sides, and Chris immediately forgot his elder brother in France to concentrate on this girl who had taken him by storm. He felt almost choked with emotion as he responded to her warmth and sparkle.

'My God, you Sheridans really are a handsome bunch!' she exclaimed in her low provocative voice. 'I had no idea you had recovered to this extent, Chris dear. They told us it would take absolutely *ages* before you'd be able to get about on your own. You must have worked like a Trojan.'

Her unconscious reference to classical history pleased him no end, but he could not take his gaze from the loveliness of her vivid pointed face, blush-tinted cheeks, wicked eyes, and the rich red tendrils of hair that lay against the white lace underbrim of her hat. What would a man have to do to win a girl like this? The answer was plain. Give his all, as Rex had too obviously done. Yet he had just been told he gave very little of himself to others.

'Hallo, Laura,' he managed. That was not an awful lot of himself to give! 'You look jolly splendid.' Oh dear, it was not as easy as Rex seemed to think!

'And so do you,' she said enthusiastically. 'I'm so used to seeing you in bed, now you're vertical you seem like an entirely different person. So much so, I almost feel shy of you.'

'Oh no,' he replied immediately. 'It's the other way around. Being able to move puts all kinds of obligations on a fellow.'

'I hear he's been chasing Matron up and down the wards,' put in Rex with a grin. 'A lad after my own heart, I can see.'

Laura smiled broadly. 'I'm sure he's much more respectable than you, darling. He's always been the soul of propriety with me.'

'That's because you're different from all the others,' said Chris with feeling. 'You're not a nurse who sees me as a rather annoying patient. And you didn't know me before—that's the most wonderful thing. You're not forever making comparisons with the old me, like everyone else does, and getting hurt when I don't remember something that means a lot to you. When I'm with you I can be what I am now without worrying.'

She smiled right up into his eyes in understanding. 'You have nothing whatever to worry about. From being a silent effigy in bed, you've turned into a sweet and worthwhile person. And I'm glad I didn't know you before. I'm such a dunce you probably would have avoided me like the plague.'

He shook his head. 'No one could ever do that . . . and I don't think you're a dunce. I mean, anyone can learn Greek or Latin by just studying books. But anyone who can fill a London theatre night after night at times like these . . . well, I think that takes something really special.'

She looked at him for a moment with a faraway look on her face. 'I think you've just paid me a very great compliment, haven't you?'

'I'll say,' he agreed fervently.

'Look, can't we sit down a moment?' she suggested. 'I had a late night and we had to set out early this morning.'

'Oh, yes,' he agreed thankfully, having just moved his sticks yet again to ease his aching arms. 'There are a couple of chairs just over there.'

Seated together along the side of the marquee, Chris realised Rex had wandered off to talk to a nearby group that included a greying churchman. They were comparatively alone, so he could broach the main subject on his mind.

'Some of the nurses here saw your show last week. When I can get around all right I'm going to come up to Town for it. It shouldn't be much more than a week or so now,' he added with false confidence.

She put her hand over his. 'That would be marvellous! There's no one I'd rather play to. Let me know when you want to come, and I'll send some front stalls for you and your friends.'

'I'd rather come on my own,' he told her quickly.

'Oh, would you?' Then she nodded gently, and smiled. 'All right, Chris, that'll be fine. You can take me to dinner afterward.'

Unable to believe she had suggested such a marvellous idea herself, he stammered, 'Won't . . . won't Rex mind?'

'Why should he? Good lord, you are his young brother.'

'Yes . . . of course.' It mattered that Rex would not mind. It robbed the meeting of all it meant to him; made it into something resembling a schoolboy treat.

She squeezed his hand. 'I had dinner with Roland before he left for France, and Rex also understood about that. He's a very special person, Chris.'

He looked down at their linked hands. 'Yes, I see.'

'Have you been doing any sketching lately?' she asked then. 'Remember how we laughed over my attempts to draw the Dean of Chapterdene School?'

In his disappointment he had almost forgotten the other important thing he had planned for today. Reaching inside his jacket he brought out a rolled sheet of thick foolscap and gave it to her.

'It's for you to keep. I thought . . . well, it wouldn't mean anything to anyone else.'

As he watched her unroll and spread it out the suspense of waiting for her reaction was almost unbearable. He would know by her expression whether or not she was just saying what she thought he wanted to hear. An age seemed to pass while she studied the drawing, and he knew the next few minutes would make the day into a triumph or a total disaster.

When she looked up at him it was with a mysterious expression he could not fathom. 'This goddess is me, isn't it . . . at the hospital concert? Except that you've transferred the scene to Greece. It is Greece, isn't it?'

He shook his head, knowing the day was a triumph. 'Not exactly. It's one of the islands we could see from Gallipoli. I used to sit behind a bush sketching it instead of the gun-emplacements I was supposed to be drawing. It was a damned sight more attractive.'

'I . . . I really don't know what to say, for once,' she told him.

'You don't have to say anything,' he hastened to assure her. 'I can tell you're pleased. Your face always shows what you feel.'

'But I had no idea you had taken in so much of that concert. It was in the early days when you were . . . were . . .'

'Like a silent effigy in bed?' he suggested, using her own earlier words. 'But I had feelings, you know, even then.'

To his astonishment the glitter of tears touched her eyes, and she looked down again at the picture. 'There's something about

445

you Sheridans that constantly takes me unawares. Just as I think I know you, I find there is something I never suspected.' Then she looked up to smile at him. 'Thank you, Chris. I think this is the most flattering present I have ever been given.'

Leaning forward she kissed him with glancing softness on his cheek. But his instinctive response was halted by a voice saying, 'Unhand that woman, or it'll be pistols for two, at dawn.'

Bill Chandler was there when Chris looked up rather guiltily. 'Come on, Chris, now's your chance to set about that meal you've been waiting for,' he said heartily. 'From all you've told me, that's more in your line than canoodling in a corner.' He made a comical bow before Laura. 'I've been sent by your beleaguered husband to escort you to the top table, ma'am. Take my arm.'

Seeing his beautiful moment about to be ruined, Chris said with a hammering heart, 'No, take mine, Laura.'

As Bill made to speak Laura silenced him with an incomprehensible look, leaving Chris to carry out what he had so impetuously suggested. That was what came of giving more of himself than usual, he thought, as he got to his feet with the aid of the sticks and turned in the right direction. It now looked a long way alongside the white-covered trestle tables to where Rex was standing at the top, surrounded by admiring ladies. But Laura slipped her arm through his and he had no choice but to set off.

His greatest difficulty was to avoid putting the sticks on the skirt of the beautiful dress that trailed the ground, but their progress was slow enough to ensure that no accidents of that nature occurred. He had never walked with a girl on his arm before, and it was an unforgettable experience that made him feel strongly protective. Then he realised that people had parted to let them through, and conversation was ceasing as their interest fastened on the progress of the fabulous Laura Sheridan on the arm of her crippled brother-in-law. The walk now turned into a marathon for Chris. Ahead he could see Rex watching them, and he began to pray nothing awful would happen.

His arms now felt weak with effort, his legs became weights he had to drag one before the other, and sweat began to bead on his forehead. Damn Rex for suggesting he should give more of himself; damn his own ego for imagining Laura would not mind going through this humiliating business; damn the sticks he needed to do something as simple as walking! Then Laura began chatting to him about the forthcoming cricket-match, saying that she hoped he would explain the rules to her, and confessing that she had never watched a game on a village-green before, just as if she was not aware that he was breathing harder with every step and had just almost stumbled. Undaunted by the silence in that marquee, she literally *talked* Chris along those last few yards to the top table, where they were all placed for the luncheon, and he made the tremendous effort because he knew he could not let her down. But he was giddy and aching all over when Rex quickly pulled out a chair for Laura to sit down, then pulled out another for his brother.

'There's nothing wrong with you that a few more helpings of strawberry blancmange won't cure,' he said softly, with a grin. 'Sit down, you've earned a rest, old lad.'

But it was to Laura that Chris gave his smile of gratitude.

Chris had been looking forward to his first glimpse of the village where he had apparently lived all his life. From the outskirts, Tarrant Royal appeared to be a beautiful peaceful cluster of thatched buildings. But he was unprepared for the size of the crowd around the green, and visitors were still flooding in only minutes before the scheduled start of the match.

'You British really take the biscuit,' marvelled Bill from beside him. 'You're three-quarters of the way to losing a war that's killing off all your men, you're so short of food there's talk of rationing it, you're being bombed in the cities and coastal towns, yet you can turn out in swarms on a day like this and pretend none of it is happening.'

'That's why we won't go *all* the way to losing the war,' came his surprising response. 'We're that sort of people.'

But he did not want to talk of serious things. A large tasty meal had helped him to recover, there was a marvellous afternoon in the sunshine ahead of him, and he had been told Rex and Laura would be staying overnight at Tarrant Hall. He had been invited to lunch with them all tomorrow, and he had decided to give Laura the cameo brooch Roland had sent him. Rex had said he should give it to a girl one day. What better girl than one who was a Sheridan, and what better day than tomorrow when all the crowds had disappeared?

Because he was who he was, Chris sat with the VIPs in a shaded enclosure, and waved his sticks triumphantly at his colleagues in hospital-blue, confined to a different enclosure with a less advantageous view. The August afternoon buzzed with laughter, conversation, and cheers as the match got underway and the heroes of the willow strolled out from the tiny pavilion, cream-clad figures making a pleasing contrast against the rich verdure of the grass.

Chris knew all about the game. He was certain he had played it himself, just as he was certain Rex was very good at it. So he was. Coming in to bat at number three, a tall muscular figure with hair even more vivid beneath the sun, he thumped the ball far and wide with daring strokes that had spectators going wild with delight and excitement. As he ran fast between the wickets it was possible to see the whiteness of his teeth where he was smiling with the pure enjoyment of doing something in which he excelled. The smile broadened to laughter as he slipped and fell, still reaching safety on his hands and knees, where he pretended to pray to the One Above who had undoubtedly been on his side.

Watching his brother, Chris grew full of pride. Rex was a man in a million, and everyone packed around that village green acknowledged the fact. He embodied all those things that were universally admired but never envied, because he seemed unconscious of them. He did what he did for enjoyment, not personal gain. He was out there as part of a team, not its star. He embraced everyone as his friend, and received universal friendship in return.

The noise and chatter became a background of sound, those around him blurred from individuals into a mass, and the sun beat down on the scene as Chris watched and applauded with enthusiasm the brother who was also a staunch friend, racing back and forth to take the score higher and higher, and acknowledging the cheers with a raised bat and broad grins in every direction. He was finally and inevitably caught out after whacking unwisely at a spinning ball, and the afternoon exploded with sound as he was cheered all the way off the field.

With interest in the match diminished until Rex came out to field, Chris reached beneath his deckchair for his book. But he was not in a deckchair, and there was no book. His heart lurched as he jumped a time-span of three years in one second. Still somewhere in the middle of that journey he stared at the strangers on upright chairs that surrounded him, at the Union Jacks everywhere, at the khaki suit he was wearing, and the partial crutches leaning against his legs. The other occasion faded completely, and he recognised present reality. But he knew what had happened and was deeply afraid. If Rex had not been caught out just then, how far would he have gone into that memory?

With rising panic he knew he had to get away. It was coming too close, that last secret he did not want to know. He had to run before it caught up with him. Sweating, knowing he was going to be sick, he struggled to his feet with the aid of the sticks.

'Where do you think you're going?' asked Bill Chandler sharply.

'To relieve myself,' he muttered. 'I don't need you to undo my buttons for me.'

He could not go into the temporary toilets formed by canvas wrapped around posts driven into the ground, because men were going in and out constantly. So he made his laboured way to a small hut used by the groundsman who looked after the green, and walked behind it to lean back against the sun-warmed wood in thankful isolation. The concentration it had taken to walk that far had removed the danger of vomiting, but he still felt that fear bordering on hysteria. Everything around him looked unfamiliar again, and that excursion into the past now seemed so vague he could hardly remember how it had felt to be there. But it had happened . . . and could happen again at any time. It *would* happen again!

Propped against the shed, his hands gripped the tops of the walking sticks because he needed to hold on to something, and he tipped his head back to gaze up at the branches of a great oak outside the village inn until they blurred with the tears welling up in his eyes. *Dear God, please don't let me remember,* he prayed. Yet it was not the truth his mind did not want to face that terrified him now. It was retreating into those lost months. He did not want to leave the world again in case it was no longer there when he finally came back.

'Are you all right, son?'

He brought his gaze from the oak branches to fasten on the face of an elderly man in shirt-sleeves and braces, who had a weather-beaten face.

'Oh . . . yes, thanks. Just resting a moment,' he murmured.

The well-wisher moved off, and Chris took off his spectacles to wipe the lenses. When he put them back on he saw a girl standing a short distance away, holding a small boy by the hand as she watched the cricket. He waited a moment or two, not sure what to do. Then he gripped his sticks and set off. There were so many people moving about, he reached her side unnoticed by her. She looked a lot thinner, and very different in a dress of soft yellow material. It was nicer, less severe than the pink nurses' outfit she used to wear.

'Hallo, Marion,' he said in subdued tones.

She turned, and for one astounding moment he thought she was going to faint. The colour drained from her face and she seemed to sway as she backed away from him, her gaze taking in every aspect of his appearance from head to foot.

'Chris!'

'I say, are you all right?' he asked in concern.

'What are you doing out of that hospital?' It came out as a whiplash accusation as she pushed the child behind her skirt. But she did not wait for his answer. Another wild glance at him, then she turned to run, gathering the child up as she went.

'Marion,' he called after her. 'What's wrong?'

Two steps and he was careless. Sprawling headlong on the grass, any further sight of her was obscured by the group surrounding him to help him to his feet.

22

THE DAY of the cricket match was one that would live in people's memories for a long time, and would go down in the chronicle of Tarrant Royal as a milestone. Laura's surprise of wearing one of her flamboyant costumes from her show, plus her willing performance in the concert afterwards, had set the seal on the carnival atmosphere that had allowed everyone to forget the war for a while, even though the proceeds were to go toward helping bereaved families. The weather had been perfect, the sideshows a huge success, and the match itself a well-fought eventful contest. The sight of Rex Sheridan once more gracing the village green with his warm personality had created a feeling that things had not really changed, and the presence of other young men of the two villages, dressed in flannels and not khaki, added to the general impression of old times which had been created by Laura in her Edwardian costume.

After the match narrowly won by Rex's team, the traditional supper and concert was riotous because all those participating released all the stresses and strains in merriment. No one wanted the day to end, so it was prolonged. The supper was eaten with great gusto, and the concert was the best ever seen at Tarrant Royal due to Laura. This time, Rex did not get off scot free. She dragged him onto the stage to play the banjo and sing a duet with her. The sight of this gorgeous flame-haired girl singing, *Hold your hand out, naughty boy,* to her equally flame-haired flirtatious husband brought the house down.

For Rex it was one of the happiest and most marvellous days of his life. He had never felt more in love with Laura than he did that day. Looking incredibly lovely she was there at his home charming people he had known and liked all his life. She was there to watch him excel in a pastime that did not involve risking his life, and she gave all she could toward making a success of a day she knew meant a lot to him.

They returned to Tarrant Hall late that evening, singing loudly all the way up the hill, and it was a sign of his complete happiness that Rex gave no thought to the news that had awaited him on his last return, very drunk, after the inter-village match.

Even so, when they were alone in his old room, and he took Laura into his arms, he discovered that she was crying.

'Darling, what is it?' he asked touching her brow gently with his lips. 'We've had such a lovely day.'

She pressed close to him whispering brokenly, 'I love you with all my heart. If I lost you, I couldn't go on.'

Too happy and contented for such a conversation he drew her away from his chest. 'What has prompted this? Not young Chris, surely? He's getting on so very well.'

She shook her head. 'He still has a long way to go, Rex. I've never stopped to think how *he* feels . . . only how I feel when I see him.'

'He wouldn't want you to cry over him, you know. I suspect he hopes for vastly different feelings.'

'I'm not crying over him . . . not really. But what has happened to him is all tied up with how I feel over you, somehow. Darling, I've never before seen you as you were today, and I feel afraid.'

'So you should,' he said lightly. 'My reputation wasn't won lightly.'

'Please don't flirt,' she begged, still tearful. 'I can't take it.'

Recognising something new about her, he sat down on the bed with her and took her hand. 'Laura, we both said things we didn't mean last night. I was tight, and you were tired and angry—our different reactions to the same thing. Our marriage is a bit like flying. We soar higher than those with their feet on the ground, but we have to come down again. Sometimes the landing is bumpy and we get hurt. But we soon take off again. I think it will always be like that for us.'

'Of course it will. I knew that from the start. That isn't what makes me afraid.'

'What does, then?'

She looked up into his face. 'How many times have you made love to a girl?'

Fearing he was entering very deep water he asked cautiously, 'Since when?'

'Since the first one?'

Whatever he said would be a lie. A man did not register his tally like shooting down Huns, and become a national hero for it.

'Laura, what is all this about? We've had a marvellous day, in every possible way. Now I desperately want to make love to you.' He kissed her deliberately and lingeringly. 'Little bitch-wife, I want you.'

'And I want you. Oh God, how I want you,' she cried. 'But I want the man I saw today, not "Sherry" Sheridan who has turned into an instinctive killer, and has to drink himself unconscious because he can't face the fact, not the man who has shot down more enemy pilots than anyone else, not the tight-lipped reluctant officer who has to talk boys into killing, too . . . and not the man who was so desperate for happiness he had to marry me because there was so little time before he returned to Hell.' She cradled his face with her hands. 'I want Rex Sheridan, cricket player, country gentleman, village flirt, amateur banjo player, jolly elder brother, and carefree virile *civilian.*' Crying in earnest now, she said, 'Darling, if I ever lose you, I shan't be able to go on alone. Whatever I say, whatever I do, whatever it appears I am feeling sometimes, beneath everything is my total need for you.'

He pulled her swiftly against him and held her tight. 'I know that. I know that, darling. But you won't lose me, I promise. I told you before that a boy called Giles Otterbourne died in my stead. I really do have a charmed life now. The Huns will never notch up my death on the way to winning the Blue Max. If I'm totally confident of that, so must you be.'

She pulled away and ran her fingers lightly against his mouth as she looked at him pleadingly. 'Rex, pretend I'm just a village girl; someone you flirted with this afternoon and coaxed up to your room tonight. Pretend the world has never heard of war, and you're just one of the Sheridans from the Hall—the one with a reputation for sexual conquests. Pretend I'm a little country virgin who has taken your fancy. Then make love to me. Take me as you took all those others before life grew so terrible. *Please,* darling.'

He did his best to comply, but she was like no little country virgin he had ever come across. All the same, it was a night he would never forget, and completed the overwhelming feeling of peace and contentment that had invaded him that day.

He had breakfast in the morning with Tessa, and Mike who had arrived halfway through the cricket-match to stay overnight. Laura remained in bed, of course. Mike was planning to return on the afternoon train with her. Rex had to give a talk at Sherbourne on the following morning, so would have to travel in the opposite direction on the evening train to the small inn where a room had been booked for him. He was not looking forward to it.

After breakfast Mike walked down to the village. Neither his sister nor Rex asked his errand. They strolled across to the stables and took out a couple of horses for a ride across Longbarrow Hill. Dressed in an old shirt and breeches from his wardrobe, Rex found the casual clothes and sun-washed country pursuit augmented that feeling of having returned to the peace of the past.

Tessa appeared to be in the same mood, and they talked about the estate and village as if war did not exist. It was clear the Australian girl was making a very good job of running the complex farming routine, and Rex thought again that she would make his brother the perfect wife. But Bill Chandler looked like snapping her up first. They would probably go back to Australia together after the war, and go out of the lives of the Sheridans as if they had never been so closely involved with them. It would all be different after the war.

Realising he was growing introspective again, he turned to Tessa. 'Come on, let's gallop. It's such a marvellous morning it deserves more than a sedate trot!'

Chris came through from the hospital just as they walked into the house from the stables. He looked rather strained, Rex thought, but his face lit up when he saw them.

'Hallo,' he greeted. 'You two look very happy.'

'We've been for a wonderful gallop right along Longbarrow Hill,' Tessa told him.

Chris's smile was rather forced. 'What did Laura think about that?'

'She doesn't know yet,' Rex said. 'She's still in bed.' Feeling so fit and invigorated after his ride made Rex more than ever conscious of how his brother must feel having to hang over two sticks just to stand for any length of time. On impulse he said, 'She'll be down soon. Her train leaves at three; Tessa and I are going to the station to see her off with Mike. Would you like me to twist Bill's arm to let you come with us?'

Strangely Chris did not jump at the suggestion as he expected. 'Yes, all right.'

It was at that point that Rex realised all was not well, and Tessa must have sensed it, too. She walked toward the kitchen saying, 'Why don't you two go and have a chat in the garden? I'll get Priddy to bring you some coffee while I change.'

Rex nodded. 'I'll just wash my hands, Chris, and join you in a couple of minutes.'

His young brother was just settling himself on a seat on the part of the terrace excluded from hospital patients when Rex joined him, and sighed with contentment as he gazed around him.

'I'm either growing more discerning with age, or else I only appreciate this place now I can't come here any time I like.' He turned at the sound of footsteps. 'Ah, Priddy, you deserve a kiss on both cheeks,' he vowed taking the tray from her. 'Were I single and of less tender years, I would whisk you away to Arcady.'

Her plump face broke into a delighted smile. 'That's the first time you've been your old self for longer than I care to remember.

454

Saucy as they come, right from a small lad . . . and you look so nice in them riding things, for a change.'

Rex put the tray down and assumed a frown. 'Not nice enough, apparently. That raisin cake is especially for Chris, not me. Shame on you, woman!'

Priddy coloured slightly. 'I never favoured any one of you boys more'n the other. But Mr Christopher isn't often here to have his favourite things. Not that you knew what you was eating half the time,' she said fondly to Chris. 'Always had your nose in a book, or doing those drawrings, you was.'

'All the more justification for my protest,' put in Rex quickly to stop her reminiscing more than she should. 'Why should he get treats when he doesn't even know what he's eating? Away with you, Priddy. I'm cut to the quick.'

When she had gone, Rex decided it was time to take the bull by the horns. 'What's up, old lad? You seem to have something on your mind.'

Looking glad of the opening, his brother said, 'A funny thing happened to me yesterday.'

'What kind of funny thing?'

'While I was watching the match I remembered something. It was another cricket-match—I don't know how long ago—and I felt as I must have done then. The whole thing went as suddenly as it had come, but the feeling stayed.' He became a little hesitant and confused. 'I'm sorry, Rex, I can't expect you to understand because I don't myself, but . . . well, what I'm trying to say is, we . . . we were pretty good chums, weren't we?'

Still unsure of what his brother was really saying, Rex put down his coffee and cake. 'Yes, and I hope we still are. Of course, we are different people, in many ways, now. I'm a grandfather, and you've been on a journey none of us can possibly imagine. But the bond is still there, Chris. It always has been.'

He nodded. 'Until yesterday I had to take your word for it. But now I know . . . in here.' He put a clenched fist on his breast. 'I still don't remember much about being here as a boy, or anything before Gallipoli. But I'm so nearly there, it's as if the sunlight is beginning to penetrate the shutters drawn against it.'

'That's marvellous,' he said with genuine enthusiasm.

'No, it isn't. It scares me to death.'

It sounded so bleak Rex felt inadequate to deal with the situation. It was too tricky for amateurs such as himself to dabble in over coffee.

'In that case, you'd better talk to Major Chandler about it.'

Chris turned away to gaze out over the terrace where his conservatory room was situated. Rex could not see his expression, but the droop of his shoulders and the prolonged silence was more than he could stand.

Putting a hand on the youngster's shoulder he said quietly, 'For a very good chum, that was a hell of a suggestion, wasn't it? If you think I can help, go ahead.'

After a moment, a quiet confession came. 'I feel most frightfully alone sometimes. It's just as if I'm the only person in the world . . . except that I'm not sure which world I'm in. Major Chandler is a doctor. He analyses every word I say and watches every move I make. He sees everything from the point of view of sanity, reason, and the wonderful blessing of normality. I'm the only one who sees things from my point of view.' Suddenly he put his head in his hands. 'I do most desperately need advice. After yesterday, I realise you are my only hope.'

Full of compassion and concern Rex got to his feet and went round to stand in front of him. 'That's a tall order, Chris. How can I advise you? I know nothing of medical matters.'

The young face looked back up at him with appeal. 'But you know about *me*. The real me. You know about that other cricket match, and those years my mind doesn't want to remember.'

Deeply sorry for his brother, yet mindful of Bill Chandler's warning that he must be allowed to recall the past without help, Rex rubbed his forehead with a worried gesture.

'I've told you all about the things we used to get up to as boys, and shown you the old photographs.'

'But that isn't part of it, is it? There's something else no one will tell me. Why? Is it very terrible?'

In a deep dilemma Rex just stood looking at him in silence. Chris took it as an affirmative, and looked down at his hands linked tightly between his knees.

'Something else funny happened yesterday. I saw Marion at the match.'

Heartbeat quickening Rex thought of a girl telling him she hoped Chris would go permanently insane and set her free. 'Marion?' he echoed in pseudo-surprise.

Up shot Chris's head again. 'Yes, Marion! You know, the nurse who isn't really a nurse,' he said aggressively. 'She took one look at me, nearly fainted, then ran away. You can drop the pretence that you hardly knew the girl, Rex. She gave me a present on my thirteenth birthday, so she must have been a pretty good friend of ours.'

Rex sighed heavily. 'You always were a damned sight too clever for your own good. How the devil did you find that out?'

'Is this terrible thing connected with Marion?' he asked.

'It isn't terrible, Chris. I swear it isn't.'

'Is it connected with Marion?'

What must he do? Bill Chandler had said Chris was still walking a tightrope. Words of his must not upset the boy's balance.

'Why don't you ask her?' he hedged.

'If she runs away when she sees me, I'll never catch her on these sticks,' came the typical Chris response as he looked away again toward his hospital room. 'So you won't tell me?'

'I wouldn't be helping you.' He sighed again. 'The dictum of the medical experts is that you must remember it yourself, and I can't go against that. I'm sorry . . . dreadfully sorry not to be of more help.'

Reaching for his sticks Chris got laboriously to his feet to stand eye to eye with Rex in one last appeal. 'I want to be part of the Sheridan family. I want to live in this part of Tarrant Hall, where I belong. I want to be a person without secrets. But I'm so afraid, I don't know what to do. They say I must be ready to remember of my own free will, but every time I do I go away somewhere and have no control over when I return. Can you imagine it, Rex? Can you imagine going to sleep tonight—this very night in August—and waking up to find it's Christmas Day? Can you imagine that same thing happening to you several times? And can you imagine being terrified to go to sleep after that in case you woke up to find you were an old man? *Or in case you never woke up again?*'

It was such a vivid dreadful description, such a desperate plea for understanding, Rex was moved beyond words. Yet, as he stood gazing at that young face that had survived burning and seen worse horrors than even he had witnessed, he knew this was his own second chance. If he had failed Chris three years ago because his flying career had blinded him to the state of despair the boy had been in, he must not fail him again now. Putting an arm across

457

his brother's shoulders he urged him forward so that they walked together across the terrace to the edge of the sunken gardens, halting at the wall that enclosed it.

'What you just described, Chris, can't be imagined. It would have to be experienced—by me, anyway. I'm a very simple chap, without your intelligence and way with words. But I know a lot about flying, and I'm good at it. So are a lot of other pilots. But they don't live very long because they hold back. I can't do that. If I had sat in my aircraft just cruising around waiting for Huns to appear, I'd have been a sitting duck because I'd be numb with fear. The unknown is always frightening. The only way I can survive is to go looking for the enemy. Then I know what I'm facing and get on with my job. Perhaps that's what you should do.'

'Go in search of my past?'

Rex nodded. 'Maybe you only retreat into this other world when recollection takes you unawares—like Fokkers coming fast out of the sun. Maybe, if you went determinedly to meet it it wouldn't seem half as frightening.' He turned to give his brother a steady look. 'The nation has dubbed me a hero, but you have vastly more courage. You've come so far in triumph, Chris, you're certain to go the rest of the way now.'

Chris thought that over for a moment or two. 'It's a good theory, but suppose it doesn't work? Suppose I only hasten that limbo that frightens me?'

He could not retreat now, so he summoned up a smile. 'You'll also hasten your return . . . and I'll do my damnedest to be here, even if it is Christmas Day.'

Things seemed to deteriorate after that. Chris said he would not go to the station with them, anyway, because he felt rather tired after the excitement of the day before, and Rex then worried about the advice he had given his brother. As he had said, suppose it hastened that limbo that led him nearer the chasm of insanity.

Saying goodbye to Laura was part of the anticlimax. They both felt it was the ending of their brief episode of bliss. Rex kissed her lingeringly at the station, heedless of the others, and said, 'After this affair at Sherbourne tomorrow I have one more visit to make before I start at the Flying School again next week. With luck, I'll be home on Thursday afternoon. If I twist an arm or two I can arrange to delay my arrival until later on Monday. That'll be three days together.'

'And three nights,' she whispered looking at him as if she were about to lose him forever. 'But they won't be as wonderful as last night, darling.'

'How do you know?' he challenged. 'You haven't had them yet.'

He felt very flat on the way back to Tarrant Hall with Tessa, and began to worry again about the advice he had given Chris. Would it be better if he never remembered the wife who wished him in Bedlam, and the child who had an amenable substitute in his doting grandfather? Because of his doubts, he went in for half an hour with Chris before leaving to catch his train. But his young brother seemed quietly content going through a book of poetry, and asked about Rex's future timetable with a composure that did not suggest a remnant of the panic of the morning.

When he got up to go Chris smiled and said, 'Don't leave it too long before you come again, will you? I might even be fit enough to gallop across Longbarrow Hill with you. I take it I do ride?'

Rex grinned. 'Not according to Roland. He used to clutch his locks in despair when you climbed onto a horse. But I could bear the experience, lad, if you're game. I'll keep you to that. Well, I'm off. Cheerio.'

'Cheerio, Rex . . . and thanks!'

The country inn seemed very lonely that night, and Rex drank too much in order to while away the time before going to bed. Then he had his recurring nightmare about burning aircraft, except that it was Chris sitting in the cockpit surrounded by flames while he had to gaze helplessly on.

On Wednesday afternoon he presented prizes at a charity garden party, declined the offers of several lonely women, then caught a train to Swindon, where he was due to address a rally designed to drum up finaneial donations from business and factory owners for the production of more aircraft. The morning dawned hot and airless, the storm that had been rolling around during the night still not having broken. Rex cursed the thick uniform he was obliged to wear, and tried to disperse a hangover by drinking a great deal of black coffee for breakfast. All this did was oblige him to excuse himself to his hosts more times than were polite during the preliminaries, and he began to count the hours to when he

459

would walk through his own front door to Laura later that afternoon.

The rally was held in the large canteen of a factory. The tables had been pushed to the sides, and chairs set out in rows on the concrete floor. There was a smell of rancid fat and boiled bones mingling with the stale smoky air that remained due to lack of any wind from the open windows to shift it. Rex felt the windows would have been better shut, since they did nothing except let in the sound of frequent trains passing along the track alongside the factory. How could any speaker compete with that?

None could, as he soon discovered during the overlong speeches made by councillors puffed up with their own importance. As he sat fidgeting on the wooden chair set on the raised platform he stared at the members of the public facing him on rows of similar uncomfortable chairs. There were elderly men in business suits and bowlers, who were plainly members of various boards, then the trim-suited, trim-moustached managers in the rows behind them. Further back were the overseers and department supervisors. Halfway to the rear were those most likely to be a group of labourers not on the morning shifts and, at the very rear of the assembly, was an astonishingly large group of women. Of course, a great percentage of factory-hands were female, these days. But they did not usually turn up *en masse* at these occasions.

Fearing that he would have to excuse himself yet again if the proceedings were not speeded up, Rex looked surreptitiously at his watch. Nearly noon already. He had planned on getting a train to London before 1 pm.

'And so, ladies and gentlemen,' the present speaker was shouting above the sound of the trains, 'I have the honour and privilege of presenting to you the greatest flying hero of our time.'

Rex winced inwardly and mentally apologised to the giants of aviation, as the introduction was concluded with, 'I give you the man who flies the aircraft we are asked to help provide. Captain "Sherry" Sheridan, D.S.O. and bar M.C., and two bars and the Croix de Guerre of France.'

Rex winced again as the foolish man recited all his awards as if they were at a Royal or highly military occasion. A man did not need medals in order to ask for money. Beggars did the same thing successfully without them. The applause gradually died away as he moved forward to the table.

'Thank you very much,' he began. 'Mr Franklin has said a number of things about me—a great deal too many for my modesty' (polite laughter) 'and ended by calling me a flying hero. But, as you see, I am not flying. The reason for this is why we are all here this morning.

'You all know that the R.F.C. went into the war with a few certified pilots and a few *certifiable* machines. Three years later we still have not redressed the balance. Although we now have a number of certifiable pilots, as well. I'm one of them,' he added with a smile, and received further laughter. 'Everyone here has someone in France—a relative, friend, a business rival, even—so I have no need to describe to you what magnificent feats our troops are doing in conditions so appalling the world will never forget. We of the R.F.C. have a vital job to do if their sacrifice is going to be worth anything, and that is to chase the Huns from the skies above them. By doing that, we protect our soldiers from an aerial enemy they cannot combat with rifle and bayonet, we protect them by putting an end to reconnaissance information on every move they make, we protect them by flying into battle above them and machine-gunning those manning the German artillery and gas-dispersal posts, and we protect them by gaining vital information on displacement of enemy forces and their movements.

'But our job is not only to protect. We attack! We attack enemy convoys, we attack their airfields, we attack their supply-dumps. And we attack their advance artillery-posts that are shelling innocent women and children in the villages of our gallant allies.' (Loud cheers and applause.)

'But, ladies and gentlemen, we cannot do our job without aircraft, and we desperately need production to be stepped up on the new designs that are capable of toppling Baron Von Richthofen and his *Kamaraden* from the skies over France and Belgium for good. I am not asking for your generous help, I am *begging* for it, so that we can do our job to let the boys on the ground do theirs and send the Huns running back to Berlin with their tails between their legs like whipped curs.' (More loud cheers and applause.)

'Or until there are no men left alive,' came a high voice from the back of the hall, making heads turn in that direction.

'Stop killing and start talking!' cried another of the women grouped together.

'End the war. End the killing!' demanded a third. 'You're no hero; you're a murderer!'

As Rex stood nonplussed on the platform, those in the front rows began shouting back at the women who were now starting to unfurl banners demanding peace and the return of the fathers of British children before they were all made orphans of war. An exchange of abuse began growing louder and louder, all pretence at decorum from the dignitaries of the front rows being abandoned as they demanded that the women be thrown out.

One particularly militant campaigner advanced down the aisle between the seats, pointing at Rex and shouting, 'He's the one to be thrown out. He tells boys to go out and kill. He visits schools and tells them war will make heroes of their pupils. He fills their innocent heads with hatred and violence. Throw him out instead!'

The councillors on the platform exchanged looks and hissed at each other, 'Get them away, for God's sake.' 'Call the police.' 'Don't let the Press get hold of this.'

But it was too late. Cameras were flashing, and notebooks were being filled with every dramatic development. The women were waving their banners bravely, and linking arms to present a united front. Their chants could be heard above the angry men and even above the trains rattling past. One young girl not much more than seventeen ducked beneath the restraining outstretched arms trying to prevent her approaching the platform, and arrived at Rex's feet, looking up at him with a tear-stained face.

'He heard you speak at the recruiting-rally and joined the R.F.C. there and then. The first time he went up a wing fell off and he was killed.' She dashed a hand across her wet eyes. *Don't you care?* Don't you care that those boys who think you are some kind of god are all going to die?'

She was dragged away, and one of the men on the platform with him touched his arm. 'Captain Sheridan, we'll slip out through the back entrance.'

Rex turned on him, his stomach churning. 'You can slip out that way, if you wish, but I'm here to help raise money for much-needed aircraft, and I'll damn well do what I came for.'

So saying he jumped down from the platform and began walking toward the women at the back of the hall, until his approach was noticed and all the voices began to die away to silence. He stopped in front of them.

'You have all flung a lot of accusations at me this morning and given me no chance to answer them,' he began in a voice that came out harsh and clipped. 'That makes you almost on a par with the Germans. They send hundreds of shells into French and Belgian villages where they know women and children can't hit back. They send Zeppelins here to drop bombs on our villages and towns, knowing we have no way of going back with bombs for theirs. They release mustard-gas on our men in the trenches, knowing it will burn and maim at a distance, while they are safely behind their big guns.'

Seeing he had momentarily got their attention he put one foot up on a chair and leant forward on his knee to say earnestly, 'You say we must stop killing and talk instead. How do you talk to men who shoot women and children as reprisals for the defence of their own country by resistance groups? How do you talk to men who march into little farming communities, take all the animals for their own food, leaving the poor peasant-folk with none, then burn down their homes before leaving? How do you talk to a nation that will use such weapons as flame-throwers, mustard-gas, and infected animals that will spread disease?'

He pointed to the woman holding the banner. 'You claimed I was a murderer. Yes, I've killed or wounded about fifty German airmen, and probably more on the ground. I shall have to pay my own toll to my conscience for that. But if I hadn't killed them, there would have been even more fatherless children in Britain now.' He indicated another woman. 'You accused me of telling schoolboys that war will make heroes of them. At eighteen every boy has to go to war. That is our government's decision, not mine. Would you rather I told them war will make corpses of them; that once they leave these shores they will never see their families and sweethearts again? Would you rather I sent them off with fear on their faces, and water in their veins, for the arrogant German boys to ridicule and scorn? *Would you?*'

He caught the eye of the tearful young girl, and said in a softer tone, 'You, my dear, should have been addressing this meeting instead. You blamed me for appealing to the courage of your young sweetheart to join the R.F.C. That he is now dead is not due to my words or to his fine courage. It is because the machine he was flying broke up in mid-air; because he was probably being taught in an aircraft that was ancient, unsuitable, and patched-up too many times. That is what is killing our young pilots more often than the Hun. If you love these heroic boys who are offering the greatest sacrifice they can make; if you want to offer your greatest support to them, give them machines that are worthy of their skill and daring.'

He turned to encompass the businessmen who had gathered behind him to hear all this. 'Gentlemen, nothing I can say will be more significant than this young woman's tears for a sweetheart lost before he could even reach France. If you can look at her and not be moved to respond to this appeal, that boy will have died in vain. Get out your chequebooks as a tribute to *him.*'

In the ensuing silence he offered his hand to the Mayor, who had been his host. 'I do have to catch a train, sir.'

Totally bemused by what had happened the man, in all the splendour of his chain of office, shook hands and mumbled, 'Thank you, Captain Sheridan. It's been . . . er . . . most interesting.'

The women with the banners seemed uncertain what to do as he walked between them to the door at the back of the canteen. But he had just reached it when a voice rang out again.

'Coward! You turn all the attention on this poor grieving girl, then run out. Are you going to let him get away with it?' came the following appeal to her militant sisters.

As he opened the door he heard a rush of feet behind him. Once outside, he was surrounded by the women who had been re-charged with aggression by their ring-leader, who could have been a pacifist, an extreme socialist, or even a Bolshevik sympathiser with orders to disrupt society at every opportunity. They all began to abuse him again, waving their banners in his face.

'You were nobody before you put on that uniform. You want the war to continue, so that you can go on enjoying yourself.'

'You're no hero; you're a killer.'

'You're a lecher! That scarf you wear is a French whore's che-mise.' That was the ring-leader again. 'It's men like you who keep wars going. While our boys are out there dying, you're safe at home bedding stupid little bitches who don't know any better!'

With his stomach churning once more he pushed his way through them, his one thought to reach the station in time to catch his train to London. The car was waiting by the kerb but, as he was about to get in it, the woman pushed to the front and confronted him defiantly, knowing members of the Press had followed and were making notes on everything that was said.

'You only want those donations so that you can continue to receive adulation and flattery . . . *and* go around in government cars,' she added for good measure. 'When the war is over, you'll have to go back to being nobody again. You'll be out of work, like the rest of those who manage to survive.' She turned to those members of the public who had gathered in curiosity with the men from the canteen who had followed into the street. 'If you give money for more aircraft, the war will go on and on. Let them run out of killer machines! The fighting will end when they have no weapons left, and only then. Hatred breeds hatred! Killing only brings further killing!' Seeing that she had the full attention of the crowd, she switched to a line that would have instant popular appeal. 'The word of Christ tells us to love our enemies and turn the other cheek. If we build more weapons of destruction we are all sinners . . . and the blood of our young manhood will be spilt because of *our* wickedness.'

Sickened and furious, Rex pushed his way to where the press reporters stood noting the whole scene with rapid scrawl. His action caused a lull in the shouting, so what he said was heard by all.

'I know what has happened this morning will be regarded by all your editors as more exciting copy than a straightforward rally. But I'm asking each and every one of you to tear up what you have there in your notebooks. If it is printed, the German newspapers will use it as propaganda to boost the morale of their troops by saying it shows the British have no more heart for the fight. But, worse than that, it will be read by our own men, standing kneedeep in mud, surrounded by the corpses of their friends, and preparing to face another winter of inhuman endurance. What do you think it will do to them to read that their womenfolk want them to put up their hands and surrender? After all they have suffered, after thousands upon thousands have died for their sakes, how do you think they'll feel to read that their wives, sweethearts and mothers who are safe, well-fed and comfortably warm at home, have had enough?' He swung round to stare at all the faces surrounding him now. 'My God, none of you has the least idea what those men are enduring out there so that you can live your well-ordered peaceful lives free of the German yoke. None of you has seen the broken villages and starvation of the French and Belgians, who are prepared to go on until the last man, woman and child, to defend their freedom.' He fixed his eye on the militant women. 'If your menfolk over there read about this, it will break them. You are not defending the manhood of Britain, you're defending your own selfish needs. They deserve better than that from the women of this country . . . and from the members of its Press.'

Gradually a cheer rose from all except the crusading women, who were mostly looking shamefaced, and Rex turned back to the car believing it was all over. But the female leader had one last shot to fire.

'What about *your* woman? Why isn't she in a munitions factory instead of prancing about a stage in next to nothing? It's quite obvious what *she's* doing for the boys in uniform . . . and it isn't supplying them with better aircraft!'

As the implication sank in Rex turned on her in overriding rage. But the police had arrived, at last, and as he seized her arms and began to shake her, an elderly constable dragged him off.

'Come along, sir. That won't do!'

Just at that moment, something hit Rex in the chest and he glanced down to see a tin fall to the ground as green paint began spreading all down his tunic and breeches. The woman who had thrown it was arrested, and Rex was bundled into the car. As it drove away he found he was shaking so much he was unable to tell the driver where he wanted to be taken.

It was evening before he reached the apartment, his final delay being a German air-raid which had resulted in a bomb being dropped just outside his London terminal, causing the train to halt while the line was cleared. He knew Laura would have already left for the theatre, but still felt overwhelming disappointment that the rooms were empty. It was their maid's evening off, so there was no hot meal for him. Not that he felt hungry. The events of the morning had left him feeling incredibly angry, with a sick feeling inside his stomach and a niggling guilt inside his head that prevented him from concentrating on anything else.

He threw his bag down in the corner and unbuttoned his tunic, feeling the elusive perfumed ghost of Laura in every part of those rooms. Longing for her washed over him. He remembered John Winters saying to him, 'Thank God there are some women who are not nurses, factory-workers, or farmhands.' Yes, Laura was supplying something to the troops that was not new weapons. But it was not what that woman had implied.

He tugged off his stained and ruined tunic in renewed anger. If that comment was reported in the newspapers he would take them all to court and sue them for every penny they owned. If nothing else, it would relieve his rocky financial situation. He took up the brandy and a glass, pouring himself a liberal measure. Then he went across to an armchair near the window. It was still light enough to read without a lamp, and he settled down with the brandy to sort through the letters on the table. There was one from his bank-manager, which he threw unopened into the waste-basket, one from Roland, another from Jake, who was still at the aircraft factory and doing well, and one from his old C.O. at Grissons. The last was official; that would be his itinerary for the coming month.

Oh God, more lectures and appeals for money! How much longer would it go on? His deep anger over the attack that morning returned. Did those women truly think he had gone rollicking through three years of war enjoying every minute of it? They had no notion of the sadness and anxiety he had suffered over his poor young brother, or the anguish of seeing friends sizzling into piles of blackened flesh. Had they ever had to witness a sight like that? Had they ever had to take off day after day to face men determined to kill? Did they have nightmares and wake up in a sweat? Did they have to live a pretence and hide the terrible truth? Did they really not know how he felt having to stand up there in front of rows of pink eager faces and have his imagination turn them into rows of corpses with black charred heads?

He realised he was beginning to shake, so he took another drink in an attempt to steady himself. Opening the letter from Jake he read of the youngster's pleasure in helping to design aircraft parts, and almost blessed his crippled leg that had kept him from being conscripted. His protégé was doing what he loved most, and thankfully did not have to face the bloody end of all his work when a machine was shot from the sky.

Roland had written at length, and the letter was mostly about Tarrant Hall and the village, as usual. When on active service, there was not a lot a man eould write anyway, without the censor cutting it all out. But there was a surprising paragraph at the end, with no preliminary explanation for it.

I have written to Cummings about my will. You may remember I originally decided to ensure that Marion would not be mistress of the Hall if Chris were ruled unfit to inherit on my death. I have reversed my decision. She is our brother's legal wife, and mother of his son. We three had such wonderful times growing up there, it would be sad if David could not do the same. Knowing the state of the mail service from the Valley of Love, would you kindly contact Cummings to ensure that he has received my letter?

Rex downed another brandy thoughtfully. What had prompted dear old dyed-in-the-wool Roland to forgive and forget? It would be the first time in his life he had done so. Events in the Valley of Love—the name he had chosen to let them know he was near Passchendaele—must be rough enough to shake even his brother's ordered nature. What a good thing he did not know Marion wished Chris permanently insane and divorced from her.

He sat for a while lost in gloomy thoughts of what would happen to Tarrant Hall in such a case. After the advice he had given Chris it was more than likely the lad would try to take on more than he could cope with and end up the way Marion hoped. If she was no longer Chris's wife, she could no longer inherit the home he would be unfit to run. Could young David still claim it?

His brain was too tired and muddled to work it out, and he sipped more brandy as he came to the maudlin conclusion that he would like to be the Squire of Tarrant Royal himself. Although he had always told Roland he did not want ownership of the place he now realised it meant a great deal to him. Last weekend had been one of the happiest in his life.

He reached for the last letter to read the schedule they had planned for him. If it took him anywhere near Dorset he would try to fit in another visit to his home. But the contents were a complete surprise! He was ordered back on active service with the new rank of Major, to command an élite squadron equipped with the new Sopwith Camel single-seat fighters that were the match of any German fighter aircraft. Due to the immediacy of his duty, he was given forty-eight hours' leave to prepare for departure. He would fly over with other returning pilots in the brand new machines on Sunday afternoon.

Mike flew back with him that Sunday, having also been recalled as part of the new squadron that was to operate over the Ypres area. The airfield was the same as any other they had known—a field with large sheds, primitive huts for accommodation, and well within the sound of enemy gunfire. It was not long before they were told why their formation had been so urgent. A massive third attempt to capture Passchendaele and its environs to mark the beginning of the final assault that would end the war was to be launched. The squadron was to be part of the air cover during the operation that had to succeed if another winter of trench attrition was to be avoided.

Rex was lucky with the members of his squadron, many of whom he already knew and respected. He was cheered into dinner on the first night because of the Gotha incident, and because of newspaper reports of his rally at Swindon. Although every word of the women's accusations had been reported, so had his strong verbal defence of the fighting men, and 'Sherry' Sheridan had become even more popular than before.

The Arrow Squadron, as it was codenamed, all voted for green stripes down their uniforms as insignia of an élite band of men. But Rex laughingly drew the line at wholesale throwing of paint at each other, and approved in its place a green stripe to be painted on the belly of each aircraft. But this brought forth a condemnation from the man in ground command of that sector, accusing the squadron of behaviour more suited to schoolboys.

But there was more than a dislike of typical R.F.C. élan behind the order issued by Lieutenant-Colonel James Ashmore. He had never forgotten the red-haired instructor at Upavon who had flown him into a haystack and put him into hospital for the whole of Christmas 1914!

23

IT TOOK Chris some days to solve his problem. Although he might manage to walk down the hill to the village with concentrated effort, he certainly would not make the return uphill. That meant he had to be transported there, and *that* meant he could not go alone. Drawback number one! The second was that he had no idea where Marion Deacon lived. Her home could be way on the outskirts of Tarrant Royal—even as far as Greater Tarrant, which he understood was some six miles off. He could not possibly knock on every door in the vicinity hoping to find her. To confront the girl at her home was essential. She could not run away then.

He reviewed the situation and listed assets against obstacles. From that list he devised a plan of campaign. His main assets were good looks and Priddy, so he set about using them both. A young nurse who had been at the hospital no more than a month had a strong fancy for him, he knew, so he began to flirt with her. Since it was a game he had never played before he was astounded at the instant success he had. Just for telling her she looked nice that morning, he was brought an extra helping of treacle tart. When he remarked how shiny her hair was, she let him stay out in the garden during Matron's inspection and told the feared superior that the patient had been called to the bathroom.

Highly delighted with this easy method of getting anything he wanted in return for a smile or small compliment, he played his trump card on the third day. With very little effort he discovered there was an elderly doctor called Deacon who lived in the village with a house and surgery almost opposite the green. Chris did not make the mistake of asking if there was a young daughter also living there. He had a feeling the source of his information would not take kindly to that!

Several more days passed as he worked out the means of getting to his destination, and this was where his other asset was put to use. Priddy doted on him, longed for a return of the old times when the three brothers had almost been 'her boys'. It was that element he must play on. Using the weapons he had only recently discovered, he went through to the house one day when the coast was clear and cornered the old soul whilst she was polishing the banisters. Within ten minutes he got her collusion in a plot to 'escape from the dreadful hospital atmosphere where he had been kept almost like a prisoner for months and months' and go for a short drive with Dawkins in the pony and trap to see the village. He added earnestly that Rex had suggested it would be the finest thing out for him, and that it would probably bring back his memory of childhood in a flash, so that he would be perfectly fit again. Priddy was no proof against such persuasion.

The clockwork running of his plan was checked when the afternoon chosen for the secret excursion was also chosen by Bill Chandler for a long session with an army expert who had journeyed to Tarrant Hall to question Chris on the secret work he had done for them. On the following day it rained heavily, so it was not until three weeks after Rex had suggested that he should go in search of the last piece of his memory jigsaw that Chris finally did so.

It was the first day of September, and the hedgerows were thick with blackberries as the trap bowled down the hill and turned into the lane leading through the village. Chris felt a sense of triumph. He had escaped unseen from his room, and persuaded a doubting and reluctant Dawkins to check that no one would see their departure from the side entrance of the house near the stables. He was out on his own and in sole charge of his actions. It was a marvellous feeling.

The village looked vastly different without the crowds of revellers there. The gala face had vanished; the flags and sideshows were only a memory. The green itself looked dry and neglected, making it difficult to believe twenty-two men clad in flannels had created such excitement there three weeks before. Yet, as they progressed along lanes where wild Michaelmas daisies grew, and the red fruits of wayside roses were bright against the green, Chris forgot the carnival village and began to appreciate the beauty of quiet rustic charm. But he was not so entranced that he missed the board on the gate of a small but attractive country house that gave the surgery hours for Dr Deacon. He took careful note of the surroundings in preparation for the return journey.

Still grumbling over the way he had been talked into doing

something of which he strongly disapproved, and which he hoped Mrs Prideaux would not have forever on her conscience if the young master suffered the consequences of going against medical rules and advice, Dawkins drove for roughly twenty minutes before turning back and heading for home at a spanking pace.

Although he had found the scene charming, none of it seemed familiar, and that little chill of loneliness began to wrap itself round Chris's heart again. This idea had been a great mistake. He should have stayed in the safe cocoon of his hospital room, looking through the conservatory glass at the world he had tried so drastically to reject. Why would a young man of nineteen feel he could not face one more day of his life? Neil Frencham had done no worse than betray his trust. It was that betrayal following on top of an earlier one that had made him want to die. It was the only logical explanation . . . and Marion Deacon was somewhere at the heart of that betrayal.

They were nearing the centre of Tarrant Royal once again, and his heart began to thud as doubts came crowding in. Did he have enough courage to see this through to the end, whatever it might turn out to be? Could he willingly and deliberately face the risk of a one-way journey into some dark mental limbo? Panic assailed him. Feeling sick and giddy he fought a battle with himself, then realised cowardice had won. He could not carry out his plan, after all. Leaning back in the padded seat in relief, he prepared to stay there until he reached home. But Fate took a hand. As the trap rounded a corner by the green and bowled along toward the Deacons' house, Marion appeared in the garden with a trug over her arm and began cutting late roses.

Almost as if it were not part of himself, he heard his voice saying, 'Stop here a minute, Dawkins!'

The coachman turned a scared face toward him. 'Here, sir? No, I don't think that's advisable. I think we should go straight up to the Hall. You've been out long enough.'

'Just do as I say,' he ordered calmly. 'I wish to speak to Miss Deacon a moment.'

'Oh lor, Mr Christopher, there'll only be trouble if I stop, mark my words,' wailed the worried old man. 'We shouldn't have come out from that hospital. I was agin it from the start.'

But Chris was already sitting forward with his hand on the small door at the back, and Dawkins must have been afraid he

472

would get out anyway, because he drew up just short of a gateway with a trellised arch. Now decisive action had been taken Chris felt very calm. Perhaps Rex had been right. Going out to meet something *was* easier than waiting for it to arrive.

But Marion's expression when she caught sight of him did not suggest it was going to be easy at all, and he believed, for a moment, that she would rush indoors. Apparently thinking better of it, she stood where she was halfway up the path, watching him as he reached for his sticks and began the hazardous business of getting to the ground from the unsteady two-wheeled vehicle. He would rather have done it without her looking on, but Dawkins hobbled round to give him a helping hand before he made a complete fool of himself. The old servant looked so worried, Chris gave him a reassuring smile.

'It's all right, Dawkins, I know what I'm doing.'

Wishing he had faith in his words, he crab-walked to the gate and stopped by the arch covered in honeysuckle, wondering what to say to the girl who was looking at him with something remarkably like fear.

'Hallo,' he began, then cleared his throat nervously. 'Now I've gone to all this trouble to find you, may I come in?'

After a long moment she nodded, but made no attempt to help him negotiate a gate on a strong spring. He bungled the job badly, and Dawkins had to extricate him from a tangle of gate and sticks so that he could start up the path toward her. Before he reached her, however, two black labradors raced from the side of the house and flung themselves on him in ecstatic greeting, nearly knocking him off balance with their frenzied leaps to wash his nose with their tongues.

'Bandit . . . Hunter, get down!' cried Marion, putting the trug on the ground and swiftly coming forward. '*Down!* Oh, you disobedient dogs!'

Hanging over his sticks Chris fondled the dogs' sleek heads, calming them with gentle hands and gentle words as they continued to take no heed of their mistress. Now safely on all fours they were still as ecstatic in their greeting.

Marion arrived before him. 'I'm sorry about that. They never take any notice of me.'

She looked different, thinner and not quite as pretty, or perhaps his memory was at fault. The irony of that thought struck him so forcibly, he had no idea what to say to her now he was face to face in her garden. As he sensed hostile resistance to what he had done, his mind teemed with confusing facts. This girl had known him well since at least his thirteenth birthday, and he was now twenty-one. She had pretended to be a nurse for reasons he had not yet discovered. She had displayed friendship, concern, and warmth during those early days when he had not even known who he was. She had helped him survive, he realised now as he searched her face for some sign of those things still. There was none.

Knowing what he now knew about her, it was possible he had hurt her by his request that she should not tend only him at that other hospital. But would it account for the way she was presently regarding him, with suppressed fear and something approaching hatred? The only feasible explanation for her complete reversal of attitude and feelings was that he had done something dreadful to her during those lost months of last winter. It would explain why she had left the hospital during that period, and why Chandler had refused to say why or where she had gone. This conclusion filled him with embarrassment and panic. He had no idea what he did during those periods when he went away from himself. Surely . . . oh no, surely he did not become a *madman!* Growing hot with the humiliation of the unknown, when he might have behaved as he had seen others in the ward behave, he stumbled over his words.

'I shouldn't have come. It must be . . . I mean, you ran away that . . . that day at the match. I'd better go.'

But he did not turn away, and neither did she. With the dogs licking his hands that clutched the sticks, he waited for her to say or do something decisive. But she seemed as unable to walk off as he did.

'I'm . . . I'm all right now,' he ventured hesitantly. 'I won't hurt you, truly I won't. Please don't be afraid of me.'

She turned away immediately and moved only a few paces to stand with shoulders bowed, as if helpless beneath some burden.

'Marion, if I hurt you in some way, I'm sorry,' he offered in continuing awkwardness, only now realising how very much he had missed her company. Just lately, he had been so obsessed with struggling to walk well enough to go and see Laura on the stage, he had put this girl to the back of his mind. 'But you should know how it is . . . how it *was,*' he amended, 'when things start . . .' He tailed off, realising she could not possibly know. No one but himself could know. 'I've asked many times to see you, and tried to find out where you had gone. But all they would tell me was that you had left the hospital.' With still no response from her, he persevered further. 'They've transferred me to Tarrant Hall . . . but I expect you know that as you live so near. I wish . . . well, I wish you had come up to see me.'

She was biting her lip, and he noticed her hands holding the sides of her blue skirt were shaking. A rush of remorse made him say, 'I owe a great deal to you. I think I might have gone insane during those first days if you hadn't been there.'

Swinging round to face him she cried emotionally, 'Oh Chris, don't. Please don't. I can't take any more.'

His heart sank. 'Is that why you ran away the other day? Oh God, did I do something absolutely dreadful to you?'

Her answer to that was to turn and hurry indoors, breaking into a run when she neared the house. When the door slammed it was like a physical blow. Hardly knowing what he was doing he turned too quickly, and overbalanced to fall headlong on the uneven path, jarring his leg so badly he felt sick with pain. He lay for a moment or two waiting for it to diminish before attempting to get back on his feet. Vaguely conscious of Dawkins bewailing the outcome of being talked into something as foolhardy as this, Chris stayed where he was, calling Rex all kinds of a fool for suggesting he should go out and meet his past. That only worked when a man flew a Nieuport . . . or when he could walk without the aid of sticks!

Then there appeared to be an altercation above him. Dawkins, and another man with crisp angry tones.

'You should have known better than to bring him here, of all places.'

'I didn't know he was a'going to do this, Doctor, or I never would've done. I'd have looked after him better'n that, believe me. But Miss Marion was in the garden, and I thought he was going to jump, if it was that I didn't stop.'

'Well, there's nothing for it but to get him up on his feet and pray he's done no damage to himself. I'm not having him inside the house, mind!'

'Oh, Daddy, we'll have to,' said Marion's agitated voice. 'That leg has had multiple fractures, and the bones had to be reset a second time when he fell out of bed.'

'To perdition with the bones!' came the astonishing comment from a medical man. 'I refuse to let him set foot inside my door.'

'He won't set foot,' came Marion's equally angry reply. 'You surely don't imagine he'll be able to walk after this. He's probably in so much pain he will have passed out. You can't just dump him in the trap for Dawkins to take up to the Hall. You're a doctor, first and foremost, and Chris is just someone in need of medical help. If *I* can go to his aid, surely you can.'

'Very well,' snapped the Doctor. 'You give Dawkins a hand on his right side . . . and I sincerely hope you don't regret this, my girl.'

They put hands on him, and Chris simulated unconsciousness while they lifted him carefully and began to carry him along. Although his leg was painful, he knew from long experience it could have sustained no more damage. All the same, Marion thought he would have passed out, so he thought it would help to pretend he had. Not only did it give him time to think, it would surely boost Marion's concern for him which seemed to have miraculously returned. It delighted and relieved him no end, and Rex was definitely back in favour again for his excellent advice.

The dogs, who began to bark at something they recognised as drama, were immediately silenced by Dr Deacon. But they were sitting beside him when Chris opened his eyes to find he was in a small surgery, lying on the examination couch behind half-drawn floral curtains. There was only Marion and her father. Dawkins had been sent to the Hall for an ambulance. Dr Deacon was examining the injured leg for tell-tale signs, but Marion was studying Chris's face in a manner he found encouraging after the way she had behaved earlier.

He smiled at her and said tentatively, 'It seems I have to be flat on my back to persuade you to stay and talk to me.'

'Are you in much pain?' she asked, deliberately adopting a nurse-like manner.

'If I'm honest and say no, you won't go off, will you? Ouch!' he cried as her father moved his ankle experimentally. 'I am now.'

'Mmm. Nothing serious. A slight sprain, that's all,' came the curt verdict. 'There's an ambulance on its way, but I'll give you a draught of something to help cope with the transfer back to the hospital.'

'I can do that, Daddy,' Marion told him in quiet tones. 'You go and wait for the ambulance.'

'And leave you here alone with him! That I won't.'

'I can manage,' came the firm assurance. 'It'll be all right.'

Dr Deacon gave a heavy sigh that puffed out his cheeks as he glared at Chris. 'You should have stayed up at the Hall. This sort of escapade does no one any good whatever, least of all those of us who have to deal with you. Just because you are on your feet, it's no sign that you are cured, believe me.'

'*Please,* Daddy,' said his daughter.

He flung her an angry look before turning to go. 'As you wish, but I'll be right next door if you want me.'

The door shut noisily behind him, and Chris said, 'You won't want him, I promise. It was the truth when I said just now that I'm better.'

'You'll need a mild pain killer before they transfer you.' She turned away to the cupboard just outside the curtains around the couch.

'I hope they take a long time in coming,' he said softly. 'I do very much want to talk to you.'

'They'll be down right away,' came her uncompromising answer, as she poured green liquid into a measure. 'You've taken a risk, and they're going to be furious because you sneaked out.'

Gingerly he struggled to a sitting position, wincing at the throbbing in his ankle that increased with movement. 'I wouldn't have had to sneak out if you hadn't run away from me at the cricket-match. I was so glad to see you that day,' he explained, taking the measure from her and drinking the contents in one gulp. 'Ugh! My intestines must be bright green by now with the amount of that stuff I've swallowed.' He handed the little metal cup back, saying earnestly, 'I was going to ask you up to the Hall. You wouldn't have to sit by my bed, you know. They let me go into the house, so we could have tea in civilised manner. There's an awfully nice window-seat with a view of the sunken gardens. But you'd already know that, wouldn't you?' he finished with experimental casualness.

She had turned back to wash out the measure at the small sink, so he could not see her expression. 'I can't come up. I have the

477

house to run, and all Daddy's filing and dispensing to do, as well as other things.'

'Like looking after people's children for them? I saw you had a little boy with you at the match.' He felt suddenly bleak. Now they were alone he did not seem to be getting any further than before. 'I suppose minding children is a lot easier than dealing with war casualties who don't know who they are.'

She nodded silently. He wanted to go over to her, but his sticks had been propped against the wall well out of his reach. Effectively stranded on the couch he wondered momentarily if it had been deliberate. Did she believe he would harm her? That brought him full circle back to the moment he had arrived, and she had run away.

'I must have done something very terrible for you to put an end to a friendship begun before I was thirteen,' he said into the silence. 'You liked me enough then to make a wonderful birthday present of pressed wild flowers.'

She shot round to face him so fast the little cup she had been washing over-meticulously was knocked to the ground. All colour had drained from her face, and she looked more afraid than ever.

'You remember!' she accused wildly. 'How cruel of you to do this!'

He shook his head slowly. 'No, you're wrong. I thought the days of pretence and confusion were past, but they remain where you are concerned. I always suspected you were not what I was made to believe. But my ideas were wildly different from the truth. Amongst a box of my boyhood possessions I found that book of flowers. I had never once suspected you had known me most of my life. How cruel of *you* not to tell me.'

'Cruel!' she cried. 'I did it to help you.'

He took in the implication of her words. 'So it's something I've done since then, not before, that has turned you against me. That means I'm back where I started. When you ran from me three weeks ago I became convinced that you were somehow tied in with the piece of my past that still remains elusive. Now, I'll have to look elsewhere for the clues.' Sighing, he told her, 'Whatever I did to you last Christmas to make you so afraid of me, I'm deeply sorry for. But if we were childhood friends and you came to that hospital to look after me, you must know I'm not really a violent person. I'm certain I'm not.' As she seemed on the verge of tears

478

again, he found himself growing more urgent with the minutes ticking past. 'Oh lord, Marion, I'm also sure I've never been very good at this sort of thing, either. What I'm trying to say is, if I abused and swore at you I did it without knowing. And I'm very upset that I've lost a friendship that must have been very close for you to go to such trouble over that beautiful book of pressed flowers.'

Her face went down into her hands, and she seemed incredibly distressed as she mumbled, 'Stop, oh stop, Chris! You don't know what you're saying. Oh, why did you come here?'

He swallowed painfully. 'To meet my fears halfway. But I've only increased them . . . and yours. Look, if you'll give me my sticks, I'll wait outside for the ambulance.'

She visibly pulled herself together as she glanced through the window. 'It's all right. It's here now.'

They came in with a stretcher, so he was forced to lie on it. It thwarted his intention of shaking Marion's hand in civilised fashion. Instead, he tried to smile, but could not manage it. How could he say goodbye to this girl when he knew he could not leave things as they were? If she were not the actual cause of the unknown drama in his life, she would at least know what it was and be able to help him solve the mystery.

But when he reached the ambulance he was so struck by something he had seen whilst being carried from the house, he heard no word of Bill Chandler's angry remonstrance. He surely had the vital clue, after all! He spent the rest of the short journey to Tarrant Hall trying to develop his theory.

Fact One: the dogs had welcomed him with the hysterical canine delight reserved for people they adore and trust, who have returned after a long absence. So he had once been a frequent and welcome visitor to the Deacons' house. Fact Two: on the wall of that small surgery he had spotted a sketch with his own signature across the corner. He must have given it as a gift, and they still treasured it. Fact Three: Deacon himself was actively hostile to him and to Dawkins. He was also protective of his daughter in their company. Fact Four: this was the most astonishing and telling one. As they had carried Chris from the surgery he had seen that same little boy Marion had had with her at the cricket-match. The child had been running about in the garden playing with a pet rabbit. At such close quarters Chris had seen he looked unmistak-

479

ably like photographs of himself and his brothers when children. There was little doubt the child had Sheridan blood in him.

Working with speed and logic, his mind had solved the mystery by the time the ambulance swung round to draw up at the impressive entrance to Tarrant Hall. The solution explained several other mysteries: why everyone was always urging him to write to his eldest brother, why the tall blond man he remembered visiting the hospital in those early days had always seemed angry and unapproachable. Yes, and now he thought about it, Marion had never been there on the days Roland had visited him.

The child looked to be around three years old, so his own age when it had happened would have been about seventeen or eighteen. Knowing now how he had felt about Rex, he realised that if he had been even fonder of his elder brother, his schoolboy admiration could have been shattered and he could have felt betrayed by such evidence.

Appalling though it still seemed he must accept that Roland had fathered that child he had just seen, and the entire Sheridan family was hated by Dr Deacon because of it. Yet not by Marion herself, apparently, because she had tried to help him in those early days at the hospital. She was also fond of Rex. Had she then believed that Roland had returned her love? Did she still love him, despite his betrayal? Was it a vain love, like his for Laura? Poor little girl!

The letter reached Roland in record time—for the army postal system, that was. Luckily, he was in reserve at the time it arrived in the Ypres sector, so he received it at the first possible opportunity. Recognising the handwriting he felt a rush of delight as he tore the envelope open. But Chris had not written at length, just one page covered in his scrawling hand. Of course, the fact that he had written at all was a tremendous boost to hope. Although Rex and Tessa had kept him up to date with Chris's progress, this factual evidence was worth its weight in gold. He had last seen his brother as a mummified stranger filled with silent hostility: to get a letter from him was so momentous Roland found his throat tightening. But the contents were as cryptic as only Chris could be.

Dear Roland—
The brooch arrived safely. Didn't quite get the link between me

480

and Bisset. Did I once know him? Rex said I ought to pass it on to some girl, so I gave it to Laura. Not sure if he knows I did. Have just discovered you meant Marion. Why me and not Rex? Sorry. Can't very well ask Laura for it now. I've seen the boy, by the way, and he looks fit and well. Hope you don't mind my mentioning the subject, but thought it might help if brought into the open. I suppose I have an aversion to secrets, these days. And I have to say I feel most awfully sorry for Marion. She's such a nice girl and has been very good to me. Found out I like Rex tremendously—at the cricket-match—so I guess it must have been the same with you before all that happened. Have decided to write because I know how I felt at Gallipoli. Hope you come through all right. I'm older now and see things differently. This letter will bear out those words. Cheerio, Chris.

Roland read it through several times and was little wiser. Whatever did it all mean? Why give Hilary Bisset's mother's cameo to Laura, of all people, and without Rex's knowledge? And what conclusion must he draw from the references to Marion and little David? 'She's such a nice girl' did not suggest he had remembered she was his unwanted wife, yet he hinted that he was older and saw things differently. As for liking Rex at the cricket-match and thinking it must be the same with him, the whole continuity of the letter was a mystery. Nevertheless, it was typical of the old Chris, who always wrote letters that were like disjointed cryptograms, and that in itself was very encouraging.

The letter strengthened Roland's longing for home leave. He had been away for eighteen months now, and rumour had it there would be a ten day trip to England after the next big push to take Passchendaele. Preparations for it were already underway. A fierce battle for the Menin Road Bridge, when artillery pounded the ground ahead in a bombardment that shattered the eardrums even of those in reserve, had been followed by two others within days of each other. Each had succeeded despite the additional torment of dust storms that had raced across the open ground.

But those who had cursed that hot gritty obscuring weapon of nature soon had cause to eat their words. By mid-October the rain was back, and it was the non-stop drenching cold rain of approaching winter. Within days the trenches had become narrow canals, where men stood waist-deep in water day and night; within days no soldier had a dry garment left to wear. If despair and desperation had been on their faces before, it now etched so deeply into their features it would never entirely disappear again. If this mammoth assault failed to set the Germans on the final run back to Berlin, there would be another winter of unspeakable misery. For a very few it would be their fourth, and it would be the one too many. They knew in their hearts they had endured all they could take. This battle *had* to succeed for them.

With the onset of the cold weather again came the inevitable bronchitis that weakened so many of the troops. These sufferers were the first victims of gas attacks and stood little chance of recovery. Roland had been a medical officer in the Ypres sector for eight months, and felt the time was equivalent to eight years' experience as a civilian doctor. His early feelings with Matt Rideaux's unit had long since gone. Used now to the sight and sound of suffering men, he knew his old vocation had been the right one for him. For every batch he lost, there were one or two he saved. It gave him a tremendous sense of responsibility and service to a community; things he had always sought and found satisfying for as long as he could remember.

It also gave him a means of communication with his fellows that he had always found difficult without some purpose in mind. Rex had struck up easy conversations and friendships wherever he went. But Roland had needed the guise of respected horseman or Squire of Tarrant Royal to help bridge the gap between himself and others. Being known affectionately by others as 'Doc' served the same purpose.

But he also acknowledged that living as he had during the past eight months had given him an insight into human behaviour that easily knocked down social or personality barriers. The tragedies of Charles Barr-Leigh, Hilary Bisset, and Rosalind Tierney had left him infinitely more perceptive, and far more tolerant than the young man of twenty-four who had caused an entire village to turn its back on him. If he was given home leave, he would do his utmost to make his peace with Tarrant Royal.

But leave would only come after battle. Meanwhile the usual proceedings would have to take place. The letters to be posted only 'if', the instructions to fellow officers regarding personal effects, and the terrible lull of waiting that somehow had to be filled in with activity. Roland had heard from Rex that his new will had been received and legalised, so his conscience was easy on that score.

His red-haired brother was back at an airfield not far from Ypres. Rex had devised his own postal system. It consisted of flying low over the front-line trenches and throwing out weighted cocoa-tins addressed to Lieutenant Sheridan R.A.M.C. which contained letters, or larger biscuit-tins in which were bars of chocolate, a cake or, once even, a brace of hares. These were passed down the line to Roland with great good humour, everyone finding the business entertaining and a good morale-booster. With 'Sherry' Sheridan in the skies above them with his 'Arrows' how could they fail? Any day, Roland expected a Sopwith Camel to land just a few feet away, and Rex to climb from the cockpit as he had at Croix Des Anges. But the R.F.C. was as deeply committed to this assault as the ground forces, and there was no time for social visiting.

Roland's battalion was ordered to the front-line again on the same day they received the news that the threatened revolution in Russia had begun, and the whole vast country was in such bloody turmoil these people who had been allies were now too busy slaughtering each other to bother about fighting the Germans. It was a terrible blow, and they all marched up to their battle positions on a night when rain fell in almost solid curtains, and a bitter wind blew back the skirts of their greatcoats, and drove the rain to sting their eyes as they stared into the darkness for the man ahead. If the front files strayed from the manufactured roads into the sea of mud, they would all surely follow.

Roland felt as heavy-hearted as anyone as he trudged through the nocturnal deluge, wondering how he had ever ridden across Longbarrow Hill in the rain and actually enjoyed the experience. When they reached the trenches they tried to settle in to wait for the dawn. But the flooded state prevented anything other than an aimless groping for a foothold or ledge that would take a man above the water level. The existing R.A.P. was useless, in Roland's opinion, and he made no attempt to enter it knowing the water would most likely reach to his armpits. By the light of star-shells intermittently illuminating the area, he set his staff to bailing-out, then stopped them after ten minutes because he realised the water just ran back in again. The job needed a pump and a deep pit to hold the drained water.

There was nothing to be done until daylight came, so he and his men hunched into their greatcoats and tried to snatch some sleep whilst leaning against the muddy walls in the torrential rain. But with the dawn came the gas-gong, and they all pulled on their respirators which always hampered vision, even in dry weather. They also hampered eating and drinking, so they had no breakfast after their cold wet night, not even a cup of cocoa or tot of rum to warm them up.

Standing there in a uniform that had soaked up so much water it felt as heavy as a suit of armour, and feeling particularly claustrophobic in the gas-mask, Roland told himself that even if he lived to a ripe old age he would never forget mornings like this—the cold, the wetness, the stink of mud, the hunger, the fear, the smell of the mask smothering his face. Would any man there be able to forget?

It was a false alarm. But, no sooner were the masks removed in great relief to the accompaniment of queries about bacon and sizzling sausages, or a jolly nice kipper or two, than the order came at speed through the tortuous corridors of that front-line to stand-to and prepare to advance.

'Blimey, sir, that's a bit sudden, ain't it?' protested his corporal. 'We ain't hardly settled in yet.'

Roland frowned. 'We can't operate in this dug-out, Sergeant Clyde. It's unusable. Go further to the rear and find a place that doesn't need a boat to negotiate, and I'll go to Headquarters to see what the situation is. If it's just a stand-to we've got time. If we're launching an attack, we're in trouble. Corporal Kenny, see that this equipment is kept out of the water, and take down that sign or the stretcher-bearers will be bringing all the casualties here.'

So saying he set off in the direction of his Headquarters with as much speed as he could muster. With the various companies manning the trenches in full strength, and their officers moving up and down behind them waiting for further orders, there was not a lot of room to pass between those high walls that had now become miniature cascades. Haste was also hampered by the obligation to wade through runny mud and slime that formed the bottom of the trenches, and which had risen above the wooden duckboards. There was that curious silence that came before an attack. Men stood facing the top of the parapets where death flitted freely and unhindered, their faces set and drawn. They smoked nervously and almost as if unaware of doing so, or they bit their fingernails, or fiddled incessantly with the straps beneath their chins that secured the tin-helmets in position. But they said nothing to each other. That would come later when it was all over, or when they were carrying their wounded friends to safety. For now, every man there was a single unit shut up within himself and his fear. The officers were the same; boys, most of them, with white faces and innocent wide eyes that held a sense of shock that all they had heard of war was now reality.

Splashing and struggling his way through to a transverse trench Roland turned into it knowing Headquarters was at the end of that stretch. Then he heard aircraft coming low and fast right overhead. Turning he saw a whole squadron of Albatross appearing out of the dawn rain that had turned to drizzle. They had one obvious target. The whole morning turned into instant hell as the machines raced at suicidal height, one behind the other, guns blazing out to rip through the trenches with perfect aim and devastate the ordered ranks waiting to go up and over.

They had come so suddenly and unexpectedly from the obscurity, everyone was taken by surprise. The soldiers fell in dozens, not knowing how death had come, or dropping wounded only to drown in the filth at their feet. Then the second wave came, spaced further apart and diving down and up again at speed to toss bombs and grenades with great accuracy into the confusion below. It was complete massacre and mayhem from the skies, and Roland was caught in it. All around him men were screaming in agony, or trying desperately to run from it. But there was nowhere to run. They were trapped in corridors in the ground that only led to other corridors.

The zooming aircraft came again, and Roland threw himself against the side wall, pressing into the mud to escape from the rain of bullets coming from the stuttering machine-guns. Two thudded against his tin-helmet with force, and he instinctively pressed even harder until he felt the mud in his nose and throat, making him cough and want to vomit. But there was no time to do anything. The bombing section was coming now, the pilots diving and releasing their bombs with as much glee as children dropping stones onto small crabs in rock-pools.

The earth behind Roland went up in a khaki spout to fall back like thick porridge all over him, leaving a gaping hole in the parapet where three men had been crouching a moment before. They were now part of the porridge falling on him. He tried to run as the next aircraft rushed headlong overhead, but the trench disintegrated leaving a great chasm that was filling with yellow-brown water that rushed into it carrying along with it partial corpses, both new and several years old.

Instinct led him to retreat, but that way was blocked by a wall of earth thrown up by another explosion. In that wall was a living man. At least, there was a living face staring at him with ghastly appeal for release from something that had become inhuman. Roland snatched up a tin-hat from a nearby head that was no longer attached to anything, and began to dig like a maniac at the earthen tomb that had swallowed all but that mudstained face that could only yet have seen eighteen years of life. There was a roaring in his head that had nothing to do with the sound of the German aircraft, or the thump of his own artillery firing at them. There was a fury inside him so great it caused him to yell all the obscenities he had ever learnt, in a voice that sounded frighteningly like Charles Barr-Leigh's.

There was something running down his face which he thought was mud, until scarlet splashes began plopping on those living features still screaming a silent plea for help. But he continued his mad frenzied digging, and the wall began to crumble until he found a torso and one leg. The other leg was missing, but both arms were there, and further digging revealed that all parts were still joined together. Mercifully, the boy was so deeply in a state of shock the ragged stump of the left leg would not be noticed by him. He clung to Roland's arm, gazing silently at him as tears welled up in his deep dark eyes to overflow onto the khaki face and leave white streaks. Then, as Roland unscrewed his water-bottle to wash the mud from the lad's face, a screaming roaring shape flashed overhead bringing a hail of lead.

Solid fire thudded into Roland's shoulder, knocking him backward with the force of it. He cried out with pain as he landed with a splash in the rushing yellowish-brown water that started to close over his head. Fear lent him strength and wits to struggle up out of danger from drowning and, clutching his upper arm, he turned back to his patient. The boy was still gazing at him in terrified appeal, but there was a neat scarlet hole in his forehead, and it no longer mattered that he had lost a leg. Nor did it matter that several others around him were torn and bleeding. Their war was over.

Breath rasping from his labours Roland scrambled up the pile of debris until he was well clear of the water, and half-lay there for a moment assessing his situation. There was blood on his trousers around what looked like a minor superficial thigh-wound, but the one in his shoulder was more serious. The bullet was still in there and would have to be extracted by someone who knew what he was doing if it were not to cause permanent damage to his muscle.

Such considerations were driven away by the sound of the aircraft returning once more, and he was about to slide to the bottom of the trench when he heard the most astonishing sound. From the mounds of earth as far as the eye could see came the faint but growing roar of men cheering.

It was soon apparent why. A formation of R.F.C. Camels had come onto the scene, and the distinctive green stripe on their underbellies identified them as the renowned 'Arrow Squadron'. Laughing somewhat shakily, Roland heard himself say, 'Damn you, Rex, who else would turn up at a time like this?'

There Rex was, easily recognisable by the famous cerise 'scarf' that streamed out in the wind behind him. But he was too busy to pick out one man on the ground as he and his pilots tangled with the German machines and began sending them out of the sky. It was difficult to follow what was going on because the cloud was so low, and the continuing drizzle made it almost impossible to identify the wheeling, zooming aircraft as enemy or ally. But the contest was quite deadly as many of the Germans, having used up their ammunition, decided to make a dash for home.

As Roland lay there he suddenly realised he was watching his own brother face death, and could do nothing to help him. He had watched numerous dog-fights, cheering or falling silent as each machine began to spiral earthward. But this was Rex, the carefree impudent brother who would give anybody anything if it were in his power to do so, and he might plunge to the ground as Roland looked on. The contest seemed much more deadly from then on; the drama almost too great to withstand. Each time an aircraft fell he caught himself praying. Some crashed too far behind the curtain of rain to be identified, and he knew the distant glow of fire could be Rex's funeral pyre.

Then one came suddenly from the clouds, twisting round and around with black smoke pouring from it. It was a Camel with half a wing hanging broken. For a nightmare second Roland thought his heart would stop and never start again, until he saw the pilot clearly. He wore no scarf.

The machine hit the ground about a hundred yards off in the middle of No-Man's-Land, but the pilot was thrown clear in a somersault action to lie face down where he dropped. The aircraft burst into sudden fire and began to burn fiercely. Then another Camel zoomed from the cloud, racing low over the area. This time it was Rex in the cockpit, hanging over the side to see the fate of his pilot. Hotly pursued by an Albatross that had dived after him, he then flew over the trenches, pointing forcibly at the crashed aircraft. Next minute, he was up and away, wig-wagging to avoid the stream of bullets coming from his enemy.

Looking back at the wreck Roland had a shock. The pilot was moving, trying to crawl away from his burning machine and away from the German lines a short distance away. No wonder Rex had been signalling so ferociously! But an Albatross was back and directed a spurt of gunfire at the man, sending up little fountains of mud in a line just ahead of him, trying to force him back. From British trenches came the sound of rifle-fire as men took aim at the German flier. But he was too quick to be caught by that, and disappeared into the clouds again.

That was when Roland, who had never done anything on impulse in his life, struggled to his feet and squelched over the broken parapet into No-Man's-Land with just one thought in his mind. That wounded man could have been his brother, and he must be brought safely in.

The flesh wound in Roland's thigh did not hurt, but it had made his leg numb so that he progressed in jerky zig-zag fashion. But his shoulder was sickeningly painful, especially when he trod in hidden dips and nearly fell. But he kept going when he heard firing once more, and realised the men in his own trenches were attacking the Albatross as it returned. Next minute, the mire ahead of him began jumping like volcanic hot springs as the enemy flashed past, a Camel almost glued to its tail, both vanishing into distant cloud next minute. But Roland realised it had not been the Albatross that had raked up the ground before him; it was rifle-fire from German soldiers in their trenches only a hundred yards or so away.

Crouching low he ran in zig-zag pattern toward the wounded pilot, and his heart sank when he discovered the man had passed out from his efforts to move with two broken legs. But Roland knew he would have to work fast if there were not to be two dead men out there. Never had he been so glad of his muscular build and strength, because the pilot must almost certainly have been a full-back in his school rugby team until a few weeks ago.

He had seen some physically impossible feats performed by men who had carried wounded comrades for miles, whilst losing blood themselves, and had marvelled at human endurance. Now he knew the roots of this were hatred and determination. War had lost its capacity for compassion. The enemy were firing on a man who very obviously no longer had the ability to fight, and another whose plain intent was to succour him. Neither of them were offering aggression and, as his hatred for the Germans increased, so did his determination to get that pilot back to safety alive.

He bent to pick up the boy over his shoulder and very nearly passed out himself with the effort. But he was remembering those others who had defied pain and weakness, telling himself he could do the same. It seemed a great deal further back to the trenches than it had going out, and the stretch of mud before him not only jumped with the hail of bullets, but seemed to be undulating as he walked.

There was a dark shape overhead again: more firing. But these bullets were directed at the aircraft, not the ground he was crossing. Vaguely aware that a machine bearing roundels was circling overhead drawing the fire from the German trenches, Roland plodded on, feeling the boy's weight on his uninjured shoulder was driving him further into the mire with every step.

Yet the trench was growing gradually nearer, and he was conscious of the sound of cheering again. How strange was human nature! In the midst of carnage, men could shout encouragement to their own side in a killing contest as if it were no more than a football match. His vision began to blur as sweat ran into his eyes. Except that it was red sweat and he had no free hand to wipe it away. He shook his head in an attempt to get rid of it, but that only made him so giddy he staggered and almost fell.

Two men loomed up in front of him. They had faces that were curiously familiar. Taking the pilot from him they placed the boy on a stretcher, asking Roland, 'Are you all right, sir?'

'Oh, yes. Be careful, he has both legs broken. There's also a wound in the neck. It's been bleeding all over me.'

They all walked the few yards to the trench. After surviving that open space it seemed almost ludicrous to get into it now. But it was the only thing to do, really. Then they all struggled and squelched along between the broken mud walls where men lay groaning, and people said things to him as he passed.

'Well done, Doc.'

'Splendid effort, old chap!'

'Wait till Fritz hears we've got another Sheridan here.'

'Take a dose of No 9, Doc. You'll soon be as right as rain!'

'Hoo-bloomin' ray!'

'If you Sheridans want to fight the war by yourselves, it's all right by me.'

Then they all scrambled into an underground ruin that reminded Roland of Croix Des Anges. Sergeant Clyde loomed up in front of him.

'This was the driest place I could find, sir.'

Propping himself up with a hand against the wall, Roland looked around and saw nothing but a blur. He was feeling very giddy and hardly able to stand the pain in his shoulder now.

'It's very nice, Sergeant.'

'Glad you like it, Mr Sheridan. But I take it you won't be staying long.'

'Not just now,' he muttered. 'Well, carry on, Sergeant.'

'Yessir.'

On the point of going with an orderly to the waiting ambulance, he turned painfully and managed to ask, 'By the way, does anyone happen to know if my brother got away safely?'

The sergeant's grin was definitely roaming all over his face as Roland studied it. 'Oh yes, sir. Major Sheridan flew over waggling his wings like mad before he took off with the rest of the "Arrows". I'd give a fiver to see his face when he finds out it was you he was protecting out there with his overhead daring to draw their fire.'

Roland's nod was nearly his undoing. 'Yes, I think I'd give a fiver, too, Sergeant. Is the assault still on?'

The N.C.O. sobered. 'At ten ack emma, sir.'

'I'll try to get back for it,' promised Roland wondering what the time was now. Surely there ought to be bacon and sizzling sausages, or a jolly nice kipper or two waiting for him somewhere.

The tiny village of Passchendaele was finally taken by Canadian troops in pouring rain on 6 November. But disasters in the other theatres of war such as the Russian Front, the Balkans, and Italy forced the Allies to abandon their plans to push on with the major campaign on the Western Front. The troops around Ypres were told to dig in for the winter. There was little else for them to do but go underground, because the entire area for miles around was a plain of cratered mud; a graveyard for men, horses and machines. There was no building, ruin, tree, stump, or human life save those that wandered wild-eyed through the ghoulish sewers of war.

The cost over the three months it had taken to gain this was two hundred and fifty thousand British lives. But the men in the Ypres sector stayed to face another winter, because they had always stayed. Despite the chorus of protest that was growing on the Home Front, they had been through too much to give up now. Each and every one of them would not go home until the enemy was totally conquered so that there would never be another war of this nature. Ypres had become to the British what Verdun was to the French. When it was eventually re-built, its foundations would be the bones of men from Britain and her Dependencies.

Roland was given ten days' leave in November. He had looked forward to going home for so long, yet now the opportunity was there it almost seemed a hurdle he was reluctant to tackle. Those last days of the third great battle of Ypres had exceeded anything he had yet experienced and had left him, like those around him, in a hiatus that made it difficult to relate with the past, or even contemplate the future. How could he adjust to such things as sitting on a train, eating a decent dinner in a restaurant, driving in a pony and trap through green country lanes bright with holly berries, lying in a real bed and hearing nothing but birdsong and the bleating of sheep outside? What could he speak of to people like Priddy and Dawkins? How would he ever find a level of rapport with Tessa, or talk to Chris in his present state? They all seemed unreal; the only people he really knew were those around him now. They had become his family, his friends, his sole reason for existence. What if he went home and found none of it as he had remembered? What if all those things he had always valued turned out to have no value at all?

So, in that state of mind, he gladly delayed his departure one more day in order to accept an invitation from the Arrow Squadron. For his rescue of the young pilot he was to be awarded the Military Cross, and the famous squadron had sent their thanks with a standing invitation to dinner and total inebriation. It had arrived by Rex's unique postal system. Accompanying it had been congratulations and surprise that it had been his own brother he had protected during the rescue, and the message ended with a comment that he supposed he would now have to suffer the tiresome business of always being asked if he was the famous *Roland* Sheridan's brother.

With his kit all packed Roland departed amidst the usual caustic and pithy remarks about the dainty little damsels waiting to lead young officers astray in London, and he climbed into the sidecar of a motor cycle in which he had begged a lift to the village near Rex's airfield. It was raining, as usual, and the only way traffic could move around in that area was on the artificial roads constructed by the R.E.'s. It was slow going, and Roland sat in the downpour hunched into the greatcoat that had not been dry for a month. But he was lost in thoughts of Rex.

It would be good to see him again after that last occasion at Croix Des Anges, when his brother had played the mouth-organ in an old cellar, and Roland had feared he might have lost touch with someone he had grown up with and loved. Now, he knew what Rex had known then; understood so much that he had never comprehended before. He would tell Rex this, show him that the gap between them had never really been there. He would also ask about Chris's strange letter. He had it with him in his pocket.

The motor cycle pulled up. There was congestion ahead. A supply-cart had slipped off the road into the mud and was stuck fast. The ancient skinny horse pulling it was struggling madly in the slime, but had no hope of shifting it, despite the lashing it was being given by the driver maddened by the curses and suggestions of all those delayed by him. Roland was immediately reminded of the horses so fiercely defended by Rosalind in Guillehoek, and climbed to the road, filled with the same hot anger he had experienced that day.

Pushing his way past the line of traffic halted in the murk of that November day, he advanced on the scene, his anger growing every minute. The poor beast was being brutally treated and was helpless to retaliate. His equine brethren had been used abominably and unforgivably in something that they could never of themselves create. The horse was a noble creature, in Roland's eyes, not a four-legged machine to be beaten, kicked, ripped apart, then left to lie bleeding by the roadside until its flesh was cut from the bones and eaten by those who had used it without compassion.

'Stop that at once,' he roared, reaching the tilting cart. 'Brutishness will solve nothing.'

The man looked round angrily, saw his accoster was an officer, and clamped his mouth over the imprecation he was plainly about to use.

'If you have that much strength and energy to spare, it might be more sensible to use it in attempting to pull the cart out,' snapped Roland. 'My God, how often do I have to point out the obvious to dolts who have less sense than the creatures they're abusing?' He looked around at all those queueing in line. 'Get off your backsides and over there, pronto!'

There was a general scramble to leave vehicles, and soldiers shambled along the slippery surface of mud, knowing in advance what they were going to be told to do. None of them had much heart for it. It was easier and drier to sit where they were and let someone else sort it out. This officer was a doctor, of all things. What did he know about horses and transport?

Having set them to pushing and heaving Roland went round to release the horse from the shafts until the cart had been righted. But it was not as exhausted as he feared, and had had enough lashing to make it want only to get away. Once free of the traces, it tossed its head in fear and lunged before Roland had a firm hold of the leathers. Unable to go forward or backward on the road, it veered straight into the quagmire, bucking and struggling against the sucking mud that brought it to a speedy halt. There it remained, rolling its eyes and whinneying with fright.

But Roland was an expert horseman. He understood and loved the creatures, knowing exactly what to do in such a situation.

Stepping off the road into the mud he began to fight his way toward the trapped horse, speaking to it in tones he knew would calm and reassure it. He spoke to it as a friend; an old beloved and trusted friend. The horse instantly responded to that instinct that tells an animal there is a bond to be had with the creature called man. Its brown eyes looked back at Roland with quiet confidence. It stopped whinneying and blew through its nostrils in a message of friendship.

Roland had just come up to it and taken hold of the bridle, when someone on the road shouted, 'Watch what you're doing, sir, that's an old mine-field.'

But his hand was on the long velvety nose, and he was renewing a never-forgotten brotherhood when the world ended.

Deeply regret Lieutenant R. M. Sheridan M.C. R.A.M.C. killed in action November eleventh. The Army council express sympathy.

24

THE NEWS of his brother's death reached Chris via Rex. He found it difficult to handle, as he confessed to Bill Chandler.

'I ought to feel as shattered as Rex plainly does, and it seems the most terrible betrayal to someone with whom I must once have had a very close relationship, *not* to feel that way. Instead, I somehow feel cheated. Roland went off to France before I had even accepted my own identity, so I've had no chance to get to know and like him, as I've had with Rex. As for his many letters, they were full of references to things I still don't remember, and told me little about him as a person. Only recently did I sense that he might have been a person of strong passions. Now, it's too late.

I think we had quarelled over something once, and I've lost the chance to put it right.'

Chandler said quietly, 'That kind of thing happens to all of us, Chris. It's not a curse of your condition. There's not a man, woman or child who hasn't regrets over something that can't be unsaid or undone.'

Due to his unease Chris turned on him. 'They at least know what it is that they regret. Have you any idea what it's like to feel most awfully guilty and not know why? Do you? I don't even know which of us was to blame.'

'Oh, come on, lad, you've got too much intelligence to trot out that piece of pathos. In a quarrel neither person is entirely in the right or wrong.'

'All right, all right,' conceded Chris, worked up by his frustration and bewilderment. 'But was it over some unimportant thing that grew out of all proportion, or had one or other of us done something almost unforgivable? *You know.* For God's sake tell me.'

The doctor shook his head. 'You have to find out for yourself.'

'You're always the bloody same! I think you *want* me to withdraw again. It would give you a holiday for a few months—or a few *years.*'

'No it wouldn't. I'd be given another patient, who wouldn't be half as interesting as you,' the older man said with his usual calm. 'Let's have a "for instance". Suppose I told you Roland had accidentally bumped into you one day causing you to knock a pot of ink over your treasured copy of Plato, and you jumped up to throw a punch to his jaw on the very day he was off to meet a very special lady friend, knocking out two of his front teeth. You both lost your tempers, ending with your vow never to forgive him for the ruined book. How would you feel? Remorseful, guilty, wanting to don a hair shirt for the rest of your days, because the book can be replaced and your brother can't?

'Or suppose I said you had taken his prize horse without his permission, and fallen at a fence causing the animal to be destroyed. He had vowed never to forgive *that.* How would you feel? Remorseful, guilty, wanting to don a hair shirt for the rest of your days?' He leant forward to look Chris in the face. 'The cause is immaterial, old son. You've got to accept this as you've had to accept everything else over the past two years. But if it helps to lash out at me, be my guest.'

Chris's wrath left him, and he got up feeling the need to move about. 'Not when you're being so damned calm and reasonable.' He walked haltingly to the end of his conservatory room with the aid of the one stick that was all he now needed, then stood gazing at the busy ward on the other side of the glass. If he could be in there with those men he might not feel so bad. If his family was going to be taken from him, he wished he had never acquired them. Rex was back at the Front. What would he do if he lost his red-haired brother, too? There would be no one.

Still gazing at the patients chatting to each other in the ward, he said, 'Are you prepared to tell me about my parents . . . or are they part of my dark secret?'

'Why the sudden interest?'

He turned round carefully. 'I just wondered if . . .' He hesitated to voice something that might sound sentimental. 'I know my mother died soon after I was born, but there are books amongst my things that were given to me by my father. The inscriptions inside them are emotionless, so he apparently had no love for me. Was it something I had done?'

'Not as I understand it. He never stopped grieving for his wife, so all his emotion went into that. He treated all three of you the same way.'

'I see.' The implications of that produced another idea. 'So it's feasible that I looked on Roland as a father-figure instead. He was five years older.'

'It's feasible.'

Chris fell silent as he walked painstakingly back across the area. It strengthened his theory regarding that little boy of Marion's who looked so unmistakably a Sheridan. A schoolboy who looked up to an older brother almost as to a parent would certainly be shocked and horrified to find he had sired a bastard, especially if the mother was a long-standing childhood friend of his own.

At that point his restlessness and complex frustration over the death of his brother he had never come to know was pushed violently aside by the realisation that Marion would probably now be heartbroken. She might be the mother of his brother's child, but she was not the next of kin. Who would tell her of Roland's death? He began to fill with compassion for her. He imagined how he would feel if Laura were killed and he heard of it through the casual conversation of others. His hands clenched into fists as he thought about the poor girl grieving alone and ignored. Would Rex have written to her? The pair were friends, and he had certainly sent a letter to break the news to Tessa, who did *not* have Roland's child, but was running his estate. Bill Chandler was apparently consoling her. But who was consoling Marion Deacon, who should rightly be Marion Sheridan?

Chris could not sleep that night, although he had actually asked for a draught of the stuff he had so often spat out in the past. He had had a bad day. It had been a long time since fears and vague unrecognisable images had left him morose and utterly despondent. After Bill Chandler had left, Chris had sat staring out at the mid-November gloom in something approaching the despair of earlier days. He had never known a mother; his father had apparently ignored him. Roland was dead just as he was proposing to reach out to him. His other brother was out there fighting in a war that seemed likely to take everyone into its jaws. Laura loved Rex to the exclusion of anyone else. Chandler regarded him simply as an interesting medical case. And his friend, Marion Deacon, had given her all to his brother and was now isolated inside her grief, no doubt. Who was left? What was the use of going on? He was again nobody from nowhere.

Lying there hour after hour in the ghostly green light of the hospital night system and listening to the rain being smashed against his surrounding glass by buffeting winds, he reviewed what he knew of himself.

Christopher Wesley Sheridan, youngest of three brothers with a close bond of love and friendship that had probably been strengthened further by lack of parental influence or interest. Christopher Wesley Sheridan, pupil of Charterhouse School, brilliant classics scholar, brilliant mathematician, brilliant linguist, amateur poet, amateur artist. Christopher Wesley Sheridan, Second-Lieutenant, unwanted interpreter, unwanted code-breaker, unwanted *anything* on the barren cliff-sides of Gallipoli. Too blind to fight, too aesthetic to cope with blood and guts, too artistic to draw useful sketches of enemy gun-emplacements, too beautiful to have a normal male friendship. *You have the most beautiful eyes of any boy I've seen.*

The serpent of a distant nightmare wriggled inside him at that. *You have the most beautiful eyes.* Why did he sense that his eyes were somehow significant beyond measure? He had been naked when Neil had said that to him. So it had not been his body alone that had attracted the man, but his eyes unmasked by spectacles. Yes, he had been swimming and had just climbed up onto a rock when it had happened. He had not seen Neil's expression, because he had been groping for the spectacles at the time. The other man's figure had been no more than a blur.

The serpent wriggled again. Those spectacles were of enormous importance. Without them, he was helpless, yet removing them was also his greatest weapon. Marion used to accuse him of 'hiding' by taking them off, but they were his means of dismissing people. Except that he saw now that it had been an illusion, like the ostrich hiding his head in the sand. They were still there, and as they retreated into blurs for him so he was somehow revealed in greater clarity to them.

Turning restlessly on his bed he stared at the changing silvery patterns made by rain gusting against the windows. Day after day, it was like looking at life without his spectacles, yet everyone else looked back and saw him with perfect clarity.

Going back over it all again he concentrated on himself as a child. It was more than likely he had seen Roland as a father-figure. Since the cricket-match he knew he had looked on Rex as his *only* friend. His *only* friend? Why? How about Marion? How about his schoolfellows?

Codrington's father is with the Foreign Office and the trip is off due to this scare in the Balkans.

Who was Codrington, and what trip was off? Something back in 1914, obviously, when the overture to the war was striking up.

He rolled his head to stare at the glass separating him from the inner ward, as the brief recollection of those words slipped back into the mists of his mind again. Nothing to glean from the child Christopher.

How about the schoolboy? A brilliant scholar; a boy with intelligence so rare it enabled him to master languages, mathematics and conundrums with ease. In addition, he was fascinated and absorbed by visual beauty as well as that of the written word. An introvert, surely. A boy, then, who would not need friends; a boy who was happiest when alone with all those things that fulfilled the desires of his mind and senses. Why would such a boy rush to the colours as a volunteer? Conscription had not been introduced until well into 1916, so joining the army must have been a voluntary act on his part. It made no sense. This boy he had apparently been would not lust for battle; would shy from violence and aggression. So why had he joined the army at the age of eighteen of his own free will? Why?

Chris reached for the glass of water beside the bed and drank thirstily. He remembered Rochford-Clarke before half his head had been blown away, saying that he had volunteered because one of his schoolfriends had won a posthumous V.C. Maybe Christopher Wesley Sheridan had done it for the same reason. Yet an introverted schoolboy aesthete would hardly have the type of friend to rush off to war and win an award for extreme gallantry in battle.

Exhausted by going over and over the same facts, Chris took off his spectacles and put them beside his pillow. He was then left with the same mist before his eyes as there was behind them. *You have the most beautiful eyes . . .* No, no, forget that strangely significant phrase and concentrate on what he had recently deduced. The oldest brother he had regarded with respect and admiration had seduced a childhood friend and sired a bastard boy. There must have been a terrible scandal, at the time, and Marion's father had understandably cut off every member of the Sheridan family from that time on. Would such a situation have been enough to drive this secret boy to go to war? Would it, together with Neil Frencham's declaration of love, have driven him to seek death at the top of a cliff? Would it? Perhaps . . . with one additional circumstance. Had that eighteen-year-old boy felt unbearably betrayed by Marion, also? Had he been so dedicated in friendship to her that her willing seduction by his own brother had been more than he could face?

He began to feel sick, and sweat broke out over his body. The clock showed it was 1 a.m. The hour when men often slipped away from the world in these hospitals. How often had he lain and watched the silent-footed men and women in white coats, their faces macabre in the dim green lights, wheel away the beds to that place from which the occupants never returned? It was the loneliest hour of the twenty-four.

All at once, he was terrified. Rex had told him to go in search of the missing piece, but he felt so close to finding it now he wanted to go no further. He recognised the signs. Flashes of images that went too fast for him to really see details; disconnected fragments of conversation by unrecognised people. He was on the edge of that abyss again. The thing that was so unfaceable he had held out for two years rather than have to live with it, was knocking on the door of his memory demanding entry. He was powerless now to refuse it. He was doomed to that limbo that yawned threateningly before him. Suppose he returned this time to find he was an old, old man, and everyone else was dead, like Roland, darling Laura, Rex, Marion, Tessa, even Bill Chandler. And that little boy with the Sheridan face would be middle-aged and fighting in another war somewhere. Suppose he never returned, and this was his last living moment?

Groping frenziedly for his spectacles he rang the bell for a nurse, then stared at her speechlessly because he had expected to see Marion. But he grasped her hand and would not let it go in case he slipped away. Another nurse came and sent the first one off in a hurry. He was feeling so ill by now he was finding it difficult to breathe. Then Dr Chandler was there speaking calmly to him, telling him to inhale to his count of ten, then exhale to another ten. The exercise was repeated until the pain in his chest began to ease, and he found he could breathe normally again. A nurse brought him a cup of tea, and he sat up to drink it. But his hands were shaking so violently he spilt most of it in the saucer. At that point he asked for a needle in his arm, but Bill Chandler told him not to be a fool.

'You've passed that stage, boy. That's sublimating the brain to the body. You now have to do the reverse. Conquer it, or it'll conquer you.'

He remained by the bed, talking in quiet reassuring manner while Chris quaked and shook throughout the time it took for the hands of the clock to reach one-thirty. By then, he was beginning to answer the grey-haired man in pyjamas and dressing-gown, who looked so much like Neil Frencham. By 2 a.m. he was talking freely. By two-thirty he even managed a laugh. By 3 a.m. he was falling asleep, lulled by the astonishing revelation that Bill Chandler did not merely regard him as an interesting medical case. The scholarly introvert who had not needed friends had turned into a

500

young man desperately seeking them. He had found one that night.

When Chris awoke he grabbed his spectacles to look at the calendar. It was still November. Thank God! Then a renewed spurt of fear made him look again, before falling back onto the pillows with a faint smile of triumph. Yes, it was still 1917.

By that mid-afternoon he could deny his resolution no longer. Waiting for the busy period when nurses were occupied with taking tea-trays round, he took his greatcoat from the locker and left by the door to the garden. Skirting the house he made his way through the shrubbery to break through into the lane leading down to the village. After the rain of the day and night before the ground was marshy, giving his boots a smearing of mud and dead leaves. The wet branches of the banks of rhododendrons dampened his thick khaki coat, and sent icy drops down his neck as he parted them on his way through. But it was a cold bright day with clouds that raced across the sun to provide a chequer-board of light and shade over the countryside around him, and he felt invigorated just to be out in it.

Although the lane was slippery where autumn leaves had fallen in patches beneath the chestnut-trees, he kept up a regular limping pace with his stick finding dry patches that provided safe support for him. But his gladness at all he saw around him began to dim as he thought of why he had made his escape that afternoon. Had he been too impetuous? There was no guarantee that Marion would be there at the end of his efforts, and even less guarantee that she would agree to see him. If her father refused to allow him in, that would be the end of it. He could hardly force entry into a house where a member of his family had brought scandal and sadness.

Halting at the bottom of the lane for a moment's rest, he wondered if he should turn back. But there was a strong urge driving him on. When he had been helpless, terrified, and in need of some anchor, Marion had apparently come to his bedside to be that anchor. If her friendship for him was still that strong despite what his brother had done, he must try to be her anchor now. It was the very least he could do.

He set off again finding the blustery wind too chilly to stand still for long. Then, as he was nearing the gate to the Deacons' house he saw Marion walking along the lane toward him carrying a shopping basket with supplies she had just fetched from the village shop. The little boy was plodding at her side, his sturdy body warmly clad in a fawn coat and buttoned gaiters, the flaxen hair covered by a woollen helmet of the same colour. The dogs trotted back and forth behind the pair, tails swinging happily in the delight of their walk.

She saw Chris and stopped in her tracks. It seemed to him that she drew the boy almost protectively behind the skirt of her blue overcoat. A pin-prick of hurt jabbed him at this sign that she feared him still. His steps slowed as he limped past her gate and up to where she stood. The resolution that had been so strong up there at Tarrant Hall began to waver now they were face-to-face. What could he say to her; how must he approach such a subject?

But she spoke first, and sounded full of apprehension. 'What are you doing in the village?'

'I was coming to see you.'

'What about?' It was very sharp, and the little boy appeared to be pushed even further behind the coat skirts.

Floundering, feeling inadequate to the task he had set himself, he said, 'Couldn't we go indoors?'

'No. I'm sorry, Chris, but I'd rather you didn't upset Daddy again. He's not very well, at present.' She looked upset herself. 'Are you supposed to be out all on your own?'

The question angered him. 'I'm not a prisoner . . . or a madman. Whatever I once did to you, it doesn't mean I go around attacking everyone I meet.'

The face that had been rosy from a brisk wind a moment before paled, and she took a step back from him.

'I'm sorry,' he offered immediately. 'Oh God, I'm making an awful mess of this. I can guess how you must feel about us all, but I *had* to come. I know what it's like to feel lost and alone. Whatever I did that you find unforgivable, we were close friends once. Rex is over there in Ypres, but I am on the spot to represent the family. I just wanted to say that if there's anything I can do for you, or the little boy, please tell me. What's his name, by the way?'

She was staring at him with wild eyes. 'You *still* don't remember?'

'No.' He reached out to put a comforting hand on her arm, but she moved back again. His own arm dropped back to his side. 'After that last time, I put two and two together. It wasn't difficult to come up with the answer. I'm more sorry than I can say, Marion.' He swallowed, conscious that he was making heavy weather of it. 'But Roland's dead now—a very honourable death —and someone has to stand in for him. I'm afraid there isn't anyone but me.'

She seemed very upset as tears began glassing her eyes. But, on the verge of trying again to touch her arm, Chris was spotted by the two labradors who rushed up to him in barking delight, leaping up to put muddy paws all over his greatcoat and upsetting his balance. All his attention was taken by them as he bent over trying to calm them and keep them on all fours. But their excitement was too great to be calmed in a moment and, next minute, one reared up to lick his nose, knocking his spectacles to the ground before he could catch them. All he could see then was a moving blur of black against the brown lane as the dogs continued to mill around him. Stooping he groped on the ground at his feet, to no avail.

He looked up at Marion. 'I say, can you see my spectacles . . . any . . . where?' He finished slowly as he saw the blurred vision of a girl who appeared to be wearing a blue bell.

Codrington's father is with the Foreign Office, so the trip is off due to this Balkans scare. You don't have much faith in my ability, do you? No one achieves anything with a negative attitude like yours, Marion.

They were by the stream, and she was standing in it with a blue dress held up free of the water. It was a hot day and he was walking home because he had forgotten to let them know he was coming. It was the long summer holiday of 1914.

The spectacles were pushed into his hand, and it was shaking as he replaced them on his nose, fastening the shanks over his ears. November had vanished, and it was high summer. The girl before him stood with her arms behind her sheltering a child, but he saw her on a carnival float chained to some railings, in that same pose, breasts outthrust. He was in a frenzy to touch them. They went somewhere dark. *I say, have you seen my spectacles? Come and get them!* Her body was now naked, and he was struggling with his trousers so that he could get on top of her. There were curtains with flowers all around them, and it was the most exciting irresistible experience of his life. They were both crying.

'Chris. Chris! Are you all right!'

He tried to move, but one leg was cumbersome. There was a stick in his hand that helped him to walk. November returned with a rush that caused vertigo.

'I . . . I didn't let them know I was coming. I'd better . . . I must go before . . .' He began to limp away.

'Can I get someone to help you?'

Oh God, those curtains with flowers were the same ones he had seen whilst lying on the couch in Dr Deacon's surgery! He tried to deny the fact, but he saw them too clearly.

'Chris, let me get someone from the Hall.'

'No. I . . . I can manage. It's not . . . far. It's not far.'

Have you been alone with Miss Deacon in her father's house under compromising circumstances? Chris, I wouldn't have said anything, but I had to.

'Please wait there. I'll get Daddy.'

'There's no need. I have to get back. If it's going to happen . . . must get back!'

'Chris, please!'

He was walking, but no number of miles would give him escape now. The voices were speaking fast and furious, condemning him, breaking him apart.

My girl is carrying your child, and it's going to have a legal father if I have to force you to church at the end of a rifle.

I can't marry her. I'm going up to Cambridge tomorrow.

You bloody little fool! You threw away your whole life when you let your body rule your head. I won't have any bastards bearing our name.

You should have learnt the golden rule that ensures you never get into this predicament.

It's so damned unfair. She asked for it.

They all do. You read enough Greek and French odes to passion to be aware of that.

None of them mentions babies and forced marriages.

Would it have stopped you if they had?

Oh God, Rex, I just don't know how I'm going to get through the next sixty years.

It was there for all the world to see—a small red-faced symbol of his lost life that screamed night and day so that he could hear it wherever he went. It smelt of vomit and urine. Before that, it had been inside that great swollen belly, and everyone knew he had put it there. In five short minutes he had put it there. Because of that, he had to talk of milk yield, lambing, manure and fertilisers; he had to tramp about in gum-boots through wind and snow, growing as dull and moronic as the sheep he had to help haul from deep drifts. She was all right. She had got what she wanted. But she had taken *everything* from him, and would continue to do so for as long as he lived. Oh God, how was he going to face the next sixty years?

He found himself leaning on that same bridge, and he felt terribly ill. His heart was thumping painfully; his arm holding the stick ached. He was much too hot, and waves of giddiness washed over him. Taking off the spectacles to wipe the lenses, he saw again that blur of a girl paddling in the stream. But it kept changing into a man in uniform, with grey hair and a friendly smile.

You look awfully different without your spectacles, Chris.

You have the most beautiful eyes of any boy I've seen.

Come and get them!

You looked so beautiful standing there naked, and those eyes with the long lashes curling over them were more than I could stand. I've grown to love you.

I didn't intend to ruin your life, Chris. I did it for love.

The voices in his head went on and on, until he also heard his own, harsh and accusing, full of emotion.

Well, I did it for lust . . . and lust has now gone cold. You'll never make love grow in me, Marion.

I gave you my eager friendship and you destroyed it all with your obscene perverted confession. You've destroyed all I had left!

He gripped the stone wall in despair that matched the other of nearly three years ago. They had turned him down at the recruiting office because of his eyes. Always his bloody eyes! But he had fooled them; fooled them for days. Except that he had not known which were men and which were bags of hay, and he had been continually afraid they would find out and send him back to Marion. *That* was why he had not written to Roland, because she was at Tarrant Hall.

Then, penetrating the past, came present grief. Roland was dead! The loyal, steadfast man with impossibly high standards which he demanded from himself as well as others, the good-looking horseman, the Squire of Tarrant Royal who dedicated himself to the village and its residents had gone forever. A beloved brother who had sacrificed his medical studies and his treasured horses in order to pay for an academic future that had been thrown away for a schoolboy's lust; that same beloved brother who had visited the hospital in the hope of being recognised, and who had written so many letters that had earned just one reply.

The cause of the quarrel is immaterial, old son. You've got to accept this as you've had to accept everything over the past two years.

But he could not accept it! Eighteen years of growing up with Roland could not be put aside easily now he had recalled them. His shoulders began to heave as he cried for those eighteen years, for all the letters he had not written, for those times he had sat in a bed silently staring at a fair-haired man in tweeds, denying brotherhood: for remembering it all too late!

In his grief he slithered and slipped down the bank to the stream and hobbled a short way into the copse, where he grew racked with sobbing as he leant against a tree. The motor cycle followed by an ambulance passed over the bridge in both directions without his being aware of them. Neither was he aware of voices calling his name from the roadside. They all moved on again shortly afterward.

Exhausted and cold Chris leant against that tree, slowly remembering all those early days before life caught up with them all. Father, remote and eccentric; Priddy a cross between aunt and servant, but the nearest to a mother any of them knew. Then Father's suicide. How well he now understood a man being driven to such means of escape. How much better it would have been for everyone if Neil had not stopped him from doing the same thing. Or if they had let him die at Gallipoli.

He moved away from the stream. It was growing cold and he had to seek refuge before they found him and took him back to Tarrant Hall. It was difficult to climb the bank back to the road. Each step was an effort, and he was shaking from head to foot. He could not possibly go back now . . . now he knew that he had a wife, and a baby that screamed night and day. Where had she put it? Had it died, like Roland? Even then, he could not go back. He had once wanted to end his life rather than do so.

Is this terrible thing connected with Marion?

It isn't terrible, Chris. I swear it isn't.

But it was! It was terrible enough to send him to war; to make

506

him, when added to an overture of love from a man he had thought of as a substitute for Rex, want to climb up a cliff to his death. His eyes and his body, that's all anyone wanted from him. They ridiculed his brain. They had humiliated him by scorning his skills at languages, his knowledge of codes, his gift of sketching landscapes. All they had wanted was another bag of hay. Knowledge counted for nothing.

You're so proud of your bloody brain, why aren't you as proud of your body? It's a very fine one.

Beautiful eyes . . . so beautiful standing there naked.

I did it for love, Chris.

. . . long lashes curling over them was more than I could stand. I've come to love you.

Come and get them!

The voices went on and on. He was trapped; tied hand and foot. His face was all bandaged because he only had half a head . . . and his body was a bag of hay. How could he have fathered a child in just five minutes behind those flowered curtains?

It was growing dark and he was drenched with sweat. Or was it rain? It was running down his face like tears. Roland was dead. Why did men die so easily when they had no wish to, yet find death out of reach when it was the only thing they wanted?

He felt so tired he wanted to drift into sleep and wake up as an old, old man. Everyone would be dead then, except a middle-aged man who looked like Christopher Wesley Sheridan. Would he also have beautiful eyes and a beautiful body? Would he be insane?

Then a new voice began repeating words in his mind, making him answer things he did not wish to say.

What would you do if I locked you in with a beautiful red-head? I'd do all she'd let me before smacking my face. What would you do with a beautiful red-head? I'd do all I could . . . What would you do with a red-head? I'd do . . . I'd do . . . Do with a red-head? I'd . . . I'd . . .

It seemed he was walking and walking forever while those words rang in his head, banishing all the others. Then, a face rose up before him. A face with whiskers, like King Edward.

'No money for a ticket, Mr Christopher. You'm always the same, sir. Since a little lad. No, sir, you cahn't get on there without a ticket. It's agin the law.'

He sat for a long while in a warm bubble and dreamed of her.

She was standing out on a terrace dressed like a goddess, with the sun on her flaming hair. He thought she looked the most beautiful creature he had ever seen. He wanted to take off her clothes and lie on top of her. But Rex stopped him. Now Marion was stopping him. But he still wanted to do it, and he must tell her before it was too late. Before she died, like Roland.

The face loomed up in front of him again, but it had no whiskers now. 'Laura Sheridan? She's halfway through the show. You can't see her now. Are you feeling all right, sir? Can I fetch someone to take you home?'

'Can't go home.' His mouth would hardly form the words. 'Must . . . must see her. Say it's . . . it's . . .'

'Say it's who, sir?'

'Sheri . . . Sheridan.'

'Sherry Sheridan? Blimey, are you her husband? Here, Jock, is this gent Miss Sheridan's husband?'

'Nah . . . but 'ee looks a bit like 'im. What's it all about?'

'Seems ill, if you ask me.'

'Well, better tell her. Just in case.'

Laura was suddenly there, her lovely face frightened, asking him all kinds of questions. But he was so tired he could no longer speak. They sat in a room full of rails with clothes hanging on them. He was there a long time, and an old woman in a black dress gave him a cup of tea. Laura came back and took him off in a car somewhere. The streets were crowded with people. The driver helped him up a great number of steps to a set of rooms. Laura gave the man money, then shut the door. When he realised why he had come, he knew she would be frightened of him, as Marion was.

'I won't hurt you,' he mumbled, swaying as he gripped the stick. 'I did it for love.'

She was smiling at him, not in the least frightened. 'What a funny thing to say. Here, drink this, my dear.'

'What is it?' He was always suspicious of glasses.

'Uncle Rex's medicine for times like these.'

To his horror he began to cry. She took the glass away from him again, and slipped her hand through his arm.

'Is it Roland, my dear?'

He was unable to answer.

'Does Major Chandler know you're here?'

He shook his head.

'Would you like me to tell him?'

He shook his head again.

'All right, let's talk about it in the morning. Come to bed. You look exhausted and drenched through.' She began leading him into an adjoining room. 'God knows how you ever got as far as London . . . but you must have been pretty damn desperate.'

Talking about how the show had gone that evening she took off his overcoat, jacket and tie. Then she pushed him gently onto the bed while she removed his boots. It was wonderful lying there beneath an amber-coloured eiderdown with the warmth and glow of a fire in the blue-tiled hearth. He no longer wanted to take off all his clothes and lie on top of her. It would give her a swollen body and a baby that never stopped screaming. She was too lovely for that, and he loved her too much.

Next minute, she was beside him beneath the eiderdown, in a soft fluffy robe that smelt of dark red roses. It was enough just to put his cheek against it and feel the softness, even though his cheeks were still wet. She seemed not to notice that as she stroked his springy hair and sighed into the flame-flickered darkness.

'I'm such a pushover for men called Sheridan. This is what comes of accepting *his* kind of four weeks.'

The words meant nothing to him. He knew he could sleep now and wake to find it was no more than the next day. All the time she was there holding him, he could not withdraw into that dreaded limbo.

Her face was the first thing he saw when he opened his eyes. It was a blur until she put the spectacles over his nose. Then he saw what he had dreamed of so many times. A pointed face, with creamy skin suggesting fragility, yet with wicked sparkling eyes that suggested all kinds of other things. It was framed by red-gold hair that caught the light as she moved, and fell in soft waves to her shoulders. For a brief moment he thought he was there with a goddess of love, until she spoke, and fantasy fled.

'I'm filled with admiration, my dear. You can out-sleep even me. It's mid-afternoon.' She put down the small tray she was holding and sat on the edge of the bed. 'Are you hungry?'

He shook his head on the pillow.

'At least drink some tea. I made it with my own fair hand, and a great many men would give a fortune for the privilege.'

'I'm most dreadfully in love with you,' he told her, knowing it had to be confessed.

She smiled gravely. 'I rather thought you might be. Is that why you came to me last night?'

'Yes.'

'Why last night?'

He lay gazing at her while he thought out the answer. 'Because it was too late to say all the things I should have said to Roland. Because Rex might never return for me to say them to him. I'm on the edge of having to surrender you forever, and I had to tell you before it was also too late.'

She gazed back at him with those marvellous green eyes now darkened by incomprehension. 'You're always far too clever for me, Chris.'

'That's what everyone says. I can't help it.'

'I know you can't . . . any more than I can help being beautiful. But beauty is no mystery. A great mind is. You should let people into it more often, my dear. It's part of that mystery that you found me last night. You were in a state of physical collapse.'

There was something he had to ask her first. 'Laura, are you frightened of me?'

'*Frightened* of you? Why ever should I be?'

'I somehow knew you'd say that,' he told her, loving her more and more with every minute. 'Yesterday I started to remember. When that happens . . . well, you know without my having to tell you. There were too many things coming at me all at once. I couldn't cope with them. That . . . that black limbo began to beckon to me. I think I almost went there, Laura, but you beckoned me even more.'

She regarded him for a moment or two, then said, 'You're shivering! Come on, drink some of this tea. I'll poke up the fire. As it's Sunday, I don't have to go to the theatre tonight, so we have all the time you want.'

He watched her as she moved across to the blue-tiled hearth to take up the poker. The dark-green velvet of her dress gleamed in the light of the flames that leapt higher as the logs split open at her touch. Her lovely curved body was outlined by the clinging material as she arched forward. *I have a wife and baby. Goodbye dreams and hopes!* Then she walked to draw aside the heavy damask curtains, and he was surprised to see the hard bright light of snow, with huge twirling flakes brushing the window. Turning to smile at him she was framed like a red-haired cameo against the winter scene. *I have a wife and baby. Goodbye happiness!*

'Snow always looks so beautiful from inside a warm room. If only we hadn't to go outside and spoil the illusion,' she said in what was almost an echo of his thoughts.

He sat up slowly and reached for the tea. She made no comment on the fact that the cup was rattling in the saucer between sips. She had returned to sit on the side of the bed, and he was not sure what to say to her now.

'Are you feeling better now, Chris?'

He nodded. 'Yes, thanks. Are . . . are you going to tell Rex I spent the night here?'

'Not if you don't want me to. It's just something between us, isn't it?'

He forgot the tea. 'You are the most wonderful person I've ever met.'

She picked up his mutilated hand from where it lay on the eiderdown. 'If that's the case, can't you tell me the real reason you made that incredible bid to reach me last night?'

It did not seem to matter that she saw his injuries that he had always tried to hide from her before. He had come to her out of terror, and now he must confess the cause of it.

'There was nowhere else to go. At Tarrant Hall there would be that limbo awaiting me. Rex told me to go out and meet it, but I'd gone far enough and baulked at the last hurdle.' He looked down at her slim hand holding his. 'He'd be disappointed in me.'

'No he wouldn't, my dear. Rex thinks you have the most tremendous courage of any person he knows. And so do I. Tell me everything that happened yesterday.'

Because he loved her, because she was somehow part of his dreams of long-ago goddesses and temples, because she was sitting there holding his hand in a warm room that was safe from the chill reality beyond the window, because she had no claim to any part of him he did not want to give, he began to speak to her as he had never been able to speak to any other person in his life.

Soon, words were pouring from him as she sat listening, her eyes shading with various emotions as he described all he had yearned for as a boy, how a girl he had known all his life had suddenly touched some chord in him that had led to the ruin of his hopes and aspirations. He told of the total despair that had led him to go to war as his only means of escape; he described the man he had sought as an anchor in his sea of fears, who had shocked him with an affection that had exacerbated the loathing of physical ravishment he then had.

When he reached the part concerning a lost terrified creature who had been given birth at the age of nineteen in a long room filled with strange people telling him strange things, he broke down, and his hands went up to cradle the head he had once thought halved and bloody. Yet nothing could dam his flood of words now, and he struggled through with a throat swollen and dry, and cheeks that were wet with the tears of remembered hopelessness.

But in the silence that lasted long after he had run out of things to say, he realised something had happened in the telling. Those long-ago boyhood hopes and scholastic aspirations seemed no more than a schoolboy's fervent dreams now. The five minutes on Dr Deacon's examination-couch showed itself as an adolescent experiment practised on the wrong girl, not a cardinal sin for which he must pay with his life. Neil Frencham struck down by a machine-gunner on that cliffside hell, now appeared as a man as desperate and lonely as he, himself, had been then, not a perverted fiend. So much had happened between; life had changed beyond recall.

'Now you have to go back and face them,' said a gentle voice breaking into his profound revelations.

He brought his head from his hands slowly. Laura was still sitting on the bed, but her eyes were overbright and glassy. He nodded, realising she meant Marion, his wife . . . and that little boy, who was his own son, of course. The baby had grown in three years.

'I don't know how,' he confessed. 'It's too sudden, too much of a shock. I hated her so much then.'

'Do you hate her still?'

He frowned. 'I don't know. I really haven't had time to think about it. I liked her very much when I didn't know who she was. I've got used to liking her, I suppose. Can a person revert to feelings of three years ago after that?'

'But she ruined your life.'

'A shell at Gallipoli ruined my life . . . for a while, at any rate.'

'It was because of Marion that you were ever at Gallipoli. She blames herself for everything.'

He shook his head slowly. 'It's too long ago to blame anyone. Now, she hates me. I think I must have hit her, or something.'

Laura got up from the bed, took a piece of bread from the tray beside it, and walked across to pick up the toasting-fork by the hearth. Sitting on the rug she held the bread out toward the flames.

'If Rex ever came back the way you returned from Gallipoli, I couldn't take it, you know. Marion makes me feel worthless. It must have taken tremendous courage to do what she did at the hospital, after the things that had happened to her. Did it ever occur to you that being made pregnant by you also ruined *her* life? She didn't have a brilliant brain and a promising academic career ahead of her, but she had a warm heart, and a vast capacity for life and love. You robbed her of all that, Chris. Even so, she went willingly when she thought her presence and caring would help you through. You sat there like a living corpse held together by bandages . . . a living corpse who didn't know her. Can you imagine her feelings, her thoughts? She stuck it for over a year, neglecting her child in the process, then broke down and was very ill.'

Put that way it made him feel selfish and tremendously guilty. 'My God, no wonder she hates me now.'

Laura turned, the firelight making her skin golden. 'Bring some more bread, will you? I don't think she hates you, my dear, it's just that she's empty of all feeling now. Women can only go on agonising for so long.'

He picked up the plate of bread, scrambled from the bed, and walked across in his socked feet to where she waited. 'If she's no feelings for me, and I've none for her, how can we possibly be a husband and wife? I haven't the first idea what to do now I know the truth. That boy is three years old, and he's my son. The whole idea is ridiculous. I'm only twenty-one.'

'You were only eighteen when you sired him.'

He sat on the edge of the low chair and absentmindedly took the finished piece of toast from her as she picked up a fresh slice of bread to spear with the toasting-fork.

'I knew who I was then. Now, I don't. While that boy has been growing up, I've been standing still.'

Her smile was warm and wonderful. 'No, you haven't, Chris. You've spent the past three years learning to be human.'

They spent the rest of the day in cosy companionship around the fire, watching the snow pile up outside. Chris knew it could not last; that he would have to go out there in the cold lonely world of reality on the following morning. But Laura seemed as anxious as he to preserve the peace and enchantment of make believe as they talked about themselves without reservations. In the process, Chris fell even deeper in love with her, but his guilt dropped away. It was no sin to love his brother's wife; it was only so if he expressed it. So he contented himself with watching her, storing up memories for when he had to leave.

They had a very special supper sitting together in the fire-glow. Maybe it was love for Laura that made the evening so full of enchantment. Maybe it was because he had to return to gigantic decisions on the morrow, or maybe it was that he was still learning to be human. Whichever it might be, he knew there'd never be another evening like it in his life.

They talked nonstop. With growing clarity he was able to recount boyhood days at Tarrant Hall and, if he suspected she listened so intently because there was so much about Rex, he tried not to feel disappointed. Once or twice he had to stop because grief over Roland grew too sharp, but she helped him over his silences.

'Don't let regret haunt you, Chris,' she advised gently. 'I think he might have been hurt at your initial inability to recognise a man you saw only as a suspicious stranger, but he had been out there for months during some of the worst battles and must have come to understand what it was like for you. He was a doctor, don't forget, who would have come across others in the same state.'

'He sent me that cameo,' Chris confessed. 'Rex told me I should give it to a girl some day. I see now he must have meant Marion. Did you tell him about it?'

'Of course. He might have thought it was from an admirer.'

'It was,' he allowed himself to say.

'Although I accept invitations to supper, I always refuse to take gifts from other men,' she went on as if he had not spoken. 'Rex knows that.'

'What did he say about the cameo?'

'Do you want the truth?' she asked.

He nodded, not wanting it at all.

'He said it was time Chandler told you you had a wife of your own.' Seeing his expression, she added, 'He's fond of Marion . . . and his nephew.'

'He always was fond of Marion,' he told her. 'I suppose he compensated for Roland and me. As for the boy, Rex always had every urchin in the village following him around. He used to give them rides on that motor cycle of his. He's that kind of person, isn't he?'

'I suppose he was once. I only saw that side of him for the first time at the cricket-match.'

'Oh, he's tremendous! Do you know, when I left Charterhouse he came to Prizegiving because Father was in Madeira, as usual, and he felt someone ought to be there to see me receive mine.' Laughing at the recollection, he went on, 'He turned up on that motor cycle, in breeches, leather jacket and goggles, frightening everyone when the engine backfired, and walked in to sit with all the toffs in morning-suits without turning a hair. That's typical of dear old Rex.' To his consternation he suddenly noticed she was close to tears. 'I say, have I upset you?'

She shook her head. 'No, it's just me being silly. I miss him so dreadfully since he went back this time.'

'He'll be all right,' he said in clumsy reassurance. 'Rex has got a charmed life. The Huns will never get *him*.'

'That's what he says, and I know he believes it. But . . . he's survived so much. I can't help feeling afraid.' She curled her legs up on the chair and leant back after putting her coffee cup down on the table between them. 'You know, Chris, I was very much like you in 1914. I knew exactly where I was going and what I wanted from life. I had abandoned my strict non-understanding family and was perfectly self-sufficient in my search for stardom. Then I arrived at my digs one night and a man who looked as stunned as I felt kissed me within the first five minutes. I tried to fight it, but I knew I had surrendered my independence, my dreams and myself. Without him I'm nothing—me, Laura Sheridan, this girl in front of you. She sits around waiting for him to appear without warning—which is what he usually does—so that she can come alive again. When that happens we live a hundred

515

years in a few days. Then he vanishes again . . . and I never know if I'm going to die because he'll never come back. I never know from day to day whether a piece of paper will arrive and tell me my life is over.'

She angled her face away to gaze into the fire. 'When that happened to you—when your confident future was smashed leaving you bewildered and afraid—you ran away and shut it from your mind. I do the same by going onto a stage and pretending it has never happened. I don't think he has ever really understood that.' She turned back, and her lovely face echoed his own present yearnings. 'But I have to come off the stage at the final curtain, and the pretence ends. Oh Chris, give me some of your courage. Tell me how to survive.'

He was overwhelmed. No one had ever asked for his help before; it was usually the other way round. 'I . . . I don't think courage is the right word,' he said hesitantly. 'It's more that there's no alternative but to go on. I used to sit there unable to move, smothered in bandages, and in the most awful pain. I felt like nobody from nowhere, and the only thing I could do was look out at the garden and tell myself those paths lead somewhere and one day I'd follow them. I didn't know what lay at the end, but it was bound to be better than where I was. I think that's how I survived.'

'Is that what you're going to do now—follow the path that leads to Marion?'

He nodded bleakly. 'I don't have much choice, do I?'

'No, Chris, no more choice than I have.' She smiled with a suggestion of closeness. 'But I'm sure you'll cope with it as you have everything else. Now you've come to terms with yourself, you're a strong person—and rather wonderful, like all the Sheridans.'

When it was midnight and the fire had burned low, she gave him some pillows and an eiderdown, together with a pair of Rex's pyjamas.

'Last night was last night,' she said gently. 'You can sleep on the sofa; or the floor if you don't fit on it.'

He took the bedding, longing to kiss her just to show his gratitude. But he did not. Instead, he said, 'I'll never forget this time I've had with you.'

'Neither shall I, my dear. You've brought him so close.'

After she had closed her door he stood for a long time gazing from the window at the snow, trying to delay sleep and the morning it would bring. She would not think he had courage if she could see the tears he could not fight.

Life should have been much easier for Chris now he was totally cured, but in one respect it was not. He had not the first idea how to tackle the problem of his marriage. He went over and over the subject without reaching any conclusion, refusing any help from Bill Chandler, who still had not forgiven him for vanishing for two days and causing great anxiety. He spent a week trying to sort things out in his mind, knowing Marion had been told that he had recalled every part of his past.

He felt it was pointless attempting to see her until he had some kind of proposal to put to her. There were the questions of where they would live now, how he would provide for her, what kind of relationship they would have. It all seemed insurmountable, until he received a visit from the family solicitor, who resolved the first two. Roland had left Tarrant Hall and the estate to him, plus the standing accumulated sum in the bank. That gave him a home and income to offer his wife. *His wife!* It was a fact he still could not assimilate or regard with any degree of acceptance. Yet he could not ignore it.

There was also Tessa to think of. Taking the news of Roland's death stoically she had agreed to remain as bailiff until Chris had sorted himself and his affairs out. But he felt awkward about installing Marion in that small part of his home that remained private, when Tessa had been virtual mistress of it for so long. He had moved into the house himself, going through to the hospital for treatment on his leg that was still causing a few problems. Bill Chandler came to him for discussions on the past, all of which he remembered with total clarity now. A decision was to be made on his future by the Army Medical Board by Christmas. Meanwhile, he had to give his word that he would not leave the house without telling the Australian where he was going.

He did not go anywhere. Snow made even a trip to the village out of the question for him, and he was too occupied with personal problems to want to go anywhere. The arctic weather reminded him of the birth of his son, delivered by Roland because the house had been cut off by snow. Yet, the years between and the things he had experienced blunted the sharp acid of that memory, as they had with all the others.

He had written a long letter to Rex full of gratitude for his excellent advice on going to meet his fears, and the wonderful outcome. It was a letter full of affection for a remembered brother, full of ramblings about his pride in having such a hero as his lifelong friend, full of praise for his flying skill and achievements. Then, inevitably, he had written of his deep sadness that recollection had come too late to enable him to write a similar letter to Roland, and how his loss seemed all the more difficult because of it.

Rex had written back in enthusiastic gladness at the news, adding that he could not wait to see Chris on his next leave—or at the end of the war, whichever came first. The letter betrayed the sender's bitterness over their older brother's death, and Chris sensed a new kind of anger in Rex's attitude toward the war and his enemies.

Soon afterward, Chris received a package containing Roland's personal effects. Amongst them were a vast number of letters, all of which appeared to have been written to David Sheridan. *I believe you should read them all very carefully, Chris,* Rex had written, *because they are meant for your son. You'll realise why they were never posted. In my opinion, it's the most telling prose I've ever read.*

So Chris sat for a whole afternoon reading a moving, vivid, brutal account of war that had reached out to touch everyone, without exception and in many different ways. He recognised himself and Marion, Rex and Laura, Tessa, and others who could easily have been Rochford-Clarke, Neil Frencham or a hundred more he had come across at Gallipoli, and in the hospital wards. Some he could not recognise—a girl who seemed to be a whore, yet who came over in the writings as one of the saddest victims of all, somehow. There were touching, warming scenes; others that were grim and bestial. One concerning a subaltern shot by his own friend who had passed beyond the limit of human suffering was totally shocking, yet it had the ring of truth about it. Another about horses, who were forced into taking part in something of which they had no equivalent understanding, almost put a lump in Chris's throat with its plea for compassion.

Chris knew literature and appreciated it more than the average man, and certainly more than Rex, who had been overcome by it. He knew that what he had in his hands in the form of letters from a soldier in the trenches to his young nephew was chillingly brilliant. It was also the expression of a complex personality that had been allowed—or forced—to emerge only when it could no longer be subdued. All his short life Roland had felt deeply and passionately over all he held dear, yet had been unable to express those feelings. Had he written those letters to young David with the intention of giving them to him when the war had become only a memory, or had he known they would be his epitaph?

Laying them aside, Chris sensed that Roland had repented his lack of caring for his nephew. So that it would not be too late, Chris must ensure that he did what his eldest brother would have done if he had lived. He sat on for the rest of that day, haunted by what he had read, and his sensitive mind went beyond the mere words into the heart of the meaning of those letters. He saw his own problem through eyes unclouded by past and present attitudes; as a small tragedy in the midst of an immense one. By the time he went to bed, he had found the resolution that had evaded him before.

As soon as the snow cleared enough to make the hill negotiable, he sent a letter to Marion asking her to the Hall. It was a formal approach, explaining that he was now fully recovered and anxious to discuss the fact with her. Since he had no wish to distress Dr Deacon further, he had asked her to come to him but, if she wished to meet elsewhere, he would be willing to comply with any request.

He was kept waiting a full week for a reply. She agreed to come to the Hall, and chose the following Monday morning at eleven. She hoped it would be convenient.

He planned and rehearsed very carefully all he was going to say, so there was no reason for nervousness. Nevertheless, he was consumed by it as he waited in the parlour by the cheerful blaze of a log fire. She arrived exactly on time, and Priddy showed her in with even more nervousness than Chris displayed. His wife wore the blue coat that had spurred his memory on that day they had last met, and a soft white scarf was thrown over one shoulder. The cold outside had flushed her cheeks attractively, and Chris was thrown totally off-balance by the rush of conflicting feelings that assailed him at the sight of her now.

From that day he had awoken in a hospital, lost and terrified, he had grown to trust and regard with fondness a nurse called Marion Deacon. She had fed him, washed him, listened to his ravings, *helped him survive*. That same girl he had seen at the cricket-match, and at her father's house in the village when he had sought her out so determinedly. He liked and respected Marion Deacon enormously; had gone out of his way to regain her friendship and approval.

Now, he was looking at a girl within a girl. She was a thin leggy creature holding up her skirts as she followed Roland and Rex through the shrubbery looking for birds' nests; she was a girl laughing up at him as he sat in a tree reading while his brothers shook the trunk in an attempt to bring him down; she was a madcap chasing across Longbarrow Hill on a pony close on Roland's heels, then arriving breathless at his own side to exclaim in admiration over his sketch of late roses in the sunken garden. She was also a young woman paddling in the stream and exclaiming on how different he looked without his spectacles; she was a blur in a storm-darkened room with a voice that urged him to pursue and catch her; she was a soft trembling naked body that pressed against him in demand. Then, she was a pale crying girl ruining his life with her accusation; a pale crying bride taking away all he had ever wanted; a pale vomiting swollen millstone around his neck. She was a screaming labouring mother producing a screaming fretful child. She was a person he hated so much he was prepared to risk death as his only escape from her. She was a wife who faced him silently in a great house that now belonged to him, waiting to hear his first words as her acknowledged husband since he had walked away from her and their child three years before.

His rehearsed speeches fled. All he did was ask her to take off her coat and sit down.

'No, thank you. I shan't be staying long,' she told him quietly.

That threw him further. He had arranged for Priddy to bring some coffee and raisin cake at eleven-thirty, when he had estimated the essentials would have been dealt with and they would be more relaxed. The old grandfather clock sounded ominous in the continuing silence, and Chris wished he had not declined Bill Chandler's help with this difficult meeting.

He tried again. 'Won't you at least sit down? I can't unless you do, and it gets very tiring if I stand for any length of time.'

She chose a chair some distance from him, and he lowered himself into another that faced her across the room.

'It was good of you to come, Marion . . . especially after the way I walked off in the village that day. It was the shock of . . . well, of too many things coming back to me at once.'

'There was a terrible commotion when you couldn't be found.'

'So I believe. I didn't think of that.'

'Why should you? You have no idea of what you're like during those periods.'

'No . . . no, I haven't,' he admitted sensing her animosity.

'But she apparently coped with it admirably.'

'She?'

'Laura . . . the girl you ran to for help.'

'Oh yes, she did. I think it was because she didn't have any idea there might be anything to be frightened about. I mean, she hadn't seen me in the hospital, as you had.' It was all going wrong; all going in a direction he had not accounted for. 'But all that is over now. I remember everything very clearly.' He had to say it. 'It was a bit of a shock, of course.'

'Yes.'

'That's why I have allowed a while to pass before seeing you. I had a lot to think over and try to make the best decisions.'

'Yes.'

It was evident she had no intention of helping him, so he plunged into his rehearsed speeches that had come back to his mind again.

'The thing is this, Marion. What happened three years ago is past, and we have both become different people. The war has changed everything, the way we all think and behave. What appeared to be important before no longer seems to matter. Social attitudes and standards won't ever be as they were then, and everyone, without exception, will have to pick up the pieces of their lives and start again. So there'll be nothing strange about our new arrangements.'

'No.'

Monosyllables still! He pressed on. 'For some unaccountable reason, poor Roland left Tarrant Hall and all that goes with it to me, not Rex. The present wording of his will is "conditional upon medical certification of his mental ability to assume responsibility for his affairs". That certification will be forthcoming by Christmas but, in any case, the house and estate are willed to you for David should I not be considered fit to run them.'

A flood of vivid colour passed over her face, then left her rather pale. 'Roland did *that?*'

He nodded. 'In a recent amendment sent from Flanders. I think he went through something akin to hell out there, you know. It made him see things in a different perspective.'

She got up and went to stand by the small casement window, looking out at the lingering snow. To his astonishment, Chris sensed that she was too overcome to speak. He rose and limped across to stand beside her. She looked round swiftly, and her eyes were bright with tears.

'Roland and I had been friends all our lives, yet we said such terrible things to each other. I sent him a white feather every week until he put on uniform. I did . . . forgive me, but I did. I felt bad enough when I heard of his death. Now *this*. I wish he hadn't.'

Chris swallowed. 'I think it was his way of saying sorry.'

'But it's too late, isn't it?' she cried emotionally. 'It's *all* too late.'

'What do you mean?'

'Oh Chris, use that brain that has been the curse of your life! Too many words have been said, too many years have passed, too many things have happened to us all! You surely haven't asked me here to suggest we try to revive something that never really lived?'

Completely taken aback, he muttered, 'It would be different now. There's the Hall, and the money from the estate. I could get work as a tutor, I expect, and I'd do my best to look after you . . . and the boy. I promise you I'm completely recovered now—ask Chandler—and I'd try to be a good husband to you now.'

'But we're both in love with someone else!'

He stared at her finding it difficult to take in what she was saying. 'I don't understand.'

'No, I don't suppose you do,' she retaliated in broken tones. 'You've been away in a world of your own for two and a half years while I've been waiting to see whether you'd go insane or not. Now the issue is settled. I'm glad for you, Chris, deeply glad. But, whichever way it had gone, I knew I could take no more. I only accepted your invitation so that I could tell you I want a divorce. I'm sure any court will understand why, and grant it.'

25

As 1918 dawned the Allies were facing their worst and direst emergency yet. The fighting troops now comprised mostly inexperienced new recruits. Those of the old regulars who had miraculously not fallen, were ill or severly shell-shocked. There were no reserves. As soon as boys were conscripted they were shipped out to the war zones in France, Belgium, Italy, the Middle East and the Balkans. The desperately-needed Americans were still only trickling through to areas where ten times their number was needed if the war was to reach a decisive stage.

In addition, the revolution in Russia had brought the fear of this huge ally making a seperate peace with Germany in order to concentrate on a civil war. This would release thousands of German troops engaged on the Eastern Front to reinforce those confronting the British and French in the Somme and Ypres sectors, and the fall of the European mainland right to the Channel coast could be a severe threat. The British would then be isolated on their small island, looking into the jaws of the ravenous Huns across a narrow stretch of water. The destruction of the British Isles by air could then be a strong possibility.

Allied air power was frantically being increased, and the severe challenge to the skill and endurance of those who repaired the aircraft as well as those who flew them, was met with great courage. But it was not only in the air that they suffered losses. The Germans might no longer have battle superiority, but they did have enviable supplies of aircraft which enabled them to launch surprise attacks on allied airfields, bombing machines as they stood on the ground, or bringing them down as pilots tried to take them airborne.

When Rex's squadron had twice suffered such attacks with the loss of four men dead, eleven wounded, and eight aircraft destroyed before they could get into the air, he knew something would have to be done. Air warfare had changed whilst he had spent the summer in England. It had become more organised. The

Germans, with typical Teutonic love of order, had devised formation flying, with entire squadrons sallying forth. To combat it, entire squadrons had to meet them. This meant the days of lone patrols, reconnaissance flights, or pairs of hunters on the prowl for a lone enemy were over. Special units had been set up for reconnaissance work, but their messages were often lost, information arrived late, or photographs showed superseded troop positions. Rex was a man who had learnt the value of the 'lone wolf' patrol; the one experienced flier who knew where to look and how to assess. In consequence, he decided to ignore an order circulated by Colonel James Ashmore forbidding unauthorised flights by single pilots, or a pair working together.

'I've heard his reasoning behind the order, and it makes sense from where he sits on his backside at Headquarters,' he told Mike one morning when rain had grounded ally and enemy alike.

'It makes sense from where *I'm* sitting on my backside, old mate,' said Mike tilting his chair back on two legs and putting his booted feet up on Rex's desk near to where his squadron commander perched on its corner, drinking brandy. 'The Huns no longer send up solo aircraft, so any fool on our side who decides on a solitary excursion is going to meet up with ten times his number.'

'Only if he goes up when they're up.' Rex waved his glass at his friend. 'I cannot and will not have my squadron decimated in these raids. We're trained to fight in the air. We don't stand a chance on the ground, and it's time they knew how it feels.'

'Hold on a moment,' warned Mike, waving his own glass back. 'If you're thinking what I think you're thinking, Ashmore will be after your guts. He already hates you for flying him into a haystack, and for ignoring his order regarding the green stripe.'

'That just proves what a simple mind he has. I've known men who have done worse than that to me, and I don't hate them.'

'Oh . . . give me an example.'

'John Winters, for one,' supplied Rex off the cuff. 'But we're getting away from my point. What is needed is a spot of retaliation to show the Hun we are not going to accept these raids meekly.' He leant forward with his elbow propped on his thigh, to look Mike straight in the eyes. 'Surprise is essential. That means taking off in the dark so arrival over their airfield is just as dawn is coming up. Or it means going up in weather conditions that usually stop all flying.'

Mike assumed an unconcerned expression. 'Like today, in fact.'

'That's right,' Rex agreed in pleasant tones. 'Just like today.'

The mechanics tried to look as though they thought nothing odd about being told to prepare two machines for flight on a day when even the birds preferred a branch in a tree, and the other squadron members pressed astonished faces to their windows to watch their Commanding Officer and senior pilot climb into rain-washed cockpits with what looked from a distance to be a basketful of grenades apiece.

They looked even more astonished an hour or so later when the pair returned, grinning all over their faces, climbing from their machines with the empty baskets over their heads as protection against the deluge. Of course, the whole squadron knew that 'Sherry' Sheridan was crazy—in the most attractive possible way, but crazy all the same. As for his long-standing Australian friend, the least said the better. The men from Down Under were known to be wild colonial boys to a man.

Neither one of them said a word about where they had been, and no one had the temerity to ask. Normal routine continued for a few days, then two aircraft were heard taking off an hour before dawn one February morning. They came back during breakfast, the two pilots bursting into the Mess in high spirits, shouting for double helpings of eggs and sausages. Although spasmodic raids on R.F.C. airfields continued, the home of the Arrows was left in peace for the next few weeks.

But these days there was a demon driving Rex. Roland's death had hit him hard. His older brother had represented all that was good about the British way of life. He had been lost in a moment, and how much had been lost with him? Chris owned it all now, and young David might have grown to love it as Roland had except that his mother was set on denying him his natural birthright. If Chris married a second time, any son of that union would be a stranger to the village and its ways. How Roland would have grieved over the coming divorce, and all it would entail.

Sometimes Rex wished he had not told Roland he did not want to take over Tarrant Hall. That weekend of the cricket-match shone in his memory as one of complete peace and happiness, and he found himself yearning for his home as he never had before. He now recognised the joys and privileges of youth he had always taken for granted. He would sit for long periods with a bottle of brandy, lost in recollections of those sunny days when he and Jake used to wheel 'Princess' from the shed, and the pair of them would float above the rolling hills of Dorset and Somerset, filled with the power and exuberance of youth.

During those periods he believed it could be the same again. But there was Laura, of course, and even if he could put an end to her theatrical career, she would never live happily in that environment. When sober and facing facts, he admitted he would not enjoy it for too long, either. Yet his restless spirit had had more than enough to satisfy it over the past three and a half years, and maybe he could be happy there so long as he had another 'Princess'. Wherever he was, he would always need to fly.

So, apart from grief and anger over Roland's death, and the concern over Chris's future now he had recovered his sanity and lost his wife, Rex felt a burning urge to arrange his own future. Those letters forwarded with Roland's personal effects haunted him. They had painted such a vivid picture of lost ideals, lost chances, lost ambitions, and lost men, he felt an overwhelming burden of responsibility to use his gift of life. In the past he had believed he was living fully and had, undoubtedly, given *something* in the process. But he now saw the young daredevil cavalier as basically selfish. Still convinced of his own survival of the war, he determined to do something truly worthwhile for the sake of all those who now could not.

Whilst in England he had come to know many of the leading aircraft designers well enough to approach them by letter, asking to join their company after the war. He had received enthusiastic replies which had sparked off a regular correspondence concerning aircraft design allied to the needs of the men who flew them. He longed for the time when he could cast off his khaki and embark on this new phase of his life. Frustration added its weight to the demon of battle within him. And there was his passion for Laura.

It was six months since he had said a difficult and strained farewell to her—the longest they had yet been apart—and the jealousy he had kept under control in England now ran riot. His wife had apparently been achieving all and more than she had dreamt possible, and Rex found it difficult to stay silent when new conscripts arrived or men returned from leave and raved about *Bows and Boaters,* with its star who was fast becoming the darling of the troops on leave. He trusted Laura—he had to or go out of his mind—but he found it difficult to accept that his wife was being discussed in trenches, ships and squadrons by men who certainly did not admire her for her personality alone. He knew the licentious soldiery and tormented himself with thoughts of the entire fighting force of the British Isles discussing what they would like to do with Laura Sheridan, given half a chance. Where would it all lead, he wondered. His longing to end the war and get back to sort it out, plus a compulsion to prove he was a better man than all the rest, augmented the most superhuman drive that propelled him, these days, and sent his personal tally toward sixty.

He soon had need of that drive. On the thirteenth of March the Russians did what had been feared and signed a separate peace with Germany, releasing hundreds of thousands of troops from the Russian Front to reinforce the depleted regiments on the Western Front. Within a week, the R.F.C. was warned to stand by for a massive German attack, which Intelligence reports believed would be launched in Flanders as the start of that year's spring offensive. Rex had the mechanics working flat out night and day to get aircraft repaired and airworthy, while aircrew waited in readiness for the battle order to come through. For three days they sat around inactive, forbidden to mount any other sorties whilst on stand-by. The news began to trickle through of a gigantic offensive far to the south at the Somme, instead, with initial advances by the enemy which had driven the Allies back over the river and lost them thousands dead and almost as many prisoners. Further reports were confused due to the rapid reorganisation of troops for a counter-attack. But it was understood the offensive had been repulsed and the danger of serious defeat averted.

The men of Rex's squadron were gathered together around his office listening to the latest information on the state of the battle, when the sound of approaching aircraft was heard by them all. It took but a moment for them to realise what was about to happen, and they all got to their feet as Rex shouted. 'Those bastards are after us again! Get into the air as fast as you can!'

Sure enough, out of the thin cloud of a grey March day came a formation of enemy aircraft and, as Rex ran with the others towards the Camels which had been lined up for three days in rows, ready for take-off, they flew low over the airfield to drop bombs slung beneath, or toss grenades, the observers in the rear cockpits using their machine-guns to advantage as their pilots climbed after the attack.

All those on the ground were sitting ducks. The field seemed to be exploding all around them, sending showers of earth over their heads, or knocking them over with the blast as they tried to reach their aircraft. Rex felt his heart pumping as he raced over the grass toward the leading Camel, furious to think they had had no warning. The mechanics were standing beside the machines in readiness but, even before any pilot reached them, three aircraft had gone up in flames and two more had been thrown on their sides with wings broken. One mechanic was almost certainly dead, and others lay wounded just out of reach of the flames. But there was no time to dwell on such things. Men had to lay dying while machines were saved. Life had become cheap; aircraft had not.

Still running Rex shouted orders to clear the wreckage away to allow those behind an unhindered path, and somehow his voice was heard and obeyed above the roar of the Germans coming in for the second time. Then men were fanning out to climb into the Camels, and an extra roar rent the air as engines were started for take-off.

Rex had scrambled into his machine and was starting to taxi forward when the next line of bombs hit the ground a few yards ahead, sending up clods of turf and leaving holes right in his path. Conscious of the looming overhead shapes he frantically changed direction, waving his arm to those behind him as a signal to fan out and take to the air in any order or manner they could manage.

From then on it was a question of fighting for survival as bullets rained down, and grenades were dropped from no more than fifty feet up. The fabric of his wings grew full of holes as Rex zig-zagged across the field unable to get up enough speed to take to the air, due to pits in the surface. All around him he was aware of the members of his squadron doing the same as he in their fight to get off the ground. Some lost the fight immediately. A grenade falling neatly inside the cockpit of one of his most valued pilots blew man and machine up in a roar of exploding fuel that raced through to the tail in a matter of seconds. Another aircraft, piloted by a boy who had only arrived to join the squadron the day before, taxied straight across the field into the trees at the edge with the dead youngster hanging over the control bar. Two more Camels collided and smashed up to block the way for others coming behind.

Yet, when Rex desperately dragged his machine up from the ground at the very last minute, he noticed others taking to the skies beside him in defiance of the buzzing Germans above.

But Rex's own flight was of short duration. As he pulled up over the tops of trees set alight by the burning Camel that had taxied into them, a spar snapped and half his lower wing tore away, weakened by the tattered fabric. His climb turned into a side-slip, and he had not nearly enough height to give him time to correct it. The ground rushed up, and he used all his strength and flying skill to come down again causing as little damage as possible to his machine. He succeeded very well, although the impact jolted him badly. But the ploughed field was muddy after the winter rains, and the wheels sank in sending the Camel straight onto its nose.

Rex must have passed out momentarily, and that possibly saved his life because the departing Germans would have taken his immobility as a sign that he was finished. As it was, he came to his senses to see them heading off into the cloud now their advantage of surprise had been outlived. He saw them from an upside-down position, and warily moved all his limbs before attempting to release his restraining belt. Dropping unceremoniously to the ground, his first action as he scrambled to his feet was to look heavenward to see how many of his squadron had survived to chase their attackers.

But the others turned into blurred dots as his scrutiny fastened on just one Camel heading straight for him in a steep glide, engine spluttering, and flames already licking around the cockpit as it came down out of control, swinging from side to side.

'Oh, my God,' he cried in a rasping breath, and felt his blood freeze as the machine hit the ploughed field no more than a few yards from him. His legs were already running before his brain told them to, but his own crash had left him shaky and uncoordinated so that he staggered unsteadily when urgency demanded swiftness. His breath was laboured when he neared the wreck that was crackling and roaring with fire that flourished on the wood-and-fabric body of the aircraft. But his laboured breathing turned to sobs of anguish when he saw, through the tongues of flame, that Mike was still alive in the middle of it. His friend was staring at him, his silvery eyes orange with the light of the flames, and his mouth wide open. The screams were drowned by the roar of flames and the crackle of wood, but Rex heard them inside his head and knew he would hear them for the rest of his life.

Tugging off his leather coat he began beating at the fire, trying to force a passage nearer the body of the machine, where his wounded friend was unable to drag himself clear. But Rex had no power against a fire that had a good hold on inflammable material and which was being fanned by a stiff breeze. His sense of unacceptable horror went into the stage even beyond that when Mike's face began to turn black and char, his dark hair became a flaming torch, and his clothes turned into a suit of fire.

Next minute, the wheel struts disintegrated; the whole machine collapsed and lost any form or identity in one huge conflagration, with Mike in the heart of it. Rex backed away, staring with eyes that were almost blinded by brightness. Then he turned and staggered over the ridged squelchy ground, vaguely aware of his own voice shouting obscenities at the sky and a terrifying feeling of thunder in his head. For a long while he stumbled about aimlessly until he fetched up hard against something and held on to it with a grip of iron, staring at it with unfocused eyes, and shaking from head to foot, until it asked him if he was all right.

They led him back to an ambulance on the perimeter of the airfield, but he refused to get in it. Someone walked beside him back across the field to his office. He noted the damage that had been done, the number of machines put out of action, and sat at his desk listing the facts. He organised burial parties for the dead, and visited the wounded in sick quarters. That evening he wrote to the relatives of those who had been lost. But when he reached the last letter, the page remained blank save for the words: *My dear Tessa.* It stayed blank for the rest of that night. He lay on his bed staring at that sheet of paper which seemed to reflect a succession of scenes. Mike featured in every one of them yet, try as he might, Rex could not remember what his friend looked like. Mike was now only a presence, without face or form.

* * *

The realisation that air power was going to be a significant element in future defence strategy had culminated in a decision to take the Royal Flying Corps away from the Army, and the Royal Naval Air Service away from the Navy, to combine the two in a separate service to be called the Royal Air Force. Although its members would continue to operate in conjunction with land and sea forces, the R.A.F. would be responsible for its own administration and combat decisions.

But behind the idea to go ahead with something that was the subject of immense wrangling and contention, lay the strength of the British public's protest and fury at being bombed again and again by the Germans, who seemed to slip through the Home Defence Squadrons with little trouble, and whose deadly raids seemed scarcely to be reciprocated. At the start of that fourth year of war, those at home had had almost enough. Maybe they could be forgiven their attitude. To stand helpless while a nation is lost on foreign soil is sometimes more of a strain than being at the heart of that loss.

So, at a time when defeat was closer than it had ever been, it was decided to strengthen the morale of the civilian population by instigating this new service, despite strong resistance to it by the members of the two separate corps. At such a vital stage it was, perhaps, unwise to embark on something which needed deep thought and concentrated planning, but those concerned went ahead. The R.A.F. was born on 1 April. It was not a painless birth. Bitter opposition and jealousy accompanied it, to remain for a long time afterward. But the men in the new service had to accept the inevitable and make the best of it.

Rex had always possessed the kind of nature that allowed him to do this, so when he was told to return to England for three days at the end of March to lend the glamour of his reputation, along with that of other aces, to the inauguration of the R.A.F. he went stifling his feelings over something he had no power to prevent. To compensate for the aviators' grudging but loyal support each of them was given complete freedom to do as he pleased during those times between official duty. It was not much, but Rex planned to make the most of it.

Reaching London after an all-night journey he had no chance of letting Laura know he was in England. She refused to have a telephone in case it disturbed her sleep, and he decided against sending a telegram for fear of frightening her. So the day dragged past, and all the while he thought of nothing else but the blessed peace of being with her and holding her in his arms to chase away the demons with which he daily lived cheek by jowl. He needed her softness, her sanity, and her unblemished beauty to drive away visions of Mike burning, men exploding . . . and his own brother blown apart over a foreign field. The minutes ticked away increasing that need for her until it was like a furnace inside him.

But, when he was finally free, he searched for a taxi in vain. Setting off on foot with the idea of buying flowers at a florist still open on a corner some fifty yards ahead, he noted that London was shabbier than when he had last seen it. With its occasional piles of rubble from air raids, sandbags around doorways of important buildings, sad-faced people wrapped against the March fog in drab coats, and a sparse array of goods in the windows, it was fast becoming like the cities of France and Belgium that had never fallen to the Germans, but were showing signs of the strain of war all around them.

The florist closed when he was ten yards from it, the sour-faced woman resolutely pulling the roller-blind over the glass door as he made frantic signs to her to let him in. Angry he turned to a newsagent and confectioner next door, which was enjoying a roaring trade. It would have to be chocolates instead of flowers.

He never bought them. Just inside the door he was halted by something he could not initially believe. Closer scrutiny showed him he must. In a glass-fronted case were the postcard pictures of film and stage stars that were extremely popular with the public. There were the great dramatic Shakespearean actors striking manly poses, film favourites who broke female hearts, shown in profile to advantage, winsome girls who partnered Charlie Chaplin, and glamour pictures of the girls beloved by the troops. Amongst the latter were some of Laura Sheridan. She smiled out at Rex from over her shoulder, which was bare along with her back down to well below her waist, and her wicked eyes invited him to study the rest of her body encased in a dark glittery clinging skirt that was slit from toe to thigh, exposing the whole of one shapely leg as she posed provocatively. It was the costume she wore for the finale of her show, but it seemed to be cut a lot lower than when Rex saw it . . . and the vibrant sexuality she had always reserved for just him, now fizzed from the picture like a star-shell.

It broke him apart as he stood looking at the girl who held his life in her graceful hands, and it was the last shock, the last betrayal, the last burden on his overladen soul. Because he had to hit out at something he smashed his fist through the glass of that case, and left. He heard nothing of the startled outcry behind him, and felt nothing of the cuts on his hand that had started to bleed so profusely.

At the junction he jumped into a taxi just as a sailor and a girl were about to get in it, and gave the address of his apartment. It was dark now, and the fog appeared to have grown thicker. Grumbling about the weather, the shortage of food, and the general character of the Germans, the driver managed quite well without answers from his passenger.

Rex left a trail of blood spots all the way up the flights of stairs he had to climb to reach his front door, and he was breathing heavily with effort and inner anguish as he reached the last set of six. Then, from the half-landing, he saw Laura come from the apartment, dressed for the theatre in a sable-trimmed evening coat. She turned, saw him, and seemed to freeze with shock that drained the colour from her cheeks. Then her face flooded with incredulous delight to make her more beautiful than he ever remembered. It broke him apart anew.

They came together at the top of the steps, and she flung herself against him in an abandoned embrace he could not begin to return. It was some while before she realised it and drew away to gaze with tear-filled eyes at his face that felt so stiff it might never move again.

'Darling, what is it?' she whispered fearfully. 'Whatever has happened? You look so . . . so *terrible!* For God's sake what has happened?'

Wanting to destroy her as she was destroying him, he heard words pour from his lips in a ceaseless stream of accusation. 'How could you do it? How could you agree to such a thing when you knew what it would do to me? I let you carry on at that theatre because I knew it meant so much to you, but you've made a mockery of all we've ever had. What more do you want, Laura? I've given you everything and you've flung it back in my face.'

Her tears had stopped; delight had been banished by shock. 'I don't understand what this is. *Please* stop looking at me that way, darling. Something's happened, but I can't think straight.' She put her hands to her temples in distress. 'I thought you were still over there. I've been living for six months never knowing if you were alive or dead. Rex, I can't take this in.' She begged for understanding. 'My God, you're actually standing there, and I can't believe it. But you're angry and hostile. What is it all about?'

'It's about postcards of you showing almost the whole of your body, which are on public sale.' His voice had risen and echoed around the hollow staircase. 'How could you degrade yourself to such an extent?'

'Degrade myself?' she repeated in bewilderment. 'I wear that costume in the show. You know I do.'

'On stage you're acting a part,' he shouted, the familiar drumming starting in his temples. 'Up there you're an imaginary creature out of reach. Those pictures are different.'

'How different?' she cried with rising emotion. 'They're only photographs.'

'Photographs that are going to be handled, defaced, and guffawed over by troops in the trenches and seamen in the sweltering depths of ships. They're going to be passed from panting subaltern to licentious colonel. They're going to circulate amidst foul-mouthed randy degenerates that even whores refuse to entertain. You've no idea where those kind of pictures end up, covered in lewd scribblings and treated in the most disgusting fashion by men who are no more than brainless lumps of flesh!' The words began to run into each other as the volcano inside him reached the point of erupting. 'You think they will bring you public veneration? All you are doing is selling yourself for tuppence to any man who wants you!'

In a fury she stepped forward and brought up her arm to strike him. But he anticipated the blow, and jerked his head back out of her reach. The movement swung him off balance, his boot slipped on the edge of the step, and he fell backward clutching at the banister. The blood on his cut hand made it slippery, preventing him from getting a firm hold. Half-staggering, half-slipping, he dropped down the flight of steps to the landing below, where he caught his forehead a mighty crack on the newel.

When he came to Laura was bending over him with fear darkening her face, and she seemed to have been crying. Their elderly neighbours were all fussing, and discussing the best way to get him up to his apartment. He could not think where he was, for a moment, and gazed at his wife as if she were a vision surrounded by a bevy of grey-haired angels.

'Are you badly hurt?' she asked him in a voice that trembled. 'Have you broken anything? There's blood everywhere. I've sent for a doctor.'

'I don't need a doctor,' he mumbled. 'Just let me lie here a moment.'

'I'll make some weak tea,' warbled one of the maiden ladies. 'Best thing in a case like this.'

'Tot of whisky would do him more good,' argued the retired mountaineer breezily. 'Wait a tick, I'll get some.'

Rex lay where he was on the concrete while Laura took off her velvet coat to fold beneath his head, and people went off to get the remedies they advocated. His vision faded and returned bewilderingly, and the volcano that had been within his breast seemed to have moved up into his head. But Laura was holding his hand and speaking softly to him in tones strongly coloured by fright, and her rose perfume wafted to him adding to his sense of confusion over time and place.

Someone put a glass to his lips and coaxed him to 'drink up'. He was not keen on whisky, but he swallowed it all. The doctor arrived and examined his body with experienced hands. Pronouncing that nothing was broken, he enlisted the help of neighbours to get Rex to his feet and up to the apartment. The bed felt marvellous after the cold concrete, and he had to fight the desire to drift away from painful reality as the doctor tut-tutted and studied the extent of the damage to his forehead.

'No abrasion, but a massive bruise coming already. You'll have a nasty headache from that,' was his hearty opinion. 'Still, that'll be nothing to a young man like you. Oh yes, I know who you are. Heard all manner of stories about your exploits. You're like the cat—nine lives. But don't throw one away on foolishness like this. Whisky has been the ruin of youngsters too often for my liking. Smelt it as I came up the steps. Holding a glass when you fell, I gather. Cut your hand badly!' He proceeded to remove splinters of glass, then bandage over the bleeding cuts. 'Well, it's no whisky for a day or two, young man. These pills I'll leave with your wife are to help you sleep. Can't drink spirits while you're taking them. Asking for trouble!'

Rex swallowed a powder the man mixed in a glass of water

fetched by Laura, but it was all automatic. Languor was fast taking him in its grip, and he had no will to fight it. In fact, oblivion seemed irresistibly attractive.

He awoke to brilliant sunshine and a blinding headache. It was a few seconds before he realised where he was. Then he worked backward to recall the whole of the previous day. Lead settled inside him as he remembered those postcards of Laura, and the quarrel that had brought her attack he had dodged. Eventually, he absorbed other facts, and looked quickly at the clock. Three-thirty! It had to be afternoon, but how could he have slept for twenty-one hours at a stretch? Sitting up swiftly he gave an involuntary shout. Every bone and joint in his body protested painfully, and the room appeared to spin in every conceivable orbit as his head thudded with agony.

Then Laura was beside him holding out a hand containing some pills, and another with a glass of water. 'Thank heavens! I've been on the verge of calling the doctor again,' she said in a voice that was very subdued, for her. 'I couldn't wake you, no matter what I did. You were supposed to take two of these at nine this morning, and another two at noon. Ought you to take four at once now?'

He stared at her, trying to marshall his thoughts. 'I'm supposed to be at a conference. No, that was this morning. I think . . . oh God, I was one of the speakers at a luncheon. It's too late now.'

She sat on the edge of the bed to put a cool hand against his cheek. In a burnt-orange dress, with her hair put up in a mass of bright curls held by a butterfly-comb of jade and pearls, she looked like the girl he had first seen enter Tessa's lodgings with her arms full of boxes.

'Darling, I've sorted all that out. The doctor has demanded that you rest for the next forty-eight hours, and I asked him to contact the appropriate people at the War Office. Stop worrying and take these.'

He looked at the pills with a frown. 'Roland used to give those to his horses!' Immense sadness washed over him. 'He'll never do it again, will he?'

Her arms stole around him and she brushed his cheek with her own, which felt wet. 'Don't, Rex! Don't think of things like that. Take the pills and lie down again.'

He did as she directed, and studied her for a while. 'Why are you crying?'

She took his unbandaged hand in hers and held it tightly. 'Because I love you so much, my dearest one, I can't contain it.'

He considered that for a while as his head continued to thud with every heartbeat. 'I feel like that sometimes. But men are not allowed to cry. They get angry, instead.'

'I know, darling.'

'Don't go away, will you?'

'No. I'll sit here while you sleep.'

'I shan't sleep.'

'All right. Just lie there and think of Tarrant Hall. I've arranged for us to go down the day after tomorrow and see Chris.'

Now he knew he must be dreaming. 'You've arranged it? How?'

'Never mind how. Just look forward to seeing him again.'

But the dream began to turn into a nightmare almost at once. Tessa was at Tarrant Hall. How could he tell her about her brother who had burnt to nothing like a candle? He tried to explain to Laura that he could not do it, could not go home. But she soothed him with soft words and her lips on his until he drifted away into deep sleep again.

Chris could scarcely contain his delight at the prospect of seeing Rex. With the old sense of brotherhood back it would be wonderful to talk over old times, despite the shadow of Roland's death which would undoubtedly darken them. It would be the first time they had met since full memory had returned, and it would add some warmth to the chill brought by his pending divorce.

It did chill him. As the weeks had passed he had become more and more disturbed over something Marion had forced on him without any discussion on the subject. There was no doubt she had a strong case, and it was probably the best solution. But, having struggled with the problem and accepted that he must take on the responsibility of a wife and three-year-old son, her sweeping demand had left him feeling peculiarly bereft—something he found quite irrational but undeniable. Over the past years he had come to terms with a wide variety of emotions that had been alien to his philosophical nature, and he was still struggling to understand this one.

The truth was, the nurse he had come to like and trust super-seded the girl he had blamed for the ruin of his life. All that recrimination seemed a lifetime away . . . and that boy was *his* son. Naturally, he experienced no paternal feelings for a child he had glimpsed only once or twice, and never spoken to, but David Sheridan was the natural heir to the house and estate. There was half of himself in that youngster. He had the Sheridan looks. Would he be clever; maybe a brilliant classic scholar? He could help the boy to achieve those goals that had seemed so important to a schoolboy back in 1914, who had allowed knowledge to stifle emotion. Surely he had a right to know how his son would de-velop; watch him grow and learn?

Marion claimed she loved someone else. Was she planning to remarry? The thought of his child being reared by another man hurt. Every time he thought of it it hurt more. Marion's new husband might be a clod-headed farmhand whose plans for David would go no further than apprenticing him to the blacksmith, or turning him into a shepherd. His son was worth more than that . . . and so was his wife! Marion could be mistress of Tarrant Hall and half the village now.

She could also be a very wealthy woman. Due to one of the strange quirks of war, the estate had made a great deal of money over the past few years by supplying grain, meat, and timber under government contracts. Tessa had managed the estate business affairs better than many a man, and had brought the Sheridan bank balance appreciably nearer its old standard. Mike's death coming so soon after Roland's had almost extinguished the spirit that drove her when she had heard the news only a week ago, but she had refused Chris's suggestion that she return to Australia or take a long break somewhere, and was losing herself in work.

Chris was also working. At Christmas he had been examined by an army medical board and declared sane, but was given immedi-ate discharge on the grounds of disability due to his mutilated hand and the leg that would always be slightly inflexible. His eyesight alone would have brought the decision, however. Im-mediately after the board he was summoned to another. As a result he was now employed, in a civilian capacity, as a translator and cipher-expert by those same people who had unthinkingly sent him to Gallipoli. He was thrilled and delighted with work that so suited all he loved to do, even though it meant a police guard on

Tarrant Hall while the war lasted. It earnt him a very large salary —far larger than he had been receiving as a second-lieutenant. And far more than whoever it was that Marion loved, he was certain. David Sheridan was entitled to the best, and he would only get it by remaining his son.

As the legal stages of the proposed divorce were being passed one by one, Chris felt more and more bleak. He liked Marion. He was sure he could like that little boy to whom Roland had written those brilliantly evocative letters. It could have worked. It could have been quite a good life. Except that Marion loved someone else —someone who was probably free to marry her. For himself, he had lost her and David, and the someone else *he* loved was married to his brother. That left him with nothing but his work, and it no longer seemed to be enough.

Bill Chandler continued to court Tessa at Tarrant Hall, and he was there on the day Rex and Laura were coming. It was a crisp sunny day. Chris strolled with him in the garden for a while, chatting about the state of the war and the many sad cases that had gone the opposite way to his own.

During a pause Chris asked, 'Is it still all right for me to seek your advice, either as a doctor or a friend?'

The other man nodded. 'Of course. But it must be bloody important for you to be so polite all of a sudden.'

Chris grinned. 'Relaxation of your influence has had a beneficial effect on my manners.'

'Cheeky sod! So what's the problem?'

'Laura.'

'Still? I thought you'd worked that affair out by now.'

'I don't think I ever will,' he retorted bleakly. 'She's not the kind of girl one can put out of one's mind easily.'

'What aspect is worrying you?'

Chris wished he had never begun the subject now, but was forced to continue. 'She's coming here today with Rex, who's over for a few days. I don't know what to do, really. It'll be the first time we've met since . . . well, since we spent those two days together. She promised not to mention it to Rex, and I'm sure she hasn't. But I wonder if it wouldn't be better to make a clean breast of it to him.'

The Australian looked at him quizzically. 'A clean breast of what? Did you go to bed together?'

'No, of course not,' he defended himself hotly. 'Betray my own brother!'

'But you wanted to?'

'Yes —*no!* I was in no state to do anything like that, you know I wasn't. But she lay *on* the bed with me all that first night. I slept on the floor on the second, in another room. But do you think I should tell Rex . . . casually, you know, as if it didn't mean a thing?'

'Didn't it mean a thing?'

He ran his hand through his hair in confusion, feeling he was getting further and further into hot water as he went. 'Of course it did. I'll never forget it. Those hours were the most marvellous of my life.'

'More marvellous than those five minutes with Marion on the surgery couch?' came the testing question. 'Chris, you are now twenty-one and, apart from natural responses to hospital attentions, you've had no sexual outlet whatever.' He stopped by the seat beneath the willow and lit a cigarette. 'When you first became rational after that shell in Gallipoli, your subconscious reaction to sexual desire was one of guilt and outrage. Until then, your own experience with a female—Marion—had brought wrath and disgust down on your head from both Roland and Dr Deacon. You were made to feel a social outcast, a filthy beast, a despoiler of innocent maidens. Even your favourite brother Rex suggested you had been something of a fool to be caught. The act itself was associated in your mind with utter delight that demanded a man's whole life in payment.' Sitting and leaning back against the trunk of the tree, he looked up at Chris through exhaled smoke. 'Your one experience with a male—Neil Frencham—had brought shock, revulsion, and a sense of betrayal. *He* became the social outcast, the filthy beast, the despoiler of innocent youth. So what were you left with? A subconscious conviction that to have such feelings was sinful and guilty, even though they gave you immense pleasure. The result? You shut yourself off from all men and women, except the one person who embodied all your subconscious ideas. To love Laura would be sinful and guilty, and also give you the delight you sought. So that's what you did.'

'*What?*' said Chris, trying to get his thoughts straight.

'Take my word for it,' the other man assured him with a confident nod. 'If Laura had taken all her clothes off and offered herself to you at any time, the whole affair would have collapsed, because the guilt of coveting your brother's wife would have been nullified. If she wasn't entirely his to covet, there'd be no point. And if you tell him today about those two nights with her, you'll see them for what they really were—a girl being kind and understanding to the frightened young brother of the husband she adores.'

Put like that it made sense—damnable sense. He turned away and looked out at the cottages dotting the outskirts of the village, and the sheep with their lambs who stood white against the lushness of the green hills rolling away toward the forest. All this was his, yet he had nobody with whom to share any of it—not even a dream—any longer.

At the first sight of Rex Chris told himself he had been foolish to imagine he had no one of his own. The reunion was emotional on several counts, not the least being that although they both realised the old bond still held, they were now different people from the two brothers who had last met on a normal footing on Chris's wedding day. As with Marion, Chris found that the feeling that had grown for an unfamiliar red-haired man in uniform, who was a national hero, somehow overlaid the careless schoolboy affection for a jolly nice older brother, making the commitment deeper and less dependent. But he was disturbed by Rex's appearance this time. There was a prodigious bruise on his forehead where he had apparently slipped and fallen when running up some steps, and he looked pale and heavy-eyed. All that was the natural result of sedation after a blow on the head. But there was the way he flinched from the fire burning in the hearth, and the absence of a smile. Even in greeting Rex had shaken his hand straight-faced. His words and tone of voice had been full of warmth, but it was as if the merry cavalier brother had been a figment of the imagination.

Chris found his mood growing bleaker still as he realised Rex had been facing almost four years of what he, himself, had experienced only briefly at Gallipoli. Was it any wonder that laughter was so hard to find for a man who had seen and suffered so much? Even so, he decided to tell Rex about the time he had spent with Laura. His brother heard him in silence, then merely said he was glad someone in the family had been on hand to help him through that difficult time.

'I have you to thank for it, Rex,' he told him warmly. 'You persuaded me to take my future by the scruff of the neck.'

'I just wish Roland had known you had pulled through all right,' was all he replied. 'I think he bitterly regretted his lack of understanding during those months following your marriage.'

'I bitterly regret doing all I did to bring such fearful results,' Chris told him. 'But *I* have to go on living with it.'

Rex looked across at him. 'You have changed, Chris. Chandler once told me if you recovered, that shell in Gallipoli might be the best thing that had happened to you. I think he's probably right.'

'He always damn well is!' They were strolling together after dinner, and an earlier shower sharpened the scent of rich earth and massed rhododendrons as they passed the stables, their footsteps crunching the damp gravel path. 'I'm glad you've come home just now,' Chris continued. 'There's something I'd like to discuss with you. I've posted a letter to you about it, so you'll get it after you arrive back, I expect. But it's nicer being able to talk it over, instead. Rex, are you listening?'

'Mmm?' He pulled his gaze away from the stables. 'Yes, go ahead.'

'I've read those letters of Roland's over and over again. They are haunting, brutal, and full of quite astonishing insight into human nature. Men like us, who have experienced war first-hand, can recognise the authority and perception with which he describes the scene.' He looked at Rex frankly. 'I was only at Gallipoli a short time, but my skin turns cold and begins to creep with the return of reality when I read some parts of those letters. As an account of war, it's masterly; as an indictment against it, it's brilliant.'

Rex nodded. 'I agree. I think I said something of the sort when I sent them to you.'

'I don't think he ever meant to post them. I don't even think they were written to his nephew. It's my belief they are really a cry to the next generation never to let this happen again. They are letters from every fighting man to every nephew all over the world. Roland never found it easy to reach out to other people, did he? But, by God, he reaches into the depths of even the darkest souls with his written words. I want your agreement to go ahead and get them published.'

Rex came to a halt and studied him shrewdly. 'Some of it is pretty strong meat.'

'So is this war.'

'You'll meet official opposition.'

'I'll fight it.'

'They won't allow that part about the subaltern shot by his own friend.'

Chris moved off again toward the corner of the house. 'I think that subaltern was Hilary Bisset, and I also think Roland tried to compensate for his feelings over me by befriending him. That's why he sent me Bisset's cameo. I realise now that he hoped I'd give it to Marion, some day.'

Rex walked slowly beside him for a moment, then asked quietly, 'Why did you give it to Laura?'

Bearing Bill Chandler's words in mind, he said with commendable ease, 'I fancied myself in love with her, at the time.'

'Doesn't every man?' It was a statement rather than a question.

'None of them have a hope with you around.'

'I know.'

'Well, what do you say about publishing those letters?'

'Yes . . . go ahead.'

'Where do you think we should send the proceeds?'

Rex thought about it a while. 'To any organisation that will use the money to buy a motor-driven vehicle to replace a horse-drawn one. Roland died trying to save one of the poor beasts, so I think it's appropriate, don't you?'

It was only as they had completed their walk and were turning back to the house because dusk was turning to night, that Rex brought up the subject of the divorce and asked how it was progressing.

'Faster than the usual speed of these things, I should imagine. Marion has a sympathetic case, and should get her freedom with ease,' Chris told him in heavy tones. 'I'll do my best to prevent the story from getting into the Press. It would sound pretty sordid in cold print, and certainly wouldn't enhance your reputation.'

'Don't worry,' Rex told him with a touch of bitterness. 'My reputation is all a myth, anyway. I'm either a hero or a murderer, depending on which way you view things.'

Chris looked at him with the concern that was growing by the minute. 'You ought to stay here for longer than a few days, Rex. I've seen enough men on the verge of cracking up, and you show all the symptoms.'

He shook his head. 'I just want to get back there and finish it off with the others. I think the Huns have just made their final bid. They're beaten and demoralised. All we need is American troops in large numbers, then we can drive them back to where they started. I just wish they'd hurry up.'

'What'll you do when it's all over?'

'Become a test pilot with Sopwith,' was the immediate reply. 'I've already been offered the job and accepted.'

'You mean to go on flying?'

The green eyes which might never have been merry for all those years looked back at him almost blankly. 'That's all I've ever wanted to do. You know that.'

Chris nodded. 'People change, though. I'm very happy doing what I do now. The Greek and Latin is more of a pleasurable pastime.'

'What about the rest of your life?' Rex asked, pushing open the door which had the lights inside burnishing his fiery hair. 'You can't live here all alone translating and inventing codes all day long.'

He answered impulsively. 'I'm going to try to obtain some kind of jurisdiction about David, so that I can teach him some things.' He stepped inside the panelled hall and shut the door behind them both. 'He's my son, so he probably has a decent enough brain to allow him to use it to advantage. Marion told me she's in love with someone, so she could marry again later on. I don't want this man . . .'

'No, she won't. He's dead,' put in Rex tonelessly. 'Burnt to ashes which couldn't be distinguished from his machine. Mike Manning is scattered all over the Ypres sector by now.'

Chris stopped dead. *Mike Manning?*

Rex stopped, too. 'That's right. While you were making sheep's eyes at my wife, he was making them at yours. They turned orange, you know, before they shrivelled out of their sockets.'

The horror of what he was saying turned Chris cold. 'Oh, my God, poor Marion!'

26

THEY PLANNED to catch the afternoon train to London, because Rex had to fly back to Belgium the following day—twenty-four hours later than expected. He had to pinch himself every so often to prove he was really at Tarrant Hall with Laura, and had not imagined all that she had said to him during the past three days.

His fall down the steps had shocked her to such an extent, she had abandoned her part in *Bows and Boaters* to her understudy while he was in England, and was indulging in behaviour completely foreign to her nature. Taking extraordinary measures to ensure she was awakened every morning at eight, she was devoting every moment to making him happy—not with erotic enticement followed by fulfilment, but quiet, deep love. He had not, in fact, taken her sexually since he had arrived home. The pills kept him drowsy so that he was very content with things as they were. As for the picture-postcards, she swore she would prevent any more being manufactured, and do what she could to have any unsold copies returned and destroyed.

Laura had helped him through the difficult meeting with Tessa, who looked thin and ill despite her determination to face up to her bad loss without giving in to feminine frailty. He was spared a conscience meeting with Marion, because Tessa informed him that Dr Deacon had taken his daughter and grandson to his sister in Bath. Rex assumed Tessa had decided whether any of her brother's possessions should be handed to the girl he had loved, but was still another man's wife.

Laura had also been very understanding over Chris, and had left them alone so that they could discuss family matters. Now, on this morning before they left, she was actually going for a walk along Longbarrow Hill with him. They went slowly hand-in-hand, enjoying the tranquillity around them as far as the eye could see.

'Does *all* this belong to Chris?' asked Laura, stopping and looking up at him.

'The land from here along the ridge to the west, and up to the far edge of the forest,' he told her waving his hand to indicate the distant boundary. 'That long line of poplars marks the southern extent, and the rest of the estate runs along that narrow section below the twin hills, then between the village and where we are standing. It used to be one of the largest estates in Dorset.'

'Why did Roland leave it to Chris, not you?'

'I get a percentage of the income. But I always told him I didn't want it.'

'It wasn't because of me?'

He looked down at her anxious face. 'No, darling. Roland could have been a doctor and Squire at the same time. Chris can be a translation expert and Squire. I was destined to fly, and the two are incompatible.'

'But you love it?'

He nodded. 'Now, more than I ever did. No, that's wrong. I always have loved it . . . but I took it for granted before.' He put his arms around her and drew her back to lean against his chest. 'We should never take anything for granted.'

She put up her hands to cover his arms as they held her. 'That's why I always seize everything with both hands. It sometimes looks like selfishness or greed. Perhaps it is, and I don't want to admit it. But when I'm old and grey I don't want to spend my days regretting my lost chances.'

He brushed her curls with his mouth. 'You'll never be old and grey. Never!' It seemed the right moment to say then, 'Why didn't you write and tell me Chris had come to you when he was in trouble?'

'Roland had just been killed, and you were having a dreadful winter out there. I couldn't see that it was important who had been there when it happened. The important thing was that he recovered.'

He tightened his hold around her, finding the distant view blurring momentarily as he whispered, 'You're really a very wonderful girl.'

'No, I'm not,' she returned quietly. 'Don't you remember my once saying it would be easy to comfort an infatuated boy, then send him away again?'

'Yes, I remember everything you've ever said.'

Her hair brushed his lips softly as she moved her head against his shoulder. 'I wish you'd forget some of them.'

He turned her within the crook of his arm, and began walking her along the hill again. 'I told you the last time we were here that our love soars high and sometimes comes down with a crash, but that we always take off again. The hurtful things are the crashes. They can't be forgotten, because they are the moments that teach us the most. Come on, just up here is the barn where I used to keep 'Princess'. She was the most wonderful piece of construction ever put together.'

He was seeing that aircraft again, and remembering the thrill of pride he had shared with Jake as they wheeled her out. It did not seem all those years ago.

'It was just as well we lived on a hill,' he said reflectively. 'It was easy to take off and let the up-currents take her right away. Better than trying to lift off over barriers of trees.'

'The people in the cottages below couldn't have been too happy, surely,' put in Laura lightly.

'Oh, yes. They used to wave as we went over.' He frowned. 'It all seemed so carefree and relaxed then.'

'It will be again, darling.'

'Yes, of course.'

They reached the barn, and he took her hand as he drew her inside the old familiar place, now empty save for some hay left from last summer. They stood together in the shaft of warm sunlight that streamed in through the open door, as he told her all about his dreams and aspirations of those days, and about Jake, who had shared them with him. He described 'Princess' in every detail, distance lending colour to her virtues and abilities so that she sounded the embodiment of every aviator's dream.

Finally, Laura squeezed his arm, causing him to look down quickly. 'Darling, I'm sure she was a wonderful machine, but you've just been describing an aircraft that could have won the war for us long ago, if we'd had enough of them.'

He looked at her earnestly. 'We're going to build one like that at Sopwith. I've already outlined some ideas to them in my letters, and they have first-class designers there. Working together we'll come up with a design men love to make, and pilots love to fly.'

She smiled at him mistily. 'Then I suggest you call it the "Sopwith Princess".'

She looked so beautiful standing there in the shaft of sunlight, he dedicated his whole life to her over again. 'I love you forever, Laura.'

Her fingers rested momentarily against his mouth. 'Of all the things there are in the world, that's one I truly believe . . . and I always will.'

He kissed her, and they both sensed there was something magical between them at that moment. The hay was warm beneath the great band of sunshine, and Rex made love to her almost reverently, and with great gentleness. Then they lay in each other's arms, listening to the sound of sheep and lambs calling to each other, the song of the skylark high and free in the bluest of skies, and the faint echo of women's voices as they worked in the fields.

Laura sighed, fanning his cheek with her breath. 'If I were to die at this very moment, I'd know I could never be more completely happy however long I lived.'

He turned his head to her. 'What about those lost chances?'

'Maybe I'd never be offered them.'

'What . . . what about my kind of four weeks?'

'What about them?'

'No regrets?'

She shook her head against the hay, and little pieces stuck to her curls. 'They were inevitable, weren't they? We belong together, Rex, and always will. We both know that.'

He drew her closer, knowing it was going to be all right. However high they soared, however bumpy the flight, they would always land safely. They drifted off to sleep in that warm caressing sunshine, surrounded by the sweet-smelling hay and soothed by the lullaby of country sounds.

The 'Arrows' welcomed their leader back, chaffed him about how he came to have such a bruise on his head, then settled into routine once more determined to retain their individuality whatever they might now be called.

But it was not so easy for Rex to forget they were part of a new organisation. James Ashmore's personality and inflexible attitude toward being cut off from the army of which he had been a part long before transferring to the R.F.C., vented its spite by swamping those under his command with all the literature, rules and regulations, and suggestions on reorganisation to suit the new demands of their rôle. He also requested returns, in triplicate, on just about every statistic the human brain could devise.

Rex recalled Chris saying he had compiled such data at Gallipoli just to give himself something to pass the time, and wished his brother were there to do it for him now. Since he was not, he put all Ashmore's communications in a drawer and out of his mind. He was a flier, not a secretary, and reading through all those official directives gave him a headache.

A week or so after arriving back a letter came from Chris. It had plainly been snarled up in the system for some while and looked decidedly crumpled and well-handled. In it, his brother put forward the idea of having Roland's letters published, and asked for Rex's approval of the scheme. So he thought it over for a few days, then replied giving the go-ahead and asking what Chris proposed doing with the royalties.

The subject was forgotten in the next few days as events moved quickly and dramatically in another German attempt to smash through to the Channel coast by attacking the area around the River Lys where, contrary to Rex's hope—and that of a host like him—hundreds of thousands more lives were lost during three weeks of grim frenzied battle, all for no strategic benefit one way or the other. The 'Arrows' were pressed to the limit during those April weeks providing air cover for their own defending troops, attacking moving columns of enemy supplies, and destroying observation balloons, aside from meeting the German *Jastas* and fighting death-or-glory battles with them.

Their exhausted spirits were cheered by the news that 'The Red Baron' Von Richthofen had been finally killed by a Canadian pilot, because they knew his legendary career had been a source of inspiration to German pilots, who could not ignore the truth that defeat was growing ever nearer. Von Richthofen's loss would be a great blow to their morale. But it would also bring about the burning desire to retaliate. 'Sherry' Sheridan's name shot to the top of the list of every German aviator when he went hunting.

It did not worry Rex. With the members of his squadron changing almost daily, he watched them burn or break apart in mid-air one after the other, knowing he was immune. But he was tired and feeling the strain of command more and more. There were things he should have done and had not, letters of condolence to be written that he had forgotten about. Too often, he would begin such a letter, only to find he could not remember anything about the dead man, could not even picture him.

Ashmore continued sending reams of orders, communiqués and other irritating rubbish, which Rex stuffed into drawers of his desk until, one morning, a motor cyclist arrived with a summons to Headquarters to explain why orders had been ignored, returns had not been filed, and certain modifications put into operation. Rex scribbled a reply saying he was too busy fighting a war to attend to such things, and declining to go to Headquarters on the grounds that he was just off to meet a flock of Albatross intent on laying eggs where they were not wanted. He then climbed into the cockpit of his Camel bearing a green stripe, and forgot all about Ashmore and his pieces of paper.

During that concentrated battle around the Lys, Rex certainly did not worry about the German determination to get him in return for Von Richthofen. But he was worried about the exhaustion that was beginning to master him. He caught himself falling asleep at all times of the day, yet no amount of it seemed to refresh him. When, after several instances of dozing in the cockpit, he went soundly asleep in mid-air to be awoken with a start when one of his squadron put a burst of gun-fire over his head, Rex decided to give up drinking. His intake had increased since Mike's death, and had plainly reached a dangerous level. He told the Mess Corporal to take it all away from his office and quarters to put under lock and key. The bewildered man had to remind him of his instructions when Rex returned two days later from a flight in which he had lost five men, and stormed over the fact that there was no brandy available.

'It was your own orders, Major Sheridan,' the corporal told him.

'*My orders!*' he repeated furiously. 'I don't give bloody stupid orders like that.'

'You told me to take it away and lock it up,' persisted the long-suffering man. 'Said it made you fall asleep.'

Rex looked at him with frown. 'Oh yes, perhaps I did. Sorry, Biggins, I'd forgotten. Look, fetch me something for this damned headache, will you? I've had it all week. At least, it seems like a week.' He threw his flying-helmet and goggles onto the desk and dropped heavily onto the chair. 'What day is it, by the way?'

'Thursday, sir.'

'Good-oh. Has the mail arrived yet?'

Biggins gave him a strange look. 'That comes on Tuesdays or Saturdays.'

'Yes . . . yes, so it does. I'm expecting a letter from my wife.'

'I had one from my missus this week. She said she'd been to see Mrs Sheridan at the theatre, and can't get over it yet. All the clothes and colour is like something in a dream, she says. Made her forget there was a war on. Cheered her up real proper, it did.'

'Good,' said Rex drowsily.

'Your lady is doing something real good back home, Major Sheridan. They need something to take their minds off all them raids, and the shortage of food. Missus's got six kids to feed. It's a problem, and no mistake.' He clomped to the door in his heavy boots. 'I'll pop over to the M.O. and get that powder for your headache.'

'No, don't bother,' murmured Rex. 'It's gone now.'

One of his senior pilots woke him as he was in the middle of a dream about Laura dancing around the stage with all the colour and costumes that made people forget about the war. But he was the only one in the audience, and her smile was just for him.

'Sherry, I think there's trouble brewing. Ashmore has arrived looking most frightfully purple around the gills, demanding to see you. He's being delayed as long as possible on his way over to your office.'

Feeling filthy and heavy-headed, Rex sat up in the wooden armchair where he had been asleep for over an hour, and muttered, 'What the hell does *he* want? Get Biggins to bring some tea or something over here, will you, Charles? I'll have it even if Ashmore declines.'

Lieutenant-Colonel James Ashmore was in anything but a tea-drinking mood when he stormed into Squadron Headquarters and saw the state of it. For the first five minutes he ranted about organisation and orderliness, concluding that he was no longer astonished that discipline was so deplorable in this particular squadron.

When he paused for breath, Rex said, 'We don't need filing cabinets with neatly labelled drawers to shoot down Huns. I hoped your visit was to tell me my replacement aircraft were on their way.'

'My visit, Major Sheridan, was to tell you I have recommended that disciplinary action be taken against you for insubordination. I've tolerated a lot from you, in the past, but you have gone too far, this time. I will not have a summons to my office treated in such infamous manner.'

Rex frowned at him. 'A summons to your office . . . when?'

Ashmore fumed further. 'Don't put on that bovine air of innocence. I have your reply here.'

'How can you have? I didn't receive a summons.'

'No? What's that then?' He threw a page from a signal-pad onto the desk, glaring at Rex.

He remembered it as soon as he saw it. 'Oh, *that* reply. It was true, I was just about to take-off.'

'You agree that you disobeyed my express command?'

'I was already obeying one from someone else—one I thought was of greater importance.'

Biggins entered with a tray of tea and poured it into two cups before departing again. Rex picked up one cup gratefully and began sipping. 'Will you have some? Sorry, but I'm off the hard stuff, at the moment.'

The offer appeared to bring the other man even nearer a state of apoplexy. 'Sheridan, we have developed considerably since the early cavalier days when men like you got away with anything. We are a unified service, not a lot of separate people doing exactly as they please. You never did understand that, did you?'

'No,' Rex replied bluntly. 'I had never been in a regiment that thrived on that kind of spirit as you had. What I do understand is flying, and I'm more use to my country at this vital time doing that than making lists of how many pairs of socks we have gone through this year. It must be important, I suppose, or you would never have spent the time on sending out such requests, but give me a clerk to cope with it while I get on with my real job. There'll be no need for all this time-wasting argument then.'

'You'll have to conform, Sheridan,' he stormed. 'In this new force there's no place for individualists.'

'I don't believe that,' he said with vigour. 'But, in any case, an old dog always knows a trick or two worth keeping.'

Ashmore studied him from head to foot. 'Some old dogs won't recognise when they've had their day. From the look of you, you've had yours.'

The man left still vowing he would demand disciplinary action with a recommendation for removal from command of a man who had been pushing his luck on the ground as well as in the air since the commencement of the war. The visit left Rex uneasy, not because of the threats but because he wondered if he *had* had his day. The old drive seemed to elude him; the old energy had gone. The need to sleep was growing dangerous when it meant he dozed at the controls of his aircraft, and his concentration wandered. Only that week he had heard from Chris, who seemed puzzled over the letter regarding publication of Roland's work, when they had already discussed it at length when he was at home six weeks before. How could he have forgotten that?

He seemed to forget so many things lately, and it was beginning to be remarked upon by the squadron. There had been too many instances of it for Rex to persuade himself they had imagined he had given them contradictory statements. Suppose he began doing so in the air; signalling first one thing, then another? It could lead to disaster. Yet he was not conscious of being muddled. His brain seemed as decisive as it had ever been.

But he did suffer from severe headaches lately. He had stopped taking alcohol of any description now, and drank gallons of black coffee instead to stimulate his brain. There was little improvement. He had toyed several times with the idea of grounding himself for forty-eight hours in order to really relax and sleep it all off. But with May halfway over, the Allies were all out to launch their *coups des grâces* before winter prolonged the war for another year. This approaching summer of 1918 would be the decisive one, Rex felt certain, and his men would need every boost they could get in the coming hot months. Any suggestion that 'Sherry' Sheridan had had enough would be fatal. Besides, he had his sights set on that job with Sopwith, and wanted to do all he could to hasten the moment he was free to take it.

He strolled across to dinner three evenings later with all that troubling his mind still, and vowing to skip any jollification afterward in order to go straight to bed. They would be off again at dawn, and he needed a long sleep after three flights that day.

When he pushed open the door of the Mess there were shouts of laughter coming from a group of rowdier youngsters in the squadron, but they all gradually faded away when Rex was spotted, and there was a great deal of furtive business behind backs that irritated him. Did they think he was like Ashmore and could not appreciate the need for letting off steam in ways more suited to schoolboys than dedicated killers? That was what they really were. He had been told enough times.

'For God's sake stop behaving like dirty-minded little third-year boys in front of a prefect,' he said brusquely. 'If there's a joke on I want to share it.'

'No . . . it's nothing,' stammered a youngster called Price.

'Hey, Sherry, come and take a look at the newspapers,' called a senior member who had known him a long time. 'They've just arrived from England, and you'll never guess what they have to say about the new Royal Air Force. If any of it is true, they won't need an army or navy any longer.'

He was walking over to the man when something fluttered to the floor from behind young Price's back, and lay face upward right in his path. Laura smiled up at him over her shoulder, and issued an invitation to pick her up. Trembling he stooped to get the postcard, and then saw what was written inside a balloon purporting to come from her curving mouth.

He launched himself at Price, grasping him around the neck and shaking him back and forth with all his strength, knowing he was a killer now. He wanted that boy never to see that picture, never write such words, never *think* of Laura ever again.

Next minute, he was being approached on all sides. Men were holding his arms, dragging him away. He fought them all, but was so tired they easily overpowered him. They took him somewhere quiet and dark, then gave him something to drink. The headache had come back in double strength as he lay on a bed, groaning softly while it thudded enough to shake his whole body.

He awoke in a strange place. It took a moment or two to realise he was in a bed in sick-bay, for some astonishing reason. Frowning he sat up and looked from the window. The Camels had gone. His own machine stood forlornly on the field in brilliant sunshine. What on earth was going on? He left the bed and walked across to open the door. An orderly got to his feet from behind a desk.

'I'll fetch the Doc, sir.'

'What the hell's happening here?' he demanded. 'Where is the squadron?'

'Gone out on patrol,' came the casual information. 'Captain Cork'll be here in a tick.'

'Where are my clothes?' roared Rex at his departing back, but the man continued on his way leaving his C.O. standing in the office totally baffled.

When the M.O. came in a few moments later, he was accompanied by a major.

'Martin, what the deuce is this all about?' began Rex immediately. 'If it's some kind of prank, I don't think much of it. Where've they hidden all the machines?'

Martin Cork looked surprisingly grave, and sighed heavily as he introduced his companion. 'This is Major Clunes, Sherry. He has come at the request of Colonel Ashmore to take you to Headquarters. I have told him I don't consider you fit enough to go, but he insists.'

'Oh, really?' put in Rex with spirit. 'Am I under arrest?'

'Good lord, no!' said the fresh-faced man with a laugh. 'Actually, I regard it as something of a joke, really. But Ashmore seemed to feel you wouldn't come if he sent a driver on his own.'

'He's right,' Rex told him. 'What does he want me for?'

'Something damned important—no, truthfully,' he added seeing Rex's expression. 'Top brass have been in conference with him for several hours, and it's urgent, apparently. My instructions were to collar you as soon as you landed.'

That reminded Rex of something. 'Where is the bally squadron, Martin?'

'Somewhere above Ypres, I should imagine. Jim's leading them.'

'Bloody nerve!' He ran his hand through his hair as he looked from one to the other. 'Forgive me, gentlemen, but I have no idea what I am doing standing in the middle of sick-bay in my underpants, when my squadron is over Ypres. Can one of you explain this phenomenon?'

'You really don't know?' asked the M.O. curiously.

'Of course I damn well don't know. I wouldn't ask if I did.'

'You weren't feeling too well.'

'Well, I can work out that much for myself. Did I hit the bottle?'

'You're on the wagon, old chap. Don't you remember?'

He frowned. 'Yes . . . yes, I suppose I am.'

Major Clunes intervened. 'I'm sorry to interrupt your guessing game, Sheridan, but I'd be glad if you'd get dressed and work it all out as we go to Headquarters.'

'Eh? Oh, all right. But I'm going to have breakfast before I go.'

'*Lunch,*' said the M.O.

'What?'

'Lunch,' he repeated. 'It's two p.m., Sherry.'

What James Ashmore wanted was important, as Major Clunes had hinted, and Rex had cause to ponder what would have happened if a driver had arrived alone to collect him, and he had refused to go. His long-standing adversary got to the point quickly, for once, which was an indication that the summons was for serious reasons.

'Sit down, Sheridan. We've never seen eye-to-eye, and I've never approved of your methods, but it seems the army has need of an old dog with a trick or two, after all. I've been detailed to call you in and explain what is wanted.' He pulled down a roller-map drawn to large scale, then picked up a pointer. 'Within the next few days, the Germans are planning to move supplies of tank fuel and ammunition to their force which is pinned down right here. As you know, this road into the village is blown to pieces, because our own columns were attacked so heavily by Hun aircraft when we held the village. This other road in was re-captured by us last week.' He tapped with the pointer. 'The open plain is impossible to cross with vehicles due to the cratered and fractured surface, so they can't approach that way. But, unless they get supplies to their troops soon, they'll be overrun by several Canadian regiments strengthened by a new large influx of Americans.' He gave a thin smile. 'They'll be overrun by us, anyway, but we'd rather do it when they have no means of defending themselves.'

Rex nodded toward the map. 'You've just proved they can't receive supplies, so what's the problem?'

'This, Sheridan,' Ashmore ran the pointer along a narrow line of blue. 'This canal is part of a large system of waterways stretching back into occupied Belgium. Army Intelligence has been following the progress of a fleet of barges purporting to contain a cargo of fruit, but a Belgian spy has discovered the real cargo and its destination.'

With some idea now of what the meeting was about, Rex asked none of the obvious questions, knowing there would be valid and comprehensive reasons as to why he was being told this highly classified information.

Ashmore anticipated him, to some extent. 'It will be obvious to you, by now, that we have been unsuccessful in destroying the fleet, and it has managed to get to within two days' journey of its destination. The men on board undoubtedly feel it will be plain sailing from now on. As you see, the canal runs, at this point, through woodland until just before the village in question. In the village and along the German positions to the west are artillery emplacements that would make concerted aerial attack very costly.'

Rex was quiet for a moment, then asked, 'How wide is the canal?'

Ashmore gave him an understanding look. 'Only just wide enough. It would take very skilled judgment, complete knowledge and confidence in the aircraft, and a pilot with daring and the luck of the Devil. But you already know that, having done something like this before.'

'Would I have complete freedom?'

Ashmore gave a tight smile. 'Even I agree you must have that. As someone who dabbled with explosives before taking up flying, can I offer a useful tip?'

Rex nodded. 'Go ahead.'

'Leaving aside the problem of flying through there without coming to grief on the trees, what I'd aim to do would be to concentrate on the leading barge. Get that alight and exploding, and a chain reaction will set the rest off.'

'How many others?'

'Five in all. Normally, they'd be well spaced out. But they'll close up in that narrow stretch.'

'Are they armed?'

Ashmore nodded. 'Machine-guns bow and stern.'

'All of them?'

'Yes.'

Rex stared at him. 'God, what a prospect!'

'It seems, on paper at least, to be a case of doing it at the first attempt, or not at all.'

'It seems to be that whichever way you look at it,' he said heavily. 'How long is there in which to study the details?'

'It'll have to be done tomorrow. You're free to decide at what hour you'll go, so long as you tell us in good time so that we can keep the skies clear for you. But, by sundown tomorrow, the convoy will be rounding this bend, and by dawn the day after will be too near its destination, which would halve your chances.'

Rex gave him a straight look. 'How do you halve anything that small?'

Ashmore sat down and laid the pointer carefully on his desk. 'I should have told you we are asking only for a volunteer on this job.'

'That went without saying,' said Rex. 'But when an old dog stops doing his tricks, he's finished, isn't he?'

He decided to go late in the afternoon, after working out the convoy's probable position at that time. It was leaving things to the last minute, but it would give him the most advantage because the sun would be going down and he would be approaching out of it. If the sky clouded over before nightfall, he would lose that advantage. But there was another one. The barges would be about to negotiate a bend in the canal and, if he failed to set up the desired chain reaction with his attack, there was every chance of the leading barge slewing across to bring about a collision, or at least block the waterway and halt the rest so that he could make a second run with more success.

He stayed in his office all that morning, studying the maps and information he had been given, and refusing to be disturbed by anyone, even the M.O. who came three times. Finally, Rex sent an orderly across to ask for a strong pill or powder to disperse the headache that had been increasing with his intense concentration since morning. The M.O. came back with it himself, declaring that when Rex got back from wherever it was he was going, he must submit to being given a complete health check.

'There's nothing wrong with me that a damn good sleep won't cure,' he declared. 'Now, go away, Martin. I'm busy.'

He ate lunch at his desk, and drank cup after cup of black coffee to stave off the sleepiness creeping over him. Even then, he had to fight to keep his eyes open. To wake himself up, he walked over to check that his machine was ready, tested the guns, and watched the fixing of the bombs into the racks beneath the fuselage. Then he went to his quarters intending to take a cold bath. On his way there, he met one of the boys in his squadron, called Price. He seemed to have a black eye.

'Hallo, Tony, been having a fight?' he asked as he passed.

'*Sir!* Major Sheridan!' called the boy, stopping Rex in his tracks. 'Yes?'

The youthful face was bright red and a picture of misery. 'I want to apologise.'

'Apologise . . . for what?'

'The . . . the picture, sir.'

Rex looked at him in incomprehension. 'Picture? What picture?'

The boy's Adam's apple rolled up and down as he swallowed several times. 'The . . . the *photograph.*'

Light dawned. 'Forget it, lad. We all make mistakes with air reconnaissance, at first. And it did look something like a lake on that photograph. No harm was done, anyway.'

Looking remarkably like a rabbit staring down the barrel of a rifle, the boy stammered, 'N-no, sir. But I just wanted to say that . . . well, that I admire you tremendously. We all do.'

Rex put out a hand and squeezed his shoulder. 'Don't waste your admiration on me. Save it for some luscious wench.' He walked off unaware that the young pilot was staring after him transfixed.

By four-thirty he was ready to leave. For some reason, the entire squadron seemed to have turned out to watch him go. After take-off he circled, and waved to them all before turning onto the course that would take him toward the canal. He felt very calm and confident, as he always did once in the air, and he thanked Giles Otterbourne once more for giving him cause for that confidence. But he cursed the pain that still thudded through his head, despite the M.O.'s draught, and the terrible sleepiness he could not seem to shake off. His eyelids kept drooping so that he had to fight to keep them open. When, after about ten minutes in the air he jerked awake to find the ground considerably closer than he intended, it gave him such a fright it proved to be a remedy.

The droning of the engines did not help, of course, and the inactivity. Once he neared the spot he would have more than enough to centre his attention on, and he would need all his wits about him. He gazed over the side at the green countryside beneath. It looked very peaceful. But it would not be long before it gave way to miles and miles of devastated brown earth with no recognisable feature on it whatever. Sometimes, from the middle of those areas something would flutter in the breeze and mark the fact that there were living creatures down there in trenches, trying to establish some kind of brotherhood with him as he passed. He turned his attention back to the map hanging on a cord around his neck and, for several seconds, found he could not remember where he was supposed to be heading. Then he saw the basket of grenades at his feet. Oh yes, they were his nest eggs for an emergency.

Thank God it was a clear day. The sun would be his ally, but he wished it did not look so fiery. It made him think of another ball of fire called Mike Manning. But that thought was too painful, and he switched his concentration to that other time he had flown through a cutting between trees. But that memory proved equally painful when he recalled why he had done it. His headache seemed to be getting worse, and his vision kept blurring. It was the worst thing that could happen just now when he needed perfect judgment. Blinking several times and shaking his head, it cleared. He breathed a sigh of relief.

The railway was in sight now, with bridges blown to block the tracks here and there. The canal would be about six miles ahead. If he hit it west of the bend he could turn to overfly it with the glow of the setting sun behind and slightly to the right of him. The men on the barges would have it full in their eyes as they rounded the bend.

Losing height when his objective came into sight, he circled looking for the break in the trees where the canal ran. Yes, there it was. God, it was narrower than he had expected. It would take a magician to fly through there. But only when he had dropped lower and lower until his wheels were almost brushing the tops of the trees did he realise the appalling difficulty of what he had been asked to do.

Gradually, carefully, he manouevred his aircraft until it was filling the width of the cutting with only a few feet to spare on either side. He was safely in, but he now had to fly the length of it without touching. Without any sense of self-aggrandisement, he realised only a superb aviator could successfully achieve what he was doing. This would be 'Sherry' Sheridan's greatest flight yet. He would look back on this in years to come, when aircraft were faster, bigger and more powerful, and still see it as something wonderful. The thrill of flight ran over him as he roared above that quiet waterway that was glittering silver and gold in the dying sunshine, and striped with dark borders of shadow near the trees.

Only when he noticed a curve ahead in that shining ribbon of water did he recall what he was really there for, and feel a thrill of a different kind. Apprehension flared strongly. It was one thing to perform a miracle of flight through a deserted cutting; quite another to do the same whilst dropping bombs in defiance of hostile machine-gunners on barges. The slightest deviation could have him catching a wing-tip on the trees and all would be over. He would need every ounce of concentration he could muster. If only his head would stop aching!

The bend seemed to be rushing toward him fast, and his hand went to the bomb-release cord. Immediately, the Camel wobbled, racing his heartbeat. The barges should be appearing round the bend now, according to his calculations. There would only be one chance, one right moment. He must not miss it: those supplies must not be allowed to reach their destination because he had been beaten by the greatest challenge of his life.

The bend was on him now, and he was misjudging the angle. The trees on the right were rushing toward him. He compensated. The machine veered wildly, shuddered, then settled level again, as his vision blurred momentarily. Tension was making him sweat. He put up a hand to dash it from his eyes just as it dawned on him that something was wrong. The water stretching ahead of him was empty, with no sign of any kind of boat.

He tried to think; rack his brains. Was it possible he had read the map wrong? No, he had found the correct landmarks. Could he have miscalculated his own speed and that of the boats? Surely not. He had been doing such things for enough years now not to make a mistake. Besides, he had double-checked all his figures before setting out. What had gone wrong? Calling all manner of curses down on the heads of Military Intelligence, who might have got it all wrong, he tried to decide what to do. Confusion teemed through his head, preventing constructive thought. What was wrong with him? He felt curiously light-headed and unconcerned with what was happening. He was no longer sure what he was doing there. It was exciting drifting through that dark-green corridor, knowing he could go on forever without touching those trees at the sides. He was master of his machine; could make it do anything he wanted. His eyelids began to droop, but through the narrowing slits he saw something like a blob on the water ahead.

Blinking himself awake, he almost came to grief as the nose dipped. Recollection rushed back. This was no pleasure trip but a vital patrol to bomb some barges. They were the blob up ahead. The sun behind him was now low enough to put a glare on the water that partially blinded him, and he accepted his job was going to be more difficult than he had thought. It looked disastrously as though the boats had stopped altogether.

He now realised how loud the roar of his engine sounded in the stillness of that waterway. They would have heard him coming a long way off. If they had any sense they would be manning the guns in readiness. That meant it would have to be the first run, or nothing. At this height, they could hit him with a revolver quite easily. Machine-guns would turn the Camel into splinters and rags in an instant.

Closer now, he saw that the barges had stopped and were drawn up alongside the right bank one behind the other. The crews appeared to be dealing with a shift in cargo on the first of the boats. But the gunners were taking no chances. They were at their posts, looking straight at his approaching aircraft. The true hazards of this job became crystal clear. The bombs would be ineffective, since he could not now fly overhead to drop them. It would have to be the grenades, which were much more chancy. He could not fly that perilous corridor, pull the pins from them all, and throw them accurately over the side all at the same time.

Swiftly revising his plans, he sped on towards the barges as the first stutter of gunfire began. Praying that the setting sun was practically blinding them, he concentrated on the closing distance between them and judged the exact moment. It had to be very quick, or he would be lost. The moment came. Pulling the pin from one of the grenades with his teeth, he dropped it back into the basket a second before pulling the bomb-release cord. Then he snatched up the basket, hung over the side of the cockpit and tossed the basket accurately onto the deck of the leading barge, hoping desperately that the timing of the fuse would allow him to get past before it went up. Bullets ripped through the fabric of his wings, and several hit the gun fairing, but he was off and safe.

The business of climbing up into the open and executing a left turn took his attention for a minute or two, so he had no real idea of the success of his plan until the sound of a gigantic explosion rent the air. He levelled and gazed over the side at the gratifying scene below. It brought a chuckle. The single live grenade had set off the chain reaction he had wanted, aided by the bombs that had exploded in the canal, rocking the barges and sending washes of water to knock over the barrels of fuel and split open boxes of ammunition that helped spread the subsequent fire that set off the rest of the ammunition.

He continued to chuckle as he circled a hundred feet or so above the cut in the trees that was starting to belch black smoke and tongues of flame. Then, as he gazed down, an almighty roar signalled the total success he had sought. Pieces of barge, boxes and barrels were flung into the air on tall spouts of water as the whole consignment exploded with a sound that would have been heard by those Germans waiting desperately for the barges. It would also be heard back at the 'Arrows' station; maybe even at Headquarters. He had done it! He had done it! And he would give a month's pay to see Ashmore's face when he heard the news.

The chuckle turned into an exultant laugh as he left the scene behind him and headed toward the sun. Nothing was impossible for man and his flying machine. The Camel had responded to his slightest touch, just as women did, and they had achieved the ultimate in skill together. He had waved his magic wand and the Camel had performed the wondrous trick. But there would be a machine even more powerful and magical than this. There would be a machine that could encompass the world, one day. He was going to help design the Sopwith Princess. Then he would fly her and, together, they would be invincible. There was nothing to compare with flying; nothing to match the feeling of conquest, or the excitement of knowing there was only a thin layer of wood and fabric between your feet and the immense sky. The flying-machine bore you along on its spread wings, while the throb of the engine propelled you to any place you wished.

He felt immensely tired now—more tired than he had ever felt in his life before. Sitting back in total contentment, he watched the sun going down in a blaze of red. It seemed very beautiful—not a bit like fire and destruction any more. As he sat there, the sound of the engine began to fade and the mysterious music of the heavens rose up around him to lull his weary brain. The headache that had been with him for so long had gone. A wonderful lightness replaced it.

He glanced over the side. Down below was Longbarrow Hill,

and Tarrant Hall stood out clearly on its crest, as it always did. It looked so very peaceful down there, with sheep dotting the hillsides, and the women waving their laundry at him in greeting. He grinned and waved back, at peace with the world. Roland would be home tomorrow; Chris at the end of the month. The long summer holidays lay ahead of them all, and 'Princess' was his and Jake's for every day of them. What more could a man want? He smiled to himself as he wandered in the realms of yesterday, tomorrow, and beyond. His eyes slowly closed.

He did not see the arrival of companions of the sky bearing black crosses on their wings; was not aware of the astonished disbelief on the faces of men who saw their most sought-after quarry flying alone and defenceless over German lines. He knew nothing of their hesitation, fearing it must be some trap, some inexplicable trick at their expense as the Camel weaved and floated in joyous dips and glides around the red-streaked evening sky.

The Albatross squadron that was returning after a raid closed in cautiously. The Camel definitely bore a green stripe; the pilot was wearing the celebrated cerise scarf and a dove emblem on his leather helmet. The German leader fired an experimental round, ripping the wing from centre to tip. The men of the squadron all exchanged looks as the British aircraft continued to glide serenely through the heavens where the first stars were beginning to twinkle. Then they closed in on their prey.

Beneath the onslaught the Camel gradually disintegrated as fabric and woodwork were blasted apart. The body of the pilot inside it grew bloody and torn as drums of ammunition were emptied into it with a blaze of uninhibited vengeance. The wreckage began to fall and, as it did, it burst into flames, plunging like a torch to the ground well inside the German sector and exploding in a shower of sparks and flames. For some while the Albatross squadron circled the spot looking down at it. Yet no man signalled in triumph to the other, and they finally turned in instinctive unison to return to base, each one very shaken and inexplicably ill at ease over what had happened.

The wreckage burned for a long time as a bright glow in the darkness. But 'Sherry' Sheridan remained undefeated. The blood that had been slowly oozing through his brain since he had hit his head on the newel outside his home six weeks before, had killed him several minutes before the Albatross squadron had come on the scene.

Deeply regret Major R. A. Sheridan, D.S.O. M.C.
Croix de Guerre, R.A.F. killed in action May eighteenth.
The Air Ministry express sympathy.

--- 27 ---

'BUT, DASH it all, she's still my wife until the divorce is granted,' said Chris heatedly, as he paced up and down that stuffy office where he had visited his solicitor. 'I have a right to know where she is.'

'You know where Mrs Sheridan is, sir. At Bath, with her aunt.'

'*Where* at Bath?'

'I cannot tell you that, Mr Sheridan, as you are well aware. Dr Deacon's solicitor will pass on any further communications from you, and he is not obliged to reveal the address. Dr Deacon has stated that his daughter is in need of peace and quiet.'

'What does he think I plan to do—rush there with a brass band and a battery of cannon?' cried Chris belligerently. 'And what about my son?'

'He is safe and well with his mother—as he has been since you relinquished responsibility for them both in 1915.'

He stopped pacing. 'I . . . I . . . my dear fellow, they were living very comfortably at Tarrant Hall, with my brother on hand.'

'The court will accuse you of abandoning them, sir, since you made no financial provision for them, either through the army or Mr Roland Sheridan, and told no one where you were.' Cummings, the family solicitor, rarely smiled at the best of times, but he looked to Chris now like a jury of twelve all accusing him without trial. 'At present, you are able to communicate with your wife through Dr Deacon's man. But, for eight months, your wife had no idea whatever where you had gone or if you had any intention of returning. I'm sorry, Mr Sheridan, but even in my book, that would be counted as abandonment.'

'I didn't leave them destitute—I would never have done that. I left a note saying I was joining the army. I suppose they could have traced me, had they really wanted to.' He pounced. 'There, you see. If they had felt abandoned, they would have contacted the army authorities.'

Cummings looked even more funereal. 'Mrs Sheridan was told to leave Tarrant Hall by your brother. In short, she was abandoned by your entire family, sir.'

Chris swallowed. 'Whose side are you on, Cummings?'

'The side of right.' He waved a hand at the leather chair. 'Please sit down, Mr Sheridan. We really cannot conduct the whole of this meeting on our feet.'

Chris eased himself into the chair. His leg still played up, especially in damp weather. 'You are conspiring to prevent me from doing right,' he pointed out angrily. 'Here I am wanting to persuade Marion she can have every comfort, a marvellous home—well, it will be when the war is over and I get it back from the Army—and considerable wealth. Added to which, the boy will get the inheritance he deserves.'

'Your son is the legal heir, whatever happens. Unless you change your will, he will inherit on your death.'

'I am only twenty-one, Cummings,' Chris reminded him with a scowl. 'It could be another sixty years until that happens. By that time, David will be a blacksmith or shepherd, with hands like hams, teeth all brown from chewing tobacco, and half a dozen grandchildren.'

The solicitor sighed, putting the tips of his fingers together to form an arch as he sat studying his wealthy client. 'Mr Sheridan, it won't help your case to lose your temper. With your medical record it . . .'

'There is nothing wrong with my sanity, if that's what you are suggesting,' he snapped.

The man looked shocked. 'Certainly not, sir! But the claimant's counsel will make a point of it.'

'I have a certificate proving I'm mentally quite sound.'

'A mere piece of paper will seem insignificant against two and a half years in a mental ward, unfortunately.'

'So much for the side of right. The law bends to suit the case.'

Cummings was shocked even further. 'The law is the law. It cannot be bent. It is sometimes . . . er . . . *coloured* to add strength to a claimant's case.' He frowned at Chris. 'Mr Sheridan, your wife is determined to bring this marriage to an end. I believe she could have done so at any time during your illness, but the fact that she waited until you were fully able to be cognisant with the case will bear even more in her favour. She is plainly not a vindictive woman, and she is surrendering a number of material benefits by her action. Her petition is entirely based on the conviction that further union with you would be impossible on the ground of incompatibility.'

Chris got to his feet again, angrier than ever. 'How the devil does she know that when she won't even try it? I'm a different person, I tell you, and the man she wanted to marry is dead.'

Cummings also rose in deference to his client, but his voice was more than usually full of woe as he said, 'If you wish to pass on a further communication to that effect, I will see that it reaches Dr Deacon's man. But I can only repeat what I have said to you from the start, sir. You will spare Mrs Sheridan and yourself a great deal of unnecessary distress by not contesting this case.'

'What about the distress of my son?' growled Chris.

'He will feel no distress at losing a father, sir. He is unaware that he has one.'

As Chris walked haltingly through the arches of Gray's Inn beneath clear skies that followed several days of rain, he thought of those last words. David Sheridan had managed for three years without a father. Why was he attaching such importance to the relationship? His own father had been no more than an occasional impersonal visitor. Had he and his brothers really suffered because of it?

Wandering through the narrow ways of old London whose ancient stone walls threw back the warmth of the sun, Chris pondered that thought. If Branwell Sheridan had been a caring parent Roland would never have taken on the responsibilities of Squire at such a young age, and instead devoted his time at home to his medical studies and his beloved horses. He would never have tried to be a substitute father to himself and Rex; never have borne the burden of keeping the estate running efficiently, even when war came. He would never have been disowned by an entire village, and branded a coward by those who meant so much to him.

If Branwell Sheridan had been a true father he would never have forced Rex to waste two years at Cambridge, but recognised his genius with machines. He would never have gambled away his sons' inheritance, then killed himself, forcing Roland and Rex to sell their dearest possessions in order to let their brilliant younger brother follow his destined course.

But Chris grew hot with shame as he realised he had been about to do the same to his own son until Neil Frencham had stopped him. Yes, he supposed he *had* abandoned the boy . . . and his mother. Small wonder Marion was not prepared to give him another chance.

Finding himself in a secluded park, he sat on a seat watching small children in sailor-suits or calico dresses, playing beneath the watchful eyes of their nursemaids. But had he really changed? Was his desire to have control of David only a bid to achieve, through his son, the academic laurels he had once prized so highly? After all, he knew nothing of the boy as an individual; had no fondness for him. Was he simply trying to recapture that golden period during the long summer holidays of 1914, when the future had appeared to stretch before him, glittering and endless?

Finally, he got to his feet and walked on, deciding not to contest Marion's petition. He owed her and the boy their freedom. He would gain freedom himself, of course. Was it too late to take up the threads and pursue that academic career, after all? Yes, possibly. Too much had happened, and he *was* a different person, no matter how people doubted the fact. Learning would not be enough for him. He wanted someone of his own. Maybe, one day, there would be another son, another girl that he could truly love. A girl like Laura. But this one would not be married to his brother.

The loneliness filling him instigated the desire to hold on to those who still belonged to him. After all, there was Rex and his beautiful wife, who both cared about him. He was not all alone in a world that had been snatched from him one day in 1915, spun around in a black frightening No-Man's-Land, then flung back into his lap last November.

He climbed the steps to Laura's apartment slowly, not as Rex would eagerly have done when he had slipped and fallen six weeks ago, bumping his head on the newel. Would there come a day, Chris wondered, when there would be a girl he would rush to meet; a girl who loved him as totally as Laura loved Rex?

The maid answered the door, saying her mistress was at the theatre for the matinée and would he care to wait. He had forgotten the matinée. It would be another two hours before it was over, and the maid was not even certain Laura would return between performances, or whether she would go elsewhere for a rest and light snack. Feeling tired and frustrated, Chris said he would wait. But he had only been sitting in the elegant room for ten minutes when memories of those nights he had spent with her began to torment him. Bill Chandler could say all he wished about being in love with the *idea* of Laura, but that was all Chris had left, and it was what he desperately wanted just then.

He got to his feet intending to go to the theatre and walked into the small square hall just as the maid was closing the door. She turned almost in fright as he appeared. Her face was white and scared. In her hand was a telegram.

'Oh, sir, this has just come for Mrs Sheridan.'

As Chris stared at it he knew what it had to be. The world turned momentarily back into that black frightening No-Man's-Land, and his whole life cried a protest that rang round his head like the scream of a shell. *No, not Rex!* Not the strong sun-browned laughing man who lambasted a cricket ball high and wide and found time to wink at all the blushing maidens as he ran between the wickets. Not the warm steadfast friend who had come to the school prize-giving on a motor cycle that back-fired continuously, and grinned with delight at the affronted well-dressed fellow visitors. Not the good-natured reckless rider who lifted small boys onto that same noisy machine for the thrill of a lifetime. Not the dashing young officer who had walked into the church behind the bride, to put some element of light into a bleak day. No, not the beloved brother who seemed to make everything come right, who ruffled his hair with careless affection, who could play a tune on anything and sing a popular song in a lusty uninhibited tenor voice. *No, no,* not Rex, who had seemed immortal!

But the words he read were irrefutable. *Killed in action.* He turned away against a wall as his shoulders began to heave. The pain now within him was greater than all the physical anguish he had suffered during the past few years. Grief was an immeasurable burden he felt unable to bear in silence. With the destruction of Rex came the destruction of hope. If *he* could not survive, how could anything?

After a while, the maid brought him a glass of brandy. Her eyes were red as she handed it to him. But he could not bring himself to drink it, because he heard Laura's voice saying: *It's Uncle Rex's medicine for times like this.*

It hit him, even through his distress. Oh God, *Laura!* His sense of loss was nothing to what Laura would feel. How would she sustain it; how would she find the strength to go on alone? In control of himself now, he knew she would be as desperately in need of help as he had been when he had made that impossible stunned journey to reach her last November. He must now be her anchor, as she had been his.

He took a taxi to the theatre and went round to the stage-door. They let him in, knowing who he was, and he went straight toward the small partitioned office of the producer. It was hot and dark backstage. Chris was sweating with the effort of controlling his own need to hit out against something he did not want to face, and the sound of a full chorus out front echoed around the dim ghostly bareness behind the glamour of the backcloth and the flats. It was a severe test to tell the man why he had come, because speaking the words meant he accepted the truth of them and declared Rex indisputably gone from the world.

'Christ,' swore the man softly. 'It'll finish her.'

'No, it won't,' Chris told him with difficulty. 'I'll stay with her and make sure it doesn't.'

The producer looked at him with deep sympathy. 'He seemed as though he would go on forever, somehow. I never thought . . . none of us ever thought . . . It must be hard for you, too. He was your brother.'

Chris swallowed. 'Rex was everyone's brother.'

Through the wings he could see Laura as she came on from the far side for her finale in the shimmering black dress. She looked superb, her vivid happiness radiating to all those beyond the footlights who had forgotten sadness and despair for a while. He clenched his hands tightly until they hurt. How could he say the words that would end that happiness; put out the bright star?

As the final number progressed, bringing that moment nearer, he knew he would stay with her forever, in whatever capacity she needed. The music was growing louder and faster as the climax approached, and Chris found a lump blocking his throat. She was shining at her brightest during this number. Would she ever shine again after today?

There was a sudden thump, near enough to shake the ground beneath his feet, but the next one came before he had had time to act on the shocked message that had reached his brain. It was in the street just outside, this time, and the blast blew in the wall containing the huge doors through which they brought the scenery. He was already running toward Laura when the third bomb landed.

It had all happened before at Gallipoli—the screams, the agony, people falling silently all around him, dust and smoke, the smell of burning, the incredible noise, fear and terror, destruction. But here, it was dark. The lights had all gone out in a moment, and there was nothing but filtering sunshine through the clouds of dust rising above debris that was still falling as walls collapsed under intolerable stress.

There was a human tide rushing toward him, trying to prevent him from going to the spot where he had last seen her standing. He fought them with all his strength as he scrambled and stumbled over bricks, beams, and broken scenery. There was a cable leaping about like a live thing with sparks flying from the broken end and, across the dim auditorium, he saw the first flicker of flames.

Out amongst the broken plush seats people were screaming, fighting their way to the exits, trampling underfoot any who lost their footing in the press. On stage and behind it heavy arc-lights, beams and great lumps of masonry were plunging down on those torn bleeding players trying to crawl to safety in their bright costumes made garish by harsh daylight beginning to penetrate as more and more of the roof collapsed.

Ignoring the fizzing cables Chris climbed over bodies trapped in the debris, coughing and retching from the dust hanging in the air, praying he would find her. As savage as any other person there, he threw off women who tried to cling to his arm, men who wanted to detain him for a rescue, and pulled aside anything that blocked his way to that spot centre-stage where Laura had been standing.

Cries for help were floating up all around him; shouts from rescuers who had come in from the street. But Chris went on with determination, as he had done on that cliffside when a gun had to be captured. As on that occasion, he had nothing left to lose. His arms did not tire, and he found superhuman strength. The whole stage was covered with masonry, wood and broken lights, but he attacked it like a man possessed, knowing she must be somewhere under there. Rex would have wanted him to get her out, not leave her to be crushed and broken by the weight pressing down. He would want her to remain beautiful. Chris prayed she would be. His lips moved in that constant prayer as he flung aside all that hid her from sight, ignoring the shouts of warning and the building that was still collapsing all around him.

Someone took hold of his arm. It was a policeman in his blue uniform and bell-shaped helmet. 'Come along, sir. It's too dangerous for that.'

'Get away,' he shouted, in a voice like many he had heard in the hospital wards. 'Take your hands off me! Get away!'

He continued his furious digging, the policeman and all else forgotten in his urgency to reach her before it was too late. But he 'was' too late, and he knelt there as tears drenched his cheeks, knowing this had been the only way for her.

Her face was cut and bruised, streaked with greasepaint and the dust of an old theatre. Those magnificent wicked eyes were closed as if in sleep, and her mouth was slightly parted in a final sigh. The vivid hair had fragments of bricks and wood caught in the curls, but it glowed in the light of the fire spreading on the far side of the theatre. He tore more debris away, sobbing with the effort, until she was free of it. Her body was still beautiful and, mercifully, it was unbroken. The glittering dress had dark red smears on it, but it caught the light to sparkle bravely as he bent and picked her up in his arms.

She felt so light and supple. He had not guessed how it would be to hold her like that, so still and belonging so totally to just one man, even now. When his lips touched hers he knew they would both understand it was just his farewell. He travelled through an aeon as he stumbled with her toward the place where rescuers and rescued were congregating by an opening onto the street. Out there, the sun was shining, and people were picking up the pieces of their lives. But Chris knew he was nobody from nowhere once more.

He saw the beam falling the instant before it hit him. Swinging round so that Laura would be unharmed, he took the whole weight of it on his back and shoulders. Even as he fell, he kept her in his arms. But they took her away just before afternoon turned into sudden night.

He awoke to a familiar scene. There was an ache across his shoulders and a burning sensation in his back. This hospital was not peaceful, as the others had been. There were at least twenty other men in the ward with him, and the windows showed a view of dirty chimneys in long rows on grey slate roofs. The nurses were mostly elderly, with stern faces, and they bustled back and forth too busy to notice that he was awake.

He had been awake several times before in this place, but they had been periods of no more than drowsy awareness. Now, he was fully alive to what was going on. As he reached for the glass of water on the locker, a nurse noticed the movement and gave him a brief smile as she hurried up the ward. A few moments later, a man he knew appeared beside his bed, studying him silently as he sat on the chair provided for visitors.

Then he said, 'There's not much of a view from these windows.'

'Better than that room at Rosemead.'

The lean face relaxed with signs of relief. 'You know who you are, then.'

'Yes. I'm not sure where I am.'

'London. All the air-raid casualties were brought here. It's the nearest hospital to the theatre. Are you ready to talk about it?'

Chris moved his head against the pillow. 'Not really.'

'You'll have to sometime, lad.'

'What is there to say? Everyone's dead.'

'You're not.'

'I wish I were.'

Bill Chandler shook his head. 'No, Chris. You fought too long and hard to have your life. You can't give up now. That wouldn't be worthy of them. You have to carry on or their sacrifice will have been in vain.'

'It's too much to ask.'

'They gave up the things they prized and valued once before for your sake, and you botched it. You can't do it a second time.'

He shook his head again. 'I'm so terribly tired . . . and I feel a hundred years old.'

'So do we all. But you are different from the rest of us, Chris. You have the gift of immense intellect which allows you to see above and beyond what is happening now. When all this ends, which it soon will, the world will need men like you to set it to rights. When the human race is bewildered, frightened, trying to return from bestiality to tranquillity, it's the men with brains and vision, the aesthetes and artists who lead the way. The warriors have their day, Chris,' he said with urgent sincerity, 'but it's the men of learning who keep the world turning. Think back on your Greeks and Romans for proof of my words.'

Chris gazed at him. 'Roland and Rex were both more worthwhile people.'

'Only because they had already proved their worth. You've been too busy trying to hang on to life to do that yet. They were also very courageous. Roland earned the Military Cross, and Rex has now been awarded a V.C. to add to his other array of medals for gallantry. It's today's headlines.'

Angling his head to look at the rows of chimneypots, Chris said, 'Rochford-Clarke told me he volunteered because his friend had been awarded a posthumous V.C. I didn't see the logic of his argument.'

'Now you do?'

'No. Rex was someone very special, and the Victoria Cross honours him as such. But going off to have half your head blown away can't honour him more . . . and it can't bring him back.'

'No, it can't. Nothing can bring him back . . . or Roland. But look at it this way. Young as your brothers were they died having achieved their aims, despite having surrendered their hopes of doing so four years ago for your sake. Roland did qualify as a doctor and more than satisfied any instinct to save life. In the process he came to terms with his fellows and set free a remarkable ability to see into the heart of human understanding which he might otherwise have kept locked inside him all his life. Those letters of his will speak for him in decades to come.

'As for Rex, he has already become a legend. In the history of aviation his name will glitter like one of the stars in the skies he graced. He died achieving the ultimate in flying skill which will be an inspiration for the generations to come. I've brought the newspaper so that you can read the details of his exploit.'

Chris hardly glanced at the folded newspaper on the bed-cover. He was still studying the chimney-pots.

The voice of his friend grew gentler. 'Chris, the men like Rex invariably die young. In a few short years they live a lifetime. They shine and dazzle, then leave a steady glow behind to guide those who come after. Can you imagine your brother as a lined and wrinkled old man with crippling arthritis, and a mind that wanders? Can you imagine him hobbling along the street muttering to himself, the butt of tormenting children who run behind him shouting out derogatory names? He was an aviator to the end. For him, life only began when he climbed up into the skies. He wanted to stay up there and never come down. He will stay up there . . . and she'll be there with him.'

Chris had to look back then at the man who had helped him through so much. 'Where is she?' he asked huskily.

'Here at the hospital. The Press is calling for a big funeral here in London. I'm very much afraid there's a likelihood of it being turned into an hysterical mass homage to both of them. The glamour of a romance that had captured a nation, and the poignancy of their united deaths is the kind of thing sorely-tried spirits use as a means of release.'

'Oh God, no!' He felt immense anger sweep over him. 'That must be stopped.'

'Maybe they would want it that way.'

'No,' he said immediately. 'Rex was never that kind of man, and even Laura would find it outrageous.'

'It's your decision. You are her next of kin.'

'It must be quietly, at Tarrant Royal. The Sheridan men all seem to die in foreign lands, so she will represent them. Besides, Rex would like that.'

'Yes, I'm sure he would.'

'It must be kept quite secret,' Chris insisted. 'I can't have . . . have . . . it will just be the few of us who . . . loved her. You'll come, won't you?'

'Of course.' He got to his feet, touching Chris's arm as he did so. 'See what I meant about a man to set things to rights when the rest of us have gone mad?'

'No one can do that,' he said heavily.

'But you can have a bloody good try, Chris. That's all any one of them would ask of you.'

The following day Chris had another visitor. He thought blue must be her favourite colour, because she wore a costume of a shade that reminded him of early bluebells.

'The only time I ever see you is when I'm flat on my back,' he greeted her quietly. 'How did you know I was here?'

'Several people told me, and it's in all the newspapers.'

'Are you going to sit down, or can't you stay long enough?'

She took the seat beside the bed. 'I'll talk for a while, until you get tired.'

He issued a challenge. 'Did someone tell you to come?'

'No, Chris. I had my own reasons. I was worried that this might start up your old trouble again.'

'I'm perfectly sane,' he told her quickly.

'I didn't mean that. It was your leg and stomach wounds. But the Ward Sister says it is only cuts and bruises, but mostly shock.'

'Funny how they'll tell visitors these things, but never the patient,' he mused, thinking how the stress of her own problems had robbed her of that country freshness she had always possessed.

She put a bunch of carnations on the locker. 'I couldn't bring the kind of flowers I knew you'd prefer, because this is London, not Somerset.'

He remembered those snowdrops she had once brought him. 'Did you come because I was a patient again and you felt you should nurse me?'

She shook her head. 'You'll be out of here in a day or two.'

'So why, then?'

'I suppose it was that . . . that I've lost people, too, and it seemed to me that we are both going to need someone to help us through for a while. Why not each other?'

He studied her pale features, trying to read what lay behind their grave expression. 'I'm not sure I understand what you are suggesting.'

'I didn't when I set out from Bath,' she confessed quietly. 'But I thought it all over on the train and there seems to be one obvious answer. Perhaps it's too soon to mention the subject, but how would you feel about abandoning the divorce?'

A week ago he would have known the answer to that. Now, he felt nothing; was drained and empty of emotion. 'I don't really know,' he said with honesty. 'Perhaps it is too soon.'

She got to her feet. 'I shouldn't have rushed up here like this.'

'No, don't go!' He took hold of her hand. 'I really am glad to see you, and you should know by now that I have few social graces. Bill Chandler is always telling me off about it.'

'He thinks you are tremendously courageous.'

'I didn't attempt to save anyone except Laura.'

She sat down again, leaving her hand in his. 'I don't think he means that, Chris.'

'Oh.' Her face looked very drawn with the harsh light from the window on it, and he found he was not as empty of emotions as he had thought. 'Marion, I'm truly sorry about Mike. I liked him.'

She looked down at their linked hands. 'It was difficult not to like him. He came along when I was lost and very frightened. He offered me all the things I had wanted from you, and I fell in love before I recognised my feelings. Chris, I must tell you that I desperately wanted to make him happy in the way he needed. The reason I didn't was not because I wouldn't betray you, but because I couldn't risk doing to another child what has been done to David.'

She looked close to tears, and he gripped her hand tightly. 'I understand. It's all right.'

'And there's dear Rex . . . and Roland,' she whispered. 'So many have gone. I thought . . . I thought those of us . . . who are left . . .'

'Bill Chandler said something like that yesterday,' he reflected. 'Something about their sacrifice not being in vain.' For a moment or two he tried to put from his mind the thought of all those he would never see again, then looked up at her. 'If we decided to abandon the divorce, could you forget all I did to you?'

'Not forget. I don't think I could ever do that. But I could put it aside, Chris, if you could do the same about what I did to you.'

'It was taken from my memory against my will,' he reminded her. 'When it returned two years later, it didn't seem half as bad.'

Her brow wrinkled in a slight frown. 'What do you feel about David now?'

'I don't know him, do I?'

'But do you want to?'

'I want to teach him things, make sure he gets the chances he deserves.'

'That's a very good start,' she told him, then hesitantly broached another point she had plainly considered during her train journey. 'I know and understand how you felt about Laura. I . . . I couldn't be a substitute for her.'

For a brief second he saw again that joyous flame-haired girl as she had been the moment before she had died, then the vision faded.

'No one could be a substitute for Laura,' he told her simply. 'She was out on her own, and always out of my reach up there with Rex. But you and I have been friends for a very long time, and survived everything the world has thrown at us. There must be something we like about each other that we can build on.'

She got to her feet then, almost as if frightened by what she had brought about. 'Think it over, Chris. I'll come back this evening when you've had a little longer to sort out your feelings.'

He nodded, feeling very tired now. 'All right. Wear that same costume, will you? It's pretty. Reminds me of the bluebells in the copse at home.'

She turned away up the ward, and he closed his eyes, still thinking of the bluebells. They would be over now, but would come again next year.

They called him the Gypsy—and Lady Campion had to trust him with her love and her life!

From the tranquil kingdom of her country house in England to the bloody heart of Revolutionary France, the beautiful, spirited Lady Campion is drawn into a deadly trap—and the bait is the one man she cannot resist.

The Fallen Angels
Susannah Kells

_____90192-5 $3.95 U.S.

"Outstanding—I loved it!" —Johanna Lindsey

"Exhilarating" —United Press International

"Spellbinding" —_Booklist_